A REALM OF SHATTERED LIES

THE SEVERED REALMS

T.A. LAWRENCE

To Alyssa Dorn and Morgan Cari,
for helping me figure out what to put in the blank spaces

PREVIOUSLY IN THE SEVERED REALMS

For those of you who read *a lot*, I know keeping up with what happened in previous books in a series can be a tad difficult. If that's you, here's a quick little summary of where we last left all our favorite heroes:

Asha and Kiran have been searching for Az, Asha's childhood best friend, for over a year now. While Az is busy hunting down humans and half-fae who possess magic, with the goal of opening the Rip, Asha and Kiran hope to find him before he succeeds...or realizes that he's the true heir to the throne. When we last saw Asha and Kiran, they were in Othian with Ellie and Evander helping them track down Blaise.

Piper and Marcus have been in hiding ever since Princess Lydia crashed their wedding and informed them that Az is still on the hunt for Piper and her Gift..

When we last saw Ellie and Evander, they were in Othian, the capital of Dwellen. Though they succeeded in finding Blaise, she abandoned them in the middle of the night to save Nox.

Blaise failed in her attempt to rescue Nox from the fate of having his body permanently overtaken by the spirit of Farin, Queen Abra's son. In a panic, Blaise placed Farin (in Nox's body) into a magical slumber, weaving both males' souls into the Fabric. She has since secretly allied herself with Az, who reminded her that opening the Rip would provide the magic necessary to rid Nox of Farin's soul for good. She now waits with Nox's body in Mystral, where she expects the rest of the group to find her.

When we last saw Nox, he had awoken in a body separate from Farin's, both of them stranded on an abandoned island in another Realm.

Content Warning:

As Blaise is still working through her past trauma in this book, the content warnings in A *Throne of Blood and Ice* still apply, though most of the references are short, single-sentence flashbacks rather than entire scenes.

ALONDRIA

MYSTRAL

DWELLEN

Vensil Forest

Kobii Mountains

The Shills

Wyndhin

Adreean Sea

AVELEA

FORGOTTEN ISLE

Edii Gulf

Evaen

The Hills

Nettlewood

Rivre

CHARSHON

Merarihi

Sea of Lythos

NAENDEN

Talens

Grythos Channel

LAEI

GLOSSARY

Characters

Abra (Mother) – Queen of Mystral; known as Mother in The Old Magic's story; mother to Farin; helped lead fae into Alondria in the past; kidnapped Nox, Zora, and Blaise; now possesses the parasite; left Mystral when Farin rejected her

Amity – Unofficially the adopted daughter of Marcus and Piper; skilled in Healing, though she has no magic of her own

Arun – Father of Asha and Dinah

Asha – Female protagonist of *A Word so Fitly Spoken*; possesses The Old Magic, who speaks to her and provides her the ability to conjure temporary illusions; married to Kiran

Azrael (Az) – Childhood best friend of Asha; illegitimate child of the previous king of Naenden; conspired with Gwenyth to take the Naenden throne in *A Word so Fitly Spoken*; now intent on opening the Rip

Bezzie – Elderly friend of Asha's; owns a tavern in Meranthi

Blaise – Female protagonist of *A Throne of Blood and Ice*; vampire (previously human); grew up in Dwellen; previously a servant in the castle in Dwellen; long-time friend of Evander's; loves Nox

Bronger – Kidnapped Piper when she was a child; organized the Coup in an effort to overthrow the fae regime; died at Piper's hand

Calias – Late King of Charshon; conspired with Azrael to overthrow Kiran; died at Kiran's hand

Casper – Cousin of Evander

Cheyenne – Sister of Marcus; kidnapped by Piper as a child, though she was taken by King Declan of Avelea and raised in his court; inhabited by magic that gives her the power to make others forget through touch

Clarissa - Stepmother of Blaise

Claudia – Victim of Nox's bloodlust

Collins - Head chef at the castle in Othian

Declan – King of Avelea; wolf shifter; raised Cheyenne; family is mysteriously absent

Derek – Male who sexually assaulted Blaise when she was a child; disappeared after discovering Blaise was pregnant

Dinah – Sister of Asha; daughter of Arun

Elias – Male protagonist of prequel novella, *A Face to Slay the Shadows*; love interest of Lydia; grew up at the Coup with Piper

Ellie – Female protagonist of *A Bond of Broken Glass*; Princess of Dwellen; glass blower by trade; married to Evander

Evander (Andy) – Male protagonist of *A Bond of Broken Glass*; Prince of Dwellen; married to Ellie

Evangeline – Queen of Dwellen; mother of Jerad, Evander, and Olwen; wife of King Marken

Farin – Son of Abra; the child from The Old Magic's story; led the fae into Alondria; soul placed into Nox's body by dark magic

Fin (Phineas) – Twin of Kiran; Prince of Talens, widower of Ophelia

Forcier – Owns a bakery in Othian

Gunter - Slave of Queen Abra; researcher; father figure and mentor to Nox; died at Nox's hand during a fit of bloodlust

Gwenyth – First wife of Kiran; conspired with Azrael to help him take the throne; died at Azrael's hand

Imogen – Servant at the castle in Othian; lady's maid to Ellie

Jerad – Late brother of Evander and Olwen; died in an accident while celebrating with Evander

Jethro – Father of Ellie; glass blower by trade

Kiran – Male protagonist of *A Word so Fitly Spoken*; King of Naenden; magical powers include the ability to control fire and the ability to control others' feelings through touch; married to Asha; twin of Fin; younger brother of Lydia

Madame LeFleur – Late owner of a shop in Othian; previously inhabited by the parasite

Marcus – Male protagonist of *A Tune to Make Them Follow*; bounty hunter by trade; married to Piper; unofficially the adoptive father of Amity

Marken – King of Dwellen; father of Jerad, Evander, and Olwen; husband of Queen Evangeline

Nagivv - Asha's feline pet

Nox – Male protagonist of *A Throne of Blood and Ice*; fae-vampire; held captive by Queen Abra since childhood; loves Blaise

Olwen – Sister of Evander; disowned by King Marken, her father; female protagonist of *Of Tangles and Tinsel*; possesses plant magic

Ophelia – Fin's late wife; coerced by Azrael and Gwenyth into their plot to overthrow the throne of Naenden; died at Kiran's hand after failing to seduce him

Piper – Female protagonist of *A Tune to Make Them Follow*; kidnapped by Bronger as a child; forced to kidnap other children for the Coup, overthrew Bronger; inhabited by Gigi, a sibling of The Old Magic; magical powers include the ability to control elements and call to others through music; married to Marcus; unofficially the adoptive mother of Amity

Quill – Married to Olwen; possesses plant magic; male protagonist of *Of Tangles and Tinsel*

Rajeen – Previous king of Dwellen; supposed father of Kiran and Fin; father of Lydia, Azrael, and Tavi

Solomon – Biological father of Kiran and Fin

Tavi – Asha's lady's maid; twin sister of Azrael; illegitimate daughter of the late King Rajeen

The Old Magic – A sentient fragment of the Fabric who lives inside Asha's mind; has several "siblings" including the parasite, who inhabited Blaise in *A Throne of Blood and Ice*, and Gigi, who inhabits Piper.

Tijan - Merchant under whom Azrael was an apprentice previously

Vizier – The vizier to the throne of Naenden; suffers from an illness that strips him of his fae anti-aging magic

Zora – Realm-walker whose soul has been woven into the Fabric; sister of Nox

Places

Alondria – The realm in which the majority of The Severed Realms takes place

Avelea – Kingdom ruled by King Declan; homeplace of Marcus, Piper, and Amity

Dwellen – Kingdom ruled by King Marken and Queen Evangeline; homeplace of Evander, Ellie, and Blaise

Ermengarde – Capital of Mystral

Evaen – Village in Avelea where Piper and Marcus celebrated Winter Solstice

Meranthi – Capital of Naenden

Mystral – Kingdom ruled by Queen Abra; homeplace of Nox and Zora

Naenden – Kingdom over which Kiran and Asha rule

Othian – Capital of Dwellen

Otho – Village in Mystral; hometown of Nox and Zora

Talens – Province in Naenden over which Fin rules

PROLOGUE

BLAISE

*N*ox is dead. Again.

This time it's in a cave, a girl with cropped golden hair cradling him in her lap as she weeps over his lifeless body.

His heart takes its last beat, but the organ itself has been displaced from his corpse, strewn across the floor of a dim cavern, a smear of blood staining its path.

The muscles in my fingers ache with strain as I pick the Rivrean thread from the tapestry, undoing my work, erasing Nox's death, and not for the first time.

My entire body trembles, and I'm so focused on unwinding the last segment of the tapestry, so rushed to undo what I've done before it cements itself into Nox's reality, I hardly notice the tears that dampen the fabric.

I drop the seam ripper I've been using to remove the thread. It clatters against the floor, glinting in the dancing light seeping through the stained windows of Abra's abandoned ballroom. Panic surges through me as I chase the instrument across the stone floor. Time ticks, numbered by the pulse drumming against my ears as the seconds I'm allotted to undo Nox's death drain away.

That's assuming you have the ability to undo his death, the voice in the back of my head whispers, but I push it away. I've survived being infested by an ancient parasite. I've kept my vampire cravings at bay to protect my friends. I tricked a monster of legends into Gunter's bedroom so I could force him into an indefinite slumber, and I *will* keep Nox from dying, even if it's through sheer obstinance.

I've already lost too much.

Where is my baby where is my baby where is my baby...

I grab the seam ripper, then scramble back to the loom, unloosing the recent stitches until the scene of Nox's death has disintegrated into a series of colorless strings hanging limp from the end of the tattered tapestry.

The sigh that escapes me provides little relief, and I try not to look at the colorless threads. The Rivrean thread is infused with magic that seeps into the ground surrounding the Rip, the fray in the Fabric that separates the Realms. Before Gunter's death, he used the magical thread to weave Nox's sister, Zora, into the Fabric itself, allowing her consciousness to slip between realms and live out a series of reincarnations while her body remains trapped in slumber.

I've been under the impression that Gunter maintained some semblance of control over the events of Zora's many lives, but I'm beginning to think I was wrong. Either that, or I'm just incompetent at weaving magical tapestries. Every time I try to weave Nox's story, the thread dyes itself whatever colors it finds necessary to conclude the story in a manner it finds satisfying.

And the Rivrean magic wants Nox dead.

Either that, or the Fates do, and they're controlling the outcome.

I don't know if it's for some eternal purpose, or their own amusement, but I won't let it happen.

Nox can't die. He can't...

The wheels clatter against the divots between the stone tiles on the floor as I push the loom away, unable to bear looking at the tapestry another moment. If I don't continue the tapestry, I figure Nox's body will be released from the slumber that ties him to the Fabric. That's problematic, since Farin is the one in control of Nox's body at the moment. Zora's in this tapestry too, so I figure I'm prolonging her captivity as well, but I don't actually know that to be the case. Gunter wove dozens of tapestries before he died. For all I know, Zora has several more to complete before she wakes up.

So I weave, hoping for, if not an alternate ending, then at least a prolongation of the inevitable. At least until Az and I can figure out a way to expunge Farin from Nox's body.

Figure out a way, the voice inside me laughs. *As if you haven't already decided what you intend to do.*

I ignore that little voice inside my head, the one that seems intent on making me feel guilty for what Az and I have planned.

I've spent enough of my life feeling guilty, allowing shame to stake me to the ground, to fill my muscles with saltwater until I'm unable to move, bloated with indecision.

I'm done feeling guilty. I'm done not getting what I want.

As if what I want is so unreasonable, so evil, that the Fates refuse to grant me my wish. As if I long for power or domination or violence or to subject others to my will.

No. All I want is Nox. And I've about decided that's not too much to ask.

I practically collapse onto the cot I dragged up here for Nox, curling into his side and tucking my ear to his chest. Each time I do, there's a moment of dread when I fear I won't hear a heartbeat. That I won't feel the steady rise and fall of his chest.

That completing the tapestry truly killed him this time. Permanently.

I don't know what will happen to Nox if he dies in another realm.

I don't intend to find out.

Thu-Thum.

I let out a breath, though there's no relief in it, and cling to the only person I'd set this world on fire for.

When I wake, it's to the creaking of the door I haven't bothered to lock in days.

I blink rapidly, uncomfortable with the idea of Az seeing me in such a vulnerable state. Usually I like to threaten his life in case he gets the idea he can double-cross me. It makes it much more difficult to be intimidating if you're found cuddled up in the arms of your indefinitely unconscious loved one, wetting their sheets with your tears.

I bolt upward in bed, but when the speckled light from the stained glass windows illuminates my visitors, Az is not among them.

"Blaise?"

Concern lines Evander's brow as he and Kiran step into a ballroom flecked with light that illuminates a pair of sleeping bodies.

And the vampire who will rip apart any seam it takes to bring them back.

"Blaise, what in Alondria...?"

Evander's sea-green eyes scan the ballroom, taking in the emerald dais on the far end, the tapestries that outline Zora's many lives.

Mostly, he stares at the two bodies, Nox and Zora laid across the cots I dragged up here for them days ago. Light speckles their faces, breathing life into Nox's pale features, his sister's warm ones.

Understanding clicks into his expression, and his gaze moves slowly to my mouth, searching for blood.

"I didn't kill them, if that's what you're thinking," I stutter, scrambling to my feet from where I was just tucked into Nox's side. I suppose it probably looked like I was feeding on his neck, with the way I was lying across him. "They're both alive. I wouldn't hurt them."

Evander's shoulders slump in relief, but Kiran approaches Zora, placing two fingers below her jawline. I suppose he locates her pulse, because he steps away and nods toward Evander.

"You left," is all Evander says, refusing to take his eyes off me.

"You don't know how dangerous Abra is. The lot of you were discussing what to do about her, like all it would take to defeat her would be a few carefully placed political maneuvers. I was afraid you didn't understand what you were getting yourself into."

Kiran crosses his arms, his tanned skin betraying divots of muscle grooved into his forearms. "So you thought it best to take on the Queen of Mystral on your own?"

I find I can't hold Kiran's molten gaze, not when it seems it might bore a hole right through me, exposing my lies for what they truly are.

4

"I just...I just can't lose anyone else."

My hand instinctively finds my belly, because at least those words aren't a lie.

"And these two?" Evander asks, still from the edge of the room. It hurts that he doesn't approach as easily as Kiran does, but then again, I've never betrayed Kiran.

At least, I haven't betrayed Kiran *yet*.

"I wasn't completely forthcoming with you back in Othian," I say, to which Evander hardly blinks. I suppose that by this point, he's used to this sort of behavior from me.

Use what they already assume about you to your advantage, Az's words echo in my ear.

"I wasn't the only prisoner Abra kept. Nox was here before me. His sister too. He and I...we formed a bond."

Evander works his jaw, clearly still hurt that I left with hardly a note, not trusting my friend enough to ask for help. "And are you and Nox involved?"

There's a protectiveness in the way he says that word, *involved*, that makes my heart ache for another time, another life. One where I might have been content with my and Evander's platonic relationship. One where I wouldn't have gotten myself into this mess to begin with.

But I suppose if I never got myself into trouble, I'd never have found Nox. So there's only so much I can bring myself to regret.

The best lies are layered into the rawest truths, Az's voice reminds me from earlier today.

I might be a vampire now, but there's not a drop of fae blood in me, meaning lies can spill from my mouth without consequence.

I allow my gaze to drop to the floor, and I trace a cluster of fuchsia and turquoise lights with my bare toe. "Nox wasn't just a prisoner. He was tasked with extracting the parasite from me. By any means possible. We grew to care for each other, but it didn't start out that way. I wanted to tell you about him. I just thought that because of what you found out, about Derek, I mean..." My throat swells at the mention of the man who stole my childhood. "I thought maybe you'd think I had..." I slam my eyes shut and swallow. "I thought maybe you'd think

5

I'd fallen for someone who hurt me. I wasn't sure you'd understand that what Nox did, what the queen forced him to do—that he was protecting his sister."

I flick my gaze back at Evander, still unable to raise my chin. In the corner of my eye, I sense Kiran tense.

Evander's jaw works, like he's trying to find something, anything, to say. Eventually he settles on, "I like to think I would have listened. Would have understood."

The words hang between us, stale as the air in this abandoned ballroom. It's not the first time I haven't come to him with the truth. Not the first time I've withheld asking my friend for help.

It's not the last, either, but it's imperative I convince him otherwise.

So I take a breath and explain. Well, I explain enough, twisting details like wisps of hair rearranged to hide the bald spots in my story. I tell Evander and Kiran that I came to Othian intent on killing Queen Abra, but that when I arrived, she was already gone. That I'd waltzed into the castle only to find she'd decided to punish my leaving by placing Nox and his sister into a magical slumber, probably with some potion she concocted.

I lie, and I sprinkle the lies with truth, and I do it so seamlessly, neither Kiran nor Evander questions my story all that much, except that Kiran asks why the castle is all but abandoned.

Thankfully, I'm able to tell him the truth, that I frightened all the servants away.

Kiran nods, and to my surprise, squeezes my shoulder. Where his rough fingers brush my neck, a splash of comfort washes over me. It fades as soon as he draws away his hand, but I'm grateful for it all the same. Why Kiran has trusted me with his secret power, his ability to manipulate emotions through touch, I'm not sure.

He really shouldn't.

"I suppose you'll want us to arrange transport for them back to Othian," Kiran says, nodding toward Nox and Zora, "until we can apprehend Abra and force her to wake them."

6

I can't allow Nox and Zora to reside under the supervision of Kiran's guards.

"Actually, I believe I know someone who can move them," I say, and when Kiran and Evander look at me with questioning eyes, I add, "You'd be surprised what sort of trustworthy fellows you can find scampering about the inns around here."

Kiran raises his brow, then reaches into his pocket and pulls out a coin purse, which he tosses in my direction. "You mean, trustworthy when provided with ample incentive."

I think the Blaise from just a few days ago would have had a worm gnawing a pit into her stomach right about now.

I think the Blaise from before might have found herself wishing the King of Naenden behaved consistently with the dreadful, murderous rumors spread about him.

But for the past several days, I've done nothing but rewrite Nox's death.

So when the guilt threatens to strike, I tuck it away.

I'll deal with it later.

Because when we get back to Othian, I'm going to kidnap Kiran's wife.

And then I'm going to make her open the Rip.

PART I

LOST

CHAPTER 1

BLAISE

I've spent over two months cooped up with the male whose life I intend to destroy.

Evander's been here too, though none the wiser.

We meant to set out for Othian, to rejoin Asha and Ellie, the day after Kiran and Evander arrived at the castle.

The blizzard had other plans.

I can't help but wonder if it's a sign from the Fates, the extension of a deadline, a plea for me to reconsider.

If it is, I'm not listening.

I've spent the past months reweaving Nox's story, keeping him from deaths that sometimes occur so suddenly, so cleverly within the Fabric, I don't always see them coming.

I fear the Fabric will outsmart me one of these days.

But the storms have finally subsided, the path between the mountains cleared as the snow melts away, leaving behind a sickly sludge.

We leave for Othian tomorrow.

As I stand at the abandoned wall on the west side of Ermengarde castle, hidden from view of the windows, Kiran's bag of coins pulls at the inside of my back pocket, weighing my coat down and dragging at my collar. Like it's going to cut off the circulation to my throat.

I haven't figured out what to do with it. Not when I'm not actually hiring anyone to take care of Nox's and Zora's bodies.

Well, I suppose I am hiring someone. It's just that his price isn't money.

Kiran and Evander think I'm going with them to hunt for Abra. They think Abra is the only one who can bring Nox back.

I can't remember if I'm the one who planted that lie, or if I just allowed them to assume.

Either way, I've had to tuck Kiran's gift away, as well as the black adamant box I've stuffed into my bags.

Just in case I happen upon Abra again.

Just in case the parasite, who now resides within Abra, needs to be contained.

Az watches me intently as he holds open the flap to the back of the wagon. "They'll be safe with me. You know that, don't you?"

"As long as I do as you ask," I say, cutting my eyes away from him and tucking my hands into my pockets, as if I have need of the extra warmth.

Az puts his hand on my shoulder, and rather than squirm away from his touch, I snap my teeth at him. He appears undeterred. He knows I want his help badly enough to control myself around him, even if his blood does smell delicious, but he removes his hand from my shoulder all the same.

The wagon is tucked within the cover of pines that border the north side of Ermengarde castle. I carried the two bodies out here by myself. They think our initial plans for transporting the bodies have changed, that instead I've hired a mercenary to protect the bodies while I'm away. Though I'm fairly certain the idea makes at least Evander nervous, he's walking on eggshells around me, so he hasn't argued too much about it.

Besides, Kiran seems convinced that the amount of coin he offered couldn't be outbought, ensuring Nox's and Zora's safety until we can find Abra, or until Kiran can send his personal envoy to look after them. At least I'd convinced him not to try to bring them back to Othian with us.

Of course, Nox's and Zora's bodies won't be here when the envoy arrives.

"We're going to get them back," Az whispers to me, and for a moment, he actually manages to sound comforting.

I don't know why it's so much easier to believe when Az says it than when Evander says it. Perhaps because Az actually possesses the ability to carry it out.

Because he's right.

We are going to get them back.

I'm going to get them back.

All it will take is Asha opening the Rip, the magic emanating from such a monumental event enough to sever Farin's soul from Nox's body.

And then I can finally let the tapestry run out, hopefully allowing Nox to wake up.

I just have to make sure the tapestry doesn't write his death before then.

"Any intel you've been able to gather while the three of you've been stuck up in that castle?" Az asks, returning to business now that he's spent his best efforts comforting me.

I shake my head, biting my lip and staring at the wagon, listening for Nox's shallow breathing.

Az frowns. "Nothing?"

I shrug my shoulders. "I can't help it if Kiran isn't exactly the sharing type."

"Maybe. But from what you tell me of Evander, he is."

"Well, that doesn't mean Kiran shares anything with him, either. I've already told you all I know. They have their sights set on Abra, which should be good news for you."

Az levels a stare at me, and I force myself to meet it, even though it makes me feel as if he'll see right through me.

But then something like sadness overcomes his expression, an anxiety I only get glimpses of.

"What?" I ask him.

His huff of air causes steam to appear in the chilled air before him. "It's just that things would be so much easier if I could find a way to depose him."

"You don't think an army of Others will be enough?" I ask skeptically, hoping to get a tad more information about how Az plans to control said Others once the Rip is opened. So far, he hasn't clued me in on many details of his plan, though I assume he has that part covered. Still, it would be comforting to know for sure that I'm not aiding someone in releasing a band of predators into Alondria unleashed.

"I just..." Az stares at the ground, tracing a path into the snow with the heel of his boot. "I just want to ensure she makes it out of this safely. Blaise, anything you know that could get her away from him..." He looks as if he's about to choke on anguish.

The air chills in my lungs. "I thought you said you and Asha no longer saw eye to eye."

Az frowns. "We don't. But it shouldn't be that way. He has a power, Blaise. The abominable type. One he shouldn't have. One that allows him to control her."

The memory of illusory comfort and ease washes over me, but it's been diluted by time. It's not as if I can access the feeling again. The feeling when Kiran picked me up and carried me out of my father's manor, plunging me into a blissful peace before he deposited me back at Othian castle.

It seemed a kindness then, and I'm not entirely ready to say that it wasn't.

Despite that, it's a dangerous power, being able to control the emotions of others. "You think he uses that power to keep her in love with him."

Az's gaze snaps toward me. "Is there another option? It's not as if Asha could love a monster like him."

Somewhere inside, my heart crunches like the topmost layer of ice beneath our feet.

"I suppose only monsters love monsters," I concede, finding my gaze drifting back to the wagon.

It doesn't seem fitting, with everything I know about Kiran, that he's controlling Asha's emotions like that. But how much do I really know about Kiran?

I know he's searching for a solution to Asha's mortality. I can't think of another reason he'd be researching liquid moonlight in the library. I also know he's doing so in secret, without alerting her to his actions. On one hand, that seems like the actions of a male who would force a woman to love him, assuming he plans to make her immortal without her permission. On the other hand, if he's controlling her emotions, why hide it from her when he could simply make her want immortality?

Unless he's not completely aware of what he's doing to her.

Unless he chooses not to be completely aware of what he's doing to her.

I know what that's like. To tuck the wrongness away. To ignore the way it mildews like forgotten crumbs in the pockets of your life, hoping if you let it alone, it will simply disappear.

I don't know whether Kiran is controlling Asha, but I do know this: he and I are the same. Both of us would do anything to save the people we love.

He won't understand when I betray him, but he should.

Because he'd do the same to me, if it was Asha stuck in an indefinite slumber.

"I'll keep my ears open," I say, and Az smiles.

The pile of coin in my pocket grows heavier.

CHAPTER 2

NOX

*B*lood doesn't taste the same here as it does in the world from which I hail.

It must be infused with more of the metallic elements than I'm used to back home, because the blood of the hare that I just strangled slides like grease in my mouth, almost stinging, it's so bitter.

I fight a gag—my throat's insistence that the blood doesn't belong —just to get it down.

I don't complain, though. I don't deserve to leech off the blood of others and have the experience remain pleasant.

"You done yet?" Farin asks, a wry look of contempt curling his lip as he watches me feed. One would think that the male who likes to feed off the screams and suffering of others would be less disgusted by my eating habits, but alas—I suppose he's nearly as self-aware as his mother.

Warm blood drips down the sides of my lips and dribbles off my chin, speckling the dirt floor of the cave within which I've been hiding during the daylight hours.

Farin was the one who brought me the hare, as well as a handful of berries that squirt red when I bite into them, flushing my mouth with a sour liquid that honestly isn't much better than the blood. He hunts for me during the day, but only because he doesn't want to waste time on it at night, the only hours in which we can travel together.

He doesn't kill the hares for me. He makes me do that myself.

There's also a part of me that wonders if he picks the berries for their color, but I'm careful with my words around Farin. There's an evil simmering within him, under the surface. Like his keeping me alive is the cracking earth obscuring a molten underground river, and I'm treading on it barefoot.

"The sunlight is fading." Farin crosses his arms and nods toward the horizon as if I hadn't noticed the harbinger of my certain death fading from view. As if I don't have an internal dial always clicking, wondering how precisely it matches up with when the sun will return.

I toss the hare to the side after draining it of blood and choking down the raw meat on its bones. Farin cooks his own meat during the day, but he doesn't bother with enough for me. Probably figures I don't mind eating it raw, though Farin's been in my head, in my body, so I suppose he should know better.

"I'm coming." I wipe my mouth on my sleeve. It's already stained a dark crimson from previous meals.

The last of the daylight fades, and we slip into the night.

THE ISLAND IS frigid at night, which I find disappointing as someone who would have preferred milder weather for a change. I can remember sitting at the feet of merchants in need of my mother's travel wares. They told stories of the beaches of Charshon and their voyages to the Forgotten Isle. I'm positive they always spoke of it being warm, especially since that was all they could think about as they shivered in the Mystral chill after being robbed of their coats by bandits on the Serpentine.

This island is a letdown at best. The nightly wind bites through my thin shirt, because apparently Blaise forgot to weave me a coat. Or maybe she just thinks all islands are warm. Which would be understandable.

The animals here are massive. A hare on this island would probably consider their counterparts from our world food. The flora is peculiar—petals and leaves have a tendency to swivel independently of the wind, like the plants themselves are eavesdropping. The greenery is sparse toward the beaches (which Farin avoids because of the cold spray of the waves, and I avoid because I'm still not confident he won't try to shove my head under the water). But toward the center of the island, it's lush with needled plants that seem well-suited to surviving the cold.

"There's something else here," Farin says as we trudge through the sand, the weight of its resistance taunting us. "Someone. Something. A mission we have to fulfill."

Farin thinks the way to get off this wretched island is to fulfill the story in whatever tapestry we're woven into before Blaise can start another. Before she traps us in a different place, a different time.

He clearly has more faith in Blaise's weaving skills than I do.

I love her, but if I'm going to be honest, I'm just glad she didn't weave us into a void.

Still, it's not in my best interest to dampen Farin's hope. As long as he expects us to beat the tapestry to its conclusion, as long as he thinks we can free ourselves from the island, he has no reason to kill me.

At least, he doesn't *think* he has a reason to kill me.

Apparently, Farin was unfortunate enough to be the first fae upon which the Old Magic placed the lying curse. Back then, the curse hadn't had time to dilute over the course of generations, and he died instantly the first time deception passed from his lips.

He's not eager to repeat the experience, and he knows if he kills me, Blaise will ask him about me when they're reunited. Then he'll have to admit the murder to Blaise, ruining his chances of stealing her from me.

It's not my pick of reasons to be left alive, but I suppose I'll work with what I have.

"What exactly do you think we're looking for?" I'm not really looking for an answer, just an excuse to keep Farin talking. I don't know why, but I feel safer when he's chattering than when he's quiet, even though I always trail him from behind.

He rips a branch from a nearby tree as we forge a path through the overgrowth.

"A story," he says, turning back to me with an obnoxiously sincere look on his face. "What else?"

I fight the urge to roll my eyes. I'm stuck on an abandoned island in a forsaken realm with a monster, and that monster also happens to be a dreamer.

Not that I'm inherently opposed to dreamers, but just about everything about Farin gets under my skin at this point.

"A story? So you think if we can get to the end of the story, fulfill our purpose on this island according to what happens in the tapestry, we'll be free?" *And you'll go back to snatching my body*, I don't add.

"You don't have to keep me talking just to keep me from contemplating killing you, you know," he says, and I have to fight the chill that snakes up my spine. "In fact, you'd think I'd be more concerned with *you* trying to kill *me* than the other way around, yet I allow you to follow at my back every night. Don't you think that's a sign of trust?"

"I suppose." I have contemplated killing Farin. Several times. Mostly utilizing graphic methods. But he's right. I won't kill him. Not when I don't know how the magic in the tapestry works. For all I know, killing Farin here would just send him straight back to my body, right back into Blaise's world. And then he'd be alone with her, and the last time that happened...

Blaise kissing him like her very soul needed it to survive...

I push the thought out of my head, but the writhing in my gut takes a moment to die down, much like the hare I strangled not an hour ago.

Farin wrenches a handful of overgrowth from the trees to make a path for us. "We have the same goal, you know."

"Is that so? And what is that?"

"Blaise's happiness."

I quirk a brow. "Her happiness? And that's really what you think you want?"

Farin smiles, and again, it's innocent enough to fool a serpent.

"Of course. Why? Is that not what you want?"

I want a great many things for Blaise, her happiness being only one of them. Farin must know that, because he has the audacity to look satisfied.

"So you think we'll make our way off this island, beat Blaise to weaving the end of the tapestry, and then we'll fight for her fair and square?"

Farin laughs. "You think I'm delusional."

I don't voice an objection to this.

"It's not as if I don't know what will happen when we return. She'll still want you over me, of course. You've had more time with her than I have, more occasions to win her affections. But I'm a patient male, and she and I are more alike than I think you want to admit to yourself."

"This isn't real."

"Does it have to be?"

Blaise kissing Farin. Blaise kissing Farin like she'd never kissed me.

My gut roils, but my years with Abra have taught me to mask my expression and my voice. "Am I supposed to expect you to play fair? Who's to say when we finish this tapestry, you won't go back to over-taking my body, trapping me in my own head? That seems like the most likely conclusion to this story, doesn't it?"

Farin pauses. I knew it was a risk to admit aloud, though perhaps not as risky as it seems. Farin isn't dull, and he's been in my head long enough to know I'm not dull either. Like it or not, Farin knows how my mind works, and he's well aware that I've already thought through how his plan is going to work out, and not at all in my favor.

"You don't know that," he says, though cautiously. He's swiveled toward me, unwilling to have his back to me any longer. "I'm in my own body now, aren't I?" He gestures to himself. A sturdy build, straw-blond hair. Fates, he looks like a born prince. "Don't you think it's possible that when Blaise wove us into the tapestry separately, she cleaved our two souls?"

Cleave. An utterly useless word, given that it can mean the opposite of itself.

I hesitate to say my next words, but I can already see the cogs in Farin's head spinning in that direction, anyway. Better we talk it through than allow his mind to carry him away. "You might have a body here, but that doesn't mean you have one back home."

Farin cranes his neck to the side. "Are you trying to convince me to kill you, Nox?"

My tongue falters in my mouth. I don't know what my aim is any longer. Except that there's a problem Farin and I both have, one that needs solving, and I don't want him working out a solution on his own.

"No," I say, rubbing the back of my neck. "I'm only saying that if we don't figure something out, we're both faced with the same problem we had before. Even if we both make it back to our world, we're still stuck together, regardless of who commands my body."

He cocks a brow. "More of a problem for you than me, considering I'm the one in control."

I shake my head. "You know that's not true. You said as much to Blaise when you admitted you were furious with the queen for putting you in my body rather than a different one. Because you know she can never love you as long as you're imprisoning me. That she's going to look at you and only ever see me."

Farin plucks a berry off a nearby vine, squeezing it between his forefinger and thumb until it bursts, staining his fingertips red. "You heard our conversation?"

"Of course I heard it. You could hear my conversations when the situation was reversed, couldn't you?"

He nods, almost imperceptibly. "Yes, but I couldn't feel you. Once I had the reins."

I don't know how to respond to that, so I don't.

"Well," he says, straightening a bit and wiping his stained fingertips on his pants. "I suppose if you were there, you know there's a flaw to your logic."

"And what's that?"

"Because if you were there, then you felt how Blaise kissed me. And you know she never kissed you like that."

Blood pounds at my brain, and where I expect a taunting grin to splay across Farin's mouth, all I get is an assessing look.

Farin putting his hands all over Blaise, lowering her onto the bed. My bed.

A vision of ripping Farin's head from his body flashes through my mind. For a moment, we exchange a glance of mutual understanding that I'm about to try.

But then I wonder if that's exactly what he wants. If he thinks his death on this island will send him back, just like I've speculated, but he can't muster up the courage to end it himself.

The thought makes the blood running through my head go cold.

It's well enough, because just then a tendril of smoke hits our noses, calling attention to the glow of a campfire in the distance.

Farin and I exchange a look that communicates we're tabling killing one another until we have a better idea of who else is inhabiting this abandoned island.

We reach the campsite quickly, our feet padding the sandy ground almost silently. The campsite is set on the edge of the beach, far enough from the waves to keep from washing away during high tide.

On a pile of rubble sits a girl who's muttering to herself in a language I don't recognize.

One silent look at Farin tells me he doesn't recognize it either. That shouldn't be surprising. We're in a different realm. There's no reason to expect to recognize any languages here.

Exhaustion mingles with exasperation in my gut. It seems there's no barrier to getting back home that the Fates won't put in our way. I'm debating whether it's even worth trying to communicate with the girl when Farin fidgets, and her neck snaps to the side, following the sound of rustling leaves.

The light of her campfire dances across her features, highlighting a tanned complexion, wide blue eyes, and hair of golden flax.

My heart stutters to a stop when my sister's eyes lock onto mine.

"Well, then," says Farin, stepping out from our hiding place in the brush and beckoning me to follow. "Seems like we've found our story."

CHAPTER 3

KIRAN

*H*umans die.

Asha is human.

Therefore, Asha...

Someone slips into the dark dungeon, the pitiful excuse for a library in the basement of Mystral Castle. According to Blaise, Nox and his mentor spent years building this "library" into what it is today.

What it is today is an insult to the concept of organization, but I can't exactly afford to be as picky as I might like.

The information I'm searching for doesn't tend to make it into civilized collections.

Besides, we're to leave for Othian tomorrow, and I won't be able to take the contents of this library with me. If I'm going to find the answer to my predicament within these volumes, I need to find it today.

The untimely blizzard has kept us trapped, confined to this dank, depressing castle where shadows writhe in the corner of my vision and the drafts from leaky windows whisper paranoia into my ears.

Evander and I have tried to send an explanation of our delay to our wives, but even the couriers refuse to weather storms such as this one.

I've spent every moment aching to return to Asha's side, but now that the storm has cleared and the time to depart draws near, I can't help but wish for more time.

More time to research.

More time with Asha.

That's the thing about being married to a human. Suddenly a resource that has always been unlimited now seems as if it's being squeezed from both sides.

A shadowy figure slinks through the piles of books, melding with the darkness.

"I can see you," I say, shutting the grimoire that's causing a sharp throbbing at my temples and placing it in my lap.

For a moment, no one moves.

"Blaise," I say, unable to hamper the annoyance in my voice.

She wriggles out from behind a stack of books, hands interlocked behind her back, looking the picture of innocence.

She is anything but, but I don't blame her for it. I don't know anyone who could, not after what I witnessed the night she killed her stepmother. We found her cradling her dead stepmother's body, drained of blood, as she cried and wept over a child she never got to name.

No, I don't blame Blaise for the flighty, untrusting woman she's become.

After all, I know what it is like to be so consumed with rage, you feel control slip from your fingertips and into the hands of someone else. Someone who doesn't simply mind spilling blood, but craves it.

That doesn't mean I like her spying on me, regardless.

"I didn't peg you for a reader," she says, swaying slightly. She has a way of doing that, carrying herself so that she seems younger, unsure of herself, boisterous and easygoing.

It's unnerving considering what I've seen her do.

Well, the aftermath of what she's done, I suppose.

"Was it my lively demeanor that dissuaded you?" I ask, sighing.

"That, and that you're usually the guy who gets pegged as the villain once the story gets penned," she says, and though her tone is teasing, her eyes are assessing, watching for my reaction. "And everyone knows villains don't read."

It's something Asha would say. In fact, I'm pretty sure Asha might have said something similar to me when she first arrived at the palace.

"That's ridiculous," I say. "If villains don't read, where do they get all their sinister ideas?"

Something flickers in her eyes, then she takes the seat across from me. It's not empty, so she has to toss aside a pile of books before she plops down onto it. I wince as one hits the floor pages first, parchment crumpling as the book splays.

"What are you doing down here?" I ask.

Blaise picks at her fingernails. "Looking for a good read. Obviously."

"Are you all packed for the journey? We're supposed to be leaving Ermengarde for Othian in the morning."

Blaise's smile is all teeth. I wonder if that's a post-vampirism thing. "Of course, Mother."

I bite my tongue to keep from reminding Blaise she's the reason I've spent months away from my wife. I hated leaving Asha, but I've hated waiting to return to her even more. Especially without means to correspond with her.

"And Nox?" I ask, wondering still how trustworthy Blaise's transport contacts actually are. "Are he and his sister taken care of?"

"Folded up and shoved into my pack."

I don't bother continuing to engage with Blaise, not if she's going to be purposefully elusive. Instead, I open the book I was reading, rifling through the pages until I get to...

"Ooooh. The history of liquid moonlight," says Blaise, now hovering over my shoulder. I jump, having forgotten how much faster she is than even the fae. "That one's a real page-turner, especially when you get to the part about undead—" She stops, her mouth working a bit, then swallows. "What has you so interested in this of all subjects?"

"I'm curious about your condition," I say, craning my neck so that it's not quite so close to Blaise's fangs.

She shoots me a knowing look. "I grew up with the fae, remember? I tend to notice when you make statements that are technically true, even if really, you're just avoiding answering my question."

"Well, it's good to know you're so clever. I'll have to keep that in mind." I return to my book.

"You know what I think?"

I let out a mournful sigh.

"I think you're interested in whether my condition makes me immortal. More importantly, I think you're wondering if my condition could make someone else immortal."

I still, Blaise's accusation lingering in the air.

"I wouldn't wish your condition on anyone I loved," I say, carefully.

"Well, you said it, so it must be true," she says, circling back around my chair and perching directly in front of me on top of a pile of books instead. "Okay, so I revise my theory. I think you want to know if there's a way liquid moonlight can give a person immortality, without tacking on the negative side effects."

I peer at her over the rim of the book. "Considering your condition involves drinking the blood of a vampire and having your neck snapped, it seems as though liquid moonlight on its own might not be the only factor resulting in the thirst for blood or the sunlight curse. Though you've yet to tell us exactly how liquid moonlight was involved."

"And if you did find there was a safe way to grant Asha immortality?" Blaise asks, ignoring my implication entirely.

"Is that supposed to be a question?"

"Would you make her do it?"

The question stuns me, but as I go to make my mouth form the word *no*, I find my tongue hesitates—the beginning of the fae curse that binds me to my vows tingling at the edge of my response.

Blaise cocks her head to the side, though I can't tell what she's thinking. I expect judgment, but when she speaks her gaze is far off, somewhere else entirely. "I'd do it, too. Because it's not fair of them, is it? To ask us to let go of them, when it wouldn't be them who'd have to suffer. When they're the ones leaving us alone, to deal with their deaths all by ourselves."

Again, I find choosing my words around Blaise similar to trying to pick which cup is hiding the coin after a performer has already jumbled up the order. "I didn't say I would take that choice away from her."

Blaise snaps her head back to me. "But you didn't say you wouldn't. In my experience, if you don't make up your mind before-hand, you'll always choose yourself when the pressure of the moment comes."

"Is this why you came down here?" I ask. "To encourage me to be the villain?"

Blaise shrugs. "Are you really the villain if you're just trying to save the people you love?"

CHAPTER 4

NOX

"Now, just remember that since I can't lie, you'll have to," Farin says under his breath, fisting his hand and tapping it against the side of my shoulder lightly as we approach Zora.

"I don't know that lying will be much use if she can't understand us," I say, though I whisper it back, which I recognize is a contradiction to my claim.

I shake my head, trying to clear the flustered haze that's invaded my eyes ever since laying eyes on my sister.

She looks different here, in this world, though I can't know if it's a true difference or just because I haven't seen her awake. Haven't had the chance to witness her demeanor, the way her eyes narrow in suspicion. The way she holds herself, like she's ready to sprint at any moment.

Either way, she spits a string of unintelligible words at us as she whips a blade from her belt.

It's a dull blade. I can tell by the way the firelight seems absorbed by it instead of glinting off the edge. I wonder how long she's gone without sharpening it. If it's even hers.

Farin and I both hold up our palms for her to see, though given the way she hisses at us, it doesn't seem to help a bit.

"Zora," I say, though I'm not sure why. I guess I'm hoping hearing her name will trigger recognition in her, but it's a groundless expectation. If she doesn't even speak our language, it's unlikely her name here is the same as back home.

Something flashes in her eyes at the sight of me. Fear, maybe? It's strange, the way her gaze lingers on me. I can smell the trepidation pumping off of her, though she pays little attention to Farin, who I consider to be the more dangerous of the two of us.

I wonder if that belief is even true.

Maybe she can scent the vampirism on me.

She yells something at us, and I shake my head to indicate I don't understand. I take a careful step forward. She flicks her knife like she intends to launch it at me, but at the last second her fingers close back over the hilt, like she's only just remembered this is her sole weapon, and she's clinging to it for dear life.

Instead, she points the blade toward the sand. Farin and I take this as a command to kneel, and we do, thinking to placate her. Hopefully, we can show her we mean no harm.

"Well, this is going well," Farin says, sounding more nonchalant than I prefer when I'm meeting my sister for the first time since childhood and have no way of communicating with her.

Something about Farin's tone must give her pause, though, because her blade falters.

"You speak Linnish?" she asks, her voice hoarse with thirst.

I've never heard the term before, and my mind is threatening to go off on a scholarly hunt for how our language could possibly have made it to another realm, but I remind myself this isn't the time for that.

"Yes," I say, and Zora swallows, blinking rapidly.

"It's dead," is all she says in return.

It's my turn to blink.

"The language," she says, emphasizing the word by conducting her blade through the air. "It's dead one."

Farin cocks his head to the side. "And yet you speak it."

Zora doesn't seem to know which one of us to point the knife toward, or whether she should be pointing it at either of us at all, because the blade is shaking and zigzagging erratically. "Not well. Not for long time. I must…" She pauses, biting her lip. "I must search for words." She points to her temple with the hand that's not holding the knife. "Some words go missing."

I frown, but my curiosity is getting the better of me. "How do you know Linnish?" I think I'm pronouncing her word for our language correctly, but I'm unsure.

"It was taught in school to me. But for reading and writing. No person speaks this language," she says again, more emphatically this time, as if remembering how suspicious she is of us. As if the curiosity of our language had wiped it from her consciousness for a moment. "Who are you?"

I look at Farin, but he only shrugs, his palms still held out in front of him. "This is all you."

Right. This Farin not being able to lie thing is going to be inconvenient. Though I suppose I should be grateful that my vampirism allows me to skirt the curse. I rifle around in my brain for a lie that might be convincing. I can't very well spout out the name of a country without her knowing I'm making it up. If Zora was taught a dead language in her schooling, I can't imagine geography wasn't part of that education.

However…

"We're voyagers from across the Great Sea," I say. "Our people search for new lands, as ours have dried up," I say, pulling from legends of the Nether. "Thanks to a storm, we were shipwrecked here. My friend and I are the only survivors, at least that we've been able to find. There could be others, but we're beginning to doubt that. We're just trying to survive. To find a way off this island."

"To explore this new world?" Zora asks.

I shake my head and fight the burning in my eyes. "At this point, we'd just like to get back home."

"You said home is dry," she says.

"That doesn't make it any less home," I murmur.

31

I try not to think about the last memory I have from home. Of Blaise kissing Farin with enough fervor that even I believed it.

"Hm." She surveys both of us with those wide eyes of hers. Fates, they hurt to look at. Everything else about her has changed so much, but her eyes are the same.

Except that they don't recognize me.

Still, she lowers her knife.

When I shoot her a questioning look, she says, "Alone? Difficult to stay alive. Not alone? Staying alive has better chances."

I hate how she sounds like she knows from experience.

"Unless you try to eat me," she says with a shrug. "Then, staying alive much harder. So don't do that."

Farin flashes her the kind of grin that makes my stomach flip. "We wouldn't dream of it, would we, Nox?"

Zora's eyes flash again with something that I can't help but hope is recognition at the sound of my name, but if there's a part of her that remembers anything connected to her original life, she doesn't mention it.

My sister brings her knife back to her side and stuffs it in a belt that clearly did not belong to her originally. She's punched an extra hole in the belt so it'll fit her waist, and now the blade rests exposed at her hip.

"That's dangerous, to keep your knife there. What happens if you slip and it twists?" Farin asks her.

Zora shoots him a look of acid, one I find immensely satisfying.

"When I stab myself on accident, here is my permission to laugh at me then," she says, and it's so much like the Zora I remember, I almost laugh. Almost.

Farin's eyes linger on my sister a tad too long for my liking. "I'll remember that. There's a cave back that way," he says, pointing into the brush. "It makes for a better shelter than the beach."

Zora immediately looks wary, and she opens her mouth to say something, but then she clamps it shut and allows a wry grin to over-take her face. She gestures in front of her. "Lead my way."

She follows us from behind, careful to stay at both of our backs.

. . .

"You never told us your name," I say, examining Zora as she scarfs down the berries I left untouched before my and Farin's expedition. She's thinner here than she is back home. Her cheeks are caverns compared to what they usually are. The sullenness of them highlights her cheekbones and makes them look as if they'll slice anyone who comes near, especially in the light of the fire we've lit in the cave. Her hair is different too. In Abra's shrine, it falls across the emerald dais in waves before cascading to the floor. Here she has it cropped short and messy, barely long enough to cover her pointed ears, as if having it any longer would only get in her way.

"Elini," she says in between handfuls of berries. "And you are Nox," she says, nodding at me. She gestures toward Farin. "And you are?"

The grin that warps Farin's lips has my fingers clenching into a fist.

"Whoever you want me to be," he says, as easily as one might expect from someone as schooled in manipulation as he is, being Abra's child.

Zora's cheeks flush red, leaving me for once grateful for the disgusting hare blood currently sloshing in my stomach. I'll have to be careful to keep myself satiated around my sister. My hunger is always worse around those whose blood I've already tasted. For years, Abra punished me by forcing me to feed on Zora. I'm just waiting for the cravings to kick in, nauseous as it makes me to consider that.

Still, whatever makes blood in this realm taste so vile must also have an appetite-curbing effect, because though I note the smattering of blood across her cheeks, my hunger doesn't stir.

My irritation, on the other hand, does.

Apparently it's not enough for Farin to gloat about taking Blaise away from me; he also feels the need to flirt with my sister while he's at it.

"Your true name will be just fine," she says evenly, schooling her voice even if she can't hide her flush.

He tells her, and she tries the name out on her tongue. "Farin," she says, as if it's familiar to her. "Kind to meet you, Farin."

"The pleasure is mine," he says back, and the curious smile that brushes his features almost makes him look sane. It's unnerving.

"What landed you on this island?" I ask, hoping to break the smoldering stare between my sister and the male who'd rather see me dead.

"A shipwreck. Same as two of you."

"Yes, but why were you on a ship?" I ask.

She raises an eyebrow at me. "To sail. Are there other reasons?"

"I think what my companion means is where were you hoping to arrive? I imagine it wasn't this island," Farin says.

"Ah. That." Zora wipes her mouth hesitantly on her tattered sleeve. "I was..." She furrows her brow for a moment before shaking her head. "The word is gone from my head." Zora makes a starburst motion with her hand before returning to her food.

Farin and I exchange a look, but we don't press her further.

"And you?" she asks. "You find cave, yet you leave it at night when caves are most useful."

That question catches me off guard, but Zora's staring at me, not at Farin, so I can't let it show on my face.

"Oh, that's to be more accommodating to Nox's sleep schedule," Farin says, not helping in the slightest. It's technically not a lie, though it only barely borders the truth.

"In our homeland, most of the game is nocturnal," I explain. "Those of us who hunt must do so under the cover of night."

I'm fairly pleased with my answer until she looks me up and down and says, "Forgive me. You don't look same as hunter." Then she turns to Farin. "You look like hunter."

A smile flickers at Farin's lips, but his eyes don't partake. "That was my father. I'm afraid I didn't inherit his skill."

It strikes me then that Farin is speaking the truth.

"Hm. Too bad," she says before looking at her berry-stained, empty hands with a forlorn expression. Then, without warning, she curls up on the ground and goes to sleep.

I decide that when I manage to wake Zora from her enchanted slumber, we're having a long talk about safety awareness.

Farin retires next, leaning against the cave wall and closing his eyes. I listen to his breath until it slows, though I don't trust him not to be faking sleep.

I spend the next several hours playing over my plan in my mind, though calling it a plan would probably be more generous than it's worth. More like the beginnings of a dozen plans, none of them actually taking form, since all of them seem to have unpleasant consequences if they go wrong.

My inclination is still to kill Farin, but there seems to be a fifty-fifty chance that this will send his consciousness back into my body. My body, which resides in the same world as Blaise. That's not exactly something I'm willing to risk. We seem to be on our way to fulfilling whatever Blaise's tapestry has in store for us now that we've met Zora. Because of the ritual Abra performed on my body, I'm still fairly certain this will end with me waking in my own body, but trapped under Farin's influence, so I'm less than enthused about his plan.

I could kill myself, hoping that would send my consciousness back to my body, but again, this seems risky, given that if I die here, I don't know that I won't die there too. Or worse, die here and allow Farin free rein of my body with me out of the way.

Free to sweep into Blaise's life and take my place.

There's a part of me that feels guilty for even thinking that way, for doubting her. For entertaining the idea that Blaise could allow herself to be entranced by a monster like Farin.

But she's fallen for a monster already, hasn't she?

She discovered I was a bloodthirsty murderer who preyed on the innocent, and she'd seen herself in me.

There's a part of me that worries Blaise loves me because of the darkness that haunts me. A part of her that loves that we're no different. That I understand her.

That same part of me worries that Farin's darkness might be just as intoxicating, if not more potent.

I try to trust her, but it's a struggle between the two sides of my consciousness, and I've never learned to master the balance.

Besides, there's no unfeeling her kiss on my lips, hungry and desperate and consuming. But that kiss wasn't for me.

It was for him.

I know I should give Blaise more credit than that. I know I should have more confidence in her. After all, that kiss hadn't been without intention. She'd used it to lull Farin into a false sense of security before she pricked him with Gunter's spindle and sent both of us barreling into this unfamiliar realm.

I asked her to kill me, and instead she bought me more time.

I understand. I really do. But I think maybe understanding, being able to walk myself through the logical sense of things, is different than believing.

It's the believing I have a difficult time with.

Blaise's kiss haunts me until the heat of it lulls me into a restless slumber.

I wake to a sharp pain cracking my skull.

CHAPTER 5

BLAISE

"I'm going to help you get him back."

Evander's voice startles me; I didn't realize he'd entered my room. I quickly stuff Nox's tapestry into my satchel as I pack my things for our upcoming journey to Othian.

"I don't know what you need from me," he says. "Where you'll need to go to get the answers about how to cure him. And I know dealing with this nonsense about Abra and the Rip takes priority. But when the time comes for you to bring him back, I'm coming with you. As long as you want it, I'll make sure you're not alone."

I blink, suddenly exhausted. "You don't have to do that, Andy."

He fidgets, his fingers tapping against the doorway. "I think that maybe I do."

My heart sinks. I know why Evander's offering this. He feels responsible for not recognizing the signs of abuse I suffered as a child. I suppose it's true, that while he couldn't have stopped Derek from assaulting me, he could have forced his way into the manor while my stepmother kept me locked in the attic during the entirety of my pregnancy. Could have recognized that something was very, very wrong.

But none of what happened to me is Evander's fault.

Still. It's nice for him to offer.

I should tell him no. Release him from his vow. Evander is sweet, but he's always been a people-pleaser. Rash. His fae curse won't let him out of his promise, even if he comes to regret it.

I open my mouth, about to tell him that I don't accept that promise. Or to tell him it's already been fulfilled by him following me all the way to Ermengarde.

But the feel of the tapestry is still at my fingertips, where I haven't closed my satchel yet. Visions of Nox's infinite deaths swirl across my vision.

And I realize I might need Andy's help getting to the Rip.

Whether he knows the treachery he's agreeing to or not.

So instead, I choke out, "Thanks, Andy."

And when the guilt threatens to swarm me, I shove it into my satchel with Nox's tapestry.

THE WAGON in which we're to travel to Othian reminds me of the kind they use in funeral processions.

In the past few weeks, Evander and Kiran managed to construct the skeleton of the wagon out of wood coated in tar, perfect for keeping out sunlight.

At first, Kiran suggested we travel by foot. Both fae and vampires have a tendency to outperform horse-drawn wagons in speed.

I wouldn't have been able to carry my loom without the wagon, so I convinced them the trip would go faster if we traveled without stopping, Evander and Kiran directing the wagon during the day while I slept. Then I could direct it at night.

Of course, I didn't bring up the loom or the tapestry.

Kiran and Evander know I work on tapestries, but they're under the impression it's to help with my nerves. It keeps up the illusion that Abra is the one holding Nox and Zora in their sleep state.

So now, when I'm alone in the wagon and supposed to be sleeping, instead I weave.

. . .

As WE REACH the border of Mystral and Dwellen, the blizzard decides it's not done with us.

Thankfully, we find a cavern in the side of the mountains large enough to pull the wagon into, protecting it from the howling storm outside.

I leave the loom and Nox's tapestry inside the wagon, not wishing to draw more attention to it than necessary. But still, I find my mind envisioning, almost obsessively, wrenching the threads from the body of the Fabric, plucking Nox from the hands of death itself.

"I can help with that, if you'd like." Kiran's voice is a low rumble coming from the shadows on the other side of the cavern.

The firelight he produced with his bare hands now dances, seemingly sourceless, in the middle of the wide space. It flickers across his features, highlighting his stern jawline, the beard he's let grow since we disembarked from Ermengarde.

It takes me a moment to understand what he means, but then he nods at my fingers. I glance down at them. They're twisted against my skin where I've been pinching myself without realizing it.

"Oh." I blink myself back to reality as I cross my arms in front of my chest. "No, that's okay."

Kiran frowns, cocking his head to the side slightly. "Are you sure?"

I'm honestly surprised Kiran is bringing up the power he seems to keep hidden from most people. But I suppose Evander is fast asleep in the corner.

I imagine it then, the surreal comfort that would wash over me with one touch from Kiran. He could take away the anguish twisting inside me. He wouldn't even have to blink.

I've already felt that kind of peace once. It's the type that could become addicting if I let it.

It's not as though I'm someone who stands easily against addictive tendencies, it's just… "The pain… I know this sounds stupid, but it helps me feel closer to him," I say, locating the bond in my heart that I sometimes think I can feel—the bloodsharing oath that binds us, even when the Fabric of realms separates us. Sometimes I think it's my imagination. Other times…

Well, I cling to it regardless.

Kiran shakes his head. Thoughtfulness stretches his lips as he leans against the wall. "It doesn't sound stupid."

I nod my head, grateful he doesn't offer it to me a second time. I'm not sure I'm strong enough to deny the offer twice, and my longing to feel close to Nox isn't the only thing causing my hesitation to accept kindness from Kiran.

I'm going to betray him, and I'd rather he not waste his time being nice to me.

"Thanks for offering anyway," I say, though my verbal gratitude means little in the face of what I plan to do.

Still, there's Az's theory. That Kiran uses his power over Asha to control her emotions. If that's true, then I suppose I have nothing to feel guilty about.

"Why do you hide it?" I ask.

Kiran raises a brow.

"Your power over emotions, I mean."

Kiran settles into the cave wall, closing his eyes as he leans against it. "At first, it was because I feared how my father"—he clears his throat on that word for some reason—"might view it. You don't have to be all that creative to imagine how he might have used it to torture his enemies."

I shudder, and my mind can't help but flash to what Kiran's touch might do to me, if he ever gets his hands on me after I hand Asha over to Az.

My mouth goes dry. "I can imagine."

"Once my father was gone, I was old enough to recognize that no one would trust someone who could manipulate their emotions. There would be no chance of diplomacy between myself and the other kingdoms."

I scoff, and his eyes shoot open.

"What?"

"I mean, you didn't seem to be too concerned with diplomacy when you decreed you'd kill your bride the morning after your wedding."

Kiran's molten eyes glaze over, as if he's far off. "No, I wasn't concerned with much else other than dousing my pain with anything that could distract me from it. Though it seems the other rulers didn't care what I did to my human subjects."

We let that thought settle uncomfortably between us.

"Do you use it often?"

Kiran shakes his head. "Not intentionally. Though I received no instruction in controlling it, so when my emotions are heightened, it seems to seep out of me, as much as I try to contain it."

Ah, there it is.

If Kiran's emotions are heightened with love when he's near Asha, is it possible he leaks his love into her, causing her to believe she loves him back?

I'm not sure that makes Kiran a villain, but it does reinforce Az's claim that Asha's feelings can't be trusted.

"If you're so bent on keeping your power a secret," I ask, "then why did you take away my pain that night?"

Kiran stares at me intently and appears to test his words before he speaks them. I'm used to that, having grown up around the fae. I know what it looks like when they're scanning their words for possible lies.

Finally, he settles on, "It wasn't difficult to take pity on you, finding you in that state."

Something about his words makes me feel naked.

Despite that, there's something he doesn't say. A truth he's had to work around.

I don't press him, but eventually he must decide it's worth telling me, because he sits up straighter, swallowing before he continues. "When I murdered Fin's wife, Ophelia, it was in a bout of rage over the fact she'd ruined my relationship with my brother by offering herself to me. The rage consumed me, so much so that when I think back to that moment, to my fire devouring her, I can't help but feel that it wasn't me. Even though logically I know it was. Even though I accept responsibility for my actions, for my loss of control. But, Blaise, I know what it is to look at the aftermath of losing control and

41

think, 'What have I done? That wasn't me.' And even then, knowing what that awful stepmother of yours did to you, I still don't know half of the pain you've endured. But I suppose I know a fraction of it, and even that was almost too much for me to bear. At least, not on my own. I just...I suppose I didn't want you to have to bear it all by yourself, especially if I could hold onto some of it for you. Even for just a moment."

A lump swells in my throat at the words that go unsaid between us.

Something cracks within me, a sliver in the fortress I've built around my heart.

All of a sudden, I'm conflicted. The urge to bare my soul to him, to admit the betrayal simmering in my heart, taps against the fissure.

Would Kiran help me, if he knew? If I admitted the truth of why I need Asha to open the Rip? That it's the only force powerful enough to separate Farin from Nox's body, the only way to free the male I love?

The part of me who is dreading going through with this plan, terrified to sacrifice not only my friends but my soul, aches to tell him. Hope, stoked by our freshly kindled friendship, flickers in my chest, whispering in my ear. *You can trust him*, it says.

But then I recall finding Kiran in the library, poring over grimoires, searching the depths of the literature on dark magic to find a cure for Asha's mortality.

And I remember that, as kind as Kiran has been to me, he will always put Asha's safety first. Of course, he will. It's only right. She's his wife, and it would be foolish of him to risk harm coming to her for my sake.

Just like it would be foolish of me to let Nox die for Kiran's sake.

Which is what will happen if Kiran learns what Az and I have planned.

Because at the end of the day, friends don't come for friends. Not when they have family and lovers who take precedence.

"We should probably be getting some sleep," Kiran says, snapping me out of my tumultuous thoughts. "Unless there's anything else you'd like to talk about?"

I blink, then swallow, shaking my head.

Kiran examines me with those molten eyes of his, and for a moment, I worry he sees right through me. But then he tucks his satchel behind his head, propping himself against the cave wall, and closes his eyes.

I can't help the relief that floods through me when his breathing slows.

I'm aware that it's a shoddy excuse—claiming I can't very well tell Kiran now that he's asleep.

But I nurse the excuse regardless.

Up to this point, I haven't allowed myself to reconsider the plan.

I need time to think.

Perhaps by morning, I'll have figured out what to do.

Perhaps the answer will come to me in a dream.

CHAPTER 6

KIRAN

Humans die, rattles a voice, one that wakes me from my deep slumber and lures me to consciousness.

Asha is human, it whispers, its gentle cadence resounding in my skull.

Therefore, Asha...

I snap my eyes open, my breathing ragged as my eyes adjust quickly to the cave. The fire I made to keep us warm through the frigid night still burns, though it waned slightly as I slept.

Humans die, whispers the voice again, and it's the first time I realize it's not my own.

Though the voice reverberates in my very bones, it's as if there's a source to it, a rope tugging me toward its owner, leading into the gaping maw of the tunnel that stretches behind us and into the depths of the mountain.

Asha is human, it whispers, sounding mournful now, its voice warbling. *Therefore, Asha...*

No. I try to shake the voice away, but I've run the words over so many times in my mind, they're etched into the very fabric of my consciousness.

I stand, placing my hand against the cool wall of the cavern. As if I need that to guide myself in the dark. As if my fae sight doesn't adjust on my behalf. As if I can't make a light source out of the air between my fingertips.

I can save her, whispers the voice, and my heart stops in my chest.

That's impossible, I mouth back, but I can't say it aloud, because I know it isn't true. Not when Blaise, living evidence contrary to my point, sleeps soundlessly across the fire from me, the flames highlighting her features. Though nothing about her pallor indicates health, at least she's alive.

Here.

With me.

It's the here with me part that Asha won't be. Not in a handful of decades, at least.

Bring the girl. She can help too, says the voice, and I find my feet crossing the cavern to obey. When I lean over and scoop Blaise into my arms, I'm shocked that she doesn't stir, but the thought quickly flees from my mind.

I step over Evander, still fast asleep on the ground, and carry Blaise into the depths of the cave.

THE VOICE CALLS ME, and the further we draw into the recesses of the cavern, the more familiar it sounds, though I can't quite place it.

Sometimes it's Asha calling to me, sometimes it's my mother from the grave. Sometimes it's a mixture of Lydia's and Fin's voices, or how I imagine they would have sounded if they held any affection for me during childhood.

My footsteps hardly make a sound against the damp floor of the cave, though moisture dripping from the stalactites does.

I can help her. I can save her, whispers the voice, and I find I believe it.

The dark tunnels break off into a series of paths, but there's no question which way is forward, not with that voice tugging on my heart like an anchor to the bow of a ship.

So I follow it into the darkness.

I'm not sure how much time passes before I arrive at what I somehow know in the recesses of my soul is my destination.

The bowels of the mountain swarm with a substance that appears as shadows one moment, a thick mist the next, depending on how the dim lights from the glowing fungi that crust the walls of the cavern shine on it.

You came, my child. You listened. I can help you.

I shake my head. "I don't need your help. It's my wife."

Ahh. Humans die, and Asha is human. This is your fear, your problem.

"Yes," I say with a shudder, staring into the gaping hole in the center of the cavern, where nothingness swarms in a void.

There's a sense that pricks at the back of my neck, one that signals that perhaps I should be afraid of this creature, but I am not afraid.

This creature knows me.

It sees and hears the darkness and does not judge me for it.

"How do I save her?" I ask, and though part of my mind wonders how I can expect this creature to know, the thought is quickly blanketed in silky sheets of trust.

Shadows lick from the creature, reaching out. At first, I think they'll consume me, but then they stop at Blaise, caressing her pale cheeks with the care of an adoring mother.

This child is one of mine, it croons. *She does not know her mother, though I wish she would.*

"I could wake her for you."

That won't be necessary, the being snaps.

"Who are you?" I ask, suddenly dying to know who this being is who promises help to my wife.

I am Marthala, says the shadows, *though I suppose it is not my name you wish to hear, but the solution to your problem.*

Shame washes over me that I've managed to offend this being, the very being who's trying to help.

You wish your wife would never grow aged, says the creature, curiosity slipping into her tone.

I shake my head. "No. No, it's not the aging process that terrifies me. I just...I can't stand the thought of her dying. My life is an eternity compared to hers, and I can't bear the thought that hers will just be a turn of the page in mine. She's my story," I add, worrying that maybe the creature won't understand. "I can't have it be over in the turn of a page. What's the point of the rest of my story if hers has already come to a close?"

Nothing, nothing is the point, muses the creature, and though it seems to understand, I can't help the dread that snakes up my spine.

Blaise stirs in my arms. I'd forgotten I was even holding her. Perhaps I should wake her. Perhaps if Marthala can save Asha, she knows how to save Nox, too.

As soon as the idea brushes my consciousness, it slips away from me.

The girl you hold embodies a scourge—the bane of the moon trapped on the earth. It is why she cannot bear the light of the sun, why she is cursed to slink in the shadows. Children of darkness cannot withstand the light. It is a wicked thing, exposing our flaws and wishing for us to be grateful to it.

"I don't wish for Asha to bear the curse," I say. "But if there's a way to give her immortality without invoking it—"

There's always a curse, my child. Always a price that must be paid, says the creature, almost contemplative.

"Then let me be the one to bear it," I whisper.

The shadows lick in curiosity around my feet, like a cat intertwining itself between my ankles.

What is your limit, my child?

"Nothing," I say. "There's nothing I wouldn't do for her."

Ah. Well, then. I suppose you'll be eager to hear the price is within your grasp.

I'm not sure why, but my gaze falls to Blaise, her eyes still and peaceful in slumber.

Immortality lies within her, but it can be severed from its master.

"How?"

What steals immortality away from a child of the night, young one?

I think back to the research I did in the libraries at Othian. "Sunlight against the skin."

Marthala hisses.

"Or separating a heart from its master's body." My gaze falls to Blaise's chest, rising and falling smoothly in slumber.

She was born of the ashes, though in the second generation, says the creature. *Your wife could be born of the ashes as well. Take the girl's heart and burn it for your wife to consume. The ashes would give life to the dead—they would certainly gift a living girl immortality.*

I frown, pain thrumming against my temple. "If it can be done with Blaise's heart, it could be done with another's, could it not?"

Mmm, says the shadows, *but when is the next time you'll find a child of the night within your grasp? When is the next time it would be so easy? This opportunity might not stumble upon you again,* says the shadow.

My ears attune to the gentle patter of Blaise's heart against her chest. There would be a certain rightness to it, I suppose. Blaise has already died, has she not? Whatever life she's been given is a bonus tacked on to the end of her mortality.

And I know Blaise suffers under the curse.

Asha wouldn't suffer, not when this manner bypasses the consequences.

Or at least, the curse—the knowledge of what I had done to Blaise —would belong to me.

Blaise said herself that she drowns herself in misery. This way, I could make it painless for her. Provide her with a hint of my powers, enough to coax her into bliss, the only bliss she might ever find in this life.

Anyone would trade a lifetime of misery for a moment of bliss.

I lay my hand across her sternum, feeling the steady thrum of her heart against my palm. Then I sneak my finger up to touch her neck.

Blaise's eyes snap open, and she attacks.

BLAISE'S FANGS shoot out from her gums as she lunges for my neck.

She's faster, but I already have her in my grasp.

All it takes is a slight maneuver of my hand. My fingers brush her skin, and then she's mine.

Blaise's body goes limp as my magic flows through her, the magic I draw from every peaceful memory I have.

Reading silently in the library with Asha's family. Falling asleep with Asha by my side at night, her body tucked into my chest. The smile on my wife's face as she plays with Nagivv.

I herd the feelings, then forward them to Blaise, soothing her wild, tumultuous rage until her eyes close and sleep descends upon her.

Once she stills, I shove my hand into her chest.

BONES CRACK and splay as my fingers close around Blaise's heart.

It's much colder than I might have imagined a beating heart to be, but this only serves to ensure my decision is the right one.

Blaise isn't truly alive, not as Asha will be.

Still, I whisper an apology to her.

I think in a different life, we might have been friends.

"Kiran," someone cries, someone who's barreling toward me. "Kiran, stop!" Evander launches himself from a raised cliff in the wall, his fall cracking stone as he lands, still sprinting toward me. I'm not sure how he found us, but I don't have time for such questions.

You mustn't stop, you must do it now. The boy wants the heart for himself, to raise his brother, whispers the shadow.

"Kiran, it's a trap. She's trying to trick you." Evander skids to a stop, his eyes going wide as his gaze slips.

"Kiran, please," Evander whispers, his gaze transfixed on my hand, plunged into Blaise's chest cavity. "Please. You're not a monster. I don't know what this creature is promising you, but whatever the promise is, it's not real. Blaise, though? Blaise is real, and if you rip her heart out, you won't be able to bring her back."

Your wife or the night stalker? whispers the voice. *Who do you choose?*

I offer an apologetic look to Evander. "I can't..." I whisper. "I can't be without her."

Something akin to understanding dawns on Evander's face. "It's offering to make Asha immortal." Evander nods, then swallows, sweat pouring down his face. "Of course it is. It told me I could bring my brother back. It's telling us exactly what it thinks we want to hear."

"Maybe it can do both." My hands tremble now, and it's getting harder to keep Blaise calm when her body wants nothing more than to send her into a flight of panic.

"No, Kiran," Evander says. "It can't bring back the dead. You know that. You know that's crazy."

"You wouldn't do it, even for him? Even for your brother?" I ask, something in my mind knocking like it wants to be let out. I try to quash the noise, because it's making it difficult to focus.

"It's in your head," Evander insists. "You wouldn't do this. It's trying to control you, and you can't let it."

"I can't let her die," I whisper, then snap my gaze back up to Evander. "Would you let Ellie die? She could have it too, you know —immortality."

Evander's face pales, but then he glances at Blaise and holds his ground.

"Ellie would never forgive me if I murdered for her. Would Asha forgive you?"

Would Asha forgive me?

She's pardoned me of so much more than I'd imagined was forgivable. She would. Asha will forgive me.

But she won't understand.

She'll do what she always does and blame herself. She'll take Blaise's death on as if it were her own.

If I kill Blaise, Asha will spend the rest of her immortal existence mourning her.

Just then, something clicks in my mind, and it's like a door being slammed open, the rest of my consciousness freed to flood back in.

My hand is still closed around Blaise's heart.

Horror overcomes me, and I uncurl my fingers, extracting my hand from her chest before I can do any more damage.

Something screams, and Evander covers his ears. It takes me a moment to realize I have, too.

Shadows swirl about the room, encompassing us, and the air is sucked from my lungs. The dark tendrils shoot into Evander's nose and mouth, and I'm brought back to the image of Calias drowning Asha and Fin.

No, no, no.

Evander's mouth widens, like he's crying out, but no sound emerges.

Another band of shadows shoots for Blaise's heart, as though Marthala will rip it out herself if she has to.

The shadows don't get to her.

Because I erupt into Flame.

CHAPTER 7

NOX

*I*t takes me a moment after the pain to absorb the facts of my current situation.

I'm at the bottom of a pit, one whose walls reach too high for me to climb.

Someone threw me down here. That explains the splitting headache.

Last of all, and most importantly, the instinct carved into the back of my consciousness—the one I never quite turn off—sounds an alarm.

Because the sun is about to rise, and there's no shade in sight.

"How did you get out?"

Zora's voice knocks me back to reality. Or, this reality, at least. I shoot to my feet, my pounding head keeping my feet from being completely steady.

"Zora, you have to help me out of here," I say, though I know immediately it's no use. No use, because she's the one who dumped me here.

She paces at the ledge of the pit, clawing her fingers through her cropped hair like she's trying to yank a realization from her mind, one she'd rather toss into this pit with me before leaving me to burn.

"How did you get out?" she asks, again spinning toward me, staring down at me from above with a crazed expression warping her typically warm features.

I choose my words carefully. "I'm not out of this pit. But I need you to help me get out, and quickly."

"Not out of *the pit*," she practically yells. "Out of my head. How did you get out of my head?"

Words fail to reach my lips. My skull is still pounding, panic making my heart race. I'm having a hard time focusing on anything other than my primal awareness of the location of the sun.

"I'll explain everything," I say, though I have no idea what she's talking about. "Just toss me a vine so I can climb out, and I'll tell you anything you want to know."

She shakes her head, her cropped hair bouncing as she does. "No. You'll tell me from down there. Right now. Then I'll decide whether you're worth letting out or not."

I grit my teeth. "You don't understand. There's not enough time. If you don't get me out of this pit before the sun comes up—"

"Then you'll burn," she says, her voice devoid of emotion. "Yeah, I know. Vampires have a tendency to do that."

The change in her speech hits me, the way she no longer searches for words or skips over simple connecting phrases.

"You didn't learn our language from a tutor, did you?" I ask.

She stares me down rather than answering.

I sigh, backing to the edge of the pit, thinking maybe the wall will provide me a few moments of shade once the sun rises.

That, and I'm exhausted enough that having the cool wall to support my back feels necessary at the moment.

"Where do you want me to start?" I ask.

"I already told you," she says. "How did you get out of my head? Are you a wraith of some sort? A dream walker? I didn't think vampires could dream walk, but maybe in other realms…"

I frown, pinching my forehead. "I don't know what you're talking about."

She lets out a disbelieving huff, propping her fists against her hips.

"You visit me in my dreams. You're a recurring nightmare of mine. Have been for years."

My stomach starts to hollow out, and the realization of what she's referring to hits me only slightly too late.

Her already sallow cheeks go sunken. "You feed on me in my dreams—"

"Zora—"

"And it's like I can't move. Can't even scream. I'm totally helpless. And then just as I think this is it, that I'm going to die, this female comes and breaks your ne—"

"Zora—"

"Stop calling me that," she snaps, and I clamp my jaw shut, shame washing over me.

"I can explain, but you have to..." I trail off, realizing now that even if there was a chance she'd let me out of this pit on trust alone, I wouldn't deserve it. Not after the torture I've put her through for years.

She seems to be thinking the same thing, because she nods at me, daring me to continue.

I swallow, squeeze my eyes shut, and try to find the words to explain.

"This isn't your world. Your original world, I mean." I open my eyes, expecting Zora to have stormed off, interpreting my words as a poorly crafted lie. A desperate grab for an escape. But she hasn't moved. Her eyes are cold as stone, but her pointed ears are perked at attention.

"You've lived many lives," I say, continuing on hesitantly. "This one isn't your first, and it's certainly not the original."

Zora blinks hard, and I can hear her heart pounding, bouncing off the walls of the pit, even from down here. "Yes, I know that I'm one of the reincarnate."

I can't help but sigh. I didn't expect her to follow me this far. "So you remember them? The other lives?"

"I'm not the one answering questions right now."

I nod. She's right. I don't have time to be interrogating her before the sun comes up. By my judgment, we have less than a quarter of an hour. If that.

"Right. I..." I swallow, struggling to corral my whirling thoughts in my panic. Calm. I have to stay calm. Logical. Like Gunter would have me do.

My heart gives a dull pang, but it's enough to propel me forward. "The realm I come from, that's your realm, too. The one you were born in. The one where your original body lies."

"So I'm dead in that realm," she says, a slight tremble in her voice, though I can tell by the strain in her throat she's trying to hide it.

I shake my head. "No. No, you're just asleep. You were enchanted —cursed, really, into a magical slumber. Those who enchanted you wished to use you, partially so you could realm-walk, partially to..."

"To what?"

I take a breath. "Partially to punish me."

There's nothing but dread in her expression, like there's something she desperately doesn't want me to say.

"Why would my fate be a punishment to you?" she asks.

"Because I'm your...family." I'm not sure why I omit that I'm her brother, her twin. Maybe it's because it makes it sound all the worse that I've spent years torturing her. When she gives me a look that says "family" is too vague a word for her liking, I add, "Your twin."

"Twins are Fates-cursed to ruin one another," she whispers.

I grimace. "That is a superstition they hold in our world."

She shakes her head. "Yours isn't the only one. If you're my brother, and if that actually matters to you, why do you feed on me?"

I fumble for the words, but they get caught in my throat. "My master seeks to punish me when I step out of line. She already has you captive, so I suppose she had to get more creative with her punishments. When I behave in a way she finds particularly displeasing, she locks me in a room with you until I break."

Zora's chin twitches. "And then?"

"And then I feed on you until she deems it time to end my punishment."

Zora looks at her toes, swallowing. "And what's her purpose for me? The realm-walking, I mean. What's my mission?"

I blink, stunned a bit. "Your mission?"

Zora chews at her cheek. "My mission. My purpose. What am I supposed to do with my lives? What are they all for?"

The anxiety, the longing that sneaks into her words, stirs something aching within me.

"I'm not entirely sure," I admit. "My master's magic isn't like some of the other rulers'. Hers comes by knowledge more than an innate gift. I think knowledge makes her feel secure. I imagine she wishes to glean information about other realms from your experiences."

Zora blinks, shifts her weight, then swallows. "That's it? That's all I was supposed to do? Gather information?"

I crane my head at her, confused by her reaction. "I'm not entirely sure. The queen never really gave me that information. I didn't even know you were realm-walking until recently. Why is what she wants important to you?"

"It's not," she says, and the words bite. Her gaze flits to the horizon, and I know before she opens her mouth what she just witnessed.

"Zora, you have to get me out of here. When the sun comes up, I'm going to burn."

"So? You'll just go back to our home realm, right?" She's pacing again, and it makes me nervous.

"I'm not sure that's how it works." I search for roots, vines, anything to get me out of this pit.

She scoffs, which I suppose is understandable.

"Besides, I don't think you want to end up alone on this island with Farin," I say.

She whips her head back in my direction. "I can't say I'm all that afraid of him when he's not the one who tortures me in my nightmares."

My legs are shaking of their own accord now, fidgeting with nervous energy as my eyes search and fail to find any footholds that might help me out of this pit. I might be able to hide in the shade for a moment, but even the shade would be subject to some amount of sunlight. If I'm interpreting my internal calculations and Zora's flickering gaze correctly, I only have a few minutes.

"Zora, please. Please trust me," I say, because it's the only thing I have left. Not logic. Not reason. Just the hope that somewhere in my twin's heart, there's a bond that won't allow me to die.

Not that the bond has ever kept me from almost killing her during Abra's punishments.

I ingest the shame that's threatening to overtake me and stare into my sister's eyes. She rips her gaze away and crosses her arms, but then her shoulders slump.

"Fine," she says. "But only because I have more questions."

I can't say relief floods my chest at that, because I'm still not confident we have enough time to get me out of this pit, but I don't complain.

"Any vines around you could toss in my direction?" I ask, though my voice is rather devoid of hope at this point.

She bites her lip and scans the area, shaking her head.

"Logs of some sort?"

"I don't see any."

"I'd accept them in all varieties at this point: bumpy, smooth, even rotting."

Zora shakes her head again, hugging her chest. She's hardly moved to look for anything, and I realize panic has frozen her in place.

"There's got to be sticks up there," I say, "something you can toss down that I can use as picks to help me climb up."

"I don't..."

"Zora, please," I say.

Her gaze flits back to me, and for that fleeting breath of a moment, it's almost like she sees me. The me that she knew before. Her childhood playmate. Her partner in mischief.

But then her gaze flickers to the horizon. Sorrow floods her features, and I know we're too late.

"Nox. Nox," she says, her legs finally moving, pacing, searching the area frantically. She tosses sticks and logs toward me, and I thrust them into the side of the pit, but they break as soon as I apply my weight to them.

"Zora," I say, pushing my forehead against the soft earth of the pit.

"Yes?"

"It was good to get to see you again," I say, just as sunlight slips over the edge of the pit and envelops me.

CHAPTER 8

BLAISE

*G*entle sunlight kisses my skin, wrapping me in a pool of warmth that soothes my aching muscles, calms my spirit.

I cannot imagine what it ever felt like not to be calm, or why I would ever choose to feel anything but this.

Faintly, I understand Kiran is going to kill me, that the hole he punched through my chest cavity is problematic, but for the life of me, I can't seem to remember why I should care.

Evander sounds frantic, and I only wish I had the energy to reach out to him and invite him to partake in the bliss that's swirling all around us.

But then Kiran's grip loosens around my heart.

Anguish takes its place.

It sprays like splintered glass through my chest, shattering any remnants of peace left within me.

I cry out, though I can't hear myself over the ringing in my ears, the buzz of pain, like a swarm of wasps in my ears.

A plume of shadows spears into my open chest, its grip cold and slimy against my heart.

And then I'm weightless and falling as light, brilliant and burning, erupts from the hands that just dropped me.

My back hits the ground as fire consumes the source of the shadow, as its tendrils writhe before fleeing my chest.

Pain.

So much pain.

It's utter agony, the way my body knits itself back together frantically. Bones spur new growths in order to reform the structure of my ribcage. Skin stretches to knit itself together.

And then there's the fire, so close overhead that it burns, slowing my healing.

Arms wrap around me, dragging me across the cavern floor and out of Kiran's way as he spews flame into the swarm of shadows.

"I've got you," whispers Evander. He picks me up, tucking me into his chest like he used to do when I was a child. In the safety of his arms, away from the flames, my muscles and bones seem to knit together more quickly.

She'll die, the creature screams as it writhes. *Your wife will die. I was trying to help, you fool. If you'd let me, I could have saved her.*

Ice coats my stomach as the creature's words ring in my head.

I watch in dread as Kiran extinguishes the only being who seems to understand what I plan to do to his wife.

"BLAISE, I'M SO SORRY," says Kiran for what must be the seventh time.

"You don't have to apologize," I say. "You weren't you. That creature, whatever she was—she was manipulating your mind."

Kiran swallows, his molten eyes doused with sorrow.

We've moved caves since the incident with the shadow creature, for obvious reasons. Part of me wonders if we should have stayed in the old one. At least we knew we had killed the monster in that one.

"Does anyone have any idea what that creature was?" asks Evander, his copper hair still disheveled from the altercation.

Kiran pinches his brow. "She called herself Marthala."

I frown. "Marthala? Like one of the three shadow sirens from the legends?"

Kiran nods.

Evander whistles. "Well, that explains why she wanted your heart, Blaise. Guess she didn't eat a nutritious enough breakfast and needed a snack."

Kiran gives Evander a strange look, like he's not quite ready to joke about the creature that almost bent him to murder.

"The legends we're told in Naenden say the shadow sirens tempt passersby with their darkest desire." Kiran watches the flames he created for us with an intentness that causes me to wrap my blanket further around me.

"Yeah, they feed off murder or wickedness, or something like that," says Evander, but then he frowns. "But I don't think it's true about the darkest desire part."

Kiran raises a brow.

"Well," Evander explains, "I don't see how it's a dark desire for you to want Asha to live forever with you. That seems pretty natural. And me...well, I don't know that it's so awful for me to wish I had my brother back."

Kiran examines him. "Perhaps not. But perhaps it targets the desires we would flirt with the darkness to obtain."

Evander blows out a puff of air, and he doesn't seem to have anything to counter to that.

"How did you know?" I ask Evander. "How did you know Marthala was trying to trick you?"

Evander becomes focused on a loose button wobbling off the sleeve of his coat. "She just stretched the illusion a bit too far to be believable, that's all." He lets out a laugh that doesn't sound a bit amused, but then he frowns and looks at me. "I wonder why she targeted both of us and not you."

The muscles in my throat freeze as Marthala's voice rings in my ear. *I could bring him back, you know.*

Kiran answers for me. "She seemed like she wanted Blaise's heart. Something about you being a night stalker. I guess she valued you dead more than any wickedness you could commit."

"Yeah, that's probably it," I lie.

Kiran goes back to staring into the fire, but Evander fixes his gaze on me. He looks like he's about to say something, but then his eyes flick behind me, toward the mouth of the cave. A smile, bright and relieved, grazes his lips.

"What?" I ask, turning to find that outside, the snow has ceased.

"I think we're going home, Blaise."

A FIRM HAND comes down on my shoulder as I perch my leg onto the wagon bed, about to step in.

I flinch.

Because it's not Evander.

Kiran clears his throat and jerks his hand back to his side. "I just wanted to apologize again for harming you earlier. That Marthala creature was in my head, but Evander saw past her, so clearly that's no excuse."

I turn to face Kiran and examine the set nature of his jaw, the molten fire in his eyes. Only hours ago, I was pondering whether to ask him for help. Wondering if perhaps he'd see in me the same love he has for Asha, and have enough sympathy for me to help.

Thanks to Marthala, I now know the answer.

"No hard feelings," I say, because it's true.

Kiran and I are the same, but that doesn't matter. Because when it comes down to which of us gets our happy ending, I know whose I'll choose.

PART II

LIAR

CHAPTER 9

PIPER

I've always prided myself on being the most paranoid person in the room.

It comes with the territory—kidnapping children for a living from the ripe age of twelve tends to do that to a person.

It seems, however, that I've been displaced.

Lydia, Princess of Naenden, also known as the Umbra—though that's supposed to be a secret—has usurped me.

The female wouldn't drink a drop of nectar from a honeysuckle without first offering it to a stranger.

That wouldn't be so inconvenient, except that she forces Marcus, Amity, and me to follow the same protocol.

As if I hadn't learned to detect poison in my goblets from the time I could taste the difference between sweet and sour. I have few things for which to thank Bronger, the man who had raised me to be his head trafficker, but survival skills definitely make the scant list.

"She really is going to do this every time, isn't she?" Marcus sits atop a tavern barstool to my left, playing with my hand under the counter, bringing a blush to my cheeks. Amity, our unofficially adopted daughter, bounces excitedly on her tiptoes before scrambling onto the barstool to my right.

Traveling with Amity has been another thing to which Lydia has had to adjust. Apparently, our guide is used to frequenting the seedier taverns and inns for daily needs, none of which Marcus or I would typically let Amity go anywhere near.

Lydia grumbles about it, of course, claiming the two of us to be overprotective. We mostly just chuckle over Lydia's stunned expression every time Amity speaks to her.

It's clear Lydia is not used to being around children and doesn't know what to make of Amity's bluntness. Which is ironic, since Lydia is probably the most blunt person I've ever met.

That, and the most insistent on checking for poison in our goblets.

That's exactly what she's currently doing, draping herself over the bar and batting her eyelashes at the male sitting beside her.

From the looks of her, you would think she's drunk, though Elias explained that Lydia can hardly stand the scent of ale. He never explained the reasoning, but I've heard enough about the late King of Naenden, known enough fathers like Amity's, to have made my own assumptions.

Lydia leans in close to the stranger, who blinks rapidly as if he's trying to decide whether this is actually happening to him, whether a female as stunning as Lydia could actually be flirting with him.

The answer is no, of course, but the male is too eager for a miracle to accept as much.

Elias sits on Marcus's opposite side, and though I exchange a glance with him—a "how do you like your female falling all over another male" kind of glance—there's nothing but sheer amusement in his expression.

Elias is considerably younger than Lydia, and one of the few true friends I made at the Coup, a league of assassins intent on overthrowing the fae regime. The Coup has dissolved since I put an arrow through Bronger's chest, but Elias remains a close friend. I was shocked to find he'd been in a relationship with the Princess of Naenden for quite a while, the two of them having kept up with one another through clandestine meetings. Like this was all a fun game of cat and mouse.

Lydia even stabbed Elias once, gifting him a collapsed lung. Apparently, he's into that kind of thing.

Yes, they're definitely a good match, I think as I look across the counter at Elias's carefree expression. There's not a hint of jealousy on his face as he watches Lydia flirt with another male.

Elias and I make eye contact. He just shrugs, as if to communicate, *It's just what she does.*

Indeed, Lydia takes a sip from her goblet (or rather, pretends to take a sip), sighing with delight and insisting to the male that this is the best-tasting wine she's ever had.

Water sloshes over the edge of the cup.

This is purposeful, of course. This way, Amity can drink it too.

Amusement mingles with shock on the male's face. Clearly he thinks she's too drunk to know what she's tasting, but when she hands the goblet to him so that he too can partake in the wonderful concoction, he draws it to his lips.

Lydia's posture shifts as she assesses everything about him. Her pointed ears perk as she listens for any changes in his pulse or breathing.

"One day, one of these poor males is going to fall over dead," Marcus grumbles.

"I saw him steal money from the coin purse of the lady with the cane in the corner," Amity whispers in a tone that suggests that, should the male fall over dead from poison not meant for him, he probably deserves it anyway.

Marcus and I exchange a look.

Our daughter has an extremely rigid moral code, another reason Lydia so often grows exasperated with her.

It used to get on my nerves, too. That was back when I was transporting Amity from her abusive home to the Coup. So much has happened since then, and in such a short time, I've grown to adore that little girl. Marcus and I plan to adopt her. We even announced it to her at our wedding, but Lydia had shown up and thrown a wrench in the process.

Still. She might as well be ours.

Marcus reaches across me and scrubs his knuckles through Amity's hair. She swats him away in annoyance for ruining her braid, which, given that it's attached to Amity, was already ruined, but he doesn't mention as much.

The male sitting beside Lydia murmurs something and walks away. He shakes his head, which must mean Lydia has employed the "disgust" segment of her protocol. It tends to be equally effective as her flirting. Especially when she sprinkles in a bit of belching and hysterical sobs in between drunken hiccups.

Looking pleased with her work, Lydia takes a swig of water, then passes the bottle down the counter, forcing us all to share since this is the only vessel in the vicinity that has been tested for poison.

"I don't know who she thinks is going to poison us," Marcus says.

He takes the bottle from me and drinks.

THE PLAN IS to sleep in tents on the outskirts of town tonight. This wasn't the original plan. More like the backup plan. But Lydia didn't like the looks the barman at the inn was giving me, so the tent it is.

I don't mind hiding out. I've been doing it my entire life, but I suppose neither Marcus nor I am used to having someone else decide for us.

Specifically, someone like Lydia.

When she and Elias first showed up, she wanted us to lie low for a while, at least until the man she called Azrael tamped down his hunt for me. That wasn't all that difficult. Elias and I still have connections that allowed us to take shelter.

Van, an old friend from the Coup, had let us stay in her new hide-out, tucked away in the ravine separating Avelea and Charshon.

Eventually, Lydia became suspicious of the lack of intel she'd been able to collect about Az's next move, and she decided that we weren't safe where we were.

That we needed the protection of royalty.

Personally, I have a sneaking suspicion the Naenden royalty needs me for something else, but Lydia always evades my questions. I'm never sure whether to trust her, but the fact that she's incapable of lying helps some. That, and the fact Elias trusts her.

Now we're on our way to Othian, the capital of Dwellen. There, we're supposed to meet up with the others who're concerned with the threat Azrael poses to Alondria. Which apparently has something to do with him wanting to open an ancient Rip between realms—a Rip he thinks my Gift is capable of opening for him.

But for now, Marcus, Amity, and I are sharing a tent, remaining rather dehydrated because of *someone's* paranoia.

We're all preparing for bed, readying to snuggle up in the far corner of the campsite, when Marcus, despite the chill of the Avelean climate, begins to sweat.

BEADS OF SWEAT pool on Marcus's forehead, settling deep within the creases on his brow as he frowns and grasps at his stomach.

"Hey. You okay?" I ask.

He blinks rapidly. "Must've been something I ate," he says, shaking it off, but I can't help the tinge of worry that gnaws at my belly.

I laugh nervously. "Well, at least we can know it's not poison."

"Yeah, at least not the intentional kind. I don't know if Lydia has found a way around food poisoning yet," he jokes, though his voice turns breathy by the end of his statement.

"Maybe I should go and see if Lydia or Elias has any tonics with them. I had some with me, but I used them on Amity last time she was ill."

I wait for Marcus to make some joke about how he's surprised Amity, who has an affinity for healing, didn't replenish our supply already, but he says nothing. He just squints and nods.

I frown, then leave the tent and cross the campsite, looking for Lydia and Elias. I find them in their tent, both already passed out on the floor, I suppose from the long day's journey. But that doesn't seem right, since Lydia insisted someone stay up at all hours to watch. We usually take shifts, and unless I miscounted, I'm almost positive it isn't my or Marcus's turn.

Unease nags at the back of my mind.

"Lydia. Elias." I don't bother whispering. Lydia wouldn't bother if she was the one trying to wake me up.

Neither of them stirs.

I'm not sure why I do it, but instinct has me grabbing a stick from outside to poke Lydia with. I do, aiming for the soft spot of her neck. When she doesn't stir, I jab her in the clavicle.

Nothing.

Fear begins to course through me, and I toss the stick to the side, leaning over Elias and pressing my finger to his neck.

A faint pulse beats there. When I check Lydia's, I find she too is alive.

Something isn't right. Poison would have been my first thought, but we've been so careful.

The image of Marcus wincing and grasping at his stomach overcomes me, and I bound from the tent, racing across the campground. I glance around for Amity, but don't see her. Worry grasps at my chest as I fling open the tent door.

What I see wrenches my heart from my chest.

Marcus is still in the tent, sweating profusely now, his tunic and trousers drenched as his entire body trembles.

Ropes bind his torso. His hands are tied behind his back, and though he strains against them, the weakness from his illness inhibits him too much for his efforts to make any impact.

Next to him sits Amity, tied up in much the same way. A gag presses into her mouth, though her brown eyes burn with clarity.

Amity, at least, doesn't appear sick.

I try to focus on that as a female garbed in a silky white robe steps out from the shadows.

She's pale from head to toe, as if she's scrubbed away at all her skin and hair and now there's no pigment left.

"Piper, dear," she says. "I've been looking for you."

. . .

"WHAT DID YOU DO TO HIM?" I cut my eyes across the tent to my husband. My gut plummets as I watch Marcus's eyes roll back in his head.

Don't die, don't die, please don't die.

Amity stares at him, too, her entire body shaking, though in fear or anger I can't tell.

The stranger clicks the overgrown nails of her forefinger and thumb together. "Poison."

My stomach clenches, worry washing over me. I find myself scanning Amity from head to toe, searching for any sign that she too might be poisoned.

"I wouldn't have hurt the child," says the female, "though I'm sure you don't understand the sentiment, given your occupation."

I clench my teeth, but I don't bother explaining myself to this female. Not when Marcus is poisoned and I need to act quickly if I want to draw information about the antidote out of this stranger.

"Who are you?" I ask.

She purses her lips, as if deciding whether revealing her identity will end up causing her trouble. "Queen Abra of Mystral," she finally says. Which I suppose means she's not concerned after all.

My mind whirs with a million questions, a multitude of facts I know about the queen coalescing in my mind, fighting for preeminence.

Queen. Cold. Widow. Suspected of poisoning her husband.

My stomach flips.

"What do you want in exchange for the antidote?" I ask.

The female raises a perfectly arched brow. "You aren't going to ask how I managed it?"

"How you managed what?"

"To poison some of you while leaving the others unharmed?"

I don't figure there's a way around the question; best to plow through it. "How?"

The female looks disappointed, but she answers anyway. "I am particularly skilled at potion-making. It's always been a talent of mine, but I possess a Gift, not unlike yours."

My Gift stirs inside me, as if waking and stretching its limbs at the sound of its name.

"I once possessed a different form of Old Magic. The kind I possess now is not like her brother, yet she offers skills I could never have dreamed of. She's done it before, you see, offered this gift to another. She taught me how to do it."

Marcus is still shaking. I'm running out of patience. "Do what?"

"Concoct potions that only affect who they're meant for. It's a hassle, you know, to try to ensure a poisoned glass gets to the right individual, especially when your goal is to poison three out of five of them. Especially when they have a princess among them who likes to stick her nose where it doesn't belong.

"So my Gift helped me. Helped me concoct a draft that would take out your guardians, at least momentarily, but the true target of the potion was your husband."

My heart pounds, rage barreling through me. That anyone would ever dare to hurt Marcus, with no reason except to get to me.

Amity is crying now, wet tears staining her cheeks as she sobs.

"What do you want?" I ask.

"I would like your assistance in a task I will reveal when it becomes relevant to you."

"In exchange for you healing Marcus now?"

The female tsks. "Don't fret. Your husband has weeks to live. As long as the task is completed before then, he'll not suffer death or permanent damage, at least not by the potion's hands."

Weeks. My heart pounds. "What do you want me to do?"

The female reaches out her hand. "I would like you to make a bargain with me. One where you'll do as I ask, whenever I ask it. Until the task is done and your husband is free."

I glance back and forth between Amity and Marcus, my heart cracking.

Since my blood is half human, half fae, I'm not cursed with the inability to lie like full-blooded fae. Still, if I enter a fae bargain with the female, I'll have no choice but to follow through. At least not without dying, should I choose to resist.

"No," I say at last.

The female lifts her brow. "No?"

I cross my arms to hide the fact that they're shaking. I'm not sure I'm successful. "No. I won't enter into a fae bargain with you."

"I must have overestimated your love for your husband then," she says, louder than she was talking previously, as if she wants to make sure Marcus hears even in his drugged state.

"No, you haven't. And if you believe I love him, as I do, then surely you know the threat of him dying is enough to motivate me to do whatever you say."

The female's lip twitches. "Perhaps you've misunderstood. Enter into the fae bargain with me, or no deal."

I stalk toward her. "Perhaps *you* have misunderstood. I'm not entering into a fae bargain with you with unnamed conditions. If I do that, my husband is as good as dead."

And I'm not providing Amity an example of entering into a messy fae bargain to get out of a temporary problem, I don't add.

Tears bead at the undersides of my eyelids, begging to spill, but I won't let them. Not when I need this female to believe my bluff.

"Fine," I say.

She slips a blindfold over me, and everything goes dark.

Amity's whimpers fill my ears.

"Wait," I say. "Deal's off unless you untie her."

The female says nothing, but I can hear her move across the tent and untie Amity's restraints.

I also hear Amity spit on her.

Fear mingled with pride lances through me, but the female gives no reaction. Not that I can tell.

I clap my fingers against my side. Our signal for "It's going to be okay."

I wonder if that's the last lie I'll ever get to tell my daughter.

CHAPTER 10

ELLIE

*W*hen I agreed to accept glassblowing lessons from my father (to relearn the skills I bargained away to save Evander's life during the third Trial), I expected him to want to go back to basics.

I just didn't expect we'd be returning to *these* basics.

We stand in my father's workshop, smoke from the furnace filling my nostrils. The overwhelming scent incites my gagging reflex, which is strange. You would think I'd be used to it by now.

I make a mental note to ask him if he's burning a different type of coal than usual.

Of course, that could just be my way of not admitting why I'm feeling ill.

I've never considered myself an anxious person, but with Blaise's disappearance and Evander's extended absence, I recently find that just about anything can turn my stomach.

Even coating cast-iron pans with enameled glass, the task my father has currently assigned me.

We've been standing here for hours. In that time frame, an enormous pile of heavy cast-iron cookware has piled up beside me. It's the new trend in Othian—enameled cookware—and my father has been all too keen to jump on it.

"Don't you get tired of this?" I ask him, wiping sweat from my brow as we work. "It's not exactly as refined as glassblowing, is it? I'm pretty sure you taught me to do this before I learned to walk."

My father shoots me a knowing look, seeing through my not-so-innocent question. "I understand that being a princess has afforded you certain luxuries, Elynore, but I wouldn't have expected the basics of the trade to be beneath you."

I level him an equally challenging glare. "It's not that it's beneath me, Papa. I'm just not sure how it's supposed to help me relearn how to glass blow."

The process of enameling cast iron is a far cry from the intricacy it takes to form a pair of glass slippers.

"Glassblowing isn't simply about skill with the hands and the torch and the furnace, Elynore. Glassblowing is about patience."

"Yes, well, I don't think my bargain took away my patience."

"It couldn't have," says my father. The grin tugging on the edge of his lip should have been foretelling when he finishes with, "given that you never possessed that particular quality to begin with."

I let out a groan, but it's the playful sort, and the low rumbles of my father's laughter warm my heart better than any furnace could.

As much as coating these pots bores me out of my mind, I've enjoyed the time it allows me to spend with my father. I'm adjusting to my life at the palace, and when Evander is home, it's downright lovely, but I've still missed my parents. I'd gone from living with them to not seeing them for weeks after the debacle with the glass slipper, and I'm more than happy for an excuse to come visit them daily.

Besides. It's an excuse not to attend King Marken's meetings with his officials.

My father-in-law and I maintain a complicated relationship. On the one hand, I'm glad he respects me enough to invite me to meetings. That he cares about my opinion.

On the other hand, the king and several of his officials hold no such respect for Evander, and they certainly don't hold back their opinions regarding my husband on my account.

It leaves me in a strange position, and though I always try to redirect the conversation away from what the king often refers to as "my offspring's numerous insufficiencies," I never seem to succeed.

Except for last week, when I told the king that if he wanted Evander to be prepared for the throne, he perhaps should have shown some forethought and trained Evander for the position from a young age.

Needless to say, I've been avoiding the meetings when I can.

"Now," says my father, wiping his sweating palms on his apron. "Why do we coat cast iron with glass?"

"You ask me this question every day."

"And?"

"And I get it right every day. One would think you'd trust that I know the answer."

"Perhaps you remember the answer because I ask you every day."

I laugh, then say, "Glass is resistant to chemicals in a way iron is not."

"Much more resistant," says my father, as if proud of the glass itself.

Indeed, he goes on with his daily ode to glass. "People underestimate glass, because they perceive it as easy to shatter. They assume iron is stronger, because iron does not break so easily. But glass is deceptively resilient, Elynore. The same chemicals which erode the iron, the glass finds to have little effect."

"You should teach philosophy at the Academy, Papa," I say, smiling up from my forty-thousandth pan this afternoon.

My father pokes out his lip and nods his head, as if he's never considered this before, but thinks it's a grand idea indeed.

"Life is like that," he continues, apparently spurred on by my encouragement. "It is often the things that appear the most delicate that, when tested, we find to be the strongest."

My father reaches out, squeezing my shoulder affectionately, and I can't help the tears that burn at my eyes.

I don't feel strong. Not anymore, at least. I haven't for a while, not since losing my ability to form art with my glass. It's not even about feeling strong, I suppose, but about feeling useful. Ever since Blaise disappeared and Asha and Kiran opened our eyes to the dangers brewing in Alondria, I've felt a sort of innate uselessness.

I'm not fae. I don't have an immortal lifespan or unworldly strength. Asha is human like me, but she has her own powers. Her Gift of the Old Magic makes her useful. She saved Kiran's and Fin's lives through an illusion she'd crafted from nothing, didn't she?

Not that I haven't tried to be of use. Asha's quick to remind me any time I feel useless that I'm the only one in our group who holds sway over the King of Dwellen, and that this is helpful in its own right. She thinks I'm the only one who can convince him of anything. Which was probably correct, up until my comment last week.

Still.

I stare down at the cast-iron pot in my hand and sigh.

It feels silly, thinking that if I could make art again, it would somehow be of assistance against the oncoming war that simmers. But in the art district, even the smallest pieces of beauty can bring joy to the downtrodden. Besides, don't they send minstrels out to war to lift the spirits of the soldiers?

I pile my finished pot atop the heap and start on the next.

THANKFULLY, Asha arrives around lunchtime to save me from completing the rest of my cast-iron pots.

She pokes her head into the workshop, crinkling her nose in displeasure at the scent of soot and enamel.

"Is it that time already?" my father asks, jumping up in delight to greet the Queen of Naenden. "Time just flies when you're lost in a train of thought."

Queen Asha curtsies to my father, and a bashful look overtakes his face. He and my mother took to Asha immediately, which I find hilarious, since my father initially pitied the girl who had ended up the sacrificial bride to the Naenden king. I'm not sure how Asha was before, but she certainly doesn't give off the aura of someone to be pitied. Even with the missing eye and the scars, there's a self-deprecation about her that's charming. One I somehow missed upon our first meeting.

She seemed so much older than me then, regal of sorts, but I've come to realize it was just part of the role of queen she plays.

In the end, Queen Asha isn't above jokes that most would consider below her station, and my parents love her for it.

"For Jethro," Asha says, pulling a parcel that smells of freshly baked bread from her pocket and handing it to my father.

Okay, so perhaps the baked goods that Asha never fails to pick up from Forcier's on the way are what endear her to my parents. But who can blame them?

My father opens the parcel, revealing marbled sweet bread, his favorite. You have to stand outside of Forcier's for an hour before he opens if you want a chance of getting any before the crowd devours it.

"You're my favorite queen; did you know that?" my father asks, his brown eyes lit with joy at the scent of the loaf.

A bemused smile touches Asha's lip. "I'll happily assume that position while we're waiting for Ellie to become a queen herself."

"Yeah, well, we both know that's never going to happen," I say, happily taking the parcel Asha hands me. "My father-in-law is immortal, remember?"

Asha shrugs. "You never know. Being a heartless boor might wear him out one of these days."

"Asha," I say, though in truth it would be nice to speak as freely as she does. There are only so many disparaging comments I can make about my own father-in-law and remain on his good side.

"What?" Asha says, pulling out her favorite order, a sticky flaxseed cake, and munching on it. "A girl can hope, can't she? Mind if I borrow Ellie for a little while?" Asha asks my father, as she always does, even though the answer is always the same—a bit of effortless grumbling about how perhaps he could spare his daughter if the queen truly needed me.

She grins and nods her head before ambling out into the yard.

· · ·

78

I CAN'T HELP but laugh at Asha's attire. It's burgeoning upon summer in Dwellen, though you can't tell based on Asha's clothing choices. She's taken to sweaters, having amassed a collection of them during her stay in Othian.

I'm not sure how she isn't sweating, though I suppose Naenden is so torrid in comparison that she truly can't stand to be out in normal clothes, even on the warmest of days.

"They're like wearing a hug." Asha gestures down to her knit sweater, as if reading my thoughts.

"You don't strike me as someone who likes hugs," I say, walking alongside her down the cobbled streets of Othian.

There's a glint of mischief in her eyes when she says, "I'm not. That's why I said they're *like* wearing one."

I'm not exactly sure why Asha makes the journey out of town to interrupt my sessions with my father every day, except that we're both missing our husbands terribly and need a distraction from their absence.

We haven't received word from them in over two months, and though that's easily explained by the late-season snowstorm that has blocked the roads out of Mystral, it's still unnerving not to have any contact with them.

I suppose we both needed a distraction.

Especially Asha, who has been screaming out in the middle of the night, awakened by cruel nightmares.

I unwrap the scone Asha got for me, but as soon as I bring it to my nose, another wave of nausea rolls over me. I wince, which Asha catches immediately with her discerning eye.

"Is it moldy?" she asks, peering over my shoulder to look at the pastry.

"No, I just..." I trail off. "I think it's making me sick, not hearing from Evander."

Asha nods. "I get pretty vomitty when I'm anxious."

So I've heard. The Queen of Naenden is rather known for her tumultuous stomach, though I think it improper to mention as much.

I change the subject. "Your nightmares seem to be getting worse," I say, which comes out not at all as the prying, gentle question that I intended. Fin is officially assigned to check on Asha during the night, but I try to relieve him when I can. The need for my presence is becoming more frequent.

If Asha is disturbed by my bluntness, she doesn't show it. "My magic is having a hard time right now. Hearing that his sister is wreaking havoc has sent him on a bit of a frenzy."

She doesn't seem all that upset about it, and if she did, it's more like she feels pity for the parasite inside her, rather than resentment.

"You don't get tired of it?" I ask. "Him projecting his fears onto you?"

She shrugs. "I figure he's gotten the nasty end of plenty of my less than pleasant emotions. Besides, I don't know how much better the nightmares would be, even if he wasn't affecting them. They aren't all about his sister."

She trails off and bites her lip. I wait for her to finish, to explain what exactly torments her in the middle of the night, but if she was going to tell me, she doesn't get the chance.

We pass Forcier's, the scent of lemon scones wafting from one of my favorite establishments in the city. Nausea churns through me, and I hardly make it to the adjacent alleyway before I vomit all over the street.

Asha follows me, seemingly undisturbed by the mess I've made. I suppose she's desensitized, though I'm not.

Embarrassment heats my cheeks. I hope no one else saw.

"Do you have a rag or something?" I ask, but Asha is already on her knees, wiping the mess from the ground with a terrycloth she pulled out of her pouch.

"You don't have to do that," I say, but she waves away my concern.

"No one should have to wipe up their own vomit," she says.

"I don't normally do this," I explain, though I do feel a bit better. "I'm not really sure what's come over me. I never throw up. Even as a child, when I had to vomit, my parents always said I would refuse to. Like I could force my body not to. I'm not sure why…"

I trail off, because Asha is looking at me strangely. In a lack of self-restraint, she glances at my belly.

"Oh." I cover my mouth with my hands, my mind immediately whirring, counting the weeks since my last cycle. "Oh."

I've been so consumed with worry over Blaise, worry over Evander not returning, I haven't even thought about my cycle in...

"Oh?" Asha says, a bit too innocently.

I let out a shocked little laugh, then throw up again in the alleyway.

CHAPTER 11

ASHA

I'm drowning. Water cascades into my mouth, dousing the pores in my lungs, stealing the air from my chest. I try to scream, but I can't seem to force the air out, not with all the pressure building in my mouth and nose.

I beg Calias to stop, but it's no use. I can hardly form words with the water shredding my throat. Besides, Calias is dead, and the laughing in the distance doesn't belong to him.

This laugh is more familiar than Calias's laugh should be.

An icy finger strokes my cheek, lifting my chin to meet a beautiful face. Az's face.

When he looks at me like that, it hurts. It aches badly enough, the pain from my drowning dissipates by comparison.

"I forgive you," he whispers. "We're going to forget all about this."

"Asha."

Az frowns, because my name is an echo on someone else's lips.

"Asha. Asha, come on. Kiran's going to kill me when the servants tell him I let you scream like this without waking you."

My eye flutters, the voice drawing me through the hazy reflection of Az's distorted face.

Don't trust him, Asha. Don't trust anyone, whispers my magic, still lost in the haze of the nightmare.

When I blink, Fin comes into focus, where Az was just now leaning over me. Concern wrinkles the corners of Fin's eyes, his light brown skin glowing in the candlelight.

Don't trust him; you can't... My magic's stupor fades a bit as he too comes to his senses.

Carefully, Fin wriggles his hand under the satin sheets. When he finds my hand, he squeezes.

"I'm sorry I woke you again," I say, wiping the sweat from my forehead with the back of my other hand.

Fin shrugs. "I don't really sleep these days, anyway."

I frown, but I don't press Fin any further. It's been a year since Fin's wife, Ophelia, died at Kiran's hand, her execution the collateral damage of a grab for the throne made by Azrael and his lover, Kiran's first wife, Gwenyth.

Lately, Fin has settled into a grim silence as far as his late wife is concerned, unless the opportunity to scathe Kiran for her death presents itself. It puts me in a strange position—Fin loathing Kiran the way he does. Fin was a friend to me even before Kiran's heart changed, before he and I fell in love. It's been difficult for Fin—watching his friend forgive the brother he so detests—but his loyalty to me has never faltered.

Except that he doesn't bother to keep his snide remarks about my husband to himself. Even around me.

"What's going on with you, Asha?" Fin asks, scanning me intently.

I blink away the sleep from my eye, and as my body settles into the fact *this* is reality, not the drowning, not Az's touch on my face, my heart rate slows. "Nothing. Well, nothing that I suppose isn't normal after suffering the trauma of drowning. I wasn't equipped for that, you know."

Fin raises a brow.

"What with growing up in a desert, and all."

"Ah," Fin says, clearly not amused. "I drowned, too, you know.

Unless you don't remember my loyally holding your hand through our shared experience. Still. I'm not the one tormented by nightmares."

A small smile grazes my lips, my eye stinging. "Of course I remember."

Fin smiles, though faintly, and it quickly turns grim again. "Kiran told me the dreams didn't start until the Old Magic learned of its sister."

He mocks, but he doesn't know the evil she is capable of, my magic grumbles within me.

I'm not sure what good it does you to worry, I tell it, though the comment is more for my benefit.

It's not easy having a being tormented by anxiety living in one's head.

And it's not easy being confined to the body of a human who rests on the lower end of the spectrum when it comes to self-preservation instinct, my magic counters.

I sigh, pushing myself up in bed and leaning against the headboard. Fin's lantern bathes the room in a warm glow, dancing off the silver-plated designs etched into the baby blue walls, causing my silver bedsheets to shimmer.

The quarters the King of Dwellen has provided during our stay in Othian are calming, pleasant. As is the style in Dwellen, most of the decor vacillates between various hues of blue, all lined with silver leaf. My room is no exception, with silver leaf depicting a mural of a lively forest on the wall, shimmering pine trees cutting across the pale blue backdrop.

The furniture is much the same, complete with a silver-plated dresser and vanity, while any cushion in the vicinity is encased in soft blue velvet.

The bed is comfortable, too. It just would be more comfortable with Kiran in it.

Months ago, when Ellie visited Blaise's rooms only to find the girl had left without a trace, Evander and Kiran set out after her, assuming a realization of some sort had dawned on her during our conversations about how Queen Abra was the Mother from the Old Magic's story. They left Ellie and me behind, figuring time was of the essence, and having two humans along would only slow them down.

It's probably true, but I don't have to like the truth, even if mentally I reluctantly agree.

Thankfully, Fin was already on his way to Othian to deliver a message from Lydia about her progress in hiding Piper from Azrael. Piper's magic, like mine, makes her capable of manipulating the Rip. Kiran, aware of my recent nightmares, had left Fin instructions to sleep in the quarters adjacent to mine and to check on me should I burst into fits in the middle of the night. I think Fin and Ellie must have developed a system, because they often alternate who comes to check on me.

Kiran and his brother might not be getting along—I'm rather shocked Fin agreed with anything Kiran commanded of him, to be honest—but they seem to possess a common interest when it comes to me.

That was over two months ago. Kiran and Evander found Blaise in Mystral all right, but that was the last we heard from them before the snowstorm hit Mystral.

Now that the storm has passed, we hope Kiran and Evander will return any day now.

Any day now isn't nearly soon enough.

"You said his name during the dream," Fin says, his voice an anchor to reality from my dreary thoughts.

I frown at him in question.

"Oh, don't look at me like you don't know who I'm talking about. You said Az's name."

My chest clenches, the feel of Az's possessive finger scraping across my face, as if it wasn't a dream at all, but a memory I can't quite quash.

"I'm suffering from nightmares. Why would my masochistic mind hold anything back from torturing me?" I ask. When Fin doesn't answer, I gesture toward my head. "Sorry if all my enemies get mixed up in here."

"You okay?"

"Yeah, you can go on back to bed now. Consider it checked off the list: Seen to the little wounded bird, otherwise known as Asha."

Fin gestures as if to strike a task off an invisible list midair. Then he stares at me. "Are you going back to bed?"

"If you get out of here, then maybe I can actually get some sleep."

He cranes his neck to the side, crossing his arms. Waiting.

"Okay, fine. It'll probably take me a while to fall back asleep."

"Same." Fin rises from the bed and extends his hand toward me. "Actually, you've pretty much ruined my hard-earned sleep for the night. I'll never make it back to bed."

I roll my eye, but stare pointedly at his hand.

He shrugs. "I figure if neither of us are going to be sleeping, we could at least be doing something productive. Besides, you owe me for waking me up. So I'm giving you a task."

"You're giving me a task."

He grins. "I'm giving you a task, my queen."

As it turns out, Fin's task involves a trip to the Othian castle library, so it's much less daunting than I previously expected.

We pad through the ornate hallways, the various portraits of Princess Olwen staring down at us as we traverse the sprawling castle.

"She just looks like she'd be a pill, doesn't she?" Fin comments as we pass a portrait of Olwen Thornwall.

"I imagine she and I could be friends."

Fin scoffs. "Just don't tell Evander."

When we arrive at the library, we're careful to shut the door behind us, leaving our lanterns with the overnight librarian and exchanging them for a set approved by the King of Dwellen himself.

I don't much like the King of Dwellen. He seems unnecessarily awful to Evander, and frequently condescending to most everyone around him, except for maybe Ellie, but the male is particular about the care his book collection receives, and that I can respect.

The specialized lanterns let off an unassuming glow that supposedly won't cause damage to the pages of the older texts contained within the library. The Othian library, much like the one in Naenden, is bedecked with books boasting all imaginable colors. It also contains at least half a dozen sliding ladders and little alcoves on the second floor of shelves, so you could settle in and read from a nook above.

It's a lovely idea, though I'm not tempted to scale them. I just like knowing the option is available to me if I so desire it.

Fin must have occupied an alcove earlier in the day, because he climbs up to one and descends with a pile of books, aware of my aversion to heights. He piles them on a desk beside a nearby window, one with Ellie's initials engraved into the side, as I examine the titles and raise my brow.

"Ah, just what I love to read for fun," I say, though I watch Fin's face carefully as I respond.

"I thought, what better to lull us back to sleep?" he says, his carefree grin never faltering.

My heart falters a bit, though. Every single book is a census record, most from Dwellen, but others are from the surrounding kingdoms. "You're still looking for him."

Fin doesn't bother to look up at me. He just settles into a seat and starts flipping through one of the books, taking notes on a parchment laid out on the table next to him.

"I thought you decided to take a break," I try again when Fin doesn't respond.

"I did."

"Then why are you looking now?"

"Isn't it within the definition of a break that the break would end at some point, and then work would resume?"

I bite my lip, but I take a seat across from Fin, nonetheless. Fin worked himself sick searching for his father when Kiran and the vizier had first told him of his and Kiran's illegitimacy. Of course, no one outside of the vizier and direct family could know. The fact that the twins are not descendants of the late king, and that Naenden law does not allow females on the throne, means that the next person in line for the throne is the king's illegitimate son.

And that son happens to be Az.

I think we all shudder daily considering what Az might do if he gets his hands on the throne. Az, the boy I was infatuated with my entire childhood. Az, who came running to rid my family's hovel of snakes and spiders anytime my sister, Dinah, or I screamed. Az, who slit the throat of his lover, just to keep her from spilling his secrets. Az, who ordered Dinah killed if I didn't do as he asked.

Az, who hates the fae despite the fact, or possibly because, they are secretly part of his heritage.

No. No one can find out that Kiran isn't the rightful heir to the throne.

Still. Fin has searched. Kiran has discouraged it, but Fin reminded him that while we were trying our utmost to keep their illegitimacy a secret, a loose end remained. It was very possible that their father was out there somewhere, well aware that his son occupied the throne of Naenden, and was biding his time until revealing such information served him.

Best we find him first, Fin had contended.

Kiran couldn't argue with that. None of us could. But in the past year, Fin's efforts turned up very little by way of his heritage, and he eventually grew discouraged.

Kiran and I thought it for the best when Fin abandoned his efforts, but now it seems he hasn't abandoned them at all.

He's just found himself a bigger library.

So I pluck a census off the pile on the desk and start to read.

WE COME up with very little in the several hours before the sun rises and dabbles sprinkles of light over the pages.

My eye starts to drift, and the sleep my body so craves begins to catch up to me.

It probably isn't for the best if I become nocturnal, but hey, if Blaise can do it, I don't see why I can't.

I'm in the middle of one of those weird falling sensations accompanied by a jerk when Fin's chair scrapes loudly against the floor.

"Asha. Asha, I think I found something—"

He is quickly interrupted by a hush from the librarian, at whom he shoots a rather disarming grin, but is met only by another round of scolding.

He rolls his eyes as she walks away.

"It really is a shame that can't work on everyone," I say. "I mean, how will you sleep tonight knowing there's someone out there immune to your charms?"

A grin tugs at Fin's lips. "What are you even talking about?"

He shoves his book at me, pointing to a piece of script. It's a list of merchants with permits to cross the Sahli and trade in Meranthi around the time Kiran and Fin were born.

"If our mother was trying to sire an heir she could claim was Rajeen's, who better to pick than a male who wouldn't stick around? Someone who had a permit to get out of Meranthi?" Fin asks.

Before I can examine the document further, someone else enters the library, alerting us to her presence with a rather squeaky cough.

Fin's eyes go wide. He quickly raises a hand, as if he's scratching the side of his face.

"You're really awful at making it look like you're not trying to hide from someone, you know," I murmur as Imogen, Ellie's lady's maid, approaches us.

"Think you could scare her off for me?" Fin asks under his breath.

"Why would you want me to do that, Phineas?" I say, imitating the way Imogen is often prone to using Fin's full name.

"You know why."

"Oh, I don't know. I think you and Imogen would make a cute couple. You both have that..." I screw up my face, struggling to find a torturous enough comparison.

"Asha." Fin is practically growling under his breath.

"You really should give her a chance, Phineas. The two of you would be adorable together. Unless, of course, there's someone else you have in mind."

Fin's eyes flash in irritation. His cheeks flush with heat at the not-so-vague reference to my sister, whom Fin has been avoiding any discussion of for the better part of a year now. Despite finding excuses to encourage the kitchen staff to leave leftovers out for my sister's food bank, happening to be in the library anytime she's there, or asking about my father incessantly, knowing the conversation will turn to news of my sister's wellbeing.

"I hate you," Fin whispers, but the lie must cause his throat to close up, because he winces and adds, "hyperbolically, of course. Just please make her go away."

"Sure. I'll just make sure to train my non-eye on her. You know, let her get a good look at the fleshy bit of skin."

"You are the best sister-in-law a male could ask for. You know that, right?"

Normally, I might feel guilty about purposefully trying to scare off one of the many girls who fawn over Fin.

Such is not the case with Imogen.

As she approaches, I make a show of waving my hand at her dramatically to get her attention.

"What are you doing?" Fin glowers at me. "You don't even act that excited to see the people you actually like."

"She's going to come over here anyway," I whisper through the side of my mouth. "Might as well make it uncomfortable for her."

THE CONVERSATION GOES ABOUT as I might have expected, with Imogen refusing to acknowledge my existence except when propriety demands a one-word answer from her.

Eventually, Fin decides he's had enough and scolds her openly for her rudeness, at which point Imogen rushes away crying.

The whole interaction leaves me with a gnawing sensation of guilt for some reason, and when I remind Fin I don't need to be defended, he tells me, "Yeah, well I've already gotten that 'I don't need you to defend me' speech from Lydia, and frankly, she's scarier than you, so I've got to take my brotherly protectiveness out on someone. Besides," he says with a sly grin as he peers up at me, "you weren't doing a good enough job scaring her off."

I throw a crumpled piece of parchment at him.

He tosses it back, hitting me in the eye—the good one, too.

CHAPTER 12

ELLIE

I like to think of myself as the type of person who comes to meetings prepared.

Attentive. Pen and parchment in hand. Ready to listen, absorb, then succinctly state my opinion.

"Princess Elynore?" says a mildly scolding voice.

I snap out of the trance I've let myself wander into. "Yes, Your Majesty?"

King Marken sits at the head of the table, looking as regal as ever in his freshly pressed blue robes. Silver cufflinks shimmer at his wrists, matching the thread woven into his sleeves and collar. My father-in-law cranes his head at me, scanning me up and down with those stone-gray eyes of his.

"We were wondering if there have been any recent developments regarding Dwellen-Naenden relations."

I blink, swallowing as I refocus my attention on the present, but the male across the table cuts me off.

"Yes, we're all wondering just what could possibly be delaying the return of your husband and the Naenden king."

From the tone of Casper Thornwall's voice, I'm guessing he's not wondering as much as he is assuming.

Casper Thornwall is Evander's cousin, the son of King Marken's sister. He's fae, too, meaning he's beautiful, but there's something sickeningly perfect about his features. He's almost dizzying to look at, with all the straight lines: the bridge of his nose, his jawline, even the way he styles his hair slicked back. Casper has Evander's coloring, tanned skin and turquoise eyes, which makes me irrationally angry. I don't particularly like the fact that looking at Casper reminds me of Evander.

I trace my fingers around a knob at the base of the oaken table at which we sit. I found the little knob the first time I attended one of these meetings, and it's been a comfort to me ever since.

"We've yet to receive contact from my husband and the King of Naenden," I say, measuring my words. "It seems most logical to assume their travel is delayed due to the winter storm that recently hit Mystral."

A cruel smile slashes across Casper's mouth. "Yes, I'm sure that's what my cousin is up to. Trying desperately to get back home to his wife. Now, if you had asked me a year ago what I thought the cause of Prince Evander's delay would be…" Casper whistles, earning several hoots and chuckles from the other advisors stationed at the table.

They like to do this. Like to imply that Evander is off warming the beds of prostitutes, his love for me quenched by nothing more than the passing of a few months.

That's fine.

Their claims would probably bother me more if I doubted what Evander was up to, but I don't. The only reason they feel the need to mock my marriage is that they're jealous of my relationship with King Marken.

Never mind that I would gladly pawn off the responsibility of having to interact with Marken if I could.

That, and I get the impression Casper considered himself next in line for the throne before I came along. I think he hoped that, since Marken possesses such hatred for his two living children, he would eventually decide his favorite nephew was a better fit for ruling the kingdom.

Poor Casper.

I ignore him, turning my attention to Marken. "There's still concern regarding the Queen of Mystral's involvement with the Rip."

Before the king can respond, Casper snorts. "The supposed Rip."

I address Evander's cousin through my teeth. "The King and Queen of Naenden can attest to the Rip's authenticity."

"Are we really going to trust what the Queen of Naenden thinks she sees with that one eye of hers?" asks Casper.

Never in my life have I witnessed such a self-satisfied grin on the face of someone so idiotic.

"Pray tell, how do you think eyes work?" I ask, never quite prepared for the conversations I'm subjected to when Casper occupies the room.

"Enough," says Marken, though he directs his statement more to Casper, whose mouth is open with a retort, than to me. "We'll await news from my son before we come to hasty conclusions regarding another kingdom's monarch."

And to think everyone else believes Marken actually listens to me.

"There's another matter to discuss, of course," says Casper, looking about the table at the other advisors, who are all nodding their heads.

I suppose this means there was a pre-meeting meeting I wasn't invited to.

Marken sighs. "And that is?"

"What should be done in the event the Heir of Dwellen does not return."

Casper has the gall to fake sobriety as he discusses the possibility of my husband's death.

I know Casper is goading me, but for once, I let it go without rebuke. My stomach flips over inside me at the idea that something has happened to Evander. It's a place I haven't allowed my mind to go, not with everything else I've been processing.

If Marken is upset by the idea that harm might have befallen his son, he doesn't show it. He simply says, as if we're discussing this morning's breakfast, "You are aware that, in the event that Evander perishes with no legitimate heir of his own, the throne would go to you, Casper."

And with the way Casper's eely gaze slips over to meet mine, I have the sneaking suspicion Casper is already aware of this.

I SPEND the afternoon with my face buried in Evander's pillow, chasing my racing thoughts around, trying to contain them. Before today I've been successful in keeping my mind from wandering down the path of worst-case scenarios, but Casper's comment in the meeting sent me over the edge.

Not that the meetings ever leave me with an overwhelming urge to skip around whistling or anything. I never feel that I handle the jeering comments well. If I ignore their jabs, I worry I seem weak. If I refuse to tolerate their unflattering comments about Evander, I worry they'll see Evander as weak.

I'm so overwhelmed that I completely forget that my mother was supposed to stop by for a visit. Of course, when Imogen brings her to my room and they find me crying, having lost my battle to remain dry-eyed, my mother sits on the bed with me and listens as I explain the events of today's meeting through a series of sniffles.

She, of course, reassures me that I'm doing just fine. But she always thinks that.

"You know, we women have power," she says once my tears have mostly subsided.

"It doesn't always feel like it," I say. "I can't exactly make them have any respect for Evander."

My mother smiles softly. "I'm sure they respect him more than you think."

I scoff. "If you heard the awful things they say, you wouldn't be claiming that."

My mother quirks a brow. "Is that so? Just last week I happened to visit the tailor's just as Casper Thornwall's wife was leaving. You wouldn't believe the unflattering things she had to say about her husband. The male was the mockery of the entire shop by the time she was through."

"I would have something to say too if I was unfortunate enough to be married to Casper Thornwall," I say, even the thought making me want to gag. I cringe in an attempt to rid myself of the notion.

"But you're not married to Casper. You're married to Evander. If Casper Thornwall's wife had the influence you do, what do you imagine she would do with it?"

A wicked smile curves across my lips. "Entertain the rest of us with a litany of Casper's worst qualities, I would hope." It makes my heart lighter just thinking about it.

"Yes, and I imagine Casper knows just that."

I shift on the bed to face her. "What's your point?"

"My point is that Casper sees you, and he sees how you talk about Evander, and he knows he could never trust his wife in the company of the king's advisors like Evander trusts you. Respect is a funny thing. We tend to give it to people who already receive it from others, whether they've earned it or not. Sometimes, respect from the majority grows or withers from the esteem, or lack thereof, of those closest to them."

I roll her words around in my mind, picking them apart and trying to decide if I agree or not. "Casper doesn't want his wife around the other advisors because Casper deserves everything his wife says about him. Besides, what you're describing isn't exactly respect," I grumble.

"No," my mother says, "but it is jealousy. Which is pretty close, if you ask me."

I JOIN Asha and Fin in the library later that day. They have a tendency to huddle together, whispering. What they're researching, I have no idea, but I don't press them about it.

Besides, I'm a tad too concerned with scrounging for information to be all that concerned with what they're up to.

I'm going to have a baby.

A baby.

Evander's baby. A half-fae, half-human little baby.

There's a deplorable lack of information out there regarding what one should expect in my situation.

Oh, sure. There are plenty of books in the library about fae pregnancies, most of them focusing on how to increase the chances of procreating, given success tends to be elusive for the fae.

Apparently not for me.

That's fine. Evander and I already knew we wanted children. I just didn't expect it to happen this quickly. Not with how difficult everyone made it out to be for fae to reproduce.

We decided from the beginning we wouldn't do anything to prevent it, for a variety of reasons. It took my parents a decade of trying to have me, and I share my mother's menstrual irregularities. That, paired with the fae's general difficulty procreating, caused us to determine that sooner than later was the best time to, if not try, then at least not *not* try.

Well, not *not* trying appears to have been effective.

Unfortunately, even the books that discuss fae gestation aren't helpful. Apparently, gestation for the fae is slightly shorter than for humans, though it varies significantly depending on the pregnancy.

Again, not that helpful to me, considering I'm human.

There are books on human pregnancy, of course, which I suppose might have been more helpful in teaching me what to expect from my body, but again, if fae gestation often depends on the levels of magic the baby's inherited…

Well, I just have no idea what to expect. Because until recent years, fae-human pairings were considered taboo, no one seems to have bothered to research what actually happens when a human becomes pregnant with a fae's child.

It's been several weeks since Asha and I first realized I was pregnant. She's been discreet and only asks about it when we're out of earshot from anyone else. Part of me isn't thrilled that she knows. If it were up to me, I'd have wanted Evander to be the first to know, but we still haven't heard from him, which has my stomach twisting further into knots. The other part of me is glad Asha figured it out, because at least I have someone to talk to about it.

Well, someone other than Peck, the royal physician, whom I told immediately.

He congratulated me, claiming he hoped the child inherited my brains rather than its father's, which he must have immediately realized was rather insensitive when I burst into a waterfall of out-of-character tears.

Peck, unfortunately, also knows little about human-fae pregnancies. So it didn't help me at all that I told him. Though he is showering me with all the treatments he can come up with for both fae and human pregnancies, meaning a strict regimen of rather contradictory advice.

The most unfortunate part is that I'm not really sure exactly how long I've been pregnant. My cycles have never been regular, which is why I didn't realize initially that something was happening. Now that I think of it, I'm not sure I've even had a cycle since Evander and I married, meaning I could be as far along as four months.

At first, I dismissed the notion. After all, my symptoms didn't appear until a few weeks ago. But Peck informed me that fae rarely experience symptoms until several months into pregnancy.

Now that I've actually started paying attention, I've noticed my clothes no longer fit as well as they used to. Imogen has had to make frequent trips to the tailor to have them taken out.

Thankfully Othian fashion has taken a turn for the poofy in the past few weeks, making it rather easy to hide my belly, which has yet to truly pop, underneath obscene amounts of tulle.

I'm already not keen on the fact that two people know before Evander; I'm not about to let other people in on the news, at least for as long as I can help it.

Especially not my father-in-law.

Fates, surely Evander will be back before anyone else notices.

My heart aches when I let myself think of it—the possibility

Evander won't be back. That I'll be bereaved of him, forced to carry and raise this child on my own.

I haven't been able to consider that version of the future, so I haven't really let myself consider *any* future. I've just plunged myself into the research of what exactly I need to be doing to keep this baby healthy, and what exactly I should expect.

After about the four hundredth book that doesn't at all mention fae-human pregnancies, I realize there may be no way of knowing what I can expect.

I'm about to give up, about to wander back to my and Evander's rooms, tuck my face into his shirt that still smells like him, and cry, when Fin jumps from the desk. "I found him," he says, running his hands through his jet-black hair.

I frown, unsure who he's talking about. Asha seems to know, because she knocks over a chair getting to the other side of the table. They both lean over an open, dusty book, Fin murmuring under his breath, Asha nodding in understanding.

I'm about to return to my fruitless endeavor when a herald bursts through the door.

"They're back," he says, and Asha, Fin, and I start.

"Who?" I ask, refusing to allow my heart to skip a beat, refusing to allow my hopes to rise.

The herald looks back and forth between Asha and me, his voice faltering. "Your...your husbands, of course."

Asha and I exchange a look, and then the two of us are both running.

WE'VE HARDLY MADE it to the cascading staircase when Evander and Kiran reach us. I jump into Evander's strong arms, memorizing the scent of him as he pulls me close and I tuck my chin into the crook of his neck.

He feels like home, and for the first time, as the tears flow freely from my eyes, I allow myself to admit how worried I've been that I'd never see him again.

"Never, ever do that again," I whisper into his ear.

He just buries his nose into the crook of my neck. "Whatever you say, Ellie Payne."

CHAPTER 13

KIRAN

*A*sha's going on about a thousand things I missed, hugging my neck and telling me I'm never allowed to leave again.

I pull her into me, savoring the curve of her back, the feel of her tiny body against mine. It hurts to touch her sometimes, to feel how fragile she is in my arms, how easily she could be taken away from me.

Humans die.

Asha is human.

Therefore, Asha...

Someone clears their throat. I look up the blue velvet–lined staircase to find Fin, hands in his pockets, looking purposefully at Evander and Ellie.

"Welcome back, old friend," he says, clapping Evander on the shoulder.

Evander immediately punches him in the face.

We all stand there in shock for a moment, Asha's eye wide as she glances up at me in faux horror, when I know she's only covering her mouth to hide her laugh.

"Evander!" Ellie cries, though more in shock than true reprimand.

My mind returns to a scene of Fin taking Ellie by the hand at her betrothal ball, leading her onto the dance floor and sweeping her away as Evander watched, fuming.

A sheepish grin overtakes Evander's face. He just shrugs, then reaches out and claps Fin on the back as if they're old pals, Fin still rubbing his jaw in confusion.

"I would say I deserve that, except I think you probably have me to thank for helping you uncover those feelings of yours," says Fin, straightening.

"Pretty sure I would have figured it out on my own," Evander says, any sign of animosity washed from his features.

Ellie gives Evander a look that he can't see—one that indicates she's not convinced. But soon the entire group is laughing, and Evander and Fin are making plans to fence in the courtyard tomorrow.

Something twists in my chest, and Evander looks over at me. "You're invited too, of course."

"Kiran hates fencing," says Fin, hastily. "I'm sure you'd rather spend your time doing something more productive, wouldn't you?"

Fin's smiling, but in his eyes is a dare, one that challenges me to see what he'll do if I ruin one more thing for him, even a stupid fencing match.

AFTER ASHA and Ellie barrage us with questions about our journey, and the two decide we've answered their questions satisfactorily, Asha's fingers interlock with mine, and she tugs me away from the group. We find ourselves in a coat closet, of all places, which is much too small for us. Well, too small for me.

"You can't wait until we get back to the room?" I ask, though not at all in judgment. My magic boils in my veins, as if I haven't been allowing myself to feel just how much I've missed her.

"No," she says, then apparently feels my magic run cold, because she corrects herself. "That's not what I meant. I'd rather not wait, but I need to talk to you about something."

"And talking can't wait?" I say, tracing my thumb around the curve of her hipbone.

She wriggles a bit, nervous energy practically spewing out of her. "No. Well, Imogen's up cleaning our rooms right now."

"Imogen? How have they not fired that woman yet?"

"That's an excellent question, and altogether beyond the point. But I don't want her overhearing this. Kiran.... Kiran, I think Fin and I did it."

"Did what?"

She takes a deep breath. "I think we found your father."

Something in my head buzzes a bit. "My father?" The word feels strange on my lips. Strange, because all my life, Rajeen was my father, or so I believed. About a year ago I discovered Fin and I were the byproduct of my mother seeking out a lover to provide the king the heir he so desperately desired.

Asha bites her lip. "I didn't tell you the right way, did I?"

I wrinkle my brow, then let out a short laugh. "No, I can't think of a better way than pulling me into a coat closet, getting me excited that you pulled me into a coat closet, then bringing up my illegitimate father."

Asha hits my chest playfully, though the contact is lighter than usual given she has no room to rear back in this coat closet. "Well, when you put it that way, it sounds worse."

"Does it?" I tease.

"Are you okay?"

I shrug. "I don't know him. It feels...strange...I suppose, knowing he's out there somewhere. But nothing more than that."

"And what happened with Fin downstairs?"

This time, an unpleasant feeling punctures my chest. I shake my head. "It's nothing different from how it always is between us."

"I hate to see him..." Asha tenses up, searching for the right word.

"Hate me like he does?"

She nods, sadness filling her eye.

"Yes, well, I don't think there's anything that can be done about it. I deserve his hatred, and there's nothing I can do to fix it. Nothing I can do that will keep him from looking at me and seeing Ophelia's blood on my hands."

Asha nods, biting her cheek and tucking her face into my chest. I'm always so conflicted when she does that. Part of me worries she does it to hide her scars. The other part of me revels in how she comes to me for protection, comfort.

"Still. I wish he'd forgive you."

"It would be nice if all it took was a punch to the jaw, wouldn't it?" I say.

Asha looks up at me. "Do you think that would help?"

"Why? Are you planning on giving Fin any ideas?"

CHAPTER 14

ELLIE

I lie in Evander's arms, burying myself into my husband's warm and familiar chest. Clinging to him feels critical, like if I let him go, this might turn out to be a dream.

Our reunion had been an emotional one.

After quite a few tears, most of them shed by me, and plenty of exchanged hugs (except for Kiran, who hugged only Asha), Asha and I had finally gotten our explanations for what had happened over the past months.

We were right. The snowstorm that had blown through Mystral had made the roads back to Dwellen impassable, leaving Kiran, Evander, and Blaise trapped in Ermengarde.

As it turned out, they'd been too late to intercept the queen. They also explained that Blaise's friend had been punished by the queen, cast into an indefinite slumber that Evander was sure Peck could somehow figure out a way to solve.

He reassured her as much, and though Blaise smiled appreciatively, I could see in her sallow eyes that she wouldn't place her hope in Peck.

The change that had overcome Blaise in the past few months was startling, though I'd encountered as much the night we found her drunk on her awful stepmother's blood.

I'd hugged her just as tightly as Evander, though I sensed she was holding back. Whether it was her newfound strength and she was afraid of crushing me, or she was trying not to sink her fangs into my neck, I wasn't sure, but the rigidness in her posture dampened my heart a bit.

"I'm so glad you're back," I'd told her. Something flickered in her brown eyes, but then she flashed me a grin, one that was all too familiar, and said, "Well, I couldn't let Collins forget how to bake pecan pastries, could I?"

I'd laughed, hugging her again, squeezing her extra tightly, and whispering, "We'll do whatever we can to help you get your friend back."

She'd given me a smile that was more knowing than reassured, then stepped backward. "Well, I'll be getting out of your way," she said, gesturing with her head between me and Evander and Asha and Kiran. "I'm guessing there's some lost time you'll be wanting to make up for in the bedroom."

The room instantly heated around us—a sign of Kiran's embarrassment, I'd come to realize in the time he'd spent in Othian—but Evander just laughed and swatted Blaise away before picking me up in his arms and carrying me to our rooms, where making up for lost time was exactly what we'd done.

"So you think she loves him, this male the Queen of Mystral punished?" I ask, tucking my head into Evander's warm chest, relishing the feel of him as we lie under the warmth of the blankets.

"I've never seen her like this, El," says Evander, placing a kiss on my forehead. "She just seems distracted, distant, all the time. I know whatever happened to her in Mystral, whatever changed her into what she is now, had an effect on her, but I think it's more than that."

My heart aches. "I can't imagine. Even just knowing how I felt when you were gone, when we hadn't heard from you..." I shake my head, shuddering until the sound of his heart against my ear settles me.

"Yeah, me neither," he says, running his hands through his hair.

My heart lurches.

In a moment, I can see them. Our child. A thousand versions of them, a thousand combinations of me and Evander, playing and laughing, giggling before my eyes.

My heart swells, and I realize I haven't let it yet. Haven't allowed myself to be excited, not with Evander gone. Not with the fear creeping in my mind that I'd never get to see him lift our child onto his shoulders or tuck them into bed.

Excitement, for the first time, barrels through me. Fear, too. Dread, really. But it all sort of feels the same, squirming in my stomach and filling me with butterflies.

"What is it?" Evander asks, his sea-green eyes swooping down on me, drunk with our reunion.

I bite my lip, grinning.

But then Evander is grabbing my waist, rolling on top of me.

"You're looking at me like you want to go for round two," he says, mischief glittering in his eyes.

I laugh, and he presses a kiss to my collarbone, making me dizzy.

The words hang on my tongue, but even as he kisses me, something feels wrong about saying them. Not here. Not now, at least.

Evander and I are going to have a baby. There's a child that will giggle and laugh and walk and have its own thoughts and opinions growing inside of me, and for some reason that doesn't seem like the sort of thing to tell your husband in the throes of desire.

No, this is the sort of thing you plan out. The kind of thing you plot, devise a clever way to surprise him with. I've been so caught up in the worry that I would never get the chance to tell him, I haven't even considered *how* I would tell him.

But then Evander kisses me again, and I realize it will be a little bit before my mind can concentrate properly.

CHAPTER 15

BLAISE

I'm pacing outside of the Othian palace library, trying to work up the nerve to ask Asha, Queen of Naenden, on a stroll.

The funny thing is, this is the sort of thing I would have found simple only a few months ago. I'm aware there are people whose consciousnesses attack them with anxiety when it comes to initiating social interactions, but of my many and various struggles, that has never been one of them.

But I'm usually not extending a social invitation with the intention of luring someone I like to their kidnapping, either, so perhaps that's the difference.

As I pace, trying to come up with a smooth way to lure Queen Asha out of the palace, the portrait of Princess Olwen that sits on the wall across from the library stares down upon me in judgment. That's exactly what Evander's pompous sister would be doing if she were here, and not holed up in a tower made of vines. Vines that probably have perfectly symmetrical flowers sprouting out of them.

I pointedly ignore her.

I suppose I could simply walk up to Queen Asha, put on a disarmingly boisterous smile, and tell her I need to stretch my legs after a long while cooped up in the Queen of Mystral's dungeon, and would she like to tag along?

But wouldn't that seem strange to her? I only just arrived at the palace two nights ago, and surely the queen would expect me to want to spend time with Ellie over her. Perhaps I could mention that I would have rather taken Ellie, but she was busy with royalty-adjacent tasks.

Except that would be rude, and just as likely to dissuade the queen from joining me.

I've about run through all my good ideas when the library doors open and someone slams into me.

"Watch where you're going, why don't y—oh!" I straighten, clearing my throat before I can spew a host of curses at the very woman I'm hoping to charm. "I apologize, Your Majesty. I didn't realize it was you. I should have been watching where I was going," I say, giving a bouncing curtsy to the queen, who looks as dazed as I feel.

She flits her hand to the side. "Don't worry about it. It's my fault, anyway. One would think at this point I'd remember to turn my head to look, but alas." She gestures to the side of her face that's missing an eye.

I'm unable to stifle my laugh, which is unfortunate. Not because the queen seems the type to be offended easily, but because it would be much more convenient for me if she weren't so stinking likable.

"Actually, I'm glad to have run into you," Asha says. "Well, not literally, of course. But here we are. I've been huddled over a pile of books as tall as I am for the past several days. My back might never straighten to its full height again. Every time I try to make my way out of the palace for a stroll, the portraits of the princess always make me feel like she's scoffing at me for going the wrong direction. Think you could point me toward the gardens?"

I straighten, shocked by my luck, but I try not to seem too eager. "I'd be happy to. But...would you mind checking out the window? To make sure the sun's already set."

Asha turns toward the nearest window, which is curtained heavily (this entire wing is, at Evander's command). She pulls it aside carefully and peeks out. "All clear," she says before she follows me heartily to her undoing.

"I'M HONESTLY surprised you want to be out here at night," I say as Asha and I stroll through the gardens. Even though summer has officially permeated Dwellen, there's still an evening chill that washes over the land once the sun sets.

I find it invigorating, but it's rather clear the queen does not. She's wrapped herself in a burgundy coat, one I'm sure Ellie gifted her, and a fur scarf obscures her neck.

It doesn't seem quite cold enough for all of that, but then again, I wasn't raised in the desert either.

It also occurs to me that the scarf covering Asha's neck might be for my benefit, though I've found my cravings, while potent, never seem to get as out of hand as they did for Nox.

As they *do* for Nox, I remind myself.

As with any time I catch myself thinking of him in the past tense, my stomach twists.

I quicken my pace, making for the tree line.

"I had it in my head that I would love the cold," Asha says, rolling her one eye at herself. "It always seemed so romantic. All the best stories have at least one scene set in the snow-capped mountains. Maybe the snow is worth it, but I've yet to see it, and I can't imagine it's worth feeling as though my joints are going to freeze together."

I let out a half-hearted chuckle, fogging the air in front of me. "Maybe you should take your walks during the day, then."

She peers down at me, only slightly taller than me, but still. Maybe it's that missing eye of hers that makes her seem so much taller. "I don't mind it so much," she says carefully.

I get the gnawing sensation that her nighttime walk was intentional. That she's been waiting for a time when I could accompany her. But why?

My gut twists inside me. Asha has a trace of the Old Magic inside her. It knows things, stories, it shouldn't. Has it seen visions of my plans with Az? Does Asha know what I intend to do, and she's simply leading me into a trap?

Panic surges inside me, and I find my senses flitting around the garden, focusing in on the rustle of birds in the trees, the gentle hum of earthworms squirming in the dirt, the padding of raccoons among the vegetables.

But I feel no one else.

No one aside from *him*, at least.

"Are you all right?" Asha's hand twitches, like she intends to take mine, but she simply frowns and says, "Kiran told me."

A lump forms in my throat. "About what?" I ask, not because I don't know, but because I want to postpone the inevitable. The moment the queen attempts to show me compassion the second before I betray her.

"About Nox. Kiran told me. Not everything, but enough."

I don't know why, but something about the fact that both Kiran and Asha have bothered to remember his name when they've never even met him has my eyes burning.

My voice is shaking, but I try my best to steady it. To maintain the nonchalant demeanor I've always found so practical. "Yes, well, then I suppose he also told you I've gone and fallen in love with my torturer. Evander hasn't said much about it, but I'm sure he's thrilled."

Asha smiles, though it's somewhat pained. "I think you'll find that Kiran is unlikely to pass that sort of judgment."

Something is squeezing at my ribcage, threatening to wrench the air out of me. Throughout Alondria, Kiran is known for his villainy. I'm not sure his sparing of Asha will ever change that. I'm not sure anything he does to atone for his sins will ever change how everyone perceives him. He has a bloodstain on his reputation, one that no launderer can cleanse.

I know what that's like.

Nox does too.

I hate relating to Kiran, hate relating to Asha. And I'm so, so tired of the shame, the guilt that only ever rots holes on my insides, never binding me up or turning me from my set path.

I shake my head; I'm being stupid. Just a few hours ago, I was fine, the wall around my heart completely intact. I don't understand why I can push these feelings away one minute, then be bombarded by them the next.

We're close to the tree line now. Close enough that the scent of pine curls in tendrils around my nostrils.

Someone's heart pumps behind a nearby tree.

I can sense him, recognize him.

I'm confident Asha cannot.

There's a faint glow coming from the lanterns strung up around the garden that highlights Asha's harsh features. Enough light that, should any of the guards patrolling the gardens walk by, they'd see everything.

More importantly, they'd see I was with her when it happened.

They'd know I didn't try to help, like I'll claim later when questioned about her disappearance.

Just a few more steps, and we'll be safely tucked away into the darkness, where no guard can contradict my story, the story Az has woven on my tongue.

I'm doing this for Nox, I remind myself.

Because that's what love is. Having no boundary you wouldn't cross, no wall you wouldn't shatter, no world you wouldn't burn for that person.

That's what love is.

It's what it has to be, because otherwise I don't think I can claim it, and I can't bear to think that perhaps I don't actually love Nox.

A memory assaults my mind, one where Farin's arms wrap around the backs of my legs, hauling me into his arms as he presses his lips to mine...

I shake it away.

"I've found some books in the library," Asha says, snatching me from my thoughts. "Some on potions, others on creatures that can inflict sleep. I don't know if there's a book out there that contains the answer to saving him, but if there is, I'll find it."

"What?" My question sounds hollow, as I'm somewhat stunned by Asha's vow. It means no more than a vow coming from my lips would, since neither of us is bound by the fae curse, but still.

"You don't have to do that." I try to keep the begging out of my voice, the please don't do this. *Please don't be kind to me. Not here. Not now. Not before I ruin you.*

"I want to." The way Asha says it makes it sound like it should be obvious.

My legs are trembling now, and I can only be thankful that Asha's human vision won't notice now that I've stepped halfway into the shadows.

Az is just behind the tree, the one to which Asha has her back turned. I can feel his heart pounding with excitement. I can feel the blood rushing to his limbs. He peeks behind the tree, just barely, and when he glimpses her, his breath catches.

Fates, I realize for the first time, *he really does have feelings for her.* Part of me has wondered if he's been exaggerating his relationship with Asha, the childhood friendship he'd claimed bound them.

I can tell now he's not exaggerating.

Maybe it's for the best. Maybe it's Az and Asha who are Fated. Maybe, if their lives were woven into a tapestry, this is how their story would always end. Maybe they're bound together by something more ancient, more primal than even a fae marriage bond.

Maybe this will not end badly for Asha.

"I can tell you're afraid," says Asha. "You're skilled at hiding it, but I recognize the signs. The jokes—they're supposed to mask the fear, aren't they?"

I swallow, the lump in my throat growing uncomfortably large. "You seem like you've gotten the best of your fears."

Asha's gaze waters over, wanders off into the dark distance. "If that's what you think, I guess I haven't lost my knack for acting."

Dread coils in my gut, and I want to scream, to beg her to stop talking, lest, lest...

"There's someone out there who wants me. Wants to use me for evil. Everyone else prefers to believe he's moved on to easier targets, but I don't think any of them quite understand. They don't know him like I do..."

Asha's still looking off into the distance, stepping backward, as if to rest her back against the tree. One more step, and the shadows will consume her.

Az shifts in the trees, readying to pounce.

Just step to the side. Into the shadows where no one will see, I tell myself.

Oh, why am I so terribly awful at listening to myself?

"Asha. Asha, you need to go back inside."

Az's heart practically stops. Then his pulse races, anger and confusion practically barreling off of him. I watch him step forward, his arms outstretched to grab Asha and steal her away, but my comment has her sidestepping into the light.

"Asha," I say, this time with enough force to my voice to alert the guard falling asleep on the balcony ahead. Voices murmur from up above, signaling to me I've got their attention.

More importantly, signaling to Az I've got their attention.

I grit my teeth, confusion washing over Asha's face.

"What's wrong?" she asks.

"Your fear." I make a careful effort to flare my nostrils, clamp my jaw. "It's making your heart race."

A breeze flutters through the gardens, and I seize the opportunity to gasp.

I let my canines out to shine. Asha's eye goes wide at the sight of them.

"Run," I beg, and she does.

CHAPTER 16

BLAISE

*I*t's no use avoiding Az.

Not since handing over Nox's and Zora's bodies back in Mystral.

I practically offered him my heartstrings on a platter.

By letting Asha go just now, I very well might have handed over Nox's and Zora's hearts as well.

My chest tightens at the thought, my canines drawing blood from where I forced them through my gums to frighten Asha away.

I don't mind that the guards on the balcony watch as I slink into the shadows. When Asha tells them I warned her that a craving struck me, they'll think I'm trying to avoid temptation. Perhaps they'll even think I'm out hunting for animal blood to satiate my thirst.

Even if they doubt my intentions, even if they think I'm a potential hazard to the human residents, I've had enough run-ins with the Othian guards to know they're unlikely to risk their own skin for the sake of the humans.

"I'm going to need a very convincing argument for why you let her get away just now," Az says, still leaning up against the back of the tree.

We're both in the shadows, but a benefit of my vampirism is a heightening of all my senses, including my night vision.

Fates, he's beautiful. His jaw perfectly cut, his black hair just messy enough to give him a wild sort of quality. He's the type of man who wouldn't have much trouble luring girls out into the woods alone late at night.

"You said you needed her alive," I say. "You should just be thankful I had the self-control not to rip her throat out just now."

Az has the presence of mind to mask his expression, but that doesn't do much to hide the way his heart races at the idea of Asha's blood spilling.

Fear for her life rolls off of him in waves.

It's a good thing too, because his relief that I didn't hurt her is the only thing keeping Nox alive right now.

"I thought you said you had your cravings under control," he counters.

I blink, fidgeting with the strands at the end of my braid. "I missed my dose this afternoon."

Az's tone goes steely. "You missed your dose." He runs his hands through his hair. "You're a wreck."

I close my eyes, gritting my teeth. "It won't happen again."

A cloud shifts in the sky, moonlight highlighting the way Az's eyes shutter with suspicion. "If your cravings are so bad right now, why do you not seem to have trouble around me?"

"Not everyone's blood is equally appealing to me. You have fae blood in your veins. It has this sour scent to it." I wince, as if even being around him makes me want to gag.

I'm not sure I've entirely convinced him, but I must have at least planted some doubt, because his shoulders slacken and he rests his forehead against the tree. "If you ever put her in danger again, remember whose life I hold in my hands."

The monster inside me envisions ripping Az's head from his body, but it would only be satisfying for a moment. An incredibly slim moment before the realization would strike that I'd never see Nox again.

"I already told you—it won't happen again," I mutter.

Az doesn't acknowledge my apology. Instead, he straightens, picking a shard of bark from the tree. "What I'm not sure will *happen again* is a better opportunity to get her alone. Do you think she'll be eager to go with you on another evening stroll after this?"

"You tell me. You're the one who claims to know her better than anyone else."

Az's expression hardens, his fingers snapping the piece of bark in his hands in half. "You need to fix this."

"I've been thinking," I say, my words pouring out of me, fearful that Az will walk away, and that as soon as he's out of sight, he'll abandon using me as part of the plan. That he'll stab a stake straight through Nox's heart and never think of us again. "And I think there's a better way to get Asha to the Rip."

Az cocks his brow and returns to defacing the tree. "You've been thinking?"

I ignore the insult to my intelligence, having gotten used to it from my stepfamily, and continue. "If we take Asha against her will, we'll incite Kiran's wrath. I don't know if you remember this, but the male burnt the King of Charshon to ashes from across the room last year."

"Kiran already has a bounty out on me," Az says, looking bored.

"Not as high as it would be if you took his wife. We both know there's nothing that incites him like jealousy."

"This isn't sounding like a plan to me. Just common observation."

"What if I could convince Asha to go to the Rip? Convince her it was her idea to begin with? Then we avoid Kiran hunting us down, intent on sprinkling our ashes on the nearest dung heap."

Az steps off of the tree upon which he was just leaning. "You think Kiran is going to allow his wife to go gallivanting across the world? To a Rip that is the weak spot between this realm and one containing vicious creatures who thirst for fae blood?"

"Maybe you're not giving him enough credit. He respects Asha, seems to let her think for herself."

Az scoffs. "And yet, you don't. You believe you can plant an idea in her head that she'll believe is her own."

I raise my chin. "Let's just say I'm highly motivated."

"And say you manage to convince Asha to come with you to the Rip willingly, and that, for reasons unknown, Kiran decides not to come with her. What then? What happens when she arrives at the Rip and realizes you've tricked her?"

I pick at my nails. "We'll cross that bridge when we get there, I suppose. But at least you won't have to drag her gagged and cuffed all the way there. Surely, you're intelligent enough to realize whatever hope you have of regaining her affection is likely to be squelched if you take that approach."

Az examines me with those sage-green eyes of his. "You really think you can do this? You really think you're just that clever? Clever enough to trick the woman who convinced an entire council of fae rulers that she'd forced her husband and brother-in-law to rip out their own hearts just at the sound of her voice?"

"Maybe not clever enough, no," I say. "But like I said, I'm highly motivated."

Az's smile is cruel. "I suppose I did make sure of that, didn't I?"

CHAPTER 17

ASHA

*L*ydia is back.

And she's back without Piper.

The library is quiet save for the librarian arguing about how she isn't keen on abandoning her station, leaving the precious books in the hands of a group partially composed of fire-wielders.

She even stands her ground in front of Lydia, which I consider fairly impressive. Eventually she seems to realize her protests are futile and she shuffles away, murmuring under her breath.

We all stand in silence for a moment. The group of us who've been waiting in Othian for Lydia's arrival take in the newcomers Lydia brought along. There's a man who stands closer to Lydia's side than I've ever seen a male, fae or human alike, dare. Are those her fingers fidgeting, as if considering taking his? He has a mess of brunette hair, sharp eyes, and a look of carefree cunning about him.

He's hardly older than me, which I have to say shocks me a bit.

It must shock Kiran and Fin too, because they keep glancing back and forth between their sister and the man. Like they're wondering if she's captured him as a pet, and if we're morally obligated to free him.

By the way he looks at Lydia, it does not appear he wishes to be freed.

I've always wondered if Lydia had a male she hid from the rest of us.

I guess now we know.

On the chaise behind Lydia lies the other man in their party. This man is clearly ill. His skin is an earthy brown, his eyes a stunning copper, though it's clear he's fighting to keep them open. His head is shaved, and atop his brow glimmers a thin layer of sweat.

He clutches his abdomen with one hand as if he might be ill at any moment. With the other, he holds the hand of a little girl. She has ghostly pale skin, a mess of a braid, and wide brown eyes that look more discerning than her years should allow.

There's an absence in the room that wafts off the pair.

Lydia looks around at the group, her lips pursed for a moment. Evander rises to meet her and introduce himself and Ellie.

Still, Lydia remains silent.

"They're trustworthy," Kiran says, recognizing the suspicion his sister holds for most everyone.

"Says the male who married a woman intent on assassinating him and taking his crown," Lydia responds, rather dryly, not taking her eyes off Evander.

Kiran sighs, rubbing his temples.

To Evander's credit, he doesn't wilt in Lydia's presence. Instead, he claps Kiran on the back and says, "Speaking from experience, I think it's those of us who've trusted the wrong people who end up being the best judges of character. We're the ones who know better than anyone what signs to look for."

He pulls Ellie close to his side, and she gives him an amused, yet slightly impressed look.

Lydia does not appear charmed.

Still, she continues on. "Very well. I found Piper months ago, deep in the villages of Avelea."

"She crashed their wedding," pipes up the child, and while I expect Lydia to look annoyed, the faintest of smiles curls on her lips.

"I suppose I did."

The man standing next to her rolls his eyes, as if that was a decision he tried and failed to talk her out of.

"I've had them hiding in Avelea with my contacts since. A month ago, we set out to move Piper and her family, as we'd gotten word her location had been compromised. During the move, we were ambushed."

Az. It was Az. It has to have been, my magic whispers.

I jolt to the edge of my seat, gripping the padding of the loveseat. "Az?" I ask, before my magic can overtake my voice.

The man lying ill on the couch jerks his head toward me at the mention of my friend.

Lydia shakes her head. "No, we believe it was Queen Abra of Mystral, though why she would want Piper, we're unsure."

Everyone who was there the night Blaise returned to Othian exchanges knowing looks.

Lydia stands, one hip out to the side. "Is anyone going to be kind enough to share what you know that I don't?"

Kiran goes on to explain Abra's identity, that she's Mother from my magic's story, the female who originally led the fae into Alondria through the Rip.

Lydia frowns. "What's our source on that intel?"

Ellie opens her mouth to explain, but at that moment, someone else speaks.

"Me." Blaise enters the library, shutting the door behind her. "They got the information from me."

Lydia looks Blaise up and down with that assessing gaze I'm all too familiar with. Blaise looks as if she might shrivel under Lydia's glare, but she bites her lip and holds her chin high.

"And what, exactly, are you?" Lydia asks.

Blaise glances down at her feet. "It's a long story."

Lydia turns back to the group. "I assume you've added this girl to your ever-growing list of people you lackadaisically assume can be trusted?"

"We trust Blaise," Kiran says, so quickly it startles me. I try to catch my husband's eye, but he gives me a look that says he'll reveal his reasoning later.

"Would anyone care to explain what Queen Abra wants with my wife?" the ailing male asks through heaving breaths.

"Yes, Marcus isn't the only one to be wondering that," says the man standing next to Lydia.

Ellie turns toward her friend. "Blaise, you know Abra better than any of us. Do you have any idea what she might want with someone gifted with the Old Magic?"

Blaise hesitates, exchanging a glance with me. She frowns apologetically, I suppose for contemplating feeding off me in the garden.

I'll have to assure her she's forgiven, later.

Sure, I'm not fond of the idea that she wanted to eat me. But that she wanted to and didn't speaks to her character in its own way.

"She needs to open the Rip," she says, her hands fisting at her side.

Kiran and I exchange a frown, even as my magic rumbles within me.

Mother hates the world of the Nether. I was there when she forced me to close the Rip.

I voice as much, and Blaise shrugs. "I don't know what to tell you, other than what I heard when I was in her dungeons."

My magic growls. *Is the night stalker calling me a liar?*

I don't think she's calling you anything, I think back.

Why are you defending someone who tried to eat you?

I'm not defending her. Well, I suppose I am defending her, but she didn't try to eat me.

Oh, she only wanted to eat you. You're right, that is much better.

Kiran shakes his head. "All we know about Mother—Abra—is that she originated from the realm that lies on the other side of the Rip. She's always been motivated to keep the Rip sutured. There's nothing for her on the other side, other than the memories of her own suffering. A time when she considers herself to have been weak. Why would she want to open the Rip?"

"Yes, child," Lydia says. "Do you have an inkling to why the queen might have changed her mind?"

Blaise hesitates, biting her lip and shuffling on her feet. "I'm trying to remember exactly what she said. I think...I think maybe it had something to do with her son Farin. The one who was dead. I don't remember everything. She had me drugged up a lot of the time, but I feel like I remember her mentioning him in connection to the Rip."

"She could have been discussing the way the boy perished," Kiran says. "He died shortly after the Rip was sutured, a victim of the fae curse, more potent in its first generation."

Blaise shakes her head. "No. No, I'm sure it had something to do with opening the Rip, not closing it."

She wants to bring him back. That vile female wants to bring him back.

"You said she kept his ashes," I offer. "Do you think she's hoping that if she's able to open the Rip, she can use the power to bring him back?"

My stomach twists at the thought.

She already has my sister to do that, my magic reminds me. *Why would she need the red-headed girl?*

I relay as much to the group, at which point Ellie answers, "The magic that infected Blaise only came out on the full moon. Maybe Queen Abra hopes to bring her son back sooner than that. Although," she pauses, thinking. "I suppose several full moons have already passed, so maybe that's not it after all."

Evander taps his knee, leaning back in his chair. "That, and it's not as if our friend Cinderella is all that cooperative when it comes to her hosts."

Kiran shakes his head. "You knew the parasite when she was bound to a human. Abra, as a fae, would have more power to bend the parasite to her will."

"Unless she made a fae bargain with it," I remind him.

"Would it have unbound the parasite from her curse to the moon when Blaise Turned?" Ellie asks me, well, my magic, I suppose.

"No," I answer for him. I'm already familiar with the answer from my magic muttering about it in my head all hours of the day. "It would have taken a different ritual to do that. Blaise, can you remember anything like that happening?"

Blaise shakes her head. "No. No, I don't think so. Not that it couldn't have happened while I was drugged. But I feel like I would have realized."

"You feel like it. How comforting." Lydia eyes Blaise with suspicion, but before Blaise can answer, Lydia turns to Marcus.

He must be prepared for the question because he says, "Piper is bound to no such curse. Her Gift works so long as she has an instrument to play."

"So this queen is taking Piper to the Rip?" the little girl whispers quite loudly to Marcus.

"It seems that's a possibility," he tells her, and I can't help but respect the way he doesn't feel the need to lie to the child. Not even under the pretense of protecting her.

"Well, at least we know where she's going," I say. "That means we can intercept her."

"That's assuming we're right about her going to the Rip, which I'm still not convinced of," says Kiran. "From what we know about Abra, it's in her core being not to allow the Rip to be opened. Remember the Council meeting? She was more than happy to assist Asha when she thought Asha was suffering under my hand. She didn't hesitate to place poison in my cup. But when Calias demanded Asha's death after her display of what she could do with her magic, Abra voted to put her to death. It seems Abra would do most anything to keep that Rip closed, even offer up someone she clearly believes to be innocent."

I nod, biting my lip. Kiran's logic is sound.

Blaise shuffles again, a bundle of nervous energy. It seems she doesn't enjoy speaking of the queen, though I can't blame her, not after the torture she suffered.

"But," Blaise says, "she's already shown she's willing to compromise what's right for something she perceives as more important. What if the game changed for her when she realized she could get her son back? What if she doesn't care what she has to do to save him?"

"That would be consistent with her behavior, based on what we know about her from the Old Magic's story," I admit. "She risked leading a host of fae into an unsuspecting realm to save Farin from infection. She'd do anything for her son."

"And who could blame her?" mutters Ellie.

Evander gives her a strange look before returning his attention back to the room.

Kiran shakes his head. "I still don't think she'd do it. Not again. Not after she sacrificed so much to close it."

Blaise addresses Kiran. "Why do you think that?"

Kiran levels a stare at Blaise, one of mutual understanding. "She's managed to lock her past, the part of her she's ashamed of, behind the Fabric, in a totally different realm. Something tells me, if we could all lock away our pasts like that, we wouldn't be keen on setting them free."

Blaise shudders under Kiran's assessing gaze, at the sheer vulnerability behind his words.

My heart gives a gentle tug toward my husband, and my hand finds its place in his.

"I don't know how to explain it," Blaise whispers to the room. "I just know in here," she closes a fist and places it on her gut, "that I'm right about this. We have to stop her."

Kiran shifts in his chair, his hand grasping tighter around mine. It's in that moment that, sound as Kiran's logic might be, I recognize why he's so unwilling to admit that the Rip might be at risk of opening.

Because if it is, I'm the only person we know other than Piper who could possibly close it.

"I'm sorry, Blaise, but it's my gut I trust, not yours," Kiran says.

"Do you have a better theory about where the queen has taken my wife?" Marcus hisses through gritted teeth.

Kiran pales at the man's anguish, his jaw set and his throat bobbing. "What exactly is it that Piper is Gifted with? Perhaps that could provide us with some answers."

"She can play songs that call out to children who are hurting," offers the little girl. "And she can drown people in floating pools of water."

Those who don't know Piper all exchange questioning looks.

"Kiran," I say, murmuring to him under my breath, "I don't think we can deny that Abra is taking Piper to the Rip. We don't have another explanation that makes sense."

Kiran tenses beside me, losing his grip on his hidden power for a moment. Dread, so potent it's almost crippling, leaks out from him and into my skin.

Horror at what he just did overcomes his face, but I stroke his arm, a silent reminder that I don't blame him for it.

"It's not enough evidence for me," says Kiran.

Lydia places a hand on her hip. "Kiran, you can't possibly be saying we should do nothing, given Abra's move against us?"

Kiran levels a glare at his sister. "You spent time with Piper. Do you think she'd betray the world by opening the Rip?"

Lydia scowls. "I hardly see how that's relevant."

"Of course she wouldn't open the Rip," says Marcus. "But if you think that means she deserves to be abandoned, just because we have confidence she won't betray us, I have to say I'm rather unimpressed by the King of Naenden. I guess you live up to your reputation, don't you?"

I expect heat to come rushing out of Kiran's hand, but that's not at all what I find.

There's no amount of anger that can drown out the crippling fear.

"I'm not saying we do nothing," says Kiran. "Between Naenden and Dwellen, we have plenty of resources to send after Piper."

"You just don't want Asha going," Blaise says, her voice warbling from across the room.

"Blaise," I hiss in warning, but she doesn't back down.

"This is bigger than any of us. Can't you see that? You weren't there, with Abra. You didn't see what I saw. You can't just ignore away the problem until it doesn't exist. Trust me, I would know. Asha," Blaise says, looking at me, "I know you understand. You're the only one who can ensure that Rip stays closed. I would go with you, I would—"

Kiran scoffs. "You almost tried to eat her, Blaise."

"Just don't let him control you like that," Blaise whispers. "Please."

Kiran's face flashes with something that almost looks like hurt.

I stand, letting go of Kiran's hand. "Thank you for your input, Blaise. But this decision is between me and Kiran, and frankly, I don't remember you being part of our marriage."

Blaise's face goes pale, and something like fury and desperation flickers behind her eyes.

"Piper is a decent person. One worth saving," is all Lydia says, directing her gaze at Kiran.

"I could go," Evander pipes up, Ellie squeezing his hand. "Lydia, Elias, Blaise. If we hurry, we might be able to intercept the queen before she reaches the Rip, assuming Piper is putting up a fight."

"Oh, I imagine she is," Marcus says, something like adoration mingled with exasperation in his voice.

"It's not going to be enough," Blaise whispers. Then she turns from the library, slipping out of the oak doors.

She's right, my magic whispers to me. *It's not going to be enough.*

CHAPTER 18

ELLIE

"*B*abe, I made a mistake."

Evander pulls his hand over his face as he paces across the floor of an empty guest room he pulled me into following the meeting in the library.

My heart sinks with anxiety, but Evander looks me in the face and continues. "I promised Blaise I'd help her. I don't know that I have a choice but to go to the Rip if she's going."

I nod my head, and though my mind is swimming with new information, I wade through it with my skirts pulled high.

"I want to come with you. I want to help."

Apparently, that isn't what Evander was expecting me to say, because his jaw works a little.

"That...that makes sense. I don't really want to have to leave you again either, El. I shouldn't have made that promise to Blaise without asking you first, though. I keep..." He grits his teeth, rubbing his sea-green eyes until they swim in pools of red.

"Making rash promises?" I ask. "In an attempt to make up for not figuring out sooner what was happening to her? Years ago, I mean? With her pregnancy, and her stepmother locking her up?"

Evander nods, his fingers still rubbing the space above his nose.

"I'm sorry, El."

I reach for the anger, feel around for it in my heart, but find none. "You'll need to stop doing that," I say, more because it seems practical than anything. "You can't be making so many promises to others that you end up putting them ahead of us."

Evander looks up at me, sorrow and regret swarming his eyes. "I know. Please know that it's not because I want to put anyone ahead of you. It's just..." He fumbles for the words.

"Guilt?" I ask.

He blows a heavy breath out of his mouth and leans against the counter behind him.

"Yeah, I think so."

I give him a soft smile, and he accepts it with a crinkle around his eyes.

"How are you not mad?"

I shrug. It's true, there's a twinge of irritation at Evander for making promises to others without me knowing about them. Promises are different for the fae. Breaking them could end up getting Evander killed. And then there's the fact that he made a promise to Blaise, of all people. Not that I haven't forgiven Blaise for all she's put us through. But sometimes I worry that Evander blames himself for Blaise's choices, and I don't want to see what could become of my husband if he places that kind of burden on his shoulders.

And no, I suppose I'm not thrilled that he made the promise to her without talking it over with me first. I knew when I married Evander that he was prone to rashness, and though it's something I hoped he'd work on, I know marriage doesn't magically change people overnight, and it wouldn't be fair of me to expect it to.

Okay.

So maybe I am angry, after all.

Maybe I want to scream that he was being stupid when he made that promise to Blaise. Maybe it makes me want to throw pillows at the wall—or okay, at him—because I don't want him leaving my side again...not when...

"What do you think about me coming with you to the Rip?"

The question sort of pops out of me.

Evander's jaw works. "I'm not going to lie, I don't like the idea. From what Asha's magic remembers about what's waiting on the other side of the Rip, I can't say I'm excited about the idea of having you anywhere near it."

My heart sinks, and I have to fight the urge to bring my hand to my belly for what has become a self-soothing habit in private. If Evander isn't fond of the idea of my going to the Rip now, certainly he won't allow me to go if he knows I'm carrying our child.

But I can't stay, I can't. "I really don't like the idea of being away from you again," I whisper, and Evander frowns.

"Evander, it's not even just that. It's that…" I squint, tears filling my eyes as all the emotions crash upon me. "It's that I've felt so, so… useless lately. Ever since I lost my ability to work glass, to make art, and especially after Blaise went missing…I couldn't do anything for her, anything to help her. And I can't make anything useful anymore. And let's just be honest, your mother doesn't need me in her meetings with the noblewomen; she's perfectly good at persuading them herself. Then there's your father. I know everyone is convinced I'm the only one he listens to, but even then, it's not very often. I just…I'm just a little lost right now, and I know I can't offer much to your expedition. I know I don't have magic like Asha and I can't fight like Blaise, and Fates, I can't really do anything of use, can I? But I just can't…I can't just stay here and wonder whether you're alive or dead. Not again."

Evander frowns again, then he pushes himself off the wall and comes near, tucking his finger underneath my chin and raising it so I can look at him. "You're not useless, Ellie."

I let out a bit of a strangled cough. "I know I'm not to you, but pretty much to everyone else…"

"I'm so sorry you lost your dream for me, El."

I shake my head. "I wasn't saying this so you would feel guilty about it. I love you, Evander. I'd do it over again if it meant saving you. I just…I just need to do *something*."

He nods, understanding. And for a moment, I think maybe he's about to tell me I can come along. A fae promise that will bind him to it, one he can't take back.

And I deserve that, don't I? He made a binding promise to Blaise without including me in the decision. It wouldn't be any different if I led him to make this promise to me without providing him all the relevant information.

But then, as he opens his mouth to tell me I can come, something wrings my gut. Because this baby is ours, not only mine, and who am I to withhold it from him just to get my way?

"You can—"

"Evander, stop," I say, twisting my fingers through his. "Before you decide, there's something you should know."

Evander cocks his head to the side, his sea-green eyes examining me.

It's not at all how I planned it, with forethought and a perfectly designed riddle for him to figure out.

Instead, I just blurt, "I'm pregnant."

Evander stares at me, and for a moment, I wonder if he isn't going to react at all. He just stands there, his fingers still intertwined in mine, though they've gone a bit limp.

"Pregnant," he says, blinking heavily.

I nod. "Pregnant."

"With a baby?"

"As far as I know, it's not a dragon or…"

And then my husband is grinning, and the stupid thing takes up his entire face, creasing the edges of his eyes, which are now glazed over with tears.

"How?" And before I can remind him just how it happened, he shakes his head. "No, I mean, when? How far along?"

"I'm not entirely sure, but I think a few months. Honestly, I'm surprised you didn't notice…earlier."

"What? When I took your clothes off?" He grins, and I laugh.

"You can definitely tell," I say, pointing to the bulge in my belly I've been trying to hide with mountains of tulle.

Evander grins, a cocky smile that has me swooning. "I just thought

131

you missed me so much that you'd turned to those pecan tarts of yours for comfort."

I gasp, but he only smiles. "I thought it was adorable."

Evander picks me up, spinning me in the air, until he seems to realize he's making me queasy, at which point he sets me down on a nearby chaise and looks at me like he doesn't quite know what to do with me.

It occurs to me that if I were Evander and our situations were reversed, this would be the time to make a dirty joke.

"Okay, so I know what you're going to say, and I understand completely why you'll want me to stay behind," I say. "But before you go and make up your mind that I'm safer here, Evander, I don't want to do this without you. I can't. Well, you know, I could technically do this without you. I mean, it would be difficult, but I'd figure it out."

Evander looks down at me, craning one eyebrow.

I take a breath in. "But the point is...I don't want to. I want you here for every moment. I want you to feel our baby kick, and I want you to be here to tell me I look sexy when I cry because my ankles have swollen to elephant-level size, and I want you to use those bat ears of yours to tell me you can hear our baby's heart beating, and most of all, I want you here, right next to me, when this baby comes. Because if you leave me alone to do this by myself while you're off adventuring with Blaise, and if you're not here to squeeze my hand and tell me I'm spectacular while I'm quite literally ripping my body to shreds to bring our child into this world, then Evander Thornwall, I'm going to be peeved."

Evander searches my face, a sly grin tugging at his lips.

"What? Aren't you going to say something?" I ask, only now realizing that my heart is pounding.

"Oh, nothing," says Evander, though the smile he's trying and failing to hide says quite the opposite.

"What?"

"Oh, nothing. It's just that you said you needed me."

"Okay, well, I qualified it quite a bit after that."

Evander wags his finger. "No, no, no. You, Elynore Payne, said that *you* needed *me.*" He points at his chest as if there were another Evander Thornwall in the room. "I would have thought you didn't need me for anything, well, other than—"

He squeezes my butt, and I can't help the laugh that follows.

"You can't distract me from this."

"I can't?" he asks, slipping his hands down to my hips and bringing his mouth to mine.

Okay, so that's a tad distracting.

"Evander," I say, pushing him away. "I need an answer. Or at least for you to tell me you're considering what I'm saying. That you're thinking up an answer. Because I could have not told you, you know. Okay, so that would have been slightly manipulative, and maybe I shouldn't hold that over your head. But..."

"Ellie," he says, taking my hands in his. His gaze dips to my belly, and his hands follow. "Something's brewing on the horizon, something big. I can't explain it, but..." He shivers, and for a moment, my carefree husband lets a spark of fear shine in his gaze. "I can't believe you didn't know."

"Didn't know what?"

"That I'm not letting you out of my sight."

CHAPTER 19

EVANDER

I'm not sure which idea is more terrifying, that I'm going to be a father, or that I'm about to transport my family to the Rip.

In hindsight, I probably shouldn't have told Ellie she could come along.

But it's not as if I can very well take it back now, not when I've given her my word.

And besides, the selfish part of me, the part of me that seems to refuse to grow up no matter how many decades pass, is glad she'll be by my side.

I've spent months away from her, all the while feeling like a piece of my chest cavity was missing. And now that I know she's carrying a child—our child—I'm even less keen to leave her.

Which leads me to the other glaring "in hindsight," which is that I likely shouldn't have promised Blaise that I'd go with her to help free Nox from his curse.

It seemed like such a noble thing at the time, to promise my aid to my friend. I already got my dream—though part of it I didn't know about at the time. And since I didn't save her from the pain she endured as a youth, I'd thought this was my chance. Not that I can ever hope to make it up to her.

There's something odd that happens when people get their happy ending. I always scoffed at it when I was younger—friends finding love and getting married, and then the inevitable...a long line of suitors hand-picked by my incredibly happy friends, just insisting that they wanted the same for me.

I'm happy with Ellie. It's like the part of me that wandered about aimlessly for so many years is finally anchored at shore.

I'm happy, and I want my friend to be happy too.

But it was stupid to promise that I'd be the guarantor of that happiness.

Again, not something I can take back now.

I rub at the back of my neck before I go to find Blaise in the library.

There's no dousing the joy in my heart at the news that I'm going to be a father. A father to Ellie Payne's child—Fates, the thought threatens to plaster a stupid smile on my face.

But I'd be lying if I said the sight of Blaise doesn't, if not dampen my joy, then at least push it to the side for a moment.

Everyone evacuated the library after Lydia's surprise arrival, pairing off with their confidants to make joint decisions about what needs to be done next. Asha with Kiran. Ellie with me. Lydia with Elias. Even Marcus with Amity.

Everyone except for Blaise, who I suddenly realize has no one to convene with.

My heart aches for my friend as I watch her, bent over in a chair, picking at the threads of a tapestry, tears spilling down her face and soaking the fabric.

She startles as I approach, stuffing the tapestry into a satchel by her side before crossing her legs, as I've never seen her do, and straightening her back.

"I didn't notice you there," she says, clearing her throat. It's the type of thing you say to make everything seem normal, though for

Blaise, whose hearing should be better than even mine, it means the opposite.

That Blaise is so wrapped up in whatever thoughts were causing those tears is not a good sign.

She gestures for me to sit across from her, in the chair directly across from the blazing hearth, but I remain standing.

"I see you're keeping up with the cross-stitching," I say, nodding toward the satchel.

Blaise wipes the tears from her eyes with the backs of her hands. "It's not technically cross-stitching, but good try. It keeps me distracted," she says. "Clarissa would have been proud to find out I'd finally learned how to do something with thread."

It's supposed to be a joke, one with a particularly Blaise brand of humor, but it falls flat.

"I just wanted you to know that I support you." The words come out of my mouth sounding wrong. Is this really what I came in here for? To excuse the stupid promise I made Blaise? The one that put her above what my family most likely needs?

I should have thought this through better.

Blaise raises a brow, and I sigh. "Earlier, when Kiran was grilling you. I supported you, and I want you to know it's because I'm your friend and I trust you."

Tear stains glisten on Blaise's cheeks as she turns to the fireplace and blinks.

"I like it here, by the fire." Her voice is lighthearted, even though it's hoarse. "It's like cheating."

I frown in question, and she laughs.

"Because I can't be in the sun, but I get to feel the fire's warmth against my skin. It's not quite the same, but if I close my eyes, I can pretend."

Blaise's eyes glaze over, like she isn't talking to me any longer, but someone far off. Someone in the past.

But soon enough she snaps back to attention, like she's banishing a thought, and folds her hands in her lap. "Thanks for supporting me.

You didn't have to do that. You're a good friend. A better one than I've been to you."

"Well, don't praise me too highly. Let's not forget that Ellie's the best friend of us all. She's coming too, you know."

Blaise's eyes flicker, or perhaps it's just the fire in the hearth dancing in the still watery lining of her eyes. "Do you think that's safe?" she asks, though hesitantly. "Ellie's human. If something were to happen, she can't heal like you and I can."

A chair sounds good right about now, so I collapse into one, placing my elbows on my knees even as my heart sinks in my chest. I already know it was a mistake to agree to let Ellie come. Blaise, of all people, being concerned with my lack of forethought feels like having a nail driven into the coffin of my stupidity.

"I know. I'm just…" Terrible at saying no? A pushover, just like my father has always complained? A boisterous, excited fool who got too wrapped up in the rush of the moment to think clearly?

"Don't worry about it too much," Blaise says, and though she's clearly backtracking after witnessing my reaction, I can't help but be comforted by it. "I'm pretty sure Lydia's coming whether we want her to or not. Between you, Lydia, and me, we can protect her. I promise."

I don't remind Blaise that without the fae curse, her promise has never meant much of anything.

CHAPTER 20

ASHA

Kiran paces back and forth in the bedroom lent to us by the King of Dwellen.

He's making singe marks on the beautiful baby blue rug, but I hold my tongue.

"Please talk to me," I finally say when I can't bear the silence anymore.

Kiran stops and glances up at me. "I don't like where all this is headed."

Something bulges in my throat. "I don't think any of us do, but we can't just sit around and ignore that the world is on the brink of falling apart."

Kiran forces his eyes shut. "I don't want to ignore it. I just don't want you getting caught up in the middle of it."

I sigh, then plop down on the bed, folding my hands in my lap. "I don't know that we have much of a choice about whether I'm in the middle of this."

Kiran's countenance falls from anger into something more desperate. "So you do want to go?"

"Want seems like a bit of a stretch. But I think I should go."

We remain in silence for a moment, the only sound Kiran's heavy breathing. "You didn't say anything in the library."

I arch a brow. "Do I need to express my opinions in front of everyone for them to be valid?"

Kiran shakes his head, running his hand through his hair. "That's not what I meant. I mean..." He swallows, and it looks as though it pains him. "Why didn't you say anything?"

I frown, watching my husband's features closely. The way his jaw has seemed permanently clenched since he returned from Othian. The worry constantly simmering in his amber eyes. He looks desperate for an answer, and it takes me a moment to recognize what he's looking for, what he's so terrified of.

Oh.

"You think that's why I didn't offer to go to the Rip? Because I feel like you control me? Because I feel like I don't have a voice?"

Kiran balls his fists. "It's how my father treated my mother. It's how he trained me to treat women. I..." He stares down at his hands. "I have this power I still can't always seem to control. Blaise might have had a point."

The sight of Kiran watching his palms like that breaks my heart, so I take my husband's hand. "I like Blaise. I pity Blaise. But Blaise has survived her entire life by learning to manipulate others. Forgive me if I don't appreciate her trying to control me by making me believe that I'm being controlled."

Kiran shrugs, chuckling, though it's somewhat pained. "She's frighteningly good at that."

I grin. "Not that good. It's not that I don't feel I have a voice—the right to my own thoughts. But I think this is the sort of thing that should be decided in private. And I don't appreciate Blaise trying to force my hand in a public conversation, before we've even had the chance to talk about it. Before we've heard each other out."

Kiran shakes his head, leaning against the desk, his weight causing it to scrape against the wood flooring. "Where did you come from?" he asks, nothing but pure adoration in his eyes.

"A windowless hovel, if you must know."

"You trust me? That I'm not trying to control you?"

"You have the ability to alter my feelings. If you wanted to control me, you could. I've doubted you before, thought you were controlling me. We figured it out, but my doubts hurt our relationship, and I don't intend on being manipulated again. I know you worry when your feelings slip out of you occasionally, but that's exactly why I think it's important that we don't feel pressured to decide anything during an intense discussion with our friends."

He swallows. "You want to go, don't you? To the Rip? I could see your self-sacrificing, lack of self-preservation wheels turning."

I let out a partially offended huff, but smile nonetheless. "I could make sure it stays closed. Or, if we're too late, I could close it back."

"If we send the others to get Piper before then, that wouldn't be necessary."

"It still is. Abra will have the power to open the Rip by the next full moon, regardless."

Kiran shakes his head. "It doesn't make sense. Abra has had the parasite for months. A full moon has passed since then. More than one, even. If she wanted the Rip open, why not do it then? Why bother taking Piper at all?"

Something squirms in my gut. The fear I've had since Lydia returned.

"What if she didn't realize the Rip could be used to bring Farin back until recently? What if someone else put that idea in her head?"

Kiran frowns, rubbing his chin. "Someone like...." He pales. "Az. Of course." He turns to me again. "If you're trying to convince me it's a good idea for you to get anywhere near that Rip, you're doing a poor job of it."

"By now, I'd have expected you to have more faith in my argumentation skills."

"I do. Frankly, that's why I'm a tad shocked."

"He wants the Rip open, Kiran. We can't let that happen. I don't know what he's planning. I don't know what he thinks he'll get out of it, but at this point he's had years to plan whatever it is, and I'm so..."

My throat constricts, my gut swirling with nausea.

Kiran pushes himself off of the desk and approaches me from behind, wrapping me in his arms as he spins me to face him. In a moment, his warmth overcomes me, thawing my skin and soothing my heart. He allows the fear to remain, however. He doesn't take that from me.

"You're still having the nightmares, aren't you?"

I nod, melting into his embrace.

"I know you fear what will happen if Az uses Piper to open the Rip. But do you know what I fear? That if we travel to the Rip, we're playing right into Az's hand. That he doesn't want Piper to open it at all. He wants you. He's always wanted you, Asha. Just on his own terms, in his own sick way. I can't help but imagine he'll find a symmetry to it, if he can force your hand."

I shake my head. "You know I wouldn't do it. I wouldn't open the Rip for him. He'd have to kill me first."

Kiran goes still behind me. "That's exactly what I'm afraid of."

We can't let him open it. We can't let it happen, my magic whispers deep inside me. In my gut, I know he's right.

"I have a responsibility, Kiran. I have the power to keep this world safe. I can't stand by and allow Az to unleash those beasts upon this world."

"I know you can't," he whispers, his warm breath rustling my hair as we sway. In the distance, out the window, the crescent moon shines down on us, holding out for our decision.

"Lydia would protect me, you know," I offer.

"Lydia already let Piper slip through her fingertips."

"And you think Lydia is likely to be fooled twice?"

Kiran shudders at the thought. "She'll rip out Abra's throat just for spite if she gets close to her."

"Exactly," I say. "She won't allow anything to happen to me."

Kiran's power rumbles, but he keeps his feelings contained, rather than letting them leak into me. "Why are you talking like I wouldn't be the one to protect you?"

I sigh, slowly pivoting in Kiran's embrace to face him. "I already told you that I think Fin and I have found a lead. One that might lead to your father."

Kiran frowns. "Then let Fin search for him."

"Kiran, it's your father."

"I already had one of those. He was disappointing enough. No need to add to the experience."

"I can see that you miss Fin."

"What's there to miss? Fin and I have never been close."

"Kiran. You killed Ophelia because you were so upset over her ruining your chances of mending your relationship with your brother. Don't pretend you don't care. Not to me, but especially not to yourself."

Kiran sighs. "You're right, but it can wait. The more pressing matter is making sure we capture Az and Abra. After that's done, I'll go with Fin to find our father."

I frown. "The lead is time sensitive. From what we can tell, the male has moved around. A lot. You might not get another chance like this. Besides, he's the only other person outside our circle who knows who you truly are. Who knows you're not the heir to the throne."

Kiran tenses, acknowledging the risk that puts him in, should that information spread.

"In my dreams, Az doesn't hurt me through the Rip, Kiran. He does it from the throne."

"They're just dreams," he says, shaking his head.

"I'm not sure they are," I whisper. "Even if they are, think of what he would do to you if he took the throne. Think of what he would do to me."

Heat surges from Kiran in a blast, though it only ruffles my hair, his powerful arms protecting me from it.

"The fact is, Az has two avenues by which he could take control. We can't afford to devote all our energy to both of them."

"Again, another reason Fin should go after our father," he says, but I can see in the flare of his molten eyes that he knows it won't be enough. That if their father is the type to betray their heritage, Kiran will need to convince him he's fit to rule.

We also both know that if need be, Kiran will be the only one of the two brothers willing to take their father out.

"I don't like the idea of being separated again," Kiran says, pressing a warm kiss against my forehead, his stubble scratching against my skin. I didn't realize until now how terribly I'd ached for that feeling while he was gone.

"Me either. But there is one benefit," I say.

He quirks a thick brow. "And what is that?"

"It means we'll have to make up for lost time tonight."

The room itself heats as Kiran stares down at me. "I've not agreed to anything," he says, stroking my cheek softly with his thumb.

"Are you sure about that? Because I'm pretty sure you did agree."

A smile, soft and familiar, curves Kiran's mouth. "You have an annoyingly precise memory, love, but I'm afraid this time you're just making things up."

I offer him an exaggerated look of confusion. "Are you sure? Because I'm pretty sure you said, 'Of course, Asha. Whatever you want, my lovely wife.'"

Kiran's fingers slip to the tie holding my robe together, playfully twisting it around his fingertips.

When he presses his mouth to mine, a smile still on his lips, warmth envelops me, and I know it has nothing to do with his Flame.

"I'd be more than happy to give you whatever you want, just in a different context," he whispers, teasing tinging his tone.

"In that case, you playing with the string of my robe like that is killing me," I say in between long kisses.

"Well, in that case," says Kiran, pulling on the tie and carrying me to the bed.

CHAPTER 21

KIRAN

"Your Majesty," says a drawling voice that grates against my very skull. "The vizier reported that your signature on these documents was time-sensitive in nature."

I look up from my book and decide I miss the days when servants trembled in my presence.

I'm in the library, searching and failing to find any books on the subject of liquid moonlight.

And apparently signing ordinances.

I allow the temperature in the library to heat just enough to make the royal courier regret his tone. Of course, the terrifying librarian, whom I'd forgotten about, shoots me a look so deadly that I quickly relent.

The courier drops a pile of scrolls on the table and hovers while I read over them. This really isn't the best time, considering I've been poring over grimoires for hours now. I barely register what I'm signing before handing it back to the courier. "There, you can go now."

He stuffs the scrolls back into his satchel and gives me a pointed glare. "I'm to wait until the week's end before I depart. The King of

Dwellen has his own correspondences that he's unable to address until the end of the week."

I let out a controlled exhale. "Then why did you make it sound as though it was of the utmost importance that I sign those immediately?"

I'm still waiting for a proper answer when the little girl who arrived with Lydia's party enters the room.

The courier uses the interruption as an opportunity to slip out of the library, though I notice he grips his stomach as he does.

The girl isn't skipping or prancing or shuffling her feet as I would expect a child to, but walking tall, her chin outstretched, her hands swaying by her side as confidently as if she were an adult.

The girl strides right up to me, drops into a curtsy so low I would consider it disrespectful if it wasn't coming from a child, and says, "Thank you, Your Highness. Or Your Majesty. I can never remember which one it is. But I think it's Your Majesty, because you're a king and not a prince, right?"

I have no idea how to respond, since I don't know what she's thanking me for. As it turns out, I don't have to, because the girl goes on talking as if she doesn't actually expect me to answer the question.

"I'm Amity. I just wanted to thank you for agreeing to help my mother. I am your humble servant"—Amity drops to a kneeling position on the floor—"and offer you my servitude as thanks for your assistance."

"That..." I say, almost forgetting I've agreed to nothing, "won't be necessary."

She doesn't seem to hear me, because she starts going on and on about all sorts of plants whose names I've never heard of. Come to think of it, I suppose I can only assume she's talking about plants.

"Yes, it will be necessary," she says, appearing quite determined. "But only if you actually save Piper," she ends up adding, I suppose in case I fail. Though I can see why a child would not want to indebt herself to the service of someone she considers a failure. I don't get a chance to reply before she adds, "Prince Fin says you're going to go on a trip with him while we journey to the Rip."

"Does he now?" Honestly, I'm surprised Fin hasn't fought this tooth and nail. Then again, Asha does hold quite a bit of sway over my brother.

"Yes, he says the male you're looking for is a merchant who specializes in illegal substances."

Amity blinks, as if now it's my turn to speak, though again, I find I have no idea what to say to this child.

"What do you know about illegal substances?" I settle on.

Amity must have been waiting for an opportunity like this one, because she yanks a crumpled piece of parchment from her pocket and hands it to me. "A bunch, actually. There are lots of illegal substances that I think might save Marcus from Queen Abra's poison. I looked up where this merchant lives."

"And?"

"And he lives in Sureth."

"I'm not sure what that means."

Amity huffs. "It means he lives at the crossroads for all sorts of trading routes. I bet he keeps stock of every illegal substance you could think of. Anyway"—she points to the crumpled piece of parchment I've yet to open—"that's a list of ingredients I need you to get for me so I can save Marcus's life."

She says it with so little emotion, it's rather alarming.

I groan inwardly. How does one explain to a child that, as much as I would love to help her father, I'll put my wife's life above anyone else's? "Amity—"

Impatient with my refusal to look at the list, Amity yanks it from my hands and unfolds it for me, smoothing it out on the table. "Here," she says, handing it back to me. "Now, are there any ingredients you don't recognize the names of? I can tell you how to pronounce them and what they look like. That way you don't get sold the wrong thing."

I open my mouth to refuse, but Amity's withering stare has me turning back to the parchment.

I'm about to tell her I don't recognize any of the materials when my gaze fixes on the fifth item on the list.

"You really think this merchant keeps stock of all these?" I ask.

Amity nods excitedly. "I told you, it's a crossroads for illegal activity. If it's crazy illegal, then it ends up in Sureth."

I check the list again, my gaze transfixing on one ingredient alone.

There, written in a child's rather neat handwriting, is the only thing that could ever convince me to let Asha go to the Rip without me.

Liquid moonlight.

CHAPTER 22

ASHA

*I*t's day three of being away from Kiran, and I already feel like I've been punched in the gut.

I thought for sure this trip wouldn't be any worse than waiting around at Othian castle, puttering about to distract myself as we waited on a message that Kiran, Evander, and Blaise were safe.

But somehow, this feels different.

There's a permanence about our separation that makes my bones ache, my muscles quiver.

My magic doesn't like it. It didn't like it when I was convincing Kiran to find his father with Fin, but I hadn't admitted as much.

If I don't want Blaise in the middle of our marriage, I certainly don't want my magic in the middle of it, either.

But still.

It was a gut feeling of my magic's that led me to sacrifice myself as a bride to Kiran in the first place—my magic's hunch that somehow, Dinah was in danger.

It's that same primal feeling that has my gut churning with every step closer to Charshon.

The first leg of the trip the group took together, with Kiran and Fin splitting off from us once we reached the border of Dwellen and

Avelea. They'll venture further into Avelea, while our party will skirt the coastline and venture into Charshon.

Kiran kissed me before he left, and I clung onto him longer than I should have.

This will not end well, my magic whispers to me with every step.

WE TAKE the path that cuts through the Kobii mountains, and I often find myself lost in the beauty of the forested mountainscapes—the lush greenery that lets off a cool glow, even in the summer months, the spray of the ocean that laps up against the cliffs as we reach the coast.

Since Blaise is with our party, we save most of our traveling for nighttime, which has my body all out of sorts. I'm feeling a bit disoriented all the time, but I try not to complain. It means that we rest during daylight hours, and since I struggle to sleep through them, I often find myself perched on a knobby log or up against a tree, breathing in the pleasant salt-flavored air and allowing the spray of the cool, white ocean to coax me into some semblance of peace while everyone else sleeps in their tents.

It's during one of these moments that Amity, Marcus's daughter, skips up to me, a handful of poorly wrapped parcels in her little grip.

When Amity first arrived, I thought her to be about ten, but Marcus quickly explained that she's thirteen, and her tiny frame is due to malnourishment when she was younger.

He rambled on about how proud he was of her for how much weight she'd gained in the past few months, though I could tell from the creases forming at the corners of his eyes that his heart was still fraught with concern over her.

Thankfully, Amity does not seem to have the abysmal energy levels of a child who is malnourished.

In fact, she seems to have the energy to talk constantly. I feel like this probably would have annoyed a younger version of myself, but I find her gregarious, if not overly candid, nature quite refreshing.

149

Or perhaps I just welcome a distraction from my magic's repetitive thoughts.

She shoves the pile of parcels into my arms, then immediately rebukes me when I drop one.

"Those are important. And fragile," she says, looking at me with disapproval as I scrape the fallen parcel off the ground. The fabric immediately goes flitting off, grasped by the playful wind, to which the poorly tied knot gives way.

"I apologize profusely," I say, to which Amity gives me a suspicious look before chattering on.

"You'll find my best mixture of healing agents in there, including my most famous concoction, ressuroot paste."

"Ooooh...what's ressuroot paste?" I try to infuse my voice with enthusiasm, which apparently falls flat on Amity's ears, because she frowns.

"You haven't heard of it?"

"Uhh..." Thankfully Marcus is walking over to us, limping a bit. My eye must be screaming HELP, because he chuckles and says, "Amity here is a little genius. Saved mine and Piper's life back at the palace in Avelea, and my sister's, too."

Amity's face falls a little. "I betrayed them, but I was only pretending. And only because I had to. I hated it the entire time."

Marcus rubs the top of Amity's already rumpled braid, only making conditions worse, but Amity seems to soak up the attention. "It was genius." He nods to the parcel, gesturing me to open it.

When I do, I find a vial of rather pungent paste that gives me the inclination to plug my nose, though I don't for Amity's sake.

"How does it work?" I ask.

Marcus opens his mouth, but Amity beats him to the explanation. He clamps his mouth shut with a smile, like he should have known better than to try.

"Well, it's kind of a long story, but it was tracked over here by the original fae. Boots are really bad about that, you know," she says, glancing at my boots in judgment. "But I guess I can be glad about it in this one instance. Anyway, the Fates cursed the ressuroot to be poisonous, but the Fates like to be ironic—ironic means different than you'd expect—so they made it so that it's only lethal if it's injected anywhere else but your heart. In your heart, it's its own antidote!"

I raise a brow. "So if you stab yourself in the heart with it…"

"It makes it look like it's killed you, but then it heals you back," says Amity, a proud grin planted on her face. "Helpful if you ever need to fake your death."

I glance at Marcus, who shrugs his shoulders and places his palms sky-up. "Believe me, I was also skeptical. Until Amity managed to outsmart all of us, including the man trying to overthrow the King of Avelea."

Amity crosses her arms. "That's not really a compliment, since James is an idiot."

Marcus lets out a deep, bellowing laugh, but coughs soon punctuate the pleasant sound. He excuses himself, claiming his throat is dry.

As he limps away, Amity's eyes trace his steps.

"He's better some days than others, but sometimes I think he's faking being better. He used to pick me up and put me on his shoulders," she says, little emotion in her voice. "He says I'm getting too big for it now, but I know that's not true, because I've grown minimally since the last time he did it, and he only stopped after Abra poisoned him."

My mouth grasps for a response, but what am I supposed to say to a child who's watching her parent die slowly?

I suppose I could tell her he's going to be fine, but Amity seems too sharp to be fooled by that. Besides, it's always felt icky to me when people treat children like they're undeserving of the truth. Like somehow their age and immaturity makes it okay to lie to them.

So I just settle on, "I bet if he could pick you up, he would."

Amity gives me a long, assessing look, then nods her head in agreement.

"There's more than just the ressuroot paste in there. The greenish paste is for if you get a fungus between your toes. There's also mandrake in there, which is supposed to be an aphrodisiac. I haven't been able to find what that means in my books, but—"

"And ressuroot paste if I need to fake my death. Got it," I say, eager to end this conversation with haste. As important as it is to me to be honest with children, that doesn't necessarily mean I want to explain what an aphrodisiac is if I can get away with it. And there is no way in Alondria I'll be shoving a knife into my chest coated with resurrection paste mixed by a child—no matter how highly it comes recommended.

CHAPTER 23

PIPER

*T*he familiar scents of winter pine and rose leaf waft over me as Abra and I ascend into the Kobii mountains. The carriage rocks against the jagged terrain of the very path I traveled with Marcus and Amity not so long ago.

Marcus.

I close my eyes, trying to breathe in his scent, trying to comfort myself with his memory.

Marcus is going to die, and I'll never get to feel the warmth of his arms holding me against his sturdy chest.

He's going to die, because I won't do what Abra asked.

I can only hope I can keep her away from them long enough for Amity to find a cure for him. That's Abra's mistake, after all. She doesn't know about Amity. About the child's gift. It isn't at all like the ones that the queen and I both possess.

Amity's gift is innate. Not the magical sort. It lies in the way her brilliant mind whirrs, making connections others can't see.

Or maybe it simply lies within her interest in the topic.

I've always wondered about that. Whether people make great strides in research because they possess superior intellect, or because they derive so much joy from the topic of study, spend so much time delving into it, they simply can't help but make discoveries.

Whatever the reason is for Amity's prodigy-level skills with potions and medicines, I can only hope they'll serve her well enough to save Marcus.

My legs itch to stretch, to run, to climb through these mountains and feel the weighty resistance of the incline against my thighs and bones.

Instead, we rattle up the spine of the mountain range like a roach on a log.

Black velvet lines the seats of the coach, making the queen's paleness even more stark, giving her a sickly look.

"Are you going to tell me what you want from me?" I ask, rubbing at the chafing my restraints cause at my wrists. They remind me of the time I spent a prisoner in Kev's cabin before I knew Marcus was coming to free me.

I don't particularly enjoy things that remind me of that time.

The queen raises her brow. "You'll find out when we arrive."

I wrack my brain, but I can hardly think what the queen could want from me. At least, not since we took the road toward Mystral rather than where I'd expected—Charshon.

The Rip is in Charshon, according to Lydia. It's where she expected Az to bring me if he ever got ahold of me. And he certainly tried, sending not only Marcus to hunt me, but a merchant to bid on me at Kev's auction.

Apparently my Gift doesn't simply offer me the ability to create music infused with magic. It also gives me the capacity to open and close the Rip between worlds. The ones through which my fae ancestors entered Alondria all those centuries ago.

When the queen threatened Marcus's life, I assumed she was taking me directly there, but we took the road to the Kobiis instead, headed toward Dwellen. My guess is that our final destination is Mystral.

Unless there's another Rip in Mystral, I have no idea what the queen wants with me.

"How do you know I can do it?" I ask, trying and failing to look her in the eye, since she often refuses to look at me.

"I'm well-informed of your skill set."

"So you want me to use my music then?" I ask. "That's going to be difficult to do given you didn't allow me to bring my flute along."

The queen waves her hand dismissively. "We both know there's nothing intrinsically magical about the flute you prefer. There are rumors you enchanted a man into freezing himself to death with an icicle when you were a child."

My back goes rigid. I was only three when the incident occurred, but it resulted in the townspeople of our Mystrian village kicking me out. My mother had left me on the outskirts of civilization, a child curled up in the snow and ready to die, when Bronger found me.

"I was three," I say, rubbing again at the restraints.

The queen hmphs. "All the better. I assume that means your skills have matured since then."

"I won't murder anyone for you."

The queen flashes me a grin, but her eyes don't participate. "Only your husband, then," she says, "should you refuse to do as I ask."

"I think I'll let you keep the title of husband killer for yourself." I lean against the wall of the coach, even as I watch for the faintest twitch at the edge of the queen's mouth.

There it is.

It's just a rumor, one that's circulated about the Queen of Mystral for years, but Bronger taught me how to read the slightest changes in facial expression, and the way she's trying to hide her reaction tells me I've hit a nerve.

"Well," I say, pushing my skull into the velvety fabric, "just because you had a less than desirable husband doesn't mean you're doing the rest of us a favor by getting rid of ours."

The queen's mouth purses. "The King of Mystral was not a cruel male. He was kind to me when no one else was. When no one else had been in a long time. I won't tolerate you speaking evil of him."

The dimple at the cleft of her chin warbles. I leaned forward. "So you didn't kill your husband then?"

She opens her mouth, then closes it, swallowing before beginning again. "No. I didn't kill the King of Mystral. Why no one believes that despite the fact I'm unable to lie about it escapes me."

I watch her for a long time after that, absorbing all the information I can.

I tell myself that it's because I want to survey my enemy, catch her in her weakness.

Really, I think I just want not to have to imagine Marcus's death.

CHAPTER 24

BLAISE

I wasn't supposed to be the villain.

I wasn't supposed to be the villain.

I'm not the villain, I remind myself as I toss pebbles into the winding creek that cuts across the lush greenery of Charshon. We arrived last night, leaving Avelea's border behind as we ventured into the place where I'll betray my friends.

I'm not the villain. I'm just a liar, a girl who's lost everything and isn't willing to lose one more person.

It's quiet here in Charshon. The streams murmur softly. The soil is soft beneath our feet, dampening the noise of our steps. Even the night is quiet, not at all like the forests of Avelea where crickets sing and hum all night long.

I wish something would hum, something would drown out the noise in my head.

My baby is dead my baby is dead my baby is dead.

My baby is dead, and so am I, in a way. At least, I'm dead enough to have severed the parasite from my body.

My baby, my poor sweet child whom I'll never get to name, never get to bury properly, is dead.

A light-haired girl, mourning over the dead brother she clutches in her lap.

A heart strewn across a cave floor.

A body swollen with salt water.

Nox is dead too, somewhere, in some realm, some reality.

My baby is dead, and I am dead, and Nox is going to be dead, and I am going to betray my friends, and the crickets can't even be bothered to drown out the noise berating my mind.

"Do you miss the light?" a tiny but self-assured voice asks from behind me.

It's enough to startle me, which is concerning. My vampire senses should have heard her approaching, but I suppose my grief, my anxiety over Nox's fate, is enough to drown out the padding footsteps of a child.

She's an odd little girl, in that she seems to possess more intelligence than should be allotted to a child. As I was trying to catch up on some sleep and avoid the sun during the day, I overheard her talking with Asha near my tent. Apparently she invented some sort of substance that has life-restoring properties if administered directly to the heart. She'd gifted some to Asha, in case she ever needs it, which seems a tad morbid for a child, especially with the clinical way she approached the topic.

I wonder if that was how Nox was as a child, too smart and serious for his youth.

Amity settles in next to me, digging her already-smudged fingernails into the dirt like her fingers are roots that drink from the earth itself. She's much too close for a child who doesn't know me, and the way she tucks herself into my side has my spine going rigid with discomfort.

The evening breeze stirs up her scent, but I don't let myself name what her blood smells like. I don't want to know.

"You didn't answer my question," she says, as if I've been unforgivably rude, which I suppose I probably have been in her eyes.

"It's not so bad," I say, slipping into my mask of a smile, the one I've molded to my face over the years. "In fact, if I close my eyes like this"

—I demonstrate, squeezing my lids shut dramatically—"I can just pretend it's daylight outside."

I open my eyes to Amity wrinkling her brow in skepticism.

"I don't think that's the same."

"Oh no?" I nudge her in the shoulder. "You've never pretended so hard that you convinced yourself something was real?"

"Not since I was little," she says, as if it's the most obvious thing in the world.

"Right. I should grow up like you then, I suppose."

For a moment, she opens her mouth like she doesn't know how to respond to that. I wonder if I've hurt her feelings, which is probably for the best, since she doesn't need to be around me right now, anyway. Not when the breeze is whipping her hair around her face, imbuing the air with her scent. I've spent very little time around Marcus, but I'm certain Amity will be in for a scolding once he finds out she snuck out here alone with me.

It's a strange realization. That parents shouldn't trust me around their children.

My heart stings a bit.

"You should go back to your tent and get some rest. We don't set off for another hour."

"I'm not tired," Amity explains. "My circadian rhythm has adjusted to being nocturnal, like you."

"Has it now?"

"Yes, but mine's the first one to adjust, meaning you're the only other person up right now, so there's no one else to talk to."

I let out a huff that's exasperated in pretense only. "Glad to know I'm your last choice."

Amity peers up at me, and there's something in her eyes that's different from the way I'm used to being looked at. Like there's more curiosity there than pity.

It's not all that unrefreshing.

"How old would your baby be now, if they had lived?"

I flinch, digging my nails into the ground as my heart gives a lurch. If Amity notices, she does nothing to amend her bluntness.

"Would they be younger or older than me?" she continues.

"I didn't know you knew about my baby."

"Sometimes adults say things you're not supposed to know when they think you're asleep."

I let out a sigh, the agitation in me dissipating somewhat. Again, there's little pity in the girl's eyes. Somehow her frank interest doesn't feel quite as suffocating as the others' empathy, and I'm tired of being pitied anyway, so what's the harm?

"Younger than you," I say, rubbing my fingertips on a blade of grass.

Amity blinks. "How much younger?"

"I don't know. I don't know how old you are."

"I'm thirteen."

"Seven years younger than you then."

"Oh," she says, like this information disappoints her somewhat.

"Why? Were you hoping for a different answer or something?"

Amity bites her lip, fighting with her braid. "No. I just think that's a long time to be missing your baby."

The breeze picks up, chilling the tears welling in my eyes until they sting incessantly.

"Yeah."

After a few moments of silence, Amity says, "I overheard them saying that you never got to figure out if it was a little boy or girl."

I'm having to fight back the tears lest they spill over onto my cheeks. "That's right," and though she doesn't ask, I find myself saying, "If she was a girl, her name was Rose. Because my mother's name was Blossom, but I couldn't stand that name, so I thought Rose would be a better way to name a girl after her. And then, if the baby had been a boy, he would have been Theo."

"Those names are all right, I guess."

I stare at the girl for a moment, mouth agape, expecting annoyance or rage to well up within me. Some appropriate reaction to this child's insensitivity.

But all that comes out is a laugh. A laugh that's somewhere between a cough and a squeal and a sob.

"I wasn't trying to be funny," Amity says.

I can no longer hold back the salty tears pouring down my cheeks as my chest spasms.

Something is terribly wrong with me. Something horribly, irreparably broken.

"I know you weren't," I say between heaves that pinch my chest. "I'm just...I'm just so used to people having no idea what to say, or saying something they mean to be kind, but's actually awful in its own way. What I'm not used to is..."

I trail off, while Amity frowns at me, confused.

"Not used to what?"

"Not used to..." I swallow. Because I know exactly who I'm not used to. Children. I'm not used to children, and that fact makes me want to scream. Instead, I steel myself and cough out a "Never mind."

"Did you have a funeral for your baby?"

Shame washes over me. "No. No, I didn't know—I thought. Well, it was a stupid thing to think, but I didn't know until—"

My teeth sinking into Clarissa's flesh. Me compelling her to fear me.

Amity says nothing. She just hops up and scampers away, leaving me alone with my miserable thoughts.

AMITY RETURNS NOT LONG AFTER, balancing a stone under each armpit. She pauses when she reaches me, her little arms shaking under the weight.

"Here," she says finally, laying the stones down in the grass beside me.

In the moonlight, I catch sight of them up close, and my throat closes up.

The rocks are smooth on the surface and almost identical, like Amity's spent the past half an hour scavenging around for the perfect pair. On each surface are scratched, in huge print with what was probably Amity's hunting knife, the names Rose and Theo.

"I thought maybe we could give your baby a funeral." For the first time since I met Amity, she sounds unsure of herself.

161

I nod, my lips unable to form words.

"And maybe Marcus could do it? I don't think he's ever done a funeral before, but I think he'd be really good at it."

I shake my head, swallowing hard. Panic rises in me at the thought of the others seeing me like this. Of them offering me their pity, their condolences, all for me to turn around and betray them.

I fumble for a reason to give Amity, a reason why I can't stand to let them bear any of my grief, but she simply says, "Or we could make it a more intimate gathering."

Relief swells in my chest, and I even let out a small smile at her tendency to use words that seem so odd coming out of a child's mouth.

"That would be perfect," I whisper. "Actually, I was thinking I would pick you to say a few words."

IN THE END, we lay the spirit of my child to rest in the soft earth, while the breeze sings my baby the lullaby I was never allowed. Amity says words I don't hear in the moment, but somehow will never forget, then sprinkles rose petals over an empty grave.

CHAPTER 25

PIPER

"You want me to enchant your son back into loving you?" I ask, trying and failing to keep my tone calm.

Abra and I have just crossed into Dwellen, but we've been skirting the border for days now. At first, I thought maybe Abra was trying to evade the King of Dwellen's forces.

But then we arrived at the warehouse.

It's a dingy but massive building. One that looks like it would house illegal goods, what with the way the windows are boarded up and the way it looms over the hillside.

It *is* the type of building that houses illegal goods, by the way.

At least, I assume the bubbling vats of shining liquid scattered across the place are illegal.

I'm not sure what we're here for exactly, but I definitely glimpsed Abra slip a vial into one of the vats and cork it before tucking it back into her robe.

I can't get a read on her. One moment she's intent on getting back to her son as quickly as possible, the next she's taking detours that end up delaying us for days.

It's almost as if Abra's not the only one making decisions.

My hands are still bound, but I've been working on this rope for

T.A. LAWRENCE

days now. I actually think I'm getting close to being able to slip my wrists through the widened gap I've wriggled.

I momentarily paused my escape attempt, though, when Abra casually dropped that, once we arrived in Mystral, I'd be enchanting her son to love her again.

Abra looks at me as if I were Amity's age and had just asked to trek across Alondria with my friends.

"He already loves me," she hisses. "All you'll need to do is to make him remember."

I huff, seeing how it is clearly my turn to talk to my conversational partner like the delusional fool she is. "That's not how my Gift works."

"Sure it does," snaps Abra. "You enchanted all those poor children into trusting you, didn't you?"

I fight the urge to tense. I've talked through this in my mind thousands of times. Marcus has talked me through this thousands of times.

I was as much Bronger's victim as his instrument. I did the best I could to only take children from homes in which they were being willfully abused, and I worked hard to keep them from suffering as soldiers at Bronger's hands.

Still. Her words sting.

Trafficker.

Kidnapper.

Child-stealer.

There aren't any words left for her to use that I haven't already used to berate myself.

I steel myself, refusing to allow Abra to get her claws into me.

This new development presents an opportunity, and I intend to take it.

"I'll need to practice," I say.

Abra's laugh is derisive.

"Like I said, I've never done anything like this before. Unless you want your son to be practice, which is fine with me."

Abra pauses, her white irises flickering with what I assume is worry. But she turns away quickly enough, dismissing me.

I use the opportunity to slip my wrists through the restraints.

164

And then I run.

THE SHADOWS ARE no help in hiding me from Abra as she and her guards chase me through the halls of the abandoned warehouse. I pound my weary feet against the creaky wooden floorboards, not even bothering to try to remain quiet.

They're going to catch me anyway.

I just need them not to catch me yet.

That's the thing about creepy abandoned warehouses: I happen to know a modest percentage of their operators. Meaning I know how they prefer to communicate their illegal dealings.

Several winding halls later, I find the office where the operator of this facility would have done business back when it was up and running. The door is locked, so I smash through the door's window, gasping in pain as the shattered glass digs into my elbow.

Then I climb through.

The office itself is a mess. Clearly looters have already turned it over. Stupid looters, given they left the most valuable substance, the liquid moonlight, alone, but still.

It's a good thing that what I need from this office isn't valuable.

I scramble toward the desk, hearing the footsteps of Abra's soldiers approaching in the hall.

Most of the desk drawers are locked, but the topmost one in the center isn't. I yank it open and gasp with relief.

Inside is a quill, the feather of which is the color of blood.

Just what I was looking for.

Bloodquills are illegal, less because of anything insidious about them, and more because they make the life of a criminal convenient.

I grab the quill and dig the pointed tip into the flesh of my arm, tracing the tattoo on my wrist.

The tattoo itself is in the shape of the cottage rooftops of Evaen, the little village Marcus and I one day dream of raising Amity in.

He bears a matching one on his chest, right over his heart.

We got the tattoos to celebrate our marriage, but they're functional as well, especially when you have a blood quill at your disposal.

Now that the link is established, I dig a message into my forearm.

By the time the guards reach me, I've stuffed the quill back into the desk, and the wounds on my arms have magically vanished.

I'm pretending to try to escape out the window when they grab me.

CHAPTER 26

ELLIE

*I*t's becoming harder and harder to keep my pregnancy from Blaise. For one, my belly has begun to bulge further. Up to this point, it's been rather easy to keep my condition hidden. The puking stopped around the time Evander returned from Mystral. Though I can feel the changes in my body, the fact that I'm on the taller side and my core is firm from years hauling around glass-blowing materials means my belly has been easy to hide underneath my parka.

Back when we were in the mountains, and a parka was appropriate attire.

Thankfully, thick, loose overcoats made sense as we cut through the Kobii mountains. But since we descended into the ravine that separates Avelea from Charshon, the weather has warmed, and it's become less and less practical for me to wear a coat.

"We have to tell her," I tell Evander one night. He sits in front of me, refusing to sleep in the cot with me, claiming the baby and I need extra room. Instead, he sleeps on a bedroll half as thick as mine.

It's all a tad ridiculous, but if I were to say it didn't make my heart all warm and fuzzy, then I would be a liar.

"I know," he says, which is his response every time I broach the subject, so I know exactly what's coming next.

"But if we could just give her a little more time," we practically sing in unison. Evander glances over his shoulder at me, then leans back on my lap as I play with his hair, the crown of his head knocking against my bump.

"I can't wear that parka any longer, Evander. If I wear it one more day, I'll overheat and melt."

"But it turns me on when you're sweaty," he says with a grin.

I tug on a strand of his hair a little harder than is necessary, and he winces.

"I know you want to protect her," I say, a little more softly this time. "Believe me, I do too. I can't imagine the hurt she's been through —is still going through. But we can't hide the truth from her forever. I try to keep in the middle of the group so she doesn't sense the extra heartbeat, but eventually she's going to notice. And besides, you're assuming she'll have a certain reaction without even giving her the chance. What if it won't bother her as much as you think it will? What if—I don't know—she'd actually be happy for us?"

"It's not that I don't think she'll be happy for us," sighs Evander. "I just think it will hurt, that's all. I know I can't predict what she'll do or how she'll feel. But I just don't want her watching us live a life that was stolen from her."

"It doesn't change anything, you know. That we're happy. I understand why you're nervous, and I don't want her to hurt, either. I certainly don't want to be a constant reminder of what happened to her. To her child." I shudder, unable to even approach what it must have felt like to lose her baby. Twice. "But you never know. We could, in trying to spare her pain, be depriving her of a little happiness too. Sometimes they go together, you know."

"That, my love, makes no sense whatsoever, and proves that you are, on slim occasion, wrong."

I laugh, but Evander's echo soon dies on his lips, and he whispers, "I'm sorry. You've been really patient with me. With this entire trip. I know it would have been better if I'd never made this promise, and I could be rubbing your feet. You could be propped up on the sofa at home right about now."

"My ankles aren't that swollen yet," I chide.

"I love you, Ellie Payne," Evander says softly.

"Yeah?"

"Yeah. You're going to be the best mother."

"I don't know. Mine's pretty good. I don't know if I can top her."

"Sure you can," says Evander. "Because she's already taught you all the things she wishes she could do over. She's basically saved you time, so you don't have to repeat the same mistakes she did. You can definitely out-mother your mother. It's simple logic."

"I can't argue with that."

"El?"

"Yeah?"

"Are you scared?"

"Terrified."

"Me too. Think we can just give it to your parents? They seem better qualified anyway."

I laugh. "I thought you said I would be a better mother than my mother."

"Yeah, but there's no way I'm exceeding your father in fatherliness. The man should write a book on it."

"Don't say that to his face. It'll go to his head."

Evander lifts himself up onto his forearms. "I'm serious, Ellie."

"About giving our child to my parents? Because I'll warn you, if we go down that path, there will be no getting them back. I'm sure my parents already have high expectations for how often our child will be at their home."

Evander doesn't smile, even at the joke. "No, I mean about being a father. I don't doubt you at all. Fates, Ellie. You'll be a natural. You're good at everything you do."

"Well, not glassblowing," I say.

"Yes, because of a magical curse that made you forget all your skill. But you'll get the ability back one of these days."

"You say that with such confidence."

"How else am I supposed to feel when it comes to you?"

I smile, linking my fingers through his. "You're going to be a wonderful father, Evander."

He shakes his head and smiles, though sadly. "You have examples of what parents are supposed to be. I don't."

"You have your mother."

Evander sighs. "Yes, but I'm not going to be the mother, am I?"

"I'm afraid you're right. That spot's taken and I'm less than eager to give it up."

"I wouldn't dare. But Ellie, I didn't have a father like yours. I don't even know what a father is supposed to do with a child."

"Well, what is it you would have liked your father to do with you?"

Evander frowns, turning away slightly, like his eyes are watering and he wants to hide it from me. "It's all silly things."

"Children are supposed to be silly. I think that's a great start."

Evander sighs. "Well, I think I would have liked it if he'd acted like he enjoyed being around me."

"I think you have a starting place," I say, though I don't mention that it's a sorry standard his father has set.

"Yeah, maybe." He smiles, seeming at least a bit comforted, then pushes my tunic up and lays his head across my belly.

"Still in there?" I ask jokingly, even though my chest always feels like it's being ripped apart from anxiety anytime he checks for the baby's heartbeat.

"Still in there," he says, and I run my fingers through his already tousled hair.

Just then, the tent flap opens and Blaise rushes in. I gasp, grabbing for my blanket to cover my belly, but it's too late.

"Oh." Blaise stares at my belly, as if to make out how it appeared like this in the hour since she'd last seen me. Her gaze darts toward the parka hanging on the clothesline, and she nods, almost as if to herself.

"That explains the extra heartbeat," she says, turning to me and Evander.

And then she plasters the most devastatingly convincing smile on her face.

"I'm so happy for the two of you," she says.

And then Blaise disappears into the night.

CHAPTER 27

ASHA

*I*t's an hour until we're to depart for the night, and I'm rubbing sleep from my eyes as I stretch my legs.

"I killed her," says a voice from behind me.

I turn to find Lydia, violet eyes staring longingly into the field of tulips that stretches out before us. Their soft petals sway in the wind, as if to a melody unheard by our ears. I remember Lydia once saying that her mother planted tulips in the Naenden palace garden. Her father had uprooted them to make room for the statue of Tionis. Lydia had replanted a section of tulips elsewhere in the garden.

"Your mother," I say, partially because I've suspected as much for a long while now. Partially because I want to give Lydia the freedom that comes with someone knowing your secret, without having to speak it into truth yourself. "I'm sorry," I add.

Lydia's face remains impassive, though I sense the slightest quaver in her voice. "You say it as if it were a misfortune that happened to me, one I had no control over."

"You loved your mother. You still do. That much is obvious," I say. "I imagine she knew that."

"She's the one who told me to do it, though my father would have

172

commanded me even if she hadn't. I think she wanted one last thing to hold for herself, one last bit of agency."

"Maybe. Or maybe she wanted to make sure you knew she understood. Maybe she didn't want you to blame yourself."

Lydia looks me over, though her eyes for once appear too tired to assess much of anything. "Maybe," she says contemplatively before turning back to the field of tulips.

"My father was a paranoid male," she continues. "He wanted to punish my mother because he believed she'd had an affair. He cited Fin's lack of magic as evidence of as much."

"He knew Kiran and Fin were illegitimate?" I ask, slightly shocked. As much as Kiran hated his father, his father was obsessed with him. Obsessed with molding him into the perfect tyrant, the perfect heir to his throne.

Lydia shakes her head, her braid wavering. "No. Well, he believed Fin to be illegitimate, but he refused to acknowledge Kiran, his heir, could be any male's but his."

I must have shown my judgment on my face, because Lydia gives a wry laugh. "There has been at least one occasion recorded in which a fae female was impregnated by two males. Twins with different fathers. I know you're thinking this is unlikely, which would make you a reasonable person. My father was not a reasonable person."

"You've known for this long that the twins had a different father from you, yet you never said anything," I say.

Lydia shrugs. "It would have only served to hurt them."

"You mean it would have hurt Kiran," I say. "Would have meant he never received the throne."

Lydia shuffles as if uncomfortable.

"I thought you believed Kiran was a dreadful ruler."

"I did. Do still, sometimes. But I suppose I hoped better for him. And as much as I hated what he had become, what my father had shaped him into…"

She pauses, and for the first time, Lydia actually looks uncertain. "Well, for one, I was truly my father's daughter. His blood, his evil, runs in my veins, not Kiran's. And Kiran… I can only imagine how much better off he'd have been if he'd had our mother's influence to guide him, even just a little while longer."

"You blame yourself for parts of Kiran's past, don't you?"

"I took his mother away from him. I couldn't take his throne, too—his identity. What right did I have, truly, to judge Kiran, when my father had made me a monster of Kiran's equal? The only difference was that Kiran took ownership of the monster inside while I choose to hide in the shadows."

I shrug. "You're a monster to the monsters, Lydia. In most stories, that makes you the hero."

She looks down at me with apprehension. "I think sometimes, Asha, you see good where it isn't."

"Then I think you see evil where it isn't."

"Well then, maybe with two sets of eyes, we can judge more clearly."

I allow her comment to hang in the silence long enough for the words to settle in.

Of course, as soon as the realization of what she said widens her violet eyes, I let out a laugh.

She does too, oddly enough.

"You should talk to Kiran," I say. "I think you might be surprised how much the two of you have in common."

Lydia rolls her eyes. "I'm not sure that's something I would like to discover about myself," she says, but underneath the derision, I can hear the fear in her voice.

"He won't hate you for telling him."

"And how can you know that?"

"Because I won't let him."

Lydia laughs again, but this time, it actually meets her eyes.

But as quickly as it appears, it's gone when Marcus comes barreling out of his tent to meet us.

Lydia and I exchange concerned looks, then run toward him, closing the distance to keep him from exhausting himself.

"It's Piper," he cries, each breath a wheeze as we meet him in the center of the field. "I just got a message from Piper."

"How is that possible?" asks Lydia, but Marcus pulls on the collar of his tunic, exposing his chest.

I've noticed Marcus's tattoos before, the typical vines and thorns that Aveleans get upon entering maturity, a time marked by profound loss.

But this tattoo is different. It looks to be the roofscape of a village, but the lines have been twisted, curled into a script that's somewhat shaky, but still legible.

She's taking me to Mystral, says the script.

"It could be a trap, a diversion," says Lydia, but Marcus shakes his head, grinding his teeth as he fights off a spasm.

"It's Piper's handwriting."

"The queen could be threatening her," I offer.

"No. Piper doesn't bend to threats," he says, and his voice is so resolute, I can't help but believe him.

Lydia strokes the hilt of her blade. "This makes no sense. Why take Piper to Mystral?"

Her gaze snaps to the side as Blaise rushes out of Ellie and Evander's tent, tears streaming down her face.

My heart plummets at the realization of what Blaise must have just discovered.

"I need to talk to Blaise," Lydia says. "Figure out what's in Mystral that the queen needs Piper for." She makes to run for Blaise when Marcus's breathing catches my attention.

"We'll need to leave as soon as possible," he says, and I nod, my heart breaking at the pain on his face.

"Right, I'll help you pack." I start toward his and Amity's tent.

I get there before he does, and when I do, Amity jolts up from her cot.

"What are you doing?" She stares at me as I start throwing her things into bags.

"You need to help me pack. Abra is taking Piper to Mystral, not to the Rip. Piper just sent Marcus a message."

Amity goes still, rather than helping. "We're turning around?"

175

I catch my breath, looking up at the child for the first time. She's shaking, large coins of water dripping from her eyes.

Marcus comes stumbling into the tent, nods at me in thanks, but before he can do much else Amity starts weeping.

"No. We can't go. We can't turn around," she says, her small voice, usually so calm, choked with panic.

Marcus goes still, then kneels in front of his daughter, holding her hands. "Your mother is in Mystral, Amity. She needs us to help her."

Amity shakes her head, almost violently. "But...but if we don't get to the Rip..."

Amity's holding her stomach now, panic washing the already pale child of any color.

"Amity, kid." Marcus wraps his arms around her and cradles her to his chest. "Talk to me. What's going on?"

Between sniffles and choking coughs, Amity manages to point to a journal atop her cot. I reach for it, flipping through the thick pages until I come across the most recent entry, at which point I realize it's not a journal at all, but a grimoire full of potion recipes.

Rivrean flax is circled in bold ink twice. My eye traces where Amity has underlined notes like, "known for its magical healing properties," and, "has been rumored to keep degenerative diseases from progressing."

"Oh." I bite my lip as I look over the top of the book at Marcus, whose brow is lined with the unspoken question, *What in Alondria is going on?*

My mouth goes dry, but I turn the book to face him. His copper eyes scan the text and he sighs, which triggers a coughing fit that has Amity's sobs intensifying.

"Please," Amity begs. "I don't want you to die. I should have told you earlier, but I was afraid I'd be wrong. And I don't... I can't—"

Marcus's face is full of shock, but he nods his head, running his hands over the back of Amity's head as she weeps into his shoulder.

"Lydia can go after Piper," I offer, though I feel extremely out of place in the middle of this emotional family moment. "Honestly, she can probably get to her faster if she doesn't have us humans slowing her down."

A flicker of anguish passes over Marcus's face, and I recognize it. The way he wants nothing more than to protect his wife.

But Marcus is level-headed.

He knows his limits, and though Marcus does better some days than others, he knows his illness has progressed.

I watch as the realization settles over his face. That even if he went after Piper, it's likely he wouldn't make the journey. "Okay. Amity, listen to me. We'll go to the Rip. We'll find this flax you're looking for."

This time, Amity's sob is one of mingled anguish and relief.

My heart cracks.

"I'll tell Lydia the plan," I say, feeling the sudden urge to give Marcus the privacy to comfort Amity.

Marcus nods and mouths a word of thanks.

I can't help but notice he's sweating again.

CHAPTER 28

BLAISE

$\mathcal{N}$ox dead on the beach.

I rip the thread from its binding and start again.

Nox dead in the cavern.

Again.

Nox dead in his sister's arms.

No.

Again.

Nox dead. Again. Nox dead. Again. Nox dead.

Not again not again not again.

Rip.

I stare down at the limp piece of torn thread in my palm. The color fades from its fibers, as if bleeding out into the surrounding air.

No.

The frayed end splays from the tapestry as if to mock me. As if to say, "This is the moment that determines Nox's death, and there's nothing you can do about it."

Maybe that's it. Maybe I simply haven't been unwinding far enough. Maybe there's something in the tapestry, something that happens earlier that ends in his death, and if I can only figure out what that moment is, I can rework it. I can change his Fate.

I can change our Fate, and then he and I can be happy. Happy, like Evander and Ellie are happy.

The sight of her bulging belly assaults my mind, and I hate myself for the way my heart sank when I saw it, detest myself for the envy that writhed within my heart at the sight of their joy.

Tears sting at my eyes as I try again with the tapestry.

Again, Nox dies.

A scream wells within me as I rip the thread away. A scream that encompasses all my pain. The pain of being without Nox, the agony of losing my baby, the sorrow of putting my child's spirit to rest, the shame that Evander and Ellie didn't tell me, because they knew, they *knew* the ugliness that would fester inside my heart at their happiness.

My baby is dead.

Nox is going to be dead, and I can't stop it, and now that Piper's contacted Marcus, informing him that Abra is taking her to Mystral, Nox is going to stay dead.

They'll turn around. They'll turn the whole caravan around, and Asha will want to go with them.

We're so close. We made it so close.

And still, I'm going to fall short of saving him.

"Blaise, I know Lydia already told you about Piper. I just wanted to let you know...Blaise?"

I turn to find Asha in the doorway of my tent. Her voice is tinged with concern, but she's not looking at me. Her gaze fixes on the tapestry, scanning the likenesses as they make their way across an abandoned island.

"What sort of thread is that tapestry made of?" Asha asks, her hand drawing toward the fabric, as if by its own volition.

I brush my braid from my neck and it swats me on the back. "I'm not sure. It's just thread I picked up back in Othian. I'll have to remember the shopkeeper's name, but I can ask her when we return."

Asha's gaze flicks between me and the tapestry.

She schools her features too late.

She knows I'm lying, and even if I hadn't glimpsed it on her face, I would have sensed it, scented it in the fear coursing through her blood.

"I'd like that." A smile lines her lips that might have been convincing to anyone else, anyone who couldn't smell her dread. "The way the dye takes to it; it's stunning. I had no idea you wove."

"It's more of a dabbling," I say, rising to my feet.

Asha's throat bobs. "Well, I just thought I'd..." But she can't seem to find the words. Either that, or she's decided perhaps I can't be trusted with the plans. "...check on you."

"Right. Keep me updated about Piper."

Asha nods her head, then makes to slip out of the tent.

She doesn't make it.

ASHA'S BLOOD tastes of anguish and Fate itself on my tongue. Any other time, I might have found the taste too intoxicating to stop, but I'm not biting her to feed.

The venom coursing through the tips of my fangs and into her bloodstream leaves a strange bile-like taste to her blood, I suppose because I made a mental note to inject more than I would normally.

Her scream stills in her throat as soon as the venom kicks in, but it's not my only safeguard. I know from the first time Nox attacked me, the night Gunter died, that my venom's effects are psychosomatic; Asha can break through her immobility if she can remind her body the paralysis isn't real.

"You're not going to scream," I whisper through blood-soaked lips. She opens her mouth, but I cut her off, the compulsion heady and soothing in my voice. "You're not going to speak either, or alert anyone that anything is out of the ordinary. Do you understand?"

She nods, though it appears taxing. I worry I was too aggressive in biting her. Blood oozes down her neck and onto my tunic at a rate I wasn't expecting, but I can't think of that now. Not when my venom will soon heal the wound without a trace of damage, anyway.

It takes more effort than it should to rip one of my tunics and roll it into a ball. I shove it into her mouth and wince when she gags and doesn't fight me, but I tie another swatch of cloth around her mouth all the same. Az warned me repeatedly of what Asha can do with her words, especially when she's near the Rip, and I'm not willing to risk her coming out of my compulsion and summoning some other-worldly beast to sic on me.

"Asha, I'm so sorry," I whisper, even as she passes out, her weight slumping against me.

It's a lie, though; I know that as soon as it leaves my tongue.

I'm not sorry. Not if Asha is the price I have to pay for outrunning the Fate woven into Nox's tapestry.

PART III

MOTHER

CHAPTER 29

NOX

*I*t takes me all of a moment to recognize death as a friend, a warm solace that frees me of my curse and allows me to feel the sunlight painting my skin one last time before I fade to nothing.

It just so happens that death is about the time the questions start.

For instance, where am I going now?

I don't mean the question as an esoteric one—though I think it's worthy of consideration—but as more of a practical one.

Is this death the end for me? Will I fade into nothingness, my consciousness untethered from my body? Will I open my eyes any moment now and find that I've beaten Farin in a footrace back to Alondria?

I decide to open my eyes and find out.

Nothing happens.

Sunlight bleeds across my exposed forearms, tickling the back of my neck, but other than that—nothing.

"So...does this mean you were lying to me about the sunlight, or about everything?" Zora asks from the pit ledge.

I crane my neck to look at her, and though that suspicion is back on her raised brow, her shoulders have slackened now that I haven't burst into flames.

My eyes sting, partly with relief at avoiding what very well could have been a permanent death, partly because it's been a long, long time since I've stood in the sun.

"Well, now that is interesting, isn't it?"

The voice is the one I least want to hear.

Footsteps shuffle, and Zora instinctively takes a step away from the rim as Farin approaches and peers over it.

"Yep. Seems like my vampirism didn't make it through the Fabric," I say, like the Fabric separating the realms is some sort of cheesecloth and my vampirism is coffee grounds that can't quite make it through the filter.

"Well, knowing that would have made things a tad easier."

"Yes, we could have traveled in the daylight, I know," I say, glad for an excuse to employ a dry sense of humor rather than tear up in front of Farin as I'm suddenly tempted to do.

"That, and I wouldn't have had to watch you feed on all those hares. It was revolting, you know. I'm afraid I'll never rinse my memory of the sound." Farin shivers, which I find a tad hypocritical, since he was the one who led me to kill so often when we inhabited the same body.

No wonder the hare's blood tasted like iron. No wonder I haven't had an overwhelming craving for Zora's blood.

I feel as though a flood of relief is about to break over me at any moment, but there's a well-crafted dam of skepticism holding it back.

I'll need to work through what this means. If it applies to my body back home. But first I need out of this pit.

"Some assistance would be nice," I yell up at both my sister and my nemesis.

Farin just stares at me, cocking his head to the side as he's prone to doing. "It is strange that your vampirism doesn't affect you here. I would have thought the curse would have clung to your very soul."

Impatience rattles within me, and I tap my foot. "Yes, well, I suppose this curse doesn't have a flair for the intangible. I'm sure it will assault me just the same once I'm back in Alondria."

Farin looks pensive. "So you think it no longer affects you because you're in a different body?"

"That does seem to be the most obvious conclusion," I spit back. "Now, if you could kindly hand me a vine."

Farin stares at me a moment, like he wants to suggest something. Instead he says, more deliberately than usual, "I'd be happy to help you."

One side of Zora's nose lifts upward, like Farin is an unfamiliar scent that she can't quite place. She and I exchange a knowing look before she draws away from the edge to look for something to help me climb up.

"You know, it's strange hearing you say that. That you're glad to help me, I mean," I say, calling up to Farin. "I might get the impression you're warming up to me."

Farin doesn't respond, and though I can sense the shuffle of Zora's feet as she searches for vines, I get the feeling Farin has hardly moved since walking out of sight.

"Farin?" I call upward. "I wouldn't have thought you'd be keen to rescue me, though I suppose you could brag about it to Bl—"

I cut myself off, a dreadful thought interrupting my line of thinking.

"You know, I was thinking," says Farin, and though I can no longer see him, his voice echoes down into the pit. "If vampirism is a curse that's tied to one's body and not one's soul, perhaps there are other curses that work similarly."

"Again," I say, "something I'd be more than happy to have an internal debate with you about once we're peacefully stuck in the same body once more."

"What?" Zora starts, almost dropping her stick.

Farin chuckles, the sound of which has the hairs on the back of my neck standing up.

Because something has occurred to me, and I can only hope that it hasn't occurred to Farin too.

"I don't see why we can't discuss it now. In fact, I believe I already possess evidence for my theory. Don't you want to hear the evidence, Nox?"

Okay, he's definitely thought of it.

"You're starting to sound like your mother, you know." It's taking every ounce of control in my body to keep my voice from trembling. If Zora can just hurry up and toss down a vine, maybe I can get out of here. But there's no way of warning her without calling attention to the problem myself.

"Would either of you care to explain what you're talking about?" Zora asks.

"Oh, I was just explaining to your brother a theory of mine. But he doesn't seem inclined to listen to the evidence."

No, no, no. "Zora, can you—"

"You see, something your brother said got me curious. If his curse isn't bound to his soul, but his body, could the same apply to other curses as well?"

"Curses like?"

"For instance, this is probably unfamiliar to you, having grown up in these lands—though I'm not sure you've been entirely honest with Nox about how much you remember of your other lives—but in the realm from which we originate, the fae are cursed with the inability to lie. For most, this curse is a minor inconvenience, but for the oldest of our kind, it's quite dreadful indeed. It can even cause death—the swift sort."

I grind out my sister's name. "Zora."

She makes to let down a vine, but Farin grabs it and yanks it back, sending her stumbling backward.

"I don't think you want to test your theory, Farin. There's no way for you to confirm it without risking your own life."

Farin shakes his head. "That's not true at all. Because it seems your sister has already lied to us, when she claimed it was difficult for her to find words in our language. If the fae curse followed her here, she wouldn't have been able to do that."

"There's a flaw in your logic, though," I say, panicking and scrambling for anything to turn Farin's course. "It's true that the curses don't reach us in this realm, but that doesn't mean they won't apply once we return. I can guarantee you I'm still a vampire back home, and that Zora's still afflicted with the fae curse. You know if you go back, you still won't be able to lie without triggering the curse. Meaning, if you hurt me, you'll have no way of hiding it from Blaise."

Farin pauses for a moment, looking thoughtful. Zora shifts on her feet behind him, clearly unsure of what to do, like she's worried moving too quickly might cause him to strike.

"I'm not sure that's true," he finally says. "I've already proven the fae curse no longer binds me. I'm sure you know that I'm not at all happy to help you, as I claimed."

I grit my teeth, irritated that Farin is too dull to get my point. There's no use making an intelligent argument with someone who is unable to follow it. "We've already been over this. Just because it didn't follow you here—"

"Doesn't mean it won't affect me over there, yes, yes. But here's the thing, Nox. We've already proven the curses bind themselves to our bodies, not our souls. And I'm not going back to *my* body, am I?"

One second, his words strike me to my core, and I'm frozen.

The next, I'm darting to the side.

It's a good thing I do, because the broken shaft of a branch pierces into the ground, where I was just standing.

Zora lets out a scream, then covers her mouth with her hands like she's surprised at herself for letting her concern for my safety slip out.

"Zora, run," I yell.

She takes one last look at me, then she does.

"Well, that's a pity. I suppose your blood connection doesn't run quite as thick through the Fabric, either, does it?" Farin asks, twirling another stick in his hand. He breaks it over his knee and hurls it at me.

I duck to the side, and it lodges in the pit wall where my head just was.

"Farin, think about this," I say, holding my palms out. "Blaise is too smart for you to trick. If you kill me, she'll know."

He quirks a smile, and I get the wretched feeling he's already thought of this. "I could always pretend to be you, you know."

My blood runs cold.

"She told me once that she would have preferred that. That it would have been a mercy if I'd lied to her, let her believe that I was you. I can't imagine why that would have changed."

The worst part is that he's not lying. I remember each and every word.

My head is spinning, but I can't let him taunt me, not if I want to make it out of this alive. "She'll probably see you do it in the tapestry. She'll see me die, and she'll know you're not me."

Farin narrows his eyes, and for a moment I think I've got him. But then a cruel grin warps his features. "Don't be frightened of death. It's dark and lonely for beings like you and me, but you're a fool if you believe the Fates forget about us. Stay interesting enough, and they might just weave you back into the story."

I don't have time to process his taunt, because something shrieks from the tree line, and the sound sends a flock of ravens hurtling toward the sky.

For the first time, I stop to consider why there's a pit dug into the ground.

Farin turns just in time to duck out of the way as a scorpion the size of an elephant launches itself into the pit.

CHAPTER 30

KIRAN

The inn we stop in to stay the night in Avelea is just the sort I would rather *not* stay in, but Fin picked it out from a noticeboard when we made it into town and I kept my mouth shut.

I'm trying my best not to antagonize him or give him any more reason to hate me than he already has, but it's proving difficult when any decision he makes is the opposite of what I would do.

This inn, for instance.

For one, it stinks of rot and vaanweed, mostly thanks to a certain inhabitant who sits behind the counter taking both food orders and payments from those who need rooms.

I don't know why we couldn't have just stayed in the simple family inn down the street. Sure, we probably would have been forced to sleep on the floor, but at least then we wouldn't have the stink of vaanweed lingering on our garments by the morning.

The innkeeper gives us curious looks, though we can't be the only ones who've stopped through this place with our hoods drawn to obscure our faces. He must assume we're assassins or mercenaries of some sort, because he uses the word "discreet" about seven times during what should have been a three-sentence exchange.

"How long are you staying?"

"Just a night."

"That'll be twelve coppers."

It isn't that difficult.

Still, by the time we've made it to our room, I'm grateful for the two beds. I claim the one by the door, though Fin immediately says, "Want to be the only one who can escape if assassins come through the window?"

I raise my brow. "Want to be the only one to escape if they come through the door?"

Red splotches appear on my twin's neck, but I just stare at the ceiling and try not to think about the critters who've likely also stayed the night in this bed.

From what others tell me, my brother is pleasant. Clever, even. Unfortunately, I never get to witness that side of him, if it even exists.

Still.

I'm probably being too harsh with him.

I turn my head to look at him and open my mouth, though I have no idea what I'm supposed to say. As it turns out, I don't have to say anything. Don't get the chance. Because Fin murmurs something about being hungry and practically flees the room, almost slamming the door behind him.

My skin heats, my magic flaring with my irritation, but I take deep breaths, doing my best to calm myself.

I don't know why I let myself get so aggravated at him when I'm the one who tore our relationship apart. There had been a time—a short, rather fleeting time—that we had actually begun getting along. Back when Gwenyth, of all people, brought us together.

Of course her apparent selflessness was actually a ploy to satisfy her own thirst for power, which I somehow find even more irritating.

I'm already not looking forward to telling Asha how this trip is going. To her asking me if I even tried. She won't ask it that way, of course. She'll be much kinder about it than I could ever manage, and it'll be immensely frustrating because I won't even be able to be mad at her for implying what I know is the truth.

That I'm not trying. Not really.

I know that. Asha will know that. Probably already knows with that extra sense of hers.

So I sigh and roll out of bed, astounded at how quickly I've already developed knots in my muscles from the lumpy mattress.

FIN'S ALREADY DRUNK, though he carries it better than I would. I'm not a drinker, never have been. Not when I know I carry my father's tendency toward rage in my veins.

I stop myself, realizing that's not true. That I don't carry any bit of Rajeen in my veins. I don't know quite how to deal with the fact that I can't blame my anger on inheriting his blood, though I'm not foolish enough to think his cruel training regimen had nothing to do with it.

Still. I wonder how long it will take me to cease thinking of the late king as my sire. I wonder if there will always be a part of me that can't quite accept it.

Fin downs a flagon of ale, his grin spread wide across his face as he sits, chair backward, legs sprawled, at the head of a band of males whose occupations I don't even want to know.

He has his hood off, drunk and forgetting that we're supposed to be hiding our identities, though even I have to admit it's unlikely anyone will recognize him.

Fin doesn't look like a prince, doesn't carry himself like a male who's been born into luxury, pampered since childhood.

He doesn't bear the weight of kingdoms on his shoulders, though he does carry his grief. But in this moment, I can't seem to find it. Perhaps that's because he's drowned it in liquor.

Fin's telling a story, one I don't recognize, about some travels he did years ago, before he married.

I don't remember him taking the trip. Don't know if he's making the story up or not. Intoxication is strange like that. It seems that so long as the drunk doesn't realize he's lying, the fae curse doesn't affect him. I decide I'd rather Fin be making up the story than hear the shenanigans he and Lydia pulled without me, on a trip I didn't even know they'd taken, while I'd been consumed with pleasing Father.

"Pull up a chair," says a male sitting at the table, gesturing toward me.

Fin swivels around to see who the man is speaking to, and as soon as his eyes focus in on me, his countenance falls. "You don't want him to sit," he drawls. "Not a people person, I'm afraid."

The group lets out a chuckle, and a few of them tug at the collars of their shirts as the temperature in the inn rises.

I hold my breath, then back away, returning to our room.

IT'S NEARLY morning by the time Fin bursts into our room, vomiting all over the floor before he collapses onto it.

My back aches from a sleepless night spent on this shabby excuse for a cot, but I make myself rise anyway, helping Fin sit up by propping him against the bed as I assist him in taking off his boots.

"Don't touch me," he says, though he can hardly get the words out.

I sigh, dropping his still-booted foot to the ground.

"Fine," I say, lifting my hands and getting back into bed.

"You...you destroy everything you touch," he says, though he's clearly having to fight to keep his head up.

I grit my teeth. "We should have this discussion when you're sober."

Fin stands, though he stumbles and has to catch himself on the cot behind him.

I only have to wait a few moments before he falls backward on it and drifts off to sleep.

THE ALCOHOL in my brother's blood must metabolize quickly, because he's ready to disembark at the appointed time the next morning. I was prepared to pay for another night, figuring he'd have to sleep away the hangover today, especially given the ale he was drinking last night smelled faerie-made. But if my brother suffers from any lingering side effects of his drinking bout, he doesn't show it.

He doesn't speak a word to me for several hours.

. . .

"I don't remember what I said to you last night," Fin finally says, speaking up past the sound of the crickets.

We've set up camp at the edge of the woods tonight, the flame I conjured in the middle of the site providing relief from the chill of the Avelean night.

"Doesn't matter. You were drunk. People say things they don't mean when they're drunk."

Fin looks at me, crinkling his brow. "Have you ever been drunk? Because in my experience, people say exactly what they mean when they're drunk."

I toss a crumbling stick into the fire and watch it burn. It's easier to watch than my brother.

"Don't worry. It's nothing you haven't expressed before," I say, and Fin goes quiet.

Several minutes pass before I find the courage to speak again. "I'm sorry, Fin. Truly sorry for what I did to Ophelia. For taking her away from you. I was just..." I take a breath, expelling the excuse. "Well, it doesn't matter. Her life wasn't mine to take."

"You think it was mine, then?"

"That's not what I said."

Silence swarms us for another long minute, when I finally collect my thoughts. "You know, I wish you would tell me. Exactly what you think of me, I mean. You hide it behind jokes and caustic comments, but I wish you would just come out and say it."

Fin huffs. "Say what? That I hate you? That I think I probably always will? Does that make you feel better, Kiran?" His voice is rising now, and he jumps to his feet. "Does it give you the closure you need if I tell you I wish Gwenyth's plan had worked? That I wish she'd succeeded?"

"If she'd succeeded, you would be dead," I say. My late wife had intended for both of us to die by the end of all her scheming.

"But Ophelia would be *alive*." Fin emphasizes his words by flexing his hands. "Or do you not understand that? Is your heart so hard that you can't imagine wanting to die for your wife? For Asha even?"

Irritation flares within me, but I keep it in check. "Ophelia betrayed you."

"Yes, for her brother. Because the life of her family was being threatened. Just like Asha was going to betray you when it came down to choosing between Dinah's life and yours."

His words strike me like a spear to the chest.

"It's the same," he says, his chest heaving. "It's the same, except you spared Asha, and you killed Ophelia. For the same crime."

My head spins, but I have nothing to say as Fin walks away, hands clasped behind his head. He doesn't come back until morning.

CHAPTER 31

NOX

*S*cales the color of a fresh bruise glimmer in the sunlight as the scorpion stares me down. Two pincers acting as a mouth clink covetously, as if it's smacking its lips. Its tail curves upward, spanning the height of the pit.

My stomach churns.

If this were a bear, I'd try to remain still, but this is not a bear, and never in any of Gunter's books have I read what to do if I were to find myself trapped in the pit of a giant scorpion.

So I do the only thing my inadequately prepped mind can think to do, and I lunge for it.

It snaps its pincers eagerly, probably delighted to have caught a prey stupid enough to actually come closer, but when I jump over its reaching pincers and land on its flat head, it rears back and shrieks again.

The force of its rearing sends me flying, but I'm ready for it. Instinctively, I wrap my arms around its tail when my torso slams against its firm scales, stealing the breath from my lungs. I have to dig my fingers into its underside to hold on as flicks its tail, but at least I don't fall.

That thought must jinx me, because the scorpion lurches and I lose my grip, sending me flying. My weight hits the wall of the pit with a sickening thud, pain shooting through my right leg and the back of my skull.

The world swims around me, multiplying the approaching scorpion in my vision by dozens.

Farin's laugh rings in the distance. I vaguely hear him say something about how Blaise won't have to see him kill me in the tapestry.

The wry part of me that still thinks Farin's an idiot is pretty sure it'll show him standing above me laughing as I get eaten, and that Blaise won't take too kindly to his standing by.

Unfortunately, I don't have the breath to say as much at the moment.

The scorpion lashes its tail at me again, but it has a crude angle on me, and its tail crashes into the wall just above me, giving me just enough time to roll out of the way before it launches at me with its pincers.

I'm on my feet in the next instant, but putting weight on my leg is agonizing. I push away the pain, trying to focus on surviving this.

Standing makes me an easier target, and the glinting barb of the scorpion's tail almost skewers me before I'm able to stumble out of the way.

It jabs again, and each time I feel as though the distance by which it misses becomes narrower.

I blink, and the scorpion multiplies in my vision again. It takes another stab at me, and since I see a dozen barbs heading in my direction, I have to take a guess at which one will strike true.

I guess correctly, but only barely. Sharp pain slices across my bicep as the barb breaks flesh.

Instant nausea washes over me.

That'll be the venom, I realize.

Great.

Yep. I'm really hoping that Farin sticks around to watch this, and that the tapestry shows him pointing his finger and laughing.

Thankfully, the fact that the barb barely broke the skin seems to keep the venom from paralyzing me completely. At least I have that to be thankful for.

Blink.

The dozens of scorpions collapse into one.

One that happens to be scuttling toward me, pincers, well, pinching in anticipation.

I suppose it thinks I'm stunned. The thought causes a giggle to escape my lips, until I realize that probably is a sign of being stunned, and I clamp my mouth shut.

Instinct cuts through the venom's haze, providing me with enough clarity of mind to stumble backward.

My back hits the wall of the pit. The pincers vibrate.

I think the venom must be swirling in my head again, because I start to wonder if maybe this is the best way I could go. The most fitting.

Paralyzed by the venom of a monster. Completely taken by its will. Ready to offer myself to be eaten.

This is how I killed the others, isn't it?

I've just happened upon a monster that's bigger than I am.

This seems fair somehow.

The scorpion rears back its stinger for the kill, but stops suddenly, as if shaken.

"Nox!"

I hear my name, and find myself searching for its source. My eyes have difficulty focusing, but when they do, they find Zora standing on the side of the pit. She's launching rather large rocks at the head of the beast.

"Well, what are you standing there for?" she screams. "Run!"

I don't have the heart to tell her there's nowhere for me to run. There must be something about the desperation in her voice that rekindles my will to live because the haze in my brain starts to dissipate. Panic—the useful kind—overtakes my limbs.

The scorpion is backing away, though it looks as if it's only doing so to get a running start at launching itself at Zora.

I use the opportunity to sidle up against the wall and sneak around to its backside. I clamber onto its back, trying to time my ascent with the moments Zora's rocks collide with the scorpion's head. So far it's working; the scorpion doesn't thrash its tail.

The climb is arduous, and I have to will myself to focus to keep my fingers from going limp. Halfway up, Zora screams a warning at me, and I have just enough time to latch myself around the tail before the scorpion attempts to fling me. My side crashes against the pit wall, but I don't fall. Zora, the scorpion, and I continue on like this—scream, thrash, cling—for a few rounds before I find myself at the tip of its tail.

The scorpion must have inched closer to Zora's side of the pit, because rather than cresting the edge of the pit like it was before, there's several feet of air between the tip and the edge.

All I can think is that I'm glad the scorpion venom dulled the aching in my leg.

I am not accustomed to my mind working this slowly, and I am not at all hoping to repeat this experience.

I take in a deep breath, fighting the fuzz that seems to block each thought.

"Nox, you need to jump," Zora screams. As if I don't already know that.

Then again, I was about to embrace death when she got here, so maybe the condescension is warranted.

I brace my limbs, preparing them to launch, but they're trembling from the combined venom and climb. I'm unsure if I can keep my balance, much less make the jump.

I'm also pretty sure if I fall this time, I'm not getting back up.

So when the scorpion rears back, readying to swing its tail at Zora, I take advantage of the momentum and jump.

CHAPTER 32

ELLIE

*I*t's minutes before anyone thinks to check.

Minutes are too long.

Lydia's gone after Piper. Elias departed soon after, intending to gather acquaintances from the Coup to assist her should Abra have an army guarding Piper. That leaves me to get Asha and Blaise, so we can get Marcus to the Rip as soon as possible.

"Blaise," I call, wishing there were a way to knock on the tent door, but of course it's made of pliant fabric, so I settle for the nearest posts.

No one answers.

"Blaise, Asha should have come by earlier. We're about to set out. I assume Asha told you, but we're going to head to the Rip. Apparently, Amity thinks there's a type of flax there that can heal Marcus. Lydia and Elias have already gotten a head start on Piper."

Nothing.

I don't like the idea of barging in on anyone, but we have to leave if we want to catch up to the others once we get what Marcus needs from the Rip.

I touch the knot on the tent door.

I know instantly something is wrong. For starters, the knot is tied. Blaise isn't exactly the modest sort. She doesn't care enough about whether her tent flap blows open and exposes her in her sleepwear to bother securing it in place, which is unfortunate for anyone who does mind.

But here the knot is, secured in place, though not neatly.

I untie it. The rope scratches my fingers, and can't help but notice the string is damp.

As the tent flap falls aside, I realize it isn't the only thing that's wet.

Blood glistens in pools inside the tent, shimmering in the lantern light. Across the tent is a tapestry, one that has been knocked over, as if in haste. Blood seeps from the floor into the fabric, obscuring parts of the story woven into it.

"Evander," I call, but my voice only rasps. I steel myself, urgency flowing back into me. "Evander!"

He's there in an instant, and when I turn to face him, there's nothing but dread in his wide eyes.

"SHE'S JUST SIGNED her own death warrant." Evander paces back and forth in the tent, trying his best to keep from stepping in the pool of blood.

Blood.

Asha's blood.

Is Asha dead? Did Blaise let herself get too hungry? I've never seen Blaise lose control before. But hadn't she almost attacked Asha the night they took a stroll through the gardens in Othian? I thought Blaise stayed on top of hunting, but if she snapped...or perhaps Asha accidentally cut herself on something.

"El. El."

I redirect my attention to Evander, but even the smell of blood is making my stomach churn.

"We have to find them."

Dread coils in my stomach. "Them? You think Asha's still alive?"

Evander stares at the blood pooling at our feet.

He doesn't have to answer.

· · ·

"Kiran's going to kill Blaise. That's what you meant earlier when you said she'd signed her own death warrant," I whisper to Evander, my back pressed against his firm chest as we ride on horseback across the Charshonian plains.

Amity and Marcus ride beside us, Amity holding the rope leading my horse. Evander has wanted me as close to him as possible, now that we know Blaise lost control. When he suggested it, I almost argued that Blaise would likely be satiated by the time we got to her, but the thought sent bile to my throat.

I vomited in the grass, and that had reminded me of Asha too.

Asha is my friend. She was my companion in Othian while we'd waited for Kiran and Evander to return. She shared in the secret of my pregnancy. She waited outside of Forcier's before sunrise just to retrieve my father's favorite bread.

I know I should feel more loss than I do, but it's like my mind refuses to process that she's gone.

But with all that blood...

"She'll have to be on the run after this," Evander says, his voice distant, his arm wrapped protectively around me as we ride.

"You think Kiran would hunt her?"

"You don't?"

I keep my voice down, noticing Amity watching us intently as she bobs up and down on her and Marcus's horse. "I think if she's hurt Asha..."

"If? You saw the blood back there."

I sigh. "I think he won't hesitate to kill her if he ever sees her again."

"Like he did his brother's wife."

"In the heat of the moment," I add.

"Are you defending him?" Evander snaps.

I go silent in answer.

"I'm sorry," he whispers.

"I know you're worried about her," I say, but I'd be lying if I said I wasn't riled. "And Evander, I don't want Kiran hunting her down any more than you do, but if she's killed Asha..."

"Then what? We abandon her? When we should have seen it coming? Should have realized she was too weak to control her cravings?"

I shake my head. "Stop."

"Stop what?"

"You have to stop taking responsibility for what Blaise does and doesn't do. You're like..." I groan, searching for the right words. "You're like one of those parents whose children grow up to be menaces to society, but you can't see them for who they've become. All you can see is a toddler who doesn't know any better than to put their hand to the stove. But Blaise isn't a child any longer, Evander. At some point, you have to stop thinking it's your fault if she reaches out and touches something that ends up burning her. That ends up burning everyone else."

"Have you given up on her?" For a moment, I think it's an accusation, a way to make me feel guilty, and anger roils up within me. How dare he? Especially after how patient I've been with all this. With his rash promises and following Blaise out here and...

"Because if so, I need to know how you do it," he says, and it's only then that I recognize the despair in his voice. That he isn't trying to accuse me at all, but that he genuinely doesn't know.

"No." I take a deep breath. "I haven't given up on her. She's my friend too, you know. And maybe I shouldn't. Maybe I only feel this way because I can't bring myself to believe that Asha is really...I do love her—Blaise, I mean. But Evander, if you try to save someone who's drowning, but they won't let you, and they grab ahold of your neck and climb onto your back, flailing...Well, you're not doing them any good, are you? You'll both just end up drowned."

"And the people I love, too." He caresses my belly absentmindedly.

"Us, too," I say, craning my neck upward and kissing him on the cheek.

"But, El? How do you let go of someone who's drowning? How do you live with yourself?"

I don't have an answer to that.

CHAPTER 33

NOX

*E*arth fills my mouth, invading the space between my teeth as I land. Coupled with the relief of hitting solid ground comes the fading of my exhilaration, which means the throbbing in my leg is about to make a reappearance. If this body were a vampire's, it would have healed by now. My fae muscles and bones and sinews will reknit themselves, but only if I can get away from the scorpion long enough to rest.

I push myself to my feet, ignoring the stab of pain that begs me not to put any weight on my leg.

Farin is nowhere to be found.

Zora has stopped throwing rocks at the scorpion. She takes one glance at me, realizes I've made it out of the pit, then spins on her heel and breaks into a run.

I follow suit.

WE RUN, our bodies cutting through the brush, even as the sound of trees rent from their roots follows close behind us. The scorpion barrels through the vegetation to get to us, but we're smaller, and maneuvering trees is a quicker feat than crushing them.

All the while, my leg aches, but running seems to be clearing the venom from my head.

Hopefully that doesn't mean I'm just providing it with a faster ride to my heart. I probably am, but there's no time to think of that now.

Zora's breath labors just ahead of me.

She doesn't turn to make sure I follow, but she doesn't have to with her fae hearing.

We race to the edge of the forest. Zora halts, holding a hand out for me to do the same. I have just enough time to dig my heels into the ground as pebbles and clots of dirt go crumbling off the cliffside directly in front of me.

My fae vision allows me to follow the pebbles' descent, but even I can't see the bottom of the canyon through the fog that swirls in its depths.

"Come on." Zora jerks her head to the side and sets off, sprinting across the edge of the canyon.

I follow, trying not to think about the crumbling density of earth at the edges of canyons like this. How well—or not—the ground adheres to itself.

After a moment, I see what she is aiming for: a bridge that connects this side of the canyon to the other.

It looks to have been made a while ago.

I try not to think about that, either.

We reach the bridge just as the tree line splinters behind us, near the spot I almost went careening over the edge.

One glance behind me reveals the scorpion, its claws digging into the ledge to keep from toppling over. It occurs to me it could probably crawl down the canyon and back up to get to us, but it hisses when it peers downward. I try not to think about what the fog obscures if even the scorpion fears it.

"Would have been nice if it had toppled over the edge," says Zora, hesitating at the entrance to the bridge.

"It never seems to work out that way, does it?"

For a moment, I think we both consider sprinting back into the forest. The bridge consists of rotting wooden slats strung together with ropes that look to be fraying at the edges. No handrails. Just a row of wooden bars, spaced out like stepping stones in a garden.

We exchange a morbid glance.

Then we run across the bridge.

THERE'S an unfortunate amount of rebound on the bridge, especially with the two of us racing across it. Every time Zora's foot lands on a plank, it sends the ones beneath my feet ricocheting toward the sky. The result necessitates an extreme feat of balance, and it impedes our progress. One can only run so quickly across an ever-changing platform without tumbling off. Still, we make it halfway across before the scorpion reaches the bridge at all.

Not that halfway is all that helpful when all the scorpion has to do to send us plummeting to our deaths is slice the ropes with its pincers.

"I don't think scorpions are that intelligent," Zora says between huffs when I bring it up.

I chance a glance behind us, which is a mistake as it almost causes me to lose my footing. The scorpion skirts around the entrance to the bridge, as if it's afraid of heights and has to work itself up to crossing it.

"Even if it were, I think it would rather eat us than kill us for spite." I have to yell over the winds that have picked up since our initial flight and are now swaying the bridge back and forth.

"How comforting!" Zora yells back. "I, for one, would pick being eaten over plummeting to a quick death with the solid ground any time."

I acknowledge her sarcasm and pick up my pace.

The other side of the canyon is in sight when we hear a crash.

The force of the scorpion launching itself onto the bridge sends both of us skyborne.

There's a moment, suspended in the air, when I feel absolutely weightless. It's as if Zora and I are frozen in time.

But then we fall.

I hit the bridge first. Something cracks beneath my weight—a rotting board that splinters upon impact. My left foot goes straight through the board, sending me toppling off balance. I fall, but my foot is still stuck.

"Hold on!" I shout at Zora, who grabs onto the ropes just in time for my weight to flip our section of the bridge upside down.

I'm hanging by my ankle, trying not to stare into the gaping mouth of the chasm beneath me. Fog swirls below, as if to welcome me into its open arms.

You would think the surprise of the flip would have sent the scorpion falling to its death. I'm not that lucky. When I crane my neck, I notice the scorpion crawling toward us, hanging upside down, unfazed by the sudden change of direction.

"Zora?" I call, having a hard time seeing her at this angle.

"Not really in the mood to chat right now," she calls back, her voice strained. She lets out a series of grunts, I assume due to the strain of pulling herself to the upright portion of the bridge.

"Are you holding on?"

"Obviously."

I fight the urge to roll my eyes before summoning enough momentum to force my torso upward. It feels as if I'm snipping the muscles in my abdomen with pruning shears, but I manage to get ahold of the ropes this way.

Zora's already waiting for me. When she extends a hand to help me maneuver right-side up, I shake my head.

"I'd rather you keep both hands on the ropes," I explain between breaths. She rolls her eyes but clamps her fingers around the ropes all the same.

Once I have my hands secure around the ropes, I swing my feet upward through a section of missing slats and wrap my legs around the ropes before pulling myself up.

Zora's gaze is fixed behind me. "Could you be any slower?"

The ropes rattle beneath my fingertips, and I don't need to turn around to understand why.

Together we scramble across the bridge on our hands and knees, not daring to stand upright lest the bridge flip again.

It slows our progress, allowing the scorpion to catch up with us until I can practically feel its pincers scraping against my heels.

Zora reaches safety first, if you can even call it safety.

Her tanned face is flushed with exertion, and I'm not sure how much longer either of us can outrun the scorpion once it's on land again.

"It's gaining on you," she says.

"Toss me your knife."

She screws up her eyebrows, but she throws me the knife all the same. The moment I have to let go of the ropes with my right hand to catch it is a less-than-pleasant experience I'm not keen on repeating.

But it's nothing compared to the bottom that falls out of my gut when I bring the knife down on the rope just below me. I don't have a good angle to cut below my feet, so I have to slice the rope directly below where I'm gripping the bridge. The ease with which the rope snaps is unsettling. I'm just going to have to think about that after I make it to stable ground. The snap of the right rope has the bridge flipping on its other side as I hold on with my left hand.

Behind me the scorpion shrieks, but as far as I can tell, it doesn't fall.

I slice at the remaining rope, but this one is more secure, and in the seconds it takes me to saw through it, I sense the scorpion gaining on me.

The rope is rubbing blisters into my left hand now. Sweat beads at my fingertips, loosening my grip. Still, the rope only frays, rather than snapping. I can't get a good angle on it, not while I'm trying to keep from plummeting.

The scorpion snaps at my foot. I have to swing it out of the way, and only barely succeed.

My abdomen feels as though it's going to rip in half.

"You have to climb, Nox!" Zora screams down at me.

I want to shout that I can't until the scorpion falls. That if it reaches steady ground, it will chase her down and kill her, but I can't find the breath for it.

It's then that I hear the sawing.

I glance up to find Zora shearing at the rope with a second knife she must have just pulled out of her boot.

"I said climb," she practically spits.

I stuff the knife into my belt and do as she says.

My muscles scream at me during the ascent. I'm not going to make it. My head is still swirling from the effects of the venom, and even if it weren't, the scorpion would still get to me before I reached land.

But I climb all the same.

I can't help but notice that Zora is on the last section of braids.

She glances at me, her knife hesitating at the last braid. Her eyes widen in horror.

"Just do it," I whisper. It's all the breath I have left, anyway.

She glances between me and the scorpion behind me.

Zora grits her teeth.

"Jump."

And then she brings the knife down on the rope.

In the half-second while it's still swinging, I yank myself up on the rope with all my might and launch myself skyward.

The rope slices in two, and for a moment, I'm weightless again. Zora's knife goes hurtling past my face, slicing me on the cheek on the way down as she drops it.

Time stands still.

And then Zora's hand clamps around mine.

She lets out a shrill cry, and something pops. My body slams against the side of the chasm, but still she doesn't let go, holding herself to the stake that once held the weight of the bridge.

I use the last of my strength to climb up her arm. I have to grit my teeth at the sound of her whimpers, but still she doesn't let go.

When I pull myself onto the ledge, I find I've never experienced ground so soft.

And when I listen for the sound of the scorpion hitting the ground to help judge how deep the canyon is below the fog, the sound never comes.

CHAPTER 34

NOX

"*I* didn't hear it hit the bottom," says Zora. We're both lying on our backs on the earth. I'm fairly sure both of us are content never to get back up, so long as we can feel solid ground underneath us for the rest of eternity.

"What?"

"I didn't hear it hit the bottom," she repeats. "For all we know, it's just lurking on the edge of the chasm wall waiting to pounce on us.

I don't bother stifling my groan. "Well, why don't you take a look and see?"

"What if it's waiting for me to do that, and as soon as I look over the edge, it plans to chomp off my head?"

I let my head flop over to the side so I can stare at my sister. She's already staring at me, looking perfectly serious.

"I'm not going near that cliff again," I say.

"Why not?"

"Because that's like flirting with death. You don't survive what we just survived, then go peeking over the edge of a chasm. It's just asking to have the ground crumble out beneath you."

She shoots me a glare. "I can't believe you won't go check for me."

"There's no scorpion waiting just below the edge," I grumble, covering my eyes with my forearm.

"Then explain to me why I didn't hear it fall."

"Because you were shrieking at the pain in your arm and couldn't hear it over your own screams? Because you were focused on making sure both of us survived, and you can't pay attention to that many things at once?"

My sister flops dramatically on the ground. "So you admit I risked my life to save you—ripped my chest muscles in half to deliver you from that monster—and you won't peek over the edge of the chasm so I can have peace of mind?"

We stare each other down for a moment. I can't believe she just used the word *deliver* in conversation. I let out a sigh. "Fine."

She looks a bit too appeased for my liking as I crawl over to the edge.

"Why are you crawling?"

"Because everything hurts."

When I get to the edge, I hesitate. "You're sure you didn't hear it hit the ground?"

"Ha! So you don't think I'm being paranoid, after all!"

I groan and force myself to look over the edge. To my relief, there's no lurking scorpion in sight. Just a glittering expanse of fog that I can't help but think looks more satiated than it did earlier.

"Well?"

"Just like I told you, it's gone." I retreat from the edge all the same.

"Then why didn't I hear it hit the ground?"

I rub my temples. "I can't say I have the energy to think about that at the moment."

"But it is noteworthy that I didn't hear it, right?"

I crane my neck to look over at her. Zora has the smuggest grin I've ever seen pasted across her face.

It makes my stomach twist, but not in such an awful way.

"It's sort of nice," I say.

She frowns. "What's nice?"

"You being insufferable. I think I might have missed that."

Zora blinks, the smug expression vanishing. In an instant, I'm wishing I could swallow the words whole, banish them from existence. But I can't, and Zora clears her throat as she stands, dusting her britches off.

I scramble to my aching feet, hurrying after her as she strides into the woods. "Please," I call after her. "Don't leave. I know you don't trust me. I know you have every reason not to. But I think…"

"Think what?" She whirls on me. "Think you could help me? It might be true. You might be my brother, but that doesn't mean you're here for me. I heard you and Farin talking back at the pit. You're chasing after a girl you fancy, which is perfectly fine. But don't act like you're here on some rescue mission for me."

I stand stunned, my words caught in my throat. What am I supposed to say to Zora? She doesn't know the entire story, of course. Doesn't know that I've spent years of my life as a slave trying to buy her freedom.

Then again, it's my fault she was enslaved in the first place.

Her calves tense, and I ready myself for her to leave me behind, but then she jerks her head agitatedly. "Come on."

"You want me to come with you?"

She runs her hands through her cropped hair and immediately gasps.

"Here, let me help," I say, remembering how lifting me out of the chasm pulled her arm out of its socket.

Zora bites her lip reluctantly, but she nods all the same.

I don't hesitate. In fact, I strike as quickly as if it were an attack; I don't want to give Zora time to anticipate the pain.

A shriek grinds through her teeth, and she pales. For a moment, I think she might pass out, but then she steadies herself, her uninjured hand on my shoulder.

"As I was going to say," she says, still heaving, "you want to get back to your girl. I want answers about who…what I am. The way I see it, we can help one another. Oh," she says, holding her palm out. "I almost forgot—I want my knife back."

· · ·

213

WE SPEND half of the day setting up a new campground in a cavern tucked into the base of one of the island's many mountains. Neither of us does much talking, at least not until our campsite is set up and we've gathered enough berries and roots to get us by for the night.

My stomach growls, eager for meat, but I have to say I'm relieved not to be eating raw hare any longer.

Once we're done eating and the last rays of sunlight fade over the horizon, Zora sits down cross-legged in front of me and clasps her hands together, as if to signal it's time to talk business.

"I'm going to need you to tell me everything," she says. So I do.

I tell her of our parents, of how Mother always had a tendency to undercharge merchants who passed by in need of cloaks after being robbed on the Serpentine. I tell her of how Father always scolded her for it, but never seemed to mean it. I tell her of snowball fights, and the loneliness of being rejected by the other children in the village, and finding friendship in each other. Then there's Abra and my false apprenticeship, and the series of foolishness that led to Zora being taken as a punishment for my disobedience. I tell her of my Turning, and she bites her lip when I get to the part about developing the ritual to bargain for her freedom. Of Gunter, how I think of him as a father-figure, but struggle with how to feel about him now that I know the pain he caused her. I tell her everything. Well, almost everything. I mention Blaise, but leave out some details I'm not quite ready to admit aloud to myself yet.

The kiss Blaise shared with Farin, namely.

"But this Blaise girl. You and Farin both love her?" Zora asks when I finish my story, apparently unsatisfactorily in the eyes of my sister.

"I love her. Farin doesn't know how to separate my feelings from his own."

"Because he was a part of you."

I shake my head. "Because he lived in my head. Leeched off my feelings, memories. That's all."

She frowns, as if trying to make sense of something.

"I know it sounds crazy, and you're probably thinking I'm out of my mind, especially with the bit about the Fabric and other realms, but—"

Zora waves me off dismissively. "I already told you, I've known for years that I've lived several lives. Though I've always attributed it to more of a spiritual reincarnation than a magically inclined fae weaving the story of my life."

Her face goes blank for a moment. I wait for her to respond, sensing whatever she's about to say isn't something I have any business pulling out of her.

"Would it bother you?" she asks.

"Would what bother me?"

"To know that all along, your actions haven't been your own. That you only thought you were making your own decisions, but really it was someone else pulling the strings all along, planning your every move. Like you're the character in a novel or a play, and your only purpose is to tell a story, or prove a point, or teach a lesson to the audience?"

I frown, choosing my words carefully as my sister stares out into the distance, toward the last glimmers of sunlight fading over the horizon.

"Of course it would bother me. I think it would bother anyone. We all like to assume that the good we do, the choices we make, can be ascribed to ourselves."

She cuts her gaze back to me so quickly, it's startling. She opens her mouth as if to say something, but then she folds her lips together, holding whatever it is in.

"You could come back, you know. You could wake up in our world. In the realm where you belong."

Zora taps her fingers against the ground. "What makes you think that?"

"The male who wove your tapestries…he's dead now. Has been for weeks. Or months. I'm not sure how time works here relative to there. I don't know how many tapestries ahead of you he was when he died, but Abra, the queen who keeps us enslaved—she made a fae bargain with me. That you would be free if I delivered an ancient magic source over to her. If you were still trapped, she'd be dead for breaking her bargain. You're free to leave this place. Free to wake up. We just have to figure out how you're supposed to do that."

Zora lets out an exasperated chuckle. "Well, when you put it that way, you make it sound easy."

I laugh and rub the back of my neck. "I wish I could say I knew where to start, but I figure there's something in your past lives that could help us figure it out. If you can remember much of them, that is."

Zora furrows her brow, and I realize I misread her meaning.

"You don't mean figuring out a way to get back, do you?" I ask, apprehension cresting inside of me.

She shakes her head, then buries her face into her knees, which she's tucked into her chest.

Abra's words echo in my head.

Perhaps she simply does not wish to return.

"You already know how to leave," I say, my realization only barely catching up to my words.

Her laugh is dry, raw. "Oh, don't sound so judgmental. As if everyone doesn't know a way to leave the life they're currently living and move on to the next. Tell me, Nox, do you believe in a life after the one you currently live?"

I blink, hardly wishing to broach this subject at the moment. "I used to. I suppose I never quite stopped."

"Do you think it's better than the one you currently live?"

My throat bulges. "For some people, I think it will be." I don't mention that such a group likely doesn't include someone who's murdered innocents. I can't imagine there being any fairness in them having to face their murderer in whatever life they currently rest in.

"Then why don't those people end their lives in order to reach the next one sooner?"

"Some do."

She shakes her head. "Only those who are in despair. But the rest who are sad, oppressed, afflicted—the ones who believe there's something better on the other side. Why don't they end it?"

"I suppose they don't believe they're finished with their current life. I suppose they believe there's something left for them to do. Some purpose they haven't yet fulfilled. Or perhaps they would miss their loved ones if they left."

Zora swallows and nods.

"And is that what you're waiting for? A purpose you feel you haven't fulfilled yet?"

It's a strange way to think of Zora. Zora, who never seemed to put much thought into the future, into anything past her current impulse.

But the Zora I knew was a child. This Zora has lived dozens of lives. How many years, how much grief, how many losses had she endured?

"I remember some of them, some of my lives. Not every detail, of course. It's funny how you forget more days of your life than you can remember. It's even worse when you've lived multiple. I remember highlights. Turning points. Beginnings and ends. First kisses. The last breaths of a lover. Not much in between. I remember every time I commit"—she stops, choosing her words carefully—"an *evil* for the first time, and my soul cracks. But there's always a purpose. I never forget those. There's always something I'm sent to do. Or so I thought."

I cock a brow at her, and she goes on. "You said back at the pit that my purpose in all my lives has been the same. To gather information. To research other worlds for your master, this queen, whoever she is. That's...that's difficult for me to accept."

I crane my head at her. "Why is that? Research, learning...those are noble ventures in their own way."

She looses a breath, curling her fingers through her short hair. "Because I've been doing more than just learning, Nox."

She peers up at me then, her blue eyes wide with mingled fear and regret. "Sometimes I'm the hero. Sometimes I'm the villain. I never quite know until it comes down to the final stand, but I've always had a role to play. But if my role was to observe, not to interfere, if there was no point to being the hero or the villain, then what in the Fates did I get my hands dirty for?"

217

. . .

THE NEXT MORNING, I wake to Zora humming as she roasts a hare over the fire.

When I get off this island, I'm never touching a hare again, but I'm grateful to my sister for at least having the kindness of heart to cook it for me.

If she's still bothered by our conversation last night, by the realization that whatever she's done to dirty her hands hasn't been Fates-ordained at all, she doesn't let it show. In fact, she seems as chipper as I've seen her since stumbling upon her campsite with Farin.

"What has you in such a good mood?" I venture to ask, hoping I won't regret it.

"Oh, nothing," she says, twirling the hare on the makeshift skewer she's made out of a loose branch. "Just that we're getting out of here."

I wait until we're eating to pursue my excited curiosity any further. It might have been years since I've interacted with Zora like this, but if there's anything I remember from our childhood, it's that her moods are prone to volatility when she's hungry, so I figure it's best to wait until she has something in her stomach before forcing her to explain herself and chancing her agitation.

Once our bellies are full of hare, I venture, "So you've figured out how to get us both back into our original bodies."

She chomps on the last bit of meat left on her skewer. "Why are you always so polite? It's sort of insulting, actually. *We* both know that *you* know that *I've* known how to get out of here this entire time. Or do you just enjoy insulting my intelligence?"

"I do take immense pleasure in it, yes," I say, to which she actually smiles, "but I didn't want to push you too hard."

"Some things need pushing," she scolds, before launching into an explanation of how she plans for us to traverse the Fabric of realms.

CHAPTER 35

ASHA

I'm drowning. Water shoots into my open mouth, the pressure too intense for me to clamp down my jaw, close the opening.

I'm drowning, and the water is filling my throat.

It's just a gag, Asha. It's not real, says a familiar voice. My magic.

Not real. It isn't real.

It's a strange sensation, swimming back to reality from the fog of mingled bliss and confusion and dread that encircles me, but my magic leads the way, his voice holding my hand through the daze until I blink, and the truth comes into focus.

"It's not real, Asha. You're not drowning," he says, except he isn't my magic at all, because my magic can't hold my hand. My magic can't stroke my cheek, can't get close enough that I could feel the heat of its breath.

Az.

No, no, no, no.

I search for my magic, for a familiar, comforting voice, but find none. Memories assault me in vibrant flashes. Blaise weeping over a tapestry. Blaise sinking her teeth into my flesh. A sharp sudden pang, then numbness. A desire for compliance washing over me.

Where are you? I call to my magic but receive no response. Is my magic still being affected by Blaise's venom?

Blaise.

I could strangle that girl.

But I can't think of Blaise now, not when Az's fingers stroke my flesh.

It's strange how a touch I had craved for so long has me wanting to crawl out of my skin now.

"It's just a gag. Just a gag. You're not drowning, I promise," Az is saying, as if his promises are worth anything.

His sage-green eyes gaze down at me in concern, his tanned face partially obscured by the shadows. Wherever we are, it's dark. But that makes sense, because if Blaise was working with Az, she would need somewhere dark to hide during the day.

The ground shakes below me, and it takes me a moment to orient myself, to realize it isn't the ground at all, but the floor of a wagon.

Az has me tied up in the back of a wagon, one that looks as though it was made to block out the sunlight. The only light in the space comes from a lantern sitting on the floorboard next to Az, who kneels above me, still stroking my cheek.

"I promise it won't be like this forever," he whispers. Like I'm a child who doesn't understand why my wound must be stitched. I want to spit at him, but the gag clogs my mouth. "We're just too close to the Rip to risk you drawing from its power and speaking. But as soon as we're back in Naenden, I promise, Asha, the gag goes. I can't—I hate—seeing you like this," he says, "but you have to understand, I don't know how long it will be until the king's powers over your emotions wear off. You're safer this way."

I can't speak with my mouth, so I give him a piece of my mind with my gaze. Not for the first time in my life, I find myself thankful for my missing eye. It makes it rather easy to communicate fury and disgust.

"I'm sorry, Asha. I really am. You'll thank me for it later, though. Once his powers over you have worn off."

I want to scream, want to shriek at Az to untie me, to never ever put his slimy hands on me again. I want to shout that he's the monster, not Kiran, and that he knows better than to think otherwise.

But I can't scream. I can't shout. I can't do anything that I want.

So I do the opposite.

I calm. I force my anger into submission, and allow a look of relief to overcome my features.

Az looks startled, but then the tears fall from my eye, and he wipes them away.

"Oh, Asha. It's okay. You're safe now. I'm going to fix things. I'm going to fix everything."

It seems he truly believes it.

It seems I'll have to make him think I believe it, too.

"I WANT you to know I've thought this through," Az says, caressing my fingers though my wrists are bound in front of me.

My back aches from the constant bumping of the wagon, but Az has reassured me it won't be much longer. That we are getting close.

"I want you to believe in me again, Asha. I've been thinking about you so much over the past year. Every stupid decision I made that cost me your trust. I was foolish, sick on a craving for power, and it blinded me to what I really needed. The only thing that's ever made me feel whole. I need you, Asha. I'm empty without you."

I force water to my eye as I watch him. It isn't all that difficult, given I have a tendency to cry when I'm enraged.

"You see, there was more to my plan than I told you last time we saw each other."

He means when he betrayed my entire family and also his lover for good measure. It's probably for the best he has me gagged, because I'm not sure I could keep from tearing into him otherwise.

"I've been doing my research on the Rip for the past couple of years. On what sort of creatures stalk the other side of it. They're massive, Asha. So much so, they almost hunted the fae to extinction."

I want to say that given such knowledge, he might want to put some thought into what such creatures might do to humans, but alas, I cannot.

"If we could have those creatures under our control, if we could raise an army of them, we could bring the fae to their knees. Their rule would be just a blip in our history. The dark ages tutors will teach future generations because they won't have to live it. We could win our world back, Asha."

Or hand this world over to a bloodthirsty race of beasts, a familiar voice says inside of me.

Oh, how glad I am to hear that voice.

My, my, perhaps I should be drugged by vampire venom more often.

We'll have to add it to our daily diet.

"I know you're thinking I'm crazy, out of my mind, but I found a way to control them, Asha. And really, it's so simple. I can't believe it took me so long to figure out."

Any chance he's going to get on with it and tell us what it is?

Doubtful. I don't think he trusts me that much.

Indeed, Az strokes my cheek affectionately before saying, "I can't wait for you to see it. I'm hoping the effects of my brother's magic wear off before then."

Well, at least he's still calling Kiran his brother, says my magic.

I figure if that's what we're feeling thankful for, we're in a pretty rough place, indeed.

"I'm sorry about biting you," Blaise says, her voice quiet as she speaks from the shadows.

I figured she was in here somewhere. Nothing else explains a wagon with zero sun access, but I haven't been keen on trying to communicate with her.

I'd promised myself and Kiran that I wouldn't allow myself to be manipulated again.

I tried my best with Blaise, tried to be her friend while still maintaining a healthy skepticism of her.

But she misled me, practically molding me like clay in her hands.

"I'm sorry about all of this, really," she continues. "Here." Something rustles, and I realize Blaise is coming closer. I stiffen as soon as she touches me. A pair of fangs flash before my mind.

She pauses for a moment, as if reconsidering, but then she hauls me upward in a fluid motion until I'm sitting up, leaning against the back frame of the wagon. "I'll adjust you every few hours so you don't have to worry about getting sores. And when it's dark out, I can take you to relieve yourself."

I just stare at her, my mouth open anyway because of the gag, but it would have been agape regardless.

She watches me for a moment, having the gall to look sorrowful, then slumps backward against the wall. The black box hooked to her belt clatters against the floorboards.

"Nox wasn't being punished by the queen. Well, he was, in a way, but that wasn't the entire story."

She goes on to explain a tale that somehow ends with Nox and Farin, once sharing a body, now banished to another realm.

Apparently that very body, as well as his sister's, joins us in the back of this dark wagon.

"Az promised to help. Once the Rip is opened, it will create enough power to separate Farin from Nox's body. I just want him back. He's all I have left. I'm sorry."

All she has left because the sniveling scoundrel has betrayed everyone else who might have taken pity on her, my magic hisses.

"For what it's worth, I won't let him hurt you," she says.

She must catch the sneer on my face, because she sighs. "I know. Not saying much coming from me. I really do like you. I'm not saying that because I want you to feel bad for me. Fates know I don't deserve your forgiveness. I just...I don't know what I need. I guess I just wish things had turned out differently. That you and I could have been friends."

I don't need to be gagged to communicate that I don't really care what Blaise would have preferred from her life.

CHAPTER 36

NOX

"So, picture the Fabric as looking something like this."

Zora's taken off her outer tunic and folded it several times, lining up the decorative eyelets at the bottom of the hem so that one could easily slide a string through them to the other side. "The Fabric is the, well, the fabric, and the realms are the spaces between the folds. The folds are what keep the realms separate; however"—she traces the series of eyelets with her fingernail—"the designers of the Fabric, the Fates in this case, sometimes create eyelets, intentional holes, in the Fabric as a way of moving between realms. The thing is, if several eyelets are lined up, you can actually traverse several realms in one go."

Zora runs her palms over the ground of the chasm until she finds a long twig. "This is you," she says, holding it up in front of her face. "You started off in one realm, but then"—she slides the twig through the eyelets so that half remains on one side of the folded tunic, the other half on the other—"your consciousness got tied into the Fabric, allowing you to slip through an eyelet. So really, you're two places at once. That's why you can have a body on both sides."

"Because my two bodies are just two sides of the same twig?"

She nods in confirmation. "Really, it's a bit more complex than

224

that, because you're actually woven into the Fabric, but I'm simplifying it for your benefit."

"Much appreciated."

"Plus, it would be difficult for me to weave this piece of twig through my coat."

"Understandable."

"Anyway, where was I? Ah, yes. Now you might be wondering why, on this side of the Fabric, you and Farin walk around as separate entities, while on the other side, you're stuck in one body." She sticks her tongue out, concentrating as she carefully peels one end of the twig in two, stopping as the twig splits at the location of the eyelet. "So on one side, you're still in one body, but on the other side, you've sort of bifurcated, presumably because of how the story is woven into the tapestry."

I nod my head, impressed by my sister's ability to explain complex interrealm travel with such a simple set of props.

"So I'm guessing what we want to do is...may I?" I ask, gesturing toward the educational contraption.

She hands it over. "It's all yours."

"What we want to do is cross the eyelet"—I bend the frayed piece of bifurcated twig back, folding it over on itself and slipping it through the hole, leaving the other frayed piece dangling—"leaving Farin's portion behind."

"And then you get your vampire body back, for whatever reason you so desire that," says Zora.

I set my jaw, less than eager to think about that reality at the moment. I won't lie to myself, I've reveled in the sunlight the past day, refusing to take for granted any moment it warmed my skin.

There's a part of me that aches to leave it behind.

But Blaise is all the sunlight I need.

I just have to hope I'm all she needs, too.

"And what's keeping Farin from finding the eyelet and crossing over, too?" I ask.

Zora shrugs. "I've missed an eyelet before. Had someone beat me to it. It closes up and opens somewhere else. It was a pain to get to, honestly. Had to traverse two oceans and a mountain range to get to it. Put me behind schedule an entire year. Well," she says, huffing a laugh, "back when I thought I had missions to complete, you know."

An uncomfortable silence settles over the cave.

"I'm glad you're coming with me," I finally say.

Zora's eyes water. She wipes them quickly on the hem of her sleeve. "Yeah, well, when your vampire brother offers you an invitation to return to a frozen wasteland where you've spent the past several years training to be a corpse, so that you can third wheel with him and his freakishly terrifying vampire girlfriend, how was I supposed to say no?"

Then she chuckles, grinning up at me with a flicker of mischief in her eyes. She nudges me in the shoulder, but I make use of the opportunity to wrap her in an embrace.

She fidgets uncomfortably, clearing her throat, but when she pulls away, she's still smiling.

"So how exactly are we supposed to find this eyelet?" I ask as we douse our campfire and prepare to go trekking across the island.

"Don't worry about it. I'll know where it is," she says.

"Am I supposed to find that reassuring?"

She flashes me a mischievous grin. "I always find them. It's like they tug at my heart. I'll just follow the pull," is all she says before she saunters out of the cave and into the brush of the island.

"So what's the tug like?" I ask, catching up to her, our feet sinking in the soft sand of the beach. "I mean, are you born feeling it, or does it hit you one day?"

"I don't know how I'm supposed to know if I'm born feeling it, considering I can't remember infanthood, but yes. I guess I can't remember a time when I didn't feel it. Of course, when I'm a young child, I have no idea what I'm feeling. To my many parents' chagrin, it usually manifests in a pull toward dangerous activities. I believe I've caused many a mother's and father's grief by launching myself off places most parents don't prefer their children to jump from. But then, as I age, some of the memories start coming back. Well, I shouldn't say start. When I'm a child, it feels the same as a wild imagination. But as I grow older, the memories separate themselves from my imagination. Like they're too detailed and...intense...not to be real. I usually find my way to some religious sect that believes in reincarnation, because they're the only ones who actually believe me. And well, the path diverges from there. But I always find my way to an eyelet. And I always step through."

"And there's always something else that happens," I say, tentatively.

She makes a noncommittal noise.

"Your purpose?" I ask.

"Yes, the Event. But it's different every time. I never know quite what it is until it's upon me. Most of the time, I don't even realize it until after it's happened." She turns toward me, punching me lightly in the shoulder. "It seems this time it's finding you."

Something flickers in her eyes when she says it, and I try to tell myself it's just a shadow from a tree overhead.

It doesn't take us long before we're back at the edge of the canyon.

Zora paces much too near the edge for my liking, stroking her chin as she thinks.

I take a peek over the edge. I'm not sure what I'm expecting to find. Maybe the decaying body of a giant scorpion at the bottom, but the fog hasn't dissipated in the heat of the day. In fact, it only seems to swirl thicker.

"Think we can walk the edge and skirt around it?" I ask. "It has to end somewhere." Of course, the end could be a cliffside over the raging ocean on both sides, but I don't know how helpful it is to mention as much.

"I don't think that's going to work," she says, staring down into the canyon, lost in thought.

Okay, so I suppose my comment about the cliffside wouldn't have been the least helpful thing spoken by either of us today.

"And why not?"

She bites her lip, glancing between me and the abyss below.

Oh.

"Because," she says, tapping her foot precariously against the cliff, "I think maybe the eyelet is in the canyon."

"WHAT DO YOU MEAN, you think the eyelet is in the canyon?"

"I mean exactly what I said. Why is that so hard to believe?"

"Why didn't you mention this earlier?"

Rage flashes across Zora's face. "Why? Are you doubting me? You think I risked my life saving you just so I could double-cross you? Just so I could convince you to jump off the edge of a canyon to your death?"

I groan. "No, of course not."

"Really? Because I'm beginning to think you really do think I'm that dumb. I get it. You're used to playing the intelligent, studious twin. Well, excuse me for not bowing before your greatness. I can't believe I didn't think to let you die when you were already hanging from the side of a cliff. Silly me."

Zora sits down at the edge, swinging her feet off the side. There's nothing I want more than to drag her backward, but she's right. She's lived dozens of lives. She's earned the right to dangle her feet off the edge if she wants to dangle her feet off the edge.

"I'm sorry," I say, sitting next to her and trying not to stare too deeply into the abyss. "I don't mean that I think you're betraying me. I just don't understand why you didn't notice the eyelet was down there before."

"I was a tad distracted by the giant scorpion, if memory serves correctly," she huffs, but there's less aggression in her voice this time. "Trust me, I don't like it any more than you do."

"So what? We're just supposed to jump?"

Apparently it's time for Zora to look at me like I'm stupid.

"Sure. Go ahead, if you think you'd get a thrill from splattering your guts across the ground."

We sit in agitated silence for a moment, before she says, "I think it's down there somewhere. "

"What makes you say that?"

She frowns and taps at her heart. "Just a feeling."

"So, how do you suggest we get down?" I ask.

Zora has always been a fidgety person, never able to stay still for long. I found it a nuisance when I was a child, but now that she's quite literally kicking her heels against the edge of the chasm, I find it abominable.

I find my gaze searching the fog below, thinking of the scorpion we never heard land.

In the end, we decide to trace the path along the chasm for a while, though after half a day of trudging, we discover exactly what I was afraid of. A cliffside whose steep descent plunges directly into a rocky surf below.

All the while, the only voice that rolls over in my head is Zora's, questioning about why we didn't hear the scorpion land.

It's a crazy thought, really. Bordering upon insanity, but this time, when I draw near the edge, the pull I feel toward the bottom of this chasm is stronger than any I've ever felt.

Not since…

Not since Blaise and I shared one another's blood.

What if the eyelet isn't in the canyon? What if it is the canyon?

"Zora?" I ask.

"Mhm?"

"That feeling of yours? The one that pulls you toward the eyelet? Has it ever steered you wrong?"

She huffs. "Well, I suppose it depends on what you mean by that. But if you mean, is there always an eyelet on the other end of the rope, then yes."

"And do you still feel it here?"

She frowns at me. "Yeeees, but—"

I don't hear the rest of what she says, because I've backed over the edge, and I'm falling.

CHAPTER 37

KIRAN

Fin and I make it to the shoddy hut on the outskirts of Sureth village just after sundown.

The boards are rotting in places, and the entire edifice is overgrown with ivy, and not the intentional, decorative sort.

The door is crooked on its hinges.

Fin and I exchange a silent look, which is about all we've exchanged since our fight. I knock on the door.

Minutes pass, and no one comes.

I knock again, this time harder.

There's a scuffle on the other side of the door, but it's muted, like someone is trying to keep their footsteps soft.

Out of instinct, I scan the dingy windows, and sure enough, I spot a shadow peeking out at us from the window to our right. It ducks as soon as it catches me watching, but the person must realize it's no use pretending no one is home any longer, because seconds later, a voice sounds from the other side of the door.

"We're closed."

"When do you open?" Fin asks, hands tucked into his pockets, though his voice is strained.

"Permanently closed," says the voice.

"Well, in that case, now seems as good a time as any," calls my brother, infusing his voice with the charm I've grown to envy over the years.

"Who are you?"

Fin gives me a questioning look.

"We're here to see Solomon," I say.

The voice on the other side of the door pauses. "What business do you have with Solomon?"

I open my mouth, ready to come up with an excuse that's not untrue, but Fin just blurts out, rather casually, as if he is telling a servant what he'd like for dinner, "We're his sons."

The person on the other side of the door stops breathing. There's a click as he unlocks the latch, and the door creaks open.

Fin's lantern casts light into the dark room, its rays reflected on the face of the male who can only be our father.

SOLOMON BECKONS us in and leads us to a table at the far end of the hut. When I pull my chair out, cobwebs come with it, spiders scuttling about, angry I've disturbed them. There's a sour scent to the house, like milk left out in the midday sun. I'm fairly certain it's wafting off our father, though it's difficult to tell when the scent is masked by several others in the room.

All the while, I can't stop looking at Solomon. I've always been told Fin and I favor our mother, but I can see now that people only said this out of ignorance of our true father's appearance. Solomon is spindly built, like Fin, and his ragged hair makes him favor my brother more than myself. As well as his eyes. His eyes belong to Fin. But his face, the set of his jaw, the firm bridge of his nose...they're all mine.

He's a good-looking male. I suppose that's rather conceited of me to think, considering the resemblance between the two of us. But he has shadows forming under his eyes that age him more than is right for the fae.

"How did you find me?" he says, and though he watches us sit, he doesn't. Instead, he stands, fingers working at his sides, ankles bobbing like he might bolt at any moment.

He keeps looking at my hands, and it takes me a moment to realize it's because they're famous for turning people into ash.

All of my magic I inherited from my mother's side of the family, though Fin got none of it. I wonder then if magic terrifies my father, considering he possesses none.

"Oh, we just followed the trail of burglary, lies, forgeries, and illegally sold items," Fin says, though there's no accusation in his tone. Only carefully crafted amusement.

Our father glances between the two of us, his eyes wary. "Are you going to arrest me? I didn't think you would have jurisdiction in Avelea."

So he knows, then, who his sons grew up to be.

"We're not here to arrest you," I say. "We simply wished to find you."

Solomon grunts, then gestures around the room. "Then consider me found."

Silence befalls us, and I realize I've made no preparation for what I intended to say to this male once we finally found him. I look at Fin, but he seems equally unprepared as I am, which I find strange since he was the one who was interested in finding our father to begin with.

"When did you find out?" Solomon taps his fingers against his sides. When he breathes, he stinks of faerie ale, though it's soured on his breath.

"A little over a year ago," I say. "We found it in the vizier's records. He swore a fae oath long ago to keep the birth records of the royal family, as well as their heritage, though he hid the records for a long while. I suppose to protect us from the king."

Solomon grunts. "So she didn't tell you, then."

Fin and I exchange a look, and Fin says, "Our mother wished to protect us. She died when we were young. Before we could have been trusted with that sort of information."

There's a defensiveness in Fin's voice, a strain I haven't noticed before.

Maybe it's just the flicker of a shadow, but I think I glimpse disappointment in my father's face.

"You're probably right about that." He kicks at a glass bottle on the floor. It clinks as it rolls back and forth across a loose floorboard.

Fin and I exchange a look, and carefully, I say, "I imagine she would have told us, had she outlived our father."

He says nothing in response.

Fin fills the silence. "So...how does one get into dealing in dark magic?"

"How does one get into royalty?" Solomon nods toward the far side of the room, where a portrait hangs, though its colors are worn with time. The portrait is of a male who must also be a relative, as he shares my and Fin's nose and coloring. "The leeching business is the inherited sort. Always wanted to pass it down to my heirs, but unfortunately they were already occupied."

He gives us the first hint of a smile I've witnessed yet, though he stares intently at his boots as he says it.

"Leeching?" I ask.

My father pulls a stone out of his pocket. It's the color of the moon, smooth as a pebble lining a creek.

"You probably wouldn't know, but magic is a coveted commodity around this place."

Fin stirs. My brother was born magicless, and though he's never shown any interest in it, I know he has to feel the lack of fairness somewhere underneath that carefree facade of his.

"Leeching is the process of, well, leeching the magic from a magic-carrying being into a calamite stone, or a leeching stone as we like to call it. It keeps the magic stable until it can be transferred elsewhere."

"And I suppose that is also highly illegal in Avelea," I say.

My father shrugs. "Is anything really illegal in this place? It's why I moved here, after all."

FIN TAKES THE GUEST ROOM, which is hardly big enough to sleep one person as it is, so I stay in the kitchen. I don't plan to sleep tonight,

233

anyway. For as much anger and hatred that my brother harbors in his heart, he's considerably more trusting than I am.

This might be our father, but he's still a criminal, and I don't have any intention of falling asleep in his abode.

It seems he doesn't intend on sleeping either, at least not through the night, for he pulls another glass bottle out of the pantry and snaps the top off of it, splintering it with his bare hands.

He takes a swig from the shattered end before handing the bottle to me.

It stinks of desperation and apathy, and I shake my head.

"Not a drinker?" my father asks, eyeing me with derision.

"I have a bit of a temper problem," I explain.

"Hm," he says. "Wonder who you get that from."

Apparently no one, I think, as I watch my father down who-knows-which-number drink for the evening.

I look around the room, noting the cabinets stocked with liquor but suspiciously lacking in food, the floorboards that boast several holes, some of which seem to have attracted wasp nests that even the insects have abandoned.

"If you need anything…" I start, not sure why I'm even saying it. This male is a drunk and will probably spend any help I offer on more ale, but if I could just help him make some repairs…

"I haven't needed anything in a long time," says my father, his eyes far away from here. "You probably won't believe me, but I do manage to make a sale here and there. Enough to get me by. I don't need the help of a pampered prince who hasn't graced this side of the sun for half as long as I have."

My neck heats, but I say nothing. At least, not until I wrench up the nerve to ask, "What do you know about liquid moonlight?"

My father's glazed eyes go sharp. "I hear you're married to a human."

I nod in confirmation, discomfort reeling in me, since he clearly sees through my intentions.

"You do that for breeding purposes?"

The room flares hot, and my father holds up his palms, sloshing ale all over himself in the process. "I didn't mean offense. Clearly, you're taken with the girl. Unless she's..." He trails off, his eyes focusing in on me, sweat beading at his brow. "I should probably be careful how I speak about your queen. I see that now. That's good in a way. It's how I felt about your mother."

My throat tightens. "In a way?"

My father narrows his eyes, like he's fighting to focus, like he feels like whatever he has to say is of the utmost importance, worth cutting through the slog of intoxication to express. "She's human. She'll fill your world full of joy, then she'll take it away in a blink of an eye."

"I can trust Asha."

"Perhaps. But she'll die on you all the same." He lifts his palms up again. "It's not her fault, I know. But I don't think the Fates built us males for that."

"For what?"

"For outliving our females."

I cock my head to the side, and he goes on.

"You see it best in humans. How the women outlive the men in most every case. I think that's for a reason. I think it's because they can handle it. Females. Women. They have a grit in them. One we males like to pretend we have by brandishing our swords and gritting our teeth through the gore and piling our money up by swindling others. Feeding off the high of the battle. The thrill of living on the run. It's all the same. But in the end, it's the quiet that gets us. It's ourselves we can't stand to face. To keep company with too long. Females are built to lose, then pick themselves up and carry on. We aren't made for that."

I stare at him a long time, not wishing to give credence to anything this drunk of a male says, but there's something in my chest that tugs in fellowship, in understanding, even as he slurs the words.

Humans die.

Asha is human.

Therefore, Asha...

"Your mother was the one I'd rather not have outlived. Fates, I hadn't seen her in years when I heard the news. I was in the middle of a sale when I found out she was dead. Killed the male who was supposed to be brokering the deal, just for mentioning her death so off-handed, like it was common gossip. He didn't see it coming...no, he didn't see it coming at all...Nothing's been the same since." His eyes snap into focus. "It'll never be the same. You'll never be the same."

Disgust roils in my gut at the thought of my father murdering a male in cold blood just for the misfortune of bearing bad news to the wrong person. But even at the thought of Asha's death, my hands heat.

Who will happen to be in the wrong place at the wrong time on the day my wife draws her last breath? Who will find themselves in the path of the Flame? Will it be the healers serving her on her deathbed? Onlookers stopping to help after an accident?

"Tell you what," says my father, tapping the bottom of his bottle against the table. "If I could have done anything to save her, I would have. Anything at all would be better than this."

He rises, lighting a bottle of incense on the counter. It smells of myrrh and is somewhat overwhelming, but I say nothing.

Then he walks to his cabinet and pulls out a dusty bottle.

When he sets it on the table and slides it over to me, I can't help but notice the shimmering milky material on the inside.

"Anything," he says again, pressing the cold glass into my palm.

The liquid moonlight sloshes about in the bottle, tantalizing to look at. It's strange, holding it in my hand. I expected it to be more difficult, convincing my father to hand this over. I at least thought he'd try to barter with me.

I could save her with this, and I feel the awe swell in my chest, that I hold the key to keeping Asha forever in the palm of my hand.

The thought is addicting, intoxicating, swirling my mind with a high I never thought attainable, a peace so deep it feels as if I couldn't crawl my way out if I tried.

The scent of myrrh washes over me again, calming every muscle in my body.

"I truly am sorry, son," says Solomon, just as he slips a mask over his face.

I realize too late where the feeling of peace hails from.

The incense weighs me down, muddling my mind.

I reach for my Flame, but it flickers out as I lose consciousness.

CHAPTER 38

ASHA

The riverside plain that stretches across the outskirts of Rivre is just as I remember it, if not slightly warmer. Last time we were here for the Council meeting, the air had been crisp with an evening chill, and though it's evening now, timed out perfectly so Blaise can walk among us for whatever nefarious purpose Az has for her, there's nothing crisp about this air.

Humidity wraps me in its blanket, as if to protect me from what's to come. As if the climate itself intends to make us sluggish, slowing us from our inevitable end.

My poor, unused legs ache as Az pushes me across the plain.

There's a patch of grass to our left, one with a jagged rock I remember sitting on as Az explained to me his plan. I search for Gwenyth's blood, any evidence that remains of her slaughter, but I find none. Of course, the weather would have washed away any evidence of her in the past year.

I wonder if her corpse was ever found by passersby, if anyone bothered to give her a proper burial, or if she was left to be food for the animals.

It's not as if I cared much for Kiran's first wife, but I'm beginning to wonder if Gwenyth and I will die for the same fatal flaw.

For loving and trusting Az.

Blaise follows close behind us, carrying Nox's body along with her.

As Az pushes me through the field, his hand at the base of my lower back, its placement makes me want to squirm. I restrain myself.

My ankles ache from disuse, and more than once I find them failing to mark the change in terrain, and Az has to catch me before I fall on my face.

He seems to cherish the moments when he catches me, caressing my hair and smiling down at me knowingly.

"You've always been so clumsy," he says, as if it hadn't begun when I lost my eye. "Do you remember tripping over Bezzie's crate of pomegranates when we were young? It sent the whole pile toppling over. We were picking them off the streets for weeks after that."

I just blink at him, allowing a smile to graze the edge of my eye.

In actuality, it's more of a grimace, but I'm betting on the assumption Az won't be able to tell the difference behind the gag in my mouth.

He smiles, a beautiful smile that lights up all his features, and I figure I assumed correctly.

The closer we get to the Rip, the more the ground underneath my feet seems to hum, aching and thrumming with an ancient power that calls to both me and my magic.

When we reach the location of the Rip, the sheer power that leaks into the air surrounding us gives me pause. I stop my feet, wishing simply to stand in awe of it for a moment.

Az won't allow that, of course. He just whispers at me that we don't have time to waste and pushes me forward.

The Rip itself isn't something I can see; at least, not since it's closed. I wonder if it will become visible once it opens again.

Except we're not opening it again, my magic reprimands.

Right.

It's not that I have any intention of opening this Rip of my own volition. It just seems Az has thought out too much of his plan at this point to overlook the simple fact that I might refuse.

My friend is clever, cleverer than I've ever given him credit for.

I can't help but assume he has a backup plan.

Even though I can't see the Rip, I can feel it. Thrumming. Whistling in the faint breeze. There's a sliver of the air in front of us that seems to call to me more brightly, and I find myself reaching for it, though I'm not sure what I'm expecting.

It's not for my fingers to find solid air, the silky sheen of a Fabric invisible to my eyes.

My entire body shudders at the chill of it. The Fabric, invisible as it is, is cold. I wonder how far I could trace the Fabric. If I clung to it, could I follow it all over Alondria, feel the Fabric that separates the realms, or could I only feel it because of the energy emanating from the Rip? Once I reached a far enough distance, would the connection then fail?

A hand traces up my arm, Az closing in on me from behind. The heat of his torso presses to my back, and my stomach turns over.

He traces his fingers up my arm until he too touches the Fabric I hold between my fingertips.

"You feel something, don't you?" he asks, his warm breath shooting shards of icicles into my ear.

I nod. Az knows anyway, and it's to my benefit that he believes I trust him. Maybe then I can convince him to remove the gag.

Wouldn't that be nice. Imagine what we could do to him, then, says my magic.

I don't particularly want to imagine, but I can't really blame my magic for its excitement over the idea of torturing Az.

"Blaise, bring me my satchel," he says. There's shuffling behind us —Blaise, doing as he says.

Tools rattle as Az reaches into his satchel behind me.

What he produces from the bag, I can't see, but he lets out the slightest of gasps, and when he brings his fingers to mine again, they're dripping with blood. His blood, I realize.

I flinch as he spreads the warm, wet substance over my fingertips, whispering hushing sounds in my ear, as if to soothe a child after a minor fall and scrape.

Once my fingers are coated in Az's blood, he takes my hand and begins to use it as a quill.

THE RUNES AZ traces on the Fabric in his own blood are unfamiliar to me.

My magic scoffs. *Are you so familiar with any runes?*

I'm not, so that's fair.

Still, these aren't like any script I've ever read, and though some of them look like pictures, others have shapes that trigger absolutely nothing in my memory.

Blaise must recognize some of them, though, because her voice goes stony. "Where did you find those?"

"Written all over the floor of that wretched dungeon they kept you in," says Az. "As well as those you couldn't seem to manage to scrub off the floor in that dazzling ballroom. I made a few modifications of my own. Do you like them?"

Blaise's expression melts back into the impassivity she seems to have perfected.

This is one of those moments when being gagged is rather inconvenient, because I, for one, would love to ask what in Alondria they're talking about.

"I don't think there's any use in binding Asha's magic to her body," says Blaise. "It seems she and her magic both like the setup they already have."

Az shakes his head, causing his cheek to brush against mine. "I'm not binding Asha's magic to her body. Like I said, I made some modifications. Besides, does it look as though I'm drawing these runes around Asha?"

When he's done, he pulls me away for a better look.

The runes written in Az's blood sear hot, then settle into a pale white circlet that hangs suspended in midair.

"You're binding the Rip? I thought you wanted to open it," Blaise says.

"All in good time," Az says.

I don't like this. I don't like this at all, says my magic.

Yeah, well, I don't like it either.

You can't open it, Asha.

Part of me wonders if I already have.

But then Az brushes a strand of my matted hair, tucking it behind my ear, and whispers, "It's time. I need you to open the Rip."

I nod frantically, as if in understanding. Perhaps Az really is delusional enough to think Kiran has been forcing me to love him, and that the separation from him will have caused the effects to fade by now.

But Az just shakes his head, and when he speaks, anger boils in his voice. "I hate what he's done to you, bending your mind like he has. Forcing you to forget how much we love each other. That you were mine first."

My entire body stills at that comment, tears of fury springing into my eye at the audacity of it.

But Az knows my allegiance isn't with him.

So how does he plan to force me to open the Rip?

Panic floods my bones as it occurs to me just what method Az employed the last time he tried to force my hand.

Dinah. Father.

My entire body is trembling, the panic of that awful night flooding back with the vigor of Calias's waves.

No, no, no, no.

"Blaise," Az says.

I'm going to kill her. I'm going to kill Blaise if she's touched them, threatened them.

But when Blaise steps in front of me, I recognize no threat in her brown eyes.

She takes my hand from Az, exposing my wrist, apology written all over her face.

CHAPTER 39

NOX

I fall.

I fall through fog and smoke. Dreams and desires.

I decide that I've plunged myself to my death.

Not for the first time, I wonder what will await me on the other end.

If it's Blaise, sitting over my sleeping body. If her voice is the first I'll hear, or if it will be Claudia's or any of the others I've murdered. Those who deserve better than to have to see me again on the other side.

Perhaps they're waiting for me.

Perhaps they always have been.

I land, but it's not on solid ground. It's in a substance that's sticky. Somehow firm and pliable at the same time. It cushions my landing, slowing me as I rip through whatever the substance is.

I find myself wondering if, in slipping through an eyelet, I've landed on the Fabric itself. If I'm tearing rips through it, shearing through separate realms to cushion my fall.

The soft, sticky substance beneath me gives way once more, and I find I'm wrapped in it. My fae vision adjusts to the fog, able to see more clearly now that I'm in it rather than looking down upon it from a distance.

Something silky, glimmering like liquid diamonds, stretches out around me, above me, below me. The material that broke my fall. It hits me that this must have been what cushioned the scorpion's fall, why we never heard it crash into the ground.

Because I haven't hit the ground yet either.

Nausea turns over in my belly when, all at once, the fog in my vision clears and I recognize exactly what I've landed in.

I've landed in a web.

I fight back the urge to gag, but my reflexes have me kicking frantically against the webbing that's tangled itself around my limbs. I don't know how far I've fallen, but I broke through several layers of the film, judging by looking upward and the fact that I'm not dead from the impact. The webbing must run as deep as the lower half of the cavern, obscured by the fog that drifts up from the ocean.

It takes me a moment, but I wrench my foot out of a tangle of web.

Of course, at that exact moment I hear a scream.

Zora's face flashes before my eyes, her mouth warped into a mingled wail of terror and howl of delight, before she comes crashing into a section of webbing above me and slightly to my left.

The weight of her fall breaks the webbing beneath her.

On the way down, she grabs onto my hand, yanking me with such force that the webbing beneath me snaps, and we go plummeting downward.

My back hits the hard earth, and soon enough Zora's splayed hand shoves into my face, blocking my nose from any chance of getting air. She shrieks and crawls off of me, but only after I practically shove her off.

"Are you crazy?" Her cheeks are flushed red with rage, the only color in this abysmally white crevasse we've found ourselves trapped in.

"Apparently it runs in our blood, considering you followed me," I hiss, yanking clots of tangled webbing off my clothing as Zora does the same. "Why did you jump?"

Zora's jaw drops. "Why did I jump? Why did you jump? You jumped first!"

"Yes, but I wasn't intending for you to come after me."

This must be the wrong thing to say, because Zora crosses her arms, water pooling and glazing over her blue eyes. "So you were just going to leave me then? The whole time, you were just going to leave me."

I run my hands through my hair, which is a mistake, because it's also caked with the filmy substance. "No, of course not. I just didn't want you to follow me into danger, that's all." As soon as the words leave my mouth, I recognize the lie in them. It's true—I wasn't intentionally abandoning Zora. I'd just been so caught up in getting back to Blaise, I'd jumped without considering that the eyelet would close behind me.

I think that might be worse.

Zora blinks away the tears, but she doesn't express any sign of understanding. Instead, she pivots, taking in our surroundings. "Well, this is new," she says under her breath.

"What, you mean the eyelets aren't usually caked over with spiderwebs?"

"If they were, I would have mentioned it, don't you think?" she says through gritted teeth. "Though I suppose this is probably a sign we're on the right track. There's always something guarding the eyelet. It's just usually not so..." She waves her hands emphatically around her.

"Disgusting?"

She answers me by flaring her nostrils. "I was going to say terrifying, but I suppose disgusting is also accurate."

"Well, tell me that homing mechanism of yours is pulsing a tad louder," I say, and she nods.

Zora clutches her chest. "We're definitely on the right track." Then my sister steps into the fog and disappears from sight.

. . .

IT SEEMS the fog that obscures the web comes as a direct byproduct of the web itself, smoke hissing at the edges of the glistening strings. It makes it rather difficult to see, and Zora and I have to stay close to keep from losing sight of one another.

Thankfully, there aren't too many webs in our way, so long as we aren't trying to ascend the canyon. The webbing itself doesn't begin for a few feet above our heads, providing us with a clear walking path.

I try not to think too hard about what else might benefit from a clear walking path down here.

After hours of searching, Zora halts in front of me, grabbing onto my hand frantically. I brace myself for a spider to come crawling out of the distance ahead.

One doesn't, but the sight that's unsettled Zora makes me almost as sick.

Just above us is a shadow. Rather, a form casting a shadow. Purple scales glisten in the reflection of the diamond webbing. Pincers splay lifeless.

The scorpion lies dead, legs splayed up in the air.

It's missing chunks of its tail and thorax.

"Well, guess we know why we didn't hear it hit the ground," I say, and though Zora lets out what I suppose is supposed to be a self-assured chuckle, she grips my hand tighter.

NOT FAR FROM where we found the scorpion remains is the entrance to a cavern, its mouth gaping at the side of the canyon wall.

"I don't suppose this lovely entrance could be the eyelet, could it?" I ask, though I hardly have the energy to infuse hope into my voice.

"Unlikely, but I imagine it is in there somewhere," says Zora, her voice strained.

Ever since we passed the scorpion carcass, she's been trembling uncontrollably. Though perhaps she's been trembling the entire time, and I've only just noticed since she grabbed my hand.

It has me wondering just how terrified of spiders Zora must be, if she's faced down whatever guarded the eyelets in other worlds, and this is what has her wobbling.

"How are you so calm right now?" she asks as we venture into the cave. Stalagmites pierce through the earth, and precipitation beads on the cave ceiling before dripping onto our foreheads. "How are you not more afraid?"

Blaise's voice rings in my ears. *I am afraid of you. I'm just afraid of me, too.*

"I am afraid," I say. "There are just things I'm more afraid of than this."

Though only barely, I don't add.

THE UNFORTUNATE THING about caves is that they have a tendency to be rather dark. Especially when the particular cave is located at the bottom of a plunging abyss in which fog blocks most of the light.

Granted, the liquid diamond webbing that decorates the ceiling of the cave gives off its own dull glow, but mentioning as much doesn't seem to provide much comfort.

Thankfully, our fae vision adjusts as we delve deeper into the tunnels, but the further we go, the sparser the diamond webbing, and the more difficult it is to see.

"Well, at least the spiders don't seem to like venturing this far," says Zora, noting our dwindling light source.

"That, or they don't like webbing getting in the way when they're trying to eat."

Zora promptly stabs me in the side with her elbow, and she shoots me a look that says, *If you scream and alert any spiders of our presence, I'll feed you to them myself.*

EVENTUALLY, the cavern breaks off into two paths, one that seems to follow an underground stream, another that's dry. When I ask Zora which way the eyelet is pulling her, she motions toward the dry path, which seems like the best luck we've had all day.

It's not.

THE TUNNEL LEADS us further into the belly of the island, the idea of which causes the hairs on the back of my neck to stand on edge.

When we reach the end of the tunnel and step into a section of cavern that branches outward into a wide alcove, Zora lets out a puff of air that hovers somewhere between a gasp and a sigh.

Of relief, I'm hoping.

When I turn the corner, I understand her reticence.

Covering the alcove is a web, much like the one that saved us from falling to our deaths only hours ago. The glow that originates from within the threads glitters across the cave, casting speckles of light upon the walls. Specks of green and pink dance in a brilliant waltz, highlighting every corner of the cave.

It reminds me of the shrine, the dazzling ballroom in which Zora's body lies dormant.

The investigator in me can't believe that's a coincidence.

"Are they all like this?" I ask, though I think I already know the answer.

To my surprise, Zora shakes her head. "No. No, they're...well, they're usually quite terrifying."

Personally, I find the light shimmering from spiderwebs alarming in its own way. I imagine the Zora from thirty seconds ago would have agreed with me. It's of no use arguing, though. Zora's face is struck with wonder, her eyes shimmering with the weblight that dances in her bubbling tears.

She reaches out, as if to touch the dancing light on the cavern wall, but she withdraws her hand, remembering that, of course, it's only a glow. Nothing tangible.

"Home looks like this, doesn't it?" she whispers as she clutches her chest.

I don't have the heart to tell her it's only her prison, the room in which Abra has her locked away. That the beautiful speckles of light that glitter in through the glass windows are simply a sorry apology, the remnants of a cold female's conscience, otherwise seared numb.

But then I remember a way it can be true.

"The land we're from—it's dreadfully cold," I say. "Everyone stays miserable most of the year. But at night the sky lights up with swirls of color. Mother, our mother, always says that's why the people in Mystral stay. Because we can't bear thinking that there are parts of the world where the sky doesn't shimmer with colors."

"Our mother sounds painfully sentimental," Zora says dryly, but she wipes her sleeves on her cheeks just the same.

"So you think we can get through this way?" I ask, unsure of where to go from here.

Zora tears her gaze away from the wall, then turns to face the web at the far end of the cave. As she approaches, she brings her sleeve to her mouth and chews on it absentmindedly.

When I examine the wall more closely, I understand why.

This web is much more intricate than the tangle of string that broke our fall. In fact, this web is a masterpiece.

The sparkling tendrils curve and cross and turn and pivot, all to form the likeness of a girl.

A girl who looks a tad too much like Zora for my comfort.

"Well. I guess that erases any doubt we might have had about this being the correct location," I say, and even as I gaze up at the portrait, my chest begins to ache.

"I used to think it was the Fates who drew these for me," Zora says, running her hand across the likeness of her fingers until she ends up pulling strands away and the fingers crumble to decay. "That they were trying to send me a message—a confirmation that I'd done their work during the times I struggled with doubt."

Zora blinks hard, then turns back to me. "Now I know it was just a curmudgeon of a male who had nothing better to do than collect knowledge of worlds unknown."

Something sharp lodges itself in my throat at the prickle of hate on my sister's tongue. There's a part of me that's still horrified by what Gunter did to her, the fact that he hid the reality of her dream state from me all these years. I wish that I could go back and ask him why he did it, if he had a good reason.

But I can't ask him. Not anymore.

"Nox? Nox."

Someone's shaking me, startling me back to reality, anchoring me until I can survive the storm of my memories, of what they say about me.

"How could I go back?" I whisper.

Zora frowns. "What do you mean, *how could you go back*? We've made it all this way. You have to go back. You have a girl to get back to, remember?"

A girl to get back to. Isn't that what Farin had said when I'd woken on this island?

Isn't that exactly the problem?

"Zora, I'm a monster where I come from. Where we come from."

She crosses her arms, looking me up and down as she sticks her foot out for balance. "Yes, I'm aware of that. You're my living nightmare, remember? A recurring one at that."

I sigh, rubbing at the crease between my brows. "You have no idea how many people I've killed."

Zora's face goes blank. "I thought you said it was him—it was Farin who killed them."

"Most of the time I had a difficult time distinguishing the difference. The line between him and me...it blurred over time. It's why he couldn't separate himself from my feelings for Blaise. It's why, when I'm in that body, I'm so desperately hungry. It's why I lose control."

"Nox, you have to go back," Zora says, resting her hand against my arm.

"There are people there...families...I'm the villain in their story, Zora. There, I hurt the innocent. I'm not good. But here..."

Zora smiles up at me, but it's a sad sort of smile, the type that makes divots in the corners of her eyes and the middle of her brow. "In this life, you get to be the hero."

I nod my head, and we stand in the silence for a while before Zora says, "I like them better, too. The lives where I get to be the hero. But that's the thing, Nox. I used to think that with each life, I could only fit one role. What if that's not how it works? What if you can be the hero *and* the villain?"

"I don't think anyone gets to be both, Zora. Not at the same time, at least."

She shrugs. "Maybe you're right. But you've still got to go back. You might not be a monster here, but Blaise isn't here either."

We pause for a moment, and it's the silence that frightens me most of all. The emptiness in the conversation where I don't have a defense, where I can't simply agree with my sister.

"What? You don't want her?" Zora asks.

The words cut, and I shake my head. "No, of course I want her. I want her everything. Every stupid little crass joke, every bruise on her heart, every laugh. I want all of her, but..."

Zora raises a brow. "But what?"

"But I'm not sure she wants me."

For a moment, Zora's expression goes blank.

Then she knocks me over the head with her fist.

"OW!" I yell, and it echoes off the cavern walls. "Was that necessary?"

"Apparently!" she says. "Now listen, you have a girl who quite literally died so you wouldn't have to choose between her life and mine. And no, don't give me that look. You might be used to being the smartest person around, but I can read between the lines too, you know. It's not that difficult to figure out. She quite literally died for you, and you're standing here wondering if she wants you?"

I grit my teeth. "During the Turning, there's something about you —something about *us*—that changes. In our souls. I know she thinks she wants me. I know she came back to Mystral intending to free me. But Zora, I was there. I was there, in his head, when she kissed him, and I know I should believe that she did it so he could let his guard down. So she could lure him into Gunter's room and disarm him. I know that's the logical thing to think. But..."

"But?"

I take in a long breath. "But...But I felt that kiss. I felt how much

251

she wanted it. You don't understand, the bloodsharing ritual. I could feel what she was feeling. What they were both feeling, and it was only feeding off of each other. She didn't just convince Farin she wanted him because she's a brilliant actor, a master deceiver. She convinced him because it was the truth."

Zora stares at me for a long while. Long enough for my cheeks to heat, as if reliving the moment the love of my life seduced my doppelgänger isn't humiliating enough as it is.

"What?" I ask, when her stare becomes unbearable.

"You need to get over that," she says.

I jerk my head backward. "Pardon?"

"Why does it matter what she wanted to do? It seems to me that you should be more concerned about what she *did* do, and that was find a way to keep you—you, Nox—alive."

"It matters because she wanted him. Can't you see why that might bother me?"

"You're allowed to be bothered," she says. "But being bothered and refusing to go back and get her are two different things."

I let out a huff, because it's the only reaction I'm able to have toward my sister. Apparently, quite little has changed.

"Listen, I've lived quite a few lives by this point, and though apparently none of them meant anything, and all my pain, loss, grief, and sacrifice have been utterly pointless, since all I was ever supposed to do was take notes, I've at least learned a bit about people. And if I've learned anything, anything at all, it's that there are few people who are willing to put their feelings aside for the people they love. And if you happen to be the person they're willing to do that for, then you had better be willing to cross realms to find them. You'd also better be willing to overlook what they might have wanted to do during a time of extreme stress and mental anguish."

I stare at my sister in a bit of shock.

"Okay," I say, swallowing my pride. "So where do you think this eyelet actually is?"

She nods toward the intricate webs again. I look, closer this time, and notice that the cave wall behind the spider silk has an effervescent

252

quality. It glistens, just slightly, and if I focus, I can glimpse the edges of a distortion.

"So we just...step through?" I ask, not sure how I feel about stepping through a cavern wall that's not actually a wall.

"Well, *you* step through, yes."

I spin on my sister.

She bites her lip, swinging her interlocked hands behind her back. "Did I not mention that I'm not going with you?"

"What do you mean, you're not going with me?"

My words rattle the cavern, echoing off the glistening walls. My hands are shaking, though if it's in anticipation of seeing Blaise again or frustration at my sister, I'm not sure.

"I mean that I'm not going with you. You know, if you would stop asking what I mean all the time and just start taking my words at face value, it would save you a lot of breath."

I squeeze my eyes shut, rubbing the bridge of my nose. It's a habit I picked up from my bloodlust headaches, a malady I suppose I'm returning to as soon as I step through this eyelet.

Without my sister.

Because apparently she's changed her mind.

Either that, or she's been lying to me from the beginning.

"Allow me to rephrase," I say, taking a steadying breath. "Why are you not coming?"

"Maybe I have a crush on your creepy body-snatching friend and I'd like to stick around to get to know him," Zora says.

I level her a deadpan expression.

"Okay, fine. I'm just not done here, that's all. I'll find another eyelet. Follow you later. I'll wake up. You'll throw a party. I suppose. Though I don't really hear you talking about friends that are still alive, so maybe you won't."

"You're not ready."

Zora exhales a huff of air, causing her cheeks to billow out. Then she lifts her shoulders, her palms face up to the ceiling. "I'm not ready."

Sorrow threatens to squeeze my heart. I'm not ready, either. Not ready to let my sister go, not when I just got her back.

"Oh, don't look so forlorn," she says, punching me in the side of the shoulder. "You're looking at me like you'll never see me again."

"I thought you'd decided there wasn't a purpose to you being here. To you living these lives. That Gunter sending you here to gather information undermined all that," I say.

"Yeah, well," she says, picking at a loose thread hanging from the tip of her sleeve, her eyes downcast as she shuffles her weight between her feet. "Maybe I don't accept that."

I open my mouth to tell her that whether she accepts it or not doesn't change reality, but when she lifts her chin and meets my gaze, there's an iron will in her expression that could level fortresses.

"All right. But you are finding that eyelet. And you are coming back home. If not for me, then at least to meet Blaise. Though now that I think of it, it's probably best you don't end up in the same room."

A wry smile tints her expression. "No promises."

I consider hugging her, but the last time I did that she wriggled out of my embrace. I suppose I have to understand. She doesn't remember our childhood like I do.

So instead I ruffle her hair, and she squirms out from under that, too, though more in annoyance than discomfort, which is somehow more comfortable for me, too.

"Bye for now," she says.

I almost choke on the words. "Bye for now."

I turn to step through the eyelet, but as I do, Zora grasps onto my arm and yanks on it, pulling me backwards as she buries her head into my chest, her cropped hair tickling the tip of my nose, threatening to make me sneeze.

"Bye for now," she whispers again.

I don't have the strength to say it again as I step out from her embrace and toward home.

CHAPTER 40

NOX

The eyelet knows I'm coming.

Where before, the cave wall appeared as a rather convincing illusion, the eyelet now curves in shadowy waves before me, smoky tendrils coming out from behind its depths. It certainly doesn't look like a way back home. For some reason, I was expecting a portal overflowing with light.

I close my eyes and clench my fists, preparing to step through. If Blaise can take on the darkness to save me, then I can walk through it to get to her.

I reach out, as if I can close my grip around the shadows and pull myself through rather than allow myself to be pulled by it.

My fingers have almost grazed the shadows when Zora screams.

Her shriek has me spinning on my heel, my instincts driving me to rip to shreds whatever has caused my sister harm.

"It doesn't look like you'd expect it to, does it?"

Farin's voice is cold, but his eyes are shimmering with a boyish excitement. "The Rip I'm familiar with appeared as a ray of light with no origin. But I suppose this isn't a Rip, now is it?"

He has Zora forced to her knees in front of him. His right hand is fisted in her hair, tugging at the skin of her strained forehead. In the other, he holds a knife dripping with fresh blood.

It matches the stain on Zora's tunic, the one ballooning at her abdomen.

The knife is missing from Zora's belt.

I don't think before I lunge, but Farin is quicker, and he drags Zora backward by her hair.

She screams in agony as the blood on her tunic continues to spread.

"Get away from her," I hiss, but Farin only flashes me an amused grin.

"I'd be happy to," he says. "I just need you to do something for me."

The bile in my stomach sours. Why do I get the feeling I know exactly what he wants?

"All you have to do is step aside. And then I won't have to hurt her any more than she already is," Farin says.

My head spins, my world turning upside down. One step behind me is Blaise, the woman I'd die for. The woman who was willing to give her life for Zora, back when she thought it was going to be a choice between the two of them.

It's like there's an invisible force pulling me between them, and either way I choose, I'll end up ripped in half, a fragment of myself.

"Nox, just go," Zora says. "Who knows? If I die, I might just wake up."

Farin's grin splits. "Who says I'm going to let you die?"

Rage splits my skull. I don't think. My limbs pump for me, and I launch myself toward Farin.

At least, he's my target.

I don't make it to him.

Because out of the shadows jumps an enormous creature, barreling on its eight legs.

Several things happen at once.

Farin glimpses the creature, just in time to yank Zora out of its way.

The spider's legs skid on the ground, thrown off by missing its bleeding target.

I don't have time to pivot before one of its flailing legs collides with my torso, sending me flying backward toward the cave wall.

Except my back never hits the cave wall.

The last thing I see is the spider lunge for Zora, and then the eyelet closes, taking me with it.

CHAPTER 41

BLAISE

I force myself not to look into Asha's eye as I plunge my
teeth into her wrist.

It's not that I need to taste blood to trigger the bloodlust that
enables my compulsion, but it certainly accelerates the process.

She winces, but only barely before the toxins in my fangs numb
the pain.

"That's enough," Az snaps, swatting me away from Asha's wrist.
Like he's worried I'll take too much blood.

I do as he says, unlatching my fangs from her skin and retracting
them into my gums. Quickly, as if he's concerned the wound won't
bind fast enough, he wraps her wrist in white gauze that turns scarlet
in an instant.

"Don't be scared," I whisper to her, and her trembling settles a bit. I
should probably feel guilty for that, for taking away her fear. It's a
reaction she has every right to possess, but guilt isn't going to get me
Nox back, so I dull it with the roar of my desperation.

"Now," I say, "I'm going to ungag you, but I need you to stay quiet
until I tell you what to say." I reach for the gag, but Az puts out a hand,
stopping me.

"Tell her to do as *I* say before you take it off."

"How about you relay to me what you want her to say, and I'll make sure it happens?"

Az shoots me an acidic glare, but he offers me the instructions, apparently not in the mood to argue.

"Okay, Asha," I breathe. "I'm going to take off your gag, and I want you to tell the Rip to open. And then I want you to call forth the Others, so they know where to flock to."

Asha's eye goes wide with fear, but in them I sense no defiance.

It's a stab to my gut to watch her comply like this.

For Nox, I remind myself. *You're doing this for Nox.*

I let myself glance at him. Give myself just a moment to examine his limp body, laid out on the grass like a corpse.

But Nox is not a corpse. And I'm going to get him back.

I turn back to Asha, reminding myself that other than a wound that's already knitting itself up, she will come to no permanent harm. Az is several awful things, but there's no doubt in my heart that he adores Asha and would be heartbroken if anything happened to her.

That's what I tell myself, anyway.

Slowly, I untie the gag, then pull the wet glob of scrunched fabric from her mouth. Asha grasps at her throat in relief, and that pesky guilt raps at the walls of my conscience again.

I'm doing this for Nox.

Just like Asha would do this for Kiran if the situation were reversed.

Would she? the voice inside my head asks.

Well, like Kiran would do for Asha, I suppose. And I know exactly what Kiran would do based on his reaction to the shadow siren.

Az licks his lips. "Tell her to say it."

"You can tell the Rip to open now," I prod encouragingly.

Asha looks back and forth between me and Az, then opens her mouth.

Except it's not Asha who speaks.

"You foolish, selfish little girl," says a voice as low and rumbling as an underground current. *"Your compulsion might be effective on Asha, but did you truly believe it would work on me?"*

259

A moment later, Az has shoved the gag back in Asha's mouth. She chokes on it, and Az's eyes widen in distress.

"I'm so sorry. This won't be forever," he says, stroking her cheek until he catches a tear in the crook of his finger. Then he whips his attention toward me, his eyes ablaze. "You said this would work."

"Don't act like bringing her here wasn't your idea in the first place," I snap right back.

He runs his hands through his hair, staring down at the ground.

Then he pulls a stake from the ground and shoves it into Nox's chest.

THE WORLD SHATTERS into a million flecks of glass, then reworks itself as Az removes the stake and Nox's chest reknits itself, tendons and skin pulling together as if woven together on one of Gunter's looms.

He missed his heart. Az purposely missed his heart.

I have to repeat those words over and over in my mind, but still my pulse refuses to calm, my breathing refuses to steady.

I thought I lost him. Truly lost him this time.

"The next one won't miss," he says pointedly, holding up the stake that still drips with Nox's blood.

"What exactly is it you want me to do?" I ask, my voice cracking at the seams.

Az shrugs. "Make her open it."

I grit my teeth, trying my utmost to clamp down on my rising panic. "I can't."

Az jerks his hand, and I scream, clutching my hand over my mouth, but the stake doesn't descend upon Nox's chest. "Are you willing to tell him that?"

Tears wet my cheeks, matching Asha's, but I don't think about her tears. Don't think about anything that threatens to make me feel guilty.

I'm so, so tired of battling that *useless* emotion.

"Please. Please, I know you don't know me," I say, addressing the Old Magic that dwells behind Asha's eye. "But I am begging you.

Anything. I'll do anything you want if you just open that Rip and use the magic it produces to split Farin from Nox's body."

Asha blinks, and with the gag in her mouth, I can't tell if the magic is even listening.

"Please, I love him. I don't know how to survive without him. I've lost everything. Everything. Surely you know what that feels like. I know you do. I've heard the stories. Heard how you lost your siblings. Please, I'm all alone. I can't...I can't..."

I can't breathe now, and Asha's dark eye goes wide with sorrow.

"Will he agree?" I ask her.

She shakes her head.

Sorrow cuts at my heart, a stray shard not meant for me, but it cuts me all the same.

I take one glance at Nox, at the male that I love, lying motionless on the ground. I listen for his steady heartbeat, dull as it may be.

And I know what I have to do.

"You know, I had one of you living inside me once," I whisper, my words sharp as the edge of a blade. "You know her, know what she's like. From what I understand, you're the one who imprisoned her, tied her up to the moon so she could no longer move about freely. They say you did it because she was careless with her hosts. That she hopped from one host to another, shredding their minds in the process. Until they couldn't even remember how to breathe. They say you couldn't understand it, couldn't fathom how your sister could be so cruel. Not when you mourned the deaths of your hosts. Not when you fretted over how helpless they were against old age..."

Asha's gaze stills, but her body begins to tremble.

"I take it you don't like losing your hosts, do you?"

My question hangs in the air between us.

"Good. Because now I think you understand. When I take this gag off this time, you're going to open the Rip. And you're going to use it to separate Farin from Nox's body. And Nox is going to wake up as himself. Because until that happens, until he wakes up and drags me away from Asha's neck, I'm not going to stop."

"Wait, Blaise." There's panic in Az's voice, but I can barely hear him.

I sink my teeth into Asha's neck, and I allow her blood to drown out the guilt.

I have no use for it anyway.

CHAPTER 42

ASHA

I can't move, can't fight back as Blaise slowly kills me, leeching the blood from my veins.

I can't move, and Calias is drowning me all over again.

At least this time it doesn't hurt, with Blaise's venom coursing through me.

I don't even care, not really. At least, I don't think I would care if my magic wasn't screaming drunkenly in my mind, his voice reverberating off the edges of my brain.

Asha. Please. I'm sorry.

He's fading slowly, I can tell. Eventually, the venom will do what it did last time, push him under.

A part of me feels a swell of wry pleasure at this, because Blaise threatened my magic with my life, telling him she wouldn't stop drinking until he did as he was told and opened the Rip.

I don't think Blaise knows what the venom does to him, that it numbs him as much as it does me.

But my magic is resisting it, fighting to retain consciousness, even as it slowly slips from my fingertips, as easily as the silky Fabric I held just moments ago.

It'll be funny, in a way, when Blaise kills me for no reason. When she realizes what she's done.

But my magic is screaming. I can't make out what exactly he's screaming, but he certainly has much more of a will for me to live than I do at the moment.

If only he'd let it work; the venom really isn't that awful. Sure, there's a certain cruelty about taking away a person's will to survive, but at least I'm not afraid.

At least I'm not hurting.

I will miss Kiran though.

Kiran.

My heart lurches at the thought of him hearing the news.

I hope that when I fade into the realm beyond the sun, I'll be able to watch over him.

No, my magic screams. I think I recognize that word.

Something rips, and it's so loud, so close to my ears, that it almost hurts.

Almost.

CHAPTER 43

BLAISE

"*B*laise. Blaise, you have to stop. You're killing her. Blaise!"

I snap my eyes open, and though I'm drunk on the taste of Asha's blood, swimming in the intoxication of the feast, there's something about that voice that catches my attention.

"Good. Good. Just like that. We just need to back away from her, okay?"

The world is swimming in darkness, but someone touches my cheeks. I blink and a face comes into view. A face with pale skin and raven hair and eyes of ice with a raging tempest underneath.

Nox.

I don't even realize I've said it aloud until he nods his head. "It's me. It's me, Nox. I came back for..." He pauses, knitting his brow. "For you."

Warm, savory blood drips from my lips, but I'm having a difficult time placing whose it is. Nox's gaze lingers on my mouth, and panic flecks across his vision.

"I can't stay here," he says, his eyes going wide. "I can't—" Nox backs away, until he's out of my vision, and then he's gone, and I'm alone.

Except I'm not alone. There's a boy standing before me. A handsome boy. The kind of handsome that makes my stomach feel as if I've consumed too many sweets. He's standing above me, glaring down at me in fury. There's pain in his eyes too, and he keeps glancing back and forth between the air and a figure slumped on the ground.

She smells like how the blood tastes on my lips.

I snap back to reality.

Asha.

My forearms find the earth, and I crawl my way to the body slumped in the grass.

"Get away from her," the handsome boy calls, but I can't hear him. Not over the ringing in my ears.

By the time I reach her, the wound on her neck has already healed, which is good, because half of my consciousness is still roiling with bloodlust.

The part of me that thinks I might have just murdered my friend is sobered up.

"Asha? Asha, please. Please wake up. Please. Come on. Don't be dead. Don't be dead." I reach for her neck to feel her pulse, but her neck snaps toward me.

"Don't you dare touch her," bellows a voice that is not at all Asha's.

"You vile, rotten, selfish creature," it roars, and I find I have no retort.

"Do you even realize what you've done, the destruction you've reaped upon the world, all because you couldn't stand to be alone?"

I blink as my hand finds my mouth.

"She's alive?" I ask. "Tell me she's still alive."

"Of course she's alive. I am speaking through her, am I not?"

I breathe out a sigh of relief, dread at what I've just done threatening to turn my gut inside out.

But my relief is short-lived, because the boiling anger in the Old Magic's voice goes stiff. Cold.

A passing breeze lifts the hair on the back of my neck.

"You spoke as if you know the stories. As if you know all about me. My origins."

My blood runs cold.

"But if you know so much about me, you must have known this is not the

first occasion on which I've been manipulated into altering the Rip against my will."

"I'll help you close it back," I whisper. "I promise. Please, I just wanted Nox back."

Nox, who is back. Nox, who held my face just now. Nox, who is probably out in the woods somewhere, writhing in pain as he tries to control his bloodlust for Asha.

"Lies," says the Old Magic. *"I've heard an assortment of them before."*

I shake my head. "Not a lie. I promise to help fix it."

"You hurt Asha."

"I know," I say. "I know, and I'm sorry, but I won't hurt her again. I just wanted Nox back."

"Yes, you keep saying that."

My heart patters to a stop, then skips.

"I did as you asked, young one. I separated your lover and the evil rot who should have been left in the ashes."

"And I'll never forget what you did for me."

"No. No, I don't believe you shall."

"Please, just tell me how I can fix it."

"I'm afraid there is no fixing it. Just like there was no fixing Farin. His death came swiftly after I cursed him. Are you aware of the stories? Did you know it was I who cursed the fae with the inability to lie?"

My mind is swimming, still numb with bloodlust.

"What is it you've cursed me with?" I dare to ask.

For a moment, I don't believe the Old Magic will answer.

But then.

"My dear, why do you assume it's you I've chosen to curse?"

CHAPTER 44

ASHA

*W*hen I open my eye again, Blaise is gone.

Az is not.

He's sideways. Well, I suppose I'm the one who's sideways, laid out like Gwenyth's corpse upon the swaying grass.

He stands there, hands clenched against his sides as he stares in front of him, his face the picture of awe.

Because of course he's awed.

I am too.

I wasn't able to see the Rip before, not when it was sutured, but I can see it now.

It's good we came at night. The reasonable part of me knows it was so Blaise could walk freely with us, but it's good all the same.

Because the sliver of light that shines through the Rip is all the more beautiful in contrast to the darkness.

Gentle rays of the sunlight of another world peek into our own, shy and glorious.

Even the runes written in Az's blood glow, purified and white in a circlet around the Rip.

I think maybe it's not so bad, this Rip, I whisper to my magic.

I don't think he answers back.

268

Probably as drunk on Blaise's venom as I am.

But then Az takes his own wrist, the one still dripping with blood from his self-inflicted wound, and dangles it in front of the ray of light.

He waits there for a moment, and then it comes.

I recognize it from my magic's visions.

Its decadent coat glistens silver in the moonlight, as if it's a fallen star that the moon itself shone down on in approval.

Its feline paws, as large as saucers, pad against the grass, long sharp fangs protruding from its maw.

Something thick and viscous drips from the end of those fangs. Where the substance drips onto the ground, the earth hisses in rejection.

Vaguely, I remember what my magic called this creature in his stories—a mere, one of the Others that haunt the Nether.

Az is reaching out for it, to touch the flat space between its sparkling eyes.

Part of me wonders if I should call out to him, warn him that the beast is as dangerous as it is beautiful. But then again, Az would have fit the same description, so he likely recognizes the monster for what it is.

But when Az reaches out for the beast, it doesn't maul him like I assumed it would.

It's perfectly still, though Az's blood drips down its snout as he pets it. Its papery tongue laps at the blood that dribbles onto its snout.

I think for sure this will be the moment it attacks. That I will watch my friend turned enemy be ripped to shreds in front of my face, as I'm unable to look away.

The beast does nothing. Not even when Az brings his blade to its forehead and slices.

Az wipes his hand on the bleeding wound, then brings the silvery substance to his mouth.

Something about Az changes then, though in my drunken stupor, my eye can't quite make sense of it.

And when Az whispers something to it, it...bows?

Then the beast turns. It roars, a command that sends a flock of ravens cawing, sprinkling the stars with darkness as they flee.

It calls, and its pack answers.

They cross through the Rip, the runes shining bright as stars as they do.

Binding runes—that's what Blaise thought they were, but Az made some modifications of his own. Then he shared blood with the beast, though that makes even less sense to me.

I remember then that opening the Rip was supposed to do something for Blaise, but I can't quite remember what. Whatever it was, it seems she must have gotten it, because she's gone.

That's when I hear the voice.

I recognize it, though it isn't Kiran's.

I guess I hoped it would be Kiran's. But Kiran is in Avelea. I should know that, since I sent him there.

So who does this voice belong to? The one that whispers in my ear, "It's going to be okay. I've got you."

Someone slips his arms underneath mine, dragging my body through the grass. He's huffing, straining under my weight.

I want to scream, want to warn this not-stranger that this won't work, to watch out for the silvery beasts. Surely he can see them? But maybe not. Az wasn't able to see the Fabric, after all.

Someone else yells ahead, and Az's gaze snaps to them. The person dragging me uses this distraction as an opportunity to haul me over his shoulder, but it's no use.

I hear someone shout my name.

There's enough possessiveness in the voice that I can't confuse it with anyone else's.

Then the Other lunges at us.

There's a scream, and I hit the ground.

I don't get to see what happens to my almost rescuer as another of the creatures approaches me, sinking its fangs into my hair and dragging me away.

CHAPTER 45

MARCUS

*S*hadows swirl about me, the product of my *paldihv* as the silvery Other crashes into me from the side, knocking Asha's limp body from my grip.

The force of the impact would have knocked the breath out of me on a normal day, but with Abra's poison necrosing my system, there's very little breath to banish.

My back hits the ground, the rear of my skull slamming against the earth, firing stars through my vision as my bow digs into my musculature.

Above me, the Other bears its paws down into my chest, yawning its fangs.

I groan, then stab upward with my dagger, missing the Other's major artery, but landing a blow to its throat all the same.

If this were a matter of my bow and arrow, the Other would have taken a blow straight through the airway. But alas. I really am better suited to long-range combat.

Still, that I'm the only one among our party who wears *paldihv* made me the obvious pick for infiltrating Az's ritual and sneaking Asha away, relying on my shadows for protection.

I stab the Other in the neck again, and this time a spray of silvery blood spatters all over my face, yet another reminder of why I don't enjoy close-range combat.

The Other sways, then slumps. It takes almost all of the strength I have left to shove its heavy body off of me. By the time I'm out from under its grip, I can hardly breathe, but I scan the perimeter just the same.

Asha is gone.

CHAPTER 46

ELLIE

*A*s I chase Amity across the field toward Marcus, I wonder if Evander and I were mistaken about whether having a child was worth it.

My heart pounds, fear racing through me as I try to catch up to the foolish, brave little girl. We were supposed to stay behind—me monitoring her and staying out of harm's way. Amity had been reluctant to agree, but she was a child and at the end of the day, Marcus's word was law.

But that was when we thought Blaise had taken Asha out of hunger.

Before we realized Blaise had simply pulled the wool over our eyes. Again.

We'd watched from behind the tree line, Az's and Blaise's voices carrying across the open field in the wind as we slowly realized what exactly was happening.

We'd observed in horror as Az stood in front of the circlet of runes that glowed peculiarly in the air, as if the rest of the field were just a backdrop painted to look like a landscape.

And then Blaise threatened the Old Magic, sinking her teeth into Asha's neck.

I had to clamp my hand over my mouth to keep from crying out. Marcus was even faster, slipping his hand over Amity's eyes so she wouldn't have to watch.

We couldn't speak, not without risking Blaise hearing us, so Marcus had taken my hand and fixed it over Amity's eyes to replace his.

Then the shadows of his *paldihv* had wrapped themselves around him, and he stepped into the open field, obscured by his magical garb.

I'd just stood there, clutching Amity's shaking body to my chest, Evander's grip firm on my shoulder, as if he were holding onto me for support lest the betrayal of his friend be too much.

At one point, I had to slip my hand over Amity's tear-soaked mouth to muffle her sobs as her fear for Marcus's life overwhelmed her.

And then there was a scream, and though it came from Asha's mouth, it didn't belong to her. It bellowed out.

And then something had Ripped.

Evander had bobbed next to me, and I could feel his muscles tensing, itching to go after Asha with Marcus, but there was no way he wouldn't be spotted in the open field.

The Rip itself was so loud, the beings that emerged from it so stunning, so earth-shattering, I almost didn't notice Nox's body move.

Evander had tapped on my shoulder and pointed him out to me, the way he pushed himself up from the ground, looking dazed, until he turned toward where Blaise was still feeding on Asha, and went completely stiff.

For a moment, I remembered Nox was a vampire too, and I worried he might attack her. But then he approached them, stroking Blaise's shoulders until she pulled away from Asha, allowing her friend's body to slump to the ground.

The three of us had watched as the faint outline of Marcus's *paldihv* reached Asha, as he wrapped his arms around her and began to drag her backward.

I'd realized too late that Amity had wriggled out from under my grip.

I'd realized too late that she was watching as the Other pounced, knocking her father to the ground.

Evander had been the first to move, rushing into the field with nothing to shield him from detection as he ran after Marcus and Asha.

Amity had been the second.

She'd sprinted off into the field, not in the direction most children would have, away from the danger.

But toward it, screaming Marcus's name.

Stupid, foolish girl.

I suppose I'm just as stupid for following her.

CHAPTER 47

EVANDER

I'm regretting never having tried to master my magic at the Academy.

My sister, Olwen, would just love to hear me admit that.

Though she would probably laugh over my dead body, telling me it's my own fault for not taking the responsibility of my magic more seriously. Still, I can't exactly be glad she isn't here, given if she were, I probably wouldn't be in my current situation.

Which is surrounded by a pack of mere, venom dripping from their ugly yellow fangs as their coats reflect the moonlight.

They're beautiful creatures, really. Stunning. The type I might be tempted to sit in awe of, if I wasn't pretty sure they're about to eat me.

The first launches, and though I parry with my sword, the only weapon I've ever felt remotely comfortable with, I'm not prepared for the weight of the mere's attack.

My sword protects me from the blow, but then the mere swipes its paw, knocking my blade from my grasp and sending it flying into the shadows.

I gesture toward the ground, and beneath the torso of the nearest creature shoots a vine riddled with thorns. It wraps itself around the beast's torso. As I fist my hand, it squeezes, sinking its thorns into the creature's skin.

The cry that bellows from the mere's mouth as the thorns slowly dig into its flesh might provoke pity in me, were I the one to attack first.

The mere currently being strangled by my singular vine writhes, flailing its paws to escape from the thorns, but the harder it resists the more I squeeze.

I'm almost impressed with my magic, which, to be honest, I haven't bothered touching in decades.

I once told Ellie that I didn't like doing things I was bad at.

I'm pretty sure that was the first moment she related to me.

Still, it seems like a petty excuse now, as the other mere, incensed by their comrade's pain, shriek in rage and advance, closing the circle they've formed around me.

It would be better if I could produce multiple vines at a time, which is exactly what Olwen would say if she were here. And probably Jerad too, if I'm being completely honest. Though his advice would come more from a place of wishing to save my life than laughing in my face and saying, "I told you so."

I keep one hand fisted, turning to the rest of the pack. With my other hand, I wield a shoot from the ground. It bursts forth from the earth, and I will it to grow.

It stops short of the length I would have preferred, and the thorns refuse to multiply with the expanded length, but it's all I have.

I flick my wrist, and it lashes toward the feet of the creatures, intending to cut off their legs from underneath them in one fell swoop.

The monsters jump, evading my vine with ease.

And then they pounce.

I barely have time to jolt out of the way before the first mere strikes, the tips of its claws a hair's breadth away from my cheek.

It comes crashing to the ground without even a thud—the creature is so light-footed.

The next attack comes in careful succession, and this time, the mere aims its maw at my torso. I might not have made it out of the way, but out of instinct my vine comes swooping in front of me, ready to protect.

It does little to harm the mere, but it slows it all the same, the mere having to claw through the stubborn little thing.

It really is thin, now that I'm getting a good look at it.

Unfortunately, looking at my pitiful excuse for a vine means I don't see the next attack coming.

Something crashes into my back, pain rippling through my entire body, sending me careening toward the ground.

My chest hits the earth with a thud, air whooshing from my lungs.

The weight of the beast falls upon me an instant later. There's the slicing of flesh as the creature paws at me. Its claws scratching at my skin without digging in. It swats at me, flipping me over on my back.

I look up to find the creature licking its maw, its tail whipping in the breeze.

Playing with its food.

It'll probably toss me around like a rag doll before this is over and done with.

I don't particularly like the idea of being anyone's food, but it feels particularly insulting to be taunted about it.

So I extend my hand, and a vine springs from the ground. The horned tip rips through the creature's neck.

My intention was to send the vine through the creature's skull, but that was unsuccessful. Apparently my vine wasn't strong enough to make it through the creature's brain.

Still, the mere slumps, its friends shrieking out in anger.

I don't make it to my feet before another is upon me.

I reach for my sword, which lies uselessly in the grass. It probably won't be much more help than the vines, considering I shirked out on those lessons, too.

The mere stomps on my hand just as my fingers brush its hilt.

Something cracks.

Actually, many things crack.

All the bones in my hand.

A terrible groan escapes my throat as the pain barrels through me. Who knew such little bones could cause so much pain?

And why are these creatures sentient enough to know when a male is reaching for his sword?

I try to summon another vine, but focusing while pain is thrumming through me, putting pressure on my skull, proves to be a task for which I am not well suited. The vine that springs up is limp, easily shredded by the mere's whipping tail. I summon another, but this one is in even worse shape.

Yeah, I really should have practiced more.

My pitiful vines lunge for the mere's legs, trying to trip the thing up, but it is of little use. The mere merely growls in irritation, swiping at the little vines as if they're gnats on the backside of an elephant.

I'm going to die.

I hope Ellie isn't watching. That she and Amity are far enough away that they can't see what is happening.

Sadness overtakes me at the idea of Ellie having to raise our child without me.

That's the one thing she'd asked of me in all this, isn't it?

If you're not here to squeeze my hand and tell me I'm spectacular while I'm quite literally ripping my body to shreds to bring our child into this world, then Evander Thornwall, I'm going to be peeved.

A pained chuckle escapes my lips. I imagine she'll be speaking my full name when she finally meets me in the afterlife, too.

It's the first time I've ever been grateful for Ellie's mortal lifespan. Perhaps I won't have to wait too terribly long for her to join me on the other side.

But no. I don't want to leave her. Don't want to watch her mourn me. Don't want to hear her screams over my dead body puncturing the veil between this life and the next.

The thought should make my stomach roil, but it doesn't.

What it does is give me strength.

What kind of things would you have wanted from your father?

I didn't have an answer then, but they all descend upon me now. I wanted my father to teach me to read, to help me build fortresses out of blocks, to sneak me out to Forcier's when I was supposed to be suffering discipline for my troublemaking.

I wanted a father who had been there.

I decide I will be there for our child.

So I let out a roar, one that expunges the pain as well as the air from my lungs, and I summon them.

The vines sprout up from the earth in droves. They're nothing compared to what my sister can produce, but they slice through flesh all the same, puncturing lungs and vital organs, until the creatures writhe.

I only manage to fell three more of them, but the rest are spooked enough that they run, and that is enough.

Pain still rippling through my hand, I stumble to my feet, scanning the area for Marcus and Blaise.

Marcus is on his feet now, releasing arrows at a group of Others who are slowly backing him toward the tree line.

Out of the corner of my eye, I glimpse more silvery beasts slink through the Rip.

Blaise... Where is she?

There.

Fighting off a pack of mere with her bare hands.

I watch as she rips the throat out of one with her teeth.

It's rather disgusting.

I step toward Marcus, concerned for his illness. Blaise seems to be handling herself just fine, and I'm still peeved that she betrayed us, even if she seems to be fighting against the Others now.

But then I hear it.

A scream.

A scream that shouldn't be here.

A child's scream.

There's a moment when the world goes still, except for Blaise, who throws the carcass of the dead mere to the side, her hungry eyes landing on me before swelling with horror. I can't seem to get my neck to turn fast enough to look. Perhaps I don't want to see, not truly, but my gaze hits Marcus, whose face has gone slack with fear, and is now bubbling with rage.

Because he recognizes that scream.

We all do.

I spot Amity, backed into the corner of two boulders as a mere races for her, then jumps.

Another scream pierces the air.

A scream that will be branded in my memory for the rest of my immortal life.

I summon the vines, but they can't reach, not from such a distance. Not when I haven't disciplined them to obey me.

So I watch helplessly as Ellie jumps in front of Amity.

I watch helplessly as the Other cuts down my wife.

CHAPTER 48

BLAISE

The agony in Evander's sea-green eyes slices across the field, searing itself into my vision.

I recognize that cry. It's the same one that's been wrenched from my own twisted throat before.

It's the cry of a mother.

There's a moment when all is still, and it's just me and Evander, his coat stained with blotches of ichor, his eyes widening, begging for it not to be true.

All around us, Others still midair, jaws frozen agape, their silvery coats glimmering in the moonlight.

Then the world snaps into action, and Evander and I run.

We weave through swarms of Others. I'm faster, nimbler, and while Evander has to muscle through several of them, I'm able to dodge their attacks with ease.

That means I get there first.

The world slows. It must be my vampire senses. They're making sense of the scene before me with such speed, it only feels slower.

Ellie lies prone on the ground, shielding both her belly and Amity beneath her weight. Sticky red blood seeps from a gash in her side where her robes have been ripped. Amity's face is flushed with exertion as she tries to wriggle out from underneath Ellie, whose entire body is trembling.

The Other still feeds from Ellie's wound, digging its venom-soaked fangs into her side.

There's a moment when this vision collides, lines up, with a memory, a dream.

Ellie crying on the floor, bleeding, her lifeblood being drained from her veins.

Ellie begging me to stop.

It's that vision that has me careening for the Other.

I grab it by the maw. There's a sickening crack as I rip the top half of its jaw from its hinges. Ellie lets out an agonized shriek as the fangs are torn from her body. The Other slumps to the ground next to Ellie, the top half of its head oozing venom and blood from where I still grasp it in my ichor-stained hand.

I only faintly hear it thud to the ground.

Amity's now out from underneath Ellie, whose body has gone limp. She must have passed out from the pain. Amity stares at me. It's only for a moment, but it only takes a moment of witnessing the utmost disappointment in a child's eyes for it to be branded into my memory forever.

"Amity, I—"

"We need to get Ellie out of here," Amity says, nodding toward our friend.

I nod in agreement, going for Ellie's underarms so I can lift her and drag her away.

"Behind you!" Amity calls, and I have to drop Ellie back into the grass to swing my body around. I turn just in time to catch a set of teeth sinking into my forearm. A cry of pain rips from my throat, but now that the Other has its jaws sunk into my arm, I use my other forearm to brace the top of its neck.

Then I take the arm onto which it's latched, and force it upward.

The Other's neck snaps in two, the crunch of its vertebrae reverberating through my skin.

Its grip doesn't slacken in death, so I have to pry its jaw open.

The pain slicing through my arm is dizzying, but at least I don't feel the effects of the venom. My vampirism must shield me from it.

Venom.

Ellie's gash contains venom.

That's why she's gone limp.

I don't have time to examine her, though, not when three more beasts cut away from the swarm, stalking us with silent padded paws as the grass waves whimsically around them.

"Amity, stay behind me," I hiss through my teeth.

The first beast lunges. I duck underneath its lithe body and thrust my hand through its neck. When I return my hand to my side, the beast's larynx comes with it.

Its body falls in a silvery heap, but the next two beasts are cleverer.

When they attack me, they do it together.

The first, I'm able to grab ahold of its throat, but at the same moment its companion barrels into my side, knocking the wind from my lungs.

My back hits the ground, the second beast rearing up in front of me. It swipes at me with its paw, but I grab onto it and twist. The beast lets out a shriek. Unable to support its weight, it comes falling atop me.

As soon as it gets close enough, I sink my fangs into the fleshy portion of its neck and shred its throat with my teeth.

Ichor sprays into my mouth, coating my tongue like bile. I spit out the mass of cartilage, shoving the weight of the creature's carcass off of me.

The last of the group whimpers before fleeing.

I allow myself a single glance at the battlefield.

Evander has gained some ground. Vines burst from the soil, tangling the feet of several of the Others, but Evander's face is strained with concentration. He has to keep producing the vines as the Others hack through them with their teeth and claws.

My heart aches to help him, but for now, Ellie's the one in the most danger, so I tear my gaze away from Andy and turn back to my friend.

284

Amity has her outer tunic wadded up. She's pressing it into Ellie's wound.

Sweat beads on Ellie's forehead, and her breathing has become labored.

Labor.

No. No, no, no, no.

I watch in horror as Ellie's slender fingers creep toward her swollen belly.

It's like she's having to fight just to move her hand.

The Others' bite contains paralytic venom.

I try not to imagine what that will do to Ellie's baby.

No, no, no, no, no.

"We need to get her to safety," says a strained voice. Marcus. He's backed his way to the three of us, firing arrows at the Others approaching. "I'll cover you while you move her. Amity, help Blaise get Ellie to safety, okay?"

Amity turns to me. "I can keep pressure applied to the wound if you can carry her."

I nod and make to lift Ellie, but Ellie grits her teeth and shakes her head. "No. No, save the baby."

Amity and I exchange concerned looks.

"We have to get you to safety first. The baby needs you living to survive," I explain.

Tears soak Ellie's warm brown cheeks. Moonlight reflects in her pupils. "I think...I think my baby is already coming."

I look toward Amity, hoping the little encyclopedia of medicine will have an argument for why that's not the case. But Amity only looks up at me with those big brown eyes of hers and nods.

Fates, no. No, no, no, no.

It's too early, much too early in Ellie's pregnancy. Even in her delirium, Ellie must realize too, because she lets out a strangled sob.

"Is there a way to stop the labor?" she asks, practically begs. "Please, please. Please make it stop."

It takes me a moment to realize Ellie isn't talking to us.

She's talking to the Fates.

So I start talking to them too.

I'm not sure whether they hear the prayers of night stalkers who betray their friends. Part of me wonders if asking will only make things worse, but the prayers come anyway, almost contrary to my will, a string of pleadings incomprehensible in my panic.

"You need to get her under cover," Marcus grumbles, face strained as he stumbles backward toward us, still letting arrows fly. My stomach plummets when I catch sight of his quiver and realize he's only got three arrows left.

I make the decision to carry Ellie into the trees.

ELLIE'S BREATHING has gotten more rapid. She keeps clenching her jaw instead of allowing herself to scream.

"It's okay; you can scream," I tell her as I set her on the ground close to where the group hid their baggage.

She shakes her head, sweat drenching her forehead. "It'll alert them."

"No more than the scent of your blood already has." I'm not sure it's the right thing to say, because Ellie's cheeks sink with horror, but the next time a contraction rips through her, she lets herself shout all the same.

"How is she having contractions? Shouldn't the venom be keeping that from happening?" I ask.

Amity shakes her head. "If it's psychosomatic like lychaen venom, it shouldn't matter. Ellie isn't in control of her contractions; her body is."

Amity's pulling vials and other materials out of her satchel, but her fingers keep fidgeting.

It's not like Amity to shake like this.

It's then that I realize Amity is preparing to deliver a child who won't be viable.

No, no, no.

I can't breathe, I can't breathe, I can't…

But no. I have to breathe. This is my fault, and I have to see it through. I have to be here for Ellie, for…

Evander comes bursting through the trees, front soaked in the inky blood of the Others.

There's a crazed look in his eyes, one that's utterly unfamiliar on his usually gentle, carefree face.

It slowly morphs into horror when he realizes what's happening.

Ellie catches his eye, and the sorrow they exchange with that one look threatens to shatter me.

"I'm sorry. I'm so sorry, baby," Ellie whispers. "I know it's too early. I couldn't…I couldn't let…"

Evander kneels on the ground next to his wife. He takes her trembling hands in his and touches them to his forehead. "I know. I know. You were so brave, and I'm so proud of you. So immensely proud to get to say you're my wife."

Ellie's brow furrows. "It's too early."

Evander's voice breaks, and my heart cracks in two. "I know."

Ellie begins sobbing.

No, no, no, no, no.

I can't breathe, I can't—

Evander's neck snaps upward, his fiery gaze meeting mine, as if noticing I'm here for the first time.

"What are you doing here?"

My voice catches in my throat. Next to me Marcus goes stiff, though he keeps his eyes trained on the wood for any prowling Others.

"What? It's not enough that you've unleashed a pack of Others on my wife? You can't even be bothered to answer my question?"

My voice trembles, even as I try to hold onto it. "Andy, I'm—"

"Don't call me that," he snaps, his face twisting in anguish. "How…" He takes in a breath, his sea-green eyes shimmering with tears. "How dare you?"

I open my mouth, but no words come out.

Evander's baby is about to die, and I'm the cause of it.

There's nothing that can fix it.

Worst of all, I know that better than anyone.

Recognize the anguish in his heart better than anyone.

My mind flashes back to the joy in Evander's and Ellie's eyes when I stumbled in on Evander listening to the child's heartbeat. The envy that settled in my stomach.

Fates, did I hope this into being?

"I didn't mean for this to happen," I whisper, and even as Evander's face hardens, it's like I can't help myself. Can't help myself from trying to force him to understand, though I have no right.

Evander swallows. "You never do."

Hurt pierces my chest at the truth of his words.

"And—Evander, I—"

I steal a glance at Ellie, but she has her eyes forced closed. The scent of her blood wafts to my nostrils.

"No." Evander shakes his head. "I don't want to hear any more excuses from you, Blaise. I'm done. I keep thinking I'm helping you, but really, I've just been enabling your selfishness."

Marcus shifts. "Evander..."

Evander barks, but not toward Marcus. "No. Blaise, do you know how guilty I felt when you were taken? How many nights I lay sleepless because I worried over what had happened to you? And I know...I know your childhood was wretched. I know Clarissa deserved what she got for what she did to you. And I'm sorry, Blaise. I'm truly sorry for what you suffered. But you know what else I'm sorry for? I'm sorry for giving so much of myself to someone who doesn't want to be helped, someone who doesn't care to get better. I put my family in danger for you. And I can't blame you for that. It was my own choice, my own doing. But you...you're so desperate to fill that void inside you, so desperate for some twisted ideal of love, that you throw away the people who actually care about you.

"I know why you did it, why you betrayed us. We all know. Even little Amity here knows. It doesn't matter what anyone else has done to prove we loved you. You're just going to throw it away for the attention of the first male who looks your way.

"So yes, you should have been nervous to tell me about Nox. And yes, I would have said you were being stupid. And I'm so, so tired of caring about whether you ruin yourself. Ruin everything you touch. Because that's what you do.

"Asha's gone, Blaise. I don't know if you've even pulled your head out of your own chest long enough to notice. You handed her over to that psychopath. Do you know how frightened she is of him? How many times Ellie had to go and sleep in the bed with her because she would wake up screaming?"

My mouth is moving, but no words are coming out.

"And now Kiran is going to have to agonize over what's happening to her. Like you've been agonizing over Nox. You can't handle your own burdens, your own pain, so you gladly hand them off to someone else."

Marcus has lowered his bow, placing a firm hand on Evander's shoulder.

Evander shrugs him off and bolts to his feet.

"Now's not the time for this, friend," says Marcus, but Evander doesn't seem to hear.

He's stalking toward me, and for the first time in my life, I see nothing but contempt in those beautiful eyes of his.

"Tell me, are you happy now? Did you find what you were looking for? Tell me it was worth it, Blaise. Tell me you got what you wanted. That the price of my child's life was worth it."

He approaches, and I find myself stepping backward, my back hitting a tree.

"Tell me. *Was. It. Worth. It?*"

I wonder for the first time if Evander is going to kill me.

I wonder if I'll let him.

He looks to be contemplating it when someone steps in front of me.

"That's enough," says a voice I ache for like the earth thirsts for water in the middle of a drought.

Nox emerges from the shadows.

Evander looks Nox up and down, and the most beautifully cruel smile warps his usually kind face. "See how long you can keep that up, defending her, before it's you who ends up in a ditch while she's onto something shinier."

Nox tenses, and for a moment, I wonder if the two most important males in my life will rip each other to shreds.

Ellie lets out a wilting cry, and the hostility melts from Evander's face. In an instant, he's back at her side, cradling her hand in his, pressing his forehead to hers as he whispers apologies in her ear.

I don't mean to eavesdrop, but I hear him beg her forgiveness for not protecting her.

Marcus's voice is steady as he addresses Nox and me. "I think it would be best if the two of you go."

It's only then I recognize the bloodlust in Nox's eyes as his gaze settles on Ellie's wound.

Nox nods and disappears into the shadows.

I take one last look at Ellie, her teeth gritted, her brow twisted in pain, and follow him into the dark.

PART IV

CURSED

CHAPTER 49

EVANDER

Our hands are clasped together, mine and Ellie's, though I can't tell which one of us is shaking. Probably both. Of course it's both of us, Ellie from the pains of labor, me from the rage boiling up inside me.

The bones in my hand are slowly knitting back together from where the Other crushed it.

I hardly notice.

Panic courses through my veins, causing my whole body to tremble, my knees to shake, though they're planted in the earth next to Ellie. Next to my wife.

She is going to die. And if not Ellie, if the Fates spare her, then our child is going to die.

I can't see a way around that, a world in which the Fates don't take our child from us, and neither can she.

How did I let this happen? Why did I place my family in danger, all in a fruitless quest to help a leech who's never wanted to be helped? A girl who's never cared about anyone other than herself?

We're going to lose our child, and I might lose Ellie too, and I can't even blame Blaise for it.

I can blame no one but myself.

How do you let go of someone who's drowning? How do you live with yourself?

That was the question I asked Ellie, unsure at the time that I could live with myself if I did.

What I didn't realize was that while I was swimming against the crashing waves, fighting with Blaise's thrashing limbs as she grabbed onto my neck and pulled, we weren't the only two in the water.

How do you let go of someone who's drowning? How do you live with yourself?

It's that you see your wife and child are in the water too, and you realize you can't save all of them.

Tears sting at my burning eyes as I watch Ellie writhe. Sweat coats her forehead. Her screams are becoming more pronounced now.

Again, Ellie asks for a cloth to bite down on, worried her wails will attract the Others. As if the blood isn't already doing that.

And there is so much blood.

Amity does as asked, though I suspect mostly to give Ellie something to do, a way to calm her anxieties.

Ellie pushes, and I squeeze her hand and tell her I love her, though that hardly seems enough.

"It's too early. It's too early," she keeps whispering, and each time it chisels away bits of my heart. By the end of this, there will be nothing left except a cavity inside my chest where our joy should have been.

All the while, Amity keeps at work, tending to Ellie's wound and checking on her progress. Marcus keeps watch. I'm not aware of a time when he lowers his bow, feeble as his poisoned muscles must be.

The Others don't come.

There are moments when my vision blurs, and all I can see is that vital moment. The mere crashing into Ellie's back, slamming her to the ground on top of Amity. I can hear the crunch of her ribs, the sound of her cries of agony.

It wasn't her shattered bones she'd wept over.

And then there were my vines, not long enough to reach, not powerful enough to protect.

All because I don't enjoy doing things I'm not good at.

Olwen could have saved her, and talented as my sister is, the same blood runs through our veins, the same magic at its core.

I just simply refused to tend to mine. Didn't care enough to bother.

And then, when Ellie said she wanted to come along with me to the Rip, I didn't consider it then, either—that I hadn't practiced long enough to protect her. I'd relied on the skills of Blaise, Lydia, and even Marcus, sick as he is, sure that any of them could best our enemies in a fight.

I hadn't bothered to train. I've had two hundred years to hone my skills, to prepare for this moment, the hour I'd need to protect my family, and I simply never cared to try.

Because I didn't let myself think about it. Just like I never let myself think about the fact that one day, Ellie will grow old and die. Just like I didn't let myself think about what would occur if the Rip were opened and the beasts got to Ellie, assuming we'd be long gone before that happened.

All I was thinking was that if I left her behind, I would miss her like I would miss my own eyesight. That I couldn't stand to be parted from her smile, her melodic voice again. I thought I needed her, and I did. But had I considered what she needed? She wanted to come, and I let myself be convinced so easily, sure that having her and our unborn child by my side would ease my anxieties. Would relieve me from worrying about whether they'd come to harm, because I could lay eyes on her any time I wanted. Hear our baby's heartbeat as I pressed my head against her belly. See the smile on Ellie's lips.

But that's always been my problem, hasn't it? For some reason, the immediate has always felt so much more real, more concrete, than the future.

But the future has a tendency of coming whether I care to consider it or not, and now I'm reaping the consequences of not taking it more seriously.

Ellie's sobbing now, the rag in her mouth soaked through, and I can't stand it. Can't stand to watch her in so much pain. Can't stand the helplessness that aches inside me.

"I can see the baby's head," Amity says matter-of-factly. Nausea washes over me.

I don't think I can stand to look, stand to watch our baby die, exposed to the elements too early, before its organs have a chance to properly develop. Will Ellie want to hold our child as it dies? I think probably so, and if she does, I'll make myself stay, planted beside her. For Ellie.

My head spins, shadows speckling the edges of my vision.

"I think it's coming," says Amity, and the blood drains from my face. I feel as though I'm going to pass out.

Amity peers up at me. "You should probably look away."

I feel weak, ridiculous, but I do as I'm told as Amity delivers my and Ellie's child.

I'M NOT sure if it takes minutes or hours, but there's a moment when the world goes numb.

And then a tiny voice creaks out into the shadows, piercing the darkness, and though it's the sound of anguish, it's also the sound of life. A first breath stolen from the air. A life wrangled from the wind by a tiny hand that flails as I make myself look into Amity's arms.

The child wriggles and writhes, very much alive, though I can hardly let myself breathe, not when I'm unsure when our child will take its last breath.

I find I don't want to miss that moment, as much as I dread it.

And then Amity's little voice calls out, as simply as if she were Peck himself, "It's a baby girl," and my entire world shatters, then mends itself right up again.

I watch in shock as Amity cuts the cord with her knife, then wipes our little girl off with a terrycloth.

Ellie is weeping, her face a strained mingling of relief and agony as she listens to the sounds of our child's screaming, tears streaming down her face.

Ellie's fingers writhe at the air. I can hardly speak, not with the wonder and shock closing off my throat, so I'm grateful when Marcus says quietly, "Amity, Ellie probably wants to hold her baby."

Even Marcus's voice is shaking, though he keeps his eyes trained on the forest.

Amity does as she's told, swaddling the baby—our baby—in her own coat, then shuffles over to Ellie's side and places our daughter in my beautiful wife's arms.

Amity has to prop up Ellie's arms because the paralytic hasn't completely worked its way out of her system.

Ellie sobs harder, the slightest gasp escaping her lips as she tucks the small, beautiful, squirming little girl into her chest, touching our daughter's tiny cheek with her thumb.

Our child continues to scream, and I wonder if perhaps I'd be content to listen to that sound for years on end.

Alive.

Our child is alive.

"Can you tell if she's healthy?" I whisper, hardly able to bring myself to look at Amity. I'm terrified her face will give her away.

The look she gives me instead is more along the lines of, "Do I look like I've done this before?," but she just shrugs.

"She's screaming, so that means she's breathing. And she's bigger than I would have thought she'd be at this point."

That's hard to imagine, given how tiny she is, clearly not ready for this world, but intent on staying here anyway.

"The gestation lengths vary from pregnancy to pregnancy," Ellie says, relief flooding down in the tears that streak paths in the grime on her face. And then Ellie is giggling, hysterically, hiccuping and coughing, and holding our child tight as she screams.

I chance a glance at the wound in Ellie's side, but Amity is already tending to it, changing the bandages and cleaning it with the salve she had in her satchel.

"The bleeding has slowed a lot. And her blood is bright again—less paralytic." Though Amity seems to be talking to herself, I figure it's more for my benefit.

"Do you want to hold her?" Ellie whispers, peering up at me with those beautiful wide eyes of hers.

I brush a tear from her cheek and shake my head. "You're the one who pushed. I just watched. I think you deserve to hold her a little while longer."

Ellie nods, not fighting me on the notion, which brings a smile to my face.

Still, I reach out to touch our daughter all the same, her little arms flailing about, like she came out of the womb ready to fight the world.

Her tiny hand finds my finger and closes around it, and I sense my heart turn its allegiance elsewhere.

In a moment, my life, my world, changes.

It's with a sudden urgency I realize that I will protect this child at any cost.

CHAPTER 50

BLAISE

*N*ox and I walk until the sound of Ellie's screams fades, lost to the howling wind and the storm brewing overhead.

Her screams might fade from my ears, but they ring in my head, scraping against my soul, reminding me of the lives I've somehow managed to crush into broken shards of lost dreams.

Dreams are like glass. They're pretty when they're still whole. So smooth and easy to the touch. But the problem with dreams is that when they shatter, they cut the skin, and even when you've swept them up, you keep finding bits of them pricking at your heels for months and years to come.

I've wrecked Evander and Ellie's dreams, and try as I might, I can't suture the glass back together. I simply don't have the skill.

Nox and I find a cave in a nearby hill that we settle into, both acutely aware of the sun approaching the horizon.

We hardly speak, at least not more than exchanging logistics about where we'll take shelter for the day.

By the time we find the cave, the protectiveness that rolled off Nox when he stepped between me and Evander has dissipated, soaking into the humid air.

When we settle into the cave, Nox takes the opposite side, leaning his back against the wall.

I lower myself to the ground, something about the feeling of sinking into the soft earth puncturing my sore heart.

We sit in silence for a long while, and for at least an hour all I can hear is the echoes of Ellie's screams.

I wonder if the baby will scream. If the Fates will grant it the taste of fresh air.

I wonder how long it will be allowed to survive outside of the womb.

Where is my baby, where is my baby, where is my baby.

I wonder if it is a little boy or a little girl. What Evander and Ellie will name their child. If they already have.

I wonder if the baby is dead.

"Blaise," Nox finally says. His voice buoys me from my spiraling thoughts, though I don't know that I deserve that—a buoy. I think I probably deserve to sink, to bury myself in Evander and Ellie's grief.

I lift my gaze to meet his. It's a struggle even raising my chin. I feel as though an ocean hangs over my head. That my skull might pop from the pressure.

"I need you to tell me what happened while I was away. What exactly you did."

The words do nothing to penetrate the numbness in my heart. I can't even bring myself to be afraid. Afraid to tell Nox what I've done.

If he heard any portion of the conversation between me and Evander, he knows I'm to blame for the death of their child.

It's not fear so much that I feel, but gratitude. I don't deserve to have this last conversation with Nox. I don't deserve to get to look at him one last time before he turns away from me in disgust. But, for some reason, the Fates have decided to grant me this mercy.

So I tell him. I tell him of Az's plan, of the friendship I developed with Asha before I betrayed her. I tell him of the lies I wove and the people I treated as stepping stones on the path to my salvation.

At least, what I thought was my salvation.

It feels a whole lot more like damnation.

I must have gotten the two confused.

When I get to the portion about threatening the Old Magic with Asha's death, of the unleashing of the Others, and how Ellie stepped in their way to keep them from attacking Amity, Nox's already pale face drains of color.

I deserve that, too.

I leave out the part about the Old Magic's curse, as I'm still not sure what it is.

Nox asks questions throughout, but they're careful, devoid of anything that might betray his revulsion.

When I'm done, he leans his head back against the cave wall and runs his fingers through his hair. He grits his teeth like he's in pain, then swallows.

"Blaise," he says, and there's no use in him hesitating, because I already know what he's about to say. "I never wanted others to suffer for me."

It shouldn't hurt as much as it does, given I'm anticipating it, but preparing my heart protects me about as much as tensing before a hundred-foot fall.

"I've caused enough suffering on my own," he says, staring up at the ceiling of the cave. "I've ripped too many people away from their families. It...it has to stop. I thought it had stopped."

There's something there behind his words, I realize, as his throat bobs.

"It was my choices that hurt them. Not yours," I say.

He rubs at his temples. Now that his and Farin's spirits are separate, I wonder if it's just habit now. "Queen Asha. I saw that man take her. Watched him drag her away. I could scent the fear rolling off of her, but I'd just woken up, and the scent of her blood was so strong...I should have saved her."

My entire being is numb. "I meant to save her, in the end. Before we arrived at the Rip, I mean. I caught the way Az was looking at Asha, the way he touched her. I told myself I wouldn't let anything happen to her. That we'd get the Rip open, separate you from Farin, and then I'd protect Asha from him. Instead, I practically handed her over."

I wonder what's happening to her now, and my gut clenches.

And then I'm back in a pantry, and Derek's hands are all over me, and…

"Nox, I've really messed up," I whisper.

He says nothing, only furrows his brow in concern. For a moment, I think it's because he can't fix it. It takes me a moment to realize it's because there's something he's not telling me.

"I know," he finally settles on.

My voice is barely a whisper. "What happened, over on the other side of the Fabric?"

Nox examines me with those piercing ice-blue eyes of his. His jaw ticks. "Zora…she helped me find a way back."

My head spins. "A way back."

I hardly have the energy to make it a question.

He pauses, pressing his lips together.

"A way back, but one that would have had you and Farin stuck in the same body, you mean."

Nox stares at me a moment, then slowly shakes his head. "No. Zora led me to an eyelet in the Fabric. I left Farin behind in the other realm."

His voice echoes off the cave walls.

"You mean…" I take in a strangled breath. Tears sting at my eyes, and I wipe them quickly away with my sleeve. "You mean you found a way back on your own? A way that would have worked without the Rip?"

Nox doesn't spare me from having to look him in the eye. "Yes."

My palm finds my mouth, and I retch. When I pull my hand away, it's covered in blood. Asha's blood.

Asha's blood in my mouth, Ellie's blood on my hands, so much blood…

Blood that wasn't necessary to shed.

My lips form the word "no," but it gets suffocated in my sobs as I bury my face in my hands.

Nothing. I've ripped my soul in two, placed Evander's baby upon the altar of my own happiness, handed Asha over to her greatest nightmare, betrayed my friends.

For no reason whatsoever.

Nox tore his way through worlds to get back to me.

And now the girl he thought he was returning to no longer exists.

Footsteps pad against the stone floor of the cave, and soon Nox's side presses into mine. He digs his fingers through my hair and pulls my head into his chest. I'm reminded of the first time he read to me aloud, how I almost fell asleep with my head in his lap, thinking that maybe Nox's embrace was what peace feels like.

Now I know better. Now I know there is no peace for me. There never will be.

And though the agony still ripples through my chest, I find myself melting into him. Find myself wanting him, wishing to drown myself in him. Aching to sear away the pain in the heat of his kiss, numb myself in his love.

It's temporary, and it's vain, and it won't last, because no happiness, no relief of mine, is meant to last. I know that now.

It makes me burn for him all the more, knowing that one day, one day sooner than I can bear to think about, I'll lose him too.

I crane my neck upward to stare into the beautiful face I know I'm destined to lose, as if somewhere, in some other world, my story is being woven into a tapestry just like Zora's, just like Nox's. But instead of my death being rewritten and rewritten, it's losing every piece of happiness I've ever tasted, all at my own hand, over and over again.

His warmth envelops me, and I find I'm alight with desire, a craving stronger than any bloodlust I've ever experienced. Nox stares down at me, his ice-blue eyes melting me with such beautiful sorrow.

I lift myself upward and press my lips to his, intent on drowning myself in him.

But something is wrong.

His mouth, once so hungry for mine, is hesitant against my lips, almost immobile. And when he kisses me back, there's something in the kiss that's sterile, like he's trying to...

Like he's trying to...

Like he's trying to convince himself he wants it.

I pull away, mortification heating my cheeks.

Fears I've been harboring for months assail me all at once.

Nox, living another life, his arms wrapped around another woman. Nox, cradling a child who only exists in another realm.

Apology paints his beautiful features, and again he rubs at his temples. "Blaise..." he tries to explain, but I'm already crawling off of him, shame threatening to suffocate me.

"Please, you don't have to explain," I say hastily. Because I don't think I'll survive it if I hear the reason escape Nox's lips. If I hear his heart belongs to another. If I hear he returned for one girl, only to realize the Blaise he thought he loved never existed.

That he's returned for a liar who betrays her friends.

Nox shakes his head. "No, it's not...I don't think it's you."

I suck in a breath. "Nox, please."

"No, there's something wrong with me, Blaise. Something that's different about me. It's like I woke up in this realm, but with something missing. I don't know if it got lost somewhere in the eyelet. But there's something..." He grasps at his chest, then looks up at me.

It's then that the memory of the Old Magic's voice returns to me.

My dear, why do you assume it's you I've chosen to curse?

CHAPTER 51

MARCUS

*M*y daughter is amazing.

My daughter is amazing, and I hate that I'm leaving her.

I watch Amity as she swaddles Evander and Ellie's baby, keeping the child tucked in close against her chest as she whispers absent-mindedly to her.

She likes to hold the child while Evander and Ellie sleep, both of them having a tendency to pass out from exhaustion despite attempting to take shifts awake with their daughter.

But they need not worry. Their little girl is in the best of hands.

Amity, of course, isn't capable of single-tasking, and I watch her rifle through her grimoire with one hand as she lays the child gently down in her lap.

My heart aches as Amity flips through the pages, underlining and circling sections with her quill.

She searches for a cure, and I don't quite have the heart to tell her there is none.

That's the thing about the Rip.

There's no flax here. At least, no flax that hasn't already been harvested. Amity reminds me that this means there's someone out there selling the flax, and that we need only locate those merchants to find the cure for my illness, but even if that's true, I know better than to think I'll make it that long.

My body is failing me.

It's a strange sensation, given I've always been so adamant about training it, bending my muscles into submission, disciplining my body rigorously to endure whatever is thrown my way.

But my strength is wilting. I managed to hold my bow while Ellie was in labor, but I was running off the thrill and necessity of the moment. Now I feel the consequences seeping exhaustion into my very bones.

I'm never quite rid of the urge to cough, which has only worsened since that mere pounced on me, crushing at least one, if not multiple, ribs.

I wish Piper were here. It's ripping my soul to shreds that I'm spending the last of my days without her. It's not that I want her to see me like this. The idea of her watching me wither away makes me sick. But I miss her laugh, her morbid sense of humor. If she were here, she'd poke me in the shoulder and make some comment about how she likes seeing my vulnerable side.

I can't stand the thought that one of these days, someone, Lydia probably, is going to bring her the news that I'm gone.

I can't stand that I won't be there to hold her in that moment.

I find myself dwelling on this thought often, mostly because my mind can't handle the alternative. That once Abra is done with her, there will be no one left to bring news of my death to. That Amity will find herself an orphan, parentless, and not for the first time.

It's that thought that keeps me fixated on the image of Piper mourning my death.

Because then at least she's alive.

At least she and Amity will have each other.

The Thornwall baby stirs, struggling against Amity's expert swaddle.

It hurts me to look at her sometimes, that baby.

I'm abundantly happy for Evander and Ellie, grateful to the Fates for that little bundle of hope they've granted us amid so much turmoil.

But when I look at the infant, I don't see her. I see the child that won't get to exist, the one I've been dreaming of since that night in Evaen when I couldn't stop searching for Piper in a crowd of dancers. Swaddled in terrycloth is the little sister Amity will never get to hold, even though Amity should get to be a sister. She'd be the best, most attentive older sister in the world.

Amity would be much better at having a little sister than I had been.

My mind flits to Cheyenne, the sister I forgot, the child who's grown into a woman who doesn't want or need my protection.

I have plenty of regrets about dying, and many of them belong to the fact that Cheyenne and I, while on civil terms, never restored our relationship fully.

I wonder if she'll regret her grudge against me when she learns that I'm dead. It's not that I want that for her. It just seems like another way that I've failed her.

Acute pain jolts through my chest, sharp enough that the world around me threatens to spin. I breathe in deeply to steady myself. That strategy worked much better before that mere crushed my ribs.

Amity's gaze jolts to attention, but I offer her a placating smile.

I'm fine, I mouth, which is a lie. The only lie I've ever felt comfortable telling her.

Well, after she learned I was a mercenary sent to capture Piper, and I vowed never to lie to the child again.

She frowns, the line between her bushy brows deepening, but then the baby starts to whine, stirring Evander and Ellie from the way they're sleeping, holding each other.

They both wipe the exhaustion from their eyes, and while Ellie sits up and props herself against our baggage, Evander rises to retrieve the child from Amity.

307

She hands the girl over eagerly, shaking her arm out rather conspicuously.

The smile that overtakes my friend's face hurts, but I'm happy for him. I truly am.

"Amity," Ellie says, her voice still hoarse but regaining its strength after a few days' rest. "Evander and I discussed something last night that we wanted to tell you together."

Amity looks rather reluctant to put down her grimoire, but Piper and I must have done something right, because she bites the inside of her cheek and turns to Ellie politely, even if her finger still taps against the tree stump in impatience.

"As you know, we didn't have a name picked out yet, so it's taken us a few days to decide..." Ellie's voice chokes up, and unable to continue, she flits a hand at Evander, signaling him to finish for her.

His sea-green eyes glisten as he looks at my daughter and says, "We've decided to name her Amity, after you."

A lump swells in my throat, immense pride welling within me.

But then I glance at Amity and...Oh no.

She's looking at Evander and Ellie blankly, like they've just informed her that the sky is blue.

"Her first name?" she asks.

Evander and Ellie glance at one another.

"Yes," Ellie explains. "We're just so grateful for all you did in helping with the delivery, we wanted to name her after you."

"Don't you think that will be kind of confusing?" my daughter, whose behavior now reflects on my parenting, asks. "I mean, if you say 'Amity,' how will anyone know which one you're talking about?"

Mortification washes over my already aching bones.

This is something no one warns you about when it comes to parenthood: how unbearably rude children have a tendency to be, and how listening to them being rude feels just as embarrassing as if the words had escaped your own mouth.

I take a deep breath, one that rather hurts, and remind myself that Amity had over a decade to develop her lack of manners before Piper and I claimed her.

Granted, even if we'd had Amity since she was an infant, would I have ever thought to bring up how she should react if anyone named their child after her?

Likely not.

"Uh," says Evander, looking rather sleep-deprived and flustered.

"Amity." I grit my teeth and will my voice to remain calm. "Evander and Ellie have done something very kind to thank you for helping them. It's a big deal to have a child named after you. Now, what do you say?"

"Thank you," Amity says, rushing through the rote phrase. "But I don't even like my name. I've always wanted to be named Cecilia. It's a much better name, especially for a princess."

I can't help it. It demonstrates a lapse in my parenting skills, but I let out a pained groan.

Evander remains still, a forced grin plastered on his face as he glances nervously at Ellie.

But then Ellie laughs, a rather neurotic cackle that sounds like something that would hurt considering the labor she just went through. Indeed, she grasps her stomach, squinting in pain, but she keeps laughing, tears pouring down her cheeks.

"Oh. I can't...I can't catch...my breath," she cries, her laughter contagious, and now Evander is laughing too, and so am I, which is unfortunate given my broken ribs.

The only one not laughing is Amity, who shrugs and goes back to reading her grimoire.

After a long while, Ellie leans her head back against the bags. "Evander, does Cecilia work for you?"

"I actually kind of like it," he says.

"Alright. It's settled then," she laughs.

"Hello, Cecilia Thornwall," says Evander, grinning down at his daughter, who appears rather apathetic regarding her naming.

Just then, Amity jumps.

"Amity, you need to say thank you—"

"Blaise's thread," she says, pointing to something in her grimoire.

I raise a brow.

"Flax is used for making thread," says Amity, rushing toward the baggage, rummaging through Blaise's things, which overprepared Amity had packed in haste in case we needed anything of hers. "I knew Blaise didn't seem like the kind of person who likes to weave for fun..."

She pulls out a bundle of thread, then throws a string into the fire, collecting the ash in a jar.

"What's she doing?" asks Evander.

"I'm saving my father, obviously," she says.

THREE DAYS LATER, Evander paces outside my and Amity's tent, rubbing a blister into the back of his neck.

I let him for a few minutes, then decide it would be kinder to put my poor friend out of his misery. I recognize the source of his anxiety and could probably give him a break by telling him I already know what he's going to say.

Evander needs to learn to say these things himself, though, so I drag my still-exhausted body out of my tent and wait.

Evander halts, sweeping his gaze over me. "How are you feeling?"

I shrug. "My muscles still feel weak, but I can tell I'm at least headed in the right direction. Better than I was a few days ago."

"So Amity's drug is working then?"

"She has me on a strict regimen. Apparently the drug isn't a cure for the poison, but it keeps it from progressing and alleviates most of the symptoms." I can't help but beam. "She's a genius, that one. Not sure where she gets it."

My joke doesn't land, which is a testament to how consumed Evander's attention is with whatever he's about to tell me.

Evander nods absentmindedly. "Ellie's getting her strength back too."

The corners of my mouth lift into a smile that I hope comes across as patient.

Evander stops and takes a deep breath. "Marcus, I...I can't tell you how much it means to me, and to Ellie, what you and Amity have done for us. For Cecilia. I don't...I can't imagine going through the past few days without either of you." He puts his hands on his hips and stares at the ground, biting the inside of his cheek as he shakes his head. "But I have to take them back home. Ellie's getting better, but she's been through so much. And Cecilia is still so young. I want both of them seen by a healer. I can't..." His sea-green eyes water with sorrow. "I can't go with you to find Piper. And I know that makes me a cruddy person, after all you've done. I know..." He trails off, looking me in the eye.

"I know," I say, clapping Evander on the back. He startles.

"You know?"

"You're not responsible for my family. I am. Piper and Amity—they come first. And you have to do the same for Ellie and Cecilia. It's what's right."

Evander looks as if he doesn't believe me. His shoulders are tensed, like he's awaiting a blow to the jaw.

"Listen to me," I say. "It's not that Amity and I won't miss your company. But it seems to me that you got yourself into this mess by putting someone else's needs above your family's. Am I right in thinking that?"

Evander clenches his teeth. He says nothing, but that's answer enough. After a moment, he swallows and says, "You stood watch. You protected us from the Others while Ellie was going into labor."

"Need I remind you that the entire reason Ellie went into labor is the fact that she threw herself between Amity and an Other? For which I am eternally grateful."

Evander nods. "Any resource you need—if I don't have it with me, I'll find a way to get it for you when I get back to Othian."

I've been considering this the past few days. "Any resources your father could spare to help me locate Piper would be helpful. I know he isn't the most amiable person, but if you could convince him, I'd be grateful. Either way, if you could use your royal influence to get a message to the Avelean court quickly, I'd be appreciative."

Evander raises his brow, so I explain, "My sister is employed by the King of Avelea. She might also be able to convince him to help."

"And what about you?" Evander asks. "What's your next move?"

I think of Piper, my lovely wife, her thoughtful ponderings, her cleverness, the beautiful way she loves Amity, the way she gets lost in her music. "Me? I'm going to track down my wife."

CHAPTER 52

BLAISE

"*Y*ou're saying that you believe the Old Magic cursed me instead of you?" Nox enunciates his words carefully, one after the other, as he stares me down.

I've backed all the way to the other side of the cave now, unable to bear the humiliation of the one-sided passion that's threatening to shred my heart into ribbons.

"I don't know for sure. But he seemed so intent on punishing me for threatening Asha's life. And he did say I wasn't the one he cursed. But think about it, Nox: I betrayed Asha to get you back. The Old Magic told me himself that when Abra betrayed him all those years ago by going back on her promise not to tell anyone about him or his siblings, he cursed the fae with the inability to lie. It's what killed Farin."

Nox flinches at the name, and I can't help but wonder what happened on the island that he hasn't divulged yet.

"The Old Magic likes for his punishments to be poetic. And what's more poetic than taking away your love for me, when you were exactly what I betrayed Asha for in the first place?"

I feel stupid as soon as the assumption leaves my mouth. "Of course, I'm not saying I deserve your love. I understand if it's just that you've realized what kind of person I am. I understand if all it is, is that you don't want to be with someone who is so willing to betray her friends…"

Nox shakes his head. "Blaise, stop, please. I think you're right. I'm not…" He winces, but continues. "I'm not happy with you right now for what you did. It makes me sick, honestly. But I crossed realms just to get to you. I sacrificed… Blaise, that kind of love doesn't just vanish overnight. The feelings I had for you before—they were gone as soon as I woke. Before I had any idea the lengths you had gone to in order to rescue me."

The smallest gasp of pain escapes my lips.

He looks up at me and frowns. "I'm being too technical, too blunt."

I cross my arms and fight back the tears, but I shake my head. "I don't want you to sugarcoat it for me."

"I think you're right, that I must be the one the Old Magic cursed."

I let out a huff, a mingled laugh and sob. "You came back for me. You stepped between me and Evander back there."

Nox's voice is steady. "I did."

"Why?" I ask.

Nox blinks, as if unsure where the disconnect between us is. "Because he was about to break you."

In other words, Nox would have done it for anyone.

WE SPEND the day discussing a plan, even though formulating one feels futile.

"I have to get Asha away from Az," I say. "I can't just let him…" My throat closes up as my imagination runs away with all sorts of violence a male like Az might enact against the object of his obsession. But there's a wicked, selfish part of me that longs to go to Asha for another reason, a part of me that hopes freeing Asha will somehow aid me in convincing the Old Magic to break the curse on Nox.

I refuse to lend credence to that motivation by acknowledging it aloud. I'm already a terrible enough person as it is. No need to share those kinds of thoughts.

"I don't see how getting Asha away from Az is possible. Not with that host of Others under his control," Nox says.

I tug at my braid. "I was able to take down several of them."

Nox shakes his head. "Several. Not a host. Even with two of us, there's too many of them to take down an army of them on our own."

On our own.

Neither of us brings up the idea of asking my friends for help.

Mostly because I don't have any of those anymore.

Neither does Nox, I realize.

"Now, if we could find a way to transfer control of the beasts from Az to us, that could present an opportunity to rescue her. Tell me again what Az's ritual was like."

I frown, but relay Az spreading his blood in ghostly runes on the thin air. Then I add, "I still don't know how that helps us, unless we find some way to corral a host of Others through the same hole."

Nox nods in agreement. "Did Az mention any other theories about how he might control them? Things he tried, but didn't work out?"

I shake my head. "No, I think he had his method of controlling them planned for a while. It was getting the Rip opened where he devoted most of his energy. He even tried to get ahold of a Gifted woman in Avelea. Thought she'd be easier to obtain than Asha. Until he found me, that is. Ironically enough, Abra got ahold of her. Apparently, the girl's Gift has to do with her music. We're still not sure what she was planning to do with her. Only that they were on their way to Mystral."

"Did Abra ever find out that you'd put Farin and me to sleep?" Nox asks.

"Not that I know of."

"Maybe it had something to do with him, then. He does seem to be the only thing in the world she cares about, and if she was headed back to Mystral instead of the Rip…"

"Yeah, maybe she was hoping Piper would enchant Farin back to loving her again." I snort.

Nox shifts uncomfortably. "I know you're joking, but it's not out of the realm of possibility."

Nox and I lock eyes for an uncomfortable moment, but then he clears his throat. "I doubt something like that would have been sustainable. I imagine the effects of the girl's music wears off over time, just as the emotions evoked by any tune would."

"Right, of course," I say, feeling stupid for hoping.

"However," Nox says, and I can practically feel the wheels in his head turning. "It does make me wonder what kind of effect her music could have on a being of lesser sentience."

"Like an Other, you mean?"

Nox sucks in a breath. "That's exactly what I mean."

CHAPTER 53

KIRAN

*B*y the time the scent of the mysterious incense my father burned fades, and I come to my senses, something is very, very wrong.

For one, I can't move my limbs. It's a struggle, but I peel my eyes open. The room is swirling with smoke, except it's the type I can't control. It covers every filthy corner of my father's cottage.

Knobs from the floorboards jut into my back, causing knots in my muscles.

How long have I lain here?

Fin.

Fin?

I have to will my muscles to obey me, but I turn my head, where I find my brother lying beside me. He's alert, his eyes boiling with rage, but he also seems to be struggling to move.

We exchange a look, and then he peels his head away from me.

"I really am sorry, kids." My father's figure appears, his silhouette a shadow forming in the haze of the smoke. "I wanted to care for you. Always thought I'd be overjoyed if you showed up at my door. But the two of you...you're just a reminder. A reminder that your mother never loved me. That she used me to get her pregnant, used me to produce heirs for her husband. I thought...I thought seeing you would change that. That I'd glimpse myself in you. But all I see is what she took from me." He swallows, then turns toward the fog, tilting his head. Another pair of figures appear from the haze. "I really am sorry. I did try," he says again, as if he thinks that means anything at all.

I reach for my fire, but hard as I try to dig for it, my hands come up empty.

Where is it? A byproduct of the magical incense, perhaps, one that hampers magic while it's being absorbed into the bloodstream?

I fight against the restraints digging into my torso, arms, and legs, but it's no use. Not when I'm struggling to even get my limbs to obey me.

The males above us wear masks that match my father's, ones that I assume filter out the effects of the incense.

"Should we dispose of the spare?" one of them asks, nodding toward Fin.

Panic rises in my chest, but the other shakes his head. "No, we have commands to bring both of them back alive. But we're allowed to torture this one if that one misbehaves," he says, glaring at me.

Commands? Commands from who?

They grab Fin first, hauling him by the ankles and shoulders until they're out of sight. The lopsided door thumps against its frame, slapping against the side of the house as the howling wind flings it around.

My father turns to look over his shoulder, then kneels down, his voice hardly a whisper. "Don't worry, son. Look to your gut for answers. It won't lead you astray."

Right. Because his gut has so obviously led him in the right direction.

He opens his mouth, as if to say something else, but before he can finish, the men return.

They haul me away and stuff me into a cart next to my brother.

Footsteps fade as they approach the house.

There's the rumble of my father's voice, sounding confused that they've returned.

Then there's a scream, and the squirting of blood.

And the sound of something wet and pliable dropping against the floor.

The sound of my father's heart, still beating as it was wrenched from his body, taps against my ears the entire journey.

CHAPTER 54

ASHA

By the time Blaise's venom wears off, we're miles away from Rivre.

From the bloodbath that surely ensued as my friends tried to rescue me.

The wagon bumps across the uneven terrain, and shooting pain darts up my back, but at least Az allows me to sit upright.

I suppose he has more room now that Nox's body is gone, though Nox's sister's body remains with us.

It makes my chest tight, thinking about her. As helpless as I am to suffer Az's whims, at least I'm awake to know what's being done to me.

Az watches me from across the dark wagon, though I can't help but feel he looks distracted, an opaque sheen covering his sage-green eyes like a chrysalis over a moth.

I knew even in my stupor that consuming the mere's blood had changed him.

There's a subtle glow to him now, as if moonlight itself inhabits his body, though it's faded somewhat in the hours we've been in transit. I'm not sure if that's because the effects of the mere blood are working their way through his system, or because we're traveling further from the Rip.

The Rip.

The Rip where my friends' bodies have surely joined Gwenyth's by now.

I try my utmost to slice through the fog that Blaise's venom wrapped around my mind during the ambush. As if remembering just who it was who tried to save me would allow me to honor them better in their death.

I still can't place the voice, hard as I try.

Fates, I just hope Amity wasn't nearby.

Amity.

My hands are still bound, my mouth still gagged, but as I wriggle around, as if to adjust myself, I can feel the bulge of a belt against my belly. Amity's survival kit.

It's a good thing Blaise never let Az search my person. Though it's about the only thing I can thank the traitor for.

Not that I'm convinced Amity's survival pack will actually help given my situation, but it's a comfort to me, nonetheless.

"I can't untie you, but I can at least offer you this," Az says, misunderstanding the reason for my fidgeting. He leans across the wagon, brushing his fingers through my hair and untying my gag. I wince at his touch. My scalp is still sore from where I was dragged across the ground by my hair by a mere.

Az frowns. "I'm so sorry it hurts. I couldn't risk the mere biting into your flesh. Their venom is also a paralytic, and I didn't know what it would do to you with Blaise's venom already in your system."

He allows the gag to fall to the floor, and I spit out the wad of fabric that's been blocking my mouth.

I don't expect to, but I let out the quietest of sobs. My jaw is still sore from the gag, and it almost feels wrong to move it. But having the gag gone...

I can't help the tears that flow freely from my eye, the hiccups that jump from my throat in laborious gasps.

"I'm so sorry I had to do that," Az says again, still stroking his

321

fingers through my sweat-matted hair. His touch, the touch I once craved, is slimy against my skin, and I want to cower from it.

I can't do that, I realize.

With my gag finally gone, there are so many things I want to scream, so many insults to hurl. I want to tell him I hate him, and I want to find daggers for words to say it. I want to take the parts of Az I know so well, the weaknesses and insecurities I know from years of idolizing his every move...I want to take them and squeeze, to lance his wounds with a scalpel and bring their rancid infection to light.

But I can't. Not if I want Az to trust me.

One last time, I reach for my Old Magic, ask him a question.

It's the faintest of movements in my chest. As if he's shaking his head *No, no, we aren't close enough to the Rip to use that sort of power.*

I continue to let the tears fall.

"That's okay. Cry as much as you need," Az whispers, and I can't help but recall the night I comforted him over my impending death.

I'll have to be smart about this if I want him to believe me. He's clearly convinced himself that it's Kiran's power over my emotions that makes me hate him. Rather than the fact that he almost caused the death of my sister. That shows he's willing, eager even, to believe there remains hope for mending our relationship.

Still, Az, deluded as he might be, is not a total idiot. Even if he is a fool, he's a paranoid one, and if I push too hard to convince him of my love, he might interpret it for what it is—an attempt to trick him.

No, I have to be smarter about this.

So I lean into the tears, welcome the urge to sob, and whisper, "I don't know what's real anymore. I don't know...I don't know what's real..."

He goes to touch me again, to comfort me, and I flinch violently. He draws his hand away with a start, and I peer up at him, widening my eye in confusion.

Az frowns, though there's a condescension to it. "That's a good sign. If you're doubting your feelings. It means the effect Kiran had over you is fading."

I allow horror to flash across my face, and he frowns again.

I squeeze my eye shut, tucking my knees into my arms, my bound hands serving as their anchor. "I'm so scared, Az. I'm so scared of what will happen to me when...when..."

"When you can finally believe it wasn't real."

I nod, hiccuping again. Then I let out something between a strangled sob and a wail.

"I don't want it not to have been real. I don't want to have not had a choice..." I shudder, and I let Az's mind run away with what exactly I was dreading realizing had not been my choice.

When I look up at him, I realize I've hit my mark. Jealousy sluices off of him in torrential waves. It's working.

He reaches for me again, but I cower, quickly biting my lip. "I'm sorry. I'm sorry. It's like I know logically that you're not going to hurt me. But the feelings swarm up, and..."

Az nods his head. "Feelings are difficult to ignore. We'll get through this, Asha. His hold over you will fade, but until then, I can be patient."

It takes all the effort in the world to give him a grateful smile, when I want nothing more than to vomit at the thought.

"Think you could distract me?" I ask.

He arches a brow, and I shrug. "I haven't talked to you in over a year. I thought maybe we could catch up." I shake my head, taking in a breath. "Not about me. I don't want to talk about...Please. Just tell me something, anything, so I don't have to think about..."

Az doesn't seem to want me to finish my sentence, because he nods and begins. "When Calias's plan failed, I made a run for it. Fates, Asha. I couldn't stop thinking about what I'd done. I thought Dinah was dead, and that it was all my fault. It had never been my intention for her to actually come in harm's way. I believed that Calias would spare her if you did as you were told, but I was still naïve then. I'd forgotten to have him specify under a fae oath that he wouldn't command any harm to come to her if you obeyed. I was sick over it for months."

Even in the dim lantern light, Az's expression seems to pale, almost as if he truly believes the lies he weaves.

"Thankfully, I'd made connections while apprenticing with Tijan, and I had my wife's dowry."

Ah. Right. I forgot about her.

The fae female Az slept with so her aristocrat parents would agree to let her marry him, ensuring wealth at Az's disposal.

I allow myself to look sick, an honest emotion given the circumstances, but one I hope Az will interpret as jealousy.

Apparently it works, because Az shakes his head. "I haven't had contact with her in over a year. Turns out running off with a female's dowry doesn't exactly strengthen one's marriage. But none of that matters. I used the funds to hire a bounty hunter to capture the Red. Blaise told me you were searching for her, too."

Ugh. Has Blaise been relaying everything back to Az?

There's a part of me that hopes her plan to get Nox back didn't work. I instantly feel guilty, as that likely isn't fair to Nox.

Though maybe he's found someone nicer than Blaise to settle down with in his other life. Or maybe he's just as backstabbing as she is and doesn't deserve happiness.

"Anyway, that plan failed, considering my bounty hunter never returned to me. I assumed he had been bought out by a higher bidder, which I suppose he had. I just wasn't expecting it to be the Red herself."

Marcus. Has the poison made its way to his vital organs yet? I feel sick.

"I'd even sent Tijan to buy her from an auction. Should have expected him not to win the bid, though. He's too conservative with money for his own good. Isn't willing to take risks. Anyway, I decided then I'd change course, try to find someone else to open the Rip for me. There were reports of a Gifted girl kept as a servant in the house of the King of Avelea, but she seemed too well-guarded to risk taking. Then there were reports of several humans who had dropped dead overnight, their neighbors suspicious that they'd been dabbling in dark magic. That trail led me to Dwellen, where I traced the parasite, as Blaise calls it, back to her. I thought I'd lost her when I realized she was in the clutches of the Queen of Mystral, but as I was searching for mercenaries who might be willing to retrieve her for me, guess who I happened upon, in an inn of all places?

"Of course, by that point, I was too late. Again. The parasite was gone, and I've heard enough about Queen Abra to know to stay out of her way. No use trying to reason with a crazy person. So I decided I'd change course again. Blaise had a connection to you, and I knew then that the Fates were smiling down on me. It was too much to be a coincidence. Asha, I've wanted so badly to fix things between us, to start over, and it was like the Fates were placing the solution in my lap. I followed Blaise back to Mystral, where I found the runes Nox had used to accidentally bind the parasite to her. I didn't know exactly what they were, of course, but I'd been researching ways to control the Others for quite a while. I thought I already had a solid plan, adapting the bloodsharing ritual of the vampires to exercise control over the Others, but the runes I found were going to make it even easier, bind the Others to me before I even began the bloodsharing ritual, so they wouldn't attack me. It was practically like receiving a seal of approval from the Fates themselves."

I open my mouth. It's going to be a delicate process, assuring Az of my shifting loyalty. I have to still be me if I'm going to convince him, which means sticking to the morals he's so familiar with me holding.

"Az, we've talked about this. Finding answers to the questions you've been searching for doesn't inherently confirm the Fates' approval. You were in the right places at the right time because you placed yourself in those situations. You were able to recognize the patterns and connections because your mind was already searching for them. It...it scares me to hear you take your own ambitions and ascribe them to the Fates."

Az takes my hand, this time ignoring my shudder at his touch. He only squeezes it tighter. "Is that really how you feel? Or is that how he wanted you to feel?"

I blink, shaking my head, as if bewildered. "I don't know. I don't know if I can tell the difference."

Az has the audacity to look pleased. "We just have to give it time, Asha. You'll see."

I won't, but at least he doesn't seem to know that.

"Let me show you something," he says, shuffling awkwardly around me, scooting me to the edge of the covered wagon, close to the flap.

The whole process of him dragging me is rather humiliating, not to mention painful, but I don't think it prudent to mention as much.

Az gives me one last look, a crazed grin overtaking his face.

He opens the flap, and my heart sinks.

Behind us, coats of silver glimmer in the moonlight. I haven't heard them, their padded steps as silent as a prayer.

The Others follow in ranks, not only mere, but other species. Some with scales and wings and fangs dripping with silvery venom.

There are legions of them.

CHAPTER 55

ZORA

I've never died before. At least, not to my knowledge.

I'm sure most people could make a similar assertion, but most people don't live multiple lives either.

At least, they don't seem to remember living multiple lives.

Not that my knowledge is perfect. It's a lot to keep up with. Honestly, one life is enough to keep up with. A friend told me once that he sometimes thinks about all the days he's lived that don't make it into his memory banks. How it was crazy that though that conversation was happening, we might not remember it at all. Entire days add up to weeks and years, all lost to our imperfect memories.

I don't remember which life I had that conversation in, but I suppose that's the point I'm trying to make.

It's a lot to keep up with, living dozens of lives, only getting glimpses of them in my memories, and even then, never quite able to sort which belongs where.

So I don't find it quite fair when others call me flighty, vapid, scatterbrained. Fleeting.

But that's also beside the point.

Where was I? Am I?

Oh yeah.

I'm dying.

There's a throbbing pain in my side where Farin's knife protrudes, and the feel of blood slipping from my veins, draining my life and consciousness with it.

I wonder what will happen to me when I die.

I wonder if I'll wake again, in another body, as I always do.

For some reason, I doubt it.

This feels final.

At least Nox gets to have his happy ending.

Mine might not be happy, but it is an ending, so there's that, at least.

"No," Farin shouts as Nox trips backward through the eyelet. Farin launches himself at it, dodging the scrambling tarantula. For a moment, I think he might make it, but then it slips from his fingertips, forming into nothing more than a wall slated with spiderwebs.

I allow myself a gargled laugh.

It's probably my last, considering the tarantula has regained its footing and is currently pivoting toward me, its pincers glistening in the effervescent light of its web.

Earlier, I thought being eaten by a giant scorpion was the worst way a person could go.

Now that I'm staring into the eight black orbs that make this tarantula's eyes, I've decided otherwise.

I scramble backward on my elbows, leaving a path of smeared blood across the cave floor.

I quickly discover this plan of action is not going to work.

The spider closes the gap between us with the ease of a single step, its long spindly legs covering the distance.

I'm not entirely sure, because my blood loss is causing my senses to fade, but I'm fairly certain I gag.

It's probably more like a retch if I'm to be perfectly honest.

Dread encompasses me, and though I try to push myself up, my hands slip on the blood-slick floor.

I hate Farin. The male doesn't even have the decency to kill me properly, and now I'm going to be eaten before I can bleed out from my knife wound in peace.

The spider clicks its pincers together greedily, then attacks.

I brace myself for a slow and agonizing death, hoping whatever goo is dripping from those pincers is an analgesic as well as a paralytic.

What barrels into my body doesn't feel like pincers, though, and it comes from the side, sending me sliding across the floor.

There's a crunch, and when I turn my head, I find that underneath the spider's massive body is Farin, whose dagger—the one he swiped from my belt and used to stab me—is twisting upward into the spider's thorax.

The spider writhes, its legs scrambling with panic as it tries to retreat, but Farin just rips the dagger from the spider's belly before stabbing it again. And again.

An image flashes over my imagination of a child torturing a spider for fun.

Black ichor sprays Farin's face as he butchers the spider's underside with his knife—no, *my knife*—a feral smile on his face.

I take it back.

I think I'd rather the spider eat me.

Since Farin and the spider are now occupied with each other, I take the opportunity to crawl away, but I don't even make it back to the tunnels before my body decides it needs to conserve blood, and that my limbs aren't what need it most at the moment.

I collapse on my side against the cave floor in time to hear the spider screech. I turn my head to watch as it crumples over, its legs shriveling up at its flayed abdomen.

Farin stands, wiping the ichor off his face.

He looks to be contemplating whether he'll hack the legs off the corpse for good measure.

Slowly, though, the high of the fight fades from his expression, and he turns toward the wall where Nox disappeared through the eyelet a few moments ago. He traces the empty wall with his careful fingers, like he thinks he'll find a secret latch that will open a hidden door.

"Looks like you're stuck here with me," I say. I'm rather certain teasing the psychopath is only going to get me killed faster, but obviously my body has redirected my blood from my brain at this point.

Farin turns, his face white with panic. He's still touching the bare wall with his fingers, though his back is now turned to it.

"No," he says again, but this time it's more of a whisper.

I might be tempted to feel bad for him, except he's the one who just stabbed me.

He brings his hand to his forehead, rubbing the spot underneath his hairline and pacing as he thinks.

Then his ears flick, and he snaps his gaze toward the wound that occurred at his own hands.

A moment later he's by my side, using his outer tunic as a bandage. The wound aches as he applies pressure to it, binding it with the fabric of his shirt.

"What are you doing?" I ask.

"What does it look like, Wanderer? I'm saving you."

My side hurts a little less now, though I'm almost certain that's not a good thing. "Why?"

Farin's eyes flit to me underneath his eyelashes, but he doesn't answer. At least not directly.

"You're still bleeding," he says. Rather obvious, if I say so myself, considering the rag is soaked through.

"That is what tends to happen when you stab someone."

"You're fae. Your body should be healing faster than this."

I frown, furrowing my brow more dramatically than the occasion finally warrants, but if this is going to be my only time to die, I think I'm warranted some dramatics.

"Ah," I say, finally understanding. My thoughts are coming to me in sloshes. "You're used to the fae healing quickly. That doesn't work here. Only in some worlds."

Farin's face goes blank, but he says nothing as his outer tunic comes off and he uses it to bandage my wound.

Then Farin lifts me into his arms and carries me away.

I fall asleep with my face tucked into his chest.

. . .

I WAKE to the scent of searing flesh. A cry escapes my lips as something burns at my waist.

"I'm sorry. I know this hurts, but it's necessary. Here," Farin says, handing me a rag that he places rather roughly in my mouth. I bite down on it, peeking through my eyelashes, still flirting with passing out.

He's holding what looks to be a brand, glowing hot as a lone ember.

Then he presses it to my bare waist.

Pain overwhelms me, but this time I force my cry into the rag inside my mouth, bearing down on my teeth like somehow I can focus on the pain there rather than the searing of my flesh.

It helps. Not by much, but I'm taking what I can get at this point.

Farin stares down at the burn site, sighing as he runs his hands through his hair. If I didn't know better, I'd say he looks distressed.

Probably just me being delusional.

Agony tends to do that to a person.

"I really am sorry," he says again, and then pain assaults my skin so completely, I lose consciousness.

WHEN I WAKE AGAIN, it's still to the scent of burning flesh, but this time it's a significantly more pleasant odor. The scent of a boar roasting over a fire, I realize, as I open my eyes and take in my surroundings.

Farin and I are still in a cave, though there's a glaring absence of spiderwebs, for which I'm grateful. He paces beyond the smoking boar, practically drilling a path in the dirt with his repetitive steps.

He glances over at me as he tugs at his sleeves, then stops in his tracks.

"You're awake," he says, to which I, probably stupidly, respond, "Your deduction skills amaze me."

331

Farin blinks, then actually lets out a huff that's suspiciously familiar to a laugh as a smile quirks at his lips. Just barely.

"How did we get out?" I groan.

"I carried you, Wanderer."

I furrow my brow. I might be disoriented, but I'm fairly sure Farin didn't strap me to his back and free climb up the side of the canyon.

He must read my mind, because he says, "The canyon levels out eventually. If the two of you had figured that out, I wouldn't have had to rush to trail you."

Huh. I suppose Nox and I should have followed the canyon in the other direction.

I go to sit up, but the aching in my abdomen prevents it, and I let out a sharp cry. Farin's at my side in the next instant, propping me up with his hands gliding down my back.

They're strangely warm, not at all the cold, clammy things I'm expecting.

I suppose he's not a vampire, though.

"You probably shouldn't do much moving around," Farin says. "I can't say I'm all that confident in my repair attempts." He nods to my waist. It's bare, Farin having rolled up my shirt to my ribcage.

"To let the wound breathe," he explains, actually clearing his throat.

"Why else would you have done it?" I ask, unable to fight the edge in my voice.

He ignores me, but he lowers me back to the floor all the same, wrapping his cloak around itself to make a pillow for my head. His fingers linger in my hair for a moment, before he quickly pulls away and returns to the other side of the cave.

"Why'd you save me?" I ask, peering at him past what I'm sure is a double chin.

Farin pokes at the boar. "I didn't mean for you to almost die. I didn't realize your body couldn't heal itself in a timely fashion."

"Yes, but why do you care?"

Farin shrugs. "I figure I'm not getting off this island, out of this world, without your help, am I?"

Oh. Right.

Well, he's not getting off this island with it, either.

"And what if there's not another way?" I ask.

Farin flashes me a grin, the same one that caught my attention the first day we met. "Well, then. I suppose you and I have this island to ourselves."

I let out a scoff, which rather upsets my still aching abdomen.

"You don't seem too worried about that outcome," I say.

His smile is as sinister as it is beautiful. "I'm not concerned about finding ways to entertain ourselves, if that's what you mean."

My cheeks heat, and I glance away, but I can only keep my eyes averted for a moment. Turning my attention from a murderer doesn't seem like the best self-preservation instinct, after all.

He's right though; I need to get off this island. And fast. I just have to figure out a way to do it without Farin tagging along.

Somehow, I doubt he'll let his guard down long enough for me to kill him.

I turn my attention back to him, hoping he doesn't notice.

That proves to be ineffective, given he's still watching me. This time, it's his turn to glance away. Just not before I catch the glimmer of concern in his assessing gaze.

CHAPTER 56

KIRAN

*T*he males who shoved Fin and me in the back of this cart must have taken the entirety of our father's incense supply, because one of them comes to burn it directly under our noses once every few hours.

I'm trying to keep up with the days, but it proves difficult when I'm unsure how long the incense knocks me out. Judging from the cycles of light and darkness I've been able to keep up with in my waking hours, I know we've been trapped in the back of the wagon for at least several days by the time the wagon comes to its ultimate stop.

"Welcome home," says one of the males, climbing atop me and Fin, not bothering to watch where he steps. Then he lights the incense, and I am lost to oblivion.

I WAKE, not in a dungeon as I expect, but on a marble balcony facing the city of Meranthi, the city I've called home my entire life. I recognize it immediately as an alcove specifically made for nobility to watch the royal ceremonies occurring on the main balcony of the palace.

The alcoves are carved directly into the marble of the palace and hewn to block the sun from the onlookers. The placement affords their tenants privacy from the crowd.

And there is a crowd.

I can tell by the murmurs the wind carries up to the balcony, along with the dust, though most of the crowd itself I can't see through the marble wall. The stage, on the other hand, is in full view below. It's been decorated with crimson sashes and a litany of rose petals.

It's a relief when, even through my grogginess, I find I can at least turn my head slightly. Doing so reveals Fin beside me, his gaze fixed on the balcony below, a sort of deadness in his eyes I've never witnessed.

"What in Alondria is going on?" he says, his voice dry with dehydration and disuse.

I stare down at the balcony below and heave a sigh. "I believe," I say, fighting the slur in my words, "that we're about to witness a coronation."

By the time the ceremony begins, Fin and I have had our faculties returned to us long enough to infer that Azrael must have figured out our illegitimate heritage. That seems to be the most reasonable explanation for what is going on, given our sleazy father sold us to the highest bidder. It seems just as likely that he also peddled the information of our heritage to Azrael's hired hands, a fact that would have easily been confirmed by demanding the vizier's records be made public.

The vizier. The acid in my gut sours at the thought of him.

At the thought of what Azrael might have done to him upon discovering the truth of my heritage.

"Is it possible that we accelerated exactly what we were trying to prevent?" asks Fin.

"Seems more probable than anything," I respond.

He sighs, leaning his head back and resting it on the back of the chair to which he's strapped.

There's a guard stationed outside the balcony, which has had bars added to it since I'd last been home, but he hasn't responded to either my or Fin's inquiries.

It appears even my guards don't answer to me anymore.

For the first time since Asha and I split our paths, I'm grateful for our separation. At least if Azrael had to discover the truth that he is the rightful heir to the throne of Naenden, Asha is far away from civilization at the moment, safe in the ambiguity of the plains of Charshon.

I don't exactly trust that the King of Dwellen wouldn't have handed her over to prevent agitating the new ruler of Naenden, had Azrael asked for her.

Trumpets sound, and the ceremony begins, Fin fidgeting in the seat next to me.

Somewhat to my relief, the vizier steps out of the double doors first, a hush going out over the crowd.

My heart leaps to see my old friend, the only true father figure I've ever had, is still alive, but something also twists in my gut at the sight of him.

How is he convincing Azrael to keep him alive?

Rule one of a coup is to wipe out all those loyal to the crown. Azrael might be inexperienced in court politics, but he's as crafty as they come, and paranoid, too. Surely he would have had the vizier swear allegiance to him, under a binding fae oath.

Something bitter wells up in me at that. Not that I wish the vizier would have died for my sake. But the change in loyalty leaves my chest tender.

The crowd quiets at the beckoning of the vizier, and when he speaks, his voice bellows across the crowd.

"I'm sure you are all wondering about the change in leadership that has recently occurred in Naenden. That is precisely why His Majesty thought it best that I present to you the records of his succession, as well as those of the previous owner of the throne."

The vizier pulls out a scroll, one I recognize even from this distance. The scroll that records my and Fin's birth, as well as our parentage. The secret the vizier kept for the sake of my mother all these years.

I'm surprised at the flush that creeps up my back and neck as he reads of my mother's relationship with Solomon. He doesn't go into detail, whether of his own volition or at the command of Azrael, I do not know.

But he reads it all the same.

The sound of my father's heart slapping the ground, still beating, thuds in my mind.

I shouldn't care, and I don't. Not really, that he's dead.

He betrayed us, after all.

So why does the sound of his heart taking its last beat reverberate in my mind? Why does it make me think of my mother, the questions that have always surrounded her death?

When he gets to the part about my mother's affair, the crowd mutters angrily, and I can't help but notice Fin shaking in the chair next to me.

"Never mind why she did it. Never mind that..." Fin stops himself, glancing at and away from me quickly.

But I don't have time to ponder about what Fin means, because the vizier continues.

"It is with great..." the vizier pauses, "obeisance, I introduce to you, one of your own, Azrael, son of Rajeen, rightful heir to the throne, the rightful King of Naenden."

There's a moment of silence, but then the doors swing wide again, and out marches Azrael, clothed in the garb not of a king, but of the city dwellers. Of the humans who dwell in Meranthi.

Fin curses.

My stomach plummets at the same time the crowd erupts into cheers.

Azrael basks in the applause for a moment, though it's all in his stance and not at all in his face. Then, with a simple gesture, he quiets the crowd and speaks.

"Friends. Family. There's a part of me that wishes I'd been trained in how to give a speech. Something that might make me sound regal.

Less like the commoner I am. But then I think...no. Because isn't that what's separated us from our leaders all this time? I stand here, the..." He acts as if struggling with the weight of what he's about to say. "The heir to the throne of Naenden. But then I look out on all of you. And I see Vinley. You sold me my first knife. Do you remember that?" He lets a brilliant smile loose on the female to whom he's speaking. "And Bezzie. How many times did you yell at me to stop leaning on your counters?"

I can't see Bezzie's reaction from the alcove, but the sound of her name strikes a chord in me. Does Asha's elderly friend support the coup?

"Arun"—the sound of Asha's father's name makes my chest want to crack in two—"how many snakes did the two of us round up together in your home?"

My eyes search for Asha's father in the crowd, but if he's there, I can't pick him out.

Azrael looks out into the distance, as if into the hovels themselves. "I'm just one of you. The offspring of a mother who worked too hard to face the end that she did. I wasn't raised for this. Wasn't groomed and brought up at the feet of tutors. I know...I know the feeling of a belly that never quite gets full. I know how it feels when the shadows are your only respite from the heat of the midday sun. I know you," he says, pointing to a child in the crowd. He reaches out his hand and lifts her up onto the stage with him, her grimy hand interlocked with his.

My fists dig into the chair to which I'm tied, my chest going hollow, as the crowd radiates love, adoration. Hope.

Hope.

Something I was never able to give them. Something I stole from them. Something Asha returned.

"Kiran." When Fin says my name, his voice is soft, possibly for the first time in years, but I can't bear to look at him. Can't bear to see the pity in his eyes. The pity I don't deserve.

Because what I deserve has finally happened, and I have the best seat in the house.

"Don't you think it's strange that he's got us up here watching, when he could be executing us to make a point?" Fin asks. Part of me wonders if my brother's trying to interrupt the guilt that threatens to strangle me, to focus my attention on the immediate problem, that Azrael has us prisoner.

"No, at least not the part about making us watch. I know exactly why he's doing that," I say, even as my chest threatens to crack.

I dive for my Flame, but it doesn't stir.

The memory of Solomon's leeching stone, smooth in my hand, chills my memory.

"I don't know how to do this on my own," says Az, and I watch him lure the people in with honey, watch as the crowd leans into him, hanging on his every word. "But we have each other. And..." He bursts into the most genuine-looking smile I've ever witnessed. "And I have some help."

He gestures, and the guards open the marble doors once again.

There's a pause as the guards retrieve whoever is standing on the other side.

When they coax the woman out onto the balcony, my entire body goes numb.

Fin strains against his bindings.

Something roars distantly in my ears.

Because out steps Asha.

Dressed head to toe in a scarlet wedding gown.

CHAPTER 57

EVANDER

I stand outside the office of a male I would have rather avoided, but desperate times call for desperate measures, and this is one of those times.

Ellie and I only made it back to Othian yesterday.

The servants have been fawning over Ellie and little Cecilia, their lips profuse with apologies for not being attentive enough to realize Ellie was pregnant. I think all the attention, including that of both sets of our parents, is driving Ellie insane.

No one has paid a speck of attention to me, which is fine. The time will come for my father to berate me about my failure to protect my family at the Rip. I'll deserve the verbal lashing I'll get once he discovers the entire story.

That's the last time I'll ever allow my father to be right about me.

I knock on the oak door, tangled with carefully manicured and pruned vines, because of course the male just has to show off his natural talents, even on his office door.

There's shuffling, and after a few minutes of what I'm fairly sure is a male pulling pants on, the door creaks open, and out peers Orion Elmroot.

He's a male several decades older than me, close to my father's age, if I remember correctly.

To be honest, I remember little about the season of my life that involved Orion.

"Your Highness," says Orion by way of greeting, though there is scant hospitality to his tone.

Orion is a fae of tall build, dark brown hair, and skin the color of tanned parchment. He has the sort of angular face that's particularly unfair, especially when he's also as naturally talented at magic as he is.

The Fates had not distributed advantages evenly when it came to this male, and I suspect he knows it.

"Has your father sent you back here for another round of 'garnering your inherited skill set'?" he asks, little enthusiasm garnishing his tone.

Immediately after Jerad's death, my father had tasked Orion with tutoring me in my magic, my father claiming he hadn't pushed the subject enough when I was in school.

Honestly, I figured my father had wished to punish me, as well as keep me busy enough with Orion's lessons that I didn't have time to bother him with my presence at family dinners. My father's always blamed me for Jerad's death and would have rather not suffered my company.

"Not this time," I say. "This time, it's me who wants the lessons."

Orion cocks an eyebrow, no amusement in the expression. "Now why would you want that, considering our previous attempts were so fruitful? Surely you have nothing left you could possibly learn from me."

I sigh. I hadn't expected Orion to agree without heavy convincing. Our "lessons," which he'd been forced into—probably because my father also hated him, though for entirely different reasons—had consisted of me showing up at his door, in the best cases hungover, in the worst, wasted out of my mind. If I remembered to show up at all, that was.

I don't remember much from our lessons, but I can't imagine I made them all that pleasant for Orion.

"Listen. I can apologize, if that's what you want," I say. "But I figure you probably don't care much for my word or my opinion, so I can't imagine an apology would be all that worthwhile to you."

"Can't argue with that," says Orion, still not bothering to open the door further.

We stand there in silence for a moment. It takes me far too long to realize Orion is waiting for me to produce an argument.

I sigh. "Listen. I know I was a horrible student. My father knew that, and that's why he stuck me with you, so he could make both of us miserable. And I know I haven't touched my magic in years, at least not until a few weeks ago. But when Ellie and I traveled to the Rip, when those things attacked her... Orion, I was helpless. It was like there was all this fear, all this pent-up energy, all this magic welling inside of me, and there was nothing I could do to channel it, control it."

"Magic is like any other muscle. If you refuse to exercise it, it withers," says Orion, going to shut the door.

I stick my hand out, stopping him. "Unless you start exercising it again. Muscle can come back, right? And magic too?"

Orion taps his foot. "It has been a very long time since you've accessed your magic, Evander. You haven't just let the muscle shrink. You've let it atrophy. Wither. Die."

"Yes, I get the idea. Believe it or not, I do know what the word atrophy means," I say. "But my magic's still there. I used it, at the Rip."

Orion frowns. "From what I've surmised, magic becomes more potent the closer it comes to the Rip. If it was weak there, it's probably close to nonexistent here. I don't have an abundance of time to waste, Your Highness."

"No, perhaps not. But it's not exactly wasted time if you're getting paid for it, is it?"

Orion stares at me. "My stipend already compensates for anything I could ever want and more. I don't have to pay for housing or food, since the crown provides as much. And believe it or not, some of us don't feel the need to douse ourselves in extravagant living."

"You live in a castle, Orion. I wouldn't exactly go about claiming you live by humble means."

"I live in the dungeons of a castle, Your Highness. And I quite like it down here. It's quiet, and I don't often receive visitors. Especially ones who are uninvited."

"Am I really a visitor if I'm technically the heir to this castle, including its dungeon?" I ask, which is apparently the wrong thing to say, because Orion goes to shut the door again.

"Wait," I say, too late this time to stick my fingers into the doorway if I don't want them squashed.

The lock bolts behind the door.

Surely there's something I can do to convince him.

"Please." I lean my forehead against the door, the vines scratching my nose. "I couldn't protect them. Ellie—I heard her screaming, and I had to watch as that thing ripped into her. I thought I was going to lose them both, and I knew in that moment that if I'd only tried, I would have had enough magic to save them. I don't know why the Fates granted me a second chance. They know I don't deserve it. Maybe they did it for Ellie and Cecilia, and it didn't have anything to do with me. But whether they meant it for me at all, I still got one. And if I don't use it to protect them, to defend my family, then what does that make me?"

After a moment, Orion's voice drawls from the other side of the door. "I suppose, the same sort of male you've always been."

The words sting, piercing through my ribs, burying their way inside my chest. I want to run off, forget this interaction ever happened. But no. Orion is only speaking the truth.

So I sit in front of his door, propped with my back up against it, pull a manual on vinecasting out of my satchel, and begin to read.

HOURS LATER, when Orion opens the door and finds my weight still against it, so that I almost fall back on him, he groans in irritation.

"How long do you plan on waiting out here?" he asks.

343

"As long as it takes to change your mind."

"You're spoiled rotten, you know that. So used to getting your way, having everything handed to you, you don't know how to be denied."

I shrug, standing to face him and wiping the dust from the dungeon floor off my pants. "So I've been told. And you know, I might have taken that as an insult. But you're correct. I am used to getting what I want. And I do expect what I want to come to me, eventually. But this time, things are a little different."

"And how is that?"

"This time, what I want is for the good of others."

"It benefits you too, you know. For your wife and child to remain safe."

"Yes, but I'm not doing this for me. I'm doing this for them. Because never again am I going to leave them unprotected simply because I've been too lazy to prepare for danger."

Orion sighs, his age showing, if not in his unfairly sculpted features, then in the weariness he carries on his shoulders. I can't help but think being cooped up in this dungeon hasn't treated him well over the years.

Why is he down here again?

Oh. Right.

He told my father off after he practically banished Olwen. Makes sense, as Orion would have seen himself in a prodigy like my sister.

"Fine. If you won't help me to save your princess and an innocent child—"

Orion opens his mouth to protest, but I won't let him finish.

"Then perhaps you'd help me for your own selfish reasons."

"I already told you I don't want money."

"I'm aware. Thankfully, I'm also aware of what you do want."

Orion scowls. "And what is that?"

"Peace and quiet." I offer him the kind of grin only a spoiled prince can perfect. "And until you train me, you won't be getting any."

. . .

THE NEXT DAY, I beat Orion to the sparring ring.

In fact, I'm so prompt, I'm already warmed up by the time he arrives.

Orion glowers at me, dressed in his training leathers.

He then proceeds to slam me in the chest with a vine.

CHAPTER 58

KIRAN

I reach inward, grasping desperately for my magic, for anything. Anything to help me burn this place, burn our home, to get to her.

To get to my wife.

But I'm grasping at the wind.

"No," Fin says. "No, she was supposed to be at the Rip. How..."

She was with Lydia. She can't be here, my mind tries to reassure me, but it's Asha on that balcony, looking out upon the crowd with numbness written all over her lovely face.

Her perfect face.

On which Az has placed a mask.

It's perfectly crafted to her features, a mask of ruby flames that traces the exact curve of her scars, down to partially covering her mouth. It's only the unmarred side of her face that shows, the rest of it glistening with jewels.

That imbecile made her cover her scars.

The thought enrages me, though it doesn't produce the fire I might have hoped.

Fin winces at the sight, jerking in his chair.

Our eyes meet one another, and something like kinship stirs between us.

THE MUSIC BEGINS, and it's the same tune that played at my and Asha's wedding.

I think I might be sick, but I can't peel my eyes off her, try as I might to fight against my restraints, break my chair, anything.

Azrael takes Asha's hands in his, and even from here, I can tell that she's shaking. Shaking like how she was when she married me.

There's no fire left in my veins, but smoke fills my lungs, suffocating me all the same.

They leeched my Flame, and I have nothing left to protect her.

The vizier begins the ceremony, except this time it's a human script, one I've never heard.

The vows are more sentimental, less transactional.

At one point, Azrael promises his body to her, and I want to claw my ears out.

"Kiran," Fin says, glancing at me. "We have to get out of here. We have to stop…" The words seem to fail him, disgust writhing on his features.

I can't hear Asha's voice as she speaks her vows. Even with my fae hearing, her voice doesn't carry like Azrael's and the vizier's.

But I can still see her shaking, still catch the glimmer of the tears streaming down her unmasked cheek.

WHEN THE CEREMONY ENDS, the crowd applauds, and Azrael cups Asha's face in his hands, drawing her in for a kiss.

Her entire body tenses, and I die on the inside.

Azrael presents his queen to the people, and they erupt into cheers.

THERE'S no fire left within me.

Nothing to burn.

I'm flickered out, left to fade.

There's nothing but emptiness where there used to be rage.

They say that fire is consuming, and I'm all used up.

"Kiran," Fin says, his tone desperate, but I can hardly hear him.

"Kiran," he says again, this time louder, and the chains bolting his arms to the steel chair rattle in emphasis.

I will my neck to crane to look at him. Anything to get the image out of my mind, the one stuck on a loop, the one where Azrael takes Asha back to his bedroom.

"Kiran. I'm sorry," says Fin, and for the first time I realize my brother's face is wet with tears. "I'm so, so sorry," he whispers.

And then we both cry.

THERE'S STILL nothing inside me, nothing but the imagined sound of Asha's quiet whimpers replaying in my mind, when the guard outside our cell makes a surprised sound.

Fin snaps his neck to the side. Mine takes longer to remember to look, but when I do, I can't help but notice both our guards are gone.

In their place is a female, one I'd recognize anywhere.

Her milkweed skin glows an even more sickly color in the reflection of the greenish lanterns. She stands there, limbs trembling, on the other side of the cell, but her eggshell eyes have a determined look about them.

Tavi. Asha's lady's maid. Azrael's twin.

Tavi wraps her fingers around the bars of our cell.

And the bars disappear.

"YOU HAVE MAGIC," says Fin, and though there's no question in his tone, I can hear the implication from a fae who was born without it.

Tavi nods her head, touching Fin's shackles until they disappear.

"We didn't know of this," I say, and it comes out more accusatory than I mean for it to.

348

"Mama said it would get me killed one day. That I must never use it. So I haven't. Not for years," she explains, working on my restraints next.

Magic has a strange way about it. For those who have both human and fae heritage, it's spotty on whether the child presents with any semblance of magic, which explains why Piper and Tavi have it and Az doesn't.

We hope.

"You made those guards disappear," I say.

She looks up at me, her eggshell eyes assessing. "I didn't kill them. Everything I make disappear shows back up somewhere."

"Please tell me you sent those guards far, far away," says Fin.

Tavi's shaking again. "I tried. Like I said, I haven't had much practice."

It's the same reason I never got much practice with manipulating the emotions of others. Tavi's adopted mother was a cook in the palace and likely had an intuition about what my father would have used Tavi for had he known about her unique abilities.

The last restraint disappears, and I lurch from my chair, but Tavi grabs me by the wrist.

"I know a passage out of the palace. You'll go undetected."

Fin and I glance at one another, and I know the determination in his eyes is mirrored on my face.

"Not without Asha," we say together.

Tavi's face falls. "There will be no getting to her. Not with how my brother has her guarded. I've heard whispers your Flame is no more?" She looks at me for confirmation. I suppose my hesitant swallow is enough, because she continues. "If you try to get to her now, you will fail. You'll need more than just the two of you to save her."

I look down at the tiny, trembling female before me and lay my hand gently on her shoulder. "Who says there's just two of us?"

WE MAKE our way through the palace, slipping through the shadows, Tavi leading the way.

349

She slinks like a ghost, her feet as soundless as a cat's as she sneaks up behind guards, then touches them, causing them to disappear.

There's no gratefulness in my chest, though I know I'll feel it later.

Right now there's no room for any emotion in my heart other than the desire to keep any harm from coming to Asha.

I can't bear them, but the imagined scenes assault me, regardless. The images of Az laying Asha out over our bed overwhelm my mind, making my stomach writhe in agony.

I have to stop it. I have to stop it from happening.

I can't let Asha hurt any more than she already has.

Fin and I wait, backs pressed against the cold marble wall, as Tavi slips around a corner to dispatch another guard.

There's the quiet noise we first heard in the cell as she makes him disappear, and Fin and I take that as our signal to move.

But then a guard emerges from around the corner across the hall, just far enough so that neither of us can reach him before he brings a whistle to his mouth and sounds the alarm.

FIN and I manage to fight off the lone guard, Fin holding him as I administer a quick jab to his head. The guard slumps, dead or unconscious, I can't tell. Fin lets his body drop to the floor, but the damage is already done.

We turn to find an array of soldiers racing down the hall.

One sends a dagger—scarlet-tipped to mark it as poisoned—spinning toward me. I dodge it with ease, my instincts taking over without having to think about it.

But where there should be a clatter as the dagger careens against the floor, there's the sickening slicing of flesh instead.

My heart fails me, but when I turn to look, I already know what's occurred.

Tavi's milkweed face drains of color as she clutches the hilt protruding from her stomach.

. . .

No.

No.

I'm sorry, I think. Or maybe I mouth it. I can't tell past the buzzing in my ears.

I'm at her side in an instant, catching her as she falls, dragging her backward into the adjacent hallway, away from the oncoming guards.

Fin races to catch up with us, his eyes wide with sorrow.

"Tavi, I'm so sorry. I didn't—I didn't realize…"

But I should have. I was so fixated on getting to Asha, I ignored my surroundings.

Of course, Tavi had stepped behind me for protection.

"I'm so sorry."

She's fighting to keep her eyes open, a dark puddle of blood forming at the edge of her lips.

"It's alright," she huffs. "Mama was right, you know. Should've listened to her."

Mama always said my magic would get me killed.

But her magic hasn't gotten her killed. I have.

I don't know what to do. Soldiers are rounding the corner, and Tavi is as good as dead, but I can't make my grip let go. Not when she sacrificed herself for us. Not when it's my fault she's dying.

"I was in love once," Tavi says, and I can hardly hear her over the rustle of soldiers in the hall. "Asha always asked me about him. I liked telling our story. But I miss him. He died, you know. It hurts." Tears puddle in her eyes. "It hurts so much. I don't…" She screws up her features, determination replacing the glassiness on her expression. "I don't want Asha to hurt. Not like that. Never like that."

Fin reaches us just as the soldiers round the corner.

Tavi's arms bolt outward, one grabbing my neck while the other wraps around Fin's wrist.

I don't realize what's happening until it's too late.

Until the world shifts, and the palace disappears.

CHAPTER 59

BLAISE

*I*t's taken us over a week to track down Abra.

Over a week. Traveling at night, sleeping in caves during the day.

I think I can admit to myself now that there was a part of me that hoped the close quarters would bring us together, remind Nox of his love for me, or at least stir up a new form of desire, but it seems to have done the opposite.

Each night of our journey, we've talked less and less. Tonight I'm certain we've only exchanged a few words, each of them logistical.

Nox is pulling away, and it's killing me not to try to stop him.

It's torture to glance over at him, only to find he's not sneaking a look at me. To address him, only for him to relay snippets of information—only what is necessary for our mission.

We finally found a lead at a village trading post in the foothills of the Kobiis, where an innkeeper had reported strange activities just over the border into Dwellen.

It struck both of us as strange that Abra would hide out here when she'd had plenty of time to get Piper all the way to Mystral while I was busy traveling to the Rip, but I'm sure Abra has her reasons.

Either that, or the parasite does.

Speaking of the parasite, the black adamant box dangles from Nox's belt. I gave it to him for safe-keeping during this mission. Figured it only made sense given Nox is the only one of the two of us who's ever used it to trap the parasite.

Of course, for the parasite to rip free of Abra, that would mean Abra was dead.

I won't mourn her if that comes to pass, but I don't want the parasite roaming about free either.

The warehouse is stiflingly warm, the scent of humidity fogging the air. There's something off about that, given we're in Dwellen during the early autumn months, but it's not as if we don't have bigger things to worry about than the climate.

Nox and I sneak through the abandoned halls, slinking through the shadows. The entire way, I can't help but remember doing this with him in the castle back in Mystral, when he took my hand and led me to see the aurora on the rooftop.

Nox doesn't hold my hand this time.

He's made it clear we're on a mission together. Our interests align, but there's no mistaking he isn't doing this for me.

Still.

He doesn't have to be here. He didn't have to come back for me after the Rip opened, and he certainly didn't have to travel all the way to Dwellen with me just to help me redeem myself.

It's not much, but it's enough of a handhold for me to cling to, like a lone root jutting out from a cliffside.

We make it to the center of the warehouse before we realize where the strange heat is coming from.

A glow ascends off the top of massive adamant vats, bright orange in hue, though some of the vats gleam white. Nox searches the large room for anyone who might be watching, then approaches the nearest vat and peers in.

"Liquid moonlight," he explains, staring down into the silvery liquid.

A chill snakes my spine. Liquid moonlight is partly to blame for Nox's vampiric condition, and I suppose mine as well, though indirectly.

"And I thought Avelea was known for underground trading," I say, sidling up next to Nox, but careful not to get close enough to touch.

My efforts don't really matter, because he stiffens anyway.

"This stuff can do worse things than cause vampirism," Nox says, glancing over to the other vats. The ones that glow orange.

"That's not liquid moonlight, is it?" I ask, chest tightening.

He shakes his head, and I follow him to the edge of the container. He glances at me before returning his attention to the vat. Then we both peer into it, and my heart jolts.

It's warm and familiar and the beauty of it, the aching for it, brings tears to my eyes and down my cheek.

It's marvelous.

It's marvelous, because it's sunlight.

"How?" I whisper, realizing this is the first time I've been able to look into anything similar to the sun without burning.

"I suppose the same way they collect the liquid moonlight," Nox says, his voice tinged with wonder. His statement reminds me of the stories I read while imprisoned. Tales of humans collecting droplets of moonlight from divots in the mountains, like one might collect dew.

I reach out my fingers to touch it, the longing to feel the sun against my skin aching, but Nox catches my wrist.

The touch is brief, over with as soon as Nox pulls my hand away from the vat and tucks his hand back into his pocket. It still sends sparks jolting through my fingertips.

"I doubt we can touch it safely."

"But it doesn't burn us like the sunlight does."

Nox shakes his head. "I imagine that's because it's contained in liquid form. Like how you might approach liquid poison without being harmed, so long as you didn't touch it, but you wouldn't dare approach it in its powder form, in case a draft stirred it up and made it airborne."

I nod, understanding now.

Still. It's nice to bask in its warmth.

"I wasn't a vampire over there, you know," says Nox, and the ease at which he provides the information shocks me. Nox hasn't been keen on talking to me throughout our journey. I try not to press, not wishing to annoy him. But it's nice for him to offer something up of his own accord for a change.

Even if that something drives a dagger through my heart.

"I didn't know that," I say, fighting my fingers, which want nothing more than to interweave themselves with Nox's. "Did it make it worse?"

Nox flicks his gaze over to me. "That's not what a normal person would ask, you know."

I shrug. "How would you know? How many normal people have you been around?"

Nox lets out a wry laugh, but his lips twist into something akin to a smile, and it's like a drug from which I've been going through withdrawal. "I suppose that's true. Still, I'm pretty sure most people would have asked if it was nice to feel the sun on my skin again."

"You can answer that question if you'd rather."

"No. You're right to ask. It made it worse."

"I thought it might. Getting a taste of something you've missed, only to have it ripped away from you again, always does."

Nox swallows, but he doesn't look at me this time.

"We should find Piper," is all he says before he walks away, leaving me alone with the sunlight I don't dare touch.

Before I follow, I grab a vial from the pouch I keep at my waist and dip it into the silky liquid moonlight.

Just in case.

THERE ARE several rooms in the warehouse containing the vats of liquid light, though the first one we stumbled upon was certainly the smallest.

It's when we approach the entrance to the largest room yet that we hear voices.

We hear them long before they can hear us, of course—vampire senses and all—but Nox and I reach out to each other at the same time, hands brushing one another's in a quiet command to tread silently.

Again, I treasure and replay that gentle touch more than I should.

It's Abra's voice that speaks the most often. It seems Nox, too, recognizes it by the way he tenses at its familiar cadence.

"I thought we were supposed to be traveling to Mystral. You know, so I could enchant your son, remember?" responds a bored-sounding woman, who must be Piper.

Abra responds with a dismissive, "That can wait."

As we peek around the corner, still disguised by the shadows, I take stock of the room. It's much like the other room in the warehouse, just three times the size, the ceiling stretching up considerably higher and supported by metal rafters.

Abra stands in the corner, staring out over a vat of liquid moonlight that intensifies her paleness.

Something stirs in me, an anxiety I can't quite get my hands on. It slips through my control, threatening to wriggle its way into my lungs until I can't breathe.

It's not the sight of Abra that frightens me.

It's knowing what dwells inside her.

The parasite.

The parasite who, should we kill Abra, would be released from her body, free to slink into mine.

No. No, that wouldn't make sense, I reason to myself. I'm a vampire, bound by the confines of night. The parasite wouldn't want someone like me, not when it's gotten used to being free from the chains of the moon.

Though I suppose she's already joined herself with Abra, and I can't imagine Abra allowed that without striking some sort of limiting bargain.

Abra stares down into the vat as she speaks, though the answering voice comes from elsewhere.

"It's taking more and more of you, isn't it?" says the female I assume to be Piper. "A little more every day. That's the deal you made with it?"

Abra doesn't answer. She just keeps staring into the vat.

"That's why one moment," Piper continues, "you're itching to get back to your son, then the next, we're off on a detour."

It takes me a moment to locate Piper, not because I can't track the direction from which her voice is coming, but because at first it makes no sense.

I recognize Piper by the red curly hair from her description, though it's rather matted from extensive travel, and the curls have turned into loose knots.

She's beautiful. Absolutely stunning, which probably shouldn't be the first thing I notice.

The first thing I should notice is that she's tied to the rafters above.

Why Abra would go to such extremes to keep Piper contained, I have no idea. Unless Abra is just being dramatic, which I suppose I wouldn't put past her.

Though apparently Abra hasn't bothered to have Piper gagged.

Nox signals to me, tapping his finger against the back of my hand. It's a signal to initiate the plan we came up with on the way here, but the touch still sets me aflame.

I douse those flames and nod back.

Then I watch him slip into the shadows.

He doesn't check to see whether I do the same.

As many inconveniences come with being a vampire, I would be lying if I said it didn't come with its benefits.

The ease at which one can climb rafters is definitely one of them.

Before the Turning, I don't think I would have had the lower body strength, much less the grip strength, to climb up here. And that's not even considering the agility required to do it quietly in the presence of Abra, whose fae hearing requires my utter silence. But with my heightened senses, I manage it. Every twitch of my musculature is

357

precise, every movement of the rafters underneath my weight measured. My body readjusts instinctively.

The problem will be signaling to Piper that I'm here without startling her and alerting the queen.

I reach the topmost rafter, still on the other side of the building from where Piper is tied, and wait in the shadows for Abra to turn her attention away. She's still staring into the vat, talking to herself now that Piper has stopped bothering to answer, but she's still facing our direction, and I don't want any signal I offer to Piper to get Abra's attention as well.

My heart pounds as I pray to the Fates that she'll somehow turn around. That she'll leave the room, rendering the backup plan Nox and I came up with unneeded.

The prayer is answered with a resounding "no," when, instead of waiting as we planned, Nox flings himself from the shadows, teeth bared for Abra's throat.

CHAPTER 60

EVANDER

*T*raining with Orion is less pleasant than I expected.

And I came in with low expectations.

Abysmal expectations, really.

Well, except for the occasions Ellie joins us. When she found out I was training, she wanted to do the same. Not with magic, but with a weapon—specifically a short sword. Peck grumbled about it, but after a few weeks of rest and a cocktail of Peck's postpartum potions, he cleared her for physical activity. Hilva, a female who retired from my father's army decades ago, now trains her in the atrium with us.

There's been more than one occasion where I've gotten smacked over the head with a rather inconsiderate vine for letting my eyes wander over to her as she trains.

What can I say?

Ellie looks hot in leathers. Especially when she's wielding a sword.

Ellie isn't training with us today, which brings me back around to my point about expectations.

First off, there's something about people who are naturally good at magic—well, good at anything—that forces them to be insufferable.

I know this well from being around Olwen, who, from the time she was eight and discovered she was better at magic than anyone

359

else, became impossible to be around. At least without wanting to claw your ears out to escape the condescending remarks—the "look, but it's so easy," before a simple flourish of the wrist and producing a functional pianoforte made exclusively of rose petals.

Orion is much the same way, though he at least attempts to be polite.

Not that he succeeds.

You see, the thing about prodigies is that because they never had to work at it, they don't understand why *you* have to work at it.

That, and they either expect way too much, or way too little of you.

If I were training with Olwen, she would expect way too little, assuming me an imbecile.

Unfortunately, I'm training with Orion, who expects way too much. Meaning I've gotten about four dozen thorn lashes to the torso from surprise attacks I can't parry.

Ow, I think in my head, Orion at least having successfully trained me not to mutter it aloud, as the consequence of a verbal slip is an additional lash.

"You're not trying," says Orion, sending yet another thorny vine my way. This one I block with my forearms as it hurtles toward my face; I know better than to think I can stop it with my magic.

My torso, Orion can beat all he wants, but I'm quite partial to my face.

Blood trickles down my skin as the thorns dig into my forearm, the vine wrapping around my wrist and yanking me to the ground, where I end up with a mouthful of earth.

"Get up," Orion says, sounding like he couldn't care less whether I do so or not.

I do anyway, shrugging away Orion's vine, which must have gotten bored with me given the way it's now scouring the soft earth for bugs.

When Orion first suggested the atrium as a place to meet for our training, I thought it made sense for teaching someone as unskilled as myself. The atrium is practically overgrown with wildlife, meaning I'll be able to practice controlling plants before we bother with sprouting them—a much more advanced task.

Still, I didn't take into consideration how public the atrium is.

Passersby frequent the area, mostly nobles waltzing around on dates, the females dangling off their arms blushing and giggling as they realize they've happened upon the Heir to Dwellen. It never takes long for their giggles to sour to snorts of derision once they've watched me unsuccessfully defend myself from something as emasculating as a rosebush.

Indeed, a couple passing by are staring at their feet, hands covering their mouths as they try to stifle their laughter at having seen me yanked to the ground by a spindly little vine.

"Of course, I'm trying. What do you think we've been out here doing since the dawn of civilization?" I ask.

Orion crosses his arms. "That's an exaggeration."

"Well, you've had me out here since before sunrise. You are aware that the fae are not nocturnal beings, are you not? The sun is rather helpful in completing most tasks."

Orion allows a wry smile to taint his features. "I would have thought you preferred practicing in the darkness, Your Highness. Less opportunity for your citizens to gawk."

He nods his head toward the couple, no longer pretending not to be watching. They both blush, then go back to examining the lilies.

"It's true. I imagine I could focus better away from prying eyes."

Orion shakes his head. "I chose this spot for a reason. Why didn't you put any effort into honing your magic at the Academy?"

I shoot him a raised eyebrow. "Because I was a youth who spent more effort chasing females than caring about my marks."

Orion shakes his head. "I don't think that's it."

"Then pray tell, why do you think I didn't try?"

"I think you're the second son. The backup. The heir your father didn't need. I think you saw your brother being groomed for the throne, and you—"

"Yes, yes," I say, interrupting my mentor. "I didn't see a need for enhancing my skills when all I was going to be was a powerless, spoiled brat, anyway." I yawn; Orion's assessment of me is so predictable.

"That's not what I was going to say. I think you were so openly criticized by your father for everything you did, you learned not to attempt the things that didn't come naturally to you. I think you learned that having your father call you lazy hurt significantly less than having him call you incompetent."

Orion goes quiet, eyeing me with curiosity, as if to watch and see whether his blow has landed.

Anger boils in my chest, seeping into my bloodstream, causing my heart to pound. It has me longing to wipe Orion's smug look off his face. Not that I have the power to get near him, which I suppose is the point.

Incompetent. That's what I am, what I've always been.

He's right. The word somehow hurts worse than being called lazy. At least with laziness, there's some agency about it.

Incompetence is something entirely more daunting.

My jaw works, and I can't seem to find the words to answer.

When Orion speaks, there's no pity in his voice, which I appreciate. "I brought you out here because if you ever want to cultivate your magic, you're going to have to get used to failing. And failing where anyone and everyone can see."

I nod, fighting the dagger that has lodged itself in my throat.

"Now," says Orion. "Where were we? Oh, right. You were trying, and failing, to stop my attacks by bending my vines backward, causing them to attack me instead."

I sigh, too exhausted to bother with a retort. Instead, I just crouch back into a defensive stance.

"Again," I groan.

Orion's smile is feral. "I thought you'd never ask."

Then he sends a vine barreling straight through my shoulder.

CHAPTER 61

BLAISE

I have to physically dig my fingernails into the metal railing to keep from flinging myself in the middle of the fight between Nox and Abra.

My heart pounds as she sidesteps his attack, hearing him even with her back turned. Nox goes flying for the vat of sunlight, his cheek almost skimming the deathly liquid's surface before he stops himself with his hands on the railing.

The weight of his impact causes the liquid sunlight to slosh over the rim, coating his hands in the stuff.

Nox lets out a strangled shout as a sizzling noise punctures the thick air, the liquid sunlight burning away his skin.

I feel as though I'm going to be sick. Though I want nothing more than to help him, though he's changed the plan, I know in my heart this is the best distraction I'm going to get for freeing Piper.

I skirt around the railing at the edge of the room, honing my senses in on the fight that's now broken out between Nox and Abra. Still, I don't let myself look, just listen.

The sizzling of flesh, the wiping of the liquid sunlight onto his coat, the stretching of skin reknitting itself. Abra's cry of anger as she lashes out at Nox.

Piper—I have to focus on saving Piper.

There's a crash down below, but I don't let myself look.

Instead, I use the sound as a cover as I sneak up behind Piper and whisper in her pointed ear that I'm here to help.

She startles, distracted by the fight breaking out below, but when I go to rip the restraints from her hands, I realize she's already clawed her way through half of the layers.

She's pretty good.

No wonder Abra tied her to the rafters. She probably hoped it would limit Piper's movement, given if she struggled too much, she would fall.

The ropes rip with ease with the talons for fingernails I can now summon at will. As soon as I cut her free, she flips herself over, hands grasping at the railing to steady herself.

Piper gives me a nod of appreciation, but she doesn't stop to ask questions as she scampers away down the long metal railing that cuts across the ceiling.

I try to hiss that she needs to wait for me, but she's already halfway across the railing.

Unfortunately, it doesn't matter how stealthy Piper is.

There's no hiding that red hair.

Abra lets out a scream from below, one that signals she's caught a glimpse of what's going on above.

That's when everything spirals out of control.

I ALLOW myself one glimpse below as Nox uses Abra's distracted attention to land a blow across her neck. She shrieks as his nails make contact, but it's short-lived. Moments later, the wound heals itself, much faster than it should for the fae.

It's then I remember the Old Magic's story.

That when Abra, then known as Mother, was infused with magic from the Rip, her power wasn't simply potions.

It was healing.

It *is* healing.

Oh no.

I go to call down to Nox in warning, but I catch myself. It's too late for that, and judging by the surprise in Nox's eyes, he's realized the problem already.

I'm still scampering after Piper across the topmost rafter when the queen sends a dagger hurtling across the room. It delves into Nox's shoulder, casting him to the floor, writhing in pain.

Poisoned. The dagger must be poisoned.

The scream that flows from my mouth is something primal. I'm going to kill her, but she's already ascending the beams of the warehouse, ready to cut Piper off before she can get down.

Amazingly enough, Piper is scrappier than she looks. I'm quickly reminded of her fae heritage when she jumps across to a neighboring beam, catching herself. It's not a graceful movement, like a vampire or a fae, but she manages the jump, which is more than a human could likely do.

Abra's face lights with fury, but before she can launch herself after Piper, I get to the queen, slamming my fist into the rafter below our feet. It trembles enough to throw Abra off her balance, allowing Piper time to slip down from the rafters and out of sight.

"You stupid little child," Abra hisses. Steam from the vats below causes her slick moonlight hair to curl in wet whips against her scalp as she regains her balance at the other end of the topmost rafter. "You should have stayed out of our way."

Our.

My blood chills as I look into Abra's eyes and find something altogether familiar and unfamiliar at the same time.

"Am I speaking to Abra or Cindy right now?" I ask, fighting to keep my voice nonchalant, though I'm rather successful. Using the nickname I gave the parasite helps ground me, strange as that is.

"We're one and the same," Abra says, which is a dead giveaway.

"So the parasite then," I say.

She lunges.

· · ·

365

THERE'S no sidestepping her on these metal bars, so I jump, grabbing at the rafters on the vaulted ceiling and swinging myself to land on the other side of Abra as she swipes at nothing but thin air.

My feet pummel the metal beams, denting them with the imprint of my boots and causing the rafter itself to moan.

I spin on my heel and find Abra charging, another poisoned dagger in hand. Its jagged tip glints in the glow of the liquid sunlight, giving the illusion that the knife itself is molten.

She swings for my head, and I duck, the whizz of the knife singing just above my hair.

The swing leaves Abra unsteady, so I take advantage of the moment and shove into her, hoping to send her toppling over the edge. She strikes faster than I'm expecting, bringing the knife down across my cheek.

Poison singes my flesh, burning away at my skin. I ignore the pain, struggling against Abra to shove her over the edge.

I'm on top of her now, pressing her back against the rafter. Unfortunately, that leaves me with nothing to hold on to but her.

A crazed look overtakes her face once she realizes this. She rolls to the side, thinking to topple me off, but something snags at my back and rips me to my feet.

Nox.

"Steady," he says from behind as he pulls me into his chest. His lips graze the tip of my ear as he whispers, "Let's finish this."

I nod and he lets go of me, launching himself between the adjacent rafters until he lands on the other side of Abra, who's back on her feet.

Abra turns to the side, monitoring both of us as Nox and I advance.

"I see you found one another," she says. For the first time, I recognize the strange timbre to her voice, like two sentiences have been melded into one. "Though there must be discontent between the two of you if you felt the need to come after me. Happy couples don't seek revenge, not when they're finally free to live out their happy, quiet lives. Tell me, Nox. Do you find the little servant girl less enticing now that you have the entire world at your feet?"

Nox growls, and Abra just laughs. "That's what I thought. I always knew being contained in that dungeon for years hampered your social skills. No wonder you wanted a girl so plain, if she was the first female to grace your presence."

"Oh, I don't know." A cruel smile forms on Nox's lips. "I saw you at your best, and I still didn't want you. How disgusting does that make you, if even the sheltered boy couldn't desire you?"

My mind does a double take. It takes me a moment to realize he's speaking to the parasite, not to Abra, though I'm not entirely sure there's a difference anymore.

Nox charges, but Abra is ready, maneuvering his attack and going airborne for a moment, until she's behind him.

She stabs at him with her dagger, and I yelp, but he's ready for it. He spins, intercepting the dagger by grabbing its hilt.

Nox faces down Abra, the female who ruined his life, both of their expressions strained as they struggle for control of the blade.

I advance, ready to jump on the other side of Abra and tear her throat out, but then she hisses, "Tell me, Nox. How's your sister?"

Nox's expression falters, just for a moment, but it's long enough for Abra to gain control, steer the dagger back toward his chest.

No.

I drop to my feet, scaling the rafter from below until I'm at Abra's back. I dig my nails into her shoulders, baring my teeth, ready to rip out her throat, when she says, "She's dead, isn't she?"

I freeze.

Abra tsks, even as Nox's face warps in pain. "That was the price you paid to get back to your little servant girl. Tell me, Nox. Is she worth it?"

Evander's voice echoes in my mind. *Tell me it was worth it, Blaise.*

No. I glance at Nox for confirmation, but he's not looking at me. Like he's refusing to.

"Oh. Oh," Abra says, a cackling delight escaping her throat. "It wasn't Farin, was it? Tell me it wasn't Farin who killed her. Because if it was, then we all know what that would mean."

No. No, no, no.

"Remind me, now. It was you who sent Farin into Zora's world, wasn't it, Blaise?"

My heart stops beating, and only now does Nox look at me.

And there's enough ice in his eyes to speak the truth without a word.

My ribs crack at the look. My fault. My fault.

Zora, unprotected Zora, dead because of me.

Because I just couldn't let Nox go like he asked.

It's then that Nox and I make a mistake.

We take our attention off of Abra. One last betrayal. One last sabotaging of one another.

I don't see the blow coming until it hits.

Well-aimed, not at my chest or neck as I expect, but at my ankles.

Abra steps forward, sending me off-balance.

My feet lose their grip on the rafter, and though my instincts have me scrambling for purchase, I'm still in so much shock from the news of Zora's death that my fingers find nowhere to grip. I fall, my body barreling through two sets of eroded rafters before I finally grip onto a loose beam.

The warehouse is burning, melting under the heat of the vats that spilled during Nox and Abra's fight below. The liquid sunlight and moonlight slink across the floor, moments away from colliding.

One glance down tells me there's another vat directly below me.

A vat of swirling liquid sunlight.

I turn to swing myself up on the beam.

Something explodes.

Liquid sunlight and moonlight blast mingled into the air, a byproduct of their collision. The vat below also explodes, making the rafter on which I've gripped groan.

It falls, and me with it. I barely catch myself on another rafter below.

Liquid from the explosion slides down the metal beam, singeing my fingertips as I try to get a grip.

I scream, a burning pain biting at my hands.

The agony is surreal, blackening the edges of my vision, and it takes every ounce of self-control I have to hold on.

It hits me then that I am going to fall. The pain is causing the muscles in my arms to seize, and even my vampire instincts can't guide me with the pain pounding in my skull.

It's then I hear a voice, and this time, there's no twinge of the parasite in it.

"Farin?" asks the queen—just the queen—peering up at Nox's face. The one that should have held her son. The fate of her son must have pushed Abra hard enough to regain control of her body, even for just a moment.

"Farin's gone," says Nox, his voice trembling with cold triumph. "I made sure of that."

Abra lets out a cry from above. It's not the cry of a villain defeated, of a conqueror put to shame. It's the scream of a mother who's lost her child not once, but twice.

It's then that I catch Nox's gaze.

Everything goes still for a moment, like Time itself stops to watch the two of us.

He's balancing on the rafter two levels above, Abra having just been sent to her knees by grief as she scrambles for purchase on the railing.

My fingers are slipping. Nox's gaze flits to them, then back to my eyes.

"Nox," I whisper, but it's no use, because Abra is down, but not for long.

"I'm sorry," he whispers back.

And rips Abra's head from her body.

It's the last thing I see before I fall.

CHAPTER 62

ZORA

"Why'd you save Nox?" I ask, trying and failing to chew the boar Farin roasted for dinner. It's rather tough, though I suppose that's more the boar's fault than Farin's. It's just more satisfying to blame Farin.

Either way, my muscles are having trouble making a dent in my portion.

Flames flicker from the fire, casting shadows across the cave, as well as Farin's masculine features. He sits across from me, having very little trouble chewing his food, though he's not the one with a knife wound in his gut, I suppose.

"Perhaps I like to keep things interesting. I'm easily bored. It's been a problem since I was a youth. My imagination's gotten me into all sorts of trouble."

"But you could have let him drown."

Farin stares at me, his crystalline eyes glowing in the firelight. "When I first woke in this world, I didn't know where I was. Who I was. I saw a male floating face first in the water, and I pulled him out. I didn't know he was my enemy at the time. Not until the memories started flooding back in."

I crane my neck at him. "And then when you realized who he was? Who you were?"

Farin sets down his piece of meat and pushes it away. "I've died once before. It isn't an experience I'd like to replicate. The forces on the other side—well, let's just say they don't like me much. The first time I died, it was due to a curse placed upon me by the Old Magic. One that prevented me from lying. Rather, it punished me for it. I thought that, should I return to my world, the curse would still apply."

"What does that have to do with Nox?"

"Because when Blaise looked me in the eye and asked me what happened to him, I wanted to be able to tell her honestly that I hadn't touched him."

"Until you learned you could lie. That the curse was broken."

Farin breathes out, though it's a subtle movement of his chest. "Until then."

"So it wasn't about not lying to the girl you claim to love. Just not having to suffer the consequences of lying."

Farin flashes me a dazzling smile. "Are you telling me you never lie?"

My lips falter, and I go back to eating my boar. Rather, attempting to eat my boar.

"You think you actually would have had a chance with her?" I ask, giving in to my incessant need to fill the silence. I might be in the presence of a psychopath, but it's still better to keep him talking.

I'm pretty sure moments of contemplation are when all the violent ideas come to people like Farin.

"Why? You don't?" He flashes me that handsome smile again, the one he has to know he possesses, and I feel my cheeks heat. I promptly blame it on the fire underneath the boar.

"She loves Nox, not you."

Farin's smile remains, though it appears effortful now. "Nox was the first male to see her for what she is and love her despite it. Of course, she developed feelings for him. That doesn't mean the two of them are right for each other."

"Oh, but you are right for her," I say.

He shrugs. "Blaise and I are the same. She simply doesn't wish to admit it to herself."

"And how are you the same?"

"Why do you care?"

"Because someone had the audacity to stab me, and I'd like a distraction as recompense."

"A distraction, eh?" Farin's eyes twinkle.

Again, I flush—stupid cheeks—but I level him a glare. "You were just talking about Blaise, the girl you claim to adore enough to cross realms for, and now you're flirting with me."

His face is unreadable, but he goes back to answering my original question. "I suppose it's the least I can do. Blaise is the type who's willing to do whatever it takes to get what she wants. She loves unconditionally, but she does so within a hierarchy. The people who outweigh the others get preference, and she'd do anything to keep them. Blaise's life has been shrouded in darkness, but her light comes from within. She can take whatever situation she's in and pretend it's something else, a better version of her life. Nox doesn't understand that about her. His mind is practical, and he only sees what's real, tangible. He doesn't see the beauty in pretending."

I chew absentmindedly on my boar bone, and between bites say, "Sounds like that's exactly what makes him better for her than you."

Farin's ears flick. "All it means is that he doesn't understand her."

I shrug. "Or maybe he understands her better than anyone else. Not because he thinks the same way she thinks, but that he can see her for what she truly is, even in ways she doesn't understand herself. Maybe being able to dream the pain away has its benefits, but maybe Blaise doesn't need someone who pretends. Maybe she needs someone to anchor her, someone to ground her to reality and help her face whatever it is her mind is trying so desperately to run away from."

Farin shifts, and for a moment I wonder if this was a stupid topic to broach. An image of Farin picking at my burns just to reopen my wound flashes through my mind. Nox did say that Farin gets a high off the pain of others.

But if Farin has an aching desire to make me scream in pain, he doesn't act on it.

"So that's the type of person you would have me be with, then?" he asks. "Someone practical. Someone who doesn't have their head in other worlds?"

My blood chills, but I don't answer him.

My lack of reply seems to please him, and he says, "If you get bored, I wouldn't mind hearing about them, you know."

I scoff, then immediately wince, grabbing instinctively at my wounded belly.

"I'd hate to give you more fodder for your imagination," I say. "It seems like a rather dangerous place."

He shrugs. "It is what got me into this mess to begin with. Though, I suppose it might have saved me too. That's the thing about pivotal moments. Did they bring disaster, or did they save you from something much, much worse? I suppose we'll never truly know, just have to wonder."

An aching hits me. The same one that tugged on my heart when Nox told me that Farin had once belonged to another world. Not this one, or the one Nox and I are originally from, but another realm entirely. Farin's a realm-walker. Like me.

"The strangest part is the way the air feels different," I whisper.

Farin shakes his head where it's propped against the cave wall and stares out into the distance. "I disagree. I think it's the way your muscles never seem to work the same in the different worlds. When I crossed from the Nether to Alondria, it was as if my muscles turned from lead to as light as a feather. Then here, I feel as though they're weak again."

I level a glare at him.

"What?" he asks.

"We're describing the same sensation, yet you claim to disagree?"

"How are we describing the same sensation? You said the difference was the air. I said it was the muscles."

"Yes, well, this realm feels like walking through air that's thick and heavy and resists you. It's the same feeling as one's muscles being weak, just blamed on a different source."

"Just blamed on a different source?" he says, before he trails off into what I believe is Farin's infamous imagination.

CHAPTER 63

BLAISE

*N*ox drops Abra's severed head as he launches toward me, but it doesn't matter.

Nox is a moment too late.

His chest hits the crooked railing a few feet above me, his hand extending.

There's just enough time for his fingers to brush against mine as I fall.

The fall is quieter than I would have thought, though I could swear I see Nox's mouth twist in agony as he bellows something.

It's probably "No."

I'm not sure why I'm as shocked as I am, but I am.

I'm going to die.

I'm going to die, and Nox didn't save me. Not because he didn't have the chance, but because he chose revenge against Abra over saving me.

There's a part of me that knows I deserve this. That this was always how my story was going to end. The betrayer justly betrayed.

It doesn't make it hurt any less.

I close my eyes, preparing for the vat of liquid sunlight to take me into its arms, to sear away the pain. Because surely it can't hurt worse than this. Than the feeling of my soul being shredded in half.

But then my hand catches on something, or rather, that something catches me, and I open my eyes.

At first, it's just a flash of red, but then Piper's face comes into focus, her face twisted in exertion as she clings to the rafter with one arm, the other keeping me suspended.

The cry that rips through the air as the weight of catching me wrenches at her shoulder muscles jolts me back to attention. Instinct takes over. I shove the image of Nox's face aside, tuck it into the corner of my mind, as I climb up Piper's arm and onto the rafters.

When I reach the top and clamber over Piper, she's whimpering in pain, but she bites it back long enough to nod her head to the side.

"We need to go," she says through clenched teeth.

"You saved me." My voice sounds lifeless.

She blinks. "Someone needed to." She pushes herself to her feet, looking like she might sway from the pain. Still, she stares up at the higher rafters, a glare of indignation pouring off her face.

Nox. She's glaring at Nox.

"Blaise," he says, and though I shouldn't, I let the sound of my name on his lips cause my heart to skip. I turn to face him, bracing myself for the agony on his face at what he'd just done. But when I look up at Nox, there's no emotion to be found.

He tosses something down at me. I catch it, and it's metallic and cool to the touch.

I stare down to find the adamant box in my hands, the echoes of a slithering fragment of ancient magic trapped inside, chilling my bones.

When I look back up, Nox is gone.

CHAPTER 64

ASHA

*N*agivv purrs, her dark snout dry and cracked with dehydration as I pet her, whispering words of comfort that I'm not sure she can understand.

Sores have cropped up around her snout, where the iron muzzle Ax had fitted to her digs into her flesh.

She whimpers as I try to soothe her. I sit in the crook of her belly and legs, swollen with dehydration, as she lies across the floor of her sanctuary.

The day of Az's coronation, he brought me here to celebrate. I suppose he thought it would be a special sort of gift to see her again.

She'd lunged for him, nearly ripping his throat out. It was only because a fae guard, sworn by his fae oath to protect Az at all costs, jumped between them that Az survived.

The guard did not.

Az had a muzzle crafted that very day.

Nagivv took down half a dozen guards before they finally succeeded in clamping it on her.

Iron mesh forms the muzzle, so technically she can still drink, but it hardly allows room for her tongue to move, and she quickly wearies of the effort it takes to drink, much less eat.

Only because I cried to Az had he commanded the kitchen staff to beat Nagivv's food into a puree that she could lick from the holes in her muzzle. I try to clean it for her between meals, but the holes are small, and a pungent odor has arisen from the patches from which I can't seem to remove the bits of food, no matter how hard I try.

I don't know what I'll do if Nagivv dies. It hurts badly enough to watch her mistreated in this way. Especially since, over the past week, the fight inside her has seemed to sputter out.

It's not something I would have ever imagined I'd witness in Nagivv, but I understand.

I understand, because the flame is dying inside of me, too.

It's been a month since the coronation, since my wedding to Az.

I've waited so patiently for Kiran to come back for me. Of course, he would have needed to regroup, rally allies who would help him sneak into the palace or overthrow Az, or whatever he's planning.

But every day that Kiran doesn't come for me, I begin to wonder if he ever will.

Sometimes, I find myself angry, petulant. Like a child unable to wield her own anger, allowing it to bubble over rather than simmer.

Just yesterday, I punched a hole in the mirror in my room. The pinprick wounds on my hand have yet to heal.

I didn't know I had it in me to punch things.

I had to lie to the guard stationed outside my room and tell him I tripped. That when I reached out to catch myself, my hand had gone straight through the mirror.

The guard seemed to believe me, but later that day, when I returned from my visit with Nagivv, I found my quarters stripped of anything that could potentially be made sharp.

I've already been moved to a windowless room.

That happened the night after the coronation. Az had me moved to quarters adjacent to his, ones with an adjoining wall, with a door between the rooms that locked from one side only. Apparently, my room once operated as servants' quarters. Previous fae royalty used these rooms should one of them fall injured and need a servant nearby at all times to tend to their wounds.

Az says he enjoys having me close by. Likes the comfort of knowing I'm safe.

My theory is that he likes that my quarters don't contain windows.

I'm not sure if he thinks I'm at risk of jumping or climbing, but he's barred almost all the windows in the palace just the same.

I've developed a strange habit of hiding unimportant things from him. Bits of food underneath the mattress. Bars of soap behind the dresser. Amity's survival kit is even stuffed in the back of the closet—Az has been careful not to undress me, so I was able to hide it under my robes—and though I've considered faking my death with that ressuroot of hers, I can't figure out a way doing so would help me.

If Az thought I was dead, he'd probably just stuff me in a marble coffin, and then I would suffocate to death.

Not ideal.

As I ponder my fate, my will to fight back slowly being chipped away from me, I nestle my head into Nagivv's dry coat and fall asleep to the hum of her gentle purr.

Az FREQUENTS my quarters at night.

Tonight is no exception, though I always hope it will be.

He never stays for long, never goes so far as to force himself upon me. A small kindness for which I thank the Fates.

But just because that threshold hasn't yet been crossed doesn't mean that Az hasn't been toeing that line.

"The guards said that you had a better day today," Az says, striding into my stuffy room. He locks the door behind him, stuffing a key into his belt.

I blink, trying to remember how I'm supposed to respond. When I first came back to the palace, I'd been playing the role of a confused girl, mind muddled by over a year of magical manipulation. I reinforced the ruse with fits of anger, coupled with long bouts of silence.

I cry myself to sleep every night, sometimes allowing Az to hold me as I drift off to sleep.

As I pretend to drift off to sleep.

But over time, I've played the part so well, infused it with so much of my own fury, my own apprehension, I fear I've forgotten where I end and this weakened version of myself begins.

I wonder if there's never been a difference.

The tears are real, after all. The darkness that sweeps over my very soul, unfaked.

"Did I?" I force a faint smile to my lips. The faint part is the easy bit, the smile itself feeling like I'm trying to lift a fallen beam off my leg at too strange an angle to fully get a grip on it.

Az nods at my plate of food, which is almost empty. "I'd say that's an improvement of its own."

I forced the food down today, only at the pestering of my magic, who refused to stop screaming in my head until I finished my meal.

It will help nothing to starve yourself, he'd told me.

I know that well enough. But it's something I can control. A simple act of defiance that even Az can't take away from me.

I'm not sure what, who that makes me, that I would harm myself just to spite him. Just to remind myself that I am my own, and not simply a pawn in his games.

It's difficult to remember when I'm too busy reminding myself to act as if I love him.

I do so now, examining the face I've memorized over the years.

Az hasn't been sleeping.

I can tell by the faint bruises that have formed underneath his eyes. I hear him pacing all hours of the night on the other side of the wall that separates our quarters.

Even in the daytime, he acts strangely. His hands have developed a tremor, his eyelids a strange twitch.

"You look ill," I say. It's effortful, but I manage to infuse my voice with concern.

Az takes in a deep breath. I don't miss how he clenches his hands to steady the tremors. "The Others are more difficult to control than I expected. It takes extreme focus to reign over their minds. I've found when I sleep, the control slips."

My heart beats wildly, and I can't decide if it's out of hope or fright. On one hand, this will be the first weakness Az has revealed. On the other…

"A pack of mere attacked a group of Meranthi citizens a few nights ago when I dozed off," he explains.

Pain swells in my throat. "Anyone we know?"

Az shakes his head. "Not personally, no. But I never meant for our own to suffer." He straightens. "I'll just have to be more vigilant."

I fight the urge to gape. "But Az, you can't just stay awake all hours."

He offers me an appeasing smile. "What? You don't have faith in me?"

No. No, I don't.

"I found a healer who specializes in this sort of thing," he says. "Turns out there's an elixir that keeps the body from needing sleep."

I find my gaze slipping to his still-twitching hand.

"That's enough about me, though," he says, sitting on the bed next to me. I tense at his nearness, the way his shoulder brushes against mine. "Do you feel…do you feel that you're getting better?"

I stare at the empty mirror frame across the room, allowing my gaze to trace the pattern of war and bloodshed the artist found fit to carve into the gold.

"Some," I say, my throat dry. "I just…" I bite my lip. It's dry too.

"You just what?" Az slips his fingers into mine, resting both of our hands on my leg. His thumb caresses my skin, occasionally slipping and brushing my thigh.

I want to vomit, bile swirling in my gut, but I hold it in.

This won't work if he knows just how disgusted I am by him.

"Well, I'm lonely, Az."

He frowns, sadness overcoming his sage-green eyes as he looks me over. "I know I've been busy with ruling matters. I've been so consumed with creating a kingdom where I can keep you safe, I haven't been here for you. That will change, Asha."

Despair constricts my throat at the idea of Az spending more time with me, but I swallow it down. "Thank you," I say, and I think perhaps it's the worst lie I've ever told. "But I know you're busy with important things. This is the beginning of your reign, the dawn of a new dynasty. The groundwork you lay now will determine the fate of Alondria for centuries to come. You can't neglect that just because I'm a wimp."

Az smiles down at me, and for a moment, he actually looks like himself. Like the Az I remember, before greed and lust for power devoured my friend's heart from the inside.

It hurts. It hurts worse than anything, seeing what can become of someone who used to be good.

"I won't neglect anything, Asha. I promise. This kingdom is somewhere our children will be safe by the time I'm done with it."

I have to stop breathing in order to keep from reacting to that. Our *children*. Az made me his queen, even if it was in a manner that utterly ignored marriage laws that had been held for centuries. Overlooked the fact that Kiran is my husband and I his wife.

Recently, I hoped Az making me his queen was more about making a public sign to the people that he'd ruined Kiran. What's a bolder statement of power than to take the previous king's bride for your own?

It was about the statement, about pretense.

Or so I thought.

I'm not so sure anymore.

He must notice my apprehension, because he adjusts on the bed to face me, this time reaching across my lap, taking both of my hands in his. "Asha, I won't pressure you into anything you're not ready for. I know you still suffer...spells. That the magic Kiran wrought on you hasn't fled entirely. I don't want..." He takes a breath, steadying himself. "I told you over a year ago that I had things I needed to work through."

I can't help but notice he isn't looking at your face right now, hisses my magic.

Indeed, Az stares at our hands, at the tattoo that swirls up my arm, binding me to Kiran. Quietly, Az takes my sleeve and pulls it further down my arm, covering the rest of the tattoo with his hand.

He breathes a sigh of relief at not having to look at it any longer.

Then he peers into my face. "I just wanted you to know that I've worked through them now. Entirely. I'm yours, Asha, through and through. Always have been. I only wish I hadn't been too dull to realize it sooner. But you know what? I can't even bring myself to regret it. Because look where it's led us, Asha. You and I? We were born to shape the world. And we're supposed to do it together."

I want to remind Az he's married, but again, he seems to have forgotten that much. The only marriage he seems to honor is the fake one he's forced me into.

"So when you're ready, I'm ready."

There's a dull aching in my heart. One that reminds me, almost dryly, how thrilled this confession might have made a previous me.

That version of me didn't possess enough respect for herself.

The self-respecting Asha might be withering away, but at least there's still some iron underneath the ashes.

I let out a shuddering sigh and allow my eye to shimmer with tears. It isn't difficult. It comes too easily these days.

And then I nod.

Az's face bursts into one of the most brilliant smiles I've ever seen.

So deceptive, that beauty of his. Has it always masked the evil lurking within, or had it contributed to it? Did that smile allow him to get away with too much as a child, rotting him slowly over the years, through trial after trial of always getting his way?

Az has always gotten what he wanted.

Always.

Well, he can't have me.

"I want it to be perfect when it happens," I say, and his smile falters a bit, but only out of disappointment. Not anger. "I don't want him lurking in the back of my mind, ruining it for us."

I swallow, emphasizing my discomfort.

Az just smiles understandingly.

And then he kisses me.

It's meant to be a reassuring, gentle sort of kiss, but I realize that too late.

Because I cringe with such disgust, there's no disguising it from Az.

When he pulls away, recognition of the truth darkens his gaze, and he shakes his head, incredulous.

"It's unbelievable—the hold he has on you."

Az jolts from the bed, leaving in a flurry of rage.

I'm not allowed to see Nagivv for three days after that.

CHAPTER 65

ZORA

*I*t's taking less time than I expected for my wounds to heal. This has me wondering whether Farin has some secret healing ability he isn't telling me about. Or maybe all the physicians are right about the salty ocean air being beneficial to one's health.

Either way, the faster I heal, the less time I have to figure out a plan for thwarting Farin's trip back to Alondria.

The other problem is, the more time my wound takes to heal, the more time Farin and I have to sit and ponder and talk. And, in a limited quantity which I monitor religiously, laugh.

That's going to be problematic.

Okay, it's already problematic, but I'm only willing to admit that to myself on certain occasions.

Now, as Farin is redressing my wound, is one of those occasions.

He does it twice a day, using the saltwater from the ocean and the few strips that are left of his outer tunic. I tell myself that I dread the occurrence. If I were to say as much aloud as a fae in Alondria, I'd likely be struck dead like Farin once was.

I have a tendency to avoid male kind. At least the ones I find attractive. It happens every time I reach the realization that there's something off about me. That I'm not meant to be a part of whatever world I'm in. That the dreams I had as a child weren't actually dreams, but memories.

It makes it difficult to attach yourself to someone, knowing you're going to have to move on without them for lives on end.

That doesn't make me immune to the male touch, though.

Farin is surprisingly respectful as he dresses my wounds, careful not to adjust my clothes any further than is necessary. It's a rather humiliating experience. For one, Farin, psychopathic as he might be, has not been punished for being so. Not when it comes to his looks and physique. And though he attempts to keep things chaste, I find his fingers often brush the skin of my torso, sending a shiver down my spine and a flush to my cheeks that I hope he doesn't notice.

"You're healing up rather nicely." He examines my wound with gratification. I crane my neck to look, which is effortful, but I'm pleased to find that he's right.

The wound, which has been oozing a rather unpleasant yellow fluid for the past several days, now looks much smaller and significantly less inflamed.

"And to think," says Farin, dressing my wound and pulling my shirt down to cover my torso. "Just a little while longer and you'll be rid of me for good."

Rid of Farin for good.

Yep. That's definitely what I want.

What any sane female would want.

To be rid of the murderer who stabbed her hoping to get back to another female.

I flash him a smile.

And hate myself for what it does to me when he smiles back.

A STORM BREAKS over the island, pelting our cave in hail and ice.

The hail doesn't make it into the cave, but the cold does.

It seeps through my thin tunic, soaking my skin and drilling into my bones, until it's less that I'm cold, and more that I ache, my limbs so brittle they feel as though they might shatter.

"You can't do this," Farin says, examining me from across the cave.

"Can't do what?" I ask, lying on my back, fighting the urge to curl into a ball in an attempt to warm myself, lest I burst the scabs that've formed on my wound.

"You won't survive the night."

"Must you narrate my death? It's a bit dramatic, don't you think?"

Farin smiles, the kind that tells me he's genuinely amused. "I could help you, you know."

I tug at the washed-up sail Farin fetched from the beach for me to use as a blanket, so that only my face shows. "I think you've done enough already."

"I'm going to take that as meaning nursing you back to health."

I sputter. "Nursing me back to health from the wound you inflicted."

He pauses. "I truly am sorry about that."

"So you've said."

"I'll say it a thousand times if I think there's the slightest chance you'll forgive me the next time around," he says.

I'd roll my eyes if they weren't so dry from the cold. "You really are enjoying this lying privilege."

Farin's lips curl. "Oh, I dunno. I can't like lying half as much as you."

I don't have energy for a response. Just a questioning look.

"You're lying to yourself right now," he says.

"Am I?"

Farin fixes his gaze on me. "Sure you are. You're telling yourself you hate me beyond what's forgivable. You're telling yourself that you don't share the same attraction for me that I hold for you. But that's not news. What's currently relevant is how you're pretending to yourself that you're not imagining me slipping into that sail with you, holding you close to me until my heat thaws your bones."

I harrumph, but it's mostly to hide the way his words would be causing me to shiver if I weren't already doing that. "You possess a rather inflated view of yourself."

T.A. LAWRENCE

He shrugs. "Who knows? Perhaps I'm secretly insecure and use my charm as a compensation method."

I can't help myself. I laugh.

His eyes glitter with satisfaction. "If I go on being self-deprecating, will you do that again?"

"Do what?"

"Laugh."

This time, I blush, and it's warm and lovely, and I'm probably only thinking it is because I'm freezing to death.

"Wanderer."

My throat goes dry. "Yes?"

"I promise if you let me hold you, I won't hurt you. Won't do anything other than keep you warm."

"I'm surprised you care anything about asking me for permission. Would have thought you'd be the type to force me into it, thinking you knew my own good."

Farin examines me for a while. "I'd rather it not come to that."

I swallow. "All right, then."

Farin doesn't hesitate. He crosses the width of the cave in a moment and slips into the sail I'm clutching around my shoulders.

Instantly, the heat of his chest warms me. Like stepping into a hot spring in the middle of winter. His heat spreads across my back, soothing the aching pain. When he slides his hand around my waist, running his fingers over it, careful to avoid my injury, I let out a sigh.

Mortification immediately overwhelms me. I wait for Farin's conceited comment about me sighing for his touch, but it never comes.

"Better?" he whispers, his breath steaming at the tip of my ear.

I nod, and he pulls me in tighter, contouring his chest to the curve of my back, wrapping his legs between mine.

As good as it feels, the shivering doesn't stop, not when the cold has seeped into my bones.

"Zora."

"Mhm?"

"There's a way we could warm you up faster."

388

My body goes rigid under his touch. I know this, of course. The first survival rule for dealing with the cold is that body heat is most efficient if it's skin-to-skin, surrounded by a blanket of some sort.

But it's bad enough allowing a murderer to wrap his arms around me, to hold me through the night.

Lying naked in his arms would feel like brandishing my bare throat to the sharp edge of a blade.

"No."

For a moment, Farin doesn't answer, and I wonder if he's contemplating forcing me to strip for my own good. Anxiety prickles my lungs, making it difficult to breathe. But then Farin just tucks his cheek into my hair and says, "Whatever you say, Wanderer."

CHAPTER 66

BLAISE

I hear Piper, the Red, speaking, but only barely. Like water's flooded my ears, and she's above the surface, calling out to me.

Autumn has settled into the outskirts of Dwellen, the trees beginning to burst into a cacophony of scarlets and yellows.

Not that I'll ever see their hues outside the shade of night.

We stalk through the forest, Piper's steps so light they hardly make a sound.

Mine don't make a sound either, which is strange, considering my entire body feels as if my veins have been filled with lead.

"We'll camp tonight, then take off first thing in the morning," Piper says, though something about that feels wrong.

"Morning?" I shake my head, bringing myself back into focus. "No. No, I can't travel in the daytime."

Piper offers me a confused look. The kind of look a female wanted in every kingdom for trafficking affords someone who claims they can't travel during the day. "We can get you a hood, a disguise even..."

I shake my head again, and it's like ridding water from my ears. "No, it's not that. I'm..." How does one explain vampirism? "I'm cursed. Sunlight burns me."

390

Piper takes that surprisingly well, though she doesn't hide the inconvenience written all over her expression. Still, she stares up at the sky while the warehouse smoke behind us fills my lungs.

Abra's body is burning in there, her head tossed casually aside from the rest of her, crumpled on the warehouse floor.

Assuming none of her landed in the vats.

I can't quite rid myself of the visual.

I would have thought I'd feel something surrounding the death of the female who made my life miserable, but I can hardly feel anything at all.

All I can feel is the pang in my chest when Nox's eyes met mine the moment he chose not to save me.

It was stupid of me not to realize why he was tagging along with me after the Old Magic cursed him not to love me anymore. I hoped there was something deeper there, something the Old Magic hadn't been able to touch.

But no. Nox just wanted Abra.

He wanted revenge, and I was the mechanism to get him there.

The strangest part is, I can't even blame him for it.

Isn't that what I used Evander, Ellie, and Asha for? To get me to the Rip so I could open it and get Nox back?

I'd known the Old Magic's punishment for me was fitting.

I just didn't realize until now exactly to what degree.

"I assume you had a cave in mind, to flee to afterward," says Piper, and my heart leaps as I remember the rendezvous point Nox and I agreed upon before entering the warehouse.

But when I lead Piper to the cave at the base of the Kobiis, there's no one there.

There's no sign anyone ever was.

Silly servant girl, no one wants the villain, whispers a voice.

A voice slithering from the adamant box strapped to my belt.

CHAPTER 67

ASHA

*A*fter an incident in which my new lady's maid, the one Az so casually replaced his sister with, found bedsores staining my thighs and torso while helping me bathe, Az has decided I'm allowed to visit the library for the afternoon.

I worry about Tavi. Az claims she's traveling the world like she always wanted, free to roam about now that her brother is king and can provide for her.

I find her sudden interest in traveling unlikely, considering the world is on the brink of war.

Tavi's disappearance isn't the only thing concerning me, though. Each night Az goes without sleep—stimulated by the magical elixir from his healer—his poise seems to slip.

Though there's part of me that hopes his exhaustion will cause him to mis-step, the other part of me worries about who will be caught in the cross fire when he finally does.

THE LIBRARY LOOKS ABANDONED, like no one has used it since Az's coup.

The thought threatens to make me sad, but it seems like a silly thing to waste my sadness on, when I can just be happy that no one thought to touch my books.

I'm not allowed by myself in the library. One of Az's guards stands at attention near the entrance, but that's fine by me. I overheard Az's instructions to him. I'm to be given the entire day to spend here, and I'm rather confident in my ability to entertain myself until the guard is lulled to sleep by boredom.

That, and the fact that I throw a few extra logs on the fireplace, causing the flames to swell jovially, thickening the air with a sickly, blanketing heat.

Granted, I'm rather uncomfortable after about an hour and find myself tugging at my collar just so I can breathe a little easier. That's no matter. The guard is faring much worse, what with all the armor piled atop him.

Beads of sweat glisten on his forehead as he stands watching me.

I'm careful to remain still as I read. No flopping about or anything that might threaten to keep the guard alert.

If he were a good guard, he could force himself awake through even the dullest, most sweltering of activities. At least, that's what Az would say.

But even guards have to sleep, and even the fae can't escape boredom.

It takes five hours and a rather heavy lunch supplied fortuitously by the kitchen staff, but eventually the guard nods off, and I sneak over to the fireplace.

MY FINGERS CARESS the stone surface, tracing the strange markings written in an ancient language.

Ah, so here we are again. They've yet to replace the vase you broke, says my magic.

Indeed, the mantel sits empty, and if I pressed my bare feet into the rug below, I'm fairly sure shards of ceramic would prick me and alert me to their presence.

393

Together, my magic and my voice meld, reading the script in the ancient language.

A quick breeze quenches the fire in the hearth as the back wall of the fireplace disappears into the shadows.

It's dark in the chamber. I'll have to find the discarded lamp somewhere on the floor if I want to see much of anything. Then again, I suppose it's not all that important that I be able to see the chamber, only that I remove some of its contents.

I shuffle around the chamber on my hands and knees, not wishing to trip and awaken the guard in the library. But when my hands touch the ground, and I reach my way to the shelves lining the edge of the room, I find nothing but dust lining the shelves.

Thinking I must have organized the scrolls on another shelf before I left, and that the turmoil of the past few months evicted it from my memory, I scale to the other side, running my hands across those shelves as well.

Empty.

A light flickers to life behind me, dread swelling in my belly.

I turn to find Az, half his face obscured in the shadows.

Even the shadows can't mask the dark circles underneath his eyes, the symptom of countless sleepless nights.

"I had them removed before you arrived," he says. "You aren't the only one who can read the ancient language. I had one of the scholars open the passageway. Sent a message ahead of us before we arrived in Naenden."

Removed. Az had the scrolls removed, anticipating I would try to use them against him.

I have the sudden urge to dig my fingernails into my skin.

Frustration threatens to boil me alive, but I won't succumb to it. Won't let Az get the best of me.

Another hope spurs within me. One I've been contemplating over the past several weeks. Opening the Rip was a substantial event, one that shook the earth itself. When I held the Fabric between my fingertips, I wondered if perhaps I could trace its path all across Alondria.

Before, I could draw power from the scrolls in the library, as they harnessed magic from the Rip through which they'd traveled.

But what if there exists more of a connection than we thought? What if, when the Rip opened, the force that caused the earth to tremble had ricocheted down the Fabric, tearing again at its weakest point?

It's a frivolous hope, but I feel for a Rip, listen for its gentle hum. A sliver of power I could draw from. Anything at all.

"Asha, dear," Az says, approaching me. I can't help but notice that he holds the lantern up to the side of my face that remains whole. "You really are beautiful," he whispers, now that the ugly side of me is obscured by the shadows.

I remember the feel of the mask plastered to my face during the coronation. That wasn't the last time I've been forced to wear it. Occasionally, he brings it to me on the nights he visits me in my quarters.

He claims it reminds him of a simpler time.

"I wish there were a way to steal you back. It's like he has his claws in you, and the harder I pull, the more at risk I am of shattering the splinter. Leaving a piece on the inside I can't hope to find, not without clawing it out. Taking muscle and flesh with it."

My magic hisses. *Is that supposed to be a threat?*

I myself am unsure. I'm beginning to wonder if sometimes Az just enjoys the sound of his own voice.

"What did you do with the scrolls?" I can't help but ask, even as my posture slumps.

I'm so tired. So, so very tired.

But keeping Az talking gives me more time to feel for the Rip I'm desperately hoping exists in this room. My fingers flex at my sides, as if trying to cling to the Fabric itself.

Nothing. I feel nothing.

Annoyance flickers in Az's sage-green eyes. "I burned them."

I stiffen. "What? Why?"

"Because of moments like this. Moments when the magic Kiran has over you became too overwhelming for you to resist. That's why you were down here, wasn't it? To draw power from the ancient scrolls, much like you would from the Rip? To use it to conjure some illusion with which to trick me into handing the kingdom back to Kiran? No, we can't risk that, can we?"

No. No, I suppose we can't.

"I was thinking, Asha," he says, bringing his hand to my unmarred cheek and whispering, "how would you feel about seeing a healer? I've found someone who specializes in your condition, and they believe they can help."

I stiffen. I know I've been depressed lately, and while I'd love to have a healer treat me, I'm suspicious of what drugs Az might command his healers to give me. Potions that would make me more compliant? The idea makes me want to hurl.

"You're beautiful, Asha. You deserve for your appearance to reflect that."

My gut clenches.

"You want to heal my scars," I say, my throat tightening.

He presses a kiss to my forehead, as if to say, *You're welcome.*

There's a numbness within me when he leads me out of the tiny alcove I had hoped might be my salvation.

The guard who fell asleep on my watch is gone. I don't want to think about what Az did with him. A messenger slips into the library, breathing heavily as he bows before Az.

"A message from the King of Dwellen, Your Majesty," says the courier, handing Az a delicate slip of parchment.

It looks like the kind of message King Marken would send, wrapped in silky thick silver parchment with a seal of blue wax hardened over the front.

Az rips it open anxiously. I watch his eyes dart back and forth, but the message must be short, because he doesn't linger on it for long.

Anxiety slips through the numb fog in my head. If Az is in contact with King Marken, that can only mean trouble. While the King of Dwellen allowed my and Kiran's extended stay in Othian, the male never bothered with the pretense that he was pleased with the situation.

I wouldn't put it past him to ally with Az, especially if Az has offered him the protection of his army of Others.

"What does it say?" I ask, infusing my voice with worry, hoping to tug on Az's sympathies.

He smiles down upon me and plants a wet kiss on my forehead. "You don't have to worry about it, love."

I don't miss the way his hands shake as he caresses my cheeks. Don't miss the crazed aura in Az's expression as he pulls away. The twitching that's returned to his left eyelid.

On the way out of the library, he rips the correspondence to pieces.

I reach for the Fabric one last time, begging it for a gap to slip through.

It doesn't reach back.

CHAPTER 68

ELLIE

Gentle rays of sunlight waft through the warped glass window —one that I suppose the palace ordered from a competitor before I married into the family, as I don't see my initials anywhere—whispering that morning has finally come.

Well, *finally* is probably a generous word.

Truth be told, I don't exactly want morning to come, not when Cecilia was up screaming all night.

Peck keeps telling me Cecilia's nocturnal sleep schedule is because I did too much riding while I was pregnant.

"Lulled the baby to sleep during the day. Taught her bad habits from the beginning," he's commented, unsolicited, multiple times.

When I complained to Evander about it, he told me that was what I got for teaming up with Peck against my husband so often.

I wasn't quite in the mood to admit that he was right, so I'd just stuck my tongue out at him wearily.

Either way, Cecilia is not a good sleeper. At all.

Which is fine, because I adore her so much my heart might explode at any moment.

Other parts of me might explode too. For instance, my bladder, which, despite Peck's potions, has yet to recover from my unfortunately traumatic labor. Then there's my patience, which I find is always ready to detonate.

It's been a rough few weeks, that's for sure.

But then there are moments like these, moments when Cecilia is sleeping, her pretty little face as peaceful as the surface of an abandoned pond, her little pointed ears poking out from underneath her dark ringlets. And I think perhaps I understand why people look back on these days so fondly.

Even if I am convinced part of the reason is that all species would cease to exist if anyone remembered these days accurately. Well, maybe not cease to exist. But there certainly would be a shortage of second siblings.

Still, as I rock Cecilia in the chair Evander made for me (complete with the comfiest pillows he could bribe out of the local seamstress), I have no choice but to feel immense gratitude. It swells in my heart just looking at her. Usually, I glance back and forth between my daughter and husband. When he isn't training with Orion, Evander is typically fast asleep across the room, exhausted from the several times he's gotten up to change her in the middle of the night between feedings.

There's something about these moments I want to keep close. We haven't officially announced Cecilia's birth yet. Enough people know about her that she's not exactly a secret, but with all the chaos surrounding her birth and Az supposedly rallying an army in Naenden, I'm not eager to share her with the world yet.

Cecilia's screaming isn't the only reason sleep evades me. Even when she's quiet, and sleep comes, it's hardly ever restful.

Nightmares, filled with images of my child's death, the lack of her screams and the continuation of mine, punctuate any slumber I might have stolen otherwise.

It tortures me when the part of me that keeps control of my mind goes off duty. During my sleeping hours, I'm at the mercy of what could have happened. What life might have been like if Cecilia had not survived.

It's in those moments that I think of Blaise, and my heart aches for my friend. My friend who's somehow made herself my enemy, though out of no malice for me.

Before, I couldn't imagine the pain she's suffered. Now, I think perhaps I can taste it, in the memories of the moments when I lost hope that Cecilia would survive. When I convinced myself the labor pains had come too early, that there was no reasonable way she could endure outside the womb.

Evander and I are fortunate. I've since found a few documents describing various gestations between fae and humans. They all varied, some lasting as long as twelve months, others much shorter. As far as I know, mine with Cecilia is the shortest recorded.

The thought makes me ill, but in more than one way. Ill, because it terrifies me thinking of what could have happened to my child. Ill, because Blaise would have been to blame if Cecilia had died.

Can I ever forgive Blaise, knowing that her actions almost caused my daughter's death? Does it make me a horrible mother if I forgive my child's potential murderer?

Not that Blaise intended for me to be caught in the cross fire. I suppose that's part of the reason she broke off from the camp. Suppose she hoped the ritual for opening the Rip would cease before the rest of the party could catch up to her and Az.

But still.

It was a betrayal, nonetheless. And after Evander gave so much of himself to prove he trusted her.

Perhaps it's my duty to hate her, to brand her as an adversary. An enemy to the family I would protect with my life.

But then, when my mind starts down that path, I always end up circling back. Back to the moments when I thought I lost my baby. Back to the shadows that surrounded me, threatening to drown me.

I'm not sure what I would have become had Cecilia died.

I don't think I would have ended up like Blaise, foolishly trusting those who seek to use her, rather than depending on her loved ones and friends.

But I likely would have hated her. Hated her in the permanent sort of way, the sort of way I wouldn't bother debating about.

I think it might have burned a hole inside me, a callus over my heart, and then I'm unsure what I would have done.

And even if I wouldn't have turned out like Blaise, losing my baby, as horrific as the thought is, wouldn't have made our sorrows equal.

No, Blaise has faced horrors in her short years, atrocities I'll likely never have to endure.

I'm not sure if that means I'm allowed to forgive her, but I think that, at least for now, I can pity her.

And that makes not hating her easier.

"What do you think?" I whisper to Cecilia, who wriggles contentedly in my arms, her tiny little body a furnace warming my soul. "Will you be mad at me if I forgive her?"

Cecilia doesn't answer. So far, my daughter is very little help when it comes to offering advice.

I'm about to tell her as much when the warped glass of the window shatters, stealing my breath and puncturing my back as I cover Cecilia with my body.

CHAPTER 69

EVANDER

*O*rion is just about to admit that I'm getting the hang of this magic thing, when shadows creep over the atrium and the blue sky turns silver.

"What in Alondria?" Orion's vines snake back to his sides as he stares into the sky, his jaw set.

Overhead, blotches of silver paint the heavens, an army of Others reflecting the sunlight like clouds carrying the warning of a storm.

These are not the mere we fought on the plains of Rivre.

These are something different entirely, called on by their kinsmen.

Wings of silver reflect the sunlight, beating torrents of wind down upon us as the plants in the atrium sway in horror. Their long, lithe bodies are coated in shimmering scales that serve as armor for the creatures.

"Wyverns," I say.

Orion glances over at me. "Wyverns are extinct."

I shrug, grasping at the hilt of my sword. "In our world, they are."

"We have to raise the alarm, alert the king," says Orion, and then he's off, and I follow.

All I can think as we sprint across the wide atrium is their names. Ellie. Cecilia. Ellie. Cecilia. Where had Ellie said they would be today?

Was she planning to take Cecilia on a stroll around the gardens? Or would they have stayed in today?

I wrack my mind, searching for what exactly she said as I left the bed this morning.

I can't think of the words.

Orion intercepts a courier. He's just shouted at him to alert the king of an attack on Othian, when the half-open ceiling of the atrium is blown to smithereens.

THE WYVERN STANDS BEFORE US, crouched on its haunches. Its tail sways, taking out pillar after pillar with its might until half of the atrium caves in. Weeping vines of greenery reach out at us from beneath the weight of the fallen stone.

The sight of it stirs something in me.

My magic, I realize.

Orion is to my left, battle ready, his hands extended at his sides as he mutters incantations.

The plants left alive in the atrium rear to attack.

Ellie. I have to get to Ellie and Cecilia. Orion can take on the beast better than I could. In fact, I'll probably just get in the way.

But then there's a cry, a child's cry, coming from behind the rubble.

My heart twists, knotting into a ball in my chest.

The nursery.

The atrium is directly above the nursery, where the servants' children stay during the day while their parents fulfill their household tasks.

Panic floods me at the sound of the cry. No, not one cry. The cries and screams of several children, trapped below the rubble.

I'm going to be sick.

My feet beg to run. To go after my wife and daughter, to search them out and lead them to the safety of the bunkers beneath the castle.

I've already tried being the hero. I've already put the needs of others before my family, and it was a mistake. It had ended with...

It had ended with Ellie, pregnant with our child, throwing herself in front of Amity.

The cries of the children ripple out into the air.

Orion spares me one glance, one nod of understanding.

I swallow, and Orion's magic attacks.

HUNDREDS OF VINES jab at the monster's throat, snaking around its neck and squeezing, but it lets out a bellow and yanks itself free. Vines splay, the wooden ones splintering and spraying shards of debris upon us.

I duck underneath Orion's next attempt to attack the creature, dodging vines and thorns as I make for the heap of rubble on the other side of the wyvern. Its tail makes a sweeping stroke. I have to jump to keep from tripping.

Orion's vines clasp on to the monster's tail, but every time one gets a grip, the spikes lining the creature's tail shear right through them.

I make my way through the tangled mess and quickly realize the stone heaps are too large to be moved by hand.

My heart races, the cries of the children growing more muffled. Are they passing out down there, unable to breathe through the dust from the debris and the weight of the stones piled atop them?

"Please, please someone help them," someone, an adult, cries from down below. "They're down here. Someone, please."

"I'm here," I bellow. "I'm coming."

Though, I'm not sure how much comfort that truly is.

I search the area, an idea springing to my mind.

I summon a nearby tangle of vines, hoping Orion won't mind if I borrow some of his, and send them snaking around the stones that are too heavy for me to lift on my own. Then, with the vines slithering through the holes in the debris and pushing upon the stone from underneath, I pull.

The boulder groans in protest, but it moves. My back aches with exertion, my muscles feeling as if they might rip with the effort, but as the vines push and I pull, the stone comes loose.

With an agonized groan, I shove the rock to the side, allowing it to tumble down the heap. The rocks underneath are smaller, though I still require the help of the vines to move them.

All the while, I keep my ears trained on the children's whimpers and the shrieks of the wyvern.

Eventually, the last of the rocks comes free, revealing a shaft of darkness below the pile.

I hadn't realized the nursery had been reinforced with iron beams, but they're holding strong underneath the weight of the rubble.

"You're safe down there?" I ask. "Is anyone injured?"

"There's a child whose leg is trapped under the rubble," calls a female's voice.

I grab hold of the lip of the hole and swing myself into the pit that used to be the nursery.

It's dark, but my eyesight adjusts quickly, revealing about a dozen children and their warden, a spindly fae female with parchment-colored skin and brown eyes that I recognize, given she's worked in the nursery for decades.

She quickly directs me to the corner, and through dust swirls in the shadows, I catch sight of a small body crumpled on the floor.

The little girl is breathing through whimpers, probably in shock from the column that seems to have crushed her knee and pinned the bottom half of her leg to the floor.

My ears attend to the fight continuing above us, but the screams of the wyvern are getting further away, like Orion is luring it out of the atrium.

To give the children a chance to escape.

His plan clicks into place in my mind, and I nod toward the warden. "Help me move this," I say, hoping that between two fae, we can move the column.

"The child will pass out once we do," says the warden, looking down at the little girl with pained eyes.

"Right." Though it kills me to do so, I climb out of the hole and direct the warden to start handing me children. She does, and together we pair the toddlers off with the older ones, instructing them to take the younger children to the emergency cellars following the lead of the warden, whom I pull out last.

"Once the children are safe, find Peck and send him to me," I say, but a dry voice clacks from the distance.

"At your service, Your Highness." Peck strolls into the busted area with his nose curled up as if he'd walked in on me and Ellie making out rather than straight into a direct assault on the castle.

I bury my annoyance, and he follows me into the hole as the children scurry off.

The little girl's whimpers have faded, and a sheen of sweat dampens her forehead.

Peck curses in his first language, his eyes widening with recognition at the child. "Why, Sonalee? Why don't you ever do as I tell you and stay out of trouble's way? This girl..." he tsks, "always stumbling into something or another, falling off precipices she's not supposed to be climbing."

He clucks, and I try to hold my tongue rather than pointing out that it's not this poor child's fault a column fell atop her.

With Peck's help, we're able to lift the column, though the girl's eyes roll back into her head immediately.

"I can carry her back to the infirmary," I say, leaning to lift her after we place the column down, but Peck shoos me away.

"Just help me get her out of this wretched hole, and I'll take her. You don't know which bed is hers, anyway."

I'm left wondering exactly how often this child has ended up in the infirmary to earn her own bed, but again, I don't question it.

Once we've hauled the girl into the atrium, I hand her limp body to Peck.

"Sure you don't need help carrying her?" I ask, though somewhat reluctantly.

Peck's voice drips with derision. "My boy, shouldn't you be looking after your own wife and child?"

I don't have time to respond before he runs off. I'm trying to remember if Ellie told me where she planned to be today, when the wyvern comes crashing back into the atrium.

This time, Orion is nowhere to be found. The wyvern licks its lips, blood staining its silvery maw, and I can't help but wonder if perhaps Orion's in front of me after all.

That thought is a bit too morbid to ponder, especially when I'm about to do battle with an Other, so I push it from my mind.

The wyvern stalks toward me, its talons clicking against the cracked marble tile.

I don't wait for it to attack. Instead, I use a technique Orion's been teaching me to summon several vines at once. They burst from the earth beneath the already cracked tile, wrapping themselves around the wyvern's scaly legs.

It cries out, its shriek rattling the half-open ceiling. It tries to stomp out the vines, but they continue coiling around its legs, and though the wyvern is panicking, its efforts are spread too thin.

I use the opportunity to run toward the beast, summoning a series of vines that serve as footholds that catapult me onto the wyvern's tail.

I was hoping for its back, right above its neck, but whatever.

The hilt of my blade glistens in the sunlight pouring through the open roof as I wield it, jumping to my feet and racing across the beast's scaly back.

It writhes against the vines, whose grip wanes as I split my concentration between maintaining them and remaining upright.

I make it all the way to the wyvern's neck and raise my blade.

When the creature extends its wings.

It flaps them, sending a gust of air through the atrium so forcefully I stumble for balance.

Two more beats of its wings, and something snaps.

My vines.

The wyvern howls in delight.

Then launches into the air.

I have half a second to dig my fingers between the scales of its neck for purchase, but doing so requires both hands. I wince as I hear my sword clank against the ground, left behind as the wyvern and I soar into the heavens.

CHAPTER 70

ELLIE

*C*ecilia is screaming, and I can't help but wonder if it will be the thing that will save us or end us.

No, if anything ends us, it'll be the Other that just burst through the window and now lurks on the floor of the nursery.

Piles of shattered glass litter the floor around its scaly, silver paws. Long claws protrude from the fissures in its paws, matching the dripping fangs extending from its long, scaly snout. Wings flake out from the reptilian creature's back, stretching themselves out, causing more glass to slide off the membranous skin and clatter to the floor.

The silver scales tip me off that this is an Other, though it's shaped like the mythical wyvern.

It stalks toward us, a razor-sharp tongue licking its silvery snout.

I'm not sure what to do. Does one scream at an Other? Likely not. If that were the answer, my bellowing child would have already frightened it away.

"Help," I call, in case the guards haven't realized Cecilia's screams aren't the routine sort, which of course they haven't, because Cecilia screams constantly. "Help. Someone, please!" I shout, tucking Cecilia closer to my chest.

My heart pounds, but the fear coursing through my veins transforms into something else, something more productive, because what I feel doesn't taste of fear at all.

No. This is something different.

I am something different.

I think perhaps I have my child to thank for that.

The Other lunges, but I am, somehow, ready. I bolt to the side, toward the nursery door. I've almost made it when I hear a clamor on the other side.

I step out of the way just in time as a line of guards comes rushing in, responding to my call for help.

Unfortunately, they have no idea what they're up against, or that the Other has just lunged for me again.

It gets two guards between its jaws, the sound of their bones cracking. That normally would make me sick, except my body seems to know that it doesn't have the option to be sick, not if I'm going to get my daughter out of this.

Instead, I retreat, hopping not-so-nimbly over the Other's swooshing tail as it focuses on the guards.

I think to hide in the closet, but then the Other opens its jaws, dropping two corpses to the floor. It hisses, spraying a silvery liquid at the remaining guards.

This time, the sound does make my stomach lurch.

Several of the guards scream, cries of pain I'd yet to hear the likes of. As I reach the closet, I chance a look over my shoulder.

I regret doing so.

The silvery spray coats the soldiers' armor, which is smoking, sizzling as the creature's spit burns holes in it, ripping through the helmets and breastplates. It doesn't slow as it reaches their skin, burning, burning, burning, until I glimpse muscle and bone and...

I look away, hearing the thud of bodies as they slump to the floor.

The creature sniffs around at their corpses, then there's the familiar crunching sound as the creature feasts.

No. No, no, no.

No, it won't get me. And it certainly won't get my baby.

Distracted. I have to get out of here while the thing is distracted, but it's blocking the doorway to the nursery with its massive body, and the only other way out of the room is the window.

That isn't going to work.

We're at least six stories up.

I could climb down, I figure. The outside of the palace is intricately designed enough that I could probably find enough footholds and handholds, if not to scale down, then to at least hide out until the Other is gone or someone can come rescue me.

I tuck Cecilia into my chest, slipping across the floor and over the Other's happily swooshing tail. There are still shards of glass left in the window, but I manage to poke my head out and get a good look.

I instantly wish I hadn't, the ground appearing so much further away than it usually does. Several gargoyles line the walls, and a few ledges too. But if I'm going to reach any of them, I'll have to jump.

The calmness I was afforded moments ago seems to vanish as reality sets in.

There's no way out of this room. Not with Cecilia in my arms.

I can't catch myself and hold on to her, too.

No. No, I won't accept that. There has to be another way. I will *make* there be another way.

Please, I pray to the Fates. *You already saved her once. Please just save her again. You don't have to worry about me.*

I blink away the tears threatening to blur my vision, swallow the fear intent on paralyzing me, then search the room again.

A sling. I have to have one around here somewhere. I used one when I took the baby on walks, but it was usually Imogen who brought it to me, and in truth, I've never paid the slightest attention to where she keeps it. In fact, I pay little attention to much of how Imogen does anything she does; I've been so exhausted.

Since when did I let myself become so helpless?

Frustration boils inside of me, but I can't let it win.

I make myself look over at the Other again, and to my dismay, I watch it lap up the last of the guards' corpses.

No, no, no, no, no.

Cecilia is still screaming. The Other will finish its meal any moment now, and it'll come straight for her.

I have to get out of here. I have to save her.

If only she could go, and I could stay, but there's no way out.

I don't realize I've been retreating until my spine hits a knob.

But there isn't a door there, my brain says, rather unhelpfully.

Still, I turn.

And almost gasp in relief.

The dumbwaiter.

Imogen sent food up on it just earlier today.

It's not large enough for me to slip into, but…

I glance down at my poor, squirming little girl.

"Mommy loves you. I know you won't remember me saying this, but I hope your daddy tells you all about it," I say, pressing a kiss to my child's forehead.

And then I place my baby in the wooden box and slam the door, tugging on the rope.

The dumbwaiter squeals.

I sense the Other turn, but I don't let myself look. I'm not going anywhere until I feel the weight of the dumbwaiter rest at the bottom of the shaft.

Fates, surely there aren't any Others in the kitchen.

Please don't let there be any Others in the kitchen, I pray.

The thought has me wanting to turn the rope the other way, to lift Cecilia back to the safety of my arms. But that's nonsensical. An idea brought on by panic and hysteria.

There's a chance the Others have reached the kitchen, but there *is* one in here with me.

I keep coaxing the rope until the weight of the dumbwaiter thuds softly, the rope stopping in my hands.

I throw myself backwards, no thought of where I might be sending my body crossing my mind. My only survival instinct is that I have to get away from where I was standing.

It turns out to be a pretty good survival instinct, because the jaws of the Other curl around the now empty space.

There's a snapping of rope as the creature's jaws cut through the pulley. Panic seizes me. I picture my baby falling, and I have to remind myself she's already reached safety at the bottom of the shaft. There is nowhere to fall.

I suck in a breath, and realize that I'm going to die.

But then, what if there's no one alive left in the kitchens? What if no one knows where to look for my baby? It's not the most reasonable of thoughts, I have to admit. Cecilia is a screamer, after all. It hasn't been my absolute favorite quality of my daughter's, if I'm being perfectly honest, but now I could have kissed the Fates' feet for blessing me with a baby whose favorite activity is alerting others of her presence.

I will die up here in the nursery, but someone will find Cecilia. Her little screams will notify her rescuer right where she is, and she will live. I hate that I'll be leaving her, but I hope that perhaps she'll understand.

The Other turns to face me, and I shudder, using what is more than likely going to be my last breath.

Evander was right. My mother is going to make the perfect mother to our child.

I decide that will be a fine alternative if this doesn't work out favorably for me. But my baby is still my baby, and to be perfectly honest, I think my mother gets plenty of time with my baby as it is.

It's with this thought that I sprint across the room, and as the Other attacks, hurtle out the window.

CHAPTER 71

EVANDER

*O*thian is beautiful from this high up.

At least, I imagine that's what I'd be thinking if I weren't currently scrambling atop the back of the wyvern, clinging to its scales for dear life as we surge into the sky.

Condensation has me choking as the wyvern cuts through the clouds, sending a spray of liquid up my nose.

I squeeze my burning eyes shut, then force them open despite the wind lashing against them.

And for a moment, as the wyvern reaches the peak of our ascent and the two of us are weightless, I peer down at the clouds beneath us, their blanket of white shining magnificently in the daylight.

There's no time to sit in awe, though.

Not when, after a single weightless moment, the wyvern twists.

My world turns upside down as the creature flips onto its back, allowing gravity to take hold and send us plummeting.

Where there was once a row of scales beneath me, there's now only clouds.

We cut through the mist.

There's only ground hurtling toward us as the wind presses my torso to the wyvern's spine.

Panic rises within me.

I really would rather not die splattered on the ground, smashed between the wyvern and a poorly placed turret.

Thankfully, the wyvern doesn't seem to realize how physics works, and that I haven't fallen faster than the wyvern itself, like the stupid creature must have hoped.

Which means it has to spin back around sometime.

That's about the only hope I have as I claw my fingers into the space between its scales and hold tight.

We fall for what feels like eternity, and just when I'm sure I'm about to become a decorative sidewalk mural in the town square, the wyvern pivots, sending me upright, then opens its wings.

We catch wind, the force of it sending us weightless again, floating upward and above the castle.

But not high enough that my vines can't reach.

I call them from the earth, sending them straight through the leathery portion of the creature's wings, biting at its membrane until its wings look like sails tattered by a storm.

The wyvern cries out, and we fall.

THE CRASH SENDS us careening through the roof of the castle.

A harsh impact rattles my bones, shooting me off the back of the wyvern. Rubble beats against my limbs as I roll across the floor, pain exploding through my muscles.

Stars blanket my vision, which doesn't seem right given it's midday, but when I go to push myself off the ground, I stumble.

Something scaly wraps itself around my torso and squeezes.

CHAPTER 72

ELLIE

$\mathcal{F}$alling is a rather unpleasant experience.

I've fallen before, back at the arena when Evander and I faced our first Trial.

Except that time, Evander was there to catch me.

Well, he'd technically been the one to drop me too, so I suppose I can't give him too much credit.

That's what I'm thinking as my body slams into the back of a gargoyle.

Its horns jam into my torso, but thankfully the artist opted for more flattened horns. I decide I'll have to seek them out in the art district and thank them later.

I'm fairly sure this is what undiluted panic feels like. Or perhaps delirium. Or maybe a combination. I don't think I'm in the mental state to make medical diagnoses at the moment.

A giggle escapes my lips, I suppose because I'm high from the fall, or maybe it's because I can still hear Cecilia's cries in my ears. (Are those real, or just in my imagination, and will the Other hear them too?)

Perhaps I shouldn't have jumped out the window. Perhaps I should have left myself in the room as bait, so that the Other wouldn't hear my baby's screams and try to burst through the shaft to get to her.

Then again, the Other probably couldn't fit.

I should probably breathe, I tell myself. I do, but then I make the mistake of looking down, thinking perhaps I can jump to another gargoyle, and then the deranged giggles begin again.

Evander never quite let go of teasing me about my fear of heights and how I clung to him like a sloth to a tree during the entirety of our first Trial.

Well, if he doesn't come provide a muscled arm for me to grab onto soon, I decide I'll never let him hear the end of *that*.

Breathe, I remind myself, looking down again.

I keep one eye closed, as if that will shield me from the truth of the height.

It doesn't.

Still, there's another gargoyle jutting from the story below. There's even another ledge to a window, but it's to the side of the gargoyle, and far enough away that I probably couldn't reach it.

So I have two options. Jump to the next gargoyle, still several stories above the ground, with few other handholds in sight. Meaning I'll have to wait up here for someone to get me.

Or I can go for the window ledge, which unfortunately has a grand total of zero gargoyles underneath it to act as a backup plan.

Above me, the Other roars with irritation. A moment later, debris litters my hair as it shoves its hideous maw through the window, its nostrils sniffing above me.

Waiting on the side of the palace for someone to find me has been withdrawn as an option.

I peer down at the ledge, which only seems to be about a hands-breadth in width. That's going to be problematic, as I'm fairly sure if I attempt to grab onto it with my hands as I fall, the result will be an Ellie splattered against the pavement below.

Not ideal.

Above me, the Other roars, stretching its apparently extendable neck to crane its head down and look directly at me.

Its moonlit eyes send a shiver through my bones, and I just have to pray it won't want to spray me with its melting venom when clearly I have nowhere else to go, and no weapon with which to fight back.

I've been keeping my sword in the training room. Not exactly helpful at the moment.

I wince as I rip the top layer of my skirt, then the second and third in succession. My hands tremble, but somehow I knot the pieces together into a rope that at least looks somewhat secure. I suppose I'll be finding out shortly.

It takes more balance than I naturally possess, but the Fates are smiling down upon me, because I manage to take the rope by both ends, looping it around the bottom of the gargoyle, then tying it in a knot at the top, leaving a long piece dangling off.

In an ideal world, I would have tied the other end of the rope around my torso, but we aren't living in an ideal world, are we? Evidenced by the fact that my baby is screaming in a dumbwaiter, a monster from another realm is dangling its head over mine, and I'm standing on a gargoyle jutting from an unfavorable height of the palace.

Yes, in an ideal world, I would have tied the rope around my waist.

But in this world, the Other opens its maw, its teeth glistening in the morning light.

So, with all the strength left in me, I grab the rope and jump.

I fall, weightless, but then the rope catches, swinging me back toward the castle wall.

Glass sprays, peppering my legs with cuts as my feet go through the window.

My backside slams against the floor of the palace. Wherever I am in the palace. A quick glance around the room tells me the spare dining hall.

I amble to my feet, thanking the Fates as I do, and run.

THERE'S no one in the kitchens when I arrive.

There's no baby in the dumbwaiter, either.

I feel as though I'm going to be sick as I take in my surroundings. Pots left boiling on the stove, aromatic soup bubbling over and sizzling in the fire below. Bowls of egg yolks left out on the counter. Milk dripping from a toppled glass onto the floor.

And no baby in the dumbwaiter.

My heart breaks in half, my mind searching for any way this might be a good thing, when I hear a cry, and it's the most beautiful sound to reach my ears.

I FIND them in the pantry, the entire kitchen staff stuffed in there. I have to pound on the door and wait for them to move the sacks of goods they barricaded the door with before they let me in.

But then I find her, my little Cecilia, crying inconsolably in the arms of Collins, the head chef. He's holding my child at arm's length like he's never held a baby in his life.

"Oh, Your Highness." He breathes in relief when he sees me, partly because I'm alive, partly because he's clearly ready to hand my baby off to me. "We thought for sure you were dead. We heard the shrieks of that creature coming down through the shaft." The whole kitchen staff shudders.

"You need to get to the bunkers," I tell them.

Collins's eyes go wide. "Surely you can't expect us to traipse through the hallways with those things on the loose."

I level a stare at him, tucking my baby into my chest and reveling in her warmth, in her shrieks.

Safe. Cecilia is safe.

"Do you really want to be stuffed into the pantry when that thing gets hungry again?"

Apparently not, because the entire kitchen staff starts to scramble out of the tiny space.

THE BUNKERS AREN'T FAR from the kitchens, so we get to them fairly quickly. It takes me banging on the metal trapdoors and using my status as princess to get the guards to open up for the kitchen staff, something I will certainly not be forgetting if ever I become queen, but eventually everyone makes it down into the dank but roomy bunker.

I search for my husband, but of course he's not down here. Anxiety rattles my chest when I realize he's probably out defending the city.

Evander.

I'd seen the determination in his eyes when he decided to train with his magic. I've witnessed how intent he's been on learning how to protect Cecilia and me.

My heart falls through my gut.

Evander has made significant gains in his magic, but these creatures are at another level entirely.

And what they did to the soldiers' armor...

I'm going to be sick.

"Collins," I say, planting a kiss on Cecilia's forehead before placing my daughter into his arms. He takes her, rather reluctantly, and she immediately starts screaming.

Then, before the guards can register whether they have the authority to stop me, I climb out of the bunker and run for the training room.

When I arrive, my sword is glinting in the sunlight, begging to be bloodied.

CHAPTER 73

EVANDER

*T*his is it. This is when I die.

I started training too late. Realized too late. Perhaps if I hadn't spent so many years with my face in a bottle, chasing after females I cared nothing for, perhaps then I would have gotten to live for Ellie. Live for Cecilia.

I just have to pray the Fates won't punish them for my lack of preparation.

I struggle against the wyvern's tail as it squeezes the breath out of me, but it's no use.

The wyvern, its mouth dripping with venom, attacks.

I brace, whether for pain or an instantaneous death, I'm not sure.

But death does not come.

The wyvern's maw halts just inches from my face. It soon begins writhing, though its tail remains wrapped around me. I struggle to free myself, but its flailing tosses me about, squeezing the air out of my lungs.

Black spots pepper my vision, but not enough that I don't glimpse what saved me, if just for a moment.

A tangle of vines wraps itself around the wyvern's neck, crushing its windpipe, wringing tighter the more it struggles.

And across the hall is my father, the King of Dwellen, staring up at the creature with delight burning in his eyes as he slowly kills my would-be murderer.

My father advances, his kingly robes whirling around him as he extends his hand.

Then squeezes.

There's a sickening crunch as the thorns shear through flesh, separating the wyvern's head from its body.

The head falls, jaw still agape in shock. It plunges toward me, but the limb of a tree slams into it, volleying it across the room.

The tail securing me loosens, my lungs gasping for breath as I fight my way out of its clutches.

I go to stand, to dust myself off and make myself less of a target for the insults that are surely coming, but before I can, a hand extends toward me.

I glance up at my father, unsure, but he nods and I take his hand. He pulls me to my feet. Where I expect mockery in his face, I find none.

"You fought valiantly," he says, his voice devoid of emotion. "There aren't many who would take on a beast of that size on their own. Few who would survive once a creature like that got them into its own territory."

"Well, I don't know that I had much of a choice," I say.

My father frowns. "There is always a choice."

I figure this is the point when my father will say something akin to, "You surprised me, boy. I would have expected you to run with your tail tucked between your legs," or, "Had you applied yourself at the Academy you might not have needed to be rescued like a child."

But he says none of these things. Instead, he studies me and says, "Your brother would have been proud of you."

My throat tightens, my mouth hanging open, but no words come out.

"Dust yourself off, son." My father nods toward the courtyard, where shrieks still rise to the sky. "We have a city to protect."

· · ·

421

WE RUN TO THE COURTYARD, my father's armor clanking around him. I try to cut toward my and Ellie's quarters, but my father informs me that Ellie and Cecilia have already reached the bunker, much to my relief. My heart aches to go to them, but I can't very well leave the city undefended while my family is safe.

On the way, my father murmurs concern that I have very little by way of armor on, but he doesn't encourage me to turn back.

There's no wasting time, not when these awful creatures are descending upon us.

"That Azrael wishes to punish me for refusing to ally with him," my father says as we hurry.

"You refused him?" I ask, a bit shocked. I would have thought that, had Azrael offered my father the power of a host of Others at his disposal, the king would have gladly accepted and claimed his duty was to his people, not the rest of Alondria.

My father grunts. "I'll be dead before I support an illegitimate sitting on a throne."

Ah. So it seems my father hasn't been overcome with some drastic personality change, after all.

Well, at least this feels like familiar footing again.

On the way, I grab an abandoned sword from the rubble and sheath it. The blood on its hilt stains my palm.

We reach the courtyard, the steps of which lead down to the closed South Gate. Residents crowd around the gates, begging to be let in, thinking the castle will provide them shelter.

They don't know it's just as dangerous inside.

Three wyverns circle overhead, picking off the archers stationed at the walls. Arrows ricochet off the wyverns' scales, showering a host of arrows upon the soldiers and crowds.

"Tell the archers to stand down. Have them search the castle for servants and children and lead them into the bunkers," I yell at a nearby soldier, who looks back and forth between me and my father, unsure.

"Well, did you hear him or not?" my father bellows.

The boy doesn't need to be told again; he sprints through the courtyards and toward the archery towers.

My father unsheathes his sword, as do I, and we throw ourselves into battle.

I COME to regret sending the archers away once the pack of mere arrive. Silver blood sprays as I slice the head off a mere that my vines caught just before it devoured me.

I cut down several mere who dug holes underneath the gates, their venom-soaked teeth often gleaming at my neck before my vines wrap around them and force them to the ground, allowing me time to stab them through.

I don't particularly like how slow my magic remains, but it's more in my control than it's ever been.

I suppose I'll have to thank Orion for that, assuming both of us survive this battle, which seems unlikely at this point.

That's fine. I don't really want to endure Orion's smug refusal to accept my thanks, anyway.

My father and I slip into a rhythm. We've never communicated well, never found a medium by which we could understand one another, but on the battlefield we come together as one. As if we're simply extensions of one another.

A mere lunges, and my vines wrap around it just in time for my father to slit its throat. Another pounces toward a child whose mother sent him scurrying under the gates, and I scoop the child into my arms and out of the way while my father cuts the beast down.

Once the child is passed off to a soldier, my father and I turn, backs facing, guarding each other.

The words we exchange are short, simple battle commands, but they might as well comprise an ardent conversation compared to the exchanges we're used to.

Because, for once, I've found something my father and I have in common, and it's not a thirst for blood or the thrill of the battle or anything I might have expected from a male so hardened.

It's that we'll do anything to protect the city we love, even if that means cooperating. Or dying.

That sentiment is cut short as a wyvern swoops over the crowd. I redirect my vines toward the rogue beast.

And miss.

Time stills, almost to a halt, as the barb of the wyvern's tail punctures my father's chest.

Shock ripples across my father's hardened features, and for the first time in my life, I witness fear in his eyes.

Buzzing swarms my ears as my father's knees buckle.

He hits the ground.

And then, in that moment of quiet, my father looks at me.

Our eyes lock; he tilts his chin downward, just slightly.

Then my father thrusts his sword upward at the same moment the wyvern's jaws encompass him.

A horrible crunching sound pierces through the fog in my ears, followed shortly by a female's screams.

My mother's screams.

They snap me back to the present, out of that horrific moment where time itself hadn't existed.

To my left, my mother cries out in anguish. She's screaming my father's name, clutching her stomach, even as swarms of vines burst out around her, strangling mere and wyverns in their fury, dashing their bodies against the stairs.

Then something replaces the rage on my mother's delicate face. The flush of battle pales from her sinking cheeks. She retches, grasping her stomach. The vines around her fall limp, dropping the strangled carcasses of the mere, but one survivor wriggles free from their grasp. It stalks my mother from behind, but she doesn't appear to notice.

It lunges, but not fast enough. Not before I send a vine shooting out of a crack in the ground, puncturing the mere's throat until a cluster of thorns protrudes from its eye socket.

The creature falls limp behind my mother.

She doesn't notice.

Murmurs echo through the crowd. *The king is dead the king is dead the king is dead*, they seem to say.

The king is dead.

My father is dead.

The words ring in my head as if in a language I don't recognize. As if I don't have the ability to process them.

My body goes still, the Others' corpses littering the courtyard.

The murmuring in the crowd grows louder, but perhaps it's just the buzzing in my own mind.

My father is dead, and I'm unsure what to do with that information.

"Evander." Ellie comes running up, her gown splattered with ink. Or no, it's not ink. It's ichor, the spray of blood from an Other she slaughtered with her still-dripping sword.

"Evander." Her hands find my jaw, gently nudging my face to look at her.

I'm not sure what she finds in my eyes, but hers water. She blinks the tears away, setting her jaw.

The mutterings in the crowd grow louder, but I can't hear them over the buzzing. Over the crunching that resonates through my mind, over and over.

I wish for another mere, another wyvern to fight, to strangle and bleed and slaughter, because then at least the noise of battle would drown out that awful sound.

Ellie turns to face the crowd, something like disgust and dread mingled on her face, but I can't hear what's causing her reaction.

She glances back at me, then my mother. My wife draws up her skirts with one hand, sword still dragging the ground with the other, and marches toward the place my father was slaughtered.

A hush goes over the crowd as she steps over the corpses of the fallen, as she grips her sword with both hands.

And separates the wyvern's head from its body, one hack at a time.

By the time she's done, Ellie is covered in ichor, the blood staining her blue gown with a silver that fades to midnight.

Carefully, with the precision it takes to etch an intricate design

425

onto a glass goblet, Ellie carves the tip of her blade into the monster's flesh, chiseling its skin and muscle away piece by piece, peeling off the scales that get in her way with her bare hands.

I hear very little of it. The only sounds I can seem to focus on are those of my mother's sobs.

When she's done, Ellie screws up her face in dreadful anticipation, then plunges her hand into the cavern she's carved in the monster's flesh.

She strains out a sob, covering her mouth with her other hand as she squeezes her eyes shut.

Then, through the hole she's made in the wyvern, Ellie Payne withdraws my father's crown.

It still drips with ichor, which she wipes with the hem of her skirt.

Then Ellie Payne marches back over to me, where I stand, ears still buzzing on the castle steps.

She looks into my eyes, hers saturated with pain and adoration. Something squeezes my frozen chest.

She ascends, the step making her of equal height to me, and places the crown upon my head.

"Long live the king," she says, her voice trembling.

Another murmur ripples through the onlooking crowd, but no one moves. No one speaks.

Determination flashes over my wife's stunning features, and a hint of icy rage as she looks out over the crowd.

Just barely, I hear my cousin Casper's voice as he leans over and whispers something to his mother. I can't hear what he's saying, but Ellie must, because her nostrils flare.

Ellie squares her shoulders, takes my hand, and kneels before me.

"No," I whisper to her. "No, I can't."

This crown doesn't belong to me. It weighs me down, threatening to strangle me. Isn't that why my father took to Ellie in the first place? Because I couldn't be trusted with the throne? Because where I lack ambition, she possesses drive. Where I lack focus, she has vision.

But Ellie just lifts her eyes, shimmering through those beautiful thick eyelashes of hers. There's no smile on her lips when she says, "Yes, Evander. You can. You can and you must."

"Long live the king," cries a familiar voice, the voice of my mother still weeping. Then she follows Ellie, kneeling. Even with her shoulders bowed, she gazes up at me with fierce determination.

Another thud as another pair of knees hits the ground. "Long live the king," says Orion, a gash along his shoulder weeping blood.

Peck is next, and slowly, the crowd bends.

All the while, Ellie's tears flow into my trembling hand as she squeezes it tight.

INTERLUDE

MARCUS

"I don't think anyone is home," says Amity, her braid looking even more ragged than usual.

Typically, Piper tries her hand at braiding Amity's hair. I wouldn't say that Piper is an expert at it, but she's certainly better than either me or Amity.

So here we are, about to make a large request to a rather irritable king, and my daughter looks like I pulled her out of a swamp.

She's still adorable though, so at least we have that going for us.

I knock again on the gated entrance to the Avelean court, my knuckles dry as they rap against the dark walnut.

Again, no answer.

There's not even a guard stationed outside.

This isn't entirely surprising, but only because things were just as eerie the last time we visited the Avelean court. King Declan of Avelea rarely makes outside appearances, and the court itself? Well, it's nowhere to be found. Last time we were here, we had the misfortune of meeting the king, but his family and courtiers were hauntingly absent.

At least there had been a festival going on then.

Now, without the jovial crowds, musical groups, and entertainment tents, the castle grounds are practically empty.

No, not practically empty. They are empty.

Except for me and Amity, of course.

"Evander probably forgot to send our letter," says Amity, and though I would typically be inclined to agree with her summation of the prince, he'd seemed determined when he told me he'd do anything to help.

I lean my forehead against the door. It's cool to the touch, mirroring the memory I have of the drafty, all but abandoned castle. The past several weeks, I've been keeping myself together for Amity. Not letting myself question whether we'll find Piper.

But my hope has rested tenuously on recruiting help from within these walls, and if no one is here...

The latch on the gate clicks.

I jump backward just in time for the gears on the sides of the gate to spin, opening the doors with a buzzing whir.

On the other side is a young woman whose face shares my nose, my smile.

When she smiles.

Which isn't often.

And certainly isn't now.

"It's a good thing I convinced Declan to let me come and see who was making such a racket," my sister Cheyenne says, examining me and Amity. "Otherwise, he might have ripped the two of you to shreds."

I tense, but Amity only laughs. "The king would never. I told him last time he needs to learn to be nicer."

At that, Cheyenne almost smiles. Almost.

It hurts, seeing how reticent she is around me. In some ways, she's still the Cheyenne I remember—light-brown skin that freckles in the sun, curly ringlets framing her face.

Those features I recognize. It's the way she carries herself as a woman—chin high, eyes discerning, shoulders squared—that's difficult for me to process.

Cheyenne gestures us inside, then leads us through the dingy castle.

Amity chats with Cheyenne on the way to the throne room. Although, it's more like Amity chats *at* her, rambling on and on about Piper's kidnapping, our travels, the chaos at the Rip, and how Cheyenne is her aunt now that Piper and I have adopted her. Cheyenne's lack of reaction tells me that she did, in fact, receive Evander's letter. All the while, I try to find places to cut into the conversation, but Cheyenne hardly even looks at me, and seems perfectly content to entertain Amity.

I remind myself that Cheyenne has no desire to have a relationship with me, and that I shouldn't push it.

Cheyenne is the youngest of my siblings and possesses a gift much like Asha's. I'm not sure where she acquired it, but since she was a child, she's had the ability to make others forget. None of us realized this, of course, not even Cheyenne, and the skill often resulted in my parents forgetting about Cheyenne altogether, even failing to feed her on many occasions.

So when Piper took Cheyenne as a child, she thought she was taking her from a neglectful family. No one realized what was actually happening.

After her disappearance, I'd spent years thinking Cheyenne was dead. So had Piper, after they were ransacked on the road.

When really, Cheyenne had been here.

Happy, and fed, and looked after.

Most of all, not forgotten.

I think I'm a reminder of a childhood Cheyenne would rather forget.

"Just remember," Cheyenne says, resting her hand on the door handle of the throne room, "he's a tad grumpier today than usual."

I knit my brow. "Was last time usual? Because I seem to remember him shifting into a wolf and attacking us."

Cheyenne shrugs, which isn't at all comforting.

She swings the door open.

431

The room is just as I remember; a long dining table cuts the space in half, though all but one seat is empty.

At the head is King Declan of Avelea.

He does not appear thrilled to see us.

Of course, Amity does not realize this. She skips right up to the king, whose blond beard has grown even more unkempt since we last saw him, and dips into a rather lopsided curtsy. "Your Majesty," she says. "I do hope you've been behaving in my absence."

I tense, but if the king is offended, he doesn't show it. He just wipes his mouth on his napkin, stares at Amity for a moment, then lifts his head to Cheyenne.

"I see your family has come for a visit," he says, sounding more resigned than threatening.

Cheyenne walks across the marble floor, hands clasped behind her back as she approaches the king and bows. "Yes, Your Majesty. They sent correspondence ahead. I believe they have a request they wish for you to grant."

"Hm." The king stares at Amity again. He has the strange look of a male who is probably quite handsome—underneath the untrimmed scruff and altogether lack of will to leave the house, at least. "And what is your request?"

I open my mouth to respond, but Amity beats me to it. "Your nose, Your Majesty."

He whips his head to me. "My nose?"

"My wife is missing, kidnapped by Queen Abra of Mystral. We request assistance tracking her. We hoped with your ability to shift, and the possessions of hers we brought along, you might be able to track her for us," I explain.

The king looks at Cheyenne, dumbfounded. "Does your family forget that I am a king and not a bounty hunter to be hired?"

"Apparently," Cheyenne says through gritted teeth, but I can't tell if the exasperation in her tone is directed toward me or the king. "But, Your Majesty, as you've already said, this is my family."

Declan examines her for a moment. "Do we not consider one another family?"

Cheyenne's face actually softens, which surprises me. I forget sometimes that Declan was the one who raised her from the time she was a child. "Of course we do. But one might say that, by proxy, that makes them your family too." Then, her voice lowers ever so slightly. "That's what we do, isn't it? Take care of each other's families?"

The king stills, and if I were the superstitious sort, I could swear I feel another presence settle upon the room.

The hair stands on the back of my neck.

"Your Majesty," Amity asks, "where *is* your family?"

I freeze, because I know instantly it's the wrong question. The king stiffens, and I know, just know, he'll deny our request. But then Cheyenne takes Amity by the hand. "They're away, but only temporarily."

Again, an icy presence coats the room. This time, Amity shivers too.

433

PART V

MARTYR

CHAPTER 74

BLAISE

I'm not sure exactly what I was expecting from Piper. The Red. Whatever she is. When I first heard of the Gifted female who made her living stealing children from their homes, a twinge of disgust had rippled through me.

Or maybe it hadn't. It had been the night I met Az at the inn, when I was on my way back to confront Farin, and I'd overheard a group of mercenaries speaking of her, debating over whether she was the head of her operation.

Actually, I think I'd been too consumed in my worry over Nox's life to have much of a reaction to the gossip.

That had been right after I Turned, and my feelings had vacillated through spells of extreme apathy, to extreme anguish, to extreme desire.

But then Kiran and Evander had spoken of Piper, how she was being transported in the care of Princess Lydia, and I suppose I had found myself disgusted with her.

I'd thought of her as Clarissa, really. Or, at least, the picture of Clarissa I'd held in my mind all those years. The woman willing to sell a stolen child for enough coin to buy herself a frilly dress.

But then I'd met Amity, seen the adoration she held for Piper, her adoptive mother, whom she missed so terribly, and I'd come to question how I felt about the other woman.

Of course, I'd had more pressing issues on my mind at the time, so if I'm honest with myself, I haven't spent too much time pondering the ethics of the woman now trudging through the woods before me.

I'd been thinking of Nox.

But Nox is gone, and I can't bear to think of him any longer.

So the ethics of a child kidnapper, it is.

"You risked your husband's life back there." My voice cracks with disuse, much like the brambles under our feet. "In saving me, rather than stopping Nox from killing Abra. Why?"

I'm not sure why the words come out so sharp, so accusatory. I don't mean for them to, but it's like the pain inside me has swollen to the point of being too big for my body. It's punching through my skin, spouting out my mouth and searching for the nearest target with a heart to shred.

Piper doesn't bother looking back at me. Even in the moonlight, she's impossible not to see. I think that would be the case even without my sharp vision, with that cascading vibrant red hair of hers. "I trust Amity will find a way to save him."

"That's a lot of pressure to put on a child."

Piper sighs, and pauses a moment with her hand on the branch she's holding out of my way. "I know. It's not my preference."

We travel in silence for a while, when she asks quietly, "How are they?"

I hesitate to reply. I've already told Piper about the Rip being opened; I just haven't mentioned the role I played.

"It's been weeks since I traveled with them," I say, but a hint of desperation peeks through her gaze and guilt floods my chest. I shouldn't have brought this up, caused her more pain than necessary. I don't even know why I did, other than the incessant need to feel that someone is hurting as much as I am. Or the need to know I'm not alone in making choices that hurt my loved ones. "But last I saw them, Amity was working on something to save him. She thought she might be close."

"And Marcus?"

"Marcus..." A lie waits on my tongue, but I find it feels crueler than even the truth. "His condition had worsened by the time I left. Though he put up quite a fight when the Others attacked. I...I imagine you would have been proud to see the way he protected Amity. The way he protected all of us." I admit it to myself more than her.

Piper's smile is strained, like she's holding back tears, but she seems grateful all the same. "He's a protector. He can't help himself. It must be killing him, knowing Amity is fretting over him."

I nod, not knowing quite what to say.

After a while and much contemplation, I find I can't hold the words in. The ones that are dying to burst through my chest.

"Why did you do it?" I ask, because the question is clawing at my insides, chewing on my very soul.

"Why did I do what?"

"Why didn't you protect the only real hope of saving Marcus?"

"Abra wasn't the only hope," Piper repeats, her tone wary. Is she wary of me, or her own motivations?

"I don't think you actually believe that."

Piper whips around to face me, her red curls blazing, but it's nothing compared to the fury in her ivy-green eyes.

As soon as the rage appears, it's gone, and her shoulders sag. "It worries me. That I didn't save his only hope of surviving."

"Then why did you do it? Why save me when you could have tried to stop Nox from killing Abra?" It feels like I'm asking for the millionth time, but I have to know, have to understand.

But that's not the right question, is it? The one I truly want to ask. *How* did you do it? That's the question that's eating away at my soul. How did you find the strength to give up the person you love the most for someone you hardly know, when I couldn't even do it for my oldest friend?

Piper shakes her head. "It was the right thing to do."

She says it like she thinks she's protecting someone innocent. I wonder if she would have saved me had she known what I've done.

Had she known it's my fault Amity was nearly ripped to shreds by an Other. That Evander and Ellie's child had died for my folly.

That a mother might have died too.

All your fault. Always your fault, sings the parasite from the adamant box at my belt. *I could make it go away, you know. The hurt. The pain. Silly silly servant girl...*

I ignore it.

As much as I can.

"Abra was a blight on this world," Piper explains. "I learned her story as we traveled. Abra was willing to go to any lengths to save her son. She allowed her affection for him to blind her to the truth of what he is. Who he might hurt if allowed to live."

I frown. "You never intended to reform him with your Gift, did you?"

Piper pauses. "No. No, I didn't."

"You were going to kill him, even though it meant Abra would refuse to save Marcus. You'd already decided on it."

Piper's pale throat bobs. "Yes."

"But you love Marcus."

Tears shimmer in Piper's green eyes. "Of course, I love him."

Then why. Then how. *Please,* I want to beg, but I don't. I simply wait for her to answer.

Instead, she turns to face me, sweeping me over with her gaze.

"How do you know that you love someone?"

I don't hesitate. "When you know you'd do anything for them."

"And what if doing anything for them means burning the world down?"

"Then you do it."

Piper looks contemplative for a moment. "But if you burn the world down, what will there be for your love to return to? What home will be left for them?"

Her words settle in my heart. "I suppose then *you're* their home."

Her eyes pierce me. "And what if, in ruining the world, you ruin yourself, too?"

I open my mouth, but I can't quite find an answer.

Piper sighs, then leans against a nearby tree. "I once had a man I would have burned the world down for. I loved him. He'd rescued me when I was a child, saved me from freezing to death in the snow. And when even my mother rejected me, he took me into his arms. Gave me a home. So I did as he asked, whatever he asked. Even if what he asked me to do chipped away at my soul. So, I suppose I burned the world for him. Is that love?"

Again, I don't think I have a response, but I try anyway. "That's manipulation. It's not at all—" I want to say it's not at all the same, to convince Piper that Nox hadn't asked me to betray my friends, to burn down the world for him. That much is true, but I get the feeling I'm missing something.

So I say nothing.

"Love..." Piper says, trailing off, like she's searching for the right words. "Love shouldn't ruin a person, Blaise. If it does, you have to start questioning whether it's love at all, or simply fear masquerading as something more pure than it can ever hope to be."

I halt, chewing my lip. "You shouldn't have saved me."

Piper looks tired. "And why is that?"

"Because I helped Azrael open the Rip."

CHAPTER 75

ELLIE

"*I* can't do this, El. I can't be king. I can't..."

Evander paces back and forth in our bedroom, the ichor from the battle still staining both our clothes. The putrid scent fills my nostrils, making me ill. The odor keeps bringing me back to the courtyard, to the devastation.

The king's body mauled by the beast, the feel of my father-in-law's hair against my fingers as I wrenched the crown from his corpse.

Asha once told me she often vomited when she was feeling anxious.

I thought it an unfortunate affliction at the time, but now I wish I could. Wish my stomach would relieve me of at least some of the weight I carry.

Cecilia coos as I rock her. My arms shake with the weight of lugging the sword up over my head and into the monster's neck as I hacked away.

That scent again.

But I hold my child, my child who is safe and fast asleep, undisturbed by the uprooting of life as we knew it.

My arms tremble, but I hold her all the same.

"Evander." His name feels limp on my tongue, mostly because it seems like such an empty thing to say to him, my husband, who just watched his father slaughtered before his very eyes, whose mother's screams still echo in both our ears. Peck gave her a draft to put her to sleep a half hour ago, after she worked herself into such devastation, he'd worried for her sanity.

She'll wake to the same amount of pain, but I'm glad for her. For the short reprieve she's currently receiving in slumber.

Evander receives none of it.

I watch, helpless, as my husband paces back and forth, muttering to himself and rubbing the back of his neck.

I don't know what to say. What I even could say. In the heat of the moment, when I watched Evander's body go into shock at the sight of his father's mangled corpse, when I heard the whisperings of the crowd, heard Evander's awful cousin Casper daring to sound pleased as he bragged to his mother... In that moment, I knew exactly what to do.

There'd been no doubt in my mind as I hacked the crown away from that awful creature's jaws, ichor spraying me in the process. There was no wondering if I was doing the right thing.

No, there'd been a quiet voice in my ear, my mother's, telling me that sometimes, respect grows or withers from the esteem or lack thereof of those closest to someone.

So I gritted my teeth and willed myself not to vomit, and I placed the crown upon Evander's head.

And then I kneeled, hoping, praying the people would follow.

There was a single moment of unease when I failed to hear their knees bend. But then Evangeline, Fates bless her, followed me. And Orion. And even Peck. And soon the entire crowd followed my lead.

And then...

And then I realized I didn't know what would come next.

I faintly heard Peck command a few of the guards to help with Evander's mother, and then Orion had been by my and Evander's sides, rushing us away before the shock from the crowd could fade, before they could bombard us with questions.

Somehow, we ended up here, both in a shocked haze, Evander more so.

Collins had brought me Cecilia, and we've been sitting here ever since, Evander pacing, me rocking back and forth, as much for my own soothing as Cecilia's.

"Evander," I say again, gesturing wearily toward the bathroom with my head. "Let me help you get out of those clothes."

Evander stops, still stunned as he looks down at the mingled silver and scarlet blood that coats him. I rise from the chair, setting Cecilia in her crib and squeezing her little hand gently before I go to him, helping him out of his bloodstained garments.

"THIS SHOULD HAVE BEEN JERAD." Evander's hair is still wet from the bath. He sits on the edge of the bed next to me, staring out the window, into the distance. His thumb rubs absentmindedly across the slick silver of the crown resting on his knee.

It aches, seeing my carefree husband like this. I've seen him mourn, seen him terrified. I watched him tremble when I went into labor and neither of us thought Cecilia would survive.

But Cecilia did survive.

I haven't watched Evander lose someone yet. Not really.

It's not the first time he's lost someone, I realize. I imagine my husband a few years ago, stumbling upon the body of his brother, dead at the bottom of a ravine after a night of Evander pushing drinks upon him.

He's always considered it his own fault. Is that how he feels about his father's death? And is it harder, losing someone you were close to, or losing someone you had longed to be close to, but never were?

"This should have been Jerad's," Evander says, ripping the crown off his lap and throwing it across the room, before burying his face in his hands. "I'm sorry. I'm sorry, I shouldn't."

The baby starts crying.

"Why did you do it? Why give me the crown?" Evander asks, anguish dripping from his eyes.

"Because," I say carefully, "it's yours."

"I don't want it."

"We don't always get to choose the responsibilities that are handed to us."

He huffs. "You act as if you're not the one who handed it to me."

I jerk my head back, tears stinging at my eyes.

Guilt washes over his face, and he reaches across the sheets for my hand. "I'm sorry, El. I shouldn't...You were spectacular back there. I don't know how you do it."

"How I do what?"

"How you always know exactly what to do."

I lean into him, tucking my cheek into his shoulder. The aftermath of his words still stings, but the sorrow in his eyes at hurting me is genuine. "The trick is *looking* like you know exactly what to do."

"Well, you had me convinced."

I tuck my face into his warmth. "It's all in the shoulders."

"El?"

"Yes?"

"I'm sorry I blew up on you."

"I know."

He laces his fingers on my shoulder, pulling me close. "I don't know how to be a king."

"I know that too. At least, I know you don't know how to be your father. But Evander, that isn't necessarily a bad thing."

He stiffens uncomfortably, and I have to move his face closer to mine to get him to look at me.

"What is it?" I ask.

"He said he was proud of me before he died. Well, technically he didn't even say that. But he said Jerad would have been proud, and coming from him, that was basically like saying he didn't wish I'd been the one to fall off that ravine."

I frown, letting out a deep exhale.

"It would have been nice of him not to leave me on such a confusing note," says Evander, shrugging.

"Well, your father did like surprises," I say, slumping back on the bed next to him.

"Hm," Evander says, pensive. "Remember me telling you about the shadow siren Kiran, Blaise, and I ran into in Mystral?"

I raise my brow. "No, the creature who got into Kiran's head and almost convinced him to yank out Blaise's heart slipped my mind."

Evander chuckles, but there's no life in his laugh. "Well, it wasn't just Kiran's head she got into."

I nod, remembering Evander telling me that the shadow siren had offered to bring his brother back. "But you didn't fall for her tricks."

Evander's cheeks drain of the little color left in them. "You know what tipped me off that it wasn't real?"

I take my husband's hand, and he strokes it absentmindedly.

"She came to me in the form of my father. Pretended to be him, then begged me to kill Blaise to bring Jerad back. I was tempted, too. But you know what the siren did that tipped me off? You know what her mistake was?"

My heart thuds, aching in my chest for my husband.

"'*I love you, son*'—that's what the vision of my father said. And I knew then it wasn't real."

Silence blankets the room for a moment, and I don't know what to say, so I do all I know to do, and sit in the pain with my husband.

"Do you regret it?" Evander finally asks.

"Regret what?"

"Putting the crown on my head?"

I snap my neck to stare at him. "Why? Are you planning on making me regret it?"

And then, blessedly, the smallest of laughs escapes my husband's mouth. "That prospect is too terrifying to consider."

Evander pulls me into him and kisses me as if our perfect little world hasn't just shattered to pieces.

CHAPTER 76

PIPER

I probably should hate Blaise a tad more than I do.

I probably shouldn't like her, either, but what can I do? Hate her for opening the Rip to bring back her kind-of-dead suitor?

That feels a little hypocritical, given I prefer others overlook the fact that I used to kidnap children for a living.

Besides, the girl is so clearly lost. And that's a feeling I recognize. I know what it's like to swim in an ocean of your own guilt, the hatred of others acting as waves crashing above your head. Your own self-talk—the current trying to pull you under.

So I decide not to feel too terrible about not hating Blaise. She's told me her story now, and though I wasn't born yesterday and know better than to assume she hasn't omitted any important information, I believe what she has revealed is probably the truth.

No one paints their own actions in such a horrible light unless it's true.

As we make our way through the forest, my heart longs for Marcus and Amity. I want nothing more than to go after them, to ensure they're safe. But if things continue to go as Blaise fears they will, I'm not sure my family will ever find safety.

It feels like my soul is being rent in two, feels like I'm abandoning them.

But logic reminds me this is just a fear response. That the idea of searching them out only feels safer. If I ever want the people I love to find peace, Az has to be stopped.

I just have to pray Amity finds a way to keep Marcus alive.

"So, does it talk to you?" she asks, seemingly out of nowhere as we pace through the words.

"Does what talk to me?"

"Your magic."

"My Gift?"

Blaise snorts. "I suppose, if that's what you want to call it."

I furrow my brow. "No. Is it supposed to?"

Blaise shrugs. "Asha's does. Mine—the parasite, I mean—never did. Not while it was inside my head, at least. When it took over my body, then it talked. But I think that had more to do with it being cursed to only be active during the full moon."

"Oh." I consider whether I've ever heard any voices. "It hums to me sometimes, sings to me. But only when I'm really emotional." I think back to the time I'd been intending to slip my blade between my ribs. I shudder, remembering the gentle tune that had carried me off to slumber before I could end my life.

"Good to know I wasn't the only one with a creepy magic," Blaise says when I relay the story.

I frown, Blaise's words bothering me for some reason. "No. It's not creepy. My Gift did it to save my life."

Something like disappointment flashes over Blaise's face, but she schools it quickly enough. "I wonder why yours doesn't talk. Asha's didn't talk to her for years, until it deemed it necessary. Maybe yours can speak, it just chooses not to. Or maybe it's cursed like the parasite was."

Something wriggles inside my chest, like a hammer bumping over a set of chimes.

"Maybe," I say, shrugging it off.

The thought, however, I can't seem to shrug away.

. . .

IT'S LATER THAT NIGHT, as we're passing through a nearby village, that we hear the news. Rather, we witness it.

Smog bears down on our lungs as the ruins of this nameless village smolder in the evening breeze. What was clearly once a town center now appears as a path of rubble and destruction.

"What do you think happened here?" I ask Blaise, but she doesn't appear to hear me.

Her ears twitch, and I remember her hearing is better than mine. What sounds like muffled voices coming from inside the few structures that are still standing are as clear to Blaise as if we occupied the same room.

"They were attacked," she says. "The villagers say it was silver monsters."

The words and their weight hang in the air between us.

The wind changes direction, slamming the stench of rotting flesh into our noses. I fight back a retch, but Blaise clamps a hand over her nose.

"Blood?" I ask.

Blaise blinks. "Yes, but I can handle it. I…"

She breaks into a run, and I follow her, though there's no use trying to keep up with her. It's hard enough just keeping her in my sight.

We end up in the ruins of what looks to be a fallen bakery. All that's left standing is the iron stove in the corner.

"Help me," Blaise commands, jumping into the pile of rubble and slinging charred planks behind her as she digs. I do as she says and help remove debris.

Underneath is the blistered corpse of a mother still clinging to her child.

An image flashes through my mind, of this mother hearing the roars of the Others. That her only thought was to wrap her child in her arms, using her body as a shield from whatever atrocities might come.

Fragments of a peasant's dress still cling to the little girl's body. I can't make out her features, not with the soot obscuring the child's face, but given her size, I imagine she's younger than Amity.

I am suddenly very sick.

"I can hear a pulse," Blaise says, reaching out for the child.

Blaise falters as her hands wrap around the child. Then she pries her from her dead mother's protective arms.

The girl doesn't move. Doesn't seem to notice.

"Blaise." Trepidation gnaws at me as she pulls the girl from the rubble. "Blaise, I don't think there's anything we can—"

"There's a healer a few houses down," she says. "We can take her to him."

I stare at the child, her body crushed under the weight of her own home, her skin blistered by flames.

I know exactly what this healer will do, will say.

One look at Blaise, and I realize she doesn't.

THE LOCAL HEALER has taken up shop in one of the few cottages left standing. The place is packed with the wounded, several laid out in rows on the floor.

Some get pallets, but most do not.

The healer is coaxing liquid into a patient's half-opened mouth when we arrive. He takes one glance at the girl in our arms and deflates.

"Erida," he says, though I have no idea how he recognizes the child in her current state.

He nods us over to the only empty spot on the floor.

On either side of the lone patch of flooring are corpses.

Blaise swallows. "No. No, she's not dead. There's a pulse."

The healer appears even more distraught by this news.

"Very well," he says. His knees creak as he stands. He's an elderly man, his face carved with the sorrows of a life acquainted with death.

He shuffles over to his workstation and pulls a vial from the counter.

Still, Blaise refuses to set the girl on the floor. Instead, she cradles her, holding her to her chest.

The healer navigates the rows of bodies, then uncorks the bottle.

Blaise's nose immediately curls. "What is that you're giving her?"

"Blaise," I say, but it's no use.

"No," she says, hugging the girl tighter, like she's protecting her from the healer. "It's opium. I can smell it. The girl's heart is barely beating. If you give that to her, it'll kill her."

The healer purses his thin lips. "I am not the one who killed this child."

Blaise is practically shouting now. *"That's because she's not dead."*

I place my hand on Blaise's shoulder, but she shrugs me off.

The healer sighs, then presses his fingers to the folds between his brows. "Erida was such a vibrant child. Thought I might take her on as an apprentice if I lived long enough. She had the disposition for a good healer. Sharp of mind, soft of heart."

Again, I can't help but think of Amity, and my heart aches for my daughter.

"Her pelvis and torso are crushed," says the healer. "Have been for days now. Her organs will have been leaking into her bloodstream, poisoning her from the inside out. If I had the resources to save her, I would try. But I don't. And even then, I'm not sure saving her would be possible. I appreciate you for pulling her out of the rubble. I would have hated for her to suffer alone at the end."

Blaise blinks, unable to hold back the tears. "There's nothing you can do?"

The healer shakes his head. "Other than ease her pain and stay with her until the end, no."

"Shut up," says Blaise, and the healer flinches.

But Blaise isn't talking to the healer.

At her belt hangs the adamant box in which the parasite is trapped.

I don't know what it's saying to her, but I can see the way Blaise's mind is whirring to treacherous places, so I place my hand on her shoulder. "There's nothing you can do, either," I say, though it makes

451

my chest feel as if it's being sawn in two. "Nothing that would give this girl her life back."

IN THE END, Blaise lets the healer place the vial to the girl's lips. Almost instantly, the muscles in the child's face relax. Heaviness overcomes her limbs.

Blaise holds the girl until her heart slows to a stop.

And for a long while after that.

WE LEARN, as we leave the healer's cottage, that just like this village, Othian was attacked, left in ruins by an onslaught of otherworldly monsters.

I watch Blaise as we overhear the whispers on the streets. She pales with each word, and I know just what she's leaning in close to hear.

"The king is dead," says another. Blaise's eyes go wide, her body rigid.

"And the prince?" she asks, breaking away from me before I can catch her arm. I follow, apprehensive. I might have made an exception for the girl, but we don't need to be interacting with people, risking being recognized. We need to listen in from the shadows, but Blaise is much too impulsive to remember that.

The male takes a swig of his ale. "There is no prince," he says.

Rage and despair boils in Blaise's eyes, and for a moment, I don't know what I'll do if she attacks the unassuming male. Am unsure what I *could* do up against a stalker of the night. But then the man lets out a belly laugh and says, "Can't be a prince, because the prince is the king now."

"And the princess?"

"Well, I suppose that would make her queen, now wouldn't it?"

Blaise's chest heaves, but something like relief seems to calm the bloodlust in her eyes. "And their child?"

The male frowns. "Haven't heard of no child, miss."

. . .

BLAISE IS quiet for the rest of the journey. She barely says anything as we set up camp in a tent so she could escape the heat of the sun come morning.

"It's my fault," she says. "I made Asha open the Rip. I'm the one who released those terrible creatures into this world. They've destroyed everything. Evander's home. My home. It's gone, and it's all my fault. Even the king." She chokes back a miserable laugh. "I always hated that male, but he was kind to my father, kind to me. If he'd let me rot on the streets, hadn't given me the job of a servant...I know he didn't do it out of kindness, but it was a favor. If he hadn't done it, he wouldn't be dead now.

"It's my fault that little girl, that Erida, died. My fault that she doesn't get to train as a healer. That she doesn't get to live. My fault that she suffered for days."

She stares off into the distance, as if still grappling with the injustice of it all. I can't help but notice the way she doesn't bring up the Prince and Princess of Dwellen's child again. That must have been the part of the story she omitted earlier. I know better than to push someone in this state, though.

"From the way they were talking in town, the creatures swept into Othian in an organized effort," I say, curious, my mind whirling in horror at that idea, but also wishing to steer Blaise away from the guilt she allows to engulf her. It rarely seems productive, and besides, I often catch glimmers of bloodlust when she's emotional. I'm not really in the mood to have my arteries bled. "I've heard the legends, just like anyone else. But I had no idea the creatures were that...sentient."

Blaise blinks back tears, and her eyes come into focus. "They're not. At least, I don't think they are. I mean, I think they have ways of communicating with each other like any animal, but it's Az who's controlling them. He performed a ritual over the Rip before we opened it, one that bound them to him. And then he..." She swallows, like the words are caught in her throat. When she finally does speak, it's like she's having to spit out the words lest they defile her mouth. "He performed a bloodsharing ritual"—she shudders visibly—"with them."

I cock an eyebrow, and she goes on to explain. "Bloodsharing is a ritual used among vampires. It gives each member full authority over the other. It's like a mating bond, or a marriage ritual. The most intimate thing a couple could experience. If it happens with a human…" She licks her lips nervously, her eyes darting to her knees. "It throws the balance of power off, giving the human more power than the vampire, because they don't have any magic to offer. I guess Az didn't have any magic to offer the Others. Either that, or his being more sentient gave him power over them, but either way, he can control them now."

I take in a breath, steadying myself as Blaise's words swim through my mind.

"So it's the control of them that's the problem?"

She shrugs.

"And what if we had a way of making that the solution?"

Blaise flares her nostrils. "I thought you said you weren't that powerful."

I had said that, back when Blaise had first informed me of her and Nox's plan. I suck in a breath, bristling, but Blaise stops walking all the same.

"Because if you're talking about what I think you're talking about," she says, "we would need enough power to lure an entire host of Others out of Az's control, across miles, to make it through the Rip."

"I'm not. Powerful enough, I mean."

Blaise narrows her eyes in question.

"But what if I knew of a way to escalate my power?"

Blaise looks skeptical. Fair enough. I'm rather skeptical myself, but still…

"You said the Rip gave Asha more power when she was close to it, didn't you?" I ask.

"Yes…but I still don't know if it gave her that kind of power."

"But that was when the Rip was closed. The Rip is open now. One would think that means there's more power to draw from. Or that it would at least be easier to access."

Blaise's gaze drifts off. "I'm still not convinced it would be enough."

I shake my head. "No. I don't think it would be either. But..." I sigh. "What have you heard about faerie-made flutes?"

"Um. Not a lot. I'm not exactly well-versed in music."

"Right," I say, rubbing at my forehead.

Then I tell her of the forest faeries.

"You mean to tell me you once had a faerie flute, basically a super flute, in your possession and you tossed it into a body of water?" Blaise asks, arms crossed as her eyes bulge. Her voice is calm, but she's bouncing up and down on her heels.

"Technically, I buried it in the ground."

"You're right. That's so much better."

"I know."

"Why? Why would you do that?"

I shrug. "The man who raised me...I had a good idea of what he would want to do with that kind of power. The kinds of things he would make me do. At the time, I still planned on going back to him, so it seemed easier to bury it than to..."

"To have to tell him no?" Blaise's tone is softer than I would have expected.

I nod, crossing my arms.

"Alright, then. So where is this flute? And more importantly, is there a series of caves along the way?"

CHAPTER 77

ZORA

"*W*hat's it like?" Farin asks. He's lying on his belly, propping his chin in his hand.

Staring at me.

I actually manage to sit myself up this time, though I have to groan and lean against the wall for support. Still. It's progress. Much better than I was a few nights ago, when the cold had me ill enough to think letting Farin hold me through the night was a good idea.

It was not.

Okay, so I suppose from a survival standpoint, it was the right move. But allowing Farin to keep me from dying from the cold is akin to asking a spider to assist you in getting untangled from its web.

"What's what like?" I ask, wishing to distract myself from the memory of Farin's warm hands wrapped around my waist.

"Having all those worlds in your head?"

I shift, though it's just as uncomfortable to do so. "Crowded," I say, to which his face lights up in the most tantalizing smile.

"Well, maybe I could help you clear out some space in there."

"You could?"

"My mind's notoriously empty. I have plenty of space to share."

I can't help but laugh at that, though it almost feels macabre.

There's no way Farin's mind is anywhere close to empty. In fact, it's probably full of treacherous murder plots. Like the six uses of the blood of virgins or how to make suffocation a less peaceful way to die.

Still.

It's nice to be asked.

"I don't remember everything about all the worlds. You know how you have all these days of your life that you don't recall a single detail about? It's like that, but worse, because I just have so many lives to keep up with."

"Then tell me what you do remember."

I laugh. "Why do you care?"

"Because I'm bored."

"And why is that my problem?"

"Because I tend to start contemplating murder when I'm bored, and since you're the only person around, and I rather fancy you, I'd appreciate it if you kept me entertained."

There's an amused dance in the way his eyes twinkle.

Should it give me the warm fuzzies that this male wants a distraction from thinking about murdering me?

Likely not.

Okay, it's a resounding no.

But coming from Farin, it's practically a bouquet of my favorite flowers.

"Fine. But only because I'm bored too."

"We don't have to tell stories, if you don't want. I'm sure we could come up with other activities to fill the time," he teases, and though my heart skips, I hasten to scold it.

Farin is a flirt.

A murdery flirt.

He's in love with Blaise. No, he's obsessed with Blaise, because that's what murdery people do. They obsess.

He just happens to have a rather flirtatious personality. It's not as if I haven't met plenty like him in my many lives—males who have their hearts set on one girl alone, yet mask their desire by flirting with any female in sight.

That's what's happening now.

Though I let myself be grateful he at least fancies me.

After all, that's better than him wanting me dead, isn't it?

"What world are you most interested in hearing about?" I ask.

He grins. "Whatever you're most interested in."

I ignore the way his smile twists my already wounded gut—the gut *he* wounded—into knots.

Ugh.

But I tell him anyway. I tell him of a realm where the ocean is such a deep indigo, it looks almost purple in the sunlight. A world in which the fae sprouted wings and soared in the heavens, making their homes in islands above the clouds.

I expect several questions about said cloud-islands, which is why I'm taken aback when instead Farin asks, "And what about males?"

"What about them?"

"Do you have one you're hoping to get back to? A Blaise to your Farin, if you will?"

I don't allow myself to dwell on how his words cause my stomach to sour.

"I don't really let myself get close to males," I say.

Farin frowns. "Why not?"

I sigh. "In each life, I start off an infant, just like everyone else. Then I grow into a child, lost in my head during the day, tortured by nightmares at night. Everyone always calls me a dreamer, says I've an imagination too big for my skull. Tutors scold me for never being able to pay attention, but really, it's like I just have too much to keep up with. And then I get older, and about the time when I would notice boys my age, that's when it hits me my dreams aren't dreams at all. They're memories. And of course, I go years without telling anyone, because obviously whoever I tell is going to think I'm crazy..."

I trail off, and Farin cocks his head to the side. "And then?"

I let out an embarrassed laugh. "And then I tread the course of many adolescent women and entrust my heart to a male, only to find him less than prepared to take care of it. You would think having gone

458

through it several times, I would learn. But they almost always decide I'm mad. Even the ones I'm convinced will believe me."

"If it makes you feel better, I don't think you're crazy."

"That's not all that comforting."

He feigns offense. "And why not?"

"Because you're crazier than I am?"

He plucks a root from the ground beneath him, twirling it in his hands. "Who knows, Wanderer. Maybe you've been looking in the wrong places for affection. Maybe crazy is just what you need."

He holds my stare for a while, and his cocky grin softens somewhat.

I'm the first to break the stare, unable to help the embarrassment climbing my cheeks.

Bad.

This is definitely bad.

CHAPTER 78

ELLIE

*A*fter the attack, I spend the mornings in the infirmaries. We've never had many in Othian. Only the one within the castle walls, and the public infirmary close to the town's square.

Tented field infirmaries popped up all over town after the attack. Peck often mutters that none of them contain proper healers, but he spends his off-time volunteering at them, so I try not to scold him for placing so much judgment on those who are just trying to help.

The infirmaries themselves are dismal. The one Other that attacked the nursery had been the only one to penetrate the castle's inner defenses. It had been cut off from the rest, and still it killed two dozen guards before it was finally put down.

The city was not so lucky.

Half of the establishments in the commerce quarter are destroyed. Forcier's bakery is gone, though he made it out alive and spends his days using the kitchens of friends to bake goods for the injured and bereaved.

Madame Lefleur's is gone, too.

Thankfully, my parents' house was spared, though the workshop took some damage. Even though Evander is dealing with his new role as king, he still finds time every day to come by the workshop and help my father with the repairs.

Overall, there's a grief that hangs over the city, one as palpable as the thick air of Charshon.

Life as we knew it, the kind we had settled into, is gone.

This is our life now—working endless hours getting supplies to and from the makeshift infirmaries, trying to keep the injured from dying of simple things like dehydration. The infirmaries are overrun and understaffed, and the burns from the Others' venom lick away at the moisture in their victims' bodies.

I take Cecilia along with me, strapped to my back. My mother keeps offering to watch her, and it probably makes more sense than suffering the knots that develop in my shoulders and neck from carrying her, but I just can't bear to leave her.

Not when any day now, those creatures might return.

Not when we are helpless.

Helpless.

Wasn't that why I told Evander I wanted to go with him to the Rip? Because I'd felt useless, helpless?

It occurs to me I didn't know the definition of those words until now.

My hands ache to do something, anything. So I do what I can, and though that mostly means lugging pails of water from the castle water reserves to the infirmaries where the healers can distribute them to patients, it's at least something. Something that leaves my palms with the calluses of *doing*.

I don't see much of Evander in the days following the attack. While I'm out lugging pails of water around, he's stuck in meetings with the nobles who escaped death or major injury. There aren't many of them, but they all have opinions, opinions that seem to contradict. Each of them feels Evander is unqualified to rule, which apparently they make evident at each meeting.

When he isn't coming up with a plan for rebuilding the kingdom or rallying allies or funding the research of weapons that could actually defend against the Others, he's busy around town. He's rebuilding cottages and helping children find their way back to their parents. Holding their hands and finding them homes when there are no parents to be found.

He's put several of them up at the palace.

Too many of them to be practical, but it isn't as if anyone is going to say anything.

Even Evander's cousin knows better than that.

Sometimes I feel a hand brush mine at the wells, catch a faint glimpse of my husband flashing me a smile when we find ourselves drawing water for the infirmaries at the same time.

We almost always arrive home at different times, one of us always discovering the other already passed out in bed.

I can hardly remember the last time we had a full conversation without either of us falling asleep.

But still. Evander leads. And Evander learns. And Evander serves. And I can hardly think about any of it without a lump forming in my throat.

ONE DAY, we find ourselves fortunate enough to be at my parents' at the same time. Mama convinced me I need sleep, and that she was perfectly capable of taking care of Cecilia for a few hours while I got some rest in my old bedroom.

I do feel better, more clearheaded, once I awake from a deathlike slumber. Part of me feels guilty though, like there are people out in the city who might have died of dehydration while I've been curled up in my old bed, succumbed to the blissful oblivion of sleep.

My mother doesn't tolerate me admitting as much, and after I feed Cecilia, she sends me out to see to my father, who she claims is equally dreadful about allowing himself rest.

Indeed, I find him in his workshop, hammering away at a loose board that came off during the attack.

He looks at me and smiles faintly. I don't say anything as I pick up a hammer and get to work alongside him.

Evander shows up not long after, placing a kiss on my forehead before grabbing a hammer and joining us.

IT DOESN'T TAKE LONG BEING in the workshop for me to transition back to helping my father with his tasks.

As we work, he asks Evander what must be an overwhelming amount of questions about what is being done about Azrael and the Others.

"Papa," I say, "Evander sits through meetings about this all day. And when he's not in meetings, he's out helping like the rest of us."

Evander rubs my shoulder. "It's okay. He's a citizen here, too. He has a right to know what's being done."

So Evander tells him. He tells him of rallying support from the other kingdoms and the troubling news of Naenden being overtaken.

My heart lurches for Asha, the idea of her being trapped in a marriage with Azrael, her nightmares coming true.

During the discussion, my mother brings me Cecilia, whom I bounce in my arms as my mother returns to the house.

"And weapons?" my father asks. "What of the problem of the Others' venom melting through our soldiers' armor, their shields?"

Evander sighs, rubbing the back of his neck. I realize it's the first time I've seen him return to the old habit in weeks.

"Honestly, Jethro, I have no idea. We have all our best weapons experts on it. I'm practically dumping out our coffers at their feet, if any of them can figure out a solution. So far, no one's been able to come up with anything. They all say the same thing: how do we fight with creatures who aren't of our world? Who don't play by our rules, the rules of our elements?"

My father crosses his arms, leaning back against a crate of cast-iron pans as he nods his head contemplatively.

He says something, but I find myself zoning out, his voice muffled in my mind.

Where my father's shoulders rest upon the crate is a spot—a hole, where the venom that sprayed on the roof of the workshop during the attack has dripped down and eaten through the wood.

"Papa," I say, scrambling over to where he's standing, reaching over him to open the crate.

"I don't know how much good those will do anybody," says my father. "Though I can't believe I didn't think of it. You're right, there probably are families who could use some cookware right about now."

I shake my head, my mouth hanging open in shock, in the hesitation that comes before hope.

"No?" my father asks.

Evander stands up straight from where he'd also been leaning on a crate behind him. "El? What is it?"

I peer down into the crate, tears stinging at my eyes as the light from Evander's lantern reveals its contents.

"Papa?" I ask again. "What are the properties of glass?"

He frowns, wrinkling his forehead, though to his credit, he rattles them off without questioning me. He ends with, "resistance to harsh chemicals."

"What was that last one?" I practically choke on my own question.

"Resistance to..."

I turn and face my father, whose eyes have gone wide. A moment later, he's peering down into the crate with me.

Where a boxful of cast-iron pans sit, unharmed by the venom that now congeals atop them.

"Evander," I say. "I think I'm going to need you to take Cecilia for a bit." I hand him our daughter, who yawns carelessly as he takes her into his arms.

"What's this about, El?" Evander looks back and forth between me and my father, the both of us probably looking high as the topmost turret at the palace.

"Oh, nothing." Papa grips Evander on the shoulder. "You just married a genius, is all."

"Well, I already knew that," he says, bouncing Cecilia and looking not at all amused that we're teasing him with this information.

"Enameled cast iron. It protects cookware from chemical elements," I say.

Evander nods, Cecilia wriggling in his arms. "Yes, so you've told me. But why exactly is that worthy of the manic grins you two have plastered on your faces?"

"Glass has properties that make it resilient against chemical damage. Meaning it doesn't erode as quickly as iron." I gesture to a pan, upon which the wyvern venom is puddled. "Meaning the Others' venom won't work on it."

"Okay, but we can't very well go around swinging glass swords, can we?" says Evander. "Unless you've figured out a way to solve the shattering upon impact problem."

"We're not going to make glass weapons," I say, my father and I exchanging those "manic" grins. "We're just going to coat the ones we already have."

CHAPTER 79

PIPER

The flute is right where I left it, buried in a hole that, now that I'm digging it up, seems much too shallow considering what I was hoping to hide.

My fists close around the flute, its white oak shaft as cool as metal to the touch, as smooth as calfskin against my fingertips.

Deep inside me, my Gift hums with delight, static prickling at my skin as I pull the flute from the dirt.

Blaise raises a brow, her arms crossed. "That's not a very deep hole."

I let out an exasperated groan, more at my past self than her. This part of the wood is mostly abandoned, but Blaise is right. It could have easily not been here when we arrived.

The full moon shines overhead, and I can't help but notice that Blaise keeps her gaze fixated either on me, the flute, or the ground.

A chill snakes through the air.

"How do you know it works? How do you know it'll amplify your powers, I mean?" Blaise asks.

I gesture with my head to the crater in the ground beyond her. She teeters at its edge, craning her neck as she peers down.

"Because that used to be a pond," I say.

"Used to be?"

"Until I summoned the water and drowned a forest faerie in it."

"Like, midair?"

I nod, and Blaise lets out a noncommittal humph of consideration.

I tap my fingers against the instrument, tracing the vines etched into its side. Inside me, my Gift bounces with excitement.

I've been paying more attention to my Gift lately, noting its mood more often than I usually do. I've always had a feeling it was sentient, but ever since learning that Queen Asha's Gift speaks to her, I can't help but wonder if my Gift is capable of the same and simply chooses not to.

What do you think? Think this will work? Think we can summon a legion of Others and march them back through the Rip?

My Gift buzzes, vibrating my ribcage, but I can't tell if it's shaking its head yes or no.

Can you use words?

Another buzz, though this time it's lower, deeper than the first.

Can you use a high note for yes and a low note for no? I ask it, feeling utterly ridiculous.

But a note, so high I feel the need to cover my ears, reverberates through me.

A resounding yes.

Okay, well, maybe you don't have to go so high, I think, though I'm pleased. My Gift is still buzzing, and this might be naïve of me, but it seems it's eager to communicate with me. Part of me has been nervous I might be infested with a magic more akin to Blaise's parasite. But no, that fear is silly. There's nothing hostile about the Gift inside me.

Can you speak with words?

A buzz, not low and not high.

Okay, so obviously that isn't the right question.

Was there a time when you used to speak?

A high note, like the smallest chime on a bell.

Were you cursed to be unable to speak?

Again, the answer is a more medium pitch. Noncommittal.

Is there a way I can help you speak?

The ambiguous noise again.

It appears my Gift doesn't know.

I groan in frustration, at which point a dirge begins playing in my ears.

I'm not frustrated at you, I quickly think, seeking to soothe the poor being trapped inside me, its voice stolen by magic or time or a curse, or something else altogether.

"Care to impart any of this conversation to me?" asks Blaise. She's staring at me as I conduct the inaudible exchange.

"Right. Sorry. It's not so much a dialogue. My Gift can communicate with me, but she uses music to do it, not words. It makes getting information a little complicated. We're trying to work out a system."

Blaise glances skyward for the first time. "Well, maybe you could work out that system while walking. I'd rather not be caught out here at sunrise."

That seems fair.

CHAPTER 80

ZORA

I stumble around the cave, holding onto the walls for support. My limbs still need practice, but it's progress.

The one time I fall, Farin is there to catch me, his sturdy arms firm but gentle around my torso.

"I'm going to have to start being careful," he says, his blue eyes assessing me, his face a mask I can't read. "One of these days, you're going to be strong enough to get away."

His tone is teasing, but a layer of ice settles over my stomach.

Because I'd already realized I could walk. Earlier today. When Farin was out hunting for our dinner.

And I'd convinced myself not to run. That I should wait until I regain my full strength.

There's a reason I'm not eager to do what it will take to get off this island. Out of this world. I'd been hoping I could avoid that eventuality by using the eyelet with Nox. Now that the eyelet has closed up, it's likely the location at which it's reopened isn't on the island.

What's also not likely is that we'll find a way to escape.

Which leaves me with only one option.

Hero or villain?

"What turned you into a monster?" I ask, not wishing to ponder the true reason I didn't run today when I had the chance.

Farin chokes, crossing the cave. "Direct, aren't we?"

I shrug.

"If you must know, I believe my father had the most to do with it, though I'm sure it's not worth blaming him over. There was a point at which I accepted my role as oppressor. I found it easier than fighting my father on the matter. Than being accused of being a weak dreamer unfit for ruling."

"And your mother?" I ask.

Farin scoffs, tossing a handful of seeds across the ground. "My mother's the worst monster of all."

I crane my neck.

"What?" he asks.

"Was she always that way? The way she was with Nox? With me?" It's odd to think that Farin's mother is partially responsible for how my many lives have turned out.

Farin shrugs. "Are any of us always that way?" There's a moroseness about his tone, a sadness I can't quite grasp.

"No, I suppose not."

"My mother was rather innocent when she was young." Farin sighs. "At least, that's how I prefer to think of her. She married my father, the leader of our tribe, thinking she could get around the tribal ordinance that prohibited members from having children."

"That's a strange ordinance."

"Babies have a tendency to scream, and the Others have excellent hearing."

I frown, imagining a society built around being quiet. Around silence. No singing or dancing or laughing.

In all my lives, I've never experienced a world like that.

"Anyway, she married my father, and though I get the impression he was kind to her for a while, all that ended when I came around. I would cry, putting the tribe in danger. He had ways of silencing me, of course, even from a young age."

A chill sneaks up my spine.

"But it was never enough. And I suppose the monster in him was always going to come out. I remember asking my mother about it once. Whether my father was always a monster. She said no, but that my grandfather had been one, and had trained it into my father. I remember asking her if I would grow up to be a monster, too." An exasperated laugh escapes his lips.

"And what did she say?"

A wry smile twists his lips. It's when he looks like this that it feels as if shards of glass are scraping against my chest. "She said no. Said that my heart was too tender. That I was stronger than my father."

Gooseflesh prickles my spine.

"I think she meant to get me away from him when she discovered we could escape to another world through the Rip. But then I was attacked by a wolf, my leg injured. She didn't know I would heal quickly, so she raced off to grab her healing supplies from our world, the Nether. My father caught her during the process. Made her lead him back to me. Imagine her terror when she found me running around on the leg that was supposed to be ruined. She'd led my father into our haven all for nothing. I didn't see her for a long time after that. By the time we met again...well, I'd say she'd changed, but I'd changed too. The monster had already been passed down."

"What kind of monster?" I can't help but ask.

Farin flicks his gaze up at me. "Why do you want to know?"

I take a step closer, feigning bravery, though I fiddle my fingers together behind my back. "Why don't you want to tell me?"

"Because," he says, "I'm getting used to someone looking at me like I'm not the villain. Maybe I like pretending."

My cheeks heat, something about the word *pretending* feeling more intimate than it should.

"Why do you want to know?" he presses again.

"Just call me curious," I say, though my breath falters a bit. Why do I want to know? So I can size up my enemy, surely. "Maybe I'd like to remind myself that you *are* the villain."

Something flashes across his face, but it's too quick for me to catch in the flickering firelight.

"And why would you need to do that?"

He's close now, and I don't know when or how it happened, at what point during our conversation he shifted toward me, lessening the space between us.

"I've already told you. I'm a rather forgetful person."

A grin snakes his lips, and they dip down to mine, ever so slightly. "Maybe I like that about you, Wanderer. Maybe I find it refreshing."

Maybe he likes that about me, but he'll always like Blaise more.

No—that's ridiculous. That should not be my number one reason to protect my heart from Farin.

I clear my throat. "Never mind," I say. "I'm sure it's a boring story, anyway."

Farin narrows his eyes in suspicion, but he creates space between us, regardless.

That's good, because I'm not sure what I might have done had he lingered close any longer.

CHAPTER 81

NOX

I hesitate at a familiar oak door, my fist brushing against the gnarled planks as I will up the courage to knock.

A set of carvings marks the door frame. Each for marking the height of a twin.

There's a slash above the shorter ones, where Zora got jealous that I was outgrowing her and pulled a stool out to the doorframe to carve her own slash when no one was paying attention to her.

My chest constricts when I see it, and in my mind, I hear another slash, the carving of a knife against her flesh.

My throat aches, a knot forming in it, and I don't know if I can bear it, showing up here at my parents' when I couldn't save her. When I didn't save her.

I didn't save either of them in the end.

A shadow flickers across the fogged windows. Before I can make the decision to run, the door creaks open.

"We're clo—Nox."

My father's voice trembles on my name, wiping away any question I had of whether he would recognize me. Before I can respond, he's practically ripped the door off its hinges, wrapping his arms around me, his strong, calloused hands grasping at the nape of my neck.

"My son. Oh, my son..."

Panic stirs through me, but it's an old reaction. Though I'm still cursed with vampirism in this body, my connection with Farin has been severed, so while the cravings for blood haven't vanished completely, they're considerably more manageable. Especially since I fed on the way.

Still, I try not to breathe too deeply as my father weeps on my shoulder.

IT'S A MORE anxiety-inducing encounter than I imagined. Mostly because I keep waiting for my father to ask about Zora, but he doesn't. I recognize soon that he's also waiting for me to ask about my mother, and my stomach plummets.

Dead. My mother is dead. She must be.

But then my father pulls away, wiping his tears from his crystal-blue eyes, and I finally get a good look at him.

He's fae, meaning he's hardly aged since I last saw him, though I suppose the same can't be said for me, since I was only a child when I was taken.

His midnight hair has grown out, and he looks less like the clean, orderly father I remember and more like a male struggling to survive alone in the wilderness.

"Your sister?" he finally asks.

I swallow, then shake my head slowly, unable to face the lingering hope in his gaze.

"Ah." It seems that's all he's able to choke out for a moment as he presses his fist to his lips and squeezes his eyes shut.

It's all my fault, I should add. *I didn't save her*, I should admit, but I don't. Can't.

"Well, we'll have to be gentle with how we tell your mother," he finally says, straightening his back, though his shoulders still droop with weariness. "She's.... Well, I suppose you'll see soon enough."

The brief relief that swarmed my chest at the news my mother still lives is replaced by an innate dread, but I've no time to ask what he means as he leads me to the back room.

I try not to, but I can't help but note the mess that's accumulated after all these years.

My parents were always the cluttered sort, mostly because they were always trading wares with the passersby that frequented the Serpentine right off of my parents' property.

This is not clutter.

It's filth.

My stomach twists at the sight, not out of disgust, but because of what I'm afraid it means.

When my father leads me to the back room, my fears are realized.

There's a lump in the bed, though I recognize immediately by her breathing patterns that my mother is not asleep. Far from it. The sun has only just set, an abnormal time for anyone to be in bed, but something about the way the closed curtains collect dust tells me this isn't an unusual occurrence.

"Merida," my father calls, and my chest constricts again at hearing my mother's name on my father's lips. I don't think I expected to hear that again. "Merida. We have a visitor."

No one answers, though I can't help but notice my mother halts her breathing. As if she can make herself unnoticeable if only she goes completely still.

"Merida." My father takes a deep breath, biting the inside of his cheek like he's afraid of telling her the truth. Not the truth that I'm alive, but of the inevitable question that will follow.

"Maybe I should just go." I'm panicking now, realizing what our loss has done to our mother. Our mother, who used to tend to the wounded who'd been robbed on the Serpentine. Our mother, who used to give too many wares for free to those upon whom she took pity.

I destroyed her by leaving, and then I took Zora away from her too. Not that I knew the consequences of my actions at the time.

You did this, a voice whispers to me in the back of my mind.

It's strange. I would have thought I blamed Abra for this. I suppose now that she's dead, there's no one left to blame but me.

The hurt in Blaise's eyes when I betrayed her flashes across my memory. At the time, I didn't think I had a choice. I entered into a fae bargain with Abra the night Blaise Turned. Vowed to be her servant eternally if she would do what she could to bring Blaise back. I'd felt good about that not being a problem as soon as I realized the parasite was the one in control, not Abra.

But then Abra had pushed through.

She was so distraught over Farin, but I knew if I didn't take my chance then, it wouldn't be long before she remembered her command over me.

I couldn't be a slave to Abra. Not again.

Still.

The hurt in Blaise's eyes scalds my soul, even if it's true that I don't love her anymore.

Blaise has haunted me since the day I left her. It doesn't seem love is a requirement for her to have burrowed inside my soul.

Because I remember loving her. Not how it felt—at least, I can't feel it in real time. But I remember there was a time when I would have clawed through heaven and earth to get to her. I remember cradling her dead body and being willing to give all of myself away just to get her back.

I push the thought of Blaise away.

"No." My father's hand grasps my shoulder as I turn to leave. "Just... just go to her. I think it will do her good."

He doesn't sound convinced of his own words, but I can't walk out on my father. So I draw near to the bed, the shadows in the pitch-black room gaping, as if they'll swallow me whole.

"Mother," I say. "It's me. Nox."

"My son is dead," she croaks out from underneath the quilt pulled over her face.

It's true. Her son died a long time ago.

I take in a deep breath. "I'm here, Mother. It's me, Nox. I'm back.

And I'm…" I can't bring myself to say safe or alright or alive, so I leave it be.

"No…" She weeps from under the blanket. I frown, hesitating as I try to move it, pull it back from her face, but she flinches and hunkers down instead.

Ice spikes my heart as she does.

What have I done to her?

What have I done to my mother?

I freeze, and I don't know what to do, but then the warmth of my father's hand clasps at my shoulder. "She often dreams that you return. She has these moments when she first wakes when she's thrilled, shaking me with excitement because our children are back. I think she thinks this is another dream. Another dream that will break her when she wakes."

"What can we do?"

My father sighs. "We'll try again tomorrow. Nighttime is difficult, and first thing in the morning is the worst, but midday is usually some better."

Some better.

That isn't encouraging.

But I follow my father out of the room regardless, my chest caving in as he shuts the door behind him.

My father has to go to town in the morning to pick up supplies, and because I'm a child and can't bear the thought of staying alone at the house with my mother who isn't my mother, I offer to come along with him.

Normally, I wouldn't be able to go along with him during the day hours, but it's reached the time of year in Mystral when the sun only shines for a few hours midday. Since my father is an early riser, it gives us plenty of time to walk to town and back before I have to worry about being scorched to death.

My father is chatty on the way to town, which surprises me. Talkative isn't a quality I remember about my father. I almost find it enjoyable, except I soon realize it stems from having no one to converse with at home anymore.

WHEN WE FINALLY REACH TOWN, I try to wait for my father in the streets. I don't really have any desire to speak to the people I haven't seen since I was a child. Most of the residents avoided Zora and me, believing fae twins to be cursed to destroy one another. Though now that I consider it, I suppose their superstitions weren't so far off after all.

My father looks disappointed though, and I realize he wants to share his excitement over my return with someone, given my mother hasn't been emotionally available. I finally give in and enter the general store with him.

It's rather empty at this hour anyway. This must be the time my father always comes, because the store owner, a female by the name of Jean with long crimson hair that's as straight as a board, purrs, "You're two minutes late, Ronan." She stares down at her ledgers from behind the counter, not bothering to look up. "I was beginning to worry I'd have to wait until tomorrow to see that handsome face of yours again."

I clear my throat, and Jean glances up, clearly startled to see my father has brought company.

That level of startled doesn't begin to match what creeps over her face when she sees me. "Nox," she whispers, her voice breathy. "You're alive."

She looks back and forth between my father and me and bites her lip, measuring her words.

Then a stunning smile curves on her full, red lips. "Why, this is wonderful, Ronan,"

Something in the way her eyes don't take part tells me it's not. For her, at least.

My father offers her a friendly smile that I find quite naïve. He puts his arm around my shoulder, pulling me close. "Showed up on my doorstep late last night. Back from the dead."

"That's delightful for you," Jean says, though she's having difficulty maintaining the levity in her tone. "I'm sure Merida is delighted."

I feel my limbs go stiff, but my father clearly doesn't see it as the fishing attempt that it is, because he answers, "I'm afraid Merida was too ill last night to recognize him, but we're hopeful that she'll feel better once the sun rises."

I mark the glimmer in Jean's eyes at the news that my return has not caused a miraculous recovery in my mother.

Farin might no longer be inside me, but that doesn't stop red from swimming in my vision.

"And your daughter?" Jean asks, ignoring my presence and focusing fully on my father.

My father blinks rapidly and shakes his head, just as he did last night.

Jean at least has the decency to look regretful at his pain. For a moment, she almost has me convinced.

"I'm so sorry, Ronan," she says, and the binding nature of the fae curse means it's true.

It doesn't stop me from wondering how her blood would taste.

ONCE MY FATHER has collected all his wares for the day, we make our way back to the cottage. The part of me that lives in dread of the sun paces quickly up the hill, though I have to remember that even my fae father isn't as swift as I am, given the advantages of my curse.

On the way, I keep opening my mouth, trying to get it to form a question, or perhaps a statement. Either way, whatever I want to say has to do with Jean. Whether father realizes her obvious feelings for him. But each time I choke on the words. Part of me doesn't want to know if my father notices and encourages them anyway.

I don't think I can bear it if my father is cheating on my mother. Because if he is, I think perhaps that's my fault, too.

CHAPTER 82

ZORA

"*A*re you going to kill me when I tell you where the eyelet is?" It's a fair question, because I'm walking with ease now. I only have a day or two at best before Farin expects me to lead him to it.

Farin raises his brow. "Would you believe me if I told you no?"

"Depends on how convincing you are."

"I like to think I can be rather convincing when I want to be." He allows his gaze to trace over me, as he so often does. "No, I don't intend to kill you."

"But you're capable of lying now."

"I told you that you wouldn't believe me, regardless."

"I'm open to the concept. I just need to be given a reason."

Farin sighs, setting down the piece of wood he's been whittling into a shiv and looking at me. "Because I like you, Wanderer. And it's a rather rare occasion that I find someone I actually do like, so no, I'd rather not kill you. Not that I wouldn't if I found it necessary, but I'd really rather you not make it necessary."

My chest caves in slightly, but if Farin is trying to persuade me, he's doing it in the best way possible. He's not trying to win me over with flattery.

There's something about someone telling you they'd kill you if they had to that makes you more willing to believe everything else they say is true, too.

Even if it hurts.

It shouldn't hurt.

Farin is not my friend.

He and I have a common goal. And personalities that jive rather well given the circumstances.

The circumstances being that he's the murderer who stabbed me so he could make it back to the woman my brother loves.

Now, as to whether I want to consider why my personality jives so well with that of a killer's, the answer is I don't. And I won't. At least not until we find a way off this island.

"The eyelet moves," I say with a heavy sigh.

Farin's brows raise.

"If someone enters it before me, it moves. I don't know how or where or why it does, but it never goes away completely."

"How do you know this?"

"Because it's happened before."

"Hm," Farin says.

"That's all you have to say?"

"It's not the most useful information you've offered me, Wanderer. Unless this world is contained to this island alone, it's not much to go off of."

"There are other ways to find it," I say.

"Is that so? And what are they?"

"If I told you, I'd have to kill you," I say, and though there's teasing in my tone, Farin turns his head slowly toward me.

He shrugs. "Dying at your hands doesn't seem like the worst way to go."

Ugh.

"What? You're not going to threaten me with my life if I don't tell you?"

A moment later, Farin is upon me, grabbing my wrists and pinning me to the wall.

"Is that what you'd like, Wanderer? For me to threaten you?"

My breath quickens, and so does my heart. The part of me that values self-preservation says it's fear that's causing my body's reaction. The part of me that knows better tells me it's something more.

His thumb finds the bone of my left wrist and traces circles into it, his forehead dropping until it's nearly resting on mine.

My head spins, dizziness overtaking me, but Farin says nothing, does nothing, like he's patiently waiting for me to make the next move.

Like a predator that lurks in the tall grass, waiting for its prey to flee, lest it cut the chase short.

This will not end well for me, I'm sure of it now.

Hero or villain?

Which role am I to play this time?

It's usually more obvious to me by this point, but now that I know I'm not here for a specific mission, everything's muddled. The feel of Farin's warm breath against my lips is not helping to clear things up.

"Sweet ones. The kind who rescue puppies on their off days," I say, to which Farin's face twists in confusion.

It's enough to break the tension between us, for which I'm rather grateful.

"You asked earlier what sort of male I find myself drawn to," I say, casually slipping out from underneath his grasp as it loosens around my wrists.

"Oh, I very much doubt that," he says, and I find myself grateful that I'm turned far enough away that he can't see the girlish smile breaking across my face.

It's rather dangerous territory I'm stepping into, helping Farin get back to the woman he so desires. Or, at least, pretending that I am.

Because there's no eyelet at the end of this journey, not that I'm aware of, at least.

It's not that there's not a way out of this world.

Nox wasn't the only memory that caused my nightmares growing up.

It's just that I have no intention of admitting to Farin how I can open up my own way out.

Hero or villain?

Which am I this time?

Lying to Farin might get me off this island, might help to ensure that my brother gets the happy ending he deserves, but it will probably end up with me dead.

But let's just say after dozens of lives lived, I'm bored, and I'm up for a novel experience.

CHAPTER 83

NOX

"Why haven't you left?"

The question hangs in the air before us, stale as three-week-old snow during the single month of summer Mystral's allotted.

My father looks up from his ledgers, shuffling uncomfortably, as if he's sure he's misheard me.

"What do you mean?"

"I mean, why haven't you left? You didn't think Zora or I were ever coming back. Why didn't you leave?"

My father sets down his ledgers, shutting them. A bloom of dust shoots out, dispersing in the air.

"Your mother isn't well enough for me to just pick up and take her somewhere new, son."

I run my hands through my hair, frustrated at my father's avoidance of the question. "No, I mean why haven't you left Mother?"

My father's throat bobs, and for the first time since I've arrived, true, unfiltered concern flickers in his eyes. "Why would you think I'd leave your mother, Nox?"

I sigh, slumping back against the chair. "How long has she been like this?" It comes out as more of a demand than I intend it to, but everything I do lately seems to be following a similar pattern.

"It comes and goes," is all he says, then thoughtfully he adds, "It's worse in the dark months."

"You live in Mystral, Father. The dark months make up most of the year."

Father sighs. "I've tried to convince her to move somewhere brighter. Even Dwellen. But she always says she wants to be right here when you and Zora find your way back home."

The bile in my stomach curdles.

"But you didn't think either of us were ever coming back."

My father frowns. "My heart hadn't given up hope. For either of you. But no. I had no expectation that I would ever see you again."

"So you stayed for nothing."

"Your mother is not nothing, Nox."

"She's a shell."

My father's chest heaves, and I can't tell if it's in frustration or anguish, or a bit of both. "What is this about?"

"I just...I just think you have the potential to be happy. I saw the way you smiled at Jean today, and I thought—"

"Jean's not my wife."

"No, but how long has it been since Mother has been that for you, either?"

My father's jaw goes slack, discomfort spreading all over his face. "Are you telling me you want me to leave your mother?"

Agony ripples through me. Because he's right. That's exactly how my words sound. "No. No, that's not what I want at all. I just...I just don't want to see you unhappy, that's all."

"My, well. Thank you, son. What a joy it is to have a child so much wiser than his own parents, that he can spend a single night with them and fix all their problems instantly."

A shard of guilt pierces my gut, and I shake my head. "That's not what I meant to do."

"Hm," is all my father says before returning to his ledgers.

"Do you still love her?" I hate how childish the question sounds when I ask it. Hate the way it pelts me with guilt, with the anguish of what I lost with Blaise. The feelings that were stripped from me, the ones I can no longer grasp, though they leave behind a gaping hole, a numbness I'm not sure can be filled.

My father peers out from over his book. Then he gestures toward the roast, my mother's favorite meal. That's why he went to the market this morning—to get the ingredients. He motions to the bowl left untouched after my mother refused to leave their room. "What exactly do you think love is, son, that you would even feel the need to ask that question?"

Shame washes over me, making it difficult to formulate the words. "You just don't seem happy, that's all. I don't...I don't want it to be because of me that you're not happy."

My father's face seems to soften at that, like he's taking pity on me somehow. And again I feel like a boy, readying to squirm underneath his scrutiny. Like I've been caught in the act of something I knew better than to do.

"Before your mother gave birth, we already knew the two of you were twins. Could hear the two distinct heartbeats from fairly early on." My father's voice trails off as he stares into the distance.

"We were so excited. We'd been trying for decades at that point. But then the day came for your mother to give birth, and the midwife told me I had both a daughter and a son, and..." He trails off again, looking down into his hands, as if remembering the children he once held there.

"They say that something changes in you when you hold your own child. That something clicks, a sort of magic that isn't magic at all, but instinctual. A bond that locks into place, quite naturally."

I shuffle in my chair, unsure what this has to do with his relation-ship with my mother, but unwilling to interrupt him all the same.

"The midwife handed you to your mother. You came first, after all. And when you hit your mother's arms, I saw it in her. That spark. The evidence something had changed. It was the most beautiful thing I'd ever seen. And then your sister came, and I remember her screaming and flailing around, already so much more boisterous than you. And the midwife wiped her off and swaddled her up and set her in my arms..."

My father takes a breath.

"And I felt nothing. Not an ounce of love, not a prick of emotion, for the child I held." He grimaces, pain evident across his face, even as my chest goes tight. "And I thought, what kind of person feels nothing when they hold their child for the first time? I hoped maybe it was just a delay. That I only had to wait a few moments for it to set in, but it had happened so quickly for your mother."

He lets out a laugh, the kind that lacks humor. "Your sister started crying, and a terrible thought rushed to my head. I thought perhaps I was just like my father after all, favoring my sons over my daughters. That I'd inherited his prejudice. But Zora was screaming, so I handed her to your mother all the same, and she just looked up at me and beamed. It took over her entire face, and I saw it again, watched that devotion set in.

"She was so proud when she handed you to me. When she told me to meet my son. But when I looked down into your tiny innocent face, still I felt nothing. No animosity, of course. And there was the desire to protect, like one might have if they were holding anyone's child. But nothing clicked for me, son. Not with you, not with your sister."

My throat goes dry. "Father, you don't have to feel guilty about any of that. It's just a natural reaction as any. You were..." My throat feels as if it's going to close up now. "Well, I've always had the best memories of you. Remember the time you taught me to build a fence? How patient you were when I was learning to whittle?"

My father nods, recollection shimmering in his eyes, but then he shakes his head as if I've missed the point. "You don't doubt my love for you, then."

"Of course not."

"But I didn't feel love for you, Nox, or your sister, when every voice in my head, every voice in the community, was telling me I should."

I shift in my chair, and the legs scratch the floor. "Yes, but I'm sure the feeling came. Just later than you expected."

Surely it came. Surely.

My father nods, conceding my point. "It took several months. Several months of watching your mother cradle the two of you like you were the moons that made the waves rise. The three of you in this little world all together, one from which I was excluded. A world I couldn't seem to reach. I helped out with the two of you as often as I could, changing your britches day and night, rocking one of you to sleep during the times your mother couldn't bear to nurse both of you at once. Yet, for months, I felt nothing."

"There's no reason for you to feel guilt."

"And why is that, Nox? Do you not feel less loved now that you know?"

I frown. "Of course not."

"And why not?"

"Because you stayed. Because you raised us as if you felt love for us. And because you grew to love us eventually, anyway. By the time it mattered. By the time we could remember."

My father nods his head. "And what of the time when I did not feel love for you?"

"You were probably in shock at the changing of your life situation..."

"But why is it you don't feel any less loved?"

"Because you kept your duty to us, anyway."

"And why should it be any different with your mother?"

My jaw works, and it takes me a moment to find an answer. "The bond between a male and wife is different than that between a parent and a child. The bond between a parent and a child is...well, it's just different. Unbreakable."

My father looks at me curiously. "I know plenty of children who have rejected their parents."

"Yes, but..."

"Do you know what I think you haven't considered, Nox? I think you haven't stopped to acknowledge that before you and Zora became the center of our worlds, your mother and I had each other for quite a long time. Decades. And if things had gone according to plan, how

488

they should have gone, you and Zora would have been in our homes for a mere two decades of it. And then you were going to leave, and it was just going to be me and your mother again, for as long as our immortality lasted. That was always the plan. Always the intention.

"It broke us, Nox. Both me and your mother when you went missing. And then, months later, Zora too. And I know it wasn't your fault, son. The Fates know because of how often I've prayed to them, how much we've both condemned ourselves, how many screaming matches we've endured blaming each other. But your mother and I made vows long ago that it was going to be me and her, come what may, and I intend to stick to that."

I pause, struck by his words. "And what if it doesn't happen?"

"What if what doesn't happen?"

"You said eventually your feelings for Zora and me developed. Over time. What if you never feel that love for Mother again?" My throat goes dry on the words. "What if it's gone forever, and there's nothing you can do to get it back?"

My father examines me with those piercing eyes of his. "Are we still talking about your mother and me?"

I sigh, rubbing my brows, and my father sets his elbows on the table.

"Nox, how do you know the sun will rise tomorrow?"

I shrug. "Because it always does, I suppose."

My father appears pleased with my response. "I already told you that your mother and I have been together for a long while. This isn't the first time she's delved into the shadows. I imagine it won't be the last. But it never lasts forever. And the female who's waiting for me on the other side..." He takes a sip of his stew, the rim of the bowl hardly obscuring his smile. "Well, you know her."

Visions of my mother as I remember her wash over me. My mother selling our wares underpriced to travelers who'd found themselves robbed and naked on the road. My mother chasing Zora and me around in the snow, then greeting us with hot cocoa when our fingers started to numb from the cold.

"Yeah," I say, unable to help my smile. "Yeah, I do."

489

"In a few months now, I'll find her out on the side of the road, handing out the last of our food to complete strangers," he says with an exasperated huff. "And then I'll fall in love with her all over again."

"How did you know the first time? The first time your feelings faded for her? How did you know they'd come back?"

My father frowns, as if he's never considered that question before. "I suppose I didn't. I suppose I just remembered the commitments I made to her and stuck to them."

I don't find that altogether helpful, but then my father leans over and says, in a whisper as if it's the secret to life, "We're all different people on the inside, son. There are lots of us running around in our heads. Different Meridas, different Noxes. But people don't change that much over their lives. We just rotate through the different versions of ourselves. Like we might our different work boots. We have a favorite, of course, one that's most worn in and comfortable. But then we have our nice pair, and the pair we wear for trekking through the ice, with all the spikes at the bottom. So far, I've determined that inside your mother are three different females. This one, the one you remember, and the one she only lets me see. Now, out of the three, I'm madly in love with two of them. The one I don't prefer...Well, she'll change it out soon enough. You'll see."

It takes me two days to decide that if my father can love two out of the three of my mother's versions of herself, I can take sixty-six percent of his advice and still respect him immensely.

It's that decision which guides me as I enter my parents' bedroom, waltz over to the bed, and drag the blankets off my mother.

"Get up," I say, though my voice sounds more weary than commanding.

My mother covers her face with her pillow, weeping into it. The sight makes my insides squirm with guilt, but I don't let it overcome me.

Instead, I wrestle the pillow away from her, which takes little effort, given my strength is an advantage.

"My little girl," my mother weeps, and though it aches my heart to do so, I pick my writhing mother up and carry her out of bed into the kitchen.

My father sits at the dining room table, looking stunned as I haul her out of her room.

He shoots up from the table. "Nox, what do you think—"

I hold my hand up to stop him. "I listened to what you said, Father. And believe me, I respect it. More than you could possibly know. But she's got to get up. Wallowing in bed all day isn't helping her."

I set my mother down, though I keep a gentle grip on her shoulders.

"My little girl..." she keeps weeping, and as gently as I can muster, I lift her chin to look at me.

"I'm so sorry that Zora is gone. But Father is here. I'm here. That's going to have to be enough."

For a moment, my mother's face goes blank, and I wonder if I've made a huge mistake, if this is the most insensitive thing that's ever been done. If I'm prowling around this realm and all the others just messing things up.

But then my mother peers up at me, and slowly, recognition flares in her eyes, flickering in the pale lantern light by which my father was penning the ledgers.

"Nox," she whispers, using my name for the first time in what I realize must be years.

I don't know what to say, so I just nod.

She lets out a strangled sob, then tucks her head into my chest. "My boy..." she cries this time.

And now that she's upright and out of bed, I let her.

CHAPTER 84

PIPER

*W*e arrive at the Rip sooner than I expect to. It took us a week to travel from Avelea, across the ravine, to Charshon.

The truth is, I haven't been sure I wanted to get here quickly.

I'm still unconvinced the power enhancement I'll receive from the faerie-made flute and proximity to the Rip will be enough to control a single Other, much less an entire army of them. An entire army that is already under Az's control.

But my feet don't stop placing one in front of the other, so naturally, we eventually arrive.

I feel it before I see it.

A gentle thrum in the soil, the reverberation of a string recently plucked.

The whistle of the wind cutting through the grass, the rattle of flax.

Marcus and Amity were here, though it's been weeks now. It's foolish and fruitless, but I search for signs of them, anyway.

I find none, of course.

Blaise pulls her hood over her head as we approach, and though there's an evening chill, I have a suspicion this is not her reasoning.

The last time Blaise was here, she betrayed her friends, the people who cared the most about her. She betrayed them for a male who left her in the end.

I imagine it can't be pleasant returning. Like if I'd tried to return to the Coup right after sinking an arrow through Bronger's chest.

I'm not sure why I do it, but I find Blaise's hand under her robe sleeves. Her skin is ice cold to the touch, but I give her fingers a gentle squeeze. At first, she goes rigid, and I think perhaps I made a mistake, but when I go to pull away, she links her fingers over my palm and squeezes back. A silent plea not to let go. Not yet.

So I don't.

Not until we reach the Rip.

IT GAPES BEFORE US, and though I can't see it, I can feel it. A chasm that rips through the very air, one that I might fall into if I get too close. It's the feeling of standing at the side of a cliff, staring down into the crashing waves and wondering if you'd survive if the edge went crumbling out from underneath you.

My heart pounds in my chest as the Fabric calls to me, a gentle but sorrowful hum. As if it were apologizing for causing us so much trouble.

There's a part of me that longs to reach out, to stroke it like one might a wounded pet, but I refrain.

Because then I see them.

The silvery runes glimmer in the darkness, forming a circlet in thin air.

"What are the chances this will actually work?" asks Blaise.

My Gift hums that noncommittal note.

"It's a toss-up," I say, and then I raise the flute to my lips and play.

TOUCHING my lips to the flute is like leaning in for a kiss, my Gift melting into the instrument, melding with its wood and the wind and producing the most lovely of songs.

493

It's a call, above all else, and as my fingers strum the keys, I lose myself in the gentle sway of the music, the notes that are not words but might as well be.

Come back, my Gift whispers into the wind. Then with a more sorrowful, drawn-out note. *You don't belong here, but I can lead you home.*

I'm not sure how long I play, the only indication of time being that my shoulders and back ache from holding the flute upright.

Nothing happens.

Nothing comes.

Eventually, either my Gift reaches the end of the tune or grows disheartened, because the music sputters out.

Blaise swallows next to me, blinking away tears.

I lower the flute, Blaise's disappointment an external manifestation of the sinking feeling in my stomach.

"I'm sorry," Blaise says, slinging the tears away with frantic swipes of her hands. "I don't know what's going on with me."

I think I probably do.

"You were hoping to make it up to them, weren't you?"

Blaise won't look at me. She just sniffles then lets out a wry laugh. "Stupid, I know. As if anything I could do could fix what I've taken away from them."

I bite my lip, debating whether to comment. On one hand, Blaise at least seems to be trying to make things right. I don't exactly want to discourage her from that.

On the other...

I think back to conversations I've had with Marcus. Times I've almost let the guilt of my past pull me under, sinking its nails into my ankles and keeping me from staying afloat. I think of what he always tells me when I consider allowing the past to drown me.

"Shame is useful, you know," I say, savoring the way Marcus's words feel on my lips. "But only for a little while. Once it prompts change, there's no need for it anymore, and if you let it sit, it only festers."

Blaise snorts. It does nothing to hide her sniffle. "Is that one of

Abra's unsolicited pieces of wisdom she forced on you when you were her captive audience?"

I smile. "No, not Abra."

"Well," she says, flitting her hand. "It's not as if I can just ignore it. Make it go away. I would if I could."

"What's the antidote for shame?" I ask, and I'm not even talking to Blaise anymore, but feeling Marcus's steady arms wrap around me as he waits for my answer. One I've memorized in the cadence of his voice.

"Pride," Blaise responds, so quickly it's clear she doesn't have to think about it.

"That's what I thought at first, too," I say. "But—"

"Piper," Blaise says, whispering my name, urgency punctuating her tone.

I allow my eyelashes to flutter open, as much as it feels like rising from bed on a winter morning during a thunderstorm.

That feeling doesn't last long. Not when my eyes lock onto what Blaise is pointing toward.

An Other, long and sleek and bright as the moon, slinks from the tree line.

IT STALKS FROM THE SHADOWS, its padded feet silent against the swaying grass.

I lift the flute to my lips and play.

My Gift buzzes inside me, heightening the tune, but I fight to keep it steady.

No sudden movements, no harsh notes.

Fear pulses in my heart as it takes a step closer, Blaise tensing at my sides, her fingers extended at her sides like she's readying a set of claws for battle.

Still, the mere draws closer, moonlight glinting off its saber-like fangs.

My Gift rears up within me, urging me to run, but I stand my ground, willing my Gift to continue lulling the beast to the other side of the Rip.

Of course, we're not positive I can keep it on the other side.

But this is really more about experimenting with this technique, anyway. To see if I can actually do it, if I can actually lure an Other out of Az's control.

As it turns out, I can't.

The mere jerks its neck, snapping its jaws.

It springs, its haunches launching it through the air with all the grace of a dancer.

Its claw aims at my throat.

Blaise aims for its.

Ichor spatters my face. I inhale it through my nose, choking on the vile taste, but the mere's body hits the ground with a thud.

My feet stay rooted to the ground, terror and relief still pounding in my stomach.

I chance a glance at Blaise, her front soaked with inky ichor.

"So I guess that settles that, then," she says.

BLAISE PACES along the edge of the cave, at the edge of where sunlight meets shadows.

I suppose that is how she's lived most of her life, though I determine it best not to mention it. Blaise has been in a state of distress ever since our plan to lure the Others back through the Rip so clearly failed.

It's been question after question. *Is there another song you can play? Are there instruments out there more powerful than that one? Did you try your hardest?*

That last one she retracted immediately, guilt swarming her face.

"I'm sorry," she says, her foot grazing the line between shadow and light. She watches it for a moment, then retreats to the back of the cave, slumping and leaning her head against the cave wall. The position leaves her neck exposed, which I suppose is something a vampire has the privilege of doing, though I find it rather ironic.

"It's a fair question," I say, shrugging. "For all you know, I could have gotten spooked and faltered."

Blaise shakes her head. "You're not the type to get spooked. You're about as level-headed as they come." She flashes me a wry grin. "I bet you even think things through before executing them."

She's right, but her comment isn't about me. It's about her, just another way for her to insult herself.

"Maybe," I say. "But obviously I didn't think this through enough."

"You think the Others are just too powerful to be controlled by your magic?"

I frown, thinking. My Gift definitely got that Other's attention. It's not as though my music had no effect on it. "It was almost like..." I sigh, trying to think of a way to explain it. "When I used to use my Gift to find children, I would focus in on their suffering. The ones who were abused. The tune I used to find them—it didn't enchant them as much as it called out to them. And then, for a while at least, if they answered the call, it formed a temporary bond between us, one that made it easy for me to track them down after the performance. It was always easy following it. Like having a rope to lead you in the dark. But with the Others, the rope is there. It's just like someone else is on the other end, shaking and pulling, tossing you around like a wave until it's impossible to hold on. I guess I lost my grip."

Blaise's eyes light up, though she tries to hide it by rubbing her forehead. "So you think you could get control back if you held on tight enough?"

I shake my head. "No. I don't think I'm powerful enough for that. Not even with the Rip and the faerie flute helping."

Blaise's shoulders deflate.

"Now, if you could take the rope out of the ocean, if you could keep the other end from shaking, then maybe."

I expect Blaise's posture to straighten, for something close to hope to spark in her eyes. Instead, she just watches the line of sunlight at the mouth of the cave, her vision fixated on it.

Blaise might as well be in another world.

"Az controls the other side. He's the one making it difficult for you to gain control," she says, her voice devoid of emotion.

I sit up straighter. "I'm not sure it's a good idea to kill Az. At least not until we know I have the Others under my control. Having them in his control is awful, but he still keeps them from roaming Alondria unfettered, at least until he needs them. I don't know how long this world would survive if they were truly unleashed."

Blaise's gaze is still unfocused, far off.

"What if we didn't have to kill Az?"

"You think there's another way to wrestle control away from him? I'm not sure how to rid the Rip of those runes."

"No, not the runes," Blaise says, shaking her head. "When Az first took control of the Others, he accidentally let one attack Asha. I watched Marcus take the blow."

"He'd only just then gained control. It's been months. I'm sure he's more practiced than he was then."

"No, I know. But what I mean is that he was distracted. When he realized the rest of the group had caught up to us, one of the mere slipped out from underneath his control."

"Again, he's probably learned to control them better now, correct? Besides, if that were the case, wouldn't he lose control of them while he slept?"

Blaise bites her lip. "I thought of that, but when I was searching grimoires for a way to rid myself of the parasite back in Mystral, I came across several magical 'remedies' for fighting sleep. I'm sure Az would have plenty of those at his disposal, especially with Naenden healers on his staff."

"You think Az hasn't slept in weeks? If that's the case, could we steal his elixir and wait until he falls asleep and loses control over the Others?" I ask.

Blaise shakes her head. "From what I read, most of these types of elixirs—"

"Have permanent effects after chronic use," I say, remembering Amity lecturing me about this one time. "So there's a possibility he won't be able to sleep again."

"Unfortunately, yes. Although he kind of deserves it. But that's not the point. The point is, what if he was so distracted, he couldn't possibly focus on controlling the others?" Blaise says.

I shake my head. "From what you've told me about Az, control is the most important thing to him. We don't often take our eyes off the things we hold dearest. If power is what he craves the most, there will be little that can rip his attention away. Unless you know of something he craves more than power."

Blaise shakes her head. "No. Not something he wants more. Just a feeling that's impossible for him to ignore."

Her face pales.

I stand to my feet. "What are you proposing we do?"

Blaise's hands fidget at her sides, pulling at the hem of her robes, the collar of her tunic. Sweat appears on her forehead, but when she turns and looks at me, there's nothing but steely determination in her eyes. "I need to get a message to Asha."

"I could reach out to some of my contacts." My words are cautious, because something crazed has overtaken Blaise's face.

She shakes her head. "There's not enough time. There's no telling when Az will attack Othian again. They're weak right now, and he knows that. I need to get the message to her before he comes back to finish what he started."

"Blaise, Asha's in Meranthi. We'd have to cross the Sahli to get to her. That would mean forging passes to get across the desert, and even then, the journey takes several days, if not weeks, even with proper escorts."

Blaise flashes me a half-hearted smile. "Then it's a good thing I'm fast."

My stomach hollows out.

"Blaise. You can't...You'll never make it."

Blaise pats my shoulder. "Well, not with a defeatist attitude like that."

My ribs constrict, my Gift humming in panic within my chest.

All in a minor key.

CHAPTER 85

BLAISE

*P*iper reaches out to a contact she has at a local inn within the town limits of Rivre.

I watch them outside, peering through the fogged window in case Piper needs me. She informed me before she went inside that the contact isn't exactly a friend. More of a friend of Bronger's—the man who kidnapped Piper as a child.

He's wearing *paldihv*, a cloak of shadows one has to kill the previous owner in order to possess.

The sight of it seems to throw Piper off. I suppose that makes sense, given Marcus owns *paldihv* himself.

When Piper meets me outside, her teeth are clamped.

I frown. "What is it?"

Piper bites back a shudder. "Nothing. That male is just a pig, is all."

When we make it back to the cave, she tells me what she learned.

The news isn't good.

Three days.

I have three days until Az unleashes the Others on Othian in a second attack.

The fastest I've ever run was when I was trying to get back to

Ermengarde before Abra completed the ritual that gave Farin complete control over Nox's body.

Even then, I wasn't fast enough.

Now I have three days to get from Rivre to Meranthi.

The distance itself would be problematic on its own. Combine that with the fact that I can only travel at night, and it's improbable I'll make it.

Then there's the complication of the Sahli.

I'm not exactly an expert when it comes to running. Never really did much of it when I was human. Something tells me miles and miles of sand aren't exactly the most conducive medium for speed.

Or endurance, now that I think of it.

I'll never make it. Piper's right about that, and shrugging off her concern doesn't make it any less true.

It doesn't have to be this way, says a voice, one that's all too familiar, even when it shouldn't be. Even when I never actually heard it back when it dwelled inside me. The parasite skitters inside the black adamant box I keep looped to my belt, tucked underneath my tunic, not because I want it close to my skin, but because I don't want to have to look at it. Piper's offered to carry it for me several times after seeing what it does to me to have it so close, but I can't bring myself to let it out of my sight. There's something about the feeling of the cold ancient metal against my skin that comforts me, reminds me that the parasite is still trapped, that it hasn't found someone to let it out.

You don't have to be a slave to the night, you know, it says again, its voice slippery against the inside of my skull.

"There's not a way to make this thing soundproof, is there?" I ask no one in particular.

Piper shoots me a concerned glance, but she shakes her head all the same. She's used to the parasite talking to me at this point, though I think it makes her uncomfortable.

That's fair.

I could help you. You and me, we could be whoever you want to be. I could give you a new body, one not cursed like yours is.

I'm not entirely sure that's true, and as much as I'd love to walk in the sun again, to be free of this cursed body, I'm not an idiot.

Well, I suppose I'm kind of an idiot.

But I'm not *that* much of an idiot.

"Shouldn't you be afraid of what I might do to you, if I absorbed you?" I ask it, ignoring the way Piper wriggles in her cot, like she's trying not to listen in but can't help that she has excellent hearing.

You're right. Your powers now might very well allow you to absorb me. Makes it seem like a good deal on your end. Just think of what you could use me for. A new body. Maybe even one Nox isn't cursed not to love. Who knows? Besides, don't you still want children one day? A new body could be useful for that as well.

No. I snap the door shut on my mind, the sliver of hope the parasite has managed to wedge between the window and its sill.

My chest aches.

It's not that I haven't considered that I won't be able to have children in this body.

It's that this seems to be the only reasonable conclusion, and the moment I realized that, I figured there was no use thinking about it any longer.

Since when has pretending gotten me anywhere useful, anyway?

Besides, I don't deserve that luxury. Not after I took Erida, the little girl from the desecrated village, from her mother's arms, still clinging to her child in death.

I might not have burned down Erida's cottage, but I opened the Rip, freeing the monsters that demolished her village, crushing the girl under the weight of her childhood home.

So no. I don't let myself think about not being able to have children.

Not when I've bereaved other parents of theirs.

Still, I know the parasite is less than convinced that my vampirism will allow me the power to absorb it like the fae can absorb the old magic. If it had any question in its mind, it wouldn't be offering, now would it?

But I allow my mind to wander—just for a moment—letting it

stretch its legs out from under the tight leash I've kept wound around it.

One last time, I let my mind slip into a world of pretend. A reality I'm aware is out of my grasp. One where the parasite lets me choose my body, and instead of turning me into Cinderella, it just lets me be me. But the me before I died. Or possibly even the me I never was, but would have been if it hadn't been for Clarissa and Derek and Abra and Madame LeFleur.

In this world, the one that doesn't exist, I'm the type of woman Nox is capable of loving. The type of woman he doesn't leave.

I know this world can't be real, because in this world, he's not a vampire either, and the two of us have children, just like the dream I used to have...

It's not real, and I know it's not real, but the image is so intoxicating, I can't help but drink.

In the morning, I'll deal with the hangover of it all, the emptiness in my chest after coveting a life that's not meant for me.

But for now, I let myself dream.

And when Piper's breathing becomes shallow and even, her body succumbing to sleep, I keep dreaming.

Even as I pack my bags and whisper a goodbye into the night.

I tug on the bond in my heart, but as always, there's no one on the other end.

I send the goodbye anyway.

CHAPTER 86

ZORA

*A*s Farin and I make our way across the beach, I keep several paces ahead of him, just out of sight. I figure he'll assume I'm trying to avoid interacting with him after our conversation last night about his probable plans to murder me.

Let him think what he wants, as long as it distracts him from the truth.

The island has the audacity to be warm today, like it's mocking me about the chill it blew into the cave last night, like the Fates are reminding me I'm as moldable as a sail in the wind in their hands.

Like all they have to do is make me shiver a bit, and they can send me straight into Farin's arms, just for their amusement.

It's growing more and more difficult not to think about how it felt that frigid night, to be tucked into his chest, to feel the strange mingling of danger and safety renewed with each step I take.

But an hour into our traipse across the sand, I stumble across something that wipes all such notions from my mind.

A body.

Worse, one that's alive.

. . .

THE MAN IS HUMAN, his breathing shallow.

Another victim of the shipwreck, perhaps? Or has another ship fallen into the snare of the rocks circumventing this island?

I fall to my knees and check his neck for a pulse. I don't know why. Of course he has a pulse; he's breathing.

Get a hold on yourself, I whisper to my shaking limbs.

My fingers linger at the man's neck, when they should be climbing to his face. All it would take would be placing my palm over his mouth and nose, and then...

"Do you have a family?" I find myself asking the man.

His black, sand-crusted eyelashes flutter. "Sara," he croaks. "My wife. Told me if I didn't come back, she'd leave me..." He chuckles, though it seems as though he's masking a sob.

My stomach wriggles.

"Children?" I ask.

He shakes his head, closing his eyes and swallowing.

Good. Good, that's good.

"Are you in pain?" I ask.

The sailor fixes a set of clear blue eyes on me. Blue like the sky, deep like the sea. His skin is weathered from what might have been decades in the sun, manning a ship's deck. No wonder his wife was irritated with him leaving again. "No pain. More concerned about that, to be honest. No feeling, either. And forget moving my fingers."

Good. That's good, too.

I'm a monster for thinking it is.

Hero or villain?

"Fell over the side when we ran aground. Knew the instant my spine hit rock that my days of walking were over." Again, he chuckles, but his voice is strained, and he begins to sob.

"I'm sorry," I say, and I mean it. My fingers twitch, his pulse still tapping against them.

"Eh. You didn't do it to me."

Normally, I would have wondered if this was true. Wondered if whoever was writing my story had snapped this man's spine specifically to transform me into the villain. I would have wondered if this man was my Event.

I don't wonder anymore.

When I murder this man, it won't be because anyone forced me to do it.

It'll be because I searched this beach, hoping to find someone I can kill easier than I can kill Farin.

I was hoping for someone I could kill with a good conscience. I'm not sure I've found that in this man, but he's as close as I'm going to get.

"I think." The man wheezes. "I think my lungs might be filling up with water."

My tongue goes dry in my mouth.

"I've been laying here for days now," he continues. "Had a lot of time to think about how I don't want to die. Been praying to the Fates that it won't be a savage animal. A couple times, the tide reached my toes, and I thought I might drown. I asked they not let me drown. That it be something quick." He offers me a sad smile. "I think they might have been listening."

I freeze, my limbs going rigid. I should be relieved, overjoyed this man wants me to kill him. It should take the burden off my shoulders completely, but still...

"What's he saying to you?" Farin asks, and his presence makes me jump. He's barefoot on the sand, so I hadn't heard him walk up.

My heart races. I shouldn't have stalled. Should have killed this man before Farin caught up to me, then I could have escaped. Without Farin.

My heart comes to that thought and halts.

That can't be why I stalled.

No, it's because taking a life is an irreversible evil. There's a reason it works. It rips the soul. And since my soul is knitted to the Fabric, it rips the Fabric, too.

"He wants me to put him out of his misery," I sigh, translating for the man into Farin's tongue. "He's paralyzed. Hit a rock on his way into the ocean."

For a moment, Farin doesn't move, and I refuse to look at him. Need to think. Need to find a way to get Farin to go away, so I can...

"Zora." Farin says my name so softly, I can't help but turn around to face him. "Don't look."

It happens so fast.

Farin grabs his dagger and brings it down behind me.

There's the sickening slicing of flesh, and a gentle thud as the dagger hits the sand.

The man doesn't have the chance to scream.

The sound makes me sick, and instinct has me craning toward the man, as if my eyes need to confirm what my ears can't seem to process.

Farin's arm lands on my shoulder, his other hand still holding the dagger, which now drips with blood. "I said don't look."

I don't.

My throat constricts, and I feel as though I might retch.

I do retch.

It doesn't take seeing it to imagine the kind sailor's head severed from his body.

"Why did you do that?" I ask, digging my fingers into the sand to steady myself. I'm still gagging, though nothing's coming out.

"So you didn't have to," he says, as nonchalantly as if he just plucked a coconut from a palm that was too high for me to reach.

"I didn't. I didn't." My throat constricts, and I feel as if I can't get air. "I didn't ask you to do that."

Farin furrows his brow, suspicion heavy on his face as he looks down at me. "You would have rather done it yourself?" Even the question sounds scornful.

I say nothing. The sound of the sailor's torn flesh still scratches against my skull. Suddenly, I feel as if I have to put an island of distance between myself and the body. I scramble to my feet, but my nausea is dizzying, and I find I stumble.

Strong hands catch me, pulling me into his chest, but I scratch at him until he lets go of me.

"Zora," Farin says, following behind me as I trudge through the sand.

"You're a monster," I say, to no one in particular.

Farin scoffs. "Are you just now figuring this out?"

I want nothing but to whirl on him, but I'm afraid of what I might accidentally see. Now that the man is dead, is he omniscient? Can he hear my thoughts, know what I would have done to him?

But I can't think about that now.

"Hey," Farin says, but I don't want to hear it. "If you were going to do it, you would have done it before I caught up to you."

"The fact that you think like that proves that you don't care. That you have no empathy, no awareness for any feelings other than your own."

Farin stops, and though I can't turn to face him, I stop too.

"If I didn't care," he says, "I wouldn't have wasted my energy. Believe it or not, it takes more effort to sever someone's head from their body than it does to walk on by."

I grit my teeth. "This isn't a joke."

"I'm not joking. Do you think I enjoyed that?"

"Oh, I don't know. Did you, or did you not, once possess a magic that got high off the pain of others?"

Farin is so quiet, I can hardly tell that he's breathing. "That man didn't feel a thing. Didn't even see it coming. I don't know what more you would have had me do for him."

I shake my head, placing my palm over my mouth, as if the man already has a stench that's following me around.

Hero or villain?

Now that the man is dead, I think I know.

"You didn't do it for him," I say. "You did it for me, and I'd rather you not."

He must think the disgust in my voice is directed at him, because he drops the bloodied dagger in the sand and walks on ahead.

He doesn't stop to ask why I'd rather he not care about me.

Doesn't stop to ask why I'm so distraught that we just killed my last chance of getting off this island.

My last chance, other than killing Farin himself.

Sand coats the spaces between my fingers as I retrieve the abandoned dagger from the sand.

CHAPTER 87

ELLIE

*C*ecilia wriggles in my arms as I stand on the castle portico overlooking Othian.

A mixture of feelings twinges at my heart. On one hand, sorrow fills me at the sight of our beautiful city, reduced to a fraction of what it once was.

On the other hand, I see the people, actually see them—their faces. For the first time in my life, it seems the people of Othian have put aside trying to become someone else.

Maybe it's just that we're all trying to survive, but I suppose that is part of it, isn't it? Realizing the cosmetics and tricks used to hide ourselves were just weighing us down the whole time.

It hurts to look out on the crowd. At the children who gather in groups too large to all have the same parents—the ones who cling to each other because they have nowhere else to go. There are men and women wrapped in tattered mourning attire.

The crowd is a sea of sorrow.

It seems no one has been left unscathed by the pain of life taken too soon.

But when I look out into the crowd, I find something else too. A determination I didn't realize was possible from a city I once considered so vain.

They wait, hushed voices echoing through the crowd.

And then the reason they've gathered arrives.

When the double doors open, and Evander steps out onto the balcony, a collective gasp ripples through the crowd.

Even I have to fight the one threatening to escape my lips.

I've gotten used to seeing Evander in royal attire. He was a prince, after all, when I met him. A lavish one at that.

But with all the excess Evander had flashed in his life before, it had only conveyed that—affluence. Wealth.

The Evander that stands before me is not that prince.

This is a king.

It's in the way he carries himself, chin held high and face set on the horizon. I know the glistening crown weighs heavy on his head, though there's no seeing that if you happen to be a casual onlooker, not with the way he holds his head steady.

His sea-green eyes, typically so full of mischief, are bright with sorrow, a rage I'd never seen until the day of Cecilia's birth. I'm surprised it doesn't frighten me, to glimpse this sort of rage in my husband, my gentle Evander.

But it's not the type of rage a wife fears.

It's the type of rage a wife's enemies fear.

Evander raises a hand, and a hush falls over the crowd. Even Evander's power-grabbing cousins shut their mouths long enough to listen.

"People of Dwellen," says Evander, his voice sounding so much older than it used to. For a moment, it unsettles me, looking up onto the stage and seeing a male I don't recognize. Like someone has taken my husband's body, and I don't know who he is anymore, and I can't even blame him for it because all he's doing is being what the Fates require of him. But then Evander grits his teeth, and a crease furrows his brow. I watch as he tries and fails to fight back the tears pooling at his lids.

I watch as Evander lets out a steadying exhale, the type that Marken would have chastised him for.

Next to me, my mother holds her breath and squeezes my hand gently.

Still, the crowd remains silent.

But then Evander's gaze finds mine, and something in him changes.

He starts again, but this time he unclasps the majestic velvet cloak from around his neck. It flutters in the wind before it falls to the stage.

Evander shakes his shoulders out, scratching his neck, but his face relaxes. "Ah, that's much better. I thought I was being strangled. I don't know if any of you have worn a cloak recently, but there's a reason they went out of style a century ago."

My father, Fates bless that man, is the first to laugh, a deep rumble that echoes through the crowd, picking up stray friends on the way until gentle chuckles sweep over the people.

My chest is still tight, and I pull Cecilia closer, finding comfort in her warm weight against my chest. But as I watch Evander, I find he already looks more himself.

He runs his hands through his hair, causing the crown to shift askew.

Evander's cousin Casper lets out a scoff, but the acrid look I shoot him is enough for him to widen his eyes and clamp his mouth shut.

This time when Evander speaks, there's not a soul in the crowd who doesn't listen. "I'm not my father. And I won't try to be. I'm not that kind of king. I suppose I could pretend I am, but you've known my reputation for quite some time now, and I know there's no erasing it from your memory. I'm not a hard male, not like he was. We all know it was my brother who was supposed to rule in my father's place, but..."

My mother tenses up next to me. Evander *is* rambling, and the temporary attention his joke wrung out of the crowd is fading. He looks at me again, and I shake my head, hoping I can communicate without words.

You don't have to put yourself down.

Evander nods, then looks out into the crowd once more. "Not long ago, my wife, Princess—I mean, Queen—Elynore, was attacked by the very creatures who invaded our city. She was pregnant with our daughter, Cecilia, at the time. For the worst several hours of my life, I was sure I would lose both of them. During that time, every moment I'd given up on myself came back to me. Every training session I skipped after a revel, every lesson I fell asleep during, every criticism of my father's that I ignored, even when he was right about me. I spent years failing myself, and I convinced myself there was no harm in it. Because it was my life and I could live it as I wished, so long as I didn't harm anyone else. But...I've come to realize just how wrong I was. That, in failing myself, I was setting myself up to fail others. My wife. My child." He swallows. "Jerad. Even Olwen..." The crowd hums at the exiled princess's name. "You. The years I wasted on ale and..." Evander steals a glance at my father, before swallowing and saying, "reckless living. I wasn't just failing myself. I was failing you, the people I would someday need to protect. I should have spent that time preparing. Instead, I spent it hiding from my responsibilities. But then..." He takes in a deep breath and looks at me...

"But then Ellie, you pulled through, and so did little Cecilia, and I knew in that moment the Fates had granted me a second chance. I didn't know at the time, of course. Had no idea that second chance would come with the weight of the crown on my head. I think... I think we all expected my father to outlive Alondria itself."

The crowd nods in unison, respectfully hanging on Evander's every word.

"I am not my father. I'm not my brother, either. I'm not the king you deserve, the one who's spent an entire life preparing to lead you. You already know that. But I'm here to tell you I know it too. And that I'm done failing myself. I'm done failing my family. And if you follow me—well—I won't say that I'll never fail, because we all know I have years of learning to make up for, but I won't give up on you, Dwellen. You're my home. And you're Ellie's home, and my daughter's home, and my wonderful in-laws' home, and if you'll have me, people of Dwellen—"

"Don't be fooled by his faux humility," says Evander's cousin, face locked into a perpetual snarl as he steps onto the stage.

My mother mutters something incoherent under her breath.

Casper speaks loudly enough that he'll probably grab the attention of the Others and lure them back to Othian. "What my cousin is about to do is ask us to fight in Naenden's rebellion against their new ruler. Their new ruler who controls the very beasts that ransacked our home. What he hasn't told you is that King Azrael wishes to ally with us. Just think of the protection his army could provide us if it were turned away from us rather than toward us. Evander has friends in Naenden he wishes to save at the cost of *your* lives."

I mark that male in my mind, and as much as I'd love to march up to the stage and slug him in the throat, my mother grasps my hand.

"Evander must learn to fight his own battles, Elynore," she whispers.

I nod, hardly able to contain the bulge in my throat.

Evander levels a cool, but unruffled look at his cousin, then slowly turns back to the people. "Those of you who wish to fight with me may. I'll be standing for the freedom of our world, whether you choose to follow me or not. But don't be mistaken. I won't be conscripting you into battle. I won't ask that of those of you who've never picked up the sword. What I will deign to ask for is your help."

The crowd mutters, and Evander's cousin scoffs. "And what is it you expect the people to do?"

Evander looks out at the crowd, and a soft smile forms on his face. "We're not a people of war. We never have been. And though I have utmost confidence that our army will battle valiantly, they'll have a fighting chance if you help them. My lovely wife, your queen, and her father have devised a plan to help defend against the Others. I only ask that you aid in making weapons to deliver to those in Naenden who stand to protect our world."

Evander's cousin scoffs, and more loudly than is likely wise, says, "What do you expect them to do? They're a bunch of preening artisans. The best of them succeeded in crafting ceramics, Evander."

That's when Forcier steps to the front of the crowd. "If you'll accept it, Your Majesty, I'd be more than happy to bake goods to send to replenish the soldiers."

Evander's eyes water. "Thank you, Forcier. That would be of the utmost help."

Forcier beams at Evander, then shoots Casper a look that could curdle milk before stepping back into the crowd.

Next to me, my mother's smirk mirrors mine as she squeezes my hand.

"Yes, and I'm sure those of us who make ceramics can learn to coat metal with glass," says the woman who owns the ceramic shop in town. My father must have told her our plan. She crosses her arms and stares at Casper, who's looking less and less comfortable by the minute.

The married couple who owns the blacksmith shop in town advances. "Our work may have been marveled at for its aesthetics, Your Majesty," says the husband, his wife finishing his sentence, "but we assure you, our blades are just as capable of slicing through flesh, and looking fashionable as they do it," she says, snapping her teeth at Evander's cousin.

Evander's smile is press-lipped. My husband is trying not to laugh.

I'm not trying that hard.

"Thank you. Your assistance is appreciated. Jethro, Ellie," Evander says, "if you'll fill the Hariwens in on the plan…"

By now several of the shop owners are filing up to the front to volunteer, and Casper looks greener by the minute.

"You fools," he hisses. "He'll fail you again. Lead you to your deaths, just like he did his brother."

The crowd goes silent.

But Evander doesn't look at his cousin. He just turns to the crowd and says, "If it is within my power not to fail you, I give you my word, I won't."

A shudder echoes over the crowd, snaking up my spine at the gravity of Evander's words.

Of the fae vow he just made.
The one that will kill him if he double-crosses it.
Fae kings don't make promises to their people.
It's simply not done.
Maybe that's why, this time, I don't have to lead the way when the people of Dwellen kneel before their king.

CHAPTER 88

NOX

I thought the bond was pulling me here.

The gentlest of tugs, an incoherent whisper that almost sounded like a goodbye.

But I was wrong.

Blaise isn't at the Rip, and I have no clue how to find her.

I take in the glow of blood runes that shimmer in a circlet, suspended midair, as I try to keep my hope from getting quashed, as I try to push away the despair.

It's proving difficult, because if she's not here, I have no idea where in Alondria she might be.

"You're too late," says a somewhat familiar voice. I spin to find a red-headed female standing behind me, arms crossed like she's the one I've forsaken.

"Piper."

Recognition slaps me across the head as my gaze adjusts easily to her unmistakable features in the glow of the starlight. Vibrant red curls, wide green eyes. She's beautiful, yet solemn.

"Something tells me it's not me you're looking for."

"Where's Blaise? She was with you last."

517

Panic crawls in my throat, worry that something might have happened to her.

"She's gone."

My breath fogs in the chill of the night. "What do you mean by gone?"

"She left in the middle of the night, two nights ago, intent on delivering a message to Queen Asha before Azrael unleashes his forces on the rest of the world."

I breathe a sigh of relief, rubbing the back of my neck. I don't miss the faint smile of vengeance on the female's lips.

"You knew saying she was gone would make me think she was dead," I say in irritation.

Piper shrugs. "What's it to you? You're the one who almost let her fall into a vat of liquid sunlight. If it weren't for me, she would be dead."

I grit my teeth, having nothing good to say to that.

Piper cranes her head at me, taking me in. "What made you change your mind about her?"

I flick my gaze at her. "How do you know I changed my mind?"

"Because when you thought she was dead, you looked like you were contemplating joining her."

I swallow, unable to look the female in her eyes. "What message is she bringing the queen?"

Piper glares at me. "I suppose if you manage to catch up with her, she can tell you herself."

"Well, then I best be leaving," I say, shrugging past the girl, headed south, though I'll need to stop in an inn on the way. By the way the stars are angled, I can tell it's almost morning.

A hand grasps on my shoulder. It's shaking as Piper spins me around to face her. I shrug her off, but there's something in the way her expression's changed that makes me regret it. It's like a mask has fallen off her features, and she's letting me see the concern underneath.

"She's going to try to cross the Sahli in a night," she says, her voice barely a whisper.

"A night?" I ask, my mind immediately swirling in calculation. "But night barely lasts five hours in the desert. And the sand..."

Piper shakes her head.

My chest constricts. "She'll never make it," I say, anxiety weaseling its way into my stomach. I find myself running my hands through my hair.

"No," Piper whispers. "No, I'm afraid she won't."

I pause, fingers halfway through my hair. It's not as though my feelings for Blaise have returned.

That doesn't mean I want her to die.

I can still see her falling, the crushing realization of my betrayal on her face in the warehouse when I chose ending Abra over saving her.

I hadn't wanted her to die then, either. But not wanting someone to die is a far cry from love.

"Why are you telling me this? I would have thought you'd want me to run after her, maximize the pain when I realized I was too late."

Piper blinks. "Because I don't want you to be too late."

I frown. "When does she plan to do this?"

"Tomorrow night."

Tomorrow night. I'll never make it in time. Not when I'll have to stop at an inn during the day.

Piper nods, biting her lip, her eyes wide as she stares down at her feet. When she finally looks at me, there's a grim determination in her eyes. "You can die and come back, right?"

I pause, the question catching me off guard. "Yes. If you snap my neck, my heart will stop for a while, but it'll always restart."

Piper stares off into the distance, tapping her foot against the ground. "How do you feel about murder?"

"It's not my preference."

Piper raises her eyebrows, bobbing her head. "And if someone probably deserves it?"

"You watched me rip the head off of Queen Abra. I think you know the answer to that question."

When Piper breathes out through her nose, it shoots streams of fog into the air. "Good. Good. Because I think I know a way for you to get to Blaise faster, so long as you don't mind a little blood on your hands."

My fangs ache, pushing at my gums at the very thought.

CHAPTER 89

BLAISE

The sand of the Sahli is surprisingly pleasant against my bare feet, the heat of the day soaked into its grains.

It will only remain pleasant for the next five hours.

Five hours.

That's how much time I have until the sun rises and scorches the ground—and me with it.

I made it across Charshon at a record pace.

Well, I assume it was a record pace. Not that I looked it up.

It took me less than a night. Of course, I had to stop in an inn during the day, but now that the sun has set and I've reached the edge of the desert, it's a race against the morning.

I could help you. Together, we wouldn't burn, whispers the voice from the box as I stare across the wide expanse, the towering dunes that block my path, cresting smoothly over the horizon as if to lie and say they'd block it for me.

"Shut up," I tell it.

And then, I run.

. . .

My LIMBS CUT across the frigid night air as my feet pound the sand. My muscles are lithe, stretching further and more efficiently than I ever could have imagined as a human.

That doesn't make the sand any less problematic.

It doesn't seem to matter how powerful my legs are, how much force I slam into the bottoms of my feet. The sand absorbs my efforts with an open mouth, like I'm pouring my energy into it with a funnel.

It's like one of those dreams where you're being chased, but suddenly you realize your legs can't run nearly as well as you thought they could, and it takes all the mental energy in the world to get them to move, but the air around you might as well have turned to water for the speed you're moving.

That's probably a dramatic example.

I am moving, much faster than I imagine anyone ever has across this treacherous terrain.

But it's not going to matter how fast I am.

Because time is fading, and I'm not fast enough.

You're NOT GOING to make it in time, whispers the parasite from inside the adamant box. Accompanying the voice is the sound of sharp fingernails tapping against the metal. *You're not going to make it, and then you'll die, and no one will even come look for your body. You'll be food for the buzzards, child. Is that how you want your pitiful existence to end? Food for the buzzards?*

Is that supposed to be a rhetorical question? I ask, not bothering to waste my breath by uttering it aloud.

Rhetorical questions are for the intelligent among you. Not those of you idiotic enough to run headfirst to their death, hisses the parasite.

You know what I think? I think you're just concerned about what will become of you if I drop dead in the middle of the desert. How much sand do you think there is in this place? And what are the chances anyone traveling through the desert would actually come across you, do you think?

The parasite goes quiet, and I get the pleasant image of Cindy, crammed in that little box, sulking.

I find my pace accelerates at the very thought.

You know what, I say, finding torturing the parasite to be more comforting than it probably should be. *That's an excellent idea, really. I could just drop you right now. Be rid of you. Sure, someone might find you, and what a problem that would cause, but then again, a sandstorm could come ripping through here any day now. How deep do you think things get buried during sandstorms?*

The parasite doesn't answer, even after several more minutes of taunting.

Eventually, even the fact that I've won this verbal sparring match doesn't keep the dread from creeping back into my chest. The sand has cooled in the chill of the desert night, but I can't help but notice the faint line of pink that taints the edge of the horizon, cresting the waves of the dunes to the east.

I strain my eyes—as if that's an effective tactic for someone with enhanced vision—for signs of Meranthi in the distance, but I see nothing but sand dunes for miles.

You'll never make it, silly servant girl, says the parasite, grinding on my nerves as it references the note Clarissa left for me after she burned all of Evander's letters. That was back when I was trapped in the attic, just after I'd lost my baby.

My baby.

My baby who has no grave, just as I won't.

We'll both be forgotten.

At least I can share that with my child.

Share something with my child.

If not a laugh or a cry or a memory or a touch, at least it's something.

I keep running, but in the distance I glimpse a strand of orange limning the horizon, replacing the pink.

No.

I glance back ahead of me, to where Meranthi should appear any moment now, but the horizon is as empty as the grave where Amity and I laid my child to rest.

· · ·

IN THE END, I don't make it.

It's sort of depressing, really, because I make it just far enough to see Meranthi shimmering in the distance when my legs give out.

As it turns out, the desert air is rather dehydrating, even at night, and the exertion of running through the sand has leeched the blood from my muscles.

I likely should have gorged myself on human blood before I tried this, but I was trying to be good.

Like that's ever gotten me anywhere.

Sand fills my mouth, crusting my dry, cracked lips as I hit the ground face-first. It's warm against my cheek, almost as if it's anticipating the rising sun.

I let myself enjoy it, just for a few seconds.

I don't think I deserve to be pleasantly warm in the few moments before I die.

So I claw my fingers into the ground, sand settling underneath my fingernails. Perhaps if I can bury myself, the layer of sand above me will protect me from the sun. I'll pass out, repeatedly, I'm sure, from suffocation. But my vampirism will wake me again, until the daylight passes and I'm free to travel at night once more.

I'll be too late for Othian by then, of course.

But then my nails scrape against something hard.

I've hit bedrock.

And the layer of sand covering it is too shallow to bury myself underneath.

Foolish child, whispers the parasite, its voice rising in panic. *Let me out, and I could help you. I could change you.*

It's trying awfully hard to sound seductive, but its panic is getting in the way.

I'm at the point now where I'll die just to spite it, just to leave it alone, trapped out here in a desert where no one will ever find it.

The spite warms my heart almost as much as the sand does.

And then the sun peeks over the horizon.

. . .

AT FIRST, death feels like burning. Like having every nerve in my skin go up in flames as the sunlight scorches my flesh.

The pain is hot, intense. Unbearable.

But nothing is permanent.

And then the fire burns through enough skin that everything goes numb.

That's when the shadows take me.

I THINK I should fear the shadows, the darkness that comes to carry me away from the world, but I'm too numb to bring myself to care.

I must be dead now. Permanently this time, because the shadows wrap their arms underneath me, pulling me into their darkness as they lift me from the ground and carry me away.

It's dark in the shadows, and my heart despairs a bit as I wonder if this is where my baby is, has been for years. But then I remember—no—my baby is somewhere full of light, and surely the shadows are reserved for people like me.

But then Death whispers my name, and the sound is so familiar, I wonder if I've belonged to him all along.

"Blaise. You're safe now," he says, and even in death, tears fill my eyes, though I can't feel whether they hit my scorched cheeks.

I failed them, I tell Death, but if he hears, he doesn't answer. *I failed my friends.*

Death carries me away, but now I'm feeling frantic. Because it's dark here, and I can't feel or see, and I can't bear the thought of my friends following me here all because I failed them.

Please send me back, I whisper. *Just long enough to warn them.*

But Death just cradles me as he leads me into nothingness.

CHAPTER 90

NOX

The shadows of the *paldihv* I stole from the man whose throat I ripped out in the inn in Charshon have carried me through the daylight hours.

I've been running for a day and night straight, my legs and back aching, the only thing propelling me my overwhelming need to reach Blaise and the human blood slowly draining from my veins.

At first, I wasn't sure what spurred the urgency. Maybe a duty I felt to my parents. Like if my father could relearn to love my mother, I was honoring them by trying again with Blaise.

Or maybe it was because I felt as if something had been stolen from me. That the Old Magic had taken not just my feelings—my feelings that belonged to me and me alone—but my future as well.

Granted, it was a version of my future that I no longer knew that I wanted.

But I suppose I didn't know I didn't want it, either.

Either way, the closer the sun came to rising, that future was racing further from my grasp.

And then there was the fact that, love her or not, I didn't want Blaise to die. But that proved nothing more than the fact that I have at least a little empathy left in my heart.

Racing across the desert, little to see or distract me by way of terrain, I've found my mind drifting to the past, percolating on memories that, while they no longer consume me, feel important all the same.

There was the time she'd folded up a scrap piece of parchment and taught me a game. I remember feeling strange about it. Like games were for children, a way for them to pass the time and befriend one another.

But I suppose that was what Blaise had been doing. Befriending me.

It occurs to me that now that Zora is gone, Blaise is my only friend.

I remember too, the time I brought her onto the roof. The feel of the fresh air had overwhelmed her after being held captive for so many weeks. I remember holding her until she knew she could breathe again, and though I can't feel anything related to that moment, I note its importance.

She'd told me about her childhood. About the man who stole it from her and the baby she hoped one day to find.

I can't grasp onto my love, but I can feel her anguish the night she learned of the baby's passing. Her stepmother had only told her the baby lived so she could blackmail Blaise into sending her family the allowance she earned as a servant.

That, I can feel.

And the night the parasite took Blaise's body permanently, when Blaise's bloodsharing bond forced me to kill her.

I can feel that, too. The snapping of her neck. The reverberation of her splitting bones. The ripping of her spinal cord.

Nausea twists in my belly.

The relief I felt when I realized she had Turned. The sorrow at the knowledge she would have to live the rest of her life in the shadows.

None of these are love, I don't think. At least not the romantic sort.

But they are the sort of thing you might feel for a friend.

It hits me then, that if nothing else, Blaise is that to me.

She has been, since the day she peered up at the male torturing her and instead saw the boy ripped from his family.

Since the day she decided she would die during the spell to separate the parasite from her body, just so I wouldn't have to choose between saving her and saving Zora.

I can't think of what else to call someone who's risked everything to keep me safe. She watched over me when I was stuck in the other realm, reweaving my tapestry, saving me from peril. In her own confused and twisted sort of way, she's given up everything for me.

And I turned around and let her fall.

So as I race across the desert, something for Blaise starts to bloom inside my chest.

It's not infatuation.

But it's something.

SHE'S ALREADY BURNING by the time I find her, the first rays of sunlight searing through her skin as she lies face-down on the ground. At first, I think I might be too late, and my chest caves in at the thought.

But then I hear her whimpering in pain, and something snaps inside of me.

The shadows of my *paldihv* catch up to her before I do, swaddling her in a thick darkness that protects her skin from further damage from the burgeoning sun.

The *paldihv's* shadows aren't enough to fully encase both of us, which is why portions of my back have been exposed to the sun the last several minutes. The shadows keep skipping back and forth, trying to douse the flames that have been popping up on my back every few seconds.

It burns, and I have to bite the urge to call out, to bring attention to the vampire set afire by the sunlight and the woman cloaked in shadows.

There's a cement bunker nearby—one of several scattered about the Sahli in case merchants encounter sandstorms. They're not exactly common knowledge, and I'm only aware of them because of the time I spent reading Gunter's books as a child.

I haul Blaise into the shelter just as the flames cut into a deeper layer of skin. I hate that I drop her to the floor, but I have to extinguish the flames, flopping around on the ground in agony as they lick at my skin.

I lie there for a long while in the dark after the flames are doused, breathing heavily and wincing as my skin reknits itself.

Blaise breathes shallowly next to me, hardly conscious after her exerted run across the desert. I had the benefit of coming from a shorter section of the vast desert, since I didn't have to worry about stopping in inns along the way. Blaise ran almost double the distance overnight.

No wonder she's passed out.

My eyes adjust well enough to the dark, and now that my skin is healing, the pain is subsiding.

When I roll over to face her, she doesn't stir. I'm struck for a moment, reminded of the first time I met Blaise. She was lying supine on Abra's dais, reeking of her own filth and face sallow with dehydration.

Still, she'd looked like she'd picked a fight and come out on top.

I'm still not sure how she managed that.

But I find myself glad that she did.

I watch her eyes dart behind her lids, reminded of how I used to try not to admire her as I worked on extracting the parasite while she slept.

But then her eyelids flutter, her chestnut eyes settling on mine. "Is this the part where you go back to watching me sleep? It's creepy, you know."

I laugh, though it's the boyish type that makes me feel as if I'm twelve years old again. Or at least the type of twelve-year-old who is granted a normal life, free of being ripped from his family.

"Or is this the part where I get to convince myself I'm dreaming?"

Her words send me back to a night not so long ago, back when she was human. Her lips feeling the blood at my wrist, drinking from me just as I sipped from her.

Desire sparks at the memory, but I have to push it away. Because it wasn't Blaise I shared that moment with. It was the parasite.

But it *was* Blaise, in a way. Her body, at least. That part I don't think either of us can deny, not when I heard her call to me just a few nights ago.

When the Old Magic cursed me, I assumed he'd shattered that bond, but then I'd felt a tug toward the Rip, the slightest prick of a goodbye, as if whispered from Blaise's lips themselves.

It's almost as if that bond has been there the entire time, but the Old Magic's curse clogged the vein that's supposed to deliver the blood flow to it.

Love. That's what I thought he took away.

But now that I'm here with Blaise, *love* seems too generic a word.

Because what does it mean to love someone, and why do we use the same word for the objects of our infatuation that we do our parents, our siblings, our friends, when those feelings are all so very different?

In fact, I'm not sure love is something the Old Magic has authority over.

Because as I study Blaise, it's true—I'm no longer infatuated with her. I don't look at her and see perfection. I'm no longer blinded to her shortcomings by intense, all-consuming lust.

I see a girl who has been so incredibly hurt that she hurts others. And I no longer see that behavior as excusable.

I see a woman who bends her morals for a taste of love—or what I thought love was only a day ago.

I see Blaise, and I find what I've always needed—a friend.

A friend I'm not sure I want to ever let go of.

A friend I'd want to be next to, regardless of whether my feelings crest in torrential waves or settle like an undisturbed pond in the center of a peaceful forest.

No, I don't think love is what the Old Magic took away at all.

I don't think he could have taken away something that wasn't wholly there yet, something that had yet to take form.

Because I don't think I knew what it was to love Blaise before. Clearly I didn't, if I felt my lack of feelings was as good an excuse as any to leave her.

As I watch Blaise, take in her beauty, it's the appreciation for how she's cared for me, the understanding between us, from which blooms something else.

The very something I thought was gone for good.

As it turns out, it seems the Old Magic took away the feelings themselves.

I just needed to find the source.

Another vein that bypassed the one the Old Magic had clogged.

"And what would you do if you convinced yourself?" I ask, surprised at the headiness in my voice.

It's because you're alone in a bunker with a female, and because you're sorely undersocalized, I remind myself.

Blaise props herself on her forearm, allowing her black hair to slip down to the floor and pool there. The dark shadows of the *paldihv* curl around her, and I can't deny the allure of it all, the way my throat tightens and my muscles tense just looking at her.

Her gaze dips down to my wrist, where she once—no, the parasite once—sipped, sealing the bloodsharing ritual between us.

Blaise wasn't there for it, of course, trapped in the corners of her own mind, though I wasn't aware of that at the time.

My neck heats with the memory of it though, the intimacy of it, before the parasite sullied it with the realization that I'd shared something so personal with a monster.

No, that wasn't what had upset me so.

It was that I hadn't shared it with Blaise.

Something stirs in me, and it's different from the protectiveness that surged in me when I found Blaise passed out in the sand, just moments away from burning.

Her gaze is still fixed upon my wrist, and I know exactly what she's thinking, because I'm thinking it too.

I can still remember last time, and I find I hate that she doesn't. That she doesn't know how good it felt, the bliss of sharing that moment.

I find I want to teach her, want her to know...

I inch closer to her, pulling her into me and offering her my wrist. She traces patterns across my veins with her fingertips, lighting me on fire as she does it.

Like she's claiming me.

I'm not exactly sure what the Old Magic did to me in taking my feelings for Blaise away. I have no idea what the parameters are.

But something within me feels as if it's going to snap.

She must sense it too, because her thumb lingers over the veins in my wrist, her lips slightly parted as she stares at the faint pulse.

It's then I realize she's holding her breath.

"Are you sure you want this?" I whisper, but Blaise's eyes are muddled over with something stronger than just desire. She slips her palm over my mouth, begging me with her eyes not to say anything.

I know then what she's thinking. Can see the agony I've caused her by abandoning her. By choosing revenge over saving her.

My chest aches for her, but then she shifts her hand, ever so slightly, so that it's not her palm grazing my lips anymore, but her wrist.

I kiss the beautiful veins and feel her pulse flutter beneath my breath.

Her breath hitches with anticipation.

The animalistic part of me, the possessive part of me that wishes to claim Blaise, to wrap her very spirit around my fingers and never let her go, tells me I should wait. That I should draw out this moment until there's nothing more in the world she could possibly want than me.

I want to consume her very being.

But then there's the part of me that knows better.

The part that knows that Blaise has waited long enough.

That I never want her to have to wait on me again.

That's the male who sinks his teeth into Blaise's perfect skin.

. . .

WHEN BLAISE TUCKS herself into the crook of my neck and bites me back, the entire world shifts. Blaise and I fall into one another, two perfectly aligned pieces of a wooden puzzle fallen under the bed collecting dust, before someone thought to join us together.

I thought the bloodsharing ritual had been effective before.

I was wrong.

Blaise and I—our bodies have been bonded for months now, ever since the parasite deceived me into the bloodsharing ritual.

That was nothing.

This? This is everything. This is two souls being knit together, so intertwined they're indistinguishable from one another. Now that Blaise is present for the ritual, we share in it together and I can feel a connection being forged, flowing in a cycle of her heart to mine and back.

It's a vow and a promise and a commitment and a covenant, one nothing in Alondria can shatter.

I tear my teeth from her wrist and run my hands through the hair at the base of her head, pulling her lips to mine, still dripping with blood.

Blaise tenses, and not in a good way.

She flicks her gaze up to meet mine. Her brown eyes shimmer golden through her thick eyelashes, but there's something other than desire there. There's a wall.

A determination.

She pulls herself from my arms and retreats toward the other side of the bunker.

I feel as though I've fallen through the ice.

"Blaise..." I say.

She tenses at her name, closing her eyes as she leans her head back against the wall.

I inch closer, but she holds up her hand to stop me, and when she stares at me, there's a gritty resolve in her eyes.

"The Old Magic took away your love for me," she says, "but it didn't take mine away for you. I had to do that myself, and it was... I can't...if we do this, there's not going to be any turning back for me," she says. "I can't spend my life pining over a male who doesn't love me back."

"Blaise, I..."

I want to tell her that it's already too late, that after what we just shared, there is no turning back. That for me, there was never really any turning back. Not in a way that wouldn't just end with me chasing her down, begging for her to give me another chance. And I want to say it, want to tell her I love her. That I love her like how my father loves my mother. But as I look at the distress in her expression, I know it won't be enough. That Blaise is a female ruled by the whims of her gut, her emotions.

And if she's convinced I don't love her, I can't simply tell her my love is different now than it was before. It will only hurt her worse in the end.

So I don't.

And we both close our eyes.

But judging from our breathing patterns, neither of us fall asleep.

CHAPTER 91

ZORA

We walked the length of the beach the rest of the day. We found no other survivors.

Because there are no other survivors.

It's just me and Farin on this island.

Meaning...

I watch him as he sleeps, his dusty hair curling slightly at the tips, his face serene as he slumbers.

He almost looks innocent, the way his chest falls and rises ever so slowly. He doesn't fear death. Or, if he does, he doesn't fear it from me.

I blink, as if that will settle the twitch in my eyelid that's overcome me ever since Farin killed the lone survivor on the beach.

That sailor was our only hope.

Our being the operative word.

There's still hope for me.

There's still hope for me. I repeat this mantra as I rise from my cot and pad toward the other side of the cave.

I pull the dagger Farin abandoned to the sand from my belt.

The hilt is cold to the touch, and I can't help but note how dull the blade appears.

This won't be clean.

But as I've said, I've never died before. I'm not eager to try it anytime soon.

This island is not the type people survive.

Farin is not the type people survive.

I seem to have forgotten that. I've allowed his charm to infiltrate my defenses, his soft touch to soothe my fear of him. But Farin is a killer by nature. He proved as much today when he severed the head from that poor sailor's body without a second thought.

Sure, I would have killed the man, given a few more moments to grieve him. I think.

But Farin hadn't flinched before taking his life. Hadn't blinked at the gore.

Because Farin is a monster. One who's spent years learning to imitate the emotions of others. No wonder he can be so charming, so gentle, when he spent so long in Nox's head, examining his every thought, every move.

It makes me sick.

Because Farin needs me if he wants off this island. He told me as much when I asked why he nursed me back to health.

But this is not how my story is going to end.

I roam worlds. I traverse the Fabric between realms. I will not be slain by a treacherous male who captured my heart with a few slick words, a night protecting me from the cold with his body.

So I turn the dagger over in my hand, careful not to make a sound as I creep to Farin's side. He doesn't stir, doesn't show any sign that my nearness disturbs him. He just sleeps, as if his conscience is clean.

I don't understand it. Not after what he did to that man on the beach. Not after the countless lives he's taken.

I don't understand it, because sleep evades me.

It doesn't matter which life I'm pantomiming, which parents I'm born to. Every parent I've ever had tells me I'm a poor sleeper, even as a baby. They all claim they don't understand why. That they tried everything to coax me into slumber.

I never quite understand until the day I realize my dreams are not dreams at all, but memories.

Even as an infant, my conscience is speckled with ink. Ink that's seeped into my very soul, blackening it with the guilt I carry from previous lives.

Here Farin lies. Unbothered. Undisturbed.

And I hate him for it.

The dagger trembles silently in my hand as I draw it over Farin's neck. I'll have to be efficient. Fae aren't as easy to kill as humans.

The crunching of the innocent sailor's spine rattles in my mind, threatening to gag me.

I rarely kill in a gruesome way, regardless of the life I've been born into.

I'm not sure I have a choice this time.

So I take the dagger, and I plunge it at Farin's throat.

It stops a hair away from his skin.

Warm fingers dig into my wrist from where Farin grabs onto me. His blue eyes, having just shot open, aren't wide with surprise as I might have expected. Just assessment. Curiosity.

"I wasn't sure you'd have the guts to actually do it, Wanderer," Farin says. He strains his jaw as I throw my entire weight into the dagger. Farin's stronger than me, though, and with a groan, he holds me off—the two of us stuck in a stalemate.

"You shouldn't have underestimated me," I say.

Farin laughs, though it's strained. "You really didn't like me stealing your thunder today, did you?"

"Oh, come on," I say, chest heaving. "We both know how this story ends. With my body in a ditch somewhere after I've shown you how to escape this world."

Farin clamps his mouth shut, then examines me carefully. His blue eyes pierce mine, and I hate feeling seen like this. I push harder on the hilt, but Farin holds me off.

"How many times do I have to tell you, Wanderer? I don't want you dead."

"The deaths of others mean nothing to you. You proved as much today," I say, though the words come out half-formed, my own guilt lancing me.

Farin frowns, cocking his head to the side, and the motion looks so nonchalant, it only inflames me.

"I don't know when you lost the ability to feel empathy for others, Farin, but you can't be allowed to live."

"You don't believe that," he says, almost slyly.

He's right. I don't believe it. Not really. But I have to believe it. Because killing Farin is the only way off this island now, and I can't... I can't...

"You're wrong, you know," Farin says. "When you claim I feel nothing for others. When I realized you wouldn't heal from the knife wound to your side...I felt something then."

I scoff. "Am I supposed to faint over how romantic it is that you regretted I wouldn't heal from the wound you inflicted?"

Farin's expression is unreadable. "No, Wanderer. No, you're not."

Deliberately, he unwraps his fingers from my wrist, clearing the path for my dagger to sever his neck.

The dagger trembles in the air.

I grit my teeth, begging my muscles to bring it down, to end this nightmare.

They don't obey.

"Why?" I ask, tears streaming down my face. "Why can't I kill you?"

Farin cocks his head to the side, still lying on the ground, so it stirs up a cloud of dust. "Believe it or not, I've been asking myself the same question about you."

This time, when Farin reaches up, he slips his fingers between mine and the dagger. Trembling, I let him pry it from my hand, and he tosses it to the other end of the cave. Then he props himself up on his elbow, his other hand finding its way to the curve of my neck just behind my ear. He runs his fingers through my cropped hair, the calloused tips gentle against my skull.

"I think, Wanderer," he says, "that I might do something foolish."

"You're a monster," I say, choking back tears, because I'm no longer talking to Farin.

Farin's eyes examine my mouth. "So I've been told."

"I just tried to kill you."

"Precisely why this is going to make me a fool."

And then he pushes himself off the ground, pulling me toward him in the same deliberate motion.

Farin brushes his lips against mine, softly at first, before deepening the kiss. It's somehow both hungry and slow, erratic and intentional.

Tiny jolts of lightning scorch my skin, lighting the path to my toes, and I find myself running my fingers through his hair, pulling him toward me with matched desire.

"We shouldn't be doing this," I whisper in between kisses, though my words are half-hearted.

"I've spent plenty of time doing things I shouldn't be doing, Wanderer," he says, pressing the name to my mouth. "Pretty sure this isn't one of them."

And it's foolish and stupid, and I'm certain I'll come to regret it, but I let him kiss me. Let myself melt into his arms, relax into his touch.

I let my guard down, and though I half expect him to, Farin doesn't use it against me. There's no dagger in his hand waiting to puncture my lungs. Just hands that intend to hold.

He's still kissing me when the ground trembles. When in the distance, something roars, shaking the entire cavern.

He's still holding me when the stalactite above our head is severed from the cave ceiling.

And then, he's not holding me at all.

My back slams against the other side of the cavern wall as Farin shoves me away from him.

When the stalactite hits, it's Farin who takes the blow.

CHAPTER 92

BLAISE

I can't seem to get last night out of my head.

Though I suppose it was technically earlier today, not last night.

The way my brain keeps time still hasn't adjusted to this nocturnal lifestyle, and I'm starting to wonder if it ever will.

I don't sleep, not with the buzz of Nox's blood fogging my mind, setting me on edge and leaving me craving more.

It was a mistake, entering into the bloodsharing ritual with him.

Not that I haven't done it before. It's just that before, I didn't know I was doing it.

Farin told me once that the bloodsharing ritual had forged something within Nox, something that felt stronger on his side than on mine. Farin attributed it to the bloodsharing ritual being stronger for the male, but now, as I remember the early hours of this morning, I'm wondering if the difference in sexes wasn't what was to blame for the inequity of the cravings.

I wonder if it's just the difference in remembering the beauty of the ritual. The feeling of giving ourselves to each other in a way that feels so complete, so full, there's something about it I don't think I can return from.

If I was pining after Nox before, I'm yearning now, and that's going to be a problem.

Because the bloodsharing ritual doesn't matter. Nox's participation in it last night is just a leftover strand of what the Old Magic didn't erase—the blood bond between us.

There was a time in my life, the old version of Blaise, who would have clung to that as an anchor for hope. Who would have been naïve enough to think the Old Magic had overlooked our bond, that he'd somehow missed it when he cursed Nox.

But I'm so, so tired of being naïve.

There's no way the Old Magic, a source as ancient as it is, missed our bloodsharing bond.

If he left it behind, left it untouched, he did it for a reason.

It's there to torture me. To lure me back into Nox's arms. It's there so that no matter how much distance I put between us, I'll still feel the tether, the hook he has in my soul.

And it'll either tear at me forever, or reel me in, only to consume me.

Not for much longer, though. Not when I likely won't make it through tomorrow.

"Did you sleep all right?" Nox asks. I flinch as his hand reaches across the bunker and finds mine, stroking the area of my wrist that still feels tender from where he fed on it earlier.

I wriggle my wrist out of his playful fingers, though it takes great effort. When I meet his gaze, there's a question there, but whatever it is, he keeps it to himself.

"We need to get a message to Asha," is all I say as I don my hood and rush out into the night.

IT'S NOT TOO long of a walk from the sandstorm bunker to the city of Meranthi, and I can't help but wonder what might have happened had I made it to the city in time. Had Nox not needed to rescue me.

The rational part of me wishes that had been the case. Then I

541

wouldn't know the taste of Nox's blood. I wouldn't be tormented by the aching that gnaws at my chest right now.

But the rational part of me has never been the strongest, and I can't help but grasp onto the memories of earlier today, letting my mind feed on them like a poison that intoxicates the drunk. I can't seem to stop.

That's the treacherous thing about the bloodsharing ritual.

It sure does feel a whole lot like love. But it's just an imitation.

It's like if Nox and I were to exchange wedding vows. Sure, we'd be bound together, but that wouldn't make him love me.

Nox tries to converse with me as we search the city walls for an opening, but I do my best to keep the conversation logistical.

He doesn't give up on the small talk, though.

"Sure you don't want to snap my neck and use this *paldihv*? It would look good on you."

I stiffen. "Of course it would. It matches my soul." The words are supposed to come out nonchalant, but my delivery is off.

Everything about Nox has me off.

"Blaise, about this morning—"

"Over here," I say, nodding toward a section of the wall that doesn't seem to be too heavily guarded.

I can't do it. Can't have him tell me that it was a mistake. That it meant nothing to him other than a lapse in self-control. A carnal desire overtaking his good sense.

Nox quiets, though that does nothing to assuage the anguish in my chest.

It takes little effort between the two of us to climb and slip over the wall into the unprotected city of Meranthi. There's an eeriness that haunts the streets that doesn't seem quite right, though I can't quite place it. It's nighttime, so it could be normal that everyone is holed up inside.

"The market is closed," says Nox, nodding down into the main thoroughfare, where booths sit abandoned for the evening.

It hits me then something Asha told me, that because of the unrelenting midday heat, business still bustled into the late hours in

Meranthi, after they'd taken a break in the hottest portion of the day.

At least, that's how it was before.

A chill snakes up my spine at the abandoned quiet of the streets.

"How do you plan to sneak into the palace?" Nox asks. When I open my mouth to tell him I was planning on playing it by ear, someone else answers for me.

"What's your business inside the palace?"

We both whip around to find a girl—human judging by the scent of her blood—standing behind us, a hood pulled low over her head.

"Who are you?" asks the girl. She brandishes a long, serrated dagger, one that really does look like the type that would be unpleasant to be cut with, even if the wound healed immediately.

There's something familiar about the girl's voice, though I can't quite place it.

"Just visitors to town." Nox holds his hands up as if that would stop him from ripping the girl to shreds if he so desired.

Everything about the girl, including her posture, drips with suspicion. "Az doesn't allow visitors anymore."

Nox and I exchange a look.

"You call your king by a shortened version of his name?" he asks.

The girl takes a moment to answer, but when she does, it's not to Nox's question. "I asked who you are, and I suggest you answer honestly."

Nox offers a questioning look at me, then takes a gamble. "We're friends of Queen Asha's."

The girl's knife hand falters, but she keeps it extended. She turns, not bothering to look at Nox.

"And you?" she asks, twisting the knife toward my chest. "Would you call yourself a friend of Queen Asha's?"

She knows, whispers the parasite in the adamant box. *She knows what you are. Not a friend, but a traitor. A snake in the grass. This girl has never met you, yet somehow she knows. The evil radiates off you, girl. Why can't you just accept that?*

I grit my teeth. "No," I say. "No, I wouldn't. She might have considered me a friend once before, but I pretty much ruined any chance of that when I betrayed her."

The girl's knife goes still, and I can't help but notice the way her breath hitches. "Then why are you here?"

Why are you here? whispers the parasite. *Do you even know?*

"I don't really know. I suppose I want to try out doing something right for once."

"Why the change of heart?" asks the girl.

It's an effort not to bite my lip. "Because I've tried the other way, and I'm learning it never works out well."

The girl's chest collapses in a sudden exhale. It takes me a moment to realize it's a gesture of exasperation as her breath fogs the air.

She slips off her hood, shooting her stunning eyes between Nox and me, looking like she knows she's going to regret whatever she plans to say next. "I suppose that's as good of a reason as any." She lowers the knife, tucking it into her belt.

Nox raises a brow, clearly shocked.

I'm a tad shocked, too. Apparently, a dash of honesty really does go a long way.

"I'm Dinah," she says, and though I don't think I've ever seen her, I recognize her now. The subtle similarities to her sister are written all over her—the curve of her nose and the deeper quality to their voices, and even the way they carry themselves. "You're Blaise, and you must be Nox," she says, nodding toward him. "Glad you made it back to this side of the Realms," she says, rather politely, especially for someone who just had a knife pointed in our direction.

She beckons us to follow her, and after we shrug at each other, we do.

"Why'd you decide to trust us?" Nox asks, clearly confused.

Dinah looks up at him and offers a sad smile. "My family believes in second chances."

Nox's eyes glow with something, and he looks at me, then quickly turns away.

"But it's really not up to me whether you're punished," she says, looking toward me with a slight bit of concern.

"What do you mean?" asks Nox.

"I mean, that decision is up to someone else." She stops, biting her lip. "I'm afraid he's not too happy with you at the moment."

Dinah slips into the shadows.

I have a sneaking suspicion I know exactly who she's leading us to.

I'm not expecting a warm reception.

CHAPTER 93

KIRAN

*L*ight from Beezie's lanterns in the main dining area streams into the cellar, highlighting flecks of dust that swirl in the air as Dinah's slight frame descends the ladder.

Fin, Lydia, and I all tense as we await the news she brings.

When Tavi used her last moments to transport Fin and me outside of the palace, she didn't send us far. We ended up dumped into an alleyway, where a beggar immediately reported to Dinah the appearance of two males who looked suspiciously like the deposed king and prince. Dinah hunted us down not long after, leading us to Bezzie, who, as it turned out, had not defected to Az, after all.

In fact, she had several choice words to say about the boy she'd always known was trouble.

We've been hiding out here ever since, in Bezzie's hidden furnished basement, devising a plan to extract Asha from the palace. It's been grueling—the waiting. The problem is that we've had difficulty finding a way into the palace that isn't heavily guarded.

Not that I wouldn't rip through hordes of guards to get to my wife. Not that I wouldn't gladly die trying.

But if we die trying, and we fail to rescue her, then Asha will be the one to truly suffer.

546

So we've waited. We've spied. We've plotted.

Lydia and Elias joined us two days ago, bringing news that the body of Queen Abra had been found separated from her head in an abandoned warehouse on the border of Avelea and Dwellen.

There was no word regarding what happened, or the whereabouts of Piper or the parasite, who we assume escaped at the moment of Abra's death.

Dinah looks at me first, holding a metallic lamp in her hands. "I think I can get into the palace in the early morning. Tonight maybe, even," she says. "There's a statue of Tionis in the graveyard quarter I doubt Az knows about. According to the guard schedule I snuck from one of their pockets, there are two gaps. The first, I'm pretty sure only I could get through. The guards on duty at that time aren't sympathetic to our cause, but they are new. There's a low risk they'll recognize me if I sneak in dressed as a servant. If we want to go as a group, though, we'll have to wait until just before sunrise, when there's a gap in coverage."

Relief lingers on the edges of my mind. It's something. Not enough to banish the anxiety threatening to rip my chest cavity in two. But it's something.

Just a few more hours, and hopefully I'll have heard from Asha.

Assuming Dinah doesn't get caught.

"But Kiran," Dinah says. "There's something else."

Fin and I exchange a worried look.

Dinah sighs. "We have visitors." She beckons to the hole in the ceiling, and two figures descend the ladder, both with too much ease to be natural.

My fingers flex into fists as the first figure lowers her hood, and none other than Blaise stares back at me.

"You."

It's as good of an accusation as I can come up with as heat boils in my head, threatening to burst the capillaries lining my skull.

I've always blamed my anger on my Flame and Rajeen. But now

547

that my Flame is gone and I've discovered my true heritage, I know better.

It's just me.

It's always been me.

Blaise opens her mouth to say something, but I get to her first.

I'm not really sure how it happens, how I outpace her and her companion. I suppose it's just the rage rolling through me.

But I blink, and then I'm pinning Blaise to the wall by her throat.

The instinct for survival flashes in her eyes. Fangs jolt from her gums, but as fast as she is with her vampirism, she's not fast enough.

Not when my skin has a grip on hers.

There's something about being bereaved of my Flame that feels unjust when it comes to destroying the female who betrayed Asha, who left my wife drained of blood on a battlefield, handed her over to the male who threatens her with his body nightly.

I should be able to make her burn.

But then again, burning is only a single feeling, an isolated sensation.

There's so much more I can do with the magic that remains. The magic my father didn't know to take.

Blaise's fangs flash, but I'm faster, as I unleash every bit of fear I've ever experienced from my fingertips, allowing it to seep into Blaise's flesh.

Her already pale face drains of its last flecks of color, her brown eyes bulging wide as I unleash dread upon her.

Her companion bellows in anger, but I can't make out his words, not with the rage buzzing in my mind. All I hear is the muffled sound of a scuffle as Fin and Lydia hold him back.

There's a flare of light behind us—Lydia's fire, I suppose, but it's hardly anchoring me to the present.

Not when all my attention is on Blaise.

It's the fear of Rajeen that I release on her first. The dread of a child at the hands of his angry father's drunken whippings. The trepidation of his father catching him in the act of weeping. The boiling tears that mar his face.

I give it to Blaise, who whimpers, her compact frame shaking underneath me.

Next, I give her the fear of when my mother took the blame for the time I broke the banister in a fit of anger, and my father made me watch as he beat her.

Tears stream from Blaise's eyes, but they're not boiling her skin, as they did mine, so I decide that's not enough.

I give her the fear of losing my relationship with Fin, the night Ophelia tried to seduce me, and when that isn't enough, the fear I felt as I watched Calias unleash waves upon Asha and Fin, drowning the two people I cared most for in the world. And even though there's a faint awareness in the back of my mind that I'm at fault, I give her Tavi, force Blaise to share in the guilt of that innocent female's death, the feel of her warm blood sticking to our fingertips.

Blaise's lips murmur something that looks like it might be a plea, but the noise in my ears is swallowing me now, drowning everything out.

So then I give her the moment the palace doors opened, and out walked Asha in a wedding gown and that dreadful mask.

"*No.*" Blaise cries out this time, and it's my own anguish I hear as she weeps for Asha, weeps for my wife.

Every moment I've laid awake, my mind racing with the possibilities of what Az might be doing to her, I funnel into Blaise. Every wicked imagining that haunts my waking moments, every sick machination that twists my dreams into nightmares.

Blaise's eyes go wide. The weeping stops, and for a moment she seems paralyzed.

And it's wrong and awful, but I want her to ache. I want her to ache like I ache, but more than that, like Asha aches. I want her to feel exactly what she's done to my wife, what she's caused.

I want her to know…

But then, somewhere in the back of the room, I hear a voice, one that's unfamiliar to me. The male who accompanied Blaise begs, "Please. Please, stop. You don't know what you're doing to her. Please."

It's then that I look down at Blaise, at the way she's gone completely still under my touch. The way she isn't fighting back.

The way she's not in the room with us anymore.

And then something else flashes before my eyes.

The girl, broken in front of her stepmother's corpse, the news of a lost baby dampening her soul.

I realize with horror that anything I might fear has happened to Asha has already happened to Blaise.

I don't think it makes me hate her any less. Perhaps it makes me hate her more, for putting Asha in a vulnerable position when she should have wanted to protect her.

"Please, just let her go," says her companion. "Do whatever you want to me instead. That's what you want, isn't it? Justice? You want to make her feel what she did to you? So torture me instead. Make her watch. Just please stop."

Blaise's eyes roll back in her head, and she begins to shake.

Too far. I've gone too far.

Again.

"Kiran," says Fin, and I see it now through his eyes, what's happening. Me pinning Blaise to the wall, consuming her with my anger, just like I did with Ophelia.

Fates, no.

Shame washes over me, and I let go. Blaise slumps, but I catch her before she hits the ground.

No, no, no.

I brush my fingers against her neck, trying to soothe what I've just unleashed upon her, the memories I've just made her relive without realizing it.

Had I realized it?

I feel as though I'm going to be sick.

But the more I try to calm her, the more I try to seep tranquility into her flesh, the more the emotion escapes me. Since I can't grasp onto it, can't remember what it feels like, it resists me, refusing to be transmitted.

"I'm so sorry," I say, the apology gravelly in my mouth.

It takes a moment for the glaze in Blaise's eyes to dissipate, and though her breathing is still heavy, she speaks with little shake in her voice.

"It's all right. That's good. That's really good," she says, to which I furrow my brow.

I have the sudden urge to look back at my siblings, to see if they're as confused as I am, but something tells me I shouldn't turn my back on the vampire whose mind I just tortured.

"I was worried that wouldn't be strong enough," she says, letting out a shiver. "But it's definitely strong enough."

I let go of her, stretching my fingers, which are sore from pinning her to the wall.

As the sounds in the room come back into focus, my ears focus in on her companion's ragged breathing behind us. The scent of burnt flesh tinges my nostrils. I turn to discover that Lydia has been holding the other vampire off by searing his skin with her Flame.

Still, she's sweating profusely from the effort of holding him back.

She finally lets go, and he runs to Blaise, scooping her in his arms, shoving himself between me and her.

"I'm okay, I'm okay," she says, her voice shaking.

"Why are you here?" asks Lydia, and while I'm still reeling from what I inflicted upon Blaise, how much further I almost went, my sister holds no pity for the girl in her voice.

Blaise untucks her face from her companion's grasp, and strengthens herself, though she's still blinking hard, like she's trying to remind herself that the emotions she was feeling were mine and not her own.

There's a bit of vulnerability there. Knowing I've let Blaise into that portion of my head.

"Because," she says, steadying herself against her companion, who's glaring at me like he wants to rip my throat out for touching her, "I know how to stop Az."

It's Fin's turn to be distrustful now. "Wouldn't it have been more convenient if you'd figured that out before you betrayed Asha?"

Blaise looks as if she's about to say something quippy, but then her

551

shoulders falter. "I'm sorry. I really am. And I wish I could be saying that to Asha right now. I can't... I know I'll never be able to make it right. That I can't undo what's happened to her these past few months. But I think I know how to stop him."

"And how is that?" Lydia asks.

"Piper can lead the Others back to the Rip," Blaise explains. "The only problem is, Az still has mental control over them. Piper thinks if we can break his focus, she'll be able to cut into the line, lure them with her magic flute."

"This all sounds very convincing," says Lydia, her tone conveying the opposite.

"Distract him? Like seduce him, distract him?" Fin asks, irritation biting his tone.

Blaise shakes her head. "No, it needs to be something more earth-shattering than that."

"You want to use me. My powers," I say.

Blaise nods.

"I would have imagined you would have already told him about my powers. Or was that the one thing you decided to keep for yourself?"

Blaise's companion growls, but she doesn't flinch from my gaze. "Az knew about your powers from your first wife, Gwenrial—Gwenyth, whatever her name was. What I'm hoping he doesn't know is that you still have them."

My mind wanders back to my now deceased father. How intentional had it been that he'd only taken my power over fire? Did he know about my ability to control emotions? I've been assuming that power came from my mother, but what if...

"You want Kiran to upset Az so much he loses a mental grip on the Others?" asks Fin.

"That would require getting close to Az, but I'm sure it could be done," says Lydia. "Assuming Kiran's powers can cause that kind of emotional distraction."

"Believe me, they can," says Blaise, standing up taller, though I can't help but notice that the tips of her fingers are still flexing and unflexing.

Guilt sluices off of me, so much so I'm shocked no one else can feel it, even though I'm not touching them.

"And how do we know this isn't just another one of your schemes?" asks Lydia. "Just another way you plan to betray us to Azrael? It's rather a convenient plan for him, don't you think? To lure Kiran back into the castle? Convenient that the only person who might challenge his throne is the only one who can use this power."

Blaise bites her lip, looking uncertain.

It's Blaise's vampire companion who speaks. "Blaise ran across the Sahli to get this news to you. She was burning in the sand, the sun cresting the horizon when I caught up with her. If that's not enough evidence that she cares for your friend's safety, I don't know what is."

"Az intends to send the Others to attack Othian tomorrow," Blaise says. "Again. If you don't believe I'm doing this for Asha, then at least believe I'm doing it for Evander. For Ellie. For—"

Whatever Blaise is about to say gets caught in her throat.

"It's better than the plan we had," says Dinah, piping in for the first time.

Lydia makes a noncommittal noise, though even my stubborn sister can't help but admit that our plan had its holes.

Like what we planned to do in the aftermath of stealing Asha out from under Azrael's nose.

I'm of two minds. There's the part of me that wants to be the one to pull my wife into my arms and carry her out from the nightmare of the palace.

Then there's the part of me that wants to have somewhere to carry her to. A home where she won't have to live in hiding, constantly hunted by the male she used to call a friend.

As much as it kills me to agree to a plan that involves me not being the one to get Asha out of the palace, I know it's the plan that gives her the best hope of a future.

One where the Others haven't taken over her home.

"Fine," I say, to Fin and Lydia's surprise. "Blaise, just tell me what I need to do."

CHAPTER 94

KIRAN

With Nox and Blaise taking Bezzie's guest room in the furnished basement, Dinah helping Bezzie out upstairs, and Elias keeping watch on the roof, that leaves me, Fin, and Lydia to share the living room.

Something tells me Bezzie arranged things like this on purpose, or that perhaps it's Dinah's doing. Though whether it's forcing Nox and Blaise into the same room, or me and my siblings, I can't tell.

We're all quiet for a while, settling onto our cots on the floor, though it's unlikely I'll sleep.

I haven't slept through the night since Asha's wedding to Azrael, my whole body squirming, my imagination torturing me with what Azrael might be doing to her during the night hours.

My stomach roils, and I find myself up and about, pacing in the middle of the night as cold sweat beads off my forehead.

"Our intel says Azrael hasn't touched her." Lydia's voice is gentle. If I've ever heard her speak that way before, it would have to have been when I was a small child.

A light flickers in the room as Fin lights a candle.

From the bloodshot veins in his eyes, I can tell he hasn't been sleeping either.

"That's a relief," he says, running his hands through his hair. My memory flickers back to something Asha told me months ago. When our relationship first progressed, Fin became visibly upset when he discovered what happened between us. Asha had thought very little of it, other than that it pained Fin to have his friend fall for the brother he hated so much.

I probably pondered it more than she did, watching the way my brother was with her, lighting up in her presence. The way he only seemed totally at ease when around her.

A pang of jealousy ripples through me at his statement of concern, though I squelch it immediately. He's Asha's friend, her brother by marriage, and he has every right to be concerned over her safety.

"I still can't sleep," I say, crossing my arms. "Just the idea of…" I feel the blood drain from my cheeks, and I wonder if I'll become physically ill.

Light from the lamp flickers on Lydia's sharp features as she sits upright and leans her back against the wall.

"It's likely at least one of us will die tomorrow," she says, looking at the ceiling rather than either of us.

I huff. "Well, I know who you're putting your hopes in, Lydia."

It's meant to be a joke, but there's too much truth in it to land properly. My sister frowns, then turns her piercing violet eyes upon me. "I don't wish for you to die, Kiran."

I cross my arms, allowing a faint smile to creep up on my face, because apparently I feel that will make this conversation less uncomfortable.

The smile must look strange on me, because she knits her brow. Fin says nothing, still standing by the candle in the corner.

"Well, I hope you don't die either, Lydia."

She doesn't smile. Not that I was expecting her to. But still, there's a sadness there in her eyes that I don't quite understand, that I can't quite grasp. Perhaps it's the knowledge of the relationship we could have enjoyed had either of us put away our pride for a moment.

"I'm not sure you mean that," she says, and now it's my turn to frown.

"Lydia, we might not get along, and you might have intended to kill me at some point, but—"

She shakes her head, shooting to her feet, urgency bleeding all over her expression. For the first time in my life, I think I find anxiety on my sister's face, especially as she chances a glance at Fin.

"There are things about me the two of you don't know," she says.

I can't help but tense, anxiety wracking me for what she might say next. I've been suspicious for a while now of what type of business my sister conducts on those long trips of hers. Granted, I rarely ask questions. Lydia's been a useful ally since we decided our goals aligned. No questions has always seemed like the best way to approach her, especially when asking for favors.

"I don't think it's going to surprise either of us if we learn you've gotten your hands dirty, Lydia," says Fin, his voice still tinged with affection.

Lydia doesn't laugh. In fact, she looks as though she's bracing herself.

I don't know what I'm expecting. Perhaps for a long-winded story slowly building us up to whatever it is she doesn't want to tell us.

That's a ridiculous thing to expect. This is Lydia we're talking about it.

Still, I'm just as shocked when she says, with no emotion imbuing her face or voice, "I killed our mother."

I tense, but Fin's the one who drops his saucer, spilling sizzling tea all over Bezzie's floor.

Anger boils within me, but it no longer flares outside of my skin, like it might have when I still possessed my Flame. Instead, it spirals inside me, mingling with confusion. "Why?" I can hardly breathe out.

All these years, I've assumed it was Rajeen who killed our mother. All these years, the reason for her death has made sense, especially since the revelation that she had an affair.

But Lydia.

My mind grapples for answers, but I find none.

"Father discovered my skill with the Flame early," she says. "As much as he hated me for not being an heir, he decided I could be put to use. So he trained me. Beat me. Used me to take care of subjects who displeased him."

Yes, that much I already know. It's the whole reason our mother had an affair to begin with. In the hopes she could bear a son and redirect our father's attention away from Lydia.

Fin still says nothing, though he's shaking in the corner.

Lydia sighs, sorrow painting her violet eyes indigo. "When Father discovered Mother had had an affair..." She takes a breath before speaking, something I've never seen my sister do. "He lost his mind to jealousy. He summoned me to the dungeons, where he was keeping Mother and..." Her eyes snap to Fin apologetically, "and you, Fin."

Fin says nothing.

Lydia pales, but when she speaks, it's nothing compared to hearing my sister, my immovable sister's voice shake. "He was lost to his own paranoia at that point. He'd convinced himself that Fin was illegitimate because of his lack of magic, but that you, Kiran, were his."

Fin and I exchange disbelieving looks.

"We're twins," I say, hesitantly.

"Yes, and I already told you he was out of his mind. I don't think he could bear believing that his favorite was not actually his heir. So he told himself the two of you had different fathers. Obviously, I don't believe that to be the case. But he'd found a report of a set of twins from centuries ago who were born to different fathers, and he latched onto that, despite the lack of evidence.

"He said I had a choice," Lydia says, and her voice goes quiet. So quiet, I can almost hear the child she was when it happened. "That I could choose between Fin and our mother."

Dread ripples through me, even though I know where this story is heading, even though I already know the ending.

"She told me to kill her, so I obeyed."

Fin's gaze transfixes on his shoes as he speaks. "I remember."

Sorrow fills Lydia's eyes. "What?"

Fin swallows. "I remember. That day. Father took Mother and me to the dungeons and made us wait for you. I always thought it was just a nightmare. Just a kid's way of explaining something that couldn't be explained."

There's a silence that creeps between the three of us, and it's thick and sweltering.

But that's all there's ever been between the three of us.

Distance.

Muggy and thick and difficult to wade through, but it's not a distance any of us created.

He created it. Rajeen. He's the one who wanted this, the hate that boils between me and my two siblings.

And he'd hated Lydia from the day she was born. From the day she left the womb and the midwife declared that my mother had borne not an heir, but a daughter.

It's why he forced her to choose. Forced her to kill, not just his enemies, but her very own mother.

Because he'd hated her from the beginning, and when she and Fin bonded, he couldn't stand for her to possess a glimmer of happiness. He'd wanted to take away that too, the relationship between siblings. He'd already been driving a wedge between us since it was discovered that I possessed magic and Fin did not.

For the first time in my life, I reach down into myself and expect to find anger, but instead find something else.

It's not as pretty and delicate as forgiveness. Not as gentle as kindness.

It's rough and calloused, and it mirrors my heart.

I reach within and find determination.

And since that's all that's left in me, that's what I use when I cross the room and take my sister in my arms.

At first she flinches, going stiff in my grasp like she expects me to reach into her chest and rip her heart out. But as I hold her, she slowly softens, her tense muscles loosening.

And then Lydia begins to cry.

Her tears are hot, boiling as they fall from her eyes and fall onto my shoulder, my neck.

Fin stands in the corner, and for a moment it strikes me as odd that it's me holding Lydia, and not the brother whose forgiveness she would sell mine for in a heartbeat, the brother she loves.

So I turn my head and urge him with my gaze.

He's stiff, his body still in shock from hearing that the nightmares that have plagued him so often are actually a memory. A leftover smudge on his mind of the truth of our mother's death.

But then I flick my neck to the side, hopefully subtly enough that Lydia won't feel.

For a moment, Fin's face hardens, and I can't help but think it's the most heartbreaking vision I've ever seen. Fin, once so full of life and joy, so, so very bitter. And I can't help but wonder if I did that. If I took the brightest star in the sky and doused it.

But even I don't have that power.

As much as he faults me for Ophelia's death, as much as I am to blame, I cannot go on bearing the burden of my brother's bitterness.

I cannot hold the blame for the darkness that swells in his heart.

I can only hold out a hand and hope he grasps it.

Fin's gaze flickers to our sister, the sight of Lydia crying, which I know he hasn't witnessed since the night of our mother's death.

A crease furrows his brow, and he takes in a deep breath, his chest expanding in reticence.

Then Fin walks toward us, putting his arms around both of us.

I don't miss it, the way he embraces me too, even if it's only for her sake.

Eventually, Lydia pulls away, slinging tears from her burned cheeks with her long fingers like she's ridding her body of spiderwebs.

There's revulsion there, on her face, at her outburst. Fin actually makes eye contact with me and smiles, an inside joke between the two of us about our sister and her disgust for actual displays of emotion.

I'm not even sure I return the smile, I'm so shocked to see it. When the moment passes and he turns back to Lydia, I can't help but wonder if I've missed my only shot.

"There's more," Lydia says with a groan.

I raise a brow. "I can't imagine it could be any worse."

She snorts, and Fin adds, "Please tell me it was you who ambushed

559

our father on the road that day. That yours was the last face he saw as he faded from this side of the sun."

Lydia's violet eyes flicker with something. "Well. I suppose I have nothing more to tell you, after all."

She watches me carefully, as the realization sets in. Rajeen was attacked by the Umbra, an assassin known for the violent murders of abusers throughout Alondria.

The Umbra, who'd saved Dinah the night Azrael had kept her hostage. The Umbra, who'd ripped the heads of the traffickers from their bodies, for some reason sparing me, the king who had threatened to kill a bride every mooncycle.

I say nothing.

By the amusement in her eyes, I don't think I have to.

CHAPTER 95

BLAISE

I wait until Kiran and his siblings are deep in conversation before I leave Nox's side and hunt down Asha's sister.

Dinah's sitting in the parlor upstairs.

She startles when I slip into the booth across from her. "You shouldn't be up here."

I can't help but notice how much harder she seems than the way Asha described her. "If anyone's coming, I'll hear them well before they have the chance to see me."

"You didn't hear me sneaking up on you in the marketplace," she counters, eyes looking rather bored.

"Yeah, well, I was distracted."

"By Nox."

I sigh, which I suppose is enough of an answer.

"The two of you aren't together," she says, and I don't know why, but I somehow feel interrogated, although she's yet to ask me a question.

"No," I half say, half swallow, misery welling up in my chest, pain that I have to quash.

"That's a shame." Somehow, Dinah sounds like she means it.

"I betrayed your sister," I remind her, taking her glass of wine and

561

taking a gulp before handing it back to her. "I would think you'd want for me to be miserable."

Dinah levels me with a stare. "If you're miserable, and you and Nox aren't together, then you betrayed Asha for nothing. The least you could do is make her sacrifice worth it."

Sadness pings at my chest. "It's not really up to me. When I betrayed your sister, I betrayed the Old Magic too. He wasn't thrilled about it, so he cursed Nox not to love me."

"Oh," she says, her gaze falling a bit. "That sounds like him. He's always been a fan of tragic stories. Unrequited love is one of his favorites." Her tone is affectionate, like how someone might speak of an ornery grandparent, but she rolls her eyes just the same. "It's not nearly as romantic as he makes it out to be."

"You mean Fin."

Dinah stiffens, but then her shoulders loosen, as if she's decided it's so obvious it's not even worth hiding. She picks at the hem of her sleeve without looking at me.

"I hold on to things longer than I should."

I flick my gaze over to the girl, assessing her, then decide to let it be. "You're not how your sister describes you."

She shifts, making herself taller in the booth. "And you're exactly how everyone describes you."

I force an amused smile to my lips. "And how does everyone describe me?"

"It would be impolite to say."

I huff a laugh. "Don't worry. Asha's never said an impolite thing about you."

"She thinks I'm soft. That being soft makes me weak," says Dinah.

I shrug. "Is she wrong?"

She blinks. "Not about the soft part. But I suppose if I tell you I'm not weak, I'll just make myself sound less credible."

I take in the girl, assessing whether she's up to the task. "I need you to get a message to your sister."

Her perfect brow shoots up. "That we're coming for her?"

"Yes. But something else, too."

Dinah's perfect features go blank for a moment. "Why did you wait to get me alone before asking me?"

I take another sip from her glass. "I think you already know the answer to that."

Her eyes turn steely. "If it's because Kiran won't like it, that means it's putting Asha in danger, which means I won't like it either."

I shake my head. "There's nothing more dangerous than going in and making decisions without all the relevant information."

Dinah narrows her eyes. "What is it you think Asha will do with the information?"

I swallow. "I think she'll make her own decisions. And that those aren't for any of the rest of us to make."

CHAPTER 96

ASHA

"*A*sha."

My name is an echo from the hall, a whisper underneath a shadow of a veil.

Kind and familiar and…

"Dinah?" I rasp, jolting from my place in the corner, where I've been… well, I'm not exactly sure what I was doing. The hours, days—they're all melding into one another around here.

My sister is disguised as a servant girl, her luxurious hair covered in a crimson veil that stretches from head to foot.

Servants, male and female alike, are not allowed to cover their faces, something Az ensures as a precaution, in case anyone thinks to sneak an assassin inside the palace unnoticed.

But other than that, Dinah doesn't look like my sister at all.

She's packed muscle onto her slight frame since the last time I saw her, like she's been out hauling crates in the desert. But that isn't what awes me. It's her face, smudged with dirt under her lids that makes her look sickly. Paint smooths out her normally almond-shaped eyes, giving them a rounder look. More paint, a few shades darker and lighter than her skin, has been applied to various features, dulling her beautiful cheekbones and making her look rather ordinary.

This is not the breathtaking girl I'd once been so confident the cruel king would take to be his beautiful human bride, only to slaughter her the next morning.

This girl is a servant. At least, she looks the part. Able to slip in and out without turning anyone's head.

"Do you like my paint?" she asks, her soothing voice as familiar as ever. So familiar that it's almost unnerving to hear my sister's voice echo from a mouth so much thinner than her own.

"You don't even look like yourself," I whisper.

This is the point when her eyes would normally twinkle, but even they seem duller. How had she managed that? "Well, that's kind of the point, isn't it?"

"How?" I whisper.

Dinah shrugs. "I've made some new...colleagues over the past few months. Some of them have marvelous skill sets that come quite in handy."

I stare at my sister, mouth agape, unable to decide what's more surprising. That my sister no longer looks like my sister, or that she's made allies of someone skilled in performing such a task.

But then her gaze takes me in, really takes me in, for the first time, and that sisterly concern swarms her face, giving away just who she is.

"Asha, I'm so sorry this has happened," she says, as if it's somehow her fault.

She closes the space between us, falling to her knees and wrapping me in an embrace. I melt into it. It occurs to me that this is the first form of welcome physical touch I've had since returning to the palace with Az, the first I don't cringe away from.

"You shouldn't have come," I say, but the words lacked vigor.

Dinah pulls back and smiles at me. "Don't lie to yourself. You're glad I'm here."

The tears that stain my cheek confirm as much.

THIS ISN'T the rescue mission I had hoped for.

"I argued to get you out of here," Dinah says, twirling nervously with her braid, "but everyone else pointed out that it wouldn't do much good to rescue you if the entire world was going to end up like the Nether."

"I have to say I agree with that," I say. "I'm not fond of the idea of having to whisper the rest of my life."

"It would be torture," Dinah adds. "But I do have a message for you, from Blaise."

"Blaise?" I practically rear back. "Tell me you don't trust her."

"Well, I wasn't particularly inclined to, to be honest." My sister blushes, as if it betrays a character flaw that she actually held a less than favorable opinion of someone. "But Kiran—"

"You've seen Kiran," I breathe.

Dinah nods, though cautiously.

"How is he?"

Sorrow lines Dinah's eyes, but something else, too. Something like hope. "It's honestly probably a good thing he doesn't have his Flame right now. He really misses you, Asha. And blames himself for what happened."

I grunt. "He should be blaming Blaise. Not trusting her."

"Well, he did almost kill her, if that's any consolation."

It was, sort of. "So what's her message?"

"She says Piper—you'll know who she is, though I thought she was from some of the Old Magic's stories when I first heard about her— has a way to lure the Others back to the Rip. Apparently, being at the location of the Rip enhances her powers, and she thinks she can call to them, even from that far away. But she can't do it so long as Az controls them."

I shake my head. "I don't know how to break his control. He's been taking a draft that makes it where he doesn't have to sleep. And I hardly have any worthwhile magic now that Az burned the scrolls behind the library fireplace."

A look of disgust overtakes Dinah's face.

"Oh, he has just gotten out of hand, hasn't he?" Dinah says, the appropriate reaction for when your childhood role model and friend goes rogue, uses you as leverage, stages a coup, and traps your sister as his forced bride.

"Did Blaise offer any ideas as to how I might sever Az's control?" I ask.

"From the tone you get when you talk about her, I would have thought you were asking so you could do the opposite."

"I am not. Though I am considering it."

Dinah sighs, long-sufferingly. "She thinks it's taking him a fair amount of concentration to keep them under control. Blaise thinks if we can distract Az thoroughly, it will give Piper the opportunity to wrestle away his reins."

"Distract him?" I ask, dryly. "And did Blaise have any suggestions for how I might do that?"

Dinah's expression darkens. "She seemed to think you would know."

DINAH CAN'T STAY LONG. Something to do with the guard shifts.

Before she leaves, I ask, "Is Tavi with you? Az says she's traveling, but I can't help but wonder if she defected."

Dinah's face falls, and she shakes her head. "No. No, she…" My sister watches my face intently, and I realize there's something she's been keeping from me. "Kiran and Fin were captured around the time of Az's coronation. Tavi helped them escape."

My heart pounds in my chest, even that much exertion making me dizzy after weeks of inactivity. "Kiran and Fin were here?"

Something about that knowledge, that they were here, and I didn't somehow know, makes me numb.

Dinah nodded. "They tried to rescue you. But they were caught by Az's soldiers. Tavi had magic, Asha. She'd kept it hidden all these years, but she used it to transport Kiran and Fin away from the palace."

"And then Az killed her for it," I say, my throat dry.

Dinah winces, tears filling her eyes. "It was a stray dagger. One of the soldiers threw it, aiming for Kiran."

My heart crumbles then, which is a strange sensation, because I assumed my heart was already rubble.

I suppose even rubble is turned to sand eventually, battered by the overbearing wind until there's nothing left of the edifice that once was.

"She deserved better than that," I say, remembering the female who had shown me nothing but kindness since she painted my face for my wedding. I remember the friend and confidant she'd grown to be.

Dinah sighs, then plants a salty, tear-soaked kiss on my forehead and tells me she has to go.

As she slips away, I wonder if I'll ever see her again.

I try not to think about it too much as I sneak into Az's empty quarters through the door Dinah left ajar, and steal his dagger out from underneath his pillow.

I lock myself back in my room and prepare for what very well might be the end.

HALF AN HOUR LATER, I'm in bed, though I can't sleep. The lock on my door clicks, and Az waltzes in. The sight of him makes my chest seize up.

"Asha," he says. "You're still awake."

My legs are trembling underneath my blankets. "I couldn't sleep."

"Well, that's for the best," he says, his smile eerily kind. "I was actually hoping you'd still be awake. Because there's someone I'd like for you to meet."

CHAPTER 97

BLAISE

The tavern owner Bezzie whistles to herself as she locks, actually locks, Nox and me in the cellar bedroom together.

I stare around at the space, which is rather tidier than I might have expected from someone as eccentric as Bezzie.

There's no vanity, though I'm not surprised. Bezzie appears to be in her seventies and not what most would classify a looker. Nor does she seem like she puts much stock in her appearance.

The rest of the room is neatly arranged with a handful of books and crafting materials.

And then there's the bed.

It's clearly the type meant to sleep only one, though my heart gives a lurch at the thought. Because this is Meranthi, and it's likely beds like this sleep multiples all throughout the city. If a family is fortunate enough to have a raised bed like this one rather than simple cots.

"You take it." Nox gestures toward the bed. He's returned to being rather distant since this morning in the bunker.

My cheeks heat as I remember the taste of his blood against my lips.

What a mess.

"Where are you intending to sleep, then?" I ask.

He nods toward the floor, where he's already rolling out a simple quilt.

Knobs from the uneven cellar floor poke out through the holes in the quilt.

I open my mouth to offer the bed to him. It would be the considerate thing to do. To share. But my chest is already halfway to cracking in two, and I know if Nox and I share this bed tonight, it'll be like striking a wedge into the crack, refusing to let it close.

It might already be too late.

So I mutter something that I hope sounds like gratitude and slip into Bezzie's bed.

I settle in and try to close my eyes and nod off, but everything about me is on edge.

My hunger especially.

"Is it just me, or does Bezzie smell delicious?" Nox asks out from the darkness.

"Ugh. I can smell her even with three doors and a floor separating us," I laugh back, though somewhat nervously.

"I mean, it's like…"

"The flavor of a good spice without the heat?" I ask.

He rolls his head to the side, his arms up above his shoulders, elbows splayed out from where he's clasped his fingers behind his head to support it. "Finishing my sentences now, are we?"

There's a gentle caress to his voice, a confidence I haven't heard since we played one of our many games back in Mystral, the feel of his hands against my waist as he picked me up and set me on the dais.

Playing.

That's all this is.

Playing, because that's a good option to distract ourselves from the fact that both of us are likely going to die tomorrow.

"Ugh. Is that what happens when people partake in the blood-sharing ritual? Because if I'd have known that, I definitely wouldn't have done it."

Nox rolls over, propping his head on his hand as he stares up at me. "It was a horribly stupid thing we did, wasn't it? Totally not enjoyable at all."

My face goes hot with the memory of his teeth pressed to my wrist, the way his eyes shone with delight as he gazed up at me.

It was stupid of us.

Very, very stupid.

"Repulsive is a better word, actually," I say, unable to stop myself from drinking in Nox's grin.

"Repulsive, huh?" he says, as if playing over the word on his tongue. "Well, if that's the word you'd use to describe it, then Blaise, I'm afraid you're looking utterly repulsive tonight."

My heart hammers, but I can't bear to look away from him, especially as his voice dips low. "Seeing you in bed like that, in that nightgown..."

Teasing shades the edge of his voice, and I stare down at the nightgown Bezzie's letting me borrow. It looks exactly like what you would expect from a seventy-year-old woman's least favorite nightgown.

"Disgusting, I'm sure," I say, trying and probably failing to maintain the lightness in my tone.

I find I can't breathe, not when he's looking at me like he's a drunk and I'm the bottle of liquor he swore he'd stay away from. But even that isn't right, because I'm the one who should stay away from him. The male cursed never to love me.

But I can tell he wants me.

And my stupid, stupid heart whispers to me that maybe that's enough.

Because this might be our last night to live, and though a relationship where Nox will never love me would rot me to the core over years... Well, desire burns fast, but if we won't be here in the morning, I'm not sure that's a problem.

"You look uncomfortable down there," I say.

Nox's eyes glint with mischief, and he scoots backward on his pitiful excuse for a cot, patting the floor in front of him as if to beckon me.

I can't help the laugh that escapes my lips. "I don't think that's going to work."

Nox shrugs. "I'm rather flexible. Willing to make anything work at this point."

"I think you're just trying to get me down there so you can steal the bed."

"I assure you I have more creative intentions than that."

My heart patters against my chest, and I feel as though I can't breathe as long as there's this gaping space between the two of us.

It physically hurts being away from him.

And now he's asking me to come down there with him.

So I do. I slip my bare feet onto the floorboards and teeter over to Nox, slipping onto the pallet with him. I drag the blanket from the bed over with me, settling it over the both of us as I lie next to him and tuck my back into his chest.

Instantly, he slips his arm around my waist, melding my body with his as warmth radiates off of him and into me.

My whole body is tingling from head to toe, and I know this is a horrible idea, one that will leave me with only bits of a memory that will fade every day once Nox is gone. If we survive tomorrow, that is.

But for now, it feels so nice to be held by him.

His fingers begin tracing patterns into my waist, and I find I can't breathe.

"Nox," I say, and it's meant as a rebuke, but my traitorous voice makes it sound like more of an invitation.

"Blaise." I can feel his lips grin as they brush my ear.

And now it's not just me that's on fire, but the bond too, the one we sutured into place, finally completed when we shared one another's blood.

And it's taut and immovable and permanent, and it's going to be the thing that kills me slowly in the end.

It takes all the willpower in my body, more than I even knew I had, to wrench myself from Nox's arms and fling myself to the other side of the room, my butt plastered to the bed as I clutch the frame of it with my fingertips.

"I can't. I'm sorry, but I can't," I say, still trying to catch my breath. But it's getting more difficult now.

Nox pulls the blankets off of himself, sitting straight up to face me. "You can't what?"

"I can't be with you. Like this. Right now. Ever," I say, even though that last word pierces my heart, even in the way it makes Nox flinch. "Nox, you're all I want. You know that. You have to know that. I handed the world over for you. There's nothing I want more than to…" My eyes trail his body. "No, that's not true. I want you, Nox. But I want you forever, not just for tonight. And I can't…I won't…" I have to dig my fingers into the mattress to steady myself, but my fingernails rip through the fabric, something I'll have to make up to Bezzie. "I can't be this person anymore, Nox."

He frowns, and I can tell he isn't following.

"I can't be someone who throws herself at anyone who pays her the slightest bit of attention. I can't be the girl who ignores the sirens in the back of her mind, the voices telling her she deserves something better than to be held for a moment. Tonight will never be enough for me, Nox. As much as I want it, I need to be loved. Not just wanted. And I've spent my whole life thinking that's what's going to fix me. I thought that if only Evander loved me back, that would somehow fix what was broken inside of me. Even with Derek…But I've been so convinced that males could fix me, I've been all too willing to take anything I can get. So much less than—well, I don't even know that I deserve more—but less than I'm willing to accept. I don't want *less than*." I breathe out. Slowly.

"And I can't do it anymore, Nox. I'm sorry, and I love you. So much more than you could imagine. But I have to have more respect for myself than this."

Nox stands to his feet, slowly, his fists shaking at his side.

And I know I should leave, break through the locked door and put myself out in the open in front of the others, because if Nox takes one more step toward me, I'm not sure I'll have the strength to resist him a second time. I've already used up all my resolve putting these few feet between us.

I'm spent, and if Nox so desires, I think I'll let him bankrupt me.

"Please," is all I have left in me to say.

Nox disregards my plea, and I know I'm done for.

He doesn't touch me. But he approaches me all the same.

"Blaise. I'm...I'm so sorry."

It's then that my heart officially cracks, because it's the confirmation of what I've feared, what I should have known from the beginning.

Nox might desire my body, but he doesn't love me, and he never will.

I shouldn't, but I meet his gaze, and his pale ice-blue eyes are melting with sorrow, and I think I might drown in the pain as I hold my breath to stop my sobs from escaping.

He doesn't love me he doesn't love me he doesn't love me.

It's the type of thing I feel I won't survive, though I know I should be stronger than that.

I stare at my hands, twiddling my thumbs like I think if I can keep them occupied long enough, I can prevent them from roaming Nox's body.

His finger slides under my chin, lifting my face to look at him.

"I'm so sorry," he says again, but this time he's not done, "that I wasn't clearer about my intentions."

My heart stutters, but I don't have the energy to stop him.

"I thought I made it clear, Blaise, when I offered the bloodsharing ritual to you again." He runs his other hand through his hair. "I see now how stupid that was of me. Of course, you'd just see that as something done out of lust. I'm realizing now I should have picked something less...passionate." His pale cheeks twinge red at that, making my chest flutter. "But Blaise, listen to me. I didn't initiate the bloodsharing ritual with you in a fit of passion. It wasn't unintentional, at least not on my part. I'm sorry...I'm sorry if it was for you. I never meant to rope you into it if it wasn't something you truly wanted." He bites the inside of his cheek, like he can't bear to ask me whether that's true. "I just...I had time to think when I was chasing you down in the desert. About all you've done, all you've given up for me. And I remembered falling for you, even if I couldn't access the feelings—I remembered the *why*. Then when I found you, and the Fates had spared you, I knew I'd be an idiot not to give my everything to you. And that's what it is, the bloodsharing ritual, to me, at least. I realize now that might not be what it is to you. I probably should have actually said that..." He smiles a bit, though it's the type that tells me he's beating himself up.

"It's not that I don't want it," I say. "It's just that I want something I can't have. And I don't want you to feel some duty to me, like you have to bind yourself to me when your heart isn't in it."

He frowns, but then he smiles, and there's something wry about it.

"Since when can we not put our heart into duty, Blaise?"

I bristle. "It's not exactly the most romantic notion in the world."

Nox sighs, then sits next to me, his thigh brushing against mine and lingering there, making it difficult to focus. "I'm sorry I left you, Blaise. I don't deserve to even be in this room with you. Don't deserve for you to let me be this close to you."

I shrug. "It's not your fault you don't love me anymore. That you never can. It's not even the Old Magic's. It's mine. I brought this upon myself."

Nox frowns. His hand goes to his pocket, and his forehead furrows, like he can't quite make a decision.

"You're wrong, you know," he says.

"About what?"

"If you think I can't love you anymore."

"Nox, you can't just will away a curse placed by the Old Magic, any more than the fae can will away the lying curse."

"I know that. But I don't think the Old Magic cursed me never to love you again."

I let out a wry laugh. "Then what is it you think he did?"

"I think he took away the feeling of being in love."

My heart feels damp. Tired. "Maybe you're right, technically it's not the same, but practically—"

"*Practically*, it's not the same at all."

"Is it not?"

"I thought that too. Until I went back home and visited my parents."

"You got to see them?" I can't help the way a smile tugs at my lips, just knowing Nox got something he's desired for so long. "How are they doing?"

His expression turns melancholy, but there's hope there. "They're...I think they'll be fine, eventually. But the reason I bring them up is that my father taught me something while I was there."

"Amazing how parents are supposed to be good at that," I say, a faint aching in my heart as I wonder what kind of advice my father would have given me about Nox, had he lived to meet him.

Nox smiles, and when he does, it melts every muscle in my body.

"Blaise, I'm sorry I haven't been clear about my intentions."

I nudge him in the shoulder, which is a mistake, because each time we touch, I feel my resolve breaking down. "You've already said that."

He turns and fixes his eyes on me. "And I'll keep saying it until you believe me."

"Until I believe what?"

"That I love you, Blaise."

My heart jolts, but it's short-lived, because it's not true. "That's impossible—the Old Magic's curse—"

"Took my feelings away. But that's all it did. But love isn't just a feeling. It's a choice. And I choose you."

I swallow, pain bulging in my throat. It's not what I want to hear, not at all. I want to hear that Nox is consumed by me. I want to hear that he feels the same way about me I feel about him.

Nox must see the disappointment in my eyes, because he sighs. "I'm still messing this up, aren't I?"

I bite my lip, nodding as tears sting at my eyes.

"Let me try again?"

"Okay."

"Blaise, I love you. I ripped through the actual Fabric separating realms to get back to you. I killed a man to get this *paldihv* to save you. Granted, he deserved it, so that's probably not the best example of a sacrifice. But then I sprinted for a day and night straight to get to you, across a desert, even. By the way, can we both agree sand is the worst substance to ever exist?"

I chuckle nervously. "It keeps falling out of my ears."

Nox grins, flicking my ear playfully, and, true to my words, a tuft of sand falls out. But then his smile falters, his expression turning serious. "And if that's not enough to convince you I love you, I'll find something to top it, I promise. The point is, you and I...we're volatile, Blaise, and even if the Old Magic hadn't cursed me, even if we'd been reunited in the way we'd wanted, then years down the road, I think there would have been times when the feelings dulled—dry spells. Because as much as we want to think we're unique, somehow immune to what everyone else seems to experience, I don't think we are. And I don't know that we'll never have difficult times, or we'll never have moments where we drive each other crazy. Or occasions where things are hard and the feelings fade for a little while.

"But Blaise. I want it to be you. I want your dry spells. I want your winters. I want your shadow seasons when the sun only shines a few hours at a time. No matter what happens, I want it to be you I'm clawing my way back to.

"It's you, Blaise. You in the shadows or you in the light. And if the Old Magic steals the way I feel about you again, it's you I want to keep crawling back to, falling in love with all over again. Today and tomorrow and the rest of our immortally nocturnal existences."

I let out a giggle, but it sounds more like a sob. "Are you trying to be romantic by talking about the times in life you'll fall out of love with me?"

"As long as it's you."

Nox bites the inside of his cheek and pulls out whatever it is that he's been twiddling with inside his pocket.

Then Nox kneels to the floor and slips something cold and metallic onto my finger.

I can hardly stand to look at it, not when Nox's eyes are filling with tears, and mine are too, blurring the moment.

"I think we're technically already married, Nox," I whisper, though it's somewhat choked. "At least, by vampire standards."

577

He lets out a chuckle, and a smile overtakes his beautiful face. "I know. I just want to be bound to you in all the ways."

"In all the ways?" I ask, playing with the band on my finger, though I still refuse to look at it, since that would mean looking away from Nox's face.

He shrugs. "One way in particular is coming to the forefront of my mind. But yes, all the ways."

"Even in the way lychaen bind themselves to each other?" I tease.

Nox winces through his grin. "If that's what you want, Blaise, then it's yours."

My heart fills with joy, and I chance a glance down at my finger, where a sole ruby ring glistens in the moonlight.

"It's the color of blood," I laugh.

Nox shrugs. "It's all Bezzie had. I figured it would work, considering my mate has a macabre sense of humor."

His mate.

The word makes my blood shiver.

"I don't know. Becoming a wife might change her a bit."

Nox holds my stare. "No one changes that much."

I let out a laugh, and it's the first time one has come freely from my chest in so very long.

"So what do you say?" he asks.

I simply grin.

CHAPTER 98

KIRAN

I wake to someone shaking my shoulders and a rather excited voice chattering my name.

"Kiran. Kiran, wake up."

I groan, wiping the sleep from my eyes. I'm fairly certain I only just fell asleep, but my muscles tense all the same.

Something's wrong.

I jolt to my feet, but when my eyes focus on Blaise, the female is practically glowing.

"Oh, don't you look agitated?" she says. It doesn't seem to occur to her she's the reason for as much.

"What's wrong?" I ask.

"What's wrong is that Nox and I aren't married yet."

She's right. Irritation swarms over me like a moth to the wick of a burning candle.

"You woke me up to tell me that?" I'm noticing now that Lydia and Fin are also grumpily wiping their eyes.

"No." Blaise punches my shoulder lightly. "We woke you up so that you could marry us."

I exchange a look with both my siblings, who appear equally

confused and irritated. Who knew the three of us had so much in common?

"No offense, but I thought the two of you were already, I dunno, blood-married or something," Fin says.

"We are," says Nox, a glint in his eyes, "but Blaise would like to be unblood-married as well."

"That seems unnecessary," I grumble.

"Well, we're probably going to die tomorrow, so I'd like it done tonight." Blaise is clearly high on whatever exchange she and Nox just had in that locked bedroom.

I really don't want to know.

I groan, wiping my forehead. "I can't marry you."

Blaise narrows her eyes. "What do you mean, you can't marry us?"

"I mean that I'm no longer King of Naenden, meaning I have no authority by which to aid you in exchanging your nuptials." What I don't add is that while I'm willing to ally with Blaise, that doesn't mean I feel like granting her joy while Asha is still trapped within Az's clutches—because of Blaise.

Still, Blaise's face actually falls, which I find surprising.

"I didn't take you to be the type to care about going by procedure," I say.

She shrugs. "I'm trying something new."

It's strange to me that this is so important to her. Blaise isn't the type to care about the rules, and frankly, I would have expected her to cast off the idea of marriage altogether.

My fingers clench at my sides, and I find myself agitated, not wishing Blaise a drop of happiness until Asha's is restored.

Still, as irritated as I am with her for betraying us, every time I try to hate her for it, my mind flashes back to the cavern and the shadow siren, my hand dripping with blood as I debated ripping Blaise's heart out of her chest to gift Asha immortality.

So, yes. As much as I'd love to hate Blaise, I think doing so would mean I'd have to hate myself.

And Asha's told me multiple times I'm not allowed to do that.

So I settle somewhere in the middle, not quite wishing Blaise harm, but not reveling in her joy, either.

"I suppose," Fin says, rubbing the back of his neck, "that I maybe could do it."

Each word drips with regret, but it's too late for my brother to take back his offer, because Blaise has already locked in on him.

"Why can you officiate a marriage if Kiran can't?" asks Lydia, skeptically.

"Because," sighs Fin, "technically, I'm still Prince of Talens."

"You're what?" Lydia and I say in unison.

"Oh, don't act so jealous," Fin says. "You both know I never had any true power. Apparently, Azrael is well aware of that too, because he didn't think it worthy of his time to go through the paperwork to depose me."

"That might be the most emasculating thing I've ever heard," says Lydia.

"Thank you for that, Lydia," Fin says, speaking through clamped teeth.

I'm not used to seeing the two of them bicker, but I can't help but find it satisfying.

Blaise just throws her arms around Fin, wrapping him in an embrace.

Fin's expression betrays that he'd like nothing more than for Blaise to get away from his neck, but when he sets her down, there's a resigned smile on his face.

When he and I lock eyes, the smile dissipates, and as Blaise scampers off to get ready, my brother leans over and whispers, eyes full of sympathy, "I'll make it quick."

My chest tightens in gratitude.

BLAISE AND NOX wanted the ceremony to happen immediately, but Bezzie insisted there had to be a reception afterward if this wedding was going to count, and she didn't want to miss the wedding for all the cooking she was going to have to do; we had to wait an hour for her to make her famous hummus.

Now that the scent of hummus is wafting in from downstairs, the ceremony can finally begin.

There wasn't any time, or anywhere, to get Blaise any sort of traditional wedding garb, so she's dressed in *paldihv*.

Apparently she had to snap Nox's neck to get it to release itself from him, but the male doesn't look any worse for wear.

Even I can reluctantly admit it's rather striking on her. As Lydia walks her into the room, the shadows melt and dance to form a black gown, complete with a train that rolls behind her in plumes.

She looks like death, but in a good way.

Nox seems to think so as well, because he stands there at the end of the cellar, looking utterly awestruck at his mate as she skips across the room.

It's a strange experience, watching a vampire cloaked in a gown of shadows literally skip across the room during a surprise wedding thrown in the middle of the night.

Not that they'd be getting married in the daylight anyway, I figure.

It's strange, and though part of me wants nothing to do with this, feels dread creeping up my throat at the idea of witnessing a wedding after the last one...

I steel myself with a deep inhale, thinking of what Asha would want.

I imagine she would find a surprise vampire wedding delightful.

So I force myself to observe, and make a note of every single detail, so I can tell her the story of it later.

Fin spent the hour Bezzie was cooking preparing his speech, and though initially he seemed irritated at being awakened in the middle of the night, I can tell he's reveling in the honor of getting to perform a wedding ceremony.

He even teasingly offered to marry Lydia and Elias if they wanted.

Lydia had flicked her wrist and informed us they'd married months ago.

Elias had shrugged in confirmation.

"We're gathered here tonight, well, I would say to celebrate the union of these two." Fin points to Blaise and Nox. "But really it's to catch up on some much needed sleep before trying to save the world, and it seems we've been roped into witnessing a wedding. Which I'm fine with, so long as you two don't try that bloodsharing ceremony in front of us. Because I might pull an Asha and throw up."

Blaise flashes her fangs teasingly, and Fin grimaces.

It's all I can do to keep from exploding as I watch Blaise and Nox exchange their vows, their world lit up in a burst of midnight light, while mine fades into the shadows of what could happen to Asha if tomorrow doesn't go as planned.

CHAPTER 99

KIRAN

*A*s it turns out, Calias did me an unexpected favor when he gifted my ignorant father all these statues of Tionis.

We've had them on our radar for weeks now as potential ways to enter the palace undetected. The statue in the gardens isn't a viable option, since that's the very statue Az once used to sneak into the palace grounds.

But Asha's innocent little sister has turned into quite the sleuth.

I would be lying if I said I expected this much of Dinah. Not that I don't hold a tremendous amount of respect for the girl. But I've always considered the way she sees the best in everyone a tad on the naïve side.

As I consider the connections Dinah made to find this statue of Tionis for us, I wonder if I've been the naïve one.

"How did you find this again?" Fin asks, looking down at the miniature version of the statue that lies in the center of a sandstone tomb on the outskirts of town.

The tomb is rather large, but it doesn't feel that way with me, Dinah, Fin, Lydia, Elias, Blaise, and Nox crammed in here.

Dinah doesn't look at Fin as she answers, though blotches of red stain her cheek. "Well, Zoph heard it from Riza, who heard it from

Bachlan, who heard it from Selda, that this was here. You can't always trust what Selda has to say, but when he's not drunk on faerie wine, he actually gives some brilliant advice."

Fin looks from Dinah to me, as if to silently ask, "Who are any of these people?"

"The beggars in Meranthi," Lydia says, a sly look of surprise on her face as she examines the younger girl.

"Oh, so you have friends in low places, do you?" Fin casually nudges Dinah in the shoulder, at which her entire body stiffens.

I frown. I know Asha teases Fin about his relationship with Dinah, but he's never expressed any intention of pursuing her romantically. I'll have to talk to him about the flirting with her problem later, especially when she's so clearly hung up on him.

"I wouldn't say that. More that I have friends in several walks of life." Dinah says this a bit stiffly. Fin frowns, then looks at me, confused.

My brother is an idiot.

Lydia and I must be sharing the same thought, because she shoots a knowing look at me. When Fin sees us, he crinkles his brow.

Dinah appears not to notice and quickly pulls out a knife, which she hastily brings down toward her palm.

Fin's hand shoots out to stop her, wrenching the knife out of her grip just as it's about to slice flesh. "Fates, did you and Asha inherit no self-preservation instincts?" asks Fin.

"The statue needs blood to operate," she says, matter-of-factly, though I don't miss the pleased smile teasing the corner of her lips.

Irritation deepens Fins's voice. "Well, let us do it. You know, since we heal."

"Actually, it would probably be best if the vampires did it. For obvious reasons," says Lydia, looking between Blaise and Nox suspiciously.

Blaise shrugs, shadows swarming around her, then brings Nox's wrist to her mouth and bites into it like one might a piece of fleshly fruit.

Distaste lines just about everyone's face but Nox's, who beams at his wife as if she had just planted a kiss on his cheek.

Fin's nostrils flare. "The two of you are disgusting."

Elias also appears to be a tad ill.

Even Dinah covers her mouth, though I can't tell if she's suppressing a giggle or a grimace.

Either way, Nox holds out his wrist, and blood trickles down, coating the statue's feet. Instead of beading at its toes, the blood seeps into the stone.

The statue swings open, leaving a gaping pit in the earth beneath.

I'm not sure what I'll find on the other side of this tunnel, not sure which Asha I'll find either.

The woman I'd seen the day of the wedding—she hadn't stood like Asha. Stiff-backed, with her chin high.

That had been weeks ago, and already it seems as if he's beaten her into submission, crushed the resolute spirit I've come to love.

THE TUNNEL LETS out behind an alcove in the South Wing, a relatively abandoned portion of the castle, which is a relief when the lot of us pile out of the hole.

The hall is empty. Quiet. There's something about it that casts an eerie feeling over our entire group.

If this goes wrong, it's likely we all die.

Even if it goes right, it's likely at least one of us will, anyway.

The realization settles over all of us and one by one, we exchange silent nods that might very well be goodbyes.

Then we sneak our way through the palace, hidden by the contoured shadows.

Down the hall, a fae clock ticks, reminding us our time is running out.

THE CURVES of the palace I grew up in are familiar as ever, and though Az has sworn my entire army into his service, he hasn't thought to change the guard postings, probably because they were well arranged already.

It gives us an advantage, as I know exactly which corners we have to be careful when rounding.

Blaise, Nox, and I fall into a casual rhythm. I grab the nearest soldier by the wrist from around the corner; the vampires sink their teeth into their neck, dousing their blood with paralytic venom.

Our goal is not to kill any of the guards. I'd rather they stand trial once I regain the kingdom, plead their case for pledging allegiance to Az. Besides, I don't know which ones stuck around to watch after Asha, and I don't want to inadvertently kill anyone who's helped her.

But if it comes down to them or her, I will.

The rest of the group pads behind quietly, Dinah the loudest with her human feet.

At one point, I hear her stifle a gasp as Fin swings her up into his arms to keep her feet from pounding so loudly against the marble floor.

The poor girl practically stops breathing.

I really am going to have to have a sit-down with him later.

It's slower progress than I'm eager for, but we reach what Dinah reports to be Az's quarters without a hitch.

The guards stationed outside his quarters would normally have been difficult to sneak up on, but it's already dark in the hallway, and Blaise's *paldihv* wedding dress cloaks her well enough.

We watch from the shadows as she sneaks up on the guards, grabs both of their wrists, and bites into them simultaneously before the guards even scream.

Nox is by her side in an instant, helping to lower the bodies to the ground without a sound.

The vampires motion for us to emerge, and we do.

Blaise and Nox part the way, and I step over the limp bodies of the guards before resting my hand on the doorknob.

I have to retract my hand, realizing it's shaking and liable to cause the metal doorknob to rattle. There's part of me that wants nothing more than to blow the door to smithereens, but now that there's only a door between me and Azrael's quarters, I'm paralyzed with dread at what I might find on the other side.

Does he take her to bed with him?

Will I open the door and find not just Azrael asleep, but my wife in his arms?

The thought itself blurs my vision, shooting pain through my temples.

It's then I feel a soft touch against my hand. I look down to find Blaise squeezing my hand, removing it from the doorknob, her stare communicating what is too dangerous to speak out loud.

Let me do this, she seems to tell me, and I find there's a gratefulness swelling in my heart.

Blaise rears back to kick down the door, but Lydia catches her by the shoulders, shaking her head then moving toward the doorknob, which she wraps her fingers around and melts off its handle.

Using two fingers, Lydia pushes the door open and beckons us into a room cloaked in shadows.

We're only in the room for a moment before Nox grabs me by the shoulder, quietly but firmly.

Panic floods through my chest as I realize why—his eyesight has adjusted faster than mine. I have to know what he sees, and also can't bear to know.

A moment later, my vision follows.

Focusing on a couple tangled underneath the sheets.

NOX'S HAND falters on my shoulder, and though at first I think he's letting me at Az, I'm mistaken.

A moment later, Blaise and Nox both have their grips on me. Nox from behind, Blaise from the front, holding me back.

Blaise shakes her head frantically but silently, her brown eyes wide with warning.

How dare she get between me and my wife?

I allow a bout of confusion to seep from my wrist where she

clutches me. It's enough to break free of her grip, and also Nox's, who goes to catch her as she stumbles to the side.

The steps I take are a blur, and then I'm at the bed, ripping the sheets from the man, terrified of what I might find underneath.

Two naked bodies lie tangled in bed.

My hand finds Az's throat, speckles of white peppering my vision.

He fights against my touch, but I don't care as I envelop him in fear, every bit of anguish I held back from Blaise bursting into the man who touched...who touched...

"Kiran, stop."

I barely register Fin's voice, his hand on my shoulder as my sense returns to me.

"It's not them. Kiran, it's not them."

I blink, and the faces of the two people in the bed come into focus.

The man writhing in my grasp. Not Az, but a male of similar build. Unfamiliar.

The woman beside him jolts upward, pulling the blanket to cover her chest.

She looks at me.

And before I can stop her.

She screams.

CHAPTER 100

ZORA

There's a moment before the stalactite spears Farin when I glimpse speckles of our life together.

Except, it's not this life—abandoned on this strange island for eternity, making the best of such an existence.

It's a dozen lives, blended together, overlapping, blurring the lines between this world and others.

But then there's the snap of Farin's bones, and the lives never meant for us fade away.

I have to battle the dizziness from where my head hit the cave wall, but I stagger over to Farin's body.

For a moment, I think he's dead, but then I catch sight of his chest, heaving barely. The stalactite juts from his shoulder, having narrowly missed his heart.

"Farin," I say, my voice frantic, but he doesn't respond. His mouth hangs slightly ajar. When he coughs, blood spews from his lips.

"No." My mind races, and I shuffle through lifetimes of memories, knowledge, searching for what I'm supposed to do. I fear removing the stalactite will only bolster the bleeding, but the cave is still trembling, and keeping him here only risks another stalactite falling on him.

I don't have time to think. I yank the stalactite from his shoulder, quickly wrapping my makeshift sail-blanket around my hand and using it to grab a stone from the border of smoldering fire. When I press it to his skin, he lets out a groan.

"Doesn't feel good, does it?" I say. The words come out biting, though I'm praying to the Fates he'll stay with me.

"You should be a healer with that bedside manner of yours, Wanderer," Farin mutters, and I let out a relieved gasp. At least he's conscious.

I drag him by his armpits out of the cave.

In the distance, smoke smolders at the top of the mountain in the center of the island.

"What," Farin says, his voice slurred, "is that?"

For a moment, I think perhaps Farin isn't as cognizant as I thought, but then it hits me. Farin describes the world from which he comes as having a flat landscape. Now that I consider it, I can't even remember enough about Alondria to know if he would have encountered any while living in Nox's head.

"That's a volcano," I explain, to which Farin frowns.

"A smoking mountain?"

"Yeah," I say, gulping. "Let's hope that's all it does."

AN HOUR LATER, soot begins to settle on the island flora, coating the leaves of the canopy overhead and mixing with the sand. That's fine with me. The more the ash settles, the easier it is to breathe.

I've found us a cave that doesn't have natural spears dangling from the ceiling, though that's going to be of little comfort if the volcano erupts again. If it spews out more than smoke this time.

I've managed to wrap Farin's wound in strips I tore from the sail, and so far that seems to have stopped the bleeding. For now. His speech has gone back to normal now that the initial shock of the wound has faded, but he's got this sparkle in his blue eyes that makes him look dazed. Almost innocent.

He catches me watching him, and his face breaks into a goofy, lopsided smile. "What is it, Wanderer? Swooning over the male who pushed you out of harm's way?"

I punch his unharmed shoulder, though lightly. "Don't flatter yourself," I say, though I hardly manage the teasing lilt I intended.

"I don't know. Seems like a fairly romantic gesture to me."

My eye twitches in response, and I avert my gaze, focusing on his wound. Already, blood has started to pool through the cloth. "We both know who you're saving the actual romance for," I say, and I'm surprised by the lack of envy in my voice.

Farin might be attracted to me, and I to him. He might even be telling the truth when he claims he has no interest in killing me. That doesn't change his reasoning for wanting to get back to Alondria.

"You jealous, Wanderer?" he asks, his chuckles broken up by the way he winces every time his chest moves.

I steady my voice. "No."

A smile brushes his soft lips. "Pity. I think I would have liked for you to be jealous over me."

The grunt I offer him is hardly an answer, but it's the best I've got.

Farin's voice is gentle. "Can I ask you a question?"

I nod, still refusing to look in his direction, to allow him to trap me with those stunning blue eyes of his. The memory of his lips on mine still burns into my skin, tempting me to slip back into a futureless daydream, a lie so easily slipped over my eyes.

"Why'd you bother pulling me from the cave? What's the point of tending to my wounds?"

I still.

"You tried to kill me only a few hours ago. I'm the one who needs you to get me off this island, not the other way around. Succumbing to a moment of passion, I can understand. This," he winces, lifting his uninjured arm to tap his wound dressing lightly. "This, I don't."

My mouth goes dry. "You can't understand fae decency? An innate respect for life?"

"No. Believe it or not, that I can understand. As I've told you, I wasn't always cruel. I remember a time when I felt compassion.

Earlier, with the man on the beach. It hurt me—considering what he had suffered. Seeing his body mangled and limp like that."

I snort. "Before or after you mutilated it?"

Farin frowns. "I already told you. I did that for you. So you wouldn't have to."

Pain constricts my chest, and I grab onto Farin's dressing and pull it tighter, partially to apply more pressure to the wound, partially because I know it'll hurt.

He winces, but there's amusement in his grimace. "Told you that you're jealous."

"There's nothing to be jealous about," I say.

"That, you're right about."

I bite my lip, my heart hammering, my mind whirring with how he must mean anything but what my heart so foolishly wishes he would mean.

But then Farin speaks, and his voice is so soft, so genuine, it's like he's a flame, and I'm the moth who knows better than to look, but simply can't help myself.

"I don't want Blaise."

The hairs on my arms stand on end, and I hate the way I flush at his words. Loathe how I've been hoping for those very words to escape his mouth. The loathing is what keeps the question lodged in my throat, keeps me from asking him why.

Instead, I consider his question from earlier. Why I can't seem to kill him, even to save myself. Why I dragged him out of the cave. Why I seared his wound to stop the bleeding.

"I guess," I say, choosing my words wisely, "I want to believe that monsters are worth saving. I guess I want to believe that the past is like the fae curse, that it doesn't make it through the Fabric. I want to believe that every time we start over in a new realm, we're washed clean of whatever happened before."

"And do you believe that?"

"It doesn't really matter what I believe," I say. Because as I look down at Farin, I realize that one way or another, if I don't get him off this island, he's going to die.

I'm not sure which way death will come, but on an island infested with giant scorpions and spiders, an island whose center is an active volcano, death will come for him one way or another.

And though I'm not confident that if I died in this world, I'd wake up in my true body, I can say for certain that Farin wouldn't.

He doesn't have a body to go back to.

"What was it like?" I ask.

He crinkles his brow. "What was what like?"

"Death?"

He doesn't hesitate. "Lonely."

That single word stirs something within me. Something I shouldn't have let fester, but now that I have, it feels too unwieldy for me to wrangle.

"What was it like?" he asks.

I offer him a soft smile. "What was what like?"

"Life?"

I open my mouth to answer, but the word gets caught in my throat.

THAT EVENING, as the volcano rumbles in the distance, looming our deaths over us, an idea comes to me.

When I tell Farin that it will involve returning to the canyon, within which lies the spot of the closed eyelet, I ask if he's willing to come along.

He just offers me a cocky grin and says, "Where you go, I go."

CHAPTER 101

BLAISE

*W*e realize too late that it's a trap.

Too easy. It was much too easy.

Sneaking through the palace, disarming the guards.

None of them saw us coming. No one put up a fight.

I reach the woman first, sinking my teeth into her wrist until a gentle numbness wafts over her, silencing her screams.

But it's too late.

There's no silencing the echo that cascades down the hall.

There's a moment when we all look at each other and realize we don't know what to do.

Not that it matters, because it was always going to end like this, anyway.

I know, because of the padding of paws, the slight scraping of talons against the marble floors outside.

The faint beating of wings just outside the window.

And a voice, the one that haunts my dreams, my consciousness, speaking from the shadows.

"Well, it's certainly nice to see the group of you have finally made amends."

Az steps from the shadows.

He knew we were coming.

Dinah and I exchange a look as the realization sweeps over me. She'd delivered the message to Asha. She'd only thought she hadn't been caught.

Dinah's face drains of color, even in the shadows.

Az snaps, and the sconces on the wall come to life.

My stomach flips.

He figured it out. Az figured out how to leech Kiran's power.

Az figured it out, and we're all as good as dead.

Kiran is the first to lunge, but a wall of fire erupts from the ground, suspended between Az and the former king, blocking his path. Az snaps again, his eyes glittering in the firelight.

Lydia tries next, but all it takes is a whistle from Az, and a mere launches through the door, tearing away the posts, fangs bared toward Elias's throat. He dodges well enough to avoid a killing blow, but the mere takes him out anyway. It swipes at his head hard enough that he clanks on the floor, head lolling to the side, unconscious with the beast bearing down on him.

Lydia makes to lunge for the beast, but Az clicks his tongue in warning. "I would remain still if I were you."

Lydia glances back and forth between Az and the beast, and I can see the calculations running through her mind.

She must doubt her speed, because she doesn't move, only scowls at Az through the fire.

"It's a shame you weren't here earlier, Kiran. You just missed Asha."

"Where is she?" Kiran growls.

Az gives him a look of derision. "Not here. Obviously."

"If you've hurt her…"

Az has the gall to actually appear infuriated by Kiran's insinuation. "Then I would have only done half of what you did to her. Picking away at her mind like you did. Do you have any idea how long it's taken me to get your claws out from underneath her skin?"

Kiran actually stills at that, though his breathing remains labored.

"I never used those powers on Asha. Not intentionally, and

certainly not without her permission. I never used them to change the way she felt about me."

Az scoffs. "So it's just time apart that has her feelings fading for you? That has her experiencing moments of clarity when she remembers it's me she wants. That it's always been me."

Nox turns toward me, a look of bewilderment on his face. I only just remember that I haven't caught him up on exactly how delusional Az has become. One look at Az tells me Piper and I were correct about our theory: he's been taking an elixir to avoid sleep. It's in the tremor of his hands, the strained tenor of his voice, the crazed glint of sage-green eyes that never rest.

I shake my head at Nox ever so slightly.

Fin surprises me when he's the next to speak. "Yes, it's always been you, and that's why you couldn't seem to get over her scars. Had 'things you needed to work through,' if I remember her account accurately."

Az turns to face Fin, his neck craning to the side in exaggerated pity. "Prince Phineas. Torn between the ghost of your late wife and your family, all of whom seem to forget who took her by the throat and snuffed the life out of her. Tell me, aren't you the tiniest bit glad that Kiran now understands a fraction of what it feels like to have your wife stolen from you?"

Nox tenses next to me, but it's nothing close to the tension going taut between Kiran and Fin. Kiran scans Fin's face for any sign that Az's accusations aren't true. But Fin has paled faster than any person I've ever seen, his cheeks a sheet of white, despite his naturally tanned skin.

"What? You're not going to deny it?" Az asks. "Oh, that's right. I forgot you fae are cursed with the inability to lie."

"You speak as though you're not the one who blackmailed Ophelia, the one whose plot ended up with her dead," Fin says through his teeth.

Az taps his fingers against his side. "Yes, but I'm not the one who touched her, am I? And as much as you'd love to hate me more than you hate him, you just can't quite burn the image out of your mind."

I don't know what I'm expecting, but it's not Dinah's voice, piping up for the first time. "Az, stop."

Az glances at his best friend's little sister, a softness overcoming his features that I've only ever seen him use when referring to Asha.

"Dinah, I know this family has taken you in over the past year. But you have to know, better than anyone, what they've done to Asha. She's changed in the time she's been with them. I know you know what I'm talking about. They took the Asha we knew and loved and replaced her with...with..."

"With someone who has enough self-respect not to fawn over the likes of you," Dinah says, each word carefully placed.

Az's eyes narrow.

"If you wanted me to support you, you probably shouldn't have kidnapped me and trapped me in a cave with a bunch of mercenaries," says Dinah.

"We both know I never would have let you come to harm."

Dinah, sweet, quiet little Dinah, scoffs.

"Though I suppose," Az says, his sage-green eyes sliding to Fin, "I can see why you feel the need to defend Fin's hatred of his brother, to change the subject. Does it remind you that you'll always be the second choice?"

Dinah and Fin both go still, but it's Lydia who speaks. "Are you going to get around to killing us, or do you have a few more souls you'd like to crush first?" She even has the audacity to sound bored.

"You're probably right." Az sighs dramatically, then turns, locking his eyes on me. "Thanks for bringing them to me, Blaise. I never would have known if it weren't for your message."

CHAPTER 102

NOX

I watch faces turn toward Blaise, Az's words replaying in my head, threatening to undo me.

He thanked her.

This monster thanked her.

"You. You tricked me." It's Dinah speaking now, her voice trembling with what I first think is despair, but now recognize as anger. The type of anger that usually gets pent up for years before truly revealing itself.

Blaise refuses to look at Dinah. Instead, she keeps her neck long, barely breathing as she looks at Az.

"I thought you might need my help one of these days," says Az, a smile staining his lips that I'd like to wipe right off of him.

"Blaise." My mate's name escapes my mouth, almost involuntarily.

The way she shakes her head is almost imperceptible in the dim torchlight.

Almost.

"I assume this is payment enough," she says, refusing to look at her friends.

Dinah's weeping now, mumbling something about her sister. Lydia curses under her breath. Fin still looks stunned from his heart being borne out for all to hear, but he wraps an arm around Dinah all the same, pulling her into his chest while she cries.

All of this, I keep track of with my peripheral senses.

But it's Kiran who I have my eyes locked on.

Because he's pinning Blaise with his stare.

I've never seen an expression so cold.

His muscles are tensed, ready to pounce, and I can see his fingers flexing, itching to tear my wife apart.

That's not going to happen.

I don't let myself consider what she's done. She has an explanation, I assure myself. She has a reason she's doing this.

"So much for the two of us understanding each other," Kiran says.

Blaise turns and looks at him, just long enough. "We both know you would have done the same to me if the situations were reversed. Or have you forgotten the way my heart felt in your hands when you almost ripped it from my chest?"

A shadow falls across Kiran's face, but Blaise isn't done. "What you made me feel, what you made me experience down in that cellar, what you made me remember—I knew then you'd never forgive me. That you'd never forget what I'd done to Asha in betraying her." Blaise turns her head to Dinah. "I'm sorry, Dinah. I truly am."

Then she turns back to Az, who says, "I would say that's quite sufficient. I'm assuming you want the curse on your lover removed."

I stiffen. No. "Blaise, we don't need—"

But Az interrupts me. "I know how it feels. To know you deserve a certain level of love, only to have magic take it away from you. I can't force Asha's magic to do anything, you know that as well as I do, but I'll ask her to convince it on your behalf."

Blaise lets out an exhale, slow and steady, visible relief loosening her shoulder blades.

The sight has a knife slicing through my heart.

I thought Blaise and I had shared everything. Our blood, our vows, our bodies, but now as I stare at the woman I love, the woman I'd rip apart the Fabric between realms for, there's a part of me that wonders if she can't help but hold some things back.

"Then I assume we're done here," Blaise says, her voice utterly devoid of emotion.

Az gives her a smile that reminds me of a serpent. "Take your lover and go. You won't be hearing from me again."

"And if the Old Magic needs us present to remove the curse?" Blaise asks.

Az's lip twitches. "If it's not gone in a mooncycle, you know where to find me."

Blaise nods, flinching as Dinah spits at her, Fin holding Asha's sister in his arms as she fights against him, lunging for Blaise.

Blaise stares at the girl for a moment, then looks up at me, pleading, sorrow filling those beautiful brown eyes of hers.

What have you done? I want to ask her. *And why, why was my promise not enough?*

She's holding her breath when she brushes past me and toward the door, where the mere guarding it steps out of her way at a simple tick of Az's head.

My feet stay planted for a second longer as I examine the broken people left in the room, the friends Blaise has betrayed time and time again.

Bitterness leeches any affection in their expressions as they watch her.

As they watch Blaise ruin herself for me.

Again.

But then something Blaise whispered to me right before we departed Bezzie's runs through my mind.

I know you love me, Nox. But can you trust me?

I'd promised her I did, and though my promise might not count for much as a vampire, it counts because it comes from me.

As long as it's you, I whisper back to her in my mind, and then I follow my wife out into the hall.

· · ·

601

WE'RE HALFWAY through the palace, mere and guards parting for us at Az's silent command, before Blaise turns the corner, then drags me into a small alcove.

"Did you really betray them?" I whisper, the words escaping my tongue, let loose by the irritation and anger swelling up within me.

She looks up at me with those big brown eyes of hers, her body pressed up to me in this small alcove, and breathes, "Yes."

My heart stumbles, and the world spins around me.

"Blaise—"

"No. I betrayed them, but not like they think."

My ears perk at that, my heart and my hopes lagging, but slowly catching up.

"Blaise, what did you do?"

She lets out a steady exhale, leaning her head back against the stone alcove, exposing her long neck, the blood at her jaw thrumming.

The sight has my heart racing. I blink my attention away and back to her.

"I might have taken a risk—I'll explain in a bit—but something must have gone wrong. I had to improvise, figure out a way for us to get away from Az so we could find Asha. I got lucky, Az thinking I meant for him to intercept the message I sent her."

I frown. "Why didn't you tell me?"

"I needed you to look shocked in case things went wrong." She blinks away what looks to be tears and shrugs. "So far, it's worked beautifully."

Guilt instantly stabs me in the chest for doubting Blaise, but then she teasingly jabs me in the shoulder. "Nah, I deserve a healthy dose of skepticism, even from you. You don't just come back from betraying the entire world without having the people closest to you question you every once in a while."

"Blaise, what did you—"

There's a scuffle in the hallway, shouts echoing through the chamber. Soldiers sound out alerts of an invasion.

Blaise and I exchange confused looks, both craning to listen.

"Alert the emperor. The King of Dwellen's army approaches. They're readying for an attack."

I glance down at my wife, whose eyes have gone wide with a series of emotions I can't seem to decipher at the moment.

"Evander," she whispers, her voice dripping with horror. "No."

"They're not prepared," she starts muttering to herself. "The mere, they're too strong. And the wyverns...their venom..."

I take Blaise by the shoulders, cupping her chin up to look at me.

"Just tell me how we help him," I say.

Her eyes clear, a plan formulating in that crafty mind of hers.

She looks as if she's about to tell me that very plan when the roof collapses, spraying morning's sunlight down upon me in a flurry of excruciating flames.

EVERYTHING IS BURNING.

I'm burning.

I'm back on the island, drowning in the fervor of the waves, saltwater soaking my lungs, except this time it's not water.

It's fire. Scorching, blazing fire, ripping me apart from the inside out.

I'm dying, and for some cruel reason, it's Farin's voice I hear, rattling unwanted in my skull. *Don't be frightened of death. It's dark and lonely for beings like you and me, but you're a fool if you believe the Fates forget about us. Stay interesting enough, and they might just weave you back into the story.*

Faintly above, I hear the echo of a roar, a scream, and then my name, over and over again.

"Nox, Nox, no. Not again not again not again. No. No, I can't lose you. Nox, please."

Blaise is begging me not to go, but the fire is feeding on me like the withering wick of a candle. I want to scream at her that I'd like to stay, that I wish we had more time, but my throat is burning.

Arms wrap around me, dragging me across the slick floor, out of the heavy rays.

Immediately, my skin starts knitting itself back together, a pain altogether worse than the burning itself. I force open my eyes and find the source of the hole in the ceiling that almost ended me.

Above us perches a wyvern, its silver scales glistening in the heat of the Naenden sun. Around us is light, reflecting off its shimmering scales, off the stark white marble of the palace.

It's beautiful, and also deadly.

"You need to run," I tell Blaise, my throat still dry despite the fact that it's healing.

"No, no. I can't leave you like this." She's shaking, grabbing onto me and pulling my back into her chest.

"I'm already healing," I say, but it's no use. It's not as if I'm going to fool Blaise into thinking I'm not defenseless should more of the ceiling cave in, exposing me to the sunlight even in the alcove she's dragged me into.

Blaise ignores me, so I try again. "You're the one wearing *paldihv*. You can still help your friends."

Blaise stills at that, and I know I've got her.

Guilt punctures my conscience for using her friends as a means to get Blaise out of here, hopefully to safety, but I can't bring myself to regret it.

Until Blaise grabs my hands, then drags them up to her face, tucking my fingers underneath her chin while another rests at the base of her skull.

"What are you do—"

A sickening crack as Blaise yanks my hands up and to the side.

A thud as Blaise's body slumps behind me.

No.

I'm still dizzy from burning, but I manage to turn around in the alcove, cupping Blaise's lifeless face as it lolls to the side. I'm back in the dungeon, cracking Blaise's neck at the force of a command I couldn't even remember until that very second.

No, no, no.

But Blaise's curse will heal her, I remind myself, digging my fingers into my knees. She'll wake up any moment now.

But why—

The shadows of the *paldihv* unfurl themselves from her face, seeping into my skin.

Oh. Oh, Blaise.

I grab her hands, intent on doing the same thing to her that she did to me, giving the *paldihv* back.

But then the wyvern shrieks, thrashing as it lands on the floor across from the alcove.

I only have time to guard Blaise's limp body with my own as it spears its barbed tail at us, skewering me through my stomach.

CHAPTER 103

EVANDER

*O*rion and I cut through the colonnades of the palace. It wasn't difficult to get in, given a wyvern had already smashed through one of the marble domes.

I can't imagine that was part of Azrael's plan.

Ellie and her father managed to rally the entire art district into forging weapons and armor that might stand a chance against the Others.

We've yet to test them.

Don't get me wrong, I'm confident in my wife's genius, but it would have been nice if we'd had time to put them through a few trials.

Oh well.

I left my wife and daughter home in Othian. I intend for this to be the last time I do that.

As we race through the palace, Orion and I fight back to back. Summoning plant life is difficult in Naenden, where the sun licks the moisture out of the air, causing my magic to groan inside of me. Getting it to function is like prodding an adolescent to get out of bed in the morning.

Still, we manage, though we quickly find that summoning succulents takes far less effort and produces much more efficient results. Spindled plants are rather effective in fighting Others.

We've just cut through the central portion of the palace, ichor already staining our enameled armor, when we spot her.

She's standing. Rather, lounging, in the middle of the palace garden, garbed in pajamas, flicking her wrist lazily as trees spring from the ground and spear through a host of attacking Others. Some trees have even sprouted high and fast enough to spear wyverns in midair.

Orion and I look at our vines, which to be honest, we were quite proud of only minutes earlier.

"Is it possible to love someone, and utterly hate them at the same time?" I ask, staring at my sister, Olwen. She yawns before snapping her fingers and producing a flytrap plant, which subsequently snaps the head off an oncoming wyvern.

"Well, it seems like she's got the gardens covered," says Orion, who frankly looks a tad relieved, when up above us a pair of servants scream.

He sprints for the steps, and I turn toward my estranged sister.

A mere jumps out in front of me, but I slash through it with ease. Moments later, I find myself fighting alongside my sister in the garden.

"Evander?" Olwen asks, voice dripping with what sounds less like sibling rivalry and more like simple derision. "What are you doing here?"

She prances off the bench, looking a bit like a ballerina as she does. Behind her shoots a stream of wooden arrows that pierces the beasts in the sky.

What a showoff.

I instantly regret the decision to come out here.

"Helping," I say, sending my own thorns twisting around the neck of a mere.

Olwen allows the edges of her lips to droop at the same time her eyebrows raise. It's the kind of expression made when someone you previously considered an imbecile does something mirroring that of someone with average intelligence.

"You've been practicing your magic. I told you that you might need it someday."

"Twelve seconds," I say, to which she raises an eyebrow.

"Twelve seconds for you to say the words 'I told you' in succession."

Her eyes don't participate in her grin. "So what? Did Father send you to die in his stead? I hear he likes that wife of yours well enough to be content to name her heir over either of us."

My throat tightens. She doesn't know. "Father didn't send me. I came of my own accord."

Olwen peers out beyond a shattered portion of the garden wall and into the desert plains, where Dwellen's army still marches on the city. "And you took his army with you? Well, I might become his favorite one of these days, after all."

"Father's dead, Olwen."

If I wasn't watching for it, I might have missed the shock that flickers across Olwen's otherwise bored features. "How?"

"Wyvern," I say, not really wishing to relive the moment.

"Hm," she says, as if told her that lip rings were now in fashion and not that our father had been slaughtered.

Before I can say as much, a formation of a half dozen wyverns swoop from the sky, nosediving directly toward us.

Olwen, of course, sends trunks skewering five of them, sparing the one nose-diving for me.

Thankfully, magic really is easier here in the gardens, though the plants are already beginning to wilt now that the climate-controlled magic barrier has been broken.

Still, when I call, the plants answer, piercing the wyvern's wings before dragging it to the ground. I spear it through its chest.

"You know," I say to Olwen, wiping the blunt edge of my blade on my trousers, "some would consider refusing to protect your king treason."

Olwen humphs. "Good thing I've already withdrawn my citizenship, then."

I roll my eyes, but then someone else comes running around the corner of a hedge, a tall male with brown hair and tanned skin who's vaguely familiar.

Olwen pierces an overhead wyvern with a jagged trunk before prancing over to the male, jumping into his arms, and planting a kiss on his cheek.

"Quill, Evander. Evander, Quill," she says.

Ah. Desidarius Quill. Olwen's old school rival.

I point the blade of my sword between the two of them. "Don't the two of you hate each other or something?"

Before my little sister can explain how she's gone from writing hate poems about this male over Solstice break to planting a kiss on his cheek, something shrieks overhead.

"Does that one seem bigger than the rest to you?" asks Quill, who sets Olwen down gently and stares at the massive wyvern above us.

The creature cranes its neck, sniffing at the wyvern carcasses Olwen and I slaughtered.

Then it bellows in rage. I have just enough time to throw my silver-coated shield over the three of us, as the wyvern sprays a pillar of flames into the sky and showers streams of acid down upon us.

The acid sizzles as it hits the shield.

But Ellie's creation holds.

Olwen coughs through the smoke. "Is it just me, or do we think that's the creatures' mother?"

CHAPTER 104

BLAISE

*W*hen I wake, Nox is gone.

So is the wyvern.

I stretch out my neck, groaning, even as panic races through me.

Shadows no longer lick eagerly around my limbs, meaning it must have worked. The *paldihv* must have joined itself to Nox.

I find what relief I can in that, considering he's gone.

When I scramble out of the alcove, careful to avoid the streams of sunlight that burst through the scattered holes in the ceiling, I can't help but cry on the inside.

Nox is gone, the voice inside my head tells me. Except it's not my voice at all, but the parasite's, whispering to me through the adamant box strapped to my belt.

The wyvern skewered him straight through his beautiful abdominals. Took him off on a ride. I do wonder where it will drop him. Perhaps it'll make a meal out of him instead.

Nausea rolls inside me, but I push the parasite's voice out of my head.

A liar, that's what she is.

But if it's not true, then where is Nox, and why would he have abandoned me?

I shake my head, reminding myself that he probably ran off to lure the wyvern away.

That's likely what happened.

That has to be what happened.

And you call me the liar, whispers the parasite, *when you're so proficient at lying to yourself. There's no need for me to even try. You'd only outdo me.*

I push it away, running through the halls, frantically searching. For who, I'm not sure. Nox? Asha? Kiran? Evander?

Evander.

He's going to die here today, and it's all my fault.

I'm going to have single-handedly wiped his name from the face of Alondria.

My footsteps pad against the ground, but I find they have no direction.

This is my fault, I realize, when another part of the roof collapses, a huddle of servants screaming out in terror as it comes crumbling atop them.

I race for them, grabbing one from the path of the oncoming ceiling, but she's screaming, screaming out for her husband, who I was too slow to save as the falling stone crushes him.

The servant screams, clawing at my neck, cursing me for saving her and leaving her husband to die.

There's a faint buzzing in my ears.

And something else.

The sound of a voice it's taking me a second to recognize.

Because it's the voice of a male shouting orders. The voice of one who protects.

The voice of a king.

I follow the voice down the hall, as if in a trance, and then I see him from the shadows where I lurk. Down, lower than the balcony, is a garden.

And in the garden is Evander.

He's arrayed like royalty, bearing the blue of Dwellen on his armor, which glistens in the sunlight, coated with a material I don't recognize.

A female stands beside him, and it takes me a moment to recognize Princess Olwen.

There's a male fighting in rhythm with Olwen, as if their tree limbs are simply extensions of one another.

I can't see the wyvern they fight from this angle, but I hear it shrieking down at the fae who fight at it from below.

I'm suspended in time as I watch him. The male who looks like Andy, but isn't. There's something about him that's changed on an innate level, something about him that's so unfamiliar, it's painful to watch.

Painful, but also beautiful.

I realize Andy has grown into himself. That I wasn't there to witness it.

There's a strength in him I don't recognize; never have I felt so disconnected.

I watch him fight. Watch him defend as I'm helpless to lend him assistance as I hide in the shadows.

I realize then what must have changed him.

Ellie's cries pierce my ears and make me want to scream.

There'd been no news on Evander's child.

No one had heard what had become of the baby.

It's changed me, and now it's changed him, except it's all my fault, and I don't even deserve to share the load of his pain.

The pain I caused.

Evander turns to look at me.

Well, it's probably not that he's looking at me. More that he's looking to the side, having glimpsed a ghost in the corner of his vision.

But his eyes settle on me. Then widen.

The shadow of the sun has crept closer on the balcony, burning my fingertips.

I step back into the shadows, panic surging through me.

Evander opens his mouth, and I scream, but it's too late. The tail of the wyvern comes crashing down into his side, sending him soaring, Olwen shouting his name.

No. No, no, no.

Always getting in the way, always ruining his life, whispers the parasite.

My hand comes to my mouth as I watch Evander's body slam against the stone garden wall.

No.

I run for him, but my skin hisses in protest as I hit the wall of sunlight.

My *paldihv*. Nox has the *paldihv*.

You made your choice, silly servant girl. Did you really think you could save them both?

The wyvern slams Evander against the wall again, and this time I hear something crack. It reverberates in my skull, deafening.

No. No, no, no.

I could help you, whispers the parasite. *Or you can stand here and watch him die. Your choice, I suppose.*

But I'm not taking any of those choices.

Instead, I do what I'm best at.

I shirk into the shadows and hide from that which frightens me most.

CHAPTER 105

BLAISE

I listen from the shadowed colonnades as the wyvern rips the palace to pieces.

The worst part is realizing there's nothing I can do.

I can hear Olwen from here, calling out orders to Evander's soldiers. Screaming her brother's name as she fights back the wyvern.

I can hear her thorns slashing at its tail as it beats Evander into the wall.

My heart aches.

Everything aches.

My friend is out there. My friend who I've made my enemy, and it doesn't matter that in the weeks since I've seen him, Evander has grown into his place as a king.

Andy is going to die out there. He's going to leave Ellie with nothing, a bereaved mother and wife, and there's nothing I can do.

His blood will be on my hands, the same as his child's, when this Other slays him.

We could help him, you know, whispers a voice from the darkness, a voice that makes my skin crawl with dread.

The voice slithers from the pocket inside my robes, the one just above my chest. *We could save Andy. It's what we both want.*

"No," I whisper. "I'm done letting you make my decisions for me."

You know it would work. I can still feel it, that desperation to be someone else. It leaks off of you, more potent than it's ever been. It has been since you betrayed your friends, since you realized what you'd done to your friend's child. You desire nothing more than to be anything other than yourself. With my help, you could transform into anyone you want. It would be so easy. Like telling your fingers to curve. Like willing your lungs to take a breath. Let me in, and you'll never have to hide from the sun again. Think of what we could transform into together. Something larger, grander than the others. I could make you a savior, Blaise.

"No, you'd take my body and run. I know you," I whisper.

You do. Which means you know how I crave the prince. How I would never let him suffer. You might have forgotten about the princeling the first moment a new set of eyes swiveled in your direction, but I am not so fickle. I do not wish the prince to perish. In this, you can be confident. I will not allow him to die.

I shake my head, fear welling inside my chest. Outside, a soldier shrieks. The noise is quickly silenced, coupled with the crunching of bones.

You know I am speaking the truth, it says.

The adamant box buzzes at my chest.

The darkness of the closet threatens to swallow me. And I'm back in the pantry with Derek, back to that sinking feeling of dread and not knowing how to say no.

"No," I cry, harsh and bitter.

Salty tears run down my cheek, coating my lips and stinging my eyes.

"No," I whisper.

You know it is the only way to save him.

"No." I'm sobbing now, fear drowning me. "You'll take me, and you'll never give me back."

I won't. I will take your body and use it for whatever I desire. It will be mine, and you will vanish from existence. Except for maybe the times I choose to allow you to exist, the times I choose to let you experience what I'm doing with your body. But your friend will live, Blaise. Or do you value your life over his? I can't say I'll be surprised if you refuse. You always have been a selfish little whore.

"No," I say again, but my voice is weak now, warbling. "No, please. Please."

Who are you begging, child? Tell me it's not the Fates. They turned their ears away from you long ago.

Sweat drips down my forehead, mingling with my tears. It's so, so dark. The closet feels as if it's closing in on me, the walls crushing my limbs. He's in here with me, touching me, pulling at my trousers, whispering to me...

Your shame, child. I know you believe me incapable of such an emotion, but it makes me pity you. I know you fear me, but just think. It could be better this way. You would be gone, erased from existence. Far, far away, where that shame that tortures you would never reach you. Doesn't that sound better?

Shame.

I hear Piper's voice in my mind.

What is the antidote for shame, Blaise?

Pride, I'd said in the moment, knowing that to be the wrong answer as soon as it fled my mouth.

I didn't know the answer then, and I don't know now, and I suppose I never will.

Because outside, the wyvern roars, and I hear it when Evander hits the ground. I feel it in the rumbling of stone when the wyvern approaches him, rearing back for the kill.

I don't know what the antidote for shame is when I burst from the safety of the shadows.

I don't know what the antidote for shame is when I unfasten the latch of the adamant box at my belt.

I don't know it until I cry out to Evander, and he turns his head to me. And in the moment before my friend is convinced he's about to die, I witness not an enemy, not the disgust I anticipate, but the warmth of a friend.

Evander's eyes welcome me, the same as the day Clarissa dropped me off at the castle years ago.

It's at that moment I understand the answer. I understand the antidote to shame.

I mouth something to him, and for a moment, I think there's no way he'll see it, but he swallows and nods all the same.

The parasite lets out a wicked laugh.

And then, for the first time in a long, long while, I step into the light.

CHAPTER 106

THE PARASITE

The parasite curls herself around the dark crevices of Blaise's mind, swimming through the current of this pitiful girl's soul.

The parasite has had a difficult time admitting it to herself, but now that she's regained Blaise's body, she can finally accept she's missed Blaise.

She's missed that intoxicating desperation, that pungent shame that consumes Blaise's inner being. As much as the parasite detested being bound by the curse of the full moon, she had savored the moments she'd been allowed control over Blaise's body.

The girl is just so…easy.

So easy, the girl doesn't even realize it about herself. It's been a pattern in the girl's life, starting with how she let her stepsister convince her that her menstruation was simply a prank, a curse purchased from Madame LeFleur's shop. Then there had been Derek, who (the parasite judges from rifling through Blaise's memories) hadn't needed very many folds on his brain to coax the stupid child into the pantry with him. Then there was Madame LeFleur, and even that dreadful Azrael character. The parasite has been forced to gather information on him from eavesdropping on Blaise's memories of conversations with the other infested girl; the one-eyed queen infested with the parasite's most naïve of siblings.

Blaise has spent her whole life under the impression that she is obstinate, stubborn, a force to be reckoned with. The parasite chuckles at the very idea, when all a person has to do is tug on the shame that seeps from Blaise's very being. It's like a bit in the foolish girl's mouth.

It's the same shame Derek used to keep her from voicing her fears —shame over the pain she'd caused her dying father in spoon-feeding him food his body could not handle. The same shame Clarissa reinforced when she locked Blaise away for the better half of the year to conceal her pregnancy. The parasite assumes Azrael used a similar technique, planting doubt in Blaise's mind about whether she could trust her friends with her secrets, her needs.

Oh, how the parasite is looking forward to taking ahold of that shame, to bending Blaise's body to her will.

Perhaps she'll use it to transform into a glorious female warrior. Use it to slay the wyvern and save the prince, then settle into her preferred form.

It won't take her long to steal the prince's heart. Before she'd been limited by the time constraint of the full moon, the only reason Ellie Payne had an advantage in stealing the prince's attentions.

Oh, yes. The parasite is looking forward to the rest of eternity.

The parasite reaches for Blaise's shame, looking forward to its familiar, dark caress.

The parasite's claws slip through thin air.

She flits around, wondering if perhaps she's misremembering where Blaise keeps her shame. She knows it was here. It was rolling off Blaise in intoxicating swells only moments ago.

But as the parasite rifles through the crevices of Blaise's mind, there is no shame, no desperation to be found.

Which is unfortunate for the parasite, as it leaves her without a handhold to grab onto when Blaise wrestles for control of her own mind.

The parasite doesn't understand, can't understand.

No, no, no. This isn't supposed to happen. The shame, the desperation—they have to be around here somewhere.

And then the parasite finds it—the desperation. At least that has been left behind, even if the shame somehow vanished. But as the parasite tries to clasp hold of it, she finds her grasp slips. Because while the shame has vanished, the desperation has transformed from something rough and prickly and easy to grasp, to something hot and slick as an iron brand.

That's not for you to use anymore, says a voice, one that sounds like Blaise, but…different somehow.

That is a ridiculous notion. Of course it can be used.

It's not for me to use anymore either. I'm giving it to my friends, Blaise's voice says, though the parasite has no idea how the girl expects to give her desperation to her friends. Stupid girl.

The parasite scrambles around, assuring herself that the shame can't have simply vanished. It has to be around here somewhere, and when she finds it, she will regain control.

Tell me, what's the antidote for shame, Cindy?

The parasite scowls at the nickname that soils her beautiful name. Cinderella is what she wants to be called. A beautiful name for a beautiful form. It belongs to her. As does Blaise.

You don't know, do you?

The parasite does not.

Perhaps that's why, when Blaise reaches for it, the parasite is not quick enough.

Perhaps that's why the parasite, much like its siblings before it, is too late to stop Blaise from absorbing her.

CHAPTER 107

EVANDER

"Come for me, all right?"

That was what Blaise mouthed to me just a moment before the inky shadows swarmed her face, and Blaise stepped into the light.

It only took that moment for me to realize that was all Blaise had ever wanted from me. Locked up in that wretched attic—for me to burst through the doors and come for her. Strapped to a dais in the dungeons of Mystral—for me to burst through the cell bars and come for her.

I didn't think before I nodded yes. Didn't need to.

Because when she opened the adamant box at her side, fear and determination engulfing her expression, I knew what she'd just released.

And in that moment, I decided I'd rip that parasite out of her myself if I had to.

And then Blaise had given herself over to it.

Or, at least, that's what I thought she was doing.

But when Blaise falls from the balcony and hits the ground, she changes, and it isn't into Cinderella or really anything I would have expected from the parasite.

There's a flash, bold enough to stun even the wyvern's attention. Something tugs at the back of my mind, reminding me that perhaps it would be best to slay the wyvern while it is distracted.

It takes effort, but I rip my eyes away from Blaise long enough to scale the length of the wyvern's wing. It realizes what I'm trying to do, but not soon enough. As soon as it whips its head back toward me, I use the opportunity to trap it with a cluster of thorny vines and slash my sword through its neck.

There's a great cry, one that pierces my ears and rumbles the entirety of the colonnade. And then the wyvern's head falls, soaking the ground in dark ichor.

Not a moment later, the body of the wyvern slumps too, launching me into the air. My feet find solid ground, and I run for Blaise, my mind whirring with how in Alondria I plan to help her rid herself of the parasite.

But I'll do it.

I will come for her.

I won't fail Blaise again.

Won't leave Blaise alone, locked up in a dark pantry, a dank attic, again.

I promised to come for her, and I'll hold to that promise.

But when I come upon Blaise, her form isn't at all what I expect. Around Blaise's body is a silvery orb that reflects the light of the sun.

And within the orb, Blaise changes.

The first image is that of a child, the Blaise I remember from when she was barely twelve. That Blaise is crying, scrubbing her long black hair full of tangles in a crusty sink, clumps of debris staining the water gray.

Within the image is a man. His gaze snakes over Blaise's childish form as if she were the prominent lady in a renowned brothel, for whom he'd just paid good money.

My gut turns over, but then there's Blaise again. Except this time she's older, the Blaise I knew before she Turned. Her shadow over-comes that of the man's, and she steps between him and the child. Then she produces a comb from her pocket, allowing her childhood self to sit in her lap as she brushes the tangles out of her hair, all the while holding the crying girl.

As quickly as it appeared, the image shifts, revealing this time a girl curled up in the shadows. Sacks of flour and sugar are stacked on the pantry shelves behind her. This time, the girl isn't crying. Instead, she lies there, a stunned expression on her youthful face. Her eyes blink rapidly, as if she thinks maybe she should be producing tears, but for some reason can't.

My stomach turns over again as young Blaise fiddles with the string at her waistband.

But then the older Blaise appears, again scooping the girl into her lap. She brushes her hair from her face and holds her younger self close. Faint whispers from the older Blaise to her younger self echo, but I can't make out what she's saying.

Only that the stunned little girl is now sobbing, shaking and trembling in her older self's arms.

There's a shift, then younger Blaise is in a small cot in a dingy attic, passed out as Clarissa and the midwife exchange frantic whispers. There's a bundle in the midwife's hand, one she refuses to hand to Clarissa no matter how much the woman insists.

But this image isn't true, because the younger Blaise wakes up, the haze over her eyes clearing as she asks the midwife if she can hold her child.

The midwife responds, but the words are too muffled to hear.

Blaise's already blood-drained face turns pale.

And then she screams, thrashing and writhing in bed. The sight makes me want to be sick. Older Blaise appears, shooing Clarissa from the room as she peers down with somber eyes at the swaddled baby in the midwife's arms.

Then she crawls into bed with the younger girl and holds her tightly as she screams.

The image swirls again, warping into the facade of the main strip in Othian. A bell rings over Madame LeFleur's shop, and into it shuffles Blaise, looking less confident than I've ever seen her, now that there's no one around for her to convince otherwise. Madame

LeFleur hunches over a piece of parchment. She doesn't bother to look up as she opens her mouth to call to the girl, but she's interrupted by a newcomer who slips into the shop.

The image changes.

Blaise coated in Ellie's blood. Blaise helping herself clean it.

Blaise murdering Clarissa. Blaise wiping the hair from her younger self's neck and holding her.

The next to appear is the image I've been dreading the most. Because it's me in the image, my expression wrought with agony as I scream at Blaise. As I tell her she's worthless. That I'm done with her.

The blood leeches from my face as I hear my words. How they sounded to her ears.

Blaise backs away, her entire body trembling, and I search the image for the slightly older version of herself. It takes me a moment, but I find her hiding and watching from beyond the trees.

I wait for her to reveal herself, to comfort the trembling girl, who it's so easy to see now is crushed, broken, but the older Blaise's face is set on Ellie.

My stomach turns over as I watch the scene play out, except it's not real, not a memory or a reflection of the past, but a conjuring of Blaise's mind, of what she assumes happened that night.

The labor happens faster than it should, and something instinctual warns me to avert my eyes as Amity pulls Cecilia from the womb.

Amity's voice warbles, her throat caught because she's just a child, a child who doesn't know how to tell parents their child is dead.

My heart breaks in half as the realization washes over me.

"No," I tell Blaise, though I'm not certain she can hear me. "No, Blaise, that's not what happened. Our baby lived. Her name is Cecilia, and she's beautiful and healthy and…"

My voice catches in my throat, because although I can't bring myself to watch the scene playing out between me and Ellie, my attention swerves to the older Blaise, observing her younger self from the trees.

"Go to her," I whisper. "Like you did all the other times."

But she doesn't. She just watches her younger self shake, barely holding herself up by a nearby tree.

The older Blaise glances at my family, then takes a step back into the shadows.

"No. No, Blaise. It's not real. It's not true. Cecilia lived," I tell her, my voice cracking with desperation as I call out to her. I go to grab her shoulders, to shake her until she listens to me, but my hands meet what might as well be iron when they slam at the orb surrounding her.

Sorrow pierces me as I watch Blaise walk away from herself, and my heart falls as I press my forehead to the glass.

"Blaise, I forgive you," I whisper to her. "I forgive you, and Ellie forgives you. We all forgive you."

I open my eyes, hesitantly, sure Blaise can't hear me, but I watch as the older Blaise appears, half of her face emerging from the shadows. She frowns as she watches her younger self with distaste.

The image shifts again.

And this time, it's another image I recognize. It's the day Blaise first returned to the palace, this time as a hired servant. I remember it well and watch as I look down on the child with a grin.

I remember how she beamed at me that day. I remember asking if she was happy to see me.

I'd been so worried about her during the time I hadn't heard from her, so eager to be convinced everything was fine when she'd arrived at the palace with that contagious grin on her face.

Knowing what I do now, that smile breaks my heart.

Blaise has been acting longer than I ever realized.

Something strange happens, and the older Blaise steps into the corridor. She pushes past Clarissa as if the babbling woman isn't even there.

Blaise kneels down next to her younger self and takes her by the hand. "You can tell him what happened to you. About Derek and the baby."

The smile remains plastered on the younger Blaise's face, and now she's whispering through her teeth. "I should have known better than to get myself in trouble. If I tell him, he'll know it was all my fault."

"It's not your fault what happened to you."

"But then he'll think I'm just a little girl."

The older Blaise brushes a hair from her younger self's forehead. "You are just a little girl. That's how he's supposed to see you. I know you're confused right now because of how Derek treated you, but Evander cares about you. He loves you like a little sister, and he wants to protect you. He can help you."

Something cracks in the younger Blaise's façade. "What if he thinks I'm gross?"

The older Blaise's throat bobs. When she speaks, her voice is hoarse but steady. "What's the cure for shame?"

The child shakes her head. "I don't know. Not caring what anyone thinks about you? Being proud of yourself?"

"That's what I used to think too. But pride's a funny thing. It makes us want to bury our problems, hide them where no one will find them. Otherwise, those we love might finally see us for who we truly are."

The child Blaise shudders.

"I know you're worried that he'll think less of you," says the older Blaise. "But that's your shame lying to you. It doesn't want you to trust him because if you do, and he still loves you, your shame worries that you might not need it anymore."

Tears stream down the little girl's cheeks. I'm vaguely aware that they're mirrored on my own.

"Trust?" she asks.

The older Blaise smiles.

A shift, and now it's Blaise, older, walking into the room with me and Ellie. She cries, telling me of what she's done, of a trip to Madame LeFleur's and a curse she can't seem to break. And now she's in the bed, the night after we discovered her with Clarissa's dead body, and she bites her lip, then tells me of Nox, the male she fell in love with during captivity.

Another shift, and we're back to the forest, and though the scene hasn't changed, and though in this reality of Blaise's my child has passed from under the sun, the older Blaise steps from the shadows, and takes her weeping self in her arms.

"I forgive you," she whispers to herself.

And when it's all over, and the orb dissipates, all that is left, is simply Blaise.

CHAPTER 108

KIRAN

"*T*ell me, Kiran. Would you like to see her one last time?"

Az's voice rings in my mind, still muddled with the residual anguish of believing I'd found him in bed with Asha. Of the realization we'd been trapped. Of Blaise's betrayal I should have seen coming.

I'm going to rip that girl's throat out if I ever get ahold of her.

Azrael's words ring in my head once again.

Would you like to see her one last time?

More than anything, though I don't know if I can bear it. Bear to see if he's broken her.

But my heart belongs to her, so I agree.

THE THRONE ROOM has been renovated since I was last here. Asha and I never had much use for it, preferring to handle foreign relations at the dinner table, with piles of aromatic foods paving the way for collaboration.

Asha always said the food made me seem softer. I wasn't sure that was a good thing when dealing with foreign diplomats, but she always assured me *softer* was quite different from soft.

It's strange, how even seemingly insignificant memories like that make me ache for her presence.

A host of guards, followed by an array of Others that follow at Az's command, lead us into the throne room. Before taking us to Asha, they bind all of us with goblin iron that keeps Lydia's fire magic at bay, as well as my ability to control feelings.

Az made sure the guards took Dinah away. He claimed seeing her sister would only upset Asha. Three guards had to restrain Fin before they managed to wrestle Dinah from his arms.

A mere drags Elias's unconscious body by the neck of his tunic, his legs limp as he smears blood from the wound in his side against the floor.

Anyone who doesn't know my sister might mistake her casual expression for indifference, but I can tell she's panicking on the inside for the life of her human husband.

"Kiran?"

My neck almost snaps as I find Asha on the other side of the room. My chest caves inward at the sight of her.

Because the woman in front of me is not the woman I'm used to seeing. Not the face whose scars I've been tracing every night in my dreams since the moment we parted.

Next to me, Fin swallows so hard it's audible.

Lydia mutters under her breath.

"What did he do to you?" I growl.

Because watching me from the throne is Asha.

She's watching me with both her eyes.

ASHA BLINKS RAPIDLY, batting tears from her eyelashes.

She's stunning, arrayed in vibrant crimson that matches her soft lips. I've always known she was beautiful, since the moment I laid eyes on her, but there's something about the lack of blemishes on her face that unsettles me, makes me want to lash out.

I'm going to kill Azrael.

It's not that I care what Asha looks like. If this is what she wanted, I'd happily have searched the ends of Alondria for a cure for her scars.

It's that I know where this is coming from. It's the same place from where Azrael told Asha in the gardens that he "had things he had to work through." The same place from which the mask he made her wear during their wedding ceremony came.

It's because he knows he can't love her, not truly, with her scars.

So instead of learning to, he's taken them away.

Taken away the scars I love to trace just before I kiss her, the scars that remind me how I almost lost her before I met her, the scars that serve as a reminder to cherish every second with her.

But what they mean to me isn't even important.

It's what they mean to her.

It's how her scars provided her freedom, honed her jagged edges, her wry sense of humor.

Her scars are her agency. Her ability to shine as simply Asha, her soul bare and beaming to a world who might otherwise allow her beauty to distract them.

Asha can take the warped features of her face and cast a spell on others with a smile. She can alter the perception of others with her words, not through any magic, but with wit and kindness. Until what they once saw as a pity, a beautiful girl marred by an unfortunate accident, they come to realize they actually prefer.

They say beauty is in the eye of the beholder, but my wife spins hearts, softens minds, until the scars on her face dance like strokes on a canvas, painting a vision so stunning, she *changes* the eyes of the beholder.

Az took that away.

Sorrow fills my wife's eyes as she looks down at me, then glances over at Elias.

"You promised you wouldn't hurt any of them," she whispers.

Lydia stiffens, like a cat whose back curls.

Fin lets out a ragged exhale.

I can't tear my eyes away from my wife.

"That one's still alive," Az says, walking up to Asha and taking her hand, pulling her from the throne to stand before us. "No harm has come to the others."

Asha nods, and there's something about her gaze that seems distant. Or perhaps I'm just not used to seeing her with both eyes intact.

"You did the right thing." Az strokes Asha's hand as she stares at the rest of us, tears still soaking her eyelashes, but still only on one cheek. "One day, you'll be free, and all of this will be behind us."

"I'm going to need you to explain what's going on here," seethes Lydia.

The faintest smile brushes Azrael's lips. "Asha and I would like to be able to go on with our lives, but there's something getting in our way, isn't there, love?"

Azrael snakes his hand over Asha's shoulder, brushing her hair behind her ear.

The sound of snapping bone rattles in my imagination as I revel in the idea of breaking his fingers one by one.

"Asha, what's going on?" Fin asks, concern for his friend evident in his voice.

Asha swallows, her throat bobbing in her thin neck.

She's lost weight.

So much of it.

I want to heave. I want to pluck Az's eyes out with my thumbs for what he's done to her.

"Asha, love. I'm so sorry," I say, my throat tightening. "I'm so sorry I failed you—"

Azrael laughs, his chuckle a cool echo across the marble floor. "Don't waste your breath, Kiran. It only makes you seem simple. Don't you know?"

When I don't flatter him with an answer, Az says, with a grin as slick as a feline's, "Asha's the one who warned me you were coming."

CHAPTER 109

KIRAN

*M*y heart falls through my chest.

Lies. That's all this boy has ever told. Lies.

"Asha?" I breathe, willing it not to be true, to be another one of Az's manipulations.

My wife swallows. "I'm so sorry, Kiran."

An arrow of doubt pierces my chest, crushing my ribs, and it's like my brain is trying to undo it, make sense of how the arrow doesn't exist, and none of this is real, and my wife is not the one who betrayed me.

Az nods to Asha. "Go on," he says.

"Yes, I think you'd better do that," says Lydia. "Go on, Asha."

Asha flinches at Lydia's words, but she turns her attention back to me, licking her perfectly full lips.

"I know you didn't mean to," she says, taking a careful step toward me. "I don't blame you for any of it. Know that, please."

Fin grits his teeth. "What's going on, Kiran?"

I shake my head, because I have no idea what she's talking about. What *my wife* is talking about. I don't even recognize her, don't...

Asha looks at my hands, bound in goblin iron. Sadness sweeps over her features, and I can't help but marvel at how different the emotion looks when it reaches the entirety of her face.

I don't recognize her. I don't recognize my wife.

Tears flow down her cheek now, wetting her flawless skin. "I didn't believe him, at first. I thought he was delusional. I fought it for so long, but…" She swallows, her throat bobbing, like there's a lump in it. "But then what he claimed started to come true. My feelings for you, Kiran. I wanted so badly for them to be real. Please know that."

My chest is caving in. I can't breathe.

"But he was right. The longer I was away from you, the more they faded. It was the case back in Othian, when you were stuck in Mystral. I ignored it then, thinking it was just my magic panicking, distracting me. And then you came back, and all was right again, because of course it was."

I hate this. I hate the way Asha's looking at the ceiling, grating her teeth like she's reprimanding herself for being such a fool. "I don't think you always realize when you're doing it, when you're leaking your feelings into others. It happens slowly, and it sticks around for a long time once it's taken hold. But the longer I've been away from you, the more empty I've felt. And Kiran, I thought it was just that I missed you. That I'd been ripped from my life, that everything was crumbling to pieces around me. I thought I was depressed. But then I realized that wasn't it. It was like…like something had drained out of me. Like I…" She swallows. "It was like when I first lost my eye, and there was a darkness there in my periphery that I wasn't quite used to, encroaching on me even when I didn't realize it. I'm sorry, but Az was right. The longer I've been away from you, the more my feelings have faded."

"Asha." Her name is a plea on my lips.

She swallows. "It's like a part of the magic is lodged in my heart. I can't quite get it to go away. Like it's taken root. I need…I need you to take it away."

My heart stops.

"What did you do to her?" I whisper, my words javelins I intend to pierce Azrael with.

633

Azrael just looks at me, and for the first time, I see no smugness in his gaze. Just desperation.

"Please, Kiran," he says. "Just let her go. Let her be happy. That's all we ask."

"What. Did. You. Do."

"He didn't do anything," cries Asha. "He didn't do anything. I asked for this. I'm so, so tired, Kiran. I just want to be whole again."

My heart fragments. "I always thought you already were."

A sad smile paints Asha's lips. "I know you did. I'll never forget that, you know. Never forget what a friend to me you became."

My world crumbles around me, and there's no one in the room. No one but me and Asha.

I always thought my worst nightmare was Asha dying.

I'm realizing I was wrong. This, what I've done to her, is so, so much worse.

"Kiran, is it true?" asks Fin.

I turn to look at my brother, but I have no answer."Please, Kiran," Asha says.

I swallow the grief in my throat as I look up at my wife and nod, slowly.

"You'll need to unbind me to make this happen," I say, my voice flat as I turn to Azrael.

He stiffens, looking back and forth between me and Asha, uncertainty flickering in his eyes.

Lydia scoffs in Azrael's direction. "Oh, we know you're not that stupid. You knew you'd have to unbind him if you wanted his magic."

The bile in my stomach sours at her words, because maybe Azrael doesn't need me at all. Maybe he has another leeching stone and can simply drain my magic from me. But my dread is short-lived, because Azrael straightens. "Of course I did. But I need reassurances," he says. "Reassurances that you won't attack us. That you won't hurt me. Not now. Not ever."

Ice skitters through my veins.

"You have my word," I say. Immediately, the fae curse snaps into place around my neck. "As long as you let my siblings go free of harm, and swear that never, until the day you die, will you lay an unwanted hand on Asha."

Az stiffens. "I'll need your word from both of you," he says to Fin and Lydia. "And you won't fight my guards as they escort you out of the palace."

"As long as Elias remains safe, you have mine," says Lydia.

Fin takes longer, surveying Asha with grief in his eyes. "Just don't make her do anything she doesn't want to, and you have mine too."

Az smiles. "Then we're all agreed."

The fae bargains snap into place, and just barely, I think I see a flicker of worry in Asha's beautiful, haunting eyes.

Several of the guards remove Lydia and Fin from the premises, carrying Elias's limp body with them.

A nearby guard removes my shackles.

I smile at my wife, just faintly, and reach for her hand, readying to take any feelings away she might have for me, searching her face for any sense she might have changed her mind.

Please change your mind. Please let this be one of your tricks, I whisper to her with the yearning in my eyes.

Tears roll down Asha's cheek.

She looks at my outstretched hand, free of its bonds, then whips a dagger from her belt and turns it on her own heart.

CHAPTER 110

ZORA

By the time we reach the entrance of the winding cavern where Nox stepped through the eyelet, the stench is almost unbearable. Farin is still having difficulty moving his left arm, a byproduct of his wound.

I can tell it hurts him by the way he swallows in between words. The way his sentences are sometimes cut short.

But he doesn't complain.

When we reach the cave that once housed the eyelet, a draft runs up my sleeve, causing the hairs on my arms to stand on edge.

"I'm guessing you felt that," says Farin.

I nod. "It was coming from the back wall of the cave, not the tunnels."

"So the eyelet is still here?"

I shake my head, unsure. Something's here all right, but I'm not confident it's anything balanced enough to provide us safe passage.

Still, I think I can fix that.

Maybe.

I cross the room, passing the corpse of the spider Farin killed. Then I run my fingers across the dangling spider silk that coats the

636

back wall. It's torn and shredded from where the eyelet closed, but the strands that remain are thick, firm to the touch.

"You really think this will work?" asks Farin, coming up behind me, his fingers gently squeezing my shoulder.

In the distance, we hear the rumble of the island, the beast of the volcano that dwells within the earth.

My throat goes dry. "It has to."

"NOX SAID Gunter was the one weaving my stories into the Fabric this entire time," I say, tying a knot between two loose strands of spider silk. "That Gunter tapped into the Fabric with thread made from the flax that grew near the Rip. Flax infused with the Fabric's magic. So what's to say," I say, stroking the silk, "we can't weave our own eyelet?"

Farin reaches from behind me, feeling the silk himself. "You think the silk is infused with magic from being near the eyelet, like the flax was infused with magic by being near the Rip? I thought the magic in the silk is what made the eyelet."

I shrug. "Does it matter which came first, as long as it still contains the magic?"

Farin hesitates.

"What?" I ask.

"It's just that, I thought you said the Fates were the ones who created the eyelets."

"So?"

Farin shuffles. "I'm not sure the Fates will be fond of me trying to replicate their artwork."

I flash him a smile, if only to hold the queasiness in my stomach in. If only so I don't have to ask what, exactly, Farin's relationship is with the Fates. "Then don't get in my way."

Farin flashes me an amused smirk, then steps backward, gesturing me forward.

I get to work.

·　·　·

IT TAKES SEVERAL HOURS, but eventually I manage to weave a portrait similar to the one we initially found here. I can't replicate it perfectly, of course. Not when part of the silk has been damaged and my memory isn't perfect, nor are my weaving skills.

But when I take a step back, I find I'm proud of my work.

"Is that your parents' home?" Farin asks, and I swallow, wiping the tears from my eyes.

Beside me, Farin gently traces the rolling hills of my parents' property, even down to a makeshift catapult in the yard.

"I thought you didn't remember them," he says.

I swallow. "I don't. But the house I remember."

"So what now?"

I bite my lip. "I think it needs to be activated with blood."

Farin goes to prick his finger with his dagger, but I grab his wrist to stop him.

"My blood. I'm the one whose soul's been here so long, it's interwoven with the Fabric, remember?"

Farin wrinkles his brow, but he places his dagger in my hand all the same.

I press it to the tip of my finger. A sharp pain, then blood buds on my swelling skin. When I glide it across the spider silk, a shiver rattles my entire body at the sensation.

Farin interlocks his fingers with mine, the tiny wound still throbbing.

Nothing happens.

The earth rumbles.

But it's not from the silk. Not from the eyelet.

In the distance, something explodes.

The ground lurches, sending Farin and me flying forward. Spider silk gags me as we're thrown through the portrait I wove.

Pain cracks through my nose as my face hits the stone wall.

My hand came loose from Farin's in the commotion, and I reach for him, still disoriented from when my head collided with the wall. When my vision finally clears, and I turn around, I find him standing back, staring at the torn spider silk canvas.

I rip the sticky substance from my face, wiping it on my pants.

Farin's expression is blank, his face white.

The earth trembles again.

"It didn't work," Farin says, no intonation in his voice.

My stomach flips. "I don't understand. I was sure it would have done something. Maybe it needed more blood. More time. I can make it again."

I spin around, frantically grabbing at loose threads of silk, but they're even more damaged than before, and few of them are long enough to tie together.

There's nothing I can do.

My hands are shaking, sweating. I'm not sure what happens now, if I die here.

I've never died before.

Never had to.

Farin turns to me, slowly, the way his expression warps telling me he's thinking the same thing.

I don't know what happens to him either, if he dies here.

I'm betting it's nothing good.

My stomach twists.

"We're stuck then," he says, his gaze somewhat distant, like he had a whole life planned out for himself, one that's just been torn from him.

"There's a chance a ship will come by," I say, though even as I say it, there's nothing convincing infusing my tone.

The ground rumbles, as if to contradict me.

We're underground. In a cavern at the base of a canyon. And if that volcano just spouted lava, it won't be long before it starts pooling into the canyon, slipping through the caverns, petrifying everything in its path.

Farin and I are going to die here, and I don't know what that means.

He blinks a few times, like he's trying to clear away a mist that's fogged his expression.

"Farin?" I ask.

I instantly wish I hadn't.

Because something in him changes.

He blinks again, but now that the fog has cleared, something else is revealed behind those brilliant blue eyes.

I'm not entirely sure why, but I take a step back.

His throat bobs. "You said this would work. You said we'd be able to get back."

"I thought we would," I say, eyes widening at the panic flaring up through him. "I don't know why it's not working."

His gaze snaps to mine, and his posture goes rigid.

He advances toward me, but it's more like an animal stalking its prey.

"You said we could make it back." His breaths are going ragged, his face contorted in whatever craze has overtaken him.

Oh. Oh, no.

It hits me then. Why he's so upset about not making it back. Perhaps part of it is fear. Dread about what will happen to him if he dies on this island. But Farin is a survivor. I recognize the type, and I doubt he has any intention of death getting in the way of what he wants.

But that's the problem.

I, inadvertently, have gotten in the way of what he wants.

And what he wants, is Blaise.

Realization washes over me in thick, salty waves, filling my nostrils and thickening the air in my lungs.

"You were just trying to get back to her. This whole time. All that's happened between us. It just made the process easier for you if I was on your team instead of fighting you," I say, my fingers clutching the sides of my trousers as anxiety and sorrow overtake me.

Something shifts in his expression, something cold and dark that he slips on as easily as one might don a mask.

Except he's not donning a mask.

He's taking it off.

"I would have thought someone who's lived so many lives would have been less naive," is all he says, and now he's looking at me like I'm the prey he's about to devour.

Fear courses through my veins, dread at the very male I fancied a kindred spirit. I'd been isolated in my experiences for so long, I'd craved someone to share them with me. I'd looked into Farin's heart and pretended I'd found a mirror when all I'd found was a ghoul capable of shifting into whatever I wished to see.

Stupid. So, so stupid.

"We'll find another way back," I say, trying to keep my voice calm, like one might do with a rabid animal you're trying not to spook.

Except Farin's not the one spooked.

My back hits the cave wall, and it's like life itself is telling me I can't go any further. That I've taken more than my fair share from it, and this is the end.

I don't know what happens at the end. I've only ever tasted beginnings and middles.

"There has to be another way. Our bodies are back in—"

I catch my breath, because Farin cocks his head to the side, a silent challenge.

Because my body is back home.

He doesn't have one if the tapestry runs out.

"You tricked me," he says, his voice a whisper, but it's trembling now. "All this time, and you were just waiting time out. Waiting for us to reach the end of the tapestry, where you get to go home, and I get to go...where, exactly, Wanderer?"

"No," I gasp, and it's true, even though the stupidity of my honesty drives a hole in my heart. "No, Farin. I didn't know this would happen. I didn't want...I wanted to save you," I say. "Wanted, hoped for a life with you."

It's the wrong thing to say, because he lets out a choked cackle, one that reminds me of a strangled animal.

"You hoped for a life with me?" he asks, his voice dripping with malice. "Well. It seems neither of us are going to get what we wanted, are we?"

He takes a step closer, and I punch at his face, but he grabs my wrist, twisting it back toward my side, pinning me up against the wall with his body.

"Tell me, Wanderer, I'm going to die here anyway it seems. What should I do with my last moments?" He presses his forehead to mine, his grip serving as iron clamps against my wrists.

I struggle against him, throwing my weight into his left side, where his shoulder is injured.

"Think that's going to help you, Wanderer? Think I don't know how to suffer a little pain?"

Slowly, like he's mocking me, he releases my wrist, then lets it fall, so that it slaps the stone wall behind us. Except it's not stone that my wrist hits. My attention fixates on my fingertips, though his are trailing up my arm, cupping my cheek in his hands and tucking my hair behind my ear.

"You don't have any suggestions?" he mocks, his lips dripping acid. "If that's the case, I think I'll just use my imagination then. Have a little fun with you. Tell me, Zora," he says, pressing his warm lips to my ear. I shudder in terror at his touch, as his voice pierces my very bones. "Do you ever fantasize about how you'd like to die? I'd be willing to let you pick. I'd—"

But he doesn't finish whatever he was about to offer.

He stumbles backward, the dagger I grabbed from his belt jutting from his chest.

From his heart.

My hands are shaking, and I step away, expecting him to lunge at me with his last breaths.

But Farin doesn't lunge.

Farin smiles.

And it's not the wicked, terrifying smile of a few moments ago.

It's the smile a husband gives his wife as she's holding his hand at his deathbed. It's a smile that says thank you for the life you've given me and I'm sorry that I'm leaving and that we couldn't have had longer.

My hand goes to my mouth, realization battering my body before it scourges my mind.

What have I done?

"No." The plea escapes my mouth in a whisper, and I find myself reaching toward Farin, like I think if I remove the dagger from his heart, I can take back the wound I inflicted too.

"No." The word comes out as a sob, and sadness creeps over Farin's smile.

He stumbles again, and this time it's toward me, pushing both of us into the cave wall as I try to support his weight, while he tries to hold himself up with his palm pressed up against the wall behind us.

"*You tricked me,*" I scream, though it's gargled with tears. I want to shove him in anger, but I can't, not when any moment now, he'll take his last breath and...

His voice is strained, weak. "Yeah. I'm told I have a problem with that."

"Why?" I ask, and I'm so angry, so enraged, that it comes out in a bed of hot tears.

"You know why," he says, and he has the audacity to give me that lopsided grin. The boyish, I've-been-up-to-something grin that makes my heart beat wildly in my chest.

He's right. I do know. Because in a few moments, Farin will die, and I'll have been the one to kill him.

Meaning a Rip will open up, one that will take me to another world. A portal out of this death-trap of an island.

"How did you know?" I breathe.

"Come now, Wanderer," Farin says, straining the teasing into his voice. "You never give me any credit. The sailor on the beach—you were so distraught... when I killed him. I couldn't figure it out. Not when you'd planned..." He squeezes his eyes shut as he fights for breath. The dagger in his chest bobs. "But then you tried to kill me. When you could have tried any time before. I knew then—how you open Rips."

I shake my head, disbelieving. "Why didn't you tell me you knew? We could have found a way off the island. We could have found a way off together. Then we could have found the eyelet and..." I stop.

Farin's straining to stand upright; he uses his finger to wipe away my tears. "You know as well as I do that this is the only way you get out of here alive."

"I don't want to go. Not without you," I say, and I'm sobbing now, and panic is overtaking my chest.

"I know. To be honest, I'm not thrilled about the situation either." Tears glimmer in his eyes, but they shine with adoration. And something I've yet to see in them. Hope.

"Please don't die," I whisper, and now it's the cave wall holding me up, and Farin pressed against me, his warmth dizzying.

"I have to. You know that," he says, and his voice is as warm and gentle as his arms the night he shielded me from the cold.

"Please. I'm so tired of being alone," I say, and now my heart is breaking, as if Farin's isn't the one with a hilt jutting out of it.

It hurts.

"We still don't know what happens if I die over here," he says, a glint of teasing in his voice. "Just think. You might be crying over nothing. I might just wake up beside you, in whatever world you end up in."

It's a stupid thought. A stupid, idiotic thought.

"You don't even have a body to go back to," I say, choking on the truth of those words.

He shrugs, though it must hurt him to do so. "A rather minor hurdle if you ask me."

I want so badly to hit him, but he lets his arm slip down to my hip as he leans on me.

"Wanderer. I've been dead before. I know we don't stop existing when we die."

"You said it was miserable where you were," I whisper.

He shrugs. "I didn't exactly have anything to claw my way back to, then."

"I'm afraid I won't remember you," I whisper, and his knees stumble, but he holds steady. "I don't always remember. Some of my lives... things get erased..."

Something glints in his eyes.

"Well, then. It's a good thing I love a good chase, isn't it?" he whispers.

And then, with all the life Farin has left in him, he kisses me, and it's fire and ice, and death and life, and sorrow and joy, and it rips my heart clean out of my chest.

Hot, salty tears stream down my cheeks, but I kiss him back all the same, and when he parts my lips and deepens the kiss, I let myself melt into him.

Just for a moment.

It's a kiss I promise myself I'll remember. One I'll claw through my memories to rediscover.

"Don't let me catch you too quickly, Wanderer," he whispers.

But then Farin's lips falter, and he lets out a shaky breath.

When his knees give out, and he crumples to the floor, I scream.

But then there's a ripping sound, and a flash of light, and I don't remember why I'm screaming at all.

CHAPTER 111

NOX

Getting speared in the stomach by a wyvern is not an event I would prefer to repeat.

Ever.

Still, I figure I've been through worse.

At least I'm not being burned to a crisp by the Naenden sun. Although it's so hot here, that might have happened anyway, regardless of my vampire curse.

If Blaise and I make it out of this alive, we're never coming back to this horrid place.

I doubt she'll object.

Sprinting across a sandy desert will do that to a person.

The wyvern lands not-so-strategically, directly into an apartment building in the center of Meranthi, spewing shattered clay bits everywhere, including my mouth.

The wyvern's talon lodges further into my gut when we make impact, but I've no time to register the pain.

I grab the scaly tail and yank it from my torso, biting through my tongue in the process.

Shadows from the *paldihv* my infuriatingly headstrong mate

passed along to me swirl around me in waves, hiding the condition of my wound.

I can still feel the muscles and organs knitting back together.

Citizens scream around me, fleeing the demolished building, as the wyvern sprays a jettison of venom out of its mouth. The silvery substance leaks through what's left of the crushed walls, hissing as it makes its way through the clay.

Excellent.

The wyvern swings its neck around to face me.

Is it just me, or does it have the gall to look pleased to see me?

If that really is a smile snaking through its ugly teeth, it really shouldn't be.

Because if I've scaled across Realms, dove into canyons, and traversed deserts to get to Blaise, I'm certainly not letting this wyvern get in my way.

WYVERN BLOOD IS DISGUSTING, in case anyone is wondering.

I highly doubt anyone is.

Especially not the screaming residents who part for me as I make my way back to the palace.

At first, I think they're probably afraid of me because of the wyvern blood dripping from my mouth, but then I remember I'm swathed in shadows from head to toe.

Yeah, the screaming is probably from that.

I MAKE it back to the palace, the pull of the bloodsharing bond tugging me toward Blaise.

As I step into the gardens, a mere pounces from the brush like it's been waiting for me.

I'm really not in the mood.

It probably isn't either, especially now that I've torn its jaw from its face with my bare hands.

Through the carnage, I glimpse a silvery orb on the mostly destroyed terrace, one that tugs at the chain intertwined with my soul.

There's a male whose forehead is pressed to the orb, and he's whispering something to it, while another pair of fae shoot vines into the sky, spearing wyverns and mere alike as they try to attack the orb.

I tread over the fallen remains of a headless wyvern, the world stilling around me as the orb dissipates, leaving my wife, my mate, fully exposed to the sun.

Fear pulses in my chest, and I'm at her side in an instant, ready to cloak her in my shadows.

The two fae manipulating the plants try to stop me, digging thorns into my flesh, but I rip through them with ease.

Only the bronze-haired male leaning before Blaise holds up a hand, not one intent on stopping me, but one that brings my attention to my wife.

To the sunlight that cuts across her face but doesn't burn.

To the blood that smells like that of a human.

Relief floods me, followed by confusion mingled with panic as I search my soul for the bloodsharing bond, but it's still there, tying us together, as strong as it's ever been.

Blaise's eyes flutter open, and though I want nothing more than to scoop her into my arms, there's something so human about her now. Apprehension that I might hurt her stops me.

"They're alive," says the male I recognize from the Rip. "Blaise, Ellie and our daughter—they both lived."

The muscles at the edges of Blaise's mouth twitch in disbelief. "Andy, I'm so sorry."

"They're alive," he repeats, and Blaise blinks.

"They're alive," she whispers back.

The male smiles.

"Nox?" Blaise groans, panic returning to her voice.

I clutch her hands in mine. "I'm right here."

This seems to settle her, and when she looks up at me, it's the Blaise I remember.

I realize I have no idea what Blaise did. What just happened.

"Nox, this is Andy," she says, rolling her head lazily toward the male kneeling over her, eyes wide with relief. "Andy, this is Nox."

"I believe we've already met." I clench my teeth at the memory of this male, of the cruel things he said to Blaise, crushing her, until I want nothing more than to rip his throat out.

Which, as it turns out, I get the perfect chance to do, because, to my shock, *Andy* embraces me.

He pulls back, a firm grip on my shoulder as he grins. "So you're the one who puts up with Blaise, here?"

I am momentarily speechless, but Blaise just crawls into my lap, letting the shadows cloak the two of us as she wraps her arms around my neck, settling herself into my grasp.

I brace myself for the bloodlust, but it doesn't come. Blaise looks human, and though I initially thought her blood smelled human, there's something about it that...isn't.

I'm about to ask what in Alondria is going on when the female plant-wielder pipes up. "Where can I get some of those?"

I turn toward her, though I realize she can't see my face. She seems comfortable in my personal space all the same.

"Pretty sure you have to kill someone to get a set," says the male standing next to her.

She turns to the male and bats the longest eyelashes I've ever seen. He crosses his arms, rolling his eyes.

"Can you please get me some?" she asks, while she snaps her fingers absentmindedly, strangling a mere that just leapt out of the shadows with a set of thorny vines.

Yep. I cannot wait to get back to the quiet, peopleless Mystral.

"Kiran." Blaise snaps back from my embrace. "I need to get to Kiran," she says, realization settling over her expression.

I stand to join her, but she shakes her head. "You should help defend the city."

I venture toward my wife. "I'm going with you."

Tears well up in her beautiful, human eyes. How is she human? And she smiles, but she shakes her head all the same.

Then she slips into the shadows, and...changes, flashing a set of glistening fangs.

Fates, Blaise can shift between her human and vampire forms.

"Do you trust me?" she asks like it's a dare.

Evander and I both groan, but we let her run off into the palace, so I suppose that means the answer is yes.

CHAPTER 112

ASHA

*E*very eye in the room swivels to me as I hold the trembling dagger to my chest.

Kiran, my sweet, sweet husband, is the first to speak. "Asha. What are you doing?"

If only I knew.

I wince at him, trying and failing at an apologetic smile.

I've been flying off script since last night. Dinah relayed Blaise's message, and ever since, I've been scrambling for purchase on a wall that has no footholds, desperately grasping for a solution to save not just myself, but everyone I love.

I spent the last few hours grappling over, not Blaise's message that they were coming to rescue me, but why she'd deemed it important to tell me.

There were multiple things that bothered me about it. Mostly that Blaise knows better than anyone how to hide important information. And that the more people who know the truth, the more difficult it is to keep hidden.

I couldn't quite believe Blaise had been so concerned over my mental wellbeing that she didn't think I could wait a few more hours to know I was being rescued.

So why?

Why inform me they were on their way? Why tell me the plan to get Kiran close enough to Az to alter his feelings?

Unless that was never Blaise's plan to begin with.

Blaise, who had spent plenty of time with Az. Enough to know that Az was already aware of Kiran's power—information he'd gotten from Gwenyth. Blaise, who knew Az would already be expecting Kiran to use it against him.

Blaise, who knew the only thing that might make it through the callus that has crusted over Az's heart.

Of course, I hadn't expected Az to bring his healer to me last night. Hadn't expected the slimy faerie to take my face in his hands, strip me of my scars with a trace of his oily fingers.

From a glance in the mirror the healer handed me, it seems my eye is back. I still can't see out of it, so consider me unimpressed.

That ordeal had thrown me off, but I'd had plenty of time to think. To figure out what Blaise wanted from me.

Plenty of time to realize that Az always wins. No matter what, he's always been so far ahead of me, I couldn't even glimpse him in the distance. And Kiran was too recognizable. He would be caught no matter what.

So I'd decided if he was going to be caught, it would be on my terms.

I'd told Az of my friends' plans to sneak into the palace. It had crushed me to do it, but I'd glimpsed it—the glimmer of trust in his eyes.

I'd known then that I had him.

I'd staged this, hoping for an opportunity to beg Kiran to take away my feelings for him.

Because if this is going to work, I don't just need Az to want me.

He has to *need* me, has to feel my love graze his fingertips.

Right before he loses me.

Az's gaze dips to the dagger, a scoff escaping his mouth. "You're not going to use that."

"You don't think so? Why is it you've had all the windows in the palace barred? What exactly is it you're so afraid I'll do?"

Az turns to Kiran. "Clearly, this male still has a hold on you. Tell me, Kiran, are you okay with Asha dying on your behalf? Is this what you intended by manipulating her feelings all this time? Though, I suppose perhaps it's useful to have a wife willing to die for you. You don't care, do you?"

"Az, please," I whisper, the point of the blade pressing into my sternum. "Don't make me do this."

"I'm not making you do anything, Asha. Just put the blade down. I can promise you, as soon as Kiran has been dealt with, you'll feel differently. I thought you were getting better, but clearly he got his hands on you at some point..." Az pales, and his attention snaps between us, as if it had just dawned on him what would have occurred if such an opportunity had presented itself.

The jealousy in his eyes rages as he kicks Kiran in the mouth. Teeth crack. Blood stains Kiran's lips, but he doesn't retaliate. He just stares up at Az, almost in disbelief.

"You never deserved her," Kiran says, and Az kicks him again.

I feel each kick as if they're to my own mouth.

"Kiran, stop," I whisper, but Kiran doesn't stop.

"I didn't either, to be frank. But at least I wasn't foolish enough to miss my chance."

This time when Az kicks, there's a snap that sounds sickeningly like Kiran's jaw.

The blade trembles in my hand. I move it to the side, feeling the notch between two of my ribs.

You can do this, you can do this, I whisper to myself.

Molten fire burns in Kiran's eyes, horror and desperation as I inch the blade toward my skin.

A tear slices through the fabric of my gown.

Tears stream down Kiran's eyes. They remind me what Kiran told me ages ago, while we talked in the palace gardens. That when he was a boy, his tears would boil, leaving burn marks on his cheeks.

653

But there's no Flame left in him. Nothing to hurt him any longer, other than me.

"I love you," I whisper.

And then I raise the dagger, preparing to plunge it into my chest.

I don't get the chance.

Something strikes me, right where I had my dagger aimed.

It takes a moment for my body to register the pain.

I glance at Az first, a smug expression on his lips. His scabbard is empty.

No.

Kiran shouts.

No, no, no.

I stare down at the hilt protruding from my chest.

My dagger, the one I coated with Amity's ressuroot last night, clatters to the floor, unused.

"No. Az, why?" My head is still spinning as I stare up at my friend. Is he this obsessed with me, that if he can't have my heart, no one can?

"You two really thought you could fool me, didn't you? Thought you could convince me you'd really hurt yourself. I'm not stupid, Asha. When will you learn that I'm not the foolish boy you've always thought me to be?"

My mouth works, but I find I can't get words to form. Not when blood is running up my throat, soaking the back of my tongue, staining my teeth red and spilling from my mouth.

My knees hit the floor, my fingers grasping at the hilt of Az's dagger in disbelief.

"You fool. I'm going to kill you," Kiran growls. "Asha, Asha, please. Please, don't go. Please."

I want nothing more than to comfort my husband, but the room is swaying, black dots swarming my vision.

"Come on, Asha," Az sings. It takes me a moment to realize he isn't looking at me. "Come out into the open, why don't you? I know you're hiding somewhere, whispering this version of yourself into reality, drawing on the magic from the Rip."

When no one appears, Az has the audacity to look inconvenienced.

He snaps his fingers at a pair of nearby guards, who go on a search. A search for me, I realize.

"No," I find the will to say, even around the blood streaming from my mouth.

I'm dying, and I have only one chance to make my death count.

"Az, it's me."

He scoffs, his beautiful features warped in derision. "I saw you, Asha—the way you acted in the compartment behind the library. The idea had occurred to me too, you know. I felt it, too—the way the entire world seemed to quake when the Rip was opened. Your magic did it so forcefully. I couldn't help but wonder if it created fissures. Fissures that might burst into canyons, especially where the deposits of other-realm magic were the strongest. Much like the scrolls hidden away behind the library. I had them burned, of course, but it hit me when you were down there that it wasn't simply the scrolls you were looking for. You were confirming there had been another Rip, another fissure between worlds from which you could draw upon. You've been having nightmares about it, talking in your sleep, screaming so loud I can hear you from the other side of the wall. I had hoped..." Az swallows, somehow looking pained. "I had hoped we were making progress. I couldn't stand to gag you again." He turns his head away from me, as if to remind himself that the true me isn't dying on the floor in front of him.

"I've been waiting, ever since, for you to summon your power in an attempt to trick me. But all is well. Once this male"—he kicks at Kiran again, who hardly seems to notice. His eyes lock upon mine, full of anguish—"is out of the way, perhaps his power over you will fail, and we can finally go back to how things used to be."

"How things used to be," I whisper.

Az can't seem to help but look at me, even if he truly believes I'm not real. His eyes are wide with hope. For a moment, he almost looks like the boy I knew and loved. The boy who dangled his feet off rooftops and dreamed of a better world.

"There's no Rip, Az. Not here," I rasp. "You're right. I was looking, hoping for one. But it was a false hope. I have no power here, other than my stories."

Az's amused grin almost falters. "This version of you will fade to ash soon enough. You might as well come out from where you're hiding."

Just then, both guards return, signaling they found no one waiting close by.

"Perhaps she's stationed by the Rip itself. Check the compartment behind the library. Bring a scribe to open it," says Az. The guards looked hesitant, but after exchanging concerned glances, they do as told.

"Az," I whisper, hardly able to maintain consciousness now. He isn't the one I wanted to be speaking to in my last moments alive, but if there's a single drop of truth in Blaise, I have one shot to make this count. "I'm scared," I say, because it's true. Because I don't want to die, not like this. Not in front of Kiran, who's known so little aside from death and destruction.

I don't want to die, but it seems I don't have a choice.

Even through the shadows encroaching on my vision, I glimpse Az's confidence falter, if just for a moment.

No, Asha. Please, stay awake. It's not your time yet, whispers my magic.

I'm not sure I can do that. Now everything is spinning.

No. No, no, no. You're too young. It's not time for you yet. You're supposed to grow old and wrinkled and horribly cynical, hisses my magic.

I'm sorry, I tell him.

That's not enough, he cries back. *Not again, not again, please, not again.*

But I can no longer hear my magic.

I can't hear anything at all.

CHAPTER 113

BLAISE

I don't watch Asha as she falls.

Instead, I watch Kiran.

I arrive too late to save her, to warn her. Kiran's face darkens in anguish. There's horror in his expression, the deep, agonizing loss that clouds his features, as his future is ripped away from him.

Her death wasn't part of the plan. When I spoke with Dinah, it was because the part of me who knew just how paranoid Az could be had worried he would already have a plan in place in case Kiran tried to use his powers against him.

I thought we could use that against Az.

Asha's involvement was supposed to be the backup plan in case we were caught.

She'd misunderstood and thought I wanted for us to get caught.

I can see now the path her mind took.

Asha's plan was to feed Az a high, just so he'd have a longer way to fall. Just so the sorrow would sting all the worse once he realized he had lost her.

She'd dangled hope of winning back her love in front of his face, just before she faked her death.

I'd only wanted Asha to be prepared if things went poorly.

But Asha had treated the escape attempt as if it were our only shot.

I recognize Kiran's pain, that agony, and I watch it from afar, feeling the loss between us go taut.

He doesn't look at me, probably doesn't even realize I've slipped into the throne room, that I've been hiding behind the velvet curtains.

The moment will come when he looks for me, though. When it settles over him that this is entirely my fault.

It won't take him long.

It's always my fault.

Something flares within me, grasping for that feeling, but no…

No. Asha knew what she was risking. It was her decision to put herself in harm's way, not mine.

Neither of us could have seen this coming. The plan should have worked. Amity's ressuroot should have worked.

I grasp against the cold marble wall, allowing the chill to stabilize me.

Az was the one to throw that dagger, not me.

Derek led me into that pantry, not me.

I swallow, then I do the only thing I can do.

Kiran lunges for Asha. At least Asha found a way to convince Az to unbind him. Az is prepared, his other dagger descending upon Kiran, aiming for his throat.

I get there first.

My fist curls around Az's blade. I feel the sting of singeing flesh, the burn of my own blood against my palm, and instead of ignoring the pain, instead of allowing it to drive me, I channel it.

Az whitens as I wrench the dagger from his grasp and push him up against the wall.

His face warps into a hateful grin, like he knows something I don't.

I clasp Kiran's goblin-iron cuffs I swiped from the floor onto Az's wrists, stifling his Flame.

"You foolish child. Let me go," he says, to which I shove his head against the marble wall just for good measure. The motion leaves him looking dazed, but not enough to slur the oncoming insults. "They'll never forgive you for betraying them."

"Well, no reason to pile on," I say.

"Asha," Kiran cries from behind me. "Asha, please. Please don't leave me. Why…"

Az lets out a laugh. "The fool believes her. Someone so dull-witted doesn't deserve—"

"Asha is dead," I say, and though Az's face falters for a moment, he regains his confidence quickly enough.

"Not you too. I would have thought you were more clever than that. Perhaps your life of lies has blinded you to them."

I shake my head, flicking my neck to gesture toward the blade Asha dropped. "I can scent the ressuroot on its tip. She doused it in the formula before she arrived. It brings a person back, but only if it's injected directly into the heart. She was trying to trick you, Az, but not in the way you thought. There's no Rip in the library, nowhere for Asha to draw on to amplify her powers. There's no illusion. No pretending. Asha is dead, and you're the one who killed her."

Az's beautiful features go still for a moment, but then he blinks, shaking his head as if to rouse himself from a nightmare. "You're lying."

"I'm not. Fates," I say, trying my best to hold it together, but I don't know if I can. Asha is dead. Fates, she's dead, and I'm the one who turned her over to her murderer.

Guilt swarms my chest, but instead of allowing it to control me, I absorb it, I own it. Just like I did the parasite.

I think of Asha. Asha, who forgave the king who planned to slaughter her the morning after her wedding. Asha, who…

Asha would have forgiven me. Fates, she probably already had.

In some ways, it makes it hurt worse, knowing that. Knowing I'd lost such a friend, even if a friendship between us had only been potential.

It's the type of pain the parasite couldn't understand, didn't know to look for, so I hold on to it, allow it to roll through me.

It only feels like I'm drowning. I take a breath to remind myself I am not.

"Only moments now," Az says, his sage-green eyes fixed on Asha's corpse. "She'll turn to dust any moment now."

"No," says a voice, ominous and familiar. One that has haunted my nightmares since the day I forced Asha to open the Rip. Since I forced him to open the Rip. *"No, Azrael. She won't."*

Az's eyes go wide, his cheeks sallow. Sweat breaks against the line between his forehead and hairline, and his lungs work rapidly underneath my forearm, where I have him pinned.

"No," he whispers. "You're just part of the illusion."

Something blue glows in the pits of Az's eyes.

I am afraid to look, but there's no pretending it away.

So I turn and stare the Old Magic in the face.

He's small. A vibrant blue light that I might have considered gentle if I didn't know any better.

"Are you happy now, young Azrael? Are you pleased with what you've done?"

Beneath my clutches, Az shakes.

"I listened, you know," says the voice, the voice that echoes not around us, but from inside of us. *"All those years, all those dreams you shared with her. Tell me, child. Was she worth it?"*

Az's eyes fix on the Old Magic.

Even Kiran's cries have gone silent.

"TELL ME!"

Az's mouth hangs open.

And then a sob escapes his mouth.

It's strangled and pitiful, and I recognize it too, just like I recognized Kiran's grief, his loss.

He doesn't speak it, but the words are written in the widening of his eyes, the slackness of his jaw—*What have I done?*

His gaze fixes on Asha, and I watch for the first time as the truth washes over him. As he looks at her body, and sees not an illusion he's outsmarted, but his childhood friend, her body splayed out on the floor, never to rise again.

It's in that moment that I realize Asha's done it.

That in her death, she's saved us all.

CHAPTER 114

PIPER

Out of the woods creep what must be three dozen Others, ranging from the feline mere to the winged wyverns.

My heart shudders, my feet wobbling on the cool earth below me.

I've been camped out by the Rip since Blaise left, waiting.

I have no way of knowing if Blaise's plan worked, whether she managed to distract Azrael enough for me to bend the will of the Others to my own.

Or if she's ashes in the desert.

What I do know is that they are coming, and as I can't fight off a host of them on my own, I have two choices.

Run, or try.

But then my Gift tugs at my heart, stoking my bloodstream like the warm glow of a hearth, the swell of a gentle flame.

Are you ready? I ask my Gift, though I wonder if I'm asking myself.

It responds with one resounding note, like a bird singing in the heavens.

I lift the flute to my lips, and together, my Gift and I play.

. . .

THE TUNE IS like the first we'd attempted to woo the Others, though different in some ways. While the other was infused with staccato notes of urgency and excitement, this one is as deep as a well and as wide as a mural.

It's the sort of song one hopes will be their last.

Their finale.

Their take a bow as the crowd erupts into applause.

This is it for us.

My Gift knows it, and I know it too.

So together we play, my fingers tapping the keys as the two of us surrender to the language we both speak.

THE SONG SWELLS AND FLOWS, and still the Others draw nearer. I don't bother looking into their eyes. If I looked and glimpsed hunger, it would only shake my resolve, and though my eyes long to look, to know whether they should scream at my feet to run, I don't let them.

Running won't do me any good at this point, anyway.

I am going to succeed.

Or I won't.

There's a peace to that, one I don't expect, and though I suspect it's my Gift's doing, I can't fault it for it.

So I play, and my Gift hums, and even the forest stops to listen as the wind carries my song to distant lands, over rolling hills, tickling the pines and stirring grains of sand as it flies.

And then I am the song, and we are one, and it's larger than the two of us, as expansive as the sky itself.

The song swells, and I fly, and suddenly my feet no longer feel the ground, my fingers no longer feel the resistance of the keys. Yet still the song plays, and it's no longer me playing it, but I'm the audience, savoring it, as surprised as the next person by the next note.

I play, or rather, the song plays me, and together we welcome the oblivion.

· · ·

SOMETHING BRUSHES AGAINST MY SKIN, stirring me from the state of euphoria, anchoring me back to this present realm, the one in which I should be torn apart.

But when I allow my drunken eyelids to flutter open, all I find is a mere. It's nuzzling up to my arm, though gently enough as not to jostle my flute. It peers up at me with wide, silvery eyes, and I can no longer tell whether the soothing hum is coming from my music or the satisfaction of my magic or the purr of the feline burrowing its snout into my elbow, wrapping its tail around my feet.

I should be terrified. But part of me is still drunk on the music. High on the performance.

It's working, I whisper in my mind to my Gift.

A high note resounds back. It sings out through the flute, and like a soldier to the sound of a trumpet, the mere stiffens.

It takes one more glance at me, those saucer-wide silver eyes glinting.

When it takes a step, its paw disappears into the void.

It cranes its neck, gesturing for the others to follow.

The mere passes through the Rip and disappears. And then, one by one, the Others follow.

First it's the Others in the field that were just surrounding me. Once those disappear, I still feel the resistance of the bonds shooting out from my flute—tethers sailing through the sky—so I keep playing until shadows form in the moonlit heavens.

Wyverns sweep in from distant lands. I shiver in the gust of their wings as they shoot by me, vanishing to dust through the Rip.

It takes longer for the rest of the mere to appear. It could take hours, it could take days, for all I'm aware.

My back throbs, my feet ache, but still I play.

I play until the last Other vanishes through the Rip, and the rope connecting us slips with it.

And with the last breaths my lungs can bear to muster, I play a note that commands the Rip to close.

It listens.

CHAPTER 115

KIRAN

*H*umans die.
      Asha is human.
Therefore... no.
Asha is dead.

I don't want to believe it. Much like Azrael, I believed in my wife. Believed she'd found a way to deceive the rest of us. A way to make it look real, when in reality, she would be hiding behind a curtain, just as Azrael expected.

Except I heard Blaise explaining to Azrael about the dagger. The one that now lies unused against the cold marble stone next to Asha, her face drained of color.

I watched her die and hoped I hadn't.

But she's gone now. Part of me knew it the moment the Old Magic separated from her body. Part of me knew it before then, the moment Az's blade punctured her chest.

When the dagger sliced through her skin, my first thought was how that couldn't be, because Az had entered a fae vow not to lay a hand on her.

My father would have beaten me for making a vow like that. One with loopholes that don't account for figurative language.

664

The curse can be so literal at times.

Even then, I don't know if I would have thought to be more specific. Because as deluded as I knew Az was, as likely as I found it that he might force himself on her having convinced himself that was what Asha wanted, never did I dream he would try to kill her.

"Asha." I crawl to her, the guards who previously detained me still in shock over their queen's death.

As I draw closer, her blood coating the slippery floor soaks my hands.

I'm transported to Rivre, where over a year ago I held the same position, cradling my wife in my arms. There was still life in her that time.

There is none now.

Her scars have returned, whatever magic the healer wrought on her skin having dissipated with her spirit.

I feel for her pulse in the crook of her neck as I brush her sweat-ridden hair away. All I find is an absence of the vitality that thrummed there only moments ago.

That's the strangeness of it all. That Asha was here, just a moment ago, looking into my eyes and trying to communicate something to me.

It's a moment so fresh in time; it feels wrong, that she's no longer here. No longer breathing. That her chest no longer rises and falls, her eye no longer sees.

It remains open, staring at the ceiling above, and I brush the side of my hand, the part that's not sticky with her blood, over her lid. There's a part of me that's selfish in doing so, like if her eye is closed, I can pretend she's sleeping. Something that's impossible to do with her staring into nothing.

It doesn't help.

Asha doesn't look like she's sleeping.

Asha looks dead.

Because she is.

Something within me cracks. Rips. An anguish I've never experienced before. I came close the day I thought I'd lost her. But she'd been hanging onto life by a thread, and I'd still been clinging to the other end.

There's nothing for me to cling to now. Nothing but her corpse, which is already cooling to the touch, and I don't even have my magic within me to warm it.

"No," I groan, but the word is fruitless, empty on my tongue. "No, you didn't die before. We saved you before."

Had we simply postponed the inevitable, then? When Asha's heart had beat again at the Council meeting, had it been because she simply hadn't fulfilled her purpose yet, and now she has, so she's been taken away from me?

I take her hand, and it hurts to touch her limp fingers.

Something comes hurtling for my head. I catch it, the vial of liquid moonlight cooling my palm.

I glance over to Blaise, who shrugs and scrapes her foot against the floor. "I swiped some from a warehouse a while back."

I stare down at the vial in my hand, and I know then I could have her back. Know that the same process that led to Farin inhabiting Nox's body could bring her back to me.

It's then that the plan unfolds. We wouldn't even have to use someone who is alive to do it. Hadn't Blaise admitted that Nox's initial plan for his spell had been to use a fresh corpse?

She wouldn't look like Asha. Talk like Asha, but I don't care. It's never been about Asha's body. It's like I told her all those nights ago in Rivre. Her body is the anchor that ties her to this side of the sun. It's what keeps her here with me.

It's what keeps her here with me.

Suddenly, I feel as though I can't breathe.

I can't be here without Asha.

I can't survive in a world she doesn't inhabit.

I know now that my father was right. That males aren't meant to outlive their females. I'm not made for this, I'm not...

The vial is cold to the touch. Silvery moonlight swirls inside the mixture, and I find it difficult to look away.

"We'd have to burn the body," says a voice from the corner. Blaise's.

I turn to look at her, to challenge the judgment on her face, but there is none.

I can tell by the set of her jaw that she understands. That doesn't mean she approves. But she won't stand in my way. It's her fault, after all. Her fault for planting the idea in Asha's mind. Her fault for putting my wife in the hands of a lunatic.

But Blaise's use of the word "we" tells me she'll help.

I can decide how I'll punish Blaise later, but first I need to know. "Is it so awful?" I ask. "Being what you are?"

Blaise looks down at herself, and for the first time I notice there's something different about her. Something I can't place. "I don't think I can answer that for anyone else."

A life without sunlight. Would Asha mind, in a place like Naenden, where most of us hide from the sunlight, anyway? In Naenden, where it's the night that is the most peaceful?

She'd do it for me, I tell myself. She'd live this life for me. But then again, I'm not so sure. In all our time together, I never asked if Asha wished to be immortal. I thought it would be better to wait on that conversation until we knew there was even an option.

I should have asked.

But if I had asked, and she had said no, would I still be grasping onto this vial, thinking of burning my wife's body to ashes so she might occupy another vessel?

Would I go against her wishes to bring her back?

But then I remember Asha walking in the sunlight back in Othian, enjoying the gentle breeze of the day. I remember Blaise describing the craving for blood, the desire to hurt others.

And I know—I *know*—this is not what Asha wants.

I crush the vial in my hand, but it's not the flecks of glass in my palm that bring the tears to my eyes.

The liquid moonlight drips to the floor, slipping through my fingertips.

It's so very cold.

"You fool," Azrael screams, but I'm not listening. "It was the only way to bring her back."

667

My head is buzzing, and I can hardly stand it.

Azrael cries out, and when I look over, blood drips from two holes in his neck, the same blood dripping from the edges of Blaise's lips.

"If you're trying to make me sleep with your venom, it won't work," Az sneers, blood slipping down his throat. "Not with the elixirs I've been taking."

Blaise drops Az. While the venom won't work to put him to sleep, it does seem to keep his legs from supporting his weight, because he crumples to the floor, his back hitting the wall.

Blaise isn't paying attention to him.

"Not the only way," she whispers to me.

My heart stops in my chest as Blaise and I lock eyes. As we're transported by a common memory, back to a cave of shadows and a creature who feeds off the darkness.

"Blaise." Her name is a warning on my tongue. Because I know what she's about to say.

And I don't know that if she gives me the option, I'll have the strength to turn it down.

Blaise's expression goes distant. "My heart. That's what the shadow told you, wasn't it? That the ashes of a night stalker's heart could grant immortality? That they could bring back the dead?"

"She could have been lying," I say, but my words come out flat. Unconvincing, even to myself.

Already I'm considering which course of action gives Asha the best chance: waiting for Blaise to offer her heart on her own, or ripping it from her chest before she has a chance to change her mind.

Blaise shakes her head. "I don't think she was lying. When I was little, my father used to tell me scary stories. Some were about shadow sirens. He always said they kept their immortality by feasting on the souls of the dead." She lets out a nervous laugh. "I guess the details got misconstrued by the time the story got to my father, but they were close enough."

In a blink, Blaise is on the ground next to me, taking my hand and placing it at her chest. Tears brim in her wide brown eyes. "What are you waiting for, Kiran? Get your wife back," she rasps.

And how I want to. How I want to pry Blaise's ribcage open before she realizes just what she's offering.

I want to whisper, "Thank you," as I quench the life from Blaise's eyes.

But I don't. Instead I whisper, "Do you truly hate yourself that much?"

Blaise takes in a deep breath, her ribs expanding underneath my hand, which she still clutches. "No. No, not anymore." She lets out a shaky laugh. "Please don't mistake this for self-pity or shame. That won't bode well for me, trust me. I just... I did this. I signed Asha's fate when I chose my happiness over her safety, when I handed her over to Az. When I forced her to open the Rip. And Asha's not the only one who's paid for what I did. So please. When Nox asks, please tell him it wasn't self-pity. I just..." She lets out a long exhale. "I just had to grow up at some point. Take responsibility, you know?"

I don't miss the double edge of her statement, and the meaning saws at my ribcage.

I nod, and Blaise coughs out a sob. She closes her eyes, straining her cheeks as she braces herself. "Just tell Nox I love him, if it's not too much trouble."

My hands tremble. For a moment I wonder if I'll have the strength to do this, so I turn and look for help from the woman who's taught me so much.

She's so still, and it's so wrong. It's not right that someone so vibrant should already be draining of color, robbed of movement.

I wonder if she knew a few moments ago what she now knows about death, if she would have been afraid.

If, over a year ago, she would have sacrificed herself, marched up to the palace like she did and demanded the vizier take her as my bride in place of the people.

Something tells me yes.

So with tears streaming down my face, I gently push Blaise away.

I don't miss the catch in her breath, the relief when I don't end her. "Why?"

A lump swells in my throat. "Because you're not the one who

669

sealed Asha's fate. You're not even second in line. It was me, when I made that wretched decree. And it was her, when she chose everyone else over herself."

Blaise doesn't say anything. She just stands, legs shaking, then treads back over to Az, keeping watch over him as he slumps against the marble floor, eyes glazed over as he stares at Asha's body.

"I love you, Asha," I say, brushing my wife's face with the back of my palm, hoping, praying to the Fates that I've made the correct choice.

I want to scream, want to burst into flames, let the anger roll off of me, but my Flame is no longer, and still the tears burn hot down my cheeks.

There is nowhere for the agony to go. Nowhere to send it. It simply burrows deeper, searing holes in my bones and tissue, devouring me from the inside, eating away at my gut.

Something about the pain sends my father's words ringing through my head.

Don't worry, son. Look to your gut for answers. It won't lead you astray.

My hand finds my stomach, as though my body feels the walls of it will burst if I don't hold them together.

For a moment, I stop breathing.

No one gasps, no one lifts a finger, no one moves, as I take the dagger from Asha's chest and plunge it into my stomach.

It stops when it hits something firm.

I pull the bloodied knife away, slipping my hand into my wound. My muscles shake as I fight through the radiating pain, but then my fingers wrap around something smooth.

When my hand reemerges, it's holding a stone.

Not any stone, I realize.

A leeching stone.

For a fleeting moment, I wonder if it's my Flame, if my father never gave the bounty hunters all they asked for, if that's why they killed him. But even as I hold it in my bare palm, I know that's not what this is. Az has my powers.

Besides, I would feel my Flame. I would know if it was contained here. It would call out to me, I'm sure of it.

Nothing calls out to me from this stone.

It's empty.

Leeching stones. Used to transfer magic from one being to another.

He must have carved me open, slipped it inside my body and allowed the wound to heal before the bounty hunters arrived to take me and Fin away.

But why give me a leeching stone with no powers?

If he had been wishing to help, why not give me something with which to defend myself?

Unless he didn't want me to take.

Unless he wanted me to give.

The leeching stone buzzes to life in my hand at the thought, but I don't know how to use it. Don't know if this ridiculous plan that's forming within my frazzled, anguished mind will even work.

I glance down at Asha, and I know I have to try.

"Will you help me?" I ask.

"Of course," Blaise answers, but I'm not talking to her.

I crane my head toward the orb floating across the room.

It seems smaller than when it first rose from Asha's chest. Like the blue flame at the tip of a dwindling wick.

"Will you help me?"

At first, I think the Old Magic isn't planning on answering me, but then it slowly drifts, stopping a hair away from the leeching stone.

I open my mouth to explain, but the Old Magic speaks first. "*I understand what you wish to do. But do you understand?*"

I nod. "Of course, I'd do anything for her."

"*It might not work. Asha is dead. The power you would need to undo that would need to be immense.*"

Something rises in my chest. "I know."

"*I am uncertain you will survive. It's not been done before,*" he says, but there's no need, because I don't care.

"I know."

671

"Kiran," Blaise says.

I offer her a faint smile. "You'll tell her I love her? That I couldn't imagine a world without her? That this was the best thing I had to offer the world, in giving her back?"

Tears glimmer in Blaise's eyes, but she nods.

I remember what the shadow siren said about Blaise's heart. That her death would save Asha's life. I thought she meant Blaise's heart could grant immortality, but I suppose the siren could simply see into Blaise's heart, the treachery she harbored there.

I have a feeling that if I killed Blaise for the shadow siren, Asha would still be alive.

I also have a feeling that if I ripped out Blaise's heart and fed it to Asha, there would be two corpses instead of one.

"And you won't betray her again," I say. This time, it's not a question.

"Never again," says Blaise, and for some reason, I believe her.

The Old Magic guides me as I place the stone on Asha's chest, her chest that guts me because it's not rising and falling as it should.

"*It might not work,*" the Old Magic whispers again.

"Are you trying to talk me out of it?" I ask.

"*No. Never.*"

I take a shuddering breath, and for a moment, I wonder what is waiting for me on the other side of the sun. Certainly not as pleasant of a place as Asha currently is.

I think I might be afraid to die. But not as afraid as I am to live without her. To wander about this side of the sun without the anchor of her presence. To die one day and face the other side, knowing I could have saved her.

So with the Old Magic's help, I close my eyes and let the stone leech away my immortality.

CHAPTER 116

ASHA

*W*armth seeps through my limbs, a gentle whisper calling me back from the darkness.

It's rather cozy here, in the darkness, but the voice pulls at my consciousness, enough for me to let go.

It's okay, whispers the darkness. *I'll be here when you're ready.*

I remember that I'm not, in fact, ready. So I open my eyes instead.

Kiran looks down at me, his molten eyes warm with affection. My cheeks are wet, but not from my own tears.

"Thanks for coming back," he says, his voice dry and cracking.

"I guess you're welcome," I respond, my voice not much better.

There's something different, an emptiness in me I can't quite place. I was dead, I'm sure of it, though the wound to my heart seems to have healed, the hilt of the dagger removed.

Did I leave my soul behind in death? Will it be waiting for me when one day I return for it?

There's something different about Kiran too. Something I can't quite place.

He presses a warm, wet kiss to my forehead, one that floods me with light.

"If I ask how I'm alive right now, will that jinx it?" I ask.

Kiran laughs, his beautiful smile lighting up his entire face, wrinkling the sides of his eyes, his forehead. Why do the wrinkles seem more pronounced than before?

"No, no jinxing," he says, then he explains everything. The journey he and Fin took to meet their father. His father's insistence that Kiran should try to make me immortal. I tense at that part, which is obvious to Kiran given that he's holding me in his lap. He shakes his head, saying he wouldn't have made me immortal, at least not without my permission, and to kindly let him finish. I do, to which he explains the leeching, how he thought that perhaps, with the help of a few friends, he might be able to leech his own magic into me.

"Kiran," I say, horror striking me. "You can't give me your immortality. You can't—"

An immortal life, one without Kiran, flashes before my eyes. Seasons and years and decades without him, watching Dinah and my father and Kiran die, while I continued unending. I can't seem to breathe, and for the first time, I recognize just what Kiran had been holding in for over a year.

"I didn't make you immortal, Asha. I'm not sure that I could have. The way it was explained to me, that kind of magic loses some of its potency when it's transferred, and that's when the recipient is alive. The power it took to bring you back..." He lets out a shudder, but he smiles through it all the same. "You're not immortal, I promise."

Now it's my tears wetting my cheek. "But you're not either? You gave it to me?"

My heart pounds in my chest. So strange, after it was so mortally wounded.

"No. No, I don't believe I am."

I expect there to be sadness in his voice, a twinge of, if not regret, then at least loss.

Kiran's voice holds no such thing.

Instead, his smile overtakes his face. "I guess we're the same in that way."

I won't have to go on forever without you, is all his eyes say.

"I love you, Asha," he says. "I don't want immortality without you. I never did."

"I love you, too," I say, "which is why I'm slightly annoyed you ever considered taking your father's advice." I jab him in the chest, but it's a fairly weak assault, given my arms still feel like jelly.

"You're a fool if you think you'll live another day," says a voice behind us, one that reminds me that Kiran and I are not alone in this room.

Kiran looks toward the sky as if it's taking everything in him not to tear Az's head from his body for having the audacity to speak at this moment.

I go to prop myself up, so I can look Az in the face. My arms tremble with weakness, but with Kiran's help, I get myself sitting upright.

Across the room, Blaise holds both of Az's bound wrists in her grasp. His hands are turning purple. She doesn't bother holding a blade to his throat, but her teeth are bared, which I figure is practically the same thing.

Hopefully, she won't decide to release him on a whim or an empty promise.

"Put him down," Az spits at the guards, nodding toward Kiran. "Or have you forgotten? The guards are sworn to me."

Fear swells in my chest. "Az, please," I whisper, but the guards don't move.

"Fools, you'll die by your oath if you don't obey."

"That's all right with us," says the guard to the left, just before he spits on Az.

Gratitude swells in my heart for these guards, who both look at me and nod. "Your kindness to us has not gone unrepaid," says the other.

Then he clenches his teeth, preparing to die.

He doesn't.

Both guards blink, but nothing happens.

"Yes, about that," says another voice, one that pricks my belly with the pang of betrayal. Out from behind the corner steps the vizier, a scroll unwound in his hands.

"They're sworn to me," Az insists, though his confidence seems to falter as he looks toward the vizier.

"They *were* sworn to you," corrects the vizier, branching the scroll and clearing his throat again.

Kiran's gaze latches on the wax seal, his emblem.

"I, King Kiran of Naenden," reads the vizier, "hereby declare that females now be eligible to claim the throne of Naenden, if such is their birthright."

My husband lets out an exasperated laugh.

My jaw drops.

Lydia waltzes in, unbound, her grin feral.

"What? No, that legislation is void, considering Kiran was never the rightful heir to the throne," Az says.

"Yet," says the vizier, wagging his finger, "Kiran still maintained the throne for a time. His declarations remain the law, unless his successor writes into law otherwise. You are lucky, young man, that our previous king was as horrible about turning in his paperwork on time as he was, otherwise your brief stint on the throne would have been nonexistent."

The vizier turns to me and offers me the softest, saddest smile, his watery eyes twinkling. "The courier tasked with carrying the document from Othian to Meranthi fell ill and was unable to commence his journey. I do apologize that this couldn't have been enacted earlier, and for my dreadful behavior as I awaited its arrival."

If I had the strength to stand, I would wrap the vizier in a hug. He must see that on my face, because the tension in his shoulders relaxes.

Az opens his mouth, but nothing comes out.

Probably because Lydia just flashed her teeth at him. "I accept my rightful place as queen," she says, flitting her hand nonchalantly, as if she were agreeing to altering a menu of chutney from mango to passionfruit. "You," she calls to the nearest guard. "Inform the healer that the Prince Regent needs attending to." She turns back toward Az, murder burning in her expression. "My first act of queen is to—"

"Wait," I say, instantly wincing. Lydia swivels her head over to me, as if she's daring me to say what she thinks I'm about to say.

"Not yet," I say, swallowing despite the dryness creeping up my throat.

Az's shoulders relax slightly, though he still taps his feet against the floor in apprehension.

Kiran tenses next to me. "Asha, he can't be left alive. He's committed treason."

"I know." I chew on my lip. "But I just..." I close my eye, not sure how to express this. "I just need some time. Besides. You and Lydia took a fae vow not to harm him. Even if you command someone else to do it, I don't want either of you ending up dead on technicalities."

"Asha, thank you," says Az, having the audacity to stumble toward me. The guard holding him twists his arm, so he has to speak through gritted teeth. "I know we've had our differences, but—"

"I don't want to ever see your face again," I say.

Az actually looks shocked. Pained even. I'm having a hard time bringing myself to care. Kiran furrows his brow at me, but I shake my head. I don't know that I can have this conversation in front of Lydia. I don't know how to explain that I want Az's execution to be a decision made not in the heat of the moment, but with a level head.

Lydia seems disappointed, but she doesn't press the issue. She just commands the guards to take Az to the dungeons and adds something about not to worry about giving him a chamber pot.

Kiran picks me up, wrapping me in his sturdy arms and tugging me into his chest.

"I can walk, I think," I say.

Kiran's amber eyes water as he looks down at me. "I think I'd like to hold you for a while, if you'll let me."

I decide I would like that very much.

On the way out, we meet the vizier by the door.

"Wait," I tell Kiran, then crane my neck toward the vizier. "If the courier fell sick, how did the ordinance finally get to us?"

The vizier's eyes sparkle. "Ah. I believe you have a servant girl to thank for that."

Kiran and I exchange a confused glance.

"Yes, apparently the girl had been waiting on return correspondence from Prince Phineas for weeks. When she realized the courier with which she had entrusted her letters had never left Othian, she alerted Queen Elynore immediately." The vizier chuckles. "Should you wish to send her a gift of gratitude, I believe her name is Imogen."

I gasp, flinging my palm to my mouth as I search for Fin who... isn't here.

"Ah, if you're looking for Prince Phineas," says the vizier, "I'll have you know that when I came to retrieve him and the princess—ahem, Her Majesty—from your friend Bezzie's, the prince immediately sprinted off to find your sister. Who is perfectly unharmed, by the way."

Kiran grunts something about "needing to have a talk with that boy."

I simply grin.

As it turns out, there were more consequences to using Kiran's immortality to bring me back than just stripping him of his.

"I want to say something, but I'm afraid it's probably the most selfish thing anyone has ever said," Kiran says. He strokes my face as I sit in his lap on the balcony in our room. Our new room.

Kiran's having the old one demolished.

I like that plan.

Not that I'll be venturing over to that side of the palace for a good long while.

I chuckle. "You've already given up your immortality for me. I think you get a temporary pass on saying selfish things."

Kiran's brow knits as he stares at my face, tracing my cheek with his thumb. "I'm glad these are back."

My heart stills as he traces the familiar pattern of scars that line the left side of my face.

As it turns out, Az's healer had been a fraud, and my scars weren't healed so much as glamoured, though the healer had explained it away by claiming he could bring back my eye, just not my vision.

The glamour had clung to my body in death but had dissipated once the Old Magic helped Kiran leech his immortality into me.

I haven't spoken to the Old Magic, of course. He disappeared after helping Kiran heal me. And apparently left an extensive list of verbal instructions about the care I would need during my recovery.

I let out a laugh.

"What?" my husband asks.

I hit him playfully on the shoulder. "You're right. That is selfish."

A smile breaks across my husband's face, and it's warm and encompassing and steals the breath from my lungs.

"Thank you," I whisper, more seriously this time.

"For what?"

Can I even count? Bringing me back? Giving years of his life away for me?

"Loving me. Me, in all my," I gesture to myself, "socially unaccept-ableness."

Kiran presses a kiss to my mouth, and I feel his lips pull into a grin as his familiar stubble scratches at my cheek. "I wouldn't want you any other way."

I yank back from him. "You mean you didn't want me when my face was all fae-like?"

Kiran sighs in exasperation.

Oh, how I've missed my grumpy husband.

"You're fun to tease, did you know that? Really, you make it much too easy."

"Tease me all you want, Asha," he says. "I'll keep a mental record of each and every time you do."

CHAPTER 117

PIPER

*I*t's morning before I wake, my eyes heavy with exertion, and when the sun beats against my face, I find my limbs aching.

I rub the sleep from my eyes, stretching my limbs until the motion reminds me of a cat. At the thought of feline creatures I shoot straight up, scanning my surroundings.

There's no sign of the Others on the plain. Just the gentle cadence of the nearby creek singing as it dances over smooth pebbles, and the sound of...

The sound of a child shouting.

"Piper? Papa, she's awake! Piper's awake!"

I don't get the chance to turn and look before something small and gangly and messy and wonderful barrels into me from behind, swinging herself around my torso until she's crushing me in her embrace.

Tears sting at my eyes, then soak Amity's hair as I rock her back and forth.

Our hug is short-lived, however, because Amity snaps her face up and quickly tells the other person behind me he's an hour late taking his medicine.

"I think it can wait a few more moments," says a voice that makes my chest want to explode with song.

Amity crawls off my lap as Marcus sidles up behind me, pulling me into his. He wraps his warm arms around me, the thorns of his tattoos poking out from beneath the long sleeves of his tunic.

"Hi," I say, leaning my head back and resting it on his firm chest.

"Hi back," he says, and then his beautiful face breaks into a grin, one that shatters my ribs and promptly puts them back together.

"How? When?"

Marcus presses a kiss to my forehead. "We had some help."

I look up and find two blurry forms escaping in the distance.

It looks like a woman riding on the back of an enormous white wolf.

"Cheyenne," I say, eyes watering, wishing I could thank my sister-in-law. But Cheyenne is a glacier we've yet to thaw, and I imagine it will take a long while yet.

Instead, I turn my attention to my own betrayal.

"I didn't save you," I blurt out. "I didn't do what Abra asked, and... and you could have died..."

Marcus chuckles. "Well, you saved the world. And since I'm included in that group, we'll say you skirted by on a technicality. Besides, technically, you saved Amity, who ended up saving me by coming up with her own remedy to help with the disease. So in a roundabout way, you really did save me."

I lean my head against his shoulder, grateful not to have to support the weight of my aching neck.

But then Marcus brushes away my hair, leaning down until his warm breath tickles my ear. "If you're feeling that guilty about it"—his fingers slip under the hem of my shirt, tracing patterns up my torso— "I can think of a few ways you could make it up to me."

A breathless giggle escapes my lips, but my response is cut off by Amity sliding her arm between the two of us, her fist stuffed with a rather pungent glob of what looks to be steamed ash.

Marcus bites back a wince and grins up at Amity. "I'm on a rather strict regimen," he explains to me, running his fingers through my hair as he massages my scalp. It only takes him one gulp to choke down the ash, which is rather impressive.

Despite the aching burgeoning in my back, I sit straight up, turning around to face him, my gaze scanning him from head to toe, searching for signs of illness.

"You're not cured," I say, and though I mean it to be a question, it doesn't come out as one.

Marcus sits across from me. It looks silly—such a large man sitting there with his legs crossed in the grass like a child. Though his smile is the weary sort, it's genuine all the same.

"Amity's still looking for a way to rid it from my system completely, but no. I'm pretty much reliant on her antidote for the time being."

My heart sinks, my gut twisting, and all of a sudden I'm back in the coach with Abra, wondering what and how I could have possibly done differently to keep her alive. To make her cure him.

"I helped them kill her. The only person who knew how to cure you," I whisper, my limbs trembling.

Marcus's forehead wrinkles. "And I wouldn't have had it any other way. You know that," he says, emphasizing his sentiment by nudging me in the shoulder. "Hey," he says as I bite the inside of my cheek and look away. He grabs my chin, his touch gentle, then turns my face to look at him. "You made the right choice."

"But if you die…"

"I have no intention of doing that anytime soon. But so what if I do? Piper, I've spent too long in the company of people—Fates bless them—who have eternity sitting at their feet, and they don't seem any better for it. You and I, we only have a finite amount of time in this world, and I'd rather it be a shortened one that leaves something good behind, than wander through life stepping on others trying to outrun the inevitable."

Amity scrunches her nose, then scrambles from my arms. She paces the area around the Rip. By the time she comes back, she looks rather forlorn.

"Well, I have one bit of bad news and two bits of good news," she says, hands on her hips. "I'll start with the bad first. The Others trampled the soil in this area so thoroughly, the crop of flax is damaged. We could plant more, but my supply is going to run out before it grows."

My soul deflates, and Marcus says, "Perhaps you should have started with the good news."

Amity shrugs. "The good news is, since I got my supply from Blaise's bag, I have a good feeling that she knows where she can get some more."

"What's the second bit of good news?" I ask.

Amity grins. "You might not know this about her, but Blaise sort of owes us."

Marcus lets out a laugh that sounds more like a wheeze, though I think it's genuinely more because he's humored than the fact that he's sick.

And suddenly, all three of us burst into laughter. Beautiful, crazed, cathartic laughter.

And somewhere deep within my soul, my Gift chimes in.

CHAPTER 118

BLAISE

bsorbing the parasite, as it turns out, has its perks.

For example, I can shift between my human self and vampire self at will now.

Handy for when I want to go about my life as normal, tasting the sun on my skin to calm my mind when it races.

Shifting is also useful when I need to impersonate someone else.

As I'm doing now, prancing down the Naenden dungeon stairs with the grace and power of Queen Lydia herself.

Lydia is not all that difficult to impersonate. Once I got the face and the form down, the general air about her was fun to master.

Oh, and the snapping my fingers and others doing as I say.

I really should focus, though.

I'm not here for fun.

Well, unless you count murder fun.

Which I probably shouldn't.

The guards at the bottom of the staircase treat me about the same way as the ones at the top did, parting way for me lest I singe them with my power. I know Lydia well enough to know she wouldn't actually discipline her guards in such a manner, but these fae must be new.

"Leave us," I say, having great fun keeping my chin held high as I state the command.

Armor clanks as guards scatter from the hallway, leaving me alone with the prisoner tucked into this hovel.

Once my hearing confirms the guards are long gone, I shift again, this time into myself. Well, the version of myself with fangs.

"Blaise," says a sly voice from within the cell. The scent of mildew and rot fills my nostrils.

It would have bothered me once.

It doesn't anymore.

"What kind of trouble are you up to these days?" asks the man in the cell.

He's sitting, perched up against the clammy wall, his disheveled hair a matted mess that falls into his eyes, obscuring his rounded ears. The type of ears someone might check to see if they were fae otherwise, given how handsome he still looks, even in a dirty cloth tunic and stinking like a pig.

People as awful as Az shouldn't get to be beautiful.

I mean, I know my record isn't exactly clean, but the Fates were fair with me and at least made me plain.

"As it turns out," I say, "the type that concerns you."

I whip out the key ring I snatched from the belt of a guard, spinning it in circles around my finger.

The grin that emerges on Az's face is the kind that used to drill a hole in my gut. "Found you couldn't live without me?"

I shrug. "We all have our own agendas. You just happen to possess more connections than almost anyone I know."

There's a twinkle in Az's sage-green eyes. "I'd be more than happy to help, assuming you know how to use that key there."

I brush aside the blatant condescension, shoving the key into the lock until it clicks.

Az stands, a bit too eagerly, and wobbles a bit. It's clear they've provided him just enough food to survive.

I wonder if he could even walk out of here on his own.

He steadies himself against the wall, then once he's gained his balance, takes a step toward the cell door.

I slip into the cell, closing the door behind me.

Metal clanks against metal.

A faint but aggravated smile grazes Az's lips. "I assume you have conditions."

I quirk a brow at him. "Whatever would have you assuming that?"

He gestures with his neck toward the door. "Why don't you get me out of here first? Then I promise I'm all yours. What I can guarantee is that I won't be much use to you when someone realizes you aren't Lydia."

I pause for a moment, still spinning the key ring around my fingers.

"I'm not worried about the guards," I say. "In fact, I can't say I'm all that worried about the royal family, either."

Az cranes his head. "Is there something you know that I don't?"

"I think we both know that Kiran and Lydia would be happy to see you dead."

Az stills, the smile still lingering on his mouth, but it's clear he's forcing it.

"If they sent you to kill me, they're idiots. Asha will never forgive them."

"I know. That is a problem, isn't it?" I say, shrugging.

"Depends on who you're asking."

"Not my problem, at least."

"You're really going to betray her. Again?"

"I'm considering it."

"She'll never forgive you, you know," he says, and, to his credit, stands his ground, though his gaze darts to the cell door behind me.

Like he thinks he has a shot of outrunning me.

It would be laughable if it wasn't so sad.

"I'm pretty sure that I've sufficiently burned any bridge of friendship Asha and I might have had. I'm less looking to rebuild than I am making sure public relations are cordial. Honestly, I don't know that I could make it any worse."

"They'll never accept you, you know," says Az. "They might claim they forgive you, but they'll never trust you after what you did."

"You mean after what you manipulated me into doing?"

Az's sage-green eyes narrow into slits. "Children don't like to take responsibility for their own actions."

"Oh, I take full responsibility. But that doesn't change the fact that you're the one who pressured me into making those decisions."

"I didn't make you do anything."

"No. No, you didn't," I say, pressing the metal key to my lips. "But you know what you did do? You saw a girl, broken and abused and drowning in shame, and you did what every other predator like yourself does. You latched on. You planted doubts into my head. You made yourself into my only source of salvation, and then you turned me against them. Cut me off from the people who cared about me. And, yes, I'll admit it, I let you. You never took my choices away from me. So there. Are you happy, Az?"

"Happy with what?" he asks.

"That when I drain your body of blood and deny you the numbing venom—I can do that now, did you know?—I will be taking full responsibility for my actions?"

Az sprints for the cell door.

I sidestep into his way, shaking my head with a tsk. Then I tap the metal key on his forehead playfully.

Nox told me before I came that I likely shouldn't play with my food.

I imagine he won't be too bothered to hear I didn't listen.

Az swallows. "I can help you."

I screw up my forehead. "You know, why do I feel like I've heard you say that before?"

"Your child," he says, clearly grasping for anything. "Your child didn't die. I know where your baby is."

I still for a moment, watching the man before me, my chest cracking a bit. It's the kind of bait I would have taken months ago, the kind that would have had me eating out of Az's hand.

I'm done eating out of other people's hands.

"No," I say. "No, you don't."

Az straightens. "If you kill me, you'll always wonder if I was telling the truth."

This time, it's me who smiles. "Well, then. You shouldn't have lied so much, should you? Seems like there should be a parable about that. Something about how, when you finally do tell the truth, no one will believe you."

Az pales, and he makes a break for it again.

This time, I let him get as far as grazing his fingers against the cell door.

When I break his leg, I make sure to cover his mouth first, muffling his scream as I clutch him from behind.

He's shaking from the pain now, and I let him wrestle his mouth free of my grip.

"If you think this will somehow free you of your shadows, the darkness swarming within you, you're wrong," hisses Az through his teeth.

My, his pulse is racing.

I'm going to miss that sound.

"That's the thing, Az. The crucial part of all this you seem to have missed."

"Oh, yeah? And what's that?"

"I'm not doing this for me."

WHEN I'M DONE with Azrael, he's nothing but a heap of soon-to-be-rotting carcass resting upon the floor.

I tried to keep it clean, for Asha's sake. There's no evidence left of how much pain I ensured he suffered. In fact, he looks rather peaceful, which he doesn't deserve and leaves me feeling a bit hollow, but it is what it is.

I didn't do this to fill a void in my chest. This wasn't about revenge.

I'm about to turn to leave, when I hear a faint shuffle in the corner.

I turn to find none other than Kiran stepping out of the shadows on the other side of the cell.

I wipe the blood staining my lips onto my sleeve.

"One of the guards tell you I wasn't Lydia?"

Kiran nods absentmindedly. He doesn't look at me. He just stares at the body crumpled on the floor. The carcass of the male who's caused him so much grief.

"Why?" he asks.

"Why what?"

Kiran levels me with an unamused glare. "Why did you kill him?"

I step out of the cell, the door creaking as I do, and transform back into the human version of myself, one without fangs or venom or speed or an unhealthy aversion to sunlight.

I shrug. "Because you couldn't."

"She'll feel betrayed," Kiran says, knitting his brow in concern.

"Eh. I'm used to it. The question is, Kiran, do you feel betrayed?"

He flicks his molten eyes down toward me. "You know I can't answer that question."

"But you know what question you *can* answer? When Asha asks if you knew anything about this, you're free, Kiran. Free to say you had nothing to do with it."

It's not quite a smile that tugs on Kiran's lips. Probably because he knows he'll have to break the news to Asha that her sadistic best friend is dead.

It's not a smile.

But it's close.

"We good?" I ask, injecting the question with way more eagerness than I intended.

This time, Kiran allows me the smallest of amused huffs, though his arms are still crossed.

"Yeah, Blaise. We're good."

CHAPTER 119

ELLIE

*M*y father and I are in the workshop, covered in sweat and coating the last bunker door with glass. We've run out of weapons to fortify, so we've taken to preparing the city shelters.

I don't let myself think about what will have happened in Naenden if these shelters become necessary.

What will have happened to Evander.

But as my father and I stare at the last of the bunker doors, waiting for the glass coating to cool, and I realize there is nothing left for me to do as far as preparing for an attack, a deep dread settles over my gut.

But then someone whistles from the doorway of the workshop, and other than Cecilia's first cries, it's the most wonderful sound I've ever heard.

"The two of you are making me grateful I had war as an excuse not to have to be cooped up in this hovel of a shop. Though, the climate of Naenden isn't much better, let me tell—"

Evander doesn't get to finish his sentence, because I've flung myself into his strong, sturdy arms and pressed what is probably a very sweaty kiss to his mouth.

If he notices, he doesn't seem at all bothered. Instead, his smile brushes my lips as he kisses me back.

I'm not sure how much time passes before my father clears his throat, quite loudly. I pull away from the kiss, a bit sheepishly, though Evander doesn't let go of me, and I don't fight him on it.

Still tucked into my husband's chest, I grin at my father as he pats Evander on the back and says, "It's good to have you home, son."

Son.

I don't think I'm imagining it when Evander's sea-green eyes glaze over with tears.

EVANDER INSISTS he see Cecilia before doing anything else. My mother's left eye twitches when he, still disgusting from his travels, takes Cecilia from her arms, but she has the good grace not to say anything.

After Evander has tossed Cecilia in the air sufficiently to get drunk on her giggles, he and I both clean up in my parents' bathing facilities.

When I bombard him with questions about the battle, my well-meaning husband chooses to inform me that Asha was murdered by Az.

He chooses to tell me this *before* he tells me that Kiran sacrificed his immortality to bring her back to life, and that all of our friends are happy and healthy.

When I complain about the momentary panic he inflicted upon me, he grins and tells me it makes for a better story the way he told it.

It's another hour before I speak to him again, but eventually he cajoles me by informing me that he's thought long and hard about it, and has decided that, should I agree, he'd like to give up his immortality as well.

I tell him that's a sweet gesture, but probably not one to be made rashly, especially when it could come in handy healing Cecilia later if need be.

In the end, he kisses me and tells me we will talk about it later.

After that, he keeps dangling the information about whether my glass coating worked.

I'M JUST SETTLING into my rocking chair in the refurbished nursery later that day, when someone knocks on the door.

Evander, sitting in his own rocking chair across from me, startles, having fallen asleep as soon as he sat down. He's more exhausted than he first let on, but I suppose that's to be expected. I'm still waiting to hear what happened during the battle. Part of me is reluctant to know. I'm not sure I want to hear about all the occasions I almost became a widow.

"Evander!" a female voice calls from beyond the closed door. "Let me in before Mother finds me and makes me speak to her!"

I shoot my husband a questioning brow. Evander drags his hand over his sleepy features. "Did I forget to mention that I brought my sister home for a visit?"

"Yes," I say. "Yes, you did."

Evander groans and drags himself from the rocking chair and to the door. When he unlatches it, a female with golden hair who otherwise looks uncannily like Evander waltzes in. A tall, trim brunette male with tanned skin and vibrant blue eyes follows close behind her.

"Ellie," Evander says, gesturing between me and the female, "This is my sister—"

"Olwen," the female says, sauntering past Evander and toward the rocking chair. "I must say, when I heard my brother had married, I didn't expect it to be to a genius whose invention would end up saving our lives. Quill and I would be sporting holes in our flesh from the wyvern acid if it weren't for Evander's shield. Say, have you ever considered becoming a professor?"

"Thornwall," drawls the male who must be Quill, still hovering at the door, "we're here to meet family, not recruit."

Olwen flits her hand before turning and flashing him a mischievous grin. "Who says we can't do both?"

I must say, I'm a bit confused regarding this interaction, considering the last I heard of Olwen Thornwall, she'd isolated herself in a tower of vines of her own making.

Evander, reading my mind, says, "Apparently, there have been quite a few developments in the past year."

I'm about to ask for an explanation, but Olwen's eyes go wide, and her rather arrogant expression softens. "I take it this is Cecilia?" she asks.

She has the look of someone who wants to hold a baby.

She also has the look of someone who's never held a baby before, and thus is too afraid to ask.

It's funny—from what I know about Olwen, she's a prodigy when it comes to magic. But it doesn't seem to matter how capable someone is in all other aspects of their lives—everyone who hasn't held a baby before seems to think it's a monumental task.

I stand and pass Cecilia to her aunt. Olwen's arms go as rigid as tree limbs, so I say, "She can support her own head now, so as long as you don't drop her or shake her too hard, you really can't go wrong."

This seems to loosen Olwen up a bit, and soon enough she's holding Cecilia like she's a little person and not a little explosive.

Of course, Cecilia *is* a little explosive, but Olwen will come to realize that soon enough, I'm sure.

"Say," Olwen says, bouncing a giggling Cecilia lightly, "do you think she has magic? You know, Quill and I could save her a spot at the Academy. If she's good enough at magic, of course. We don't want to be too nepotistic."

"Only a little nepotistic," Quill says, rolling his eyes slightly.

I look at Evander, who is shaking his head. As much as I want to ask how Olwen ended up pulling strings at Dwellen's most prestigious magic school, it seems as though Evander's heard an earful of this story on his journey.

"We don't know if she has magic yet," I say. "From what we understand, some children with both fae and human heritage are born with magic, others aren't."

"Hm," Olwen says, conjuring a flower in front of Cecilia's face, as if to probe for any magical ability.

Evander groans in the corner, but Olwen soon makes the flower open and close, playing peek-a-boo with Cecilia, which makes my daughter laugh uncontrollably, so I allow it.

Olwen and Quill stay long enough that night falls, while Evander returns to his rocking chair and falls asleep.

Left alone with my sister-in-law and her husband, I'm about to ask how they met, wondering if this will lead me to understand why Olwen left her tower and how they both seem to have influence at the Academy, when Quill's ears flick.

"Someone's outside the door," he says.

I frown and rise from my rocking chair. When I open the door, no one is there.

My heart thuds, and I turn to look at Evander, who looks as if a jolt of lightning striking the castle wouldn't wake him.

I turn to check on Cecilia, who is fast asleep in Olwen's arms, and inform my family I'll be right back.

When I step into the hall, a draft sends a chill up my arms, and I wrap my chemise tighter around my shoulders, hastening down the corridor.

The hooded figure is already halfway down the next hallway by the time I turn the corner, but I recognize her gait.

"Blaise."

The hooded figure stops, then rises to the balls of her booted feet.

I wonder then if she'll run, but she doesn't. Instead, she slowly pivots on her heel to face me, slipping her hood off.

She's not as she was when I last saw her, gaunt and devastatingly beautiful at the same time. Evander told me earlier that Blaise absorbed the parasite, and with it, the ability to shift into her human form.

But she's not that version of Blaise anymore, either.

"I'm sorry," she says, and her voice cracks. "I shouldn't have come. Evander told me the baby was okay. I just needed…" She trails off, biting her lip.

My next words come as a shock to both of us. "Would you like to see her yourself?"

Blaise blinks, like she might have imagined the offer.

"Assuming you have control over your human form and aren't going to shift by accident."

Blaise shakes her head. "No. No, it doesn't work like that. I'm..." She closes her eyes, as if to fight off tears. "It doesn't control me anymore."

I wonder then if she's talking about the parasite, or something else entirely.

I gesture with a flick of my head for her to follow. She does, catching up to me in the hall.

"I'm so sorry, Ellie," she says. "I know my apology doesn't mean anything. Doesn't fix anything. But I am sorry. I never meant for you or Cecilia to get hurt. Not that that excuses anything I did."

We stop outside the door to the nursery, and though I'm fairly sure Olwen and Quill can still hear us with their fae hearing, I keep my voice hushed anyway.

"You know, I've thought long and hard about what I would do if I ever saw you again. Wondered if I could ever forgive you, or if doing so would be betraying Cecilia in a way. I've spent a long while dwelling on what could have happened to my child because of you." I sigh. "But if there are different versions of history, if there's a version of myself where Cecilia came to harm because of you—well—I pity that Ellie, but her load is not mine to carry. Me? I have to deal with the woman who caused my city great suffering"—Blaise flinches—"but if I'm not mistaken, gave herself up to her greatest fear in order to save my husband. So, let's not dwell on the choice I might have had to make. Instead, you can help us rebuild Othian, and I'm sure Evander will consider amnesty."

Even as the words come out, they ache a bit. Sound too harsh. When I open my mouth to soften them, Blaise puts her hand on my forearm and stops me.

"No," she says. "Don't take anything back. I'm the one who built this wall between us. Let me worry about climbing it."

I nod, already feeling bits of the wall crumble. When I open the door, it creaks, and Blaise lets out the tiniest of sobs when she glimpses Cecilia cradled in Olwen's arms.

"Do you want to hold her?" I ask.

But Blaise shakes her head, a sad smile spreading on her face. "No. No, I don't think so. I just wanted to see her for myself."

Olwen looks up, curious, but Blaise doesn't follow me into the room.

"I plan to help you rebuild here, but first I need to help Marcus. Amity's running out of flax for his medicine, and I know where to get plenty more."

I nod, glad to hear that there's hope for Marcus as well.

She gives me a curt, shy nod, then makes as if to go, but before she can, I clear my throat. "Blaise?"

She turns, even as she pulls her hood over her head.

"The wall—" I say, biting my lip. "It's the type with moss on it. And several askew bricks. In case you need a foothold or two."

Blaise smiles.

It's strange, because though I've seen her smile before, it was never quite like this.

She's already gone by the time I realize why.

It's the first time I've seen her smile when the intention is to show rather than to conceal.

CHAPTER 120

KIRAN

*M*ortality is not as awful as I imagined it would be.

Though my body is technically only twenty-five years old, Marcus keeps telling me to enjoy the next five years, so I'm assuming it only gets worse from here.

I look down at my coronation robes and smile.

It's not my coronation we're celebrating today. No, that was taken care of months ago when Lydia decided after a week that possessing the throne of Naenden was too restrictive for her tastes, and she passed a law that allowed the ruler to appoint their successor.

She then abdicated the throne to me, just before declaring she and Elias would be away on an extended vacation for a long while.

No, the coronation clothes are customary for when one ruler is crowning another.

I let out a soft little laugh. I might have given up my mortality to bring Asha back, but apparently the Old Magic didn't bother to leech me of my fae curse as well.

He's fond of his curses, that Old Magic is.

Which means that the fae curse still binds me to my vows, even the ones made in fits of protective rage.

697

Like how I vowed to Calias over a year ago that if he harmed Asha, I would personally coronate his nephew.

So here we are, Asha looking dazzling in a gown of sparkling peridots, ready for me to place a crown on the crown prince's head.

He's only just now reached the age of maturity in Charshon, meaning that for the past year, his uncle has been acting as king's regent. The male wasn't exactly thrilled to give up the ability to crown his own nephew king, but apparently Lydia stopped by on her extended holiday and "spoke" with him about it. Even though I don't want to know what that involved, I'm grateful to my sister for looking out for me nonetheless.

Music sounds, and the princesses and princes of Charshon make an impressive display of moving wheels cut into the facade of the palace balcony walls with a roar of rushing water they control. The wheels whir, turning gears, the motion of which opens the doors.

Out steps the crown prince, garbed in sea-foam robes that match the color of the ocean that sparkles beyond the palace.

The people of Charshon cheer, and though I've always found the crown prince a bit of a sniveling child, it seems that in the years since I've seen him, he's learned to hold his head high.

When he glances between me and Asha, he offers Asha a smile, and he looks her in the eye as he does it.

I decide the Naenden-Charshon relations might have a chance at being mended after all.

And then I keep the promise I made to Calias, and crown his nephew the king of Charshon, while behind us, the crowd roars.

LATER THAT NIGHT, Asha rolls over in bed, her eye fixed on me.

She's so funny when she wants to ask me something serious. She's always worried she's come about the topic too abruptly. As if the fact that she's been staring at me strangely, opening her mouth every once in a while before clamping it shut, hasn't already tipped me off.

"You haven't told me much about what happened when you went to see your father," she finally says.

Ah. That.

Well, I suppose I understand why she's been hesitant to broach the topic. I let out a breath, then prop myself up, my elbow digging into the mattress.

"There's not exactly much to tell. We met; he betrayed Fin and me to Az's soldiers. Sold Az the information about our true identity. He must have felt somewhat guilty about it, because he inserted that leeching stone into my stomach. And then he died."

Asha blinks, waiting.

I groan. "Which, I suppose, I might feel an inkling of regret over. Not that I crave a relationship with a father who was willing to betray me for coin."

"But it would have been nice to have a father worth forming a relationship with."

I rest the side of my head against the headboard. "Something like that."

"You and Evander have that in common, you know," Asha says.

I grunt, fixing a skeptical eye upon my wife. "Are you suggesting I take Evander out for tea so we can share the tragic stories of how both of our fathers *almost* made amends just before their deaths?"

Asha flits her hand. "No, that sounds like a terrible idea. Why would I recommend that when you could bury the feelings and carry them all the way to your dea—" She stops, the word caught in her throat.

"Asha."

My stunning wife blinks back unnecessary tears.

"Hey." I cup her chin in my hand, lifting her head so that our gazes meet. "You're not allowed to feel guilty about that."

She chuckles, though her laugh comes out choked. "Careful. If you talk like that I might start to wonder if you're going to take the guilt away yourself."

I jerk my hand away from her chin dramatically, and she actually laughs this time.

"I didn't want an eternity if you couldn't be in it," I say.

Asha lies back on her pillow, staring at the ceiling. "Is that why you spent all that time searching for a way to make me immortal—before your father brought it up?"

My heart stills, my mind whirring. "Who told you?"

Asha snorts. "The perfectly functional part of my brain that houses deductive reasoning skills. Of course I expected you to be searching for a way to make me immortal."

My words catch in my throat. "I... Why didn't you say anything?"

She shrugs. "I thought it would be good for you if you learned to bring it up first."

I narrow my brow. "But *you* just brought it up."

"Yes, well, you ran out of time. I was getting impatient."

I roll my eyes, but before I can tell Asha I wouldn't have made her immortal without her permission, she coughs.

"Besides, bringing up something you've been nervous to tell me provides the perfect segue for a topic I've been nervous to tell you."

I raise a brow. "Which is?"

Asha sighs dramatically, causing her shoulders to hunch.

Then she places both of her hands on her belly.

My gaze follows the way she strokes it protectively.

I think my heart stops in my chest.

Asha just grins up at me maniacally. "You know, I think I'll just wait and tell you in the morning."

CHAPTER 121

NOX

Ermengarde castle is abandoned when Blaise and I arrive.

I suppose I shouldn't be surprised, as I killed its queen.

You can really tell how tiny the population is in Mystral given our queen is dead and life seems to have gone on as usual in all the towns we've passed through.

I'm sure eventually someone will make a claim for the throne.

It's strange being back here, and when I step through the gate, left ajar, it occurs to me that this is the first time I've done so willingly.

The castle itself still looks just as menacing as it was the day Abra and the king stole me from my family, the turrets just as sharp as they pierce the heavens.

A chill snakes my bones that has nothing to do with the Mystrian climate, the howling wind that cuts through the grounds, rifling up loose bits of freshly fallen snow.

"You ready?" Blaise asks me.

"No," I say, but I take her hand, and we step forward anyway.

We make our way to Gunter's room first. He's half of the reason we're here. Apparently, among Blaise's companions who accompanied her to the Rip was a human by the name of Marcus, whom Abra had poisoned in an attempt to coerce his wife.

Somehow, Marcus's daughter had figured out how to use Rivrean flax to treat his illness, though he'll need to take it his entire life unless they can find a permanent cure.

Unfortunately, the flax only grows in Rivre, and the onslaught of Others damaged the grounds. They think it might be years before the field is restored to health. Blaise heard of the problem through correspondence with Amity and immediately thought to come here.

We'd needed to make our way back here eventually, anyway.

As we enter Gunter's room, I find myself flinching at the scent. It's been months since Gunter burned his familiar incense here, but the fragrance permeates the room, as well as my childhood, and even a whiff of it feels like being slammed over the side of the head with Gunter's presence.

Gunter, whom I killed because I couldn't get control of Farin.

Gunter, whom I failed.

Just like I failed Zora.

As Blaise and I carry Gunter's sacks of flax up the dungeon stairs and to the wagon we parked just outside the entrance, the incense follows me, reminding me of the male who raised me when my father couldn't. The male whose blood I drained from his veins.

He'd begged for my forgiveness when he died. I didn't know at the time that he'd been apologizing for weaving Zora's mind into the Fabric, for placing her in an indefinite slumber.

As we grab the last of the sacks, Blaise must sense my discomfort being back here, because she says, "He wrote about it in his journals. I think he feared what Abra might have done to Zora if he disobeyed her."

My throat goes dry as I scan the room. Gunter's organized chaos. His piles of journals and books. His desk in the corner, the candle atop it burned to its base. The spinning wheel in the corner, which he used to put my sister to sleep.

My chest clenches, because it doesn't matter—the one secret Gunter kept from me.

In the end, he could only protect us in the way he knew best.

I forgive you, I think on the way out.

And as Blaise closes the door behind us, I think I hear him reach from the past and whisper it back.

WE'RE silent as we wind our way up the staircase that leads to the abandoned ballroom. The door, left ajar, creaks, beckoning us into the glittering space that held Zora's body for so many years.

We don't know where she is.

The last anyone still living saw her was Asha, when she was being dragged from the Rip in Az's wagon.

We don't know what Az did with Zora once they returned to Naenden.

Blaise still feels guilty about it—ending him before she made him tell where he hid Zora's body. I've told her not to.

Because I already know what happened.

And I doubt it had anything to do with Az.

Because I left Zora alone with Farin. Meaning Zora is dead.

I always wondered what would happen if you died in the Fabric.

If I had to guess, there was no body for Az to hide.

The ballroom is too stunning to have been a prison. The floor still sparkles with flecks of multicolored light through the stained glass windows.

Still, even though I'm confident Zora is gone, that I failed her one last time, Blaise convinced me to come back. To collect the tapestries at least.

"To honor her many lives," is what Blaise had said.

So here we are.

They line the far wall, tapestries of black, woven with Zora's story in multicolor fabric. I've never really looked at them closely. Even when I believed Gunter was weaving the tapestries for me, I couldn't bear a glance at them. Not when it was my fault my sister was being held captive.

Now it's my fault she's dead, and you would think that would make me want to look less. It does, in a way. But I feel it's my duty. That even if it hurts, I owe her to look.

I owe my sister that—seeing her.

"You know," Blaise says, slipping her hand through mine, "when I was trying to change your ending, the Fabric kept altering the color of the thread. Like the Fates themselves were controlling it. Like they wanted to be the ones to write the ending."

A knot swells in my throat. "Good to know they prefer me dead."

Blaise frowns. "Maybe. I guess now that I think of it, I'm not sure how much of the story was the Fates, how much of it was what I rewrote, and how much was yours, Zora's, and Farin's."

A pained smile tugs at my cheeks. "I suppose that is the age-old question—how much control do we have over our own fate? Who knew my wife was such a philosopher."

Blaise tugs at my hand, and though my chest feels tight, we walk across the room to read the many stories of my sister. When we get halfway across the room, I stop, closing my eyes. "You go on ahead. Look first?" I ask.

It's a silly thing to ask, because Blaise has already seen the tapestries.

Blaise squeezes my hand. "Of course."

I wait as she patters to the other side of the room. Soon, her heart begins to race, her breath turning ragged.

No.

Something is wrong.

"Nox," Blaise says, her pitch heightened. "I think you should look at this."

I steel myself and join my wife, following to the portion of the first tapestry, where she's pointing.

"This one's changed," she says. "I used to stare at these when I sat in here with your and Zora's bodies."

"You're sure it's different?" I ask.

"I'm telling you, I would have remembered this."

That's when I look.

Because woven into the tapestry, holding a child, is Zora.

Except she's had twins.

And holding the second child is Farin.

"No." The word slips from my mouth without my permission. "No," I say again, this time more firmly. I take the tapestry by the hand, feeling the sudden urge to rip it to pieces. To pluck the story away, thread by thread, just like Blaise did with my deaths.

Blaise turns to me, her silky black hair framing her face as she knits her brow, and takes my hand, uncurling my fingers from the thick tapestry.

"Why don't we look at the rest?" she asks.

My ears are buzzing with Zora's screams as Farin shoved the knife through her gut.

No, he can't...

But the next tapestry is the same. A different setting, this one a mountain cottage, but by the fire are Zora and Farin, grasping their children in their arms.

"They look happy," says Blaise, and then she scoffs a bit. "Well, maybe not to begin with." She points toward the top of the tapestry, where Zora is holding a knife to Farin's throat.

The next tapestry tells the same story, and the next, until in dozens of realms, Zora and Farin are brought together, sometimes by sea, sometimes by land, sometimes by war, sometimes by wind.

But by the middle, they're always together.

And by the end...

Well, the endings vary.

No matter what, Farin always finds her.

"But he's a..." I stop myself, swallowing the word.

Blaise gives me a knowing look. "A monster?"

I grimace. "I was going to say a murderer."

Blaise cringes, but we do it together. "Well, I suppose he fits right into the family then."

But then my wife adds, "But I want to know how he did it."

"What do you mean?"

She shakes her head. "He wasn't here before—in the tapestries. I would have noticed, I'm sure of it."

I shrug. "You said the Fabric has a mind of its own."

"It does," she says. "But how can it change itself without a weaver? Unless…"

She claps her hand over her mouth and races to the end of the line of tapestries, where the last, pitch-black tapestry has always hung.

Except the tapestry is no longer blank.

Within it, woven in the silver of a ghost, is the spirit of a male who looks suspiciously like Farin.

Farin isn't who catches my attention.

It's the three figures, tall as looming shadows, hands folded before them, hoods drawn.

Behind them is a loom.

Farin's voice rattles through my mind. *Don't be frightened of death. It's dark and lonely for beings like you and me, but you're a fool if you believe the Fates forget about us. Stay interesting enough, and they might just weave you back into the story.*

"Blaise," I ask, my breath fogging the frigid air, "whatever happened to the tapestry you wove me into?"

Blaise frowns. "I left it behind when I kidnapped Asha. I was in such a daze, such a rush to get her to the Rip, I didn't think to bring it. Didn't think it would be any use to me, since I was running out of time."

"So it's just sitting abandoned in a field in Charshon somewhere?"

Blaise furrows her brow, then her eyes go wide. "No. No, it isn't." She rummages through her satchel, yanking out a crumpled letter. Her eyes dart across the page, scouring the text. "I didn't know what she was talking about… Thought she was just being childish."

Blaise shoves the letter into my hands, points to a section of text toward the end.

Oh, and by the way, I really liked the love story you left behind. I tried to tell it to Marcus, but he didn't think it was romantic at all. He says villains don't make for good love interests. Though I will say, the ending left me hanging. I thought for sure that wasn't how you planned to end it—it's kind of a cliffhanger, you know—and that you got interrupted, but the final stitches are all done.

    -Amity

"THIS HAS to be talking about the tapestry I left behind, doesn't it? What else could she be talking about?" Blaise asks.

"I thought you said you didn't finish the tapestry," I say.

Blaise gazes up at the previously blank tapestry. At the image of Farin kneeling before the three hooded figures.

"I didn't."

CHAPTER 122

ASHA

I find him just where I expected, follow his pull into an abandoned alleyway in Meranthi that no one else seems to notice.

Tucked away, as if trying to be forgotten.

As if waiting for someone to remember.

Dramatic as ever.

"I'm not climbing up there, you know," I call from down below, my voice echoing up over the wall.

No one passing by on the street seems to notice.

When I don't receive an answer, I start picking up pebbles and slinging them overhead.

"Listen, you're the one who instilled within me a fear of heights. Stop sulking and come down here yourself."

Again, silence.

I shrug, then back away, leaning against the warm clay wall of the building behind me.

I once had nightmares about this place, about the flash of pain that had seared up my back and side, taking my eye with it. This is the first time I've come back here, and as I look around, examining the alleyway that technically doesn't exist, I find myself surprised.

Surprised at the lack of shadows, the lack of terror swelling in my heart.

By all accounts, it's just a normal, non-existent alleyway.

I wonder if perhaps I should have come back sooner. If facing it on my own terms would have stopped the nightmares.

Or perhaps it would have been equally as terrifying, if I'd come any earlier.

I suppose I'll never know.

Still, I wait, yawning.

Eventually, an orb of bluish light peeks over the rooftop.

I wink at it, and it flits backwards, out of sight, but when it peeks again, I wave.

The light forming it whooshes, giving the striking impression of an exasperated sigh.

Then the strange orb of light drifts downward, floating to a halt in front of my face.

"You're much cuter than I imagined you'd be," I say, at which the blue orb flares orange for a second, or perhaps it's just my imagination.

I do not appreciate being disturbed, says the orb, the familiarness of the deep, cranky voice causing my heart to swell.

I cross my arms, then point to my missing eye. "Yes, I'm aware of that."

Is there something you wished to say to me that was important enough to wake me from my slumber?

"Oh, don't act like you didn't want to be found. Otherwise you wouldn't have hidden exactly where you knew I would find you."

I didn't know you would find me, drawls the familiar voice. *I didn't even know whether you would think to look.*

I level my most annoyed stare. The orb flickers. "So this was a test? To see if I'd come looking for you?"

It was no such thing.

"If you wanted me back so badly, you know you could have come to me and just asked."

I am perfectly content with my solitude. I was content with it before a meddling child came and disturbed my peace all those years ago, and I'm perfectly content with it now.

"Right," I say. "And that's why you hid where you knew I'd be able to find you."

I don't see why I should abandon a perfectly good dwelling place on your account, my magic says. *Though now that you seem intent on coming here and torturing me, I believe I might be forced to emigrate elsewhere.*

The orb flicks upward, in a way that somehow I know he's turned his back to me, but not so quickly that he can't hear me saying, "I miss you, you know. I'd like for you to come back."

The orb halts. *Wherever I go, I only bring trouble. Death always comes to those whom I attach myself to.*

"That's because you attach yourself to humans who are going to die with or without you. It's a little self-absorbed of you to assume you're the reason, don't you think?"

The orb bristles. *It matters not whether I am the cause. Humans always die, and there is nothing I can do to change that. So what is the use of me trying?*

I step forward, off the wall, craning my head to the sky. "Maybe that's just it. Maybe you stop trying, and just accept it."

I've done that plenty, thank you, said the orb.

"Then you're experienced enough for the job. That's a good thing, isn't it?"

The orb stills, then whispers, *I cannot watch you die again, Asha. And you will die.*

"I know," I say, testing my words. "But you'll hear about it, regardless. I'm the Queen of Naenden. You won't be able to escape knowing when the time finally comes."

No one but you knows to disturb me up here, says the Old Magic.

"Well, then I'll come and visit once a year. You'll know the year I don't come that I've died."

That's incredibly cruel of you.

"What? Dying? I'm sure I won't be able to help it."

He's still floating away.

"Nagivv misses you," I try. Although I'm fairly certain that if

Nagivv found the Old Magic in his orb-like state, she'd swat at him with her paw.

I pull out the last of my leverage. "I'm pregnant!" I blurt. "You can say no to me, but we both know you're curious to see how this little baby will turn out."

The Old Magic halts. He lingers for a moment before turning back around to face me. *You will torture me, regardless?* he asks. I can't help but note the hope in his voice.

"With equal measure that you've tortured me all these years," I reply with reverence.

Very well, then, says the Old Magic.

The blue orb rushes into my heart before I have the chance to change my mind.

CHAPTER 123

BLAISE

I have to take time off from shifting for the better part of the year.

Nine months, to be exact.

We're not actually convinced it would hurt the baby, but Nox has entire chalkboards full of theories on why it might, so I try not to stress him out too much.

That means no vampire hearing to spy on our neighbors. It also means I still have to suffer the back pain as the baby kicks at my spine.

Worth it, though.

When I first realized I was missing my cycle, I wondered if it was just a byproduct of my not-quite-human, human form.

But no.

It pretty much meant what it tends to mean.

The vomiting had confirmed as much.

Telling Nox had been the fun part. He'd spent an entire hour in silence, looking stunned.

Then he'd retreated to his chalkboards and notes, talking to himself as he tried to figure out the science and or magic behind exactly how a vampire had managed to impregnate a not-quite-human female.

I offered to help him reenact the exact method I suspected was to blame, but he was dazed enough that he didn't catch on to my not-so-subtle methods of seduction.

Eventually, he decided that it was, in fact, possible, and though vampirism is considered a sort of undead curse, everything about him works properly, other than the going out in the sun part.

After that was settled, he took me up on my previous offer.

I watch him now, my hand absentmindedly caressing my belly as he scribbles furiously in a notebook by the light of a waning candle.

If I know my husband, it's either got something to do with our child, or tracking down his sister's body.

He hasn't quite come to terms with the fact that Zora seems happy falling in love repeatedly with a killer.

"Figured out yet how to keep our child from being a murderer before it's developmentally appropriate?" I tease, rocking back and forth in the chair Nox's parents made for me the week after we told them they'd be having a grandchild.

"I've tracked down a few vampire covens in the mountains," he says, pressing the pen to his temple as he scribbles something else. "So far, I've failed to make contact, but I'm thinking if I show up and prove I'm one of them, they won't turn me away."

I frown, disliking the sound of this. "Yes, and I'm sure none of them will covet the *paldihv* that allows you to move about freely in the sun."

Nox looks up at me, as if surprised at himself for not considering this earlier. Then he shrugs. "If it's a risk we need to take to get answers…"

It takes great effort, but I haul myself out of the rocking chair. Eventually. Though my poor swollen ankles don't seem to like the vertical position too much.

I practically have to waddle over to my husband, who looks as if he's about to pull the skin from his temples with how hard he's stretching them.

"What if…What if we just play it by ear?" I ask.

Nox swivels to face me, like I've just recommended we feed our baby opossum blood in place of breastmilk.

"You're not worried?" he asks.

"Oh, I'm terrified of our little monster baby. But what you seem to be forgetting is that the two of us are monsters too. I'm sure whatever this child throws at us, we'll still be bigger than them for quite a few years."

"What if the baby can't go out in the sun?"

"Our village gets three hours of light during the peak summer months. I think it will be okay."

Nox slumps back in his chair, leaning his head back. "None of the other parents are going to let anyone near our kid."

"That's what you're worried about?"

He shrugs. "I just don't want our child to grow up..." He swallows. "Alone." Then he gives me a rather serious look with those pale blue eyes of his. "Not having friends as a child is a recipe for psychopathy, you know. That, combined with a thirst for blood..."

"Nox."

"Yeah?"

"This child won't have the childhoods we had."

Nox swallows, looking up at me with those beautiful eyes of his. "We can't know that for sure."

"No, but probability-wise, being kidnapped by an evil queen seems unlikely, now doesn't it?"

Nox shrugs, conceding with a nod.

"And," I add, "as long as you don't marry a money-grubbing wench to replace me when I die, then I don't think our child will have my childhood either."

Nox actually smiles at that. "But you know how attractive I find money-grubbing wenches."

WHEN THE UMBRA comes for me, at first I think perhaps it's to punish me for my sins.

The moment in the Naenden colonnade didn't cleanse me of my

shame entirely. Only made it manageable. Something I could grasp onto and use. I'm not sure the parasite recognized that my shame was still there.

I still hear Ellie's screams at night. I wake to Nox murmuring my name, holding me in his arms until I stir from my nightmares. The nightmares in which Ellie's baby doesn't survive.

But the guilt is manageable, and I've found I can channel it into more useful endeavors than self-sabotage.

Still, I'm not entirely surprised when the Umbra comes to hand me my sentence.

The cloaked assassin is accompanied by a human woman, one who looks familiar though I can't quite place her. The type of familiar that reminds me of a fever dream.

I don't entirely feel that I deserve the Umbra's mercy, but I won't go down without a fight. Not with what it would do to Nox if I died.

I have found I am worth quite a lot to the ones I love, and I'm not willing for them to suffer over me any longer.

That, and I'll protect the baby inside me with my life.

I tell the Umbra as much, and brace for a fight, but the figure only shakes his head and nods toward the human woman.

She curtsies to me, which I find strange. I haven't been curtsied to in a long while, not since my father was still alive and working as an ambassador for the king.

"Miss Blaise," she says, and her eyes go glassy at my name. Her voice tightens, and she apologizes, clutching at her chest. "It's just, it's just so nice to see you doing so well. With a family of your own and all," she says, nodding toward the glow coming from our cottage window, as well as the swell of my belly.

I frown because this woman seems so familiar, and still I can hardly place her. "I'm sorry, but might you remind me how I know you?"

She smiles. A hearty, wholesome smile that wrinkles her entire face. "Your stepmother hired me. I was the midwife who assisted with your child's birth. I'm so sorry for your loss—that horrible day I'll never forget." She wipes her watering eyes with her sleeve, and I find

I'm not breathing. My head swims, roaring with white noise, but the Umbra nods at her to continue. "When your stepmother saw that the child had already passed on, she told me to—" The woman's words seem caught in her throat, and fury threatens to well in me, but the Umbra catches my shoulder and squeezes gently. "Well, I didn't think the baby deserved what your stepmother intended, but I knew your stepmother would kill me if she found out I disobeyed her orders, and I…"

"A little boy or a little girl?" I find my lips asking, though I can't recall telling them to.

The midwife blinks, and she gives me a reassuring, if pained, smile. "A little girl. You had a daughter, Miss Blaise."

I try to choke back a sob, and fail.

"Rose," I say, sucking in a breath even as my eyes burn.

The midwife smiles. "Yes. She looked like a Rose. I…" She pauses, as if not sure what she's about to say is appropriate. "I paint, on the side. Always have. Helps me process life. I painted your daughter— Rose—many times over the years. Her beautiful face has been in my memory all this time. I brought some of the paintings, if you'd like them."

I can't quite find the words, so I just nod my head, mouth slightly ajar.

She pulls a small portrait from her satchel. I take it in my hands and stare at my daughter for a long while.

EVENTUALLY, I learn that the midwife faked her own death after Rose's birth. She knew Clarissa knew nothing of her disobedience. But she also knew of Clarissa's paranoia that someone would spread the gossip that Blaise had been with child.

As it turns out, the midwife wasn't the adulteress Clarissa had claimed her to be. Clarissa had made that part of the story up. She'd lied to the midwife's husband, who was known for being a jealous drunk, in the hopes that he would finish the midwife off in a drunken rage.

Instead, the husband had killed himself.

The midwife had found him hanging from the rafters and, wise to Clarissa's schemes, had used the opportunity to fake her own murder.

Her brother was the coroner, and as she and her husband had no other family, no one questioned when the coroner claimed to have found both of them dead.

With the help of her brother, the midwife ran, starting life anew in a small village of Mystral.

Where she now paints portraits of my little Rose.

When she finishes her story, I hardly know what to say.

So I invite her in for tea.

She stays for a long while.

EPILOGUE

THE OLD MAGIC

*T*he Old Magic finds the holidays to be quite the ordeal, especially Winter Solstice when everyone and their cousin's sister decides whatever climate they live in is not a preferable way to spend the holiday. Asha and Kiran, of course, believe that a Winter Solstice is not a Winter Solstice without snow, despite the Old Magic reminding both of them that they always hate the snow as soon as the first flake melts upon their skin, burning their hands frozen.

Since Kiran's Flame died with Azrael, the Old Magic supposes the poor male doesn't have a manner in which to warm himself.

Ellie and Evander are the opposite. They suffer the displeasure of snow multiple months out of the year, and by the time Solstice comes around, they want nothing more than to escape to somewhere with a warmer climate.

This almost always results in at least one person complaining about the weather, no matter where the group decides to meet for the Solstice that particular year.

Of course, on the years they meet in Naenden, everyone complains about the weather.

The children are also an ordeal.

In fact, last year, the interruptions had gotten so bad, so frequent, the Old Magic is considering withholding story hour.

Thankfully, since this would have meant that the Old Magic would have missed story hour as well, he's come up with a better plan for punishing the insolent children. Blaise and Nox's children especially. When they're not getting their sticky hands into the blood sausage, they're skirting around rules as if they're suggestions, and always, always interrupting the Old Magic's stories.

That, and the Old Magic gets the strangest feeling around Aysel, Blaise and Nox's oldest.

There is something familiar about her, something that reminds him of...but that can't be.

In fact, the Old Magic can't help but eavesdrop through Asha's ears on Nox and Marcus's nearby conversation.

"So, Sasha's magic talks to her?" Nox asks Marcus as they sit around the fire.

Marcus leans back in his chair, chewing on the flax Amity brought him a few minutes earlier.

Marcus chuckles. "It's the strangest thing. We had no idea what was happening at first. Sasha kept getting into trouble, then telling us it was the voice that was telling her to do it."

Nox stiffens. "What kind of trouble?"

"Oh, nothing too sinister. Mostly getting into the kitchen and trying to make things a three-year-old should not be attempting. I can't tell you how many fires I had to put out before we finally figured out what was going on."

Nox sits on the edge of his seat now. "Which was?"

"Apparently, when the fae absorbed magic all those generations ago, it got passed down with each generation, fracturing each time. Except when Piper was born, since she had human blood in her veins, a fraction of her magic sort of woke up. At least, that's how Sasha explained it to us. When Sasha was born, there was even less fae blood, meaning Sasha's fragment can actually speak to her."

Nox chooses his words carefully. "And that doesn't...disturb you?"

"Oh, it does. Immensely. But it's not as if I can really do anything about it, can I? Other than lay down ground rules about what is and isn't allowed in the kitchen."

Nox glances at Aysel, and his expression softens. "No, I suppose not. But what if...what would you do if the voice Sasha was hearing wasn't inclined toward good?"

If it were me, I'd drop her off at the vampire clans in the north and be done with her, thinks the Old Magic to himself, though this is one of the less self-aware things he has thought, since he secretly holds a tenderness for Aysel.

Marcus furrows his brow. "What do you mean?"

Nox leans forward, propping his elbows on his legs as his tone goes hushed. "It's just that Piper's magic, Asha's magic—they both have a sense of morality. I just can't help but worry that passing fragments of the parasite onto our children..."

"Is going to ruin them irreparably?" Marcus asks.

Nox grimaces. "Well, yes."

Marcus shrugs. "It's called being a parent. We all worry about that." He goes to stand from his seat to refill his drink and glances at Aysel, who's trying to coax a beetle into the fire. "Though, I would make an extra attempt to socialize her with other children if I were you."

Nox's shoulders deflate slightly, but then he takes a deep breath and goes to his daughter, smiling gently and whispering something in her ear. She groans, looking forlorn at being forced to abandon her attempt at beetle extermination, but she does as her father says, scampering off to play with the other children.

Cecilia quickly welcomes her. "Oh good!" she exclaims, her black ringlets bobbing underneath the cone of paper she's turned into a princess hat atop her head. "You can be the villain!"

Aysel's eyes glitter with delight.

Nox sinks into the couch, tipping his head back in exaggerated despair. "I give up," he says.

Marcus, having returned with his drink, slaps Nox on the shoulder. "Well, if it's any consolation, she does make a pretty adorable villain."

The Old Magic could not agree more, though he'd be loath to admit it.

He returns his attention to Asha, who has been silently chuckling as she also eavesdrops on the conversation happening across from her.

You shouldn't laugh, the Old Magic scolds. *That child might very well be the death of us one day. Growing up with my wicked sister knitted to her soul.*

Asha internally flares her nostrils. *A fragment of your sister,* she reminds him. *Besides, it's not really the dark urges someone has that make them good or evil. It's which has control over the other.*

The Old Magic is about to retort that it's much easier to be good if you don't have evil urges whispering in your ear, but then his gaze fixes on little Aysel. "No," she whispers to herself, shaking her head vehemently. "Cecilia is my friend. Friends don't steal friends' princess hats."

Asha smiles. *See?*

The Old Magic is forced to admit that he does.

Asha has that way about her, being able to see the best in people, sometimes even when the Old Magic is convinced it's not truly there.

Like Blaise, for example. Over the years, Asha has come to forgive her for her betrayal, despite the Old Magic's constant skepticism and warnings.

Oh, well. He supposes that is in Asha's nature.

Though he hasn't said a negative thing about Blaise since he got suspicious that perhaps she had been the one to kill Azrael.

That boy needed to die.

Still, Blaise and Asha keep their distance from one another, even at these gatherings. The Old Magic knows that Asha suspects Blaise of the same.

It's not that Asha blames Blaise for ending the life of the man who tortured Asha and held her captive, for keeping Kiran from being the one to do it.

In fact, part of her is grateful, but when she approaches Blaise, she sometimes feels she can smell Az's blood on her, and it makes Asha sick.

As for why Blaise keeps her distance, the Old Magic suspects it's more to do with a fear of him and his curses than it is for Asha.

The Old Magic finds satisfaction in knowing Blaise is afraid of him, though it's a tad unwarranted. He might have cursed away Nox's feelings for Blaise once upon a time, but again—Az needed to die.

And if Blaise was the only one willing to get his blood on her hands, the Old Magic could respect that.

Blaise sits in the corner, speaking with Piper. They've kept in touch over the years, and from what the Old Magic can tell, Blaise looks to Piper like a slightly older sister.

Asha swivels her head, searching for Fin and Dinah, but neither are anywhere to be found. At least not in the vicinity.

"You know, I always expect you to try to set them up at these things," says Kiran, taking his place on the loveseat with his wife. Asha smiles and tucks herself into her husband's chest.

Normally, the way Asha's heart flutters in Kiran's presence disgusts the Old Magic, but even he is not immune to Winter Solstice cheer.

"It's just such a romantic time of year," Asha says. "Especially when we're somewhere cold like Othian. I guess I keep hoping they'll find themselves chilly and in need of one another to warm them up."

Optimistic view, for something that has yet to occur, even after years of being in one another's constant proximity, the Old Magic scoffs.

Asha grunts, though Kiran is so used to her talking to the Old Magic in her head that he doesn't mistake her displeasure for being directed at him this time.

The Old Magic can't help but notice that Asha can't help but notice that Kiran's hair is going gray on the sides, just above his ears.

The sight fills Asha with a mix of emotions: gratefulness for Kiran's sacrifice, guilt over his lost years.

Oh, don't be so dramatic, the Old Magic scolds. *Kiran hasn't yet reached his thirtieth year. His hair is just graying early, that's all.*

But it wouldn't be graying at all if he hadn't given his immortality to save me, Asha thinks back.

You're right, says the Old Magic, *because he would have died of heart-break or some equally ridiculous malady, and then he'd be rotting in the ground, growing no hair at all.*

Asha swats him away, but she tucks her head into her husband's chest and savors each rise and fall.

Her moment of peace is soon interrupted by Evander, who waltzes up behind the sofa and clasps his hands on Kiran's shoulders. "You know, Kiran, it's pretty inconsiderate of you to be going gray this early. You could at least have the decency to wait until I've settled into my mortality for more than a few months."

Kiran lets out an exasperated sigh. "I miss the days when you were afraid of me."

"Shouldn't have lost that fire magic of yours then," Evander says, dragging a chair next to Kiran's side of the sofa.

The Old Magic thinks that's quite a bold thing to say, for someone who recently lost his immortality. Ellie must think so too, because she appears at Evander's side, then plucks a hair from his head. Evander jumps, eyes wide as he examines the hair for any hint of gray. When the King of Dwellen discovers the plucked hair retains its copper hue, and his queen is offering him a mischievous grin, he grabs her by the waist and yanks her onto his lap as she laughs.

"I think I see a wrinkle," Ellie teases, tracing the corner of Evander's eye with her forefinger.

The Old Magic decides to ignore them, even if Asha isn't. Ellie and Evander are much too affectionate in public for the Old Magic's liking. Though he secretly finds it admirable that Evander gave up his immortality earlier this year to save Cecilia from an illness that came close to taking her life.

The Old Magic notices that Ellie is wearing a set of intricately designed glass slippers.

Eventually, the children gather together, Cecilia and Aysel hobbling over the rest to sit in the front, facing Asha; Kiran and Asha's oldest child squeezes between them.

Even Amity joins them, herding the younger children like a mother hen before settling down behind them with a cup of hot cocoa.

The Old Magic is glad Amity still joins. He worries every year that this will be the year she's outgrown story hour.

He suspects Amity has, in fact, outgrown story hour, but that she stays to appease him, which warms his borrowed heart almost as equally.

Once Blaise's daughter finally shuts up, Asha asks, *You ready?*

It's a silly question, of course. The Old Magic has spent the better part of the past year crafting this particular tale. This will be the story to finally teach these impertinent children a lesson, after all.

So Asha opens her mouth, and out from it pours the melodious voice of the Old Magic as he spins a tale, all the while intoxicated on the children's unbreakable attention.

It's a tale of bravery and loss, misery and triumph.

It's the story of a girl whose soul had somehow gotten itself woven into the very Fabric of the Realms. A girl who belongs nowhere and everywhere at once.

It's the story of a girl who's never died before.

The story of a girl who bridges Realms.

And the villain who follows her to the ends of them.

It's the Old Magic's best work so far, if he does say so himself.

He ends it, of course, on a cliffhanger.

AUTHOR'S NOTE

It's hard to believe this little story I wrote the first chapter of on a plane on the way to Hawaii over two years ago is finally finished. That being said, I know some of y'all are wondering about the future of a few of our favorite side characters. Don't worry—I haven't forgotten about them. Fin and Dinah's story is one that's been bouncing around in my mind when I'm supposed to be working on other things. (Cheyenne's too). Right now, I think their stories belong in A Swoony Solstice, my holiday fantasy rom-com series. Because let's be honest— they've been through enough stress already and deserve some coziness in their lives.

Farin and Zora, on the other hand...

Well, they've been through a lot of stress too, but why not put them through a little more?

I already have plans for our favorite realm-walking couple, but I'm not telling you when or where (or *who*) they'll show up. Because yes, I am mean like that.

Oh! And that holiday fantasy rom-com series I mentioned? The first book in the series is already out, and it's called *Of Tangles and Tinsel*, for those of you who want to read about Olwen and Quill's story.

If you're wondering what's next for T.A. Lawrence books, I'm ridiculously excited to announce a project that's been begging me to write it for over a year now. I've been telling it no, of course, much to its chagrin, but now that The Severed Realms series is finished, I'm finally ready to write the story that's already captured my heart.

Be looking for *Losing Wendy* in 2024.

I'm pretty sure you've already figured out what it's about.

FREE PREQUEL NOVELLA

Curious about how Lydia and Elias fell in love? Sign up to my newsletter to receive a free prequel novella!

Get *A Face to Slay the Shadows* at **talawrencebooks.com**

ACKNOWLEDGMENTS

There are so many things I could thank God for when it comes to these books, but today I've settled on thanking the Lord for time. Books are endurance projects—series even more so. This is the first series I've completed, and I couldn't have done it without the God who has chosen to grant me the days and health to do it.

Jacob, thanks for believing in me enough to tell me to go down to part-time in my day job while I was still in the red. Dad, thanks for convincing me that this book needed a glossary. I'm sure my readers are thanking you too. Mom, thanks for all the hours you spent teaching me to read and for your patience with my horrible handwriting.

Rachel Bobo, thanks for constantly lifting me up when I'm drowning in self-doubt.

Alyssa Dorn and Morgan Cari, thanks for bearing with the blank spaces and helping figure out what to put there.

Christine, thank you so much for your attention to detail and for agreeing to take on such an enormous project.

Maci, I hope Blaise and Nox's conclusion was everything you hoped it would be.

Rachel Broadway, thanks for convincing me to change my outline. Unless readers end up hating that particular sub-plot, in which case, Aimee Turner, I guess I should have listened to you instead.

ABOUT THE AUTHOR

T.A. Lawrence is the author of The Severed Realms, a series of fairytale retellings that feature mystery, danger, romance, and, of course, fae. T.A. Lawrence also writes the middle-grade series The Astoria Chronicles, the story of a girl who frequents a fantasy world through a portal in her neighbor's cotton field. T.A. lives in Alabama with her loving and supportive husband Jacob, who occasionally convinces her to leave the house.

ALSO BY T.A. LAWRENCE

The Severed Realms

A Word so Fitly Spoken

A Tune to Make Them Follow

A Bond of Broken Glass

A Throne of Blood and Ice

A Realm of Shattered Lies

A Swoony Solstice

Of Tangles and Tinsel

The Astoria Chronicles

The Keeper of the Threshold

The Secret of Atalo

Made in the USA
Las Vegas, NV
15 January 2024

84400170R00433